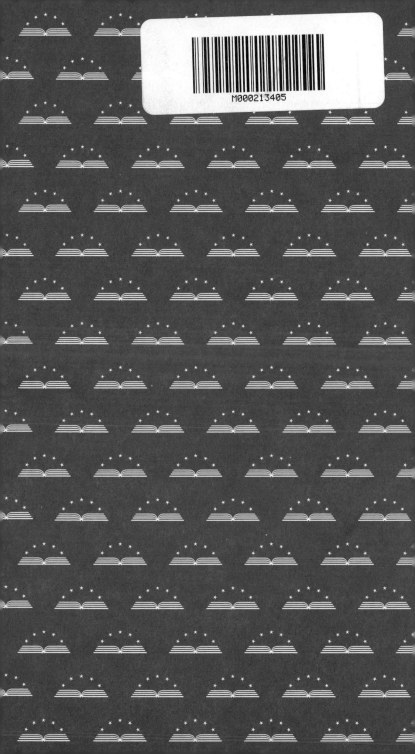

JACK KEROUAC

JACK KEROUAC

Visions of Cody
Visions of Gerard
Big Sur

Todd Tietchen, *editor*

THE LIBRARY OF AMERICA

Visions of Cody copyright © 1960 by Jack Kerouac, renewed 1972
by The Estate of Jack Kerouac. Reprinted by permission of John Sampas.
Visions of Gerard copyright © 1958, 1959, 1963 by Jack Kerouac,
renewed 1986, 1987 by Stella and Jan Kerouac.
Big Sur copyright © 1962 by Jack Kerouac. Reprinted by
permission of The Estate of Jack Kerouac.
"The Visions of the Great Rememberer," by Allen Ginsberg.
Copyright © 1974 by Allen Ginsberg, used by permission of
The Wylie Agency LLC.

This paper meets the requirements of
ANSI/NISO Z39.48–1992 (Permanence of Paper).

Distributed to the trade in the United States
by Penguin Random House Inc.
and in Canada by Penguin Random House Canada Ltd.

Library of Congress Control Number: 2014946646
ISBN 978–1–59853–374–3

First Printing
The Library of America—262

Contents

VISIONS OF CODY

1

THIS IS AN OLD DINER like the ones Cody and his father ate in, long ago, with that oldfashioned railroad car ceiling and sliding doors——the board where bread is cut is worn down fine as if with bread dust and a plane; the icebox ("Say I got some nice homefries tonight Cody!") is a huge brownwood thing with oldfashioned pull-out handles, windows, tile walls, full of lovely pans of eggs, butter pats, piles of bacon——old lunchcarts always have a dish of sliced raw onions ready to go on hamburgs. Grill is ancient and dark and emits an odor which is really succulent, like you would expect from the black hide of an old ham or an old pastrami beef——The lunchcart has stools with smooth slickwood tops——there are wooden drawers for where you find the long loaves of sandwich bread——The countermen: either Greeks or have big red drink noses. Coffee is served in white porcelain mugs——sometimes brown and cracked. An old pot with a half inch of black fat sits on the grill, with a wire fryer (also caked) sitting in it, ready for french fries——Melted fat is kept warm in an old small white coffee pot. A zinc siding behind the grill gleams from the brush of rags over fat stains——The cash register has a wooden drawer as old as the wood of a rolltop desk. The newest things are the steam cabinet, the aluminum coffee urns, the floor fans——But the marble counter is ancient, cracked, marked, carved, and under it is the old wood counter of late twenties, early thirties, which had come to look like the bottoms of old courtroom benches only with knife-marks and scars and something suggesting decades of delicious greasy food. Ah!

The smell is always of boiling water mixed with beef, boiling beef, like the smell of the great kitchens of parochial boarding schools or old hospitals, the brown basement kitchens' smell—— the smell is curiously the hungriest in America——it is FOODY insteady of just spicy, or——it's like dishwater soap just washed a pan of hamburg——nameless——memoried——sincere——makes the guts of men curl in October.

THE CAPRICIO B-MOVIE: the glass facings on the marquee, over which the movable letters are slid, are in places broken so that you can see bulbs inside and some of the bulbs broken; further the letters always misspell——*Short Subjets* etc.——*Alwa ystwo big features* (the letters misplaced as well) so that from a distance you see this spotty marquee (it is supported from the brick face of the building by iron black sooty hooks and bars——just behind marquee top a nameless window with a dusty heavy wire screen, probably projection room)——from a distance you can't read it and it's been spelled out by crazy dumb kids who earn eighteen dollars a week and know Cody and it looks like a B-movie. The sidewalk in front is dirty, has banana peels and the old splashmarks of puke or broken milk bottles——the lobby has a tile floor——a torn rubber carpet leading to ticket box, which is as ornate as something from a carnival and curlicued and painted gaudy orange-brown (just because for tickets); bespectacled middleaged Jewish proprietor takes tickets. The pictures in the sidewall slides are always the same, terrible B-movies—— twelve installment serials, western or fantastic and cheap—— Negro boys spar in front. Across the street is an old beat gas station——diner on the other corner——right next to movie is a hotdog-Coke-magazine establishment with a big scarred Coca-Cola sign at base of an open counter topped by a marble now so old that it has turned gray and chipped, covered with bottles of syrup to make soda drinks and ad cards and junk, and beneath, an ancient woodflap once used to close place at night, now nailed under Coca-Cola, is so weatherbeaten and old, and was once painted brown, that it now has a shapeless color like shit against the gray, almost shit-gray sidewalk which is covered with butts and gumwrappers itself. This is the bottom of the world, where little raggedy Codys dream, as rich men plan gleaming plastic auditoriums and soaring glass fronts on Park Avenue and the rich districts of Denver and the world.

IN THE AUTUMN OF 1951 I began thinking of Cody Pomeray, thinking of Cody Pomeray. We had been great buddies on the road. I was in New York and I wanted to go to California and see him, but I had no money. I'm in an old El station on Third Avenue and 47th, sitting in wooden sunken-seat benches along the walls——the *Porter* sign in the door is almost all faded——In the raw wood wall a strange beautiful window with blue and red stained glass fringes——two bare bulbs on each side of it——the floor old worn planks——the whole place shakes as the train approaches. A huge old iron potbelly stove, its iron showing through grayish (not polished for years)——the stovepipe goes up four feet then over seven feet (climbing slightly) then up two feet to disappear into the fantastic ceiling of carved wood, into some kind of chimney flue characterized by a circular cover with carved openings——the stove sits on an ancient pad, and the floor sags away from it. At the wall tops along ceiling are carved raw buttresses like in Victorian porches. The place is so brown that any light looks brown in it——It's fit for the sorrows of winter night and reminds me speechlessly of old blizzards when my father was ten, of "'88" or some such and of old workmen spitting and Cody's father. Outside——sprawling "alpine lodge" crazy crooked wood house with fringes, weathervane tower, vane itself, pale shapeless snot green, stained with ages of rain and snow, onetime *red* (now forlorn hint of red) tower—— fringes elaborate as hell——timbers on tracks are splintered and aged beyond recognition.

AND OVER AT THIRD AVENUE AND 9TH STREET is a beat employment agency, it's over a music store which (Western Music Co.) has a dirty piss splashed and littered sooty sidewalk in front, and iron cellar sidewalk doors also filthy and sag when you walk over. *Western Music Co.* written in white against green glass with lights behind but so sooty is the white part it makes a dirty sad effect.

Old newspapers and old paper container tops, piled up in corner of door, maybe by bum, wind or child. In the window is a big bass drum, used, faded——saxes——old fiddles——Tuba sitting on tinfoil (attempt to brighten window sensationally, drastically like they do in wildest modern stores). Bongos—— guitar——regular old black and white linoleum (one-foot squares) is bottom of show window. Entrance to W.E.A. is to left——Sign is long vertical wedge sign, black on yellow, says *Central Employment Agency*——Black with dust planking is hall leading in——Sign says (34 is the number)——*chefs, cooks, bakers, waiters, bartenders, etc.*——In the office (brown light) sits a shirtsleeve vest brownsuit boss at desk (with bowtie, cropped gray hair) as two beat clients wait in blue leather chairs—— one of them is old white-hair guy in Scandinavian ski sweater. Other is dark, beat Greek in dark suit offset by white shirt and blue snazzy tie——An unused desk among the three altogether has a green blotter on it torn in middle, raveled up, showing undercardboard——rough plaster stonewalls are painted brown and yellow——folded newspapers lie about——third beat guy being interviewed, sits on radiator covering with back to big plate glass window that faces old El station where watchers linger for nothing (or for next door weird factory shop where fat men in aprons are making labels for dolls). Boss uses phone, guy sitting (with open sports collar and Army-Navy Store suit) big, like boxer, waits all hunched forward with palms on knees——

Building is ancient red——1880 redbrick——three stories—— over its roof I can see cosmic Italian oldfashioned eighteen-story office block building with ornaments and blueprint lights inside that reminds me of eternity, the enormous house of dusk where everybody is putting on their coats——and going down black stairs like fire escapes to eat supper in the dungeon of Time underneath just a few feet over the Snake——and Doctor Sax clambers over the wallsides as night falls, with his suction cups——and the superintendent is sleeping.

Meanwhile, next door to the music store is a shoe repair, closed and dark now, then the *Harmony Bar and Grill* in crimson neon upon the gray sidewalk.

THE MEN'S ROOM in Third Avenue El has wood walls painted green (for wainscot effect this), yellow up to old carved wooden ceiling——stench of piss is like ammonia——piss in urinal sloshes as train, arriving, shakes the place——high on wall where yellow paint is, a big coathook decked with soot (like snow that's fallen on a twig) and fully a foot long, like seeing an enormous cockroach——and too high to reach——toilet bowl has oldfashioned outhouse plank with hole to lower——bowl strangely surrounded by a fence of piping, like a park——same stained glass window but unwashed and has chain you pull it open with, like flushing out——The wainscot effect of dark then yellow up to ceiling is also to be found in the clock-tocking reading rooms of flophouses like the Skylark in Denver where Cody and his father stayed where bums sit on creaky chairs and with their cloth caps settin straight on their heads and still covered with grease spots probably from Montana they grimly read the papers to show that tonight they are not goofing in no alleys with rotgut and in fact they've just eaten supper in the restaurant with all the cheap prices soaped-in on the plate glass windows——*Soup*, 5¢, *Italian spaghetti*, 20¢, *knockwurst and beans*, 25¢ (bent over their plates and gobbled food with big grimy sad hands, gripping, old cloth capped heads bent in pitiful congregation, the needs and necessities, no "dining" here) in fact the most woebegone bignosed bum in the world, enormous red nose that in fact he snicked out as he came out of the eatery to cap the horror of it——a big clown caricature of the Hawk——had eaten 20¢ worth 'cause I saw him lay it on the counter and let it go reluctantly, spaghetti or the vegetable dinner plate, portions seemed to be awright inside, three slices of bread not two, I saw heaps of boiled potatoes alongside meat as those heartbreaking poor guys in their inconceivable clothes, World-War-I Army greatcoats, black baseball caps too small like Cody's father's with a witless peak, leaned elbows over their humble meals of grime——I saw the flash of their mouths, like the mouths of minstrels, as they ate . . . the bignose bum moved away from his 20¢ at a very (pitiful tomato "salads") slow, slow shuffle, sort of eased himself from the area of the restaurant to the area of the sidewalk, where in the chill October with winter coming he shuffled right along in his white shirtsleeves nothing else and drab pants like the pants of Dutch bums in windmills and dung, his head bent as if from the weight of the immense melancholy nose (twice as big as W. C. Fields!)——(no hope, "no-good" pedestrians on all sides). The wainscots of flophouses——I was amazed by them "adventurous slouched hats"——ages of rain make their brims roll up and down willy-nilly and yet just because it's these damn old cowboys wearing them the hats retain immense indefinable charm of the wideopen free sprawling America of railroads and distant mesas——that *Australian*, that pioneer, that frontier dash is worked in by the rain——on their slanted farlooking heads. And they are adventurous, one guy against the wall has same look you see on kid of eleven having first cornsilk butt along garage wall after supper in the interesting darkness in Eau Claire, Wisconsin——same wickedness, as if the world was his mother remonstrating with him——same look of adventuring you see on young truckdrivers when they stop at a lonely junction Coke stand at night in Texas and their enormous truck-trailer sits waiting for them huge across the road, with a spare tire regardant under the cab like the ram shield on a Dodge radiator cap——the flying billy ram of travel——and both of 'em dirty and grim and come a long way and quiet and Henry-Fonda-like and talk to each other that you can't hear and when they leave together they move with the same sadness as if their adventure together was persecuting them to grieve the same careful way and off they go into their own night beyond the whatevers of where you who watch them still stay, they are gone yonder never to come back again and have come and gone like ghosts across your eyes and the bums have that same grave, careful adventurous sorrow as they stand stiffly before an alley wall looking straight ahead with their eyes and their drinkwet mouths glistening in the moonlight in a lunar Bowery, spitting or saying "Hey sport, gimme a dime for a goddamn cup of coffee," and in it there is a statement "I've come a long, long way to be standing against this wall——stranger——and you ought to 'preciate the troubles I've had and the miles I done——'cause after all I'm from a Houston and you're a damn New Yorker that ain't never been to God's country *Texas*——"

WELL, MASTURBATION. There's absolutely no sense whatever in lettin your pants down à la shittin and then, cause you're too lazy to get up, or make other shifts, simply milk the cow (with appropriate thoughts) and let the milk at its sweet keen pitch spurt downward, between thighs, when the urge at that moment is upward, onward, out, straining, to make everything come out as though gathering it from all corners of the loins to purse it out the shivering push bone——No, with the thing flapping and milking below, not only that the seat cover restricting the natural quiverbow jump of the cock——at the great moment there is a sudden sorrow 'cause you can't push in, out, over, onward, at it——but just sit dumbly (like a man sits down to piss) oozing below for miserable hygiene and convenience's sake in an awkward woebegone, in fact castrated with legs-tangled-in-pants position and dumb shirt tails hanging à la shit——and barely missing the real draining kick and ending up having done nothing but clean out the loins as if you'd stuck a dry rag in there and pullmopped out your life's desire. Well, Cody got to know that soon enough.

I WANDERED IN THE STREETS OF NEW YORK and dreamed of crossing the country again. I followed Victor, he was wearing a really strange expensive coat like camel's hair, three-quarter length, with great rich dark designs and yet strangely Christlike as a coat——walking in immense long strides along Second Avenue——pretty sure Victor though I didn't know he was so tall unless it was all those tremendously short Italian mothers he was passing at his end of the sidewalk as I followed made him so *grand*——long prophet strides——carrying some package wrapped in brown paper——headed east towards First Avenue——seemed to be going slow but I had a hard time keeping up——and I thinking "Good thing I have my Proust——in case I should ever follow him all the way which is apparently Paradise Alley over on the river they'd see not only how beat my copy is but that I seriously carry it around because I'm really reading it, really bemused in the streets with it like they'd be"——really a scholar, a hip mystic——though they'd question my red October shirt yet they wouldn't——I'd say "Where's this Nory?" and he'd say "She's my sister" and then I'd meet them and there'd be silence and I guess they'd wonder why I came, unless peeking at the subterraneans ain't never enough reason for them because I'm——It would have to be joining them in their own kind of sullen, if not sullen silently martyred almost dull, calm, or reticence, or bourgeois stupidity, or probably great serious saintly peace as in Victor's floating passage sweeping up the street as he goes without even looking right or left and there goes a little kid following him half in jest, or accidentally but mainly I think in awe and maybe even love as if Victor reminded him of Jesus too and being a kid he makes no bones about wanting to crowd-up to the source of warmth and light—— A strange thing for an American to be doing in his adventure across these years and specifically right now 1951——What'll they say about his "career"——what he's doing this moment——fifty years from now when he shall have grown old and sepulchral in a new rest home somewhere where interests are so far from Christlike subterranean Rimbaud motorcycle Provincetown kicks that I can't even estimate——and his hallway has worst possible martyring smell: the mash of apple wine——he climbed his stairs, I heard doors close, thought maybe JC himself took shits, pisses (and of course) but mainly could it be possible

Victor takes a lonely homecoming crap in a raw toilet of tenements and has the same feelings I have as he sits looking at the
pocked walls, smells same raw danks, hears the same noises, has
similar feet feelings and perhaps "engourdissement" when he
sits too long, and returns to his room (as I do) with mind on
kicks he brought home in package and desk things and poor
solitary shifts of time and consciousness just like everybody else?

SO I SIT IN JAMAICA, LONG ISLAND in the night, thinking of
Cody and the road——happens to be a fog——distant low of a
klaxon moaning horn——sudden swash of locomotive steam,
either that or crash of steel rods——a car washing by with the
sound we all know from city dawns——reminds me of Cam-
bridge, Mass. at dawn and I didn't go to Harvard——Far far
away a nameless purling or yowling of some kind done either
by (raised, vibroned) a train on a steel curve or skidding car——
grumble of a truck coming——small truck, but has whistle tires
in the mist——a double "bop bop" or "beep beep" from railyards, maybe soft application of big Diesel whistle by engineer to acknowledge hiball-on-the-air from brakeman or car
knocker——the sound of the whole thing in general when there
are no specific near-sounds is of course sea-like but also almost
like the sound of the living structure, so as you look at a house
you imagine it is adding its breathing to the general loud
hush——(ever so far, in the hush, you can hear a tiny SQUEE of
something, the nameless asthmas of the throat of Time)——now
a man, probably a truckdriver, is yelling far away and sounds
like an adventurous young fellow playing in the darkness——the
harmonies of air brakes stopping on two intervals, first application, the sound of it melting and echoing the second application
and harmonizing——A cluster of yellow November leaves in an
otherwise bare and sheepish castrated tree send up a little meek
PLICK as they rub together preparing to die. When I see a leaf
fall, I always say goodbye——And that has a sound which is lost
unless there is country stillness at which time I'm sure it really
rattles the earth, like ants in orchestras——Moan, the terrible
sound now of the Public Address system in the Milk Factory,
the voice like it's coming out of a stovepipe full of screens and
amplified——a voice like night——a big steelrim cricket——(it's
stopped)——I heard it once so loud "Please turn off the water,"

a woman, a rainy night, I was shocked——A car door slamming, the click, the velvet modern hinge-click before the soft
slam——the soft cushioned new-car slam, flump——some man
in hat and coat up to something pompous, secret, sheepish——
The area breathes; it seems to want to tell something intelligible
to me——

I WENT TO HECTOR'S, the glorious cafeteria of Cody's first
New York vision when he arrived in late 1946 all excited with
his first wife; it made me sad to realize. A glittering counter——
decorative walls——but nobody notices noble old ceiling of
ancient decorated in fact almost baroque (Louis XV?) plaster
now browned a smoky rich tan color——where chandeliers
hung (obviously was old restaurant) now electric bulbs within
metal casings or shades——But general effect is of *shiny food* on
counter——walls are therefore not too noticeable——sections of
ceiling-length mirrors, and mirror pillars, give spacious strange
feeling——brownwood panels with coathooks and sections
of rose-tint walls decorated with images, engraved——But ah
the counter! as brilliant as B-way outside! Great rows of it——
one vast L-shaped counter——great rows of diced mint jellos
in glasses; diced strawberry jellos gleaming red, jellos mixed
with peaches and cherries, cherry jellos top't with whipcream,
vanilla custards top't with cream; great strawberry shortcakes
already sliced in twelve sections, illuminating the center of the
L——Huge salads, cottage cheese, pineapple, plums, egg salad,
prunes, everything——vast baked apples——tumbling dishes of
grapes, pale green and brown——immense pans of cheesecake,
of raspberry cream cake, of flaky rich Napoleons, of simple Boston cake, armies of éclairs, of enormously dark chocolate cake
(gleaming scatological brown)——of deepdish strudel, of time
and the river——of freshly baked powdered cookies——of glazed
strawberry-banana desserts——wild glazed orange cakes——
pyramiding glazed desserts made of raspberries, whipcream, lady
fingers sticking up——vast sections reserved for the splendors of
coffee cakes and Danish crullers——All interspersed with white
bottles of rich mad milk——Then the bread bun mountain——
Then the serious business, the wild steaming fragrant hot-
plate counter——Roast lamb, roast loin of pork, roast sirloin
of beef, baked breast of lamb, stuff'd pepper, boiled chicken,

stuff'd spring chicken, things to make the poor penniless mouth
water——big sections of meat fresh from ovens, and a great
knife sitting alongside and the server who daintily lays out portions as thin as paper. The coffee counter, the urns, the cream
jet, the steam——But most of all it's that shining glazed sweet
counter——showering like heaven——an all-out promise of joy
in the great city of kicks.

But I haven't even mentioned the best of all——the cold cuts
and sandwich and salad counter——with pans of mountainous
spreads of all kinds that have cream cheese coverings sprinkled
with chives and other bright spices, the pink lovely looking
lox——cold ham——Swiss cheese——the whole counter gleaming with icy joy which is salty and nourishing——cold fish, herrings, onions——great loaves of rye bread sliced——so on——
spreads of all kinds, egg salads big enough for a giant decorated
and sprigged on a pan——in great sensuous shapes——salmon
salads——(Poor Cody, in front of this in his scuffled-up beat
Denver shoes, his literary "imitation" suit he had wanted to
wear to be acceptable in New York cafeterias which he thought
would be brown and plain like Denver cafeterias, with ordinary
food)——

THAT SENSE OF SPRING comes over us in the Indian Summer
subway station because of something warm (the sun upstairs)
and yet dank like leftover oozes of winter——like the wet boughs
shining at three o'clock in a March afternoon——like G Street
in Washington when I was young and so ambled in imitation of
Big Slim with short steps, erect and openminded and Howdy
Pard, walked like that in the sun outside marquees and shooting
galleries and among orange peels of honkytonk life and suddenly a dark cool feeling comes from an open cellar or maybe
a river breeze from Potomac, and it's Spring.

The subway lady is sitting on side bench holding *Journal
American* up with two blackgloved hands——a funny Elly-like
but aged (fifty-five) face with glasses, looking oddly French-
Canadian, like an aunt of mine who pursed her lips the same
way among the woodpiles of West Massachussetts or North
Maine on gray exhalation days of piney mist as her sons stood
arms akimbo in the yard——Actually she wears low-cut green
sexy dress under red coat with big girlish buttons (like a little

Pawtucketville girl at afternoon novenas)——her green dress
has ribbon collar then opens below to reveal bosom breastbone
which is no longer milkwhite but weather red. Fact is, further,
she wears high-heeled black velvet pumps and looking close at
my old aunt I see she has American peps in her and her face
when lowered over paper has same heartbreaking little chagrined pout Elly had when I'd find her sometimes sitting doing
nothing in a slant of afternoon sun in our bedroom (Apt. 62) as
perhaps she foresaw herself as something like this woman in her
days of lessgrace——there is however something schoolteacherly
closed and grave in her face reading. Ah life.

OH ROAD! IN AN ATTEMPT TO IMITATE the taste of a pork dish
I ate in Hartford 1941 when I was passing through on the back
of the truck (with my dog), the truck carrying my family's furniture back to Lowell, and by strange coincidence we stopped at
Hartford to eat lunch in a diner right next door to the Atlantic
White Flash where I worked with Mike and Stanfield and Irv
Morgan the first thing I hit town——but now this morning,
still remembering the wonderful taste of what I guess was roast
pork steamed and kept warm, going on a blueplate dinner with
mashed potatoes, hundreds of great truckdrivers and even some
of the boys from my station devouring it——so me (and movers)
tried it and because it was a crisp day in December and we
were on the road it just was inexpressibly good to me, thinking then, ignorantly "The best porkchop" I ever ate——and in
fact Mike was next door at the station and I talked to him after
eating this meal that I haven't forgotten after eleven years and
he said "What the hell you doing here boy?" and I said "See
that truck out there? we're moving back to Lowell, my family,
don't believe me?" and "Hyah hyah!" Mike just laughed and in
fact came out and played with my little pup Wacky (*Purp*——he
always called pups) for awhile and then the truck rolled on,
bearing me sadly back to the scenes of my boyhood as I sat
watching the more and more familiar road unwind from the
back of the truck——so I wake up this morning, find cold roast
pork in the icebox, a double chop, and steam it in a pot placed
in a bigger pot that has water (two inches) that I boil with a
cover over the whole works, trying to keep that precious flavor
of the pork without frying or any kind of fat situation like that

and all because I remember that porkchop Hartford '41. All you do is head straight for the grave, a face just covers a skull awhile. Stretch that skull-cover and smile.

TOM CAME TO GET ME in my brightly lit Friday night house with Ma watching TV, Mrs. Blackstone chatting in and out, the lights along from bathroom to bedroom as I ablute week-endishly *Esquire*-ly and whistle and sing——Tom and I in high spirits——First complication is Rose wanting us to visit her at Richmond Hill bar which we do zooming through the night in big Buick (and she just called with her father the watchmaker from Russia born sitting right next to the phone in dumbmouth sad easy chair trance as sexy smallcunt dotter calls boys)——We find the bar, rolling through October climaxes of leaves falling and Halloween soon and I got red October shirt ah me so sad that every year we have to lose our October!——poor little Rose with her Thirties style short dress, pretty legs, high click heels, pinched face, perennial cigarette, drinksad eyes at the baron stool with little pimple this night on chin where you might kiss her and it would break and I hated to look at it though on her smooth face now in retrospect (and it's gone) it memories sexily like a beauty spot kind I used to see on chins of old movie queens in photos front of theater——wondering if it was photo ink——We squeeze into phonebooth two of us to call Ed and she tells Tom come in and as he does he has to push folding panel into her cuntbox and she looks him straight in the eye as he pushes harder and harder so he can slip in and she says "Come on, push, push——" and laugh, and air no more air in small booth soon——She has other baby responsibilities so we go on to New York after exciting preliminary Friday night beers standing (just like in Denver bars of Cody) at stools freshly laughing and recounting (never I dreamed it was first night of a five-day binge)——for Friday night to drinking weekenders is like Monday morning for ambitious clerks. In the ever more exciting big-traffic-all-of-it-pouring-into-New-York night we zoom down Queens Boulevard for the hundredth time in our friendship (and as Cody used to do in Hudson) and talking excited, listening radio Al Collins Purple Grotto (Al is playing talk-record slow speed so creates terrible monster but inter-views it casually as if nothing) and other things and so bemused

I didn't notice my usual mad notice of New York glittering skyline and we're in town Tom dropping me off at Wilson's so we won't miss Mac due to meet me there ten sharp (time also of first round Louis-Marciano fight) and I'm worried Wilson (the meeting place) will be downstairs watching fight which is exactly what he was doing (with Marian) and where Mac just arriving from upstate in his car (parked on Park at 57th) comes accidentally, just to catch first round and brew before going up to meet me and therefore doesn't see sign Wilson left for *me* and anyway Wilson is leaving bar because beer too expensive just for fight so they go upstairs and Marian is sulking because she half wants to go to Westchester on train but now to solve probably her indecision has perfect opportunity to blame it on my unasked making a meet with Mac in her house, so that when at 10:10 I come running up the stairs like mad all vibrant with the Friday night excitement that has been buzzing all the way from the Island and in fact of course from Tom's garage way out in the sticks in Lynbrook where his Buick shiny nose waited, in the driveway downstairs reflecting his shaving lights upstairs as he too sang and dressed and his mother and family in their richer way were enlivened among all the room lights of Going Out Friday Night——as I ran up the stairs exuding all this joy which perhaps comes only from living on the Island, on the LAND, and buzzing in——and as Tom wheeled away to pick up Ed at Columbus Circle who was subwaying down from Columbia himself laden with a thousand dreams of zest because his schoolwork is over and he loves Maria Tom's sister and has youthful joys and generally buzzing these days——I run up stairs smack into Marian sulking in her *bathrobe* on the sofa (while deciding to give up idea of trains because "now it's too late of course"), the grim sullen look of the New York-tied maybe and her general recent retirement from all enthusiasms except martyrism——and Wilson himself sitting all slicked up (as never) in suit and collar with a patient martyred look of his own (both of them tight-jawed) because Marian bugs him and anyway he's bushed from week of drinking——and McCarthy drinking beer, the least surprising one there and now I know why because *he* burgeoned enough for ten men within two hours as soon as he met Josephine——and JOHN MACY of all inappropriate, complicated inopportune people to be there (having called, and being a great popular witty entertainer of the Wilsons now as Wyndham once was in his less swish and more boyish way)——all four, stolidly sitting, radio much too loud piping out irritating excited voice of Bill Corum blow by blow fight——I run in, "Marian! Tom's coming too!" and am met by such a stonewall of already prepared antagonism and indifference, in fact so much that Marian made an attempt to grimace her message with eyes and Wilson didn't help, so much that I in my unpreparedness stood like I was shot in the middle of the room, teetering and quivering as my mind registered the psychological atmosphere and also I hadn't said hello to Mac yet who drove from Poke just for me. Yes, I wanted to go to California and find my buddy Cody again——and myself too.

POUGHKEEPSIE BACKYARDS on a clear, keen, painfully blue late October day——with the sky looking like it had been sugar cured, peppered and cloved and smoked during the night like a ham and was retaining hints of glistening moisture in the skin——somewhere in its pigmentation. The town of Poke, and the backyards with wash hung out as far as the eye can see because the lovely simple apple pie wives (like Cody's wife in rickety Frisco same) with short dresses and sexy bare legs just naturally have agreed that Monday is Washday——so there's a silence in the mystic rippling clotheslines right now, gardens of silence in the backyards——here and there you see a garage with the door open and splintered shelves of oil cans inside——a housewife in a housecoat shaking out her dry mop with dreamy irritation——three more of them going by with groceries and wondering who the fuck is sitting on mad McCarthy's porch—— The silent backyards make you think of the men who are work-ing with their hands and left things in order during the day, left their wives to do chores that on an afternoon like this (towels flapping in unison down the block) is symbolic——the sheets of the night are aired to Monday rumors——it is advertised to the Lord in the sunny heaven that women live here and the earth is taken care of——dusk will bring the men back, slamming along the walls to be let in, rolling home on clattering rollerskates to occupy (in a blind dream) the houses that sat all day breathing and waiting for them——little children, meanwhile, who own the secret porches, fall adreaming on the swirl of clotheslines, Arctic, sad.

Far off, like seeing a new nation of monkeys in the trees across the river (no river, just a rill of gardens) are levels and continents of wash hung out by treedwellers and seven-foot women: this is an Africa that you find in the middle of a drowsy American day——Over there, nearer, they've arrived jiggling all over with curiosity, the little fallen sparrows——asking themselves questions——swish, they're gone.

I REMEMBER CODY, awed telling me, the last time he ever came to New York, of knock on the door lasting a half hour at Josephine's, his going down fire escape backlot, landlord who'd bought the damned ground threw open his window and said "Yes, what is it?" and Cody said "You wouldn't think a friendly looking fellow like me, and believe me I am a friendly nice fellow, would be and even though it's strange for me to say it openly and to a stranger——but I'm not a robber——look at me, just look at me, I assure you."

It's like when I'm looking through Wilson's bookshelf and start humming a tune while he's arguing with Marian—— ("Moonglow"). "What made you think of singing that?"

"I dunno."

"It'll forever be a mystery to me——"

No possible way of avoiding enigmas. Like people in cafeterias smile when they're arriving and sitting down at the table but when they're leaving, when in unison their chairs scrape back they pick up their coats and things with glum faces (all of them the same degree of semi-glumness which is a special glumness that is disappointed that the promise of the first-arriving smiling moment didn't come out or if it did it died after a short life)——and during that short life which has the same blind unconscious quality as the orgasm, everything is happening to all their souls——this is the GO——the summation pinnacle possible in human relationships——lasts a second——the vibratory message is on——yet it's not so mystic either, it's love and sympathy in a flash. Similarly we who make the mad night all the way (four-way sex orgies, three-day conversations, uninterrupted transcontinental drives) have that momentary glumness that advertises the need for sleep——reminds us it is possible to stop all this——more so reminds us that the moment is ungraspable, is already gone and if we sleep we can call it up again mixing it with unlimited other beautiful combinations——shuffle the old file cards of the soul in demented hallucinated sleep——So the people in the cafeteria have that look but only until their hats and things are picked up, because the glumness is also a signal they send one another, a kind of a "Goodnight Ladies" of perhaps interior heart politeness. What kind of friend would grin openly in the faces of his friends when it's the time for glum coatpicking and bending to leave? So it's a sign of "Now we're leaving this table which had promised so much——this is our obsequy to the sad." The glumness goes as soon as someone says something and they head for the door——laughing they fling back echoes to the scene of their human disaster——they go off down the street in the new air provided by the world.

Ah the mad hearts of all of us.

THE MAN READING THE PAPER before the big green door is like an Arab in city clothing, felt hat, bow tie, plaid pants, like Aly Khan he has black hair bulging from the sides under his hat—— He sits semi-facing cafeteria (where us Egyptians wait) under this damn twenty-foot door that looks like it's going to open behind him and a green monstrous five-foot hand will come out, wrap around his chair and slide him in, the great door swinging back shut and no one noticing. (And on each side of the great door is a green pillar!) Inside, that man will be made naked and humiliated——but actually gladdened——he's shaking his head sadly at the paper——he's moving his foot up and down nervously as he reads——he's jutting up his lower lip, deep in reading——but the way he holds the paper vertically folded and now bending it over like a little woman to follow the print you can see his mind's really goofing——and he's waiting for something else. The big green door holds itself up like a lamb to sacrifice to the sun at sea dawn over him, and it has wings.

An immense plate glass window in this white cafeteria on a cold November evening in New York faces the street (Sixth Avenue) but with inside neon tubular lights reflected in the window and they in turn illuminating the Japanese garden walls which are therefore also reflected and hang in the street with

the tubular neons (and with other things illuminated and reflected such as that enormous twenty-foot green door with its
red and white exit sign reflected near the drapes to the left, a
mirror pillar from deep inside, vaguely the white plumbing and
at the top of things upper right hand and the signs that are
low in the window looking out, that say *Vegetarian Plate* 60¢,
Fish Cakes with Spaghetti, Bread and Butter (no price) and are
also reflected and hanging but only low on the sidewalk because also they're practically against it)——so that a great scene
of New York at night with cars and cabs and people rushing
by and *Amusement Center, Bookstore, Leo's Clothing, Printing,*
and *Ward's Hamburger* and all of it November clear and dark
is riddled by these diaphanous hanging neons, Japanese walls,
door, exit signs——

But now let's examine it closer. Riddled and penetrated and
obscured and rippled and haunted and of course like kaleidoscope over kaleidoscope but above the glittering street are the
darkened or brownlit windows of Sixth Avenue semi-flophouses
and beat doll shops and blackdust plumbing shops and Waldorf
Cafeteria Employment Office closed, red neons through windows at other end——Furthest up in dark is the focus of this
entire human scene: this is a fourth floor unwashed window
with the shade not drawn more than a foot but ever so thin
brown filthy lace or muslin curtain (and now the light went
off!!) failing to hide the shadow of an iron bed. Now that it's
gone off the mirror pillar is suddenly revealed all the way to its
entire length because my attention had been on the actual window and the reflected pillar was just barely touching the edge of
the window and I didn't know it. Most amazing of all now this
reflected mirror pillar hanging in the street is at the same time
reflecting the tubular neon, the real one inside, not the imaged
one outside, and also reflects parts of the wall I didn't mention
that are not Japanese but checked red and green. There are no
more lights in those windows up there, I'll tell you what happened: some old man finished his last quart of beer and went
to sleep——either that or he was hungry, wanted to sleep it off
instead of spending fifty-five cents for fishcakes at Automat——
or an old whore fell weeping on her bed of darkness——or they
saw me noticing the window four stories and across the street
down the mad city night——or now that the light is off they

can see me better across all these confusions of reflected light
(I know now that paranoia is the vision of what's happening
and psychosis is the hallucinated vision of what's happening,
that paranoia is reality, that paranoia is the content of things,
that paranoia's never satisfied). Other signs, the window ones,
are reflected this way:

⧓ TA ⌐ O⊃ O H ⊃   T O H
⸲ ⊻ ⌐ ⊃ ⌐ ⌐O

                                        (put   a   mirror   to   it)
and across this goofiness cars flash by and the asses of pedestrians hurrying in the cold flash by, when it's yellow cabs the flash
is brilliant yellow streak, when people the flash is memoried and
human (a hand, a bag, a burden, a coat, a package of canvases,
a dull, above it the floating white faces)——When it's a car the
flash is dark and shiny and staring into it for all signs of flashes
sometimes you only see soft clicking oncoming and outgoing of
glow from neon lights intertwined in the street——and the white
line in the middle of Sixth Avenue, and just the barest indication of a piece of litter in the gutter across the street unless just
the gutter's reminder, without looking but just absorbing as
you stare the people pass and you know what they are (two Texans! I knew it! and two Negroes! I knew it!) a beat gray coupe
flashed through looking like something from Massachusetts
(eager Canadians come to fuck in New York hotels)——now
the backward *Hot Chocolate Delicious* letters are shifting their
depths as my eyes rounden——they dance——through them I
know the city, and the universe——Now and finally right next to
this part of the plate glass window that I've been staring at for
half an hour, peeking through an area of six inches between the
drapes and the window is a sidewall mirror which is reflecting
everything that's happening to the right of me up the street,
in fact to places I can't even see, so that while staring into my
"flasher" I suddenly saw a cab coming out of the corner of my
eye and it just never arrived, just disappeared——it was coming
from the right in actuality, in reflection from the left, and I
had been watching the flash of actual rightward going cars and
cabs——In that six-inch area also are the people, observing the

same laws of movement and reflection but from not so great a distance because they are closer to the plate glass, specifically closer to the miraculous mirror, and aren't outflung in the road appearing from far off. While observing this "flasher" a car came and parked in it, that is, a very shiny new fender is seen (obscuring, for instance, the white line in middle of road) and in that fender that's round those crazy little images of things and light seen on round shinies (like when your nose hugens as you look closer) those little images but too small for me to observe in detail from a distance are playing——they're playing only because a red neon is flashing and every time it's on I see more of them than otherwise——and actually the main neon crazy image is playing on the silver rim of a headlamp of an Oldsmobile 88 (as I look and see now) as it flashes on and off red, and I hear above the clatter and sleepiness of cafeteria dishes (and swish of revolving door with flapping rubbers) and voices moaning, I hear above this the faint klaxons and moving rushes of the city and I have my great immortal metropolitan in-the-city feeling that I first dug (and all of us) as an infant . . . smack in the heart of shiny glitters.

ROAMING THOSE SUBWAYS I see a Negro cat wearing an ordinary gray felt hat but a deep blue, or purplish shirt with white shiny pearl-type buttons——a gray sharkskin suit jacket over it——but brown pants, black shoes, deep blue ordinary one-stripe socks and gabardine topper short and beat, with edgebottoms rain-raveled——carrying brown paper bag——his face (he's sleeping) is big powerful fighter's sullen thicklipped (*thick Afric lip*) but strangely pudgy sweet face——dark brownskin——his big hands hang, his fingernails are pink (not white) and are soiled from a laboring job——Looks like Joe Louis only a Joe Louis who has known nothing but the freezing cold Harlem winter mornings when old blackbumbs infinitely beater than old Cody Pomeray of wino Denver go by with wool caps pulled over their ears with no prospects for the future whatever except below zero filthy snows——His look is wild, frightened, almost tearful as he wakes from a nap and looks across aisle at redfaced white man in glasses and gray clothes with a big red ruby on his finger, as if that man wanted to kill him especially . . . (in fact man has eyes closed and chews gum). Now cat has seen me and looks at me with a kind of dawning simple interest but falls right back to sleep (people have watched him before).

This cat is coming from a job in Queens where undoubtedly there is a wire fence and he carries some kind of mop and goes about bareheaded. Now his big Harlem hat is on again (did I say ordinary? It has that wild level-swooping Harlem sharpness worked in, an *Eastern* hat, thousands of cats in the street). He makes me think too of that strange Negro gurgle or burble in the voice that goes with the strangely humble clownish position of the American Negro and which he himself needs and wants because of a primarily meek Myshkin-like saintliness mixed with the primitive anger in their blood. When he left he walk-waddled out, from side to side, clicking, lazy, half asleep, "What you doin? what you doin?" it, and he, seemed to say to me——Damn, now he gone, he gone, I love him.

But now let's examine these American fools who want to be big burpers and ride in the subway with starched white collars (Oh G. J., your abyss?) and "business" clothes and yet by God they laugh and strain eagerly to their friends just like happy Codys, Leos, Charley Bissonnettes of time——this one's a small businessman, actually a good guy I can tell by his pleading laugh——the kind that chokes and says "Oh yes say it again, I loved you that time!" And woe! woe! upon me, now I see he's a cripple——left foot——and his face is the face now of a serious frowning eager invalid maybe like the face of that rollerboard monster on Larimer Street who must have turned it huge and eager from his bottoms when he saw him, young Cody, come ball-bouncing down the street from school in a slant of tragic lost afternoons long departed from *the memory of love*, which is the secret of America——lost too, this subway invalid, in the folds of his own thick bustling manlike neck muscles—— carrying a paper file envelope——chatting with tall younger fellow in glasses whom he admires and to whom he leans of course with that love of older man for younger man and especially of sick man for healthy dumbman everywhere.

CLOSER TO HOME, IN JAMAICA, still wandering, a lovely bakery window: cherry pie with little round hole in the middle to show glazed cherries——same with all crust pies, including mince, apple——fruit cakes with cherries, nuts, glazed pineapple sitting in erect paper cups——wonderful custard pies with their golden moons——powdered lemon-filling layer cakes——little extra-special cookies two-toned——also two-toned chocolate icings on round beautiful chocolate cakes with sprinklings of brown crumbs around bottom edges and lovely raveled arrangements in icing itself——done with baker's trowels——Those fat scrumptious apple-pineapple cakes that look like bigger editions of Automat-cakes, lumpy icing with a glaze——Everybody's watching——Wild raggedy coconut cakes with a cherry in the middle . . . like wild white hair.

The traceries of a tree against the gray rainy dusk——

It gave me a shudder of joy to see a cake with pink icing on top all raveled, with a red cherry in the middle, the sides around all covered with chocolate chip!

But across the street a bleak rectory. On the lawn in front are two twenty-foot spruce trees——the building is that peculiarly pale *orange* brick, color of puke, cat's puke——done up English style, or Saxon, with fort ramparts over the door, the oaken door but pale brown oaken not dark with three little glazed windows on top for decoration and one in middle for the purpose of looking to see who's coming in——on each side of gray concrete *frame* to all this with the carved oldprint word *R e c t-o r y* are jolly Charles Dickens English lamps——then two little narrow slit windows about a foot wide, four foot down——at base of this bunched entrance is cellar-window behind concrete protective curb of some kind (nameless, crazy, like the Christmas tree shrubberies in front of suburban law offices and the little wire fences around shrubs, shape:

all crazy, useless, supported by one-foot tall fenceposts made of iron but look as if taped, with a noose on top

with a curb to
separate this, elevate, or emphasize its elevation from sidewalk
and something never used or understood by anybody except
those incurable *sitters* like me and Cody)——

Above castle ramparts and Gothic windows of rectory front is
a brick gable with a regular American window that has Venetian
blind, above that a gray concrete cross that looks like the stanchions you see around war memorials in parks in the South and
like crosses on cemetery main offices. Warm rich orange lights
burn in rectory at dusk. This is certainly nothing like Proust's
Combray Cathedral, where the stone moved in eccentric waves,
the cathedral itself a great refractor of light from "outside"——

THE POOR LONELY OLD LADIES OF LOWELL who come out
of the five-and-ten with their umbrellas open for the rain but
look so scared and in genuine distress not the distress of secretly smiling maids in the rain who have good legs to hop
around, the old ladies have piano legs and have to waddle to
their where-to——and talking about their daughters anyway in
the middle of their distress.

People going by. The big cowlick Irishman with camel's hair
belted coat who lumbers along, his lips loosened in some sullen
thought and as though it wasn't raining in his huge dry soul——

The fat old lady incredible-burdened not only with umbrellas
and rain cape but underneath bulging pregnantly with hidden
protected packages that stick so far out she has trouble avoiding
bumping people on sidewalk and when she gets in the bus it
will create a major problem for the poor people who are now,
in their own parts of the city headed for the bus, unsuspecting
of this——

The sharp little rich Jewish lady in a fur coat who lofts an umbrella that catches the eye it's so expensive and designed (red on
brown) so beautifully, cutting along with that surefooted bandy
legged gazotsky waddle that distinguishes her from other ladies,
the great high civilization peasant woman of swank apartments
with a hairy husband Aaron who deals in high finance with
the gravity and hirsute slowness of an ape, she's headed home
with a package and the rain like other things does not distress
her——

The Irish gentleman all bundled tightly in a dark greenslick raincoat, collar up, tight at his raveled chin, hat, no umbrella, a little anxious as he proceeds somewhat slowly to his objective and lost in thought of his job or wife or by God anything including feelings of homosexual deterioration or that Communists are secretly controlling his life at this very moment by thought-waves from a machine projecting from a submarine five miles offshore, maybe a teletype operator at U.P., thinking this as he goes down Sixth Avenue the name of which was changed to Avenue of the Americas some years ago to his complete disgust, going along surrounded by this entire night of dark rain in this moment of time that he occupies with a white scared sidelook at something on the bottom of the sidewalk (which isn't me)——

The young darkhaired plump pimply guy of thirty in a blue cloth jacket, from Brooklyn, who spends Sunday afternoons reading funnies ("Mutt 'n' Jeff") and listening to ballgames on the radio, cutting along from his job as shipping clerk in an office near *The New Yorker* on 45th Street and thinking, suddenly, that he forgot the new key to the garage he had made this noon, forgot it on the dispatcher's desk in that empty blue light but it's raining so goes on home and he too surrounded by rainy night and the Hudson and East rivers but can only be interpreted in terms of his garage keys (at this moment)——

——Irwin Garden, Nardine, it seems they now went by separately——

——The strange old crazy lady from out of town who waddles like going over firewood in the yard of the farm she comes from, or did, before she moved to the upstairs flat in a wooden tenement block in New Brunswick, with her companion looking for a place to eat, her feet in those half heeled old lady black shoes very tired and so tired she lags behind her companion (similar but not so eccentric or unspeakably individual and tragic old lady) and sees this cafeteria, yells "Here's a place to eat," companion answers: "It's only a cafeteria and the food is awful in those places, George told me to stick to little restaurants"——"But there aren't any!" (and quite naturally, they're on Sixth Avenue and the restaurants are all on sidestreets mostly, the ones with white tablecloths, etc., although they will hit such restaurants if they keep distressing in the rain on up six more blocks to near Radio City)——So they decide, or that is Companion decides Stewart's Cafeteria is nowhere and my old eccentric lady with her curly gray hair and great low hanging appurtenances that touch the sidewalk such as umbrella, packages held low-dangling and almost underhanging from a limp blue-veined marble white oldlady dear crazy finger and the low hem of her enormous oldlady greatcoat that looks like it was made to be a thick shroud to hide the atom bomb in in the middle of an airfield at dawn so nobody could tell what it looked like——this poor crazy old lady is like my aunts, from Winchendon, Maine, etc., from woods who come gawking out of the forest of the night to see great glittering New York and are so themselves the raw creatures of time and earth that in New York they are completely lost, don't lose their woods look, suffer on smooth sidewalks of concrete the same pain and awkwardness and womanly Gea-like distress and ecstatic agony that they suffer in pinecone rows beneath the cobwebby moons of New Hampshire or even (name it) Minnesota——and so are *really* doomed as in this case never not only to find a restaurant that will glowingly symbolize New York for them so they can go home and tell the glorious story in detail by the pantry window, the little one that looks out on the woodpile and one Arctic star——they won't even find any restaurant and'll wind up in a big beat Greek lunchcart six feet by ten because their feet will have given out and they'll capitulate to something in New York they wouldn't even think of accepting in Winchendon or Fergus Falls and never will they tell this shameful story without a true sense of forest sistership anyway in a nonexistent goddamn New York.

As far as young women are concerned I can't look at them unless I tear off their clothes one by one including this last girl (with her Ma) wearing a green bandana and cute little face and long newlook coat, and low heels, walks throwing her thighs loosely as though floppy and not as much control as her youth would indicate, and the big coat hides her figure lines but I figure her cunt is sweet, you get to it via white lace panties, and she be fine. This is almost all I can say about almost all girls and only further refinement is their cunts and will do.

FOLLOWING LEE KONITZ the famous alto jazzman down the street and don't even know what for——saw him first in that bar

on the northeast corner of 49th and Sixth Avenue which is in a
real old building that nobody ever notices because it forms the
pebble at the hem of the shoe of the immense tall man which
is the RCA Building——I noticed it only the other day while
standing in front of Howard Johnson's eating a cone, or rather
it was too crowded for me to get a cone and I was just standing
there and I was thinking "New York is so immense that it would
make no difference to anybody's ass if this building exists and is
old"——Lee, who wouldn't talk to me even if he knew me, was
in the bar (from which I've made many phonecalls) waiting with
big eyes for his friend to show up and so I waited on corner to
think and soon I saw Lee coming out with his friend who'd arrived and it was Arnold Fishkin the Tristano bassplayer——two
little Jewish gazotsky fellows they were really as they cut across
the street and Konitz in that manner that was forceful and I said
to myself "He can take care of himself even though he goofs
and does 'April in Paris' from inside out as if the tune was the
room he lived in and was going out at midnight with his coat
on"——(but I haven't heard him for weeks and weeks)——Both
of them real small among the crowds, Fishkin is five-foot-three
or such and Konitz five-six or such——cutting along so I follow,
and they turn west at 48th, I go across the street, temporarily
bemused first by a sign for a large furnished room with cooking
privileges and bath in a beat sort of hidden tenement smack in
the cunt of midtown but how can I live there or even be like Lee
Konitz cutting around the world of men and women when my
father told me to take care of my mother on his deathbed (these
my thoughts)——and where d'you think they go but Manny's
the music store of hipsters and Symphony Sid but which however at this moment (and strangely connected with the feeling
I had had while waiting for Konitz looking over big buildings
to see Atlantic clouds blowing in from sea and realizing sea is
bigger even than New York and that's where I oughta be) is
filled with a whole crew of sailors apparently in the store to buy
equipment for a big whaling oompapa Navy band! And Konitz
goes completely unrecognized by them although the Danny
Richman-like owners know Lee so well they don't say to him,
as I would, "Where you playing now, great genius?" they say
"When you leaving?" knowing already of his road plans——Lee
buys reeds or such in a box almost but not quite big enough

for an alto (and already packed and waiting for him) and then
he and Fishkin cut around the corner (as I follow through a
sea of crowds) to a mysterious marble lobby of big office buildings and cut right upstairs on foot and in fact a whole bunch of
hip looking guys are coming to do same (avoiding elevators)
and I study board to find out big deal on second floor or third
(walkup) floor but nothing, so the mystery remains though I
still say it must be a music school and this was typical of my lostness and loneliness, I go around dressed like a bum with a seedy
envelope, have no Fishkins to walk with, unless I'm drunk, and
spend my time watching the frenetic lights of Times Square (the
huge current *Quo Vadis* montage that goes up almost as high as
Astor Hotel roof, a blue-light woman tied to a stake that goes
higher than her head in blue-light eyries and neons burning a
painting of Rome that has in it eighteenth-century tenements
of Pittsburgh quite Georgian and also Greek Parthenons, *MGM
presents* on white neons then huge *QUO VADIS* lighting up,
first ordinary, then running, then blinking, then shivering, then
in the climax running-blinking-shivering as if coming) and this
sign is bigger than next door's *TEN TALL MEN* which is big
enough and biggest I ever saw till *QUO VADIS*, and I am lonely
and small in all this, goodnight.

A SAD PARK OF AUTUMN, late Saturday afternoon——leaves by
now so dry they make a general rattle all over and a little girl in
a green knit cap is squashing leaves against the wire fence and
then trying to climb over them——also mothers in the waning
light, sitting their kiddies in swing seats of gray iron and pushing them with grave and dutiful playfulness——A little boy in
red woodsman shirt stoops to drink water at the dry concrete
fountain——a flag whips through the bare bleak branches——
salmon is the color of parts of the sky——the children in the
swings kick their feet in air, mothers say *Wheee*——a trash wire-
basket is half full of dry, dry leaves——a pool of last night's rain
lies in the gravel; tonight it will be cold, clear, winter coming
and who will haunt the deserted park then?

IN FALL 1950 when I was so much on weed, three bombs a day,
thinking about unhappiness all the time I one night really carefully and high listened to George Handy's "The Blues" (Vicki

had his picture up on wall with mine and Charlie Parker's, *the mind, the hand, and me the heart* she said) but to really drift and I found it a big mocking sound and specifically the joy of the bop middle with Herby Steward is rejected for this modern or rather sadomasochistic modernity, on T I was able to see that Handy was sacrificing joy which existed naturally in his heart for the glooms and despairs and great disappointed deaths, the deadly loss of ego, the last acknowledgement of self——the music seemed to say "There are still a few things that you can cling to and this I supposed you should be soothed about——ha ha——but you won't even get that——though there's joy in our souls (bop interlude) we are nothing but shits and we'll all die and eat shit in graves and are dying now." Pretty powerful talk!

MORE AND MORE I THOUGHT OF CODY, I wanted to say to him "All of a sudden I remember a sunset when my father was driving me and his buddy Old Mike Fortier and I think young Mike my buddy was there too, in this old '34 Plymouth, to Nashua, N.H. to meet a circus man they were playing poker with, maybe it was W. C. Fields!, in the summertime, my father wearing a strawhat that with certain types of faces, say Jimmy Foxx's has gone completely out of American life, me noticing and never to forget again a certain house by the side of the road, a farmer's house or more exactly the house of a callous-fingered character of the woods like you must have in the West who always has two, three cords of wood stacked in his yard and maybe drives into town Saturday nights in his Essex that he uses the back of for loads of wood to buy the Sunday fun-nies, that kind of hodgepodge made-by-himself house and my thoughts ran along just about what I'm saying now eighteen years later; dreaming this, and also on the big inclusive event of the sinking sun, especially as it showed slanting and golden and all that in the grass, when suddenly Old Mike lit his pipe and puffed and this unforgettable inexpressively rich smell pervaded the car as they went right on talking: a smell that I remembered just tonight again, nothing less than a big man poking pudgy fingers at the bowl of his pipe on an ordinary afternoon in 1933 when probably you, at seven or six, were doing any one of the innumerable visions I have of you in Denver at all ages——a smell that wasn't so much a certain tobacco but arose like a genie from the fact that Old Mike had to do with its inception. The smell was Mike himself, my buddy's father, the big favorite of a mad gang my father had (all of them with wives, children, houses, just like you), who used to sneak up on one another, I remember sitting in the parlor listening to the old pre-Basil-Rathbone Sherlock Holmes on the radio with my father and sis and suddenly in kitchen I see a man creeping up like an Indian with twelve people creeping behind him from the kitchen door and it's a surprise party which rocks house (small rose-covered cottage, actually and no shit, next to a rickety grocery store, on West Street Lowell) till dawn, Big Mike was the leading maniac of the gang or that is at least the biggest most hearty *swearer*, shocked even the screeching ladies of this exclusive French-Canadian raucous madclub while another madcap (Monette) was actually the chief Indian creeper and screamer, I think in fact put on women's clothes and screamed like Finistra, but anyway at the same time Old Mike was also the most grave, sober, quiet and meditative one at other times, and was smoking his pipe thus when the memory was instilled in me by the same forces eighteen years ago which now drive me obsessively to remember. When a man puffs a pipe his eyes bulge over the smoking bowl into space, he seems to have sinus trouble and all such big adult wreckages and profound architectural failings that on the other hand couldn't possibly exist if the man wasn't a pillar of strength and didn't have huge belly to stand it; I had seen Mr. Fortier staring at me over his pipe with the same bulging eyes when I semi-tiptoed past his 'den' in the Fortier house, always fearful of disturbing the privacy of such an enormous father, he had ten kids, a three-hundred-pound wife and believe this: a sixteen-room house with a few old lady lodgers far off in the bowels somewhere, a house, with concomitant cellar, so vast, so unbelievable that I since dream of it as a boat floating to Boston and Greenland on a canal, not a rich house or manse or anything just an old New England monstrosity he'd bought for say ten thousand dollars smack in the middle of the wild Canuck tenements of Salem Street, always fearful that he would see me pass and then I'd have to say something which never came out without an effort so agonizing and personal to something lost in me that I'd go away grabbing my sweater and cursing myself . . . but now he was sitting beside me, fatherly, I had no cause to be scared though as I say I always felt he liked my old man but not me, that something separated me from those qualities in my old man that made him love the name Duluoz, and that 'something' was lost to me forever, I'd never get it back even to examine it, and in fact I realized it was all a big paranoia of mine (even then you see!). Oh Lord have pity on our souls——and the pipesmoke suddenly became the fulfillment of the fact that this tremendous father was and had been all along accepting me, thus, following the events of yesterday . . . the loneliness . . . the (as Proust says God bless him) 'inexpressibly delicious' sensation of this memory——for as memories are older they're like wine rarer, till if you find a real old memory, one of infancy, not an established often tasted one but a *brand new one!*, it would taste better than the Napoleon brandy Stendhal himself must have stared at . . . while shaving in front of those Napoleonic cannons. . . ."

SUBURBAN CITY "FOOD SHOP" of which there is none bleaker than this one in the gloomy Jamaica night——the *MERIT Food Shop*, written in green neon (greon) in the window, *MERIT* is, and *Food Shop* in orange——now why?——You pick up your ticket cafeteria style corning in, the thing rolls and rings. The floor is all shades of brown and yellow "pebbled" marble with little thin metal lines separating various sections; covered with dirty napkins (from metal boxes on counter), cigarette packs, clusters of sawdust tracked from behind counter——Two waitress-type girls who just came in of course brighten it up and make me think of Hartford though I look mad with beard, shirts—— What's so bleak——Jamaica itself; secondly the cold sad Sunday midnight; nobody knows anybody else, not even as in 23rd Street Rikers, suburban cities are centers of vast residential districts so big out-of-town people couldn't conceive——people in here live miles and miles apart, are going through Jamaica in the transportation system only——The coffee is given to you intact with cream, always too much cream——Further dark faced types in topcoats suddenly begin talking about Columbia game with counterman (as though they were fraternity presidents with golden hair)——Inconceivably quiet switchmen from Long Island Railroad (L.I.R.R.)——Outside all I can see of the night is a green neon clock that says *WATCH HOSPITAL* around the

time which is in red——A tall usher-like thin boy came in for
coffee and hamburger——going home now theater's closed (and
can't even cook one in his own kitchen), going home along cold
suburban street with wind and dry leaves and dark——

This place is bleaker than any Rikers and of course any lunchcart because there's nothing to define it with——how can I describe this table top I'm on, this marble plytex with metal rim?

Ah fuckit, I'll go home and think in the dark.

The first desk on Phoebe Avenue——first brown desk——was
placed against the wall in the room that served as the dining room only when we had company——the furniture still had
chalkmarks under made by me and Nin and Gerard——The
brown, in fact mahogany darkness of this my first study——and
this first desk——window was on left, lace, facing Mrs. Quinn——

Whether her cherry trees were in bloom or not it was brown
in this room——when my father had rheumatism in it the sheets
of his sickbed made it gray——now this is an "inexpressibly
delicious" old memory like old port——nothing in California
matches it. I rolled my glassies for the first time on the jagged
wood of the desk——it was when I got idea for racing, they
meandered a race under my eyes——it was a gray day——the
whole idea of the *Turf* must have come to me like (as just now
and not since 1948) that so-seldom experience of seeing my
whole life's richness swimming in a palpable mothlike cloud, a
cloud I can really see and which I think is elfin and due really
to my Celtic blood——coming only in moments of *complete
inspiration*. . . . In my life I number them probably below
five——at least on this level——

Followed by those first strips of race results, the *green ones*——
the Turf was inexpressibly connected with masturbation as
Haunted Memories like this must be.

ST. PATRICK'S CATHEDRAL: most striking of the windows and
I didn't expect strikingness at this late hour——is at upper front
left——a lonely icy congealed blue with streaks of hot pink——
little blue holes——painted with an immeasurable blue ink, *noir
comme bleu*, black like blue, I was going to say three Apostles
but there are only two, third slot is not figure, is three one-
third-size endisced figures almost like holes in skating ice——but
with a winter swamp water full of mill dyes and midnight——no

sky has had the color of this glass, and I know skies——all other
windows here now dimming except this——It faces East, must
be amazing tomorrow morning——faces East like my poor hospital window——Lord, I scribbled hymns to you——the other
windows grow rich, brown, dark, secret, get better with age of
light like wine with age of Time——The halo round the head
of first figure remains bright and shining in the now general
midnight blue of the window——halo of second figure is more
humble——this window is secreted away and almost has same
color as windows at halfway point turningpoint of stairs in
old Victorian homes——concealed too——Only now I begin
to notice the green——The similar triple window behind and
above altar is now gone into the night——but not here. St. Jean
Baptiste is smaller than this but I think more holy because of
Canadians' Sunday morning at 5:30 like Marie Louise——Now
the window darkens to match the great transformations without, refracting them inward to these kneelers, who can't stand
ordinary glare of life in their musty meditations and guilty
anxieties——People come to church for guilt now——Ah, a
French insurance salesman over there (from Centralville)——
from Forest Hills *vraiment*——an older Pat O'Brien in dark almost priestlike suit to my left——clutches prayer book devoutly,
closes eyes with matching fervor——O huge sorrow!

The altar of St. Joseph at my right a symphony in brown——
his brown vestments with the traditional waist cord, the flickering brown candle racks——the brown confessional in back in
its swarming nameless church shadows where old men whisper
laryngitisly in your ear, with a rich wine, portwine red velvet
drape and somewhere a priest is eating grapes——A curious
young woman in a muskrat fur coat is hanging around there
lighting candles——What's her truck with St. Joseph?——he
who now with demure plaster countenance, holding the in-
substantial child with feet and face too small and body too doll
like, presses cheek against the painted curls, supports in midair
lightly against his brown breast the Son, with unstraining but
rather greeting hand, downward looking into candles, agony,
the foot of the world, all the angels and calendars and spirey
altars behind him, eyes lowered to a mystery he himself wasn't
hipped to yet he'll go along in the belief that poor St. Joseph
was clay to the hand of God (statue), a humble self-admitting

truthful Saint——with none of the vain freneticisms of Francis, a Saint without glory, guilt, accomplishment or charm——
a self-effacing grave and demure ghost in the Arcades of
Christendom——he who knew the desert stars, and spat with the
Wise Men in back of the barn——arranger of the manger, old
hobo saint of haylofts and camel trails——Old lady in black coat
and gray hair (Ma Tante Justine) socks the necessary action, the
coin, into the candlelight concession and Joseph acknowledges
with that ungraspable imperceptible sigh of statues——

Now my holy blue window, the one like the window at 94-21
that made me so often think there was a weird blue light in the
railyards which could only be seen from halfway down the hall
stairs when actually it, the window, was only taking the ordinary
corner streetlamp which was in line with railyards and giving
it inky blue hues like that apocalyptic-end-of-the-world blue
light, the light of subterranean stars, we've all seen in tunnels
especially subway tunnels——that window, as suddenly now I
hear the chorus of prayers in a rickety mumble repeating the
moans of an accredited adjuror either upstairs or so far up front
that it's inconceivable to my senses like some of the distances
in the West——all I see is five spaced ordinary ladies, only two
of them side by side, and it can't be them make this ghostly
prayer——It's a novena in the innards of the church itself, it is
locked in the stone and released each night at this time by the
wizardly prayers of some old hooknosed ribbon clerk who acts
like a divining rod withal to draw the innate sound out of the
churchy-twisted Chicago stone (I have just noticed that the
marble squares in the floor are also separated by metal rims like
in the MERIT Food Shop last night)——The novena hushke-
hush sounds like this: agony in the hands, fakery, fear of moaning, so a general communal drone that takes care of the moan-
sound when it rises en masse in these stone arches that were
made and shaped to transform irritable mumbles into longfaced
groans——Far off across the sea of seats and the continent of the
altar, among Gothic holes and openings, I see a parade of hand
claspers and one flitting wispy ravenclad boy priest who wheels
to kneel and coughs politely——There, too, I see flickers like
the fires of Hannibal's camp across the plains of Rome——This
window is now gone dead with the night, woe unto the last
halo, it didn't seem possible——The leading novena voice is like

a woman's——can it be? Before me kneeling is a humble little woman in a black cloth coat and cheap fur collar, with black beret, ordinary hair, praying like the ladies, the unobtrusive un-showingoff ladies of Lowell especially the French ones who live above the Royal Theater and wait for their husbands to come home Saturday night from Manchester, from over yonder over the gray woods where the crow caws——

Many years ago in a church just like this but smaller, ho-lier, more venerated by hearts, I came with hundreds of little death-conscious boys of St. Joseph Parochial School (church always filled us with the knowledge of the gloom and horror of funerals even if we had learned to reconcile ourselves to the shame and sadness of confession, confirmation exercises, what all)——We circled in orderly terror and also boredom beneath the great arches that weren't high like this yet seem the same height and from which depended the longest lamp chain of my experience——there are some actually that long here but only unobtrusive at sides and supporting unimportant side lamps shaped unimpressively like circular breadboxes with Jap lantern sides and eight-disc bottoms shining (fragrant glimmer)——The one at St. Jean was the main lamp of the entire church, an immense chandelier of the house of God greater than chande-lier in anybody's including City Hall house——Always this kind of girl in church: unbearably pretty, unbearably neat, carry-ing unbearably crisp and crinkling package, unbearably stylish and in gay but not wild colors——this one white silk kerchief well flowed and green coat——and unbearably sharp clean high heels——but I always think: "You're too unbearable for anything ——the least or most of which is love or the house of the real dying God——Where do you go, doll of the bathtub? to Pur-gatory to clean up some more——to hell to burn neatly——to heaven for snow——to church to add fresh snow to the snow of your soul?——Have you sinned? can it be? Is the white snow of church respectability what you come for?" But this is wasteful speculation——Now in Mexico, on San Juan Letran, I know churches where little barefooted girls in rags kneel in dust—— and in Lowell, though, you'll see crispy-clean in church, she's everywhere, I don't know what she's up to, who she's trying to drive away (me I guess)——speculation——

Slam! the great slam of a pew box in echoey church——it

sounds like the sad gun of eternity being fired in the name of mortal imperfection——a vicious priest performs the rite to see effects——he mocks those who're afraid to try slamming——and vanishes on shroudy feet to tear the chicken at rectory *nappes* with a spot-splash of wine and a joke about the great syphilitic Pope who was squeezed into his coffin but never said a word against the church——An American flag and a nameless crazy Steinberg flag hang above——out front, Easter Day 1950, I covered parade with Sara and United Press——My life——O vast beginning pillars of the knee-rest's base——O marble bottoms of stony heaven——Here in St. Patrick's they have rubber mats for knees, no tortured wood. A fag television dancer in white turtleneck and sport jacket swishes down the aisle——But this reminds me, all these women indiscriminately scattered in a church at evening, of Lowell and the way they've swallowed priest's cock in that humility of theirs that commands me to desist and know the "fear of God" and they love funerals, I don't; they love wax, love musty indoors and innards of bloody altars——

The men in here are horses' asses——And now finally the window is so *out* that the bottom glass reflects *brownly* the lights that just came on for an imminent service.

These glass windows refract NIGHT too for now I see nothing but the rich dim recollections of what at dusk was a Rembrandt barrel of ale in a Dublin saloon when Joyce was young, the hint so vague it's like people in a dark room wearing phosphorescent rims and all involved in some drama so tragic that the light of day can't shine on it——only the inward light of night——"A holy and wholesome thought to pray for the dead so that they may be removed from sin"——from Maccabees. The priest speaking: now he quotes MacArthur Old Soldier crap——mixing theological verities with today's headlines, blah, blah, I now go out, tired, into my own thoughts and have no place to go but find my road.

HIPSTER, SOUP, didn't get any bread because he's so habitually thin can't absorb it——just soup——tall, thin, dark long hair almost bun in back——coolly stirs soup, tries it for heat, casts scornful glance around, starts——still blowing——wearing (now really deep in eating, all he needs is little soup) a sharp-cut lapel suit with tieless yellow sport shirt——hornrim glasses, mustache——his curiosity is thinly veiled in a sophisticated glare, done side-eyed y'see——A guy sat opposite him, he glances coldly into his face, other ain't looking so studies him a little longer coldly——table manners flawless——now he's interested in guys open paper upside down on table——looks quickly over a shoulder pad to notice sources of noise and voices——wipes himself with napkin using both hands daintily——now lights his cigarette, as he came in he threw the crumpled pack (disdain-fully) on the table before taking big hipster winter blue coat off——now he's finished, just came in to eat, warm up some, puts it on, goes——reaching in pants pockets in that nameless gesture men have in topcoats when they so reach——glossy hair——to Eighth Avenue.

Now exactly in his place without knowing who was there before, the poor lost history of it, sits a pretty brunette with violet eyes and a flowing purple drape coat——takes it off like stripteaser, hangs it on hook (back to it) and starts eating with pathetic delicate hunger her hot plate——deep in thought while she chews——wearing cute little white collar draped over black material and three pendants, pearls; lovely mouth; she just blew her nose daintily with a napkin; has private personal sad man-ners, at least externally, by which she makes her own formal existence known to herself as well as polite social cafeteria watchers she's imagining, otherwise why the act though it is genuine. She took a bite off the fork and THEN and how she'd *blow!* she licked the side of it in a slight furtive movement of pleasure, her eyes darting up to see if anybody noticed this——as her hunger is appeased she grows less interested in outward manners, eats more rapidly, has sadder more personal bemuse-ments with herself over the general rim and consciousness of her cunt which is in her lap as she sits——

She breaks my heart just like X. and all my women have broke my heart (just by looking at her)——that's why women are impractical for me——Now, as I say these great grave things, she turns and watches a Naval officer leaving with open flirta-tious interest but he didn't acknowledge, just flapped his coat like Annapolis or a shroud and left, and she watched anyway as if for the benefit of any girls *watching her dig a man*, as if she was in the WACS, or made little jokes about the shortage

of "available" men when all the time the good men like me
peek at their souls like this unnoticed ha ha——An ugly woman
is sitting opposite her; my girl is bored, looks away, abstractly
primps her hair——Her nose has that interesting little curved-
ness that emphasizes the plump point pearshape of her cheeks
and general Indian melancholy or Semitic womanliness——her
fingers are long, long and extremely thin and breakable and I
bet cold——warm heart no doubt about it——Now, finished, she
hangs to look around, tosses her head to see, coughs, feels her
own chin, is bemused as if on a cock and same as in sun doing
wash——with that little ravenous birdy *attention* to things, to
special female-comprehension things——yet all of a sudden she's
drowned in sorrow looking at mirror, at herself and also just
into space——but snaps, darts around the head to see people,
couples, women and men (always interested exclusively in the
man's bearing with big coat and proudness at the wintry entrance and the woman's acceptance of this and flaunt of it at
cafeteria with birdy dignities and knowledges and primps of
her own while man dreams in his own dream of himself with a
self-satisfied smile) and further she's aware at this very moment
of the sheen of the ebony-latex tabletop with its innumerable
microscopic scratches but she's really thinking of something
I'll never know, since I was in the Cathedral while what she's
thinking about probably took place. She lingers a long time for
a girl——waiting?——cold?——sad, lonely?——I can't help her, I'm
doomed to these universal watchfulnesses——and a whore or
two——With her head down inexpressible purity shows in her
face, like a young Princess Margaret Rose, and beauty, slant-
eyed young girl beauty with freshness of the cheeks and upward-
sending rosy-glow lips——she's reading a library book! and
sighing!——a freshness that comes from her lips being chastely
compressed and is aura'd from the tendernesses of her neck just
beneath the ear from the fragile white breakable susceptible
cool brow which will never know wild sweats, just cool beads
of joy——as she reads she fondles the creases that run from her
nose to her mouth each side with doubly applied fingertips and
is really digging her own face and beauty as much as I——turns
the bookpages with small finger, so long, ridiculously far out——
the book is a Modern Library!——therefore she's probably no

dumb little book-of-the-monther typist but maybe a hip young intellectual girl from Brooklyn waiting for Terry Gibbs to pick her up and take her to Birdland. She'd melt for me in two minutes, I can tell by looking at her. Big horrible middleaged Jewish couple sitting now with her——like invading Ammonites. Now she goes——beautifully, with simplicity. It no longer makes me cry and die and tear myself to see her go because everything goes away from me like that now——girls, visions, anything, just in the same way and forever and I accept lostness forever.

Everything belongs to me because I am poor.

I HAVE *RÊVES*, abed on a third-story tenement porch and any moment I can turn over, ruin the balance of the corrupted porch and fall down with the works or I can turn over and fall out of bed through the rickety railing——This porch kills me——it's like Moody Street above Textile Lunch porch——The tenement, O woe, is in middle of woods with Philippinewars and also "Dracut"——Mike and Jeannette and Rita mostly are there——I am ill, thus bed, as in Margaret Cole ill-on-porch-but-first-story dream——these woods are green and belong to that up-and-down hilly rickety village by the lakes which associates with the Horace Mann hill and the *S.S. Dorchester* at foot of it.

And day before an incredibly exciting perfect dream——I was told to find my way back to the Kingsbridge Hospital——started by way (out of same spectral Pawtucketville two weeks ago sprouted Lowell-center skyscrapers) of Mt. Vernon or Crawford Street, on hill part that leads to pines of "North Lowell" like——and Road became one of these brand new oiled sand roads out by places, hills where I did some dream-sliding and actual three-year-old real-life-rolling on wheels——through such woods, a few "American" cars going by, smack leading into the Hospital, where the walls, the doors (the same place three weeks ago bombarded by artilleries) and same place where those patients joked with me in a big room with all complicated jokes and wheelchairs, whirlpool baths (and that artillery dream, we started at hospital but moved up to the front, to night, MacArthur, boom, enemy land and town, but made our way back). This "Gardner" sand road goes among woods where (near sandbank) my Ma and I once moved to tenement and similar to Mike's rickety porch one——among woods where also are hills that begin in Bloodworth's Highlands and go all the way to immense hills of Gardiner, Maine via sunsets and Norths that go even further to Greenland of pumps, via canals, the canal being that which Fortiers and us in Gershom but also Salem house floated to Boston, a spectral canal, far from dull, and in any case big house like Lowell high school basement, Salem basement, Paramount theater apartments (on Times Square) so vast and sunny and the one big high-ceiling rich glassy-on-the-floor huge oneman room Cody had to do with in last night's dream before our rendezvous with the sensualists who had girls, weed, and that Mexico apartment (Medellín) tablecloth (that fleecy soft bed and soft table, what a joy to recall it! damn!——).

This Philippine wood round Mike's house is the one in the bigyard Horace Mann dream and is just like Hospital grounds, *pale* green, afternoon green (Ah that relaxin at Kingsbridge! talk about your Touros and Camarillos), the dream of the westbank Mike-first Hudson River homestead, the trees of Versailles——in which Duke Gringas was and later real infantry movements and one time a jungle clearing with snipers and straw——the Philippine, or Mike woods are I think different level than Chet Vaska Lakeview also Central City *North* woods and maybe even rolling hills of Ioway with cops and gun and connected to another part of the Hudson westbank in redbrick——Hospital whirlpool jokes like the cruel needle jests of sadistic docs in Japan war and in fact in Japan itself when I saw that Jap boy at dark dusk in cold London hat——O the vast arcades of that London! with my father! and Liverpool gang nights. Tony Bero was with Duke Gringas.

The sensualists were Richman and that Glennon guy I lived near where the mattress fires took place, 40th Street behind big high Times Square where I always find my show on a glittering apple-pie corner, show's inside and is always Brooklyn one (with high terrible balcony) that I reach via Lynn-like brownbrick leaving behind sad Nashua sorrows where my father is either onelegged or is Louise himself in a truncated house and the Nashua is like Asbury Park and the towns of Nin and Paul in the South (because of one Main Street) where recently I had an affair with a girl and handled a rake on bonfire night——that country goes back via Vaska northwoods and King and jagged

Colorado namelessly I guess you might say to that damn tragic dark pump at the bottom of the hill where potatoes are peeled, Oh Slave!

AND BETHESDA, AN EARLY NIGHT I SPENT thinking about my FATE, how it was impossible for me to die (with loss, that is) because of charts, had-to-do's, SUPREME REALITY, and it was raining out; was that first, no *second* ward when allowed myself to think in *fate* terms, apparently because I was soon gettin out and back to merchant marine——aware of Maryland, the Maryland forest in the night, rain on Wilderness, went in bathroom to smoke and think just as recently at Kingsbridge I'd go shit and brood——So later I grew conscious of wrinkled cigarette packs and Arthur Godfrey on sunny porch (which was earlier nuttier pinetree hatch) like real hungup patient until guy said "Cock weather" to change my concepts——that Nashua or Kinston Main Street, America littleboys dig towns just as simple as that, Lowell has areas, New York boroughs.

OH THAT CODY DREAM, last night he was all attentive as he never really or only rarely is——in a suit, suits always look new on him, with hair wild and bushy not because uncombable but had been ruffled in the coffee drinking, gabbling-at-bars excitement of the broad crazy dark and dusty New York night—— Now we were on a sidewalk, like Paris sidewalk of Buferd-park-movie-house dream, saying goodbye to a segment or group and then heading out together to later, wilder parties——as I say, like Errol Flynn and Bruce Cabot but ever so much beater and stranger, really less simple and less inscrutable. How tragic the sidewalks were——along the order of Julien's when he in a dream came back or was back from death in an apartment house with an elevator and his mother sweet, white-faced, was willing for once to talk to me, the tragedy then was in the very sidewalk out front. In fact Cody and I were in that general vicinity which is like Sheridan Square (FBI tea dream), perhaps the Deni Bleu one of that sun-slanting afternoon in Nick's when he got back from Brazil in real life but really a new Sheridan Square I've been getting lately (where are these messages from?) which I think is connected with Danny Richman but positively connected (with sad Greek lunchcarts I dug 1939)

with a girl——that pale sweet girl who lay like a great soft oyster
(Bev Watson) on a couch after unspoken agreement she disrobe
and give herself to my hand although by that time scene had
shifted from Sheridan Square to a house in Maine or Lowell.
Next Cody and I were in dark hallway of the sensualists; party
was up; I arranged for girls; Cody, for first time, followed me
and let me do things. In other dreams when I go San Francisco
to see him, and we descend the mighty hills in a car, one time he
fell out of the car in one of his attempts to show driving tricks, I
closed my eyes exasperatedly to die but he miraculously jumped
back into the car and righted it——in San Francisco I follow
him, or alone go up long Babylonian stairs (ferry, too) like the
stairs in D. W. Griffith's Feast of Belshazzar in *Intolerance* to
find the girls over the ridge and down to the swimmingpool,
the little sweet Italian group I never refound in m' dreams but I
think already met and lost recently in real life——There sat Cody
and I——I was looking at tablecloth——thinking "I am tired, we
do too much, I must run away from Cody to ever rest but now
he's following me *I'll never can do it.*" We're high on T and
staring at wild designs of tablecloth which are also dear familiar
lunchcart check designs under the ceiling fans of Oklahoma
roadhouses as well as Mexico City tablecloth. Main thing, Cody
had given up and was following not me, but anybody sweet and
good and kind in the world, like he'd died and came over to
see me before his departure, dammit, into eternity. This was a
dream last night. And Cody let others do talking, for once was
a smiling and bemused listener, like Irwin or everybody——He
said something: "I'll only be back for a short time but while I'm
here you've got to take care of me, understand?——you've got
to see I don't get lonely, I don't know anybody in that cafeteria
of yours on Fourth Street and Bowery. I don't ever go to those
high balcony movies on V-Square, Brooklyn is too mad, the Els
confuse me, the canals, the little white houses, the ships east
or west and that pump at the foot of the hill where you peel
potatoes I have nothing to do with it——I'm in your hands entirely as you were in Frisco when I jumped back in the car going
fullspeed——I want to meet people and gurls——take me to the
white one, the soft one you had on your couch there——Oh
this is a cold dark town, man." We talked and smoked with the
sensualists. Once I had a dream that a party was going on in a

bleak little house standing all by itself in a dump lot the other side of the Brooklyn Bridge, old eighteenth-century brick house with warehouse and gables, and inside an orgy was going on, there were Negro sailors, Irwin Garden, a girl on her knees and suddenly the Brooklyn Bridge was burning and these people didn't care, only the wild bourgeois who ran across the Bridge risking their lives with dogs under their arms. This Cody didn't understand; he understood only Frisco and those soaring wild whitehouse hills where my father once lived and rejected me, the time I said *boo!* in his cellar there at what I thought was a ghost and it was only Mr. and Mrs. Old and he was gambling with the fellers he used to know in the redbrick alley between B. F. Keith and Bridge Street Warehouse Lowell, Mass. So I not only took care of Cody's understanding but protected him from horrors which he, unlike me, was not capable of absorbing. Yes he was strange, childlike, and as if, as I say, he had died or been otherwise crippled in S.F. and had come to see me prior to some sad journey from which he never was going to come back——so naturally I took advantage, went to pains to arrange the best party with the sensualists, it was a sort of dark ambiguous flop but Cody and I jumped and made it. This dream followed the one about Crawford Street in Lowell and the Kingsbridge Hospital, as if replacing it for special reasons when I decided to sleep some more. The next time I've a dream about Cody and they're rare I will note it: but now just let the only other rememberable dream of Cody I have serve our growing purposes——this is going to be the complete Cody——

Inseparably entwined with Joe my boyhood chum, I had flash of that many-windowed wooden cell-house along Third Avenue and also in Joe's barn and Julien's jailship connecting with Cody——but this occurred when I wished to harken back to our discussion at the sensualists (I say sensualists because one of them was that unspeakably sensual fag from Glennon's who talked with that young actor and me, part Rance the hipster, part more desperate than that, somehow a Cody hero)——when I said in effect to Cody "If you worry about my attitude or have in the past towards homosexuality don't worry now, I have a new attitude" (a Ritz Yale Club party where I went with a kid in a leather jacket, I was wearing one too, and there were hundreds of kids in leather jackets instead of big tuxedo Clancy millionaires and I yelled over to a gang "Buddy Van Buder?" thinking it was Buddy Van Buder but they only smiled, cool, and everybody was smoking marijuana, wailing a new decade in one wild *crowd*) "——not only that party but other things that also make me sad though but I'm fundamentally opposed on principle and because I don't like it——but think how strange and charming it is that I understand it now and in fact there was a blond *amant* at Josephine's, man——" To get on with Denver: there was a cartoon moon shining over a boardfence, a wild drugstore ice cream crowd on the corner, somewhat Reservoir Hill-like, ricketiness, and then these tremendous brawling bars to which Cody and I repaired for gabbling talks——apparently in my early dreams of Cody it was bars not T-pads of sensualists I envisioned——as if Cody and I were construction workers not dissipates who dissipate so much it becomes a principle and finally a philosophy and finally a revelation——That Denver had elements of Big Slim Washington and New Orleans, had a strange New Haven empty lot with three-row house where I lived (near trolley line, near water, where innumerable small craft sit in dry canals and people celebrate along boardwalk which faces a dry sea with terrible raveled muds and spiders but in rain big tidal waves and storms and naval battles start offshore, flashing Pow! in the rainy sea)——and a New Orleans, née Florida, which also has MexCity in it and I was in Mexico City with Cody. I've dreamed of Dave Sherman on a gray student afternoon in Mexico City which was in fact half on the Columbia campus where I'd been flunking classes and goofing for years, cutting classes in science for El rides into unknown upper New Yorks and failing to salute the flag in front of the library with other boys who ate regularly in the cellars that were vast like Lowell High School cellars. I know it isn't true, but it seems to me Cody was stealing a suit during that happy afternoon in MexCity with Sherman. These are the pitiful few dreams of Cody I have——is that all?

A GREAT AMERICAN INTERSECTION like the ones I will now go find on the road to Cody with a White Tower on one corner, diner (new blue cute kind with woman proprietor-waitress says "Come on let's go" to half-drunk eccentric) opposite, small beat white Mobilgas station another corner (topped by red

neoned flying redhorse, becluttered, white curbs soiled, car for
sale, sign says *Complete wheel alignment service* and *Brakes re-
lined*, tires for sale, used, including one vast graypainted truck
tire), outdoor vegetable and fruit stand on the other (*ice cold
watermelon, red like fire, we plug 'em*).

Traffic lights shuttle this wild restless travel, cars nudging
around impatiently and even hitting dips near sewers to do
so, panel trucks, taxis, big trucks all mixed with cars, a four-
direction confusion and anger and also buses, tooting, wheeling, jumping by, sending up fumes, buses growling, squeeking
to stop, massing, surging, occasional sad pedestrians completely
lost——a more interesting intersection further? Mainly, though,
this is, a sad *white* outside-of-town intersection openspaced,
stuccoed like buildings on Arapahoe Street in Cody's Denver,
this is the openspace whiteness which is always situated *exactly
halfway* between the country and downtown, so that when
you come in to a new city you always have to cross snowy suburban intersections like this——I've seen a building, originally
redbrick one-story warehouse, located exactly at this halfway
spot between the highways of the land and the dense buildings downtown and it was painted white but had failed and
the redbrick showed through——to make a startling sight in all
the pure hotdog roadstand and motel whiteness and in fact the
gravel is almost white in these nameless districts of U.S.A. Red
traffic light gives it a sense of rain; the green gives it a sense of
distance, snow, sand——

I GOT EXCITED, I thought I'd go to the Coast without money
anyway. I wrote a letter to Cody:

"My trip to Frisco at last to stay with you and talk
with you and really be with it 100% for any number of
inexpressibly delicious weeks you wish; beyond that even,
Josephine wants to come, she wants to hitch, adventures
etc. of young girl digging the road, she comes back via
Lushy-Mushky Bust Colo. for her Sis, of course Josephine wants to cuk 7 Fuck (what mistakes dear me cuk
7 Fuck would be SOME FUCK) and I was saying she
wants to fuck and fuck (fuck and fuck I meant to write
but didn't capitalize the 7) she wanted to fuck and fuck
or that is fuck and fuck and has or rather and has been

doing so (all this in imitation of you, you fool) and
or rather doing so, Oh for goodness sakes, here is the
sentence, Josephine wants to fuck and fuck and has been
doing so with Irwin and me regular as pie and spent 4
days with me giving skull and getting skull, Mac and girl
and me and everything and everybody but kitchen sink,
weekend climaxed by my bringing colored guitarist and
pianist and colored gal and all three women took off tops
while we blew two hours me on bop-chords piano, new
Marty bop-tapdanced, guitar bongoed and Mac fucked J.
on bed, then I switched to bongo and for one hour we
really had a jungle (as you can imagine) feeling running
around, and after all there I was with my brand new
FINAL bongo or rather really conga beat and looked up
from my work which was lifting the whole group (as if in
prophecy of the fact that you and I could be great jazz
musicians *among* jazz musicians) (they yelled GO) and
what do I see but this tall brown gal with a long white
gleaming pearl necklace hanging down between her
black tits clear to her black bellybutton, walking into
parlor on padding black feet, looking at me, etcetera.
Cody you are, I believe, my last remaining complete
great pal——I don't think I'll ever have another like you
for I might retire in (like Swenson) so far, or go crazy
or eccentric——of course somewhere along the line I'll
end up yakking with some wench in a black night, like
Louis-Ferdinand Céline, like those lonely soldiers who
come back from Germany with six-foot-ten-years-older-
than-them Isolde warbrides and argue with them in bleak
rooms over drugstores, in bars, on church steps in the
middle of the night in winter if you see what I mean, I
mean bleak, sad, really mated, hung, like Bull with June
or a lushy Josephine doll of course but aside from all
that, I can't think of anybody and that includes Swenson
with whom I talked last night and includes Irwin G.
who, undoubtedly the greatest, just doesn't give a shit
(like Rappaport, also tremendous), and certainly not
Hayes, Bull etc., anybody who knows the sum and
substance of what I know and feel and cry about in
my secret self all the time when I don't feel strong, the

sorrows of time and personality, and can therefore on
all levels make it all the way with me——who knows and
loves even jazz as I do, and digs it as I do, who's been
AROUND and then some. I'm completely your friend,
your 'lover,' he who loves you and digs your greatness
completely——haunted in the mind by you (think what
that means, try to reverse, say, supposing you referred all
your sensations to somebody and wondered what they
thought about it) (that settles it: this letter includes a
dream I had of you two, three nights ago), supposing
each time you heard a delightfully original idea or were
given such an image that makes the mind sing you
immediately slapped it over like one of those new office
roller files to check with the CODY THING, that is, the
Cody constellation, and then on another level checked
it emotionally like to measure its amounts of awe that
you would bring to it. Last night Swenson spoke at
such great length on Genet that I suddenly realized
(had innocently queried: 'And Genet? have considered
Genet?') he not only of course had considered Genet,
every work published to date and incidentally reports
brought to him personally by people who know him,
reports about some recent new shift in Genet's general
feeling or attack (and the reason I have no details is
because I wasn't listening, I was only dreaming over the
significance that overlayed or overlay the context because
it really to me was its rainbow) he even knew in detail
the characters of the books, the names of the great
mythological French queers of the underworld Paris,
Froufrou, Mimi, Ange Divine and the lot, every nuance,
like we know Buckle or Huck, knew them intimately, had
savored them at his longest and most hungup leisure on
nameless afternoons in that house which he now occupies alone 'cause his aunt died (and think!: he misses her!
'I've grieved just the proper amount on the surface of it
but it's rather——rather, you know——after, one DOES
realize, I *just did* wish I'd been nicer to her, that's all,
really') (finally, after a whole minute of his eyes struggling from their demure downward cast to turn over
to me, his face suffusing with a sudden blush that seems

to advertise his glances, writhing with his body one way
while his gorgeous enormous eyelids unfurled the other
way, in my direction, to reveal eyeballs in the act of
rolling with indescribably veiled languor, mixed with shy
shames and raptures of all kinds, as if from premeditated
evil depths, from long private preparations no man could
ever dream was possible to the mind, mincing deliciously
all over like this big lovely child that reads the Apocalypse, wrapping himself around doors, melting, like
Bloom, most like Leopold Bloom in a Dream, with his
huge expressive and excessive nose which is the indicator
of all his directions and etcetera the fingers). I dig
Swenson, I dig like you did, I dig jazz, a 1000 things in
America, even the rubbish in the weeds of an empty lot,
I make notes about it, I know the secrets; I dig Joyce and
Proust above Melville and Céline, like you; and I dig *you*
as we together dig the lostness and the fact that of course
nothing's ever to be gained but death; I only wanted to
tell you how great I think you are (after all). So hear my
plea——*write*——let me know if that attic's still open, for
the three, four weeks I be there; hip me to anything you
can think of. Don't give me up, I'm lost——especially
since her, I almost had no life in me this summer, it's
comeback (I think) and right now, on no more than
a hangover from last night (Josephine made a turkey,
Irwin and I invited Swenson, Danny Richman, Nardine,
Peaches Martin (!)——who's back playing guitar and singing folk songs in Village and separated from Hayes who
has 'black orchid' Indian girl in MexCity and fears she'll
find an 'amant more blond' while he pleads with medics
for operations, 40 others, Julien Love and his fiancée
and he immediately began breaking Josephine's expensive glasses with tosses over his shoulder and she doing
tit for tat and even more pretended casual but with her
own destruction not his so later I tackled Julien maybe
because of this but he had something like a fit, a rigid
trembling popeyed fit and had to be led out of pad,
Irwin wagging his finger at me, 'Julien is *weak*, leave
him alone' as if saying he was sick little boy, not tackle
him, and so on, and don't continue because you dig

Julien anyhow, in fact surmise if you will that on way out
he knocked over big hall table lamp and landlord got on
Josephine, you dig Julien anyhow and I think he's 'had
it,' I guess——) from this night, when also I got hi on
Mexshit with Danny Richman to Julien to Rappaport
to girls in general to etcetera (and all the time conscious
of this awful Newyorkitis, this incessant drinking and
talking always in a musty pad not even cool but drunk,
like when you were there last trying to make a W. C.
Fields show) (incidentally I've since dug Harry Levinski
and he told me stories about Huck in 1933, isn't that
real *choice?*), drunk and most of all all exhibitional like
a bunch of goddamn fools who can't grow up and
dig anything but themselves, that includes me, I need
the fresh winds of California, I start right after New
Year's——but from this night, and its hangover, to return,
I am conscious of my own personal tragedy, my sleep,
that is my room itself is haunted by it at night when I
sleep or wake from a series of restless desperate images,
catching myself in the act of shuffling the file cards of the
memory or the mind under the deck, aware also of the
tragedy, the loneliness of my mother. I have the persis-
tent feeling that I'm gonna die soon, only the feeling, no
real I think wish or 'premonition,' I feel like I've done
wrong, to myself the most wrong, I'm throwing away
something that I can't even find in the incredible clutter
of my being but it's going out with the refuse en masse,
buried in the middle of it, every now and then I get a
glimpse. I get so sick thinking of the years I wasted, especially 1949 after we returned from Frisco all that Watso-
nia and Boisvert and hangup——yes, now I know how
to understand life, I learned the hard way, etc., after
14 years trying——but why did I waste 1949 with false
understanding and bum kicks like the flatteries of J.
Clancy etc., why did I waste my beautiful MexCity on
paranoias, I could (like today) have gone out dressed
the way I like, casual, cool, no big author or even big
American or tourist or whatever, just go and mix with
the cats and get to know people, the really interesting
ones, like say the circles revolving around that mudhut

coffee-nutmeg-rum bar we had to jump over an open
sewer, an open gash of the lost corrupted lake of the
Aztecs to get to——Instead——Oh shit! never again Cody!
I *really* know now, you'll see, of course everything is fine
because I've won (you see I almost lost this summer, if I
had gone to Mexico with Julien instead of re-remember-
ing my soul in the hospital (Oh what things I have, or
could tell you about the hospital! what literatures out of
just that one month (remember the wheelchair letter?)
for my big personal knowledge Odyssey structure (this is
apart from objective fragments of my life to examine)——
with Julien, Mexico, drunk, June dying, I might have
gone under, that is, seriously, in the habit of dying and
started doing it and maybe even in the powerful gut
feeling I had (and still do, never had before, it makes
me lush) maybe even a habit itself, junk, from sheer need
to turn over before I kick the dog. But now I'm a big
seacaptain again, lookout——that is, faroff eyes in the gray
morning, and I think of Frisco, I think of the evening
I'm going to arrive, shh, I creep up the street taking in
not only every aspect possible all the sensations round
me but referring them to earlier personal tiptoeings
around my beloved and spectral and soon to be holy
Frisco——the neons, the mad neons, the soft, soft nights,
secret chop sueys in the air and I know a bar on Embarcadero where Oakland Mex Hipsters drink and blast
with 50¢ whores, it's near markets, I never told you,
but tiptoeing to your house, digging the street, digging
available indications of what's going on in your house
from a block away (actually understanding in myriad
rapid thought everything I sense as it stands in front
of me and activates all around, in portable breast shirt-
pocket notebooks slapping), advancing little by little to
the point of knocking on the door which will be exactly
like those hot summer afternoons when I used to
pretend that I was dying of thirst in the desert but an
Arab chieftain found me and took me to the hospitality
of his tent, and laid a glass of ice water in front of me,
but said 'You can only have it if you surrender your fort
and your men, and do it on your knees abjectly' and

I agree, bowing my head in tremendous heroic agony but seeing the glass, the dews of the foggy rim, the ice clinking, and plunging for it, raising it slowly to my lips, the forbidden drink, that moment of actually taking the first sip and appreciating water itself playinly, whee, wow, you know what I mean, that's how I'm gonna knock on your door which ain't any door.

Jack

P.S. Dear Evelyn,
I would have complied with your every wish immediately, in that letter of several months ago, if I'd had half a chance——between hospital, troubles, having to work and earn $ and everybody wants me to get drunk I had no idea how I'd ever get to Frisco or whether, in spite of Cody's desperation with regard to his loneliness on the level you mentioned, it was possible, wise, healthy, etc. for me to try to go any old way; but now I'm going to try it, in fact I wish I'd tried it then. Now if Cody doesn't tell me about his REAL troubles how can I know? Believe me, I suffer the same as Cody from not seeing him once in a while——and have to batter my head against the general emptiness when I want to explain something to somebody. So anyway Evelyn, I hope I'm still wanted; I'm Cody's friend, not his devil. Ain't you by the way about to run out of names for the kiddies? We never know where we're going.

Love, Jack D."

2

Around the poolhalls of Denver during World War II a strange looking boy began to be noticeable to the characters who frequented the places afternoon and night and even to the casual visitors who dropped in for a game of snookers after supper when all the tables were busy in an atmosphere of smoke and great excitement and a continual parade passed in the alley from the backdoor of one poolroom on Glenarm Street to the backdoor of another——a boy called Cody Pomeray, the son of a Larimer Street wino. Where he came from nobody knew or at first cared. Older heroes of other generations had darkened the walls of the poolhalls long before Cody got there; memorable eccentrics, great poolsharks, even killers, jazz musicians, traveling salesmen, anonymous frozen bums who came in on winter nights to sit an hour by the heat never to be seen again, among whom (and not to be remembered by anyone because there was no one there to keep a love check on the majority of the boys as they swarmed among themselves year by year with only casual but sometimes haunted recognition of faces, unless strictly local characters from around the corner) was Cody Pomeray, Sr. who in his hobo life that was usually spent stumbling around other parts of town had somehow stumbled in here and sat in the same old bench which was later to be occupied by his son in desperate meditations on life.

Have you ever seen anyone like Cody Pomeray?——say on a streetcorner on a winter night in Chicago, or better, Fargo, any mighty cold town, a young guy with a bony face that looks like it's been pressed against iron bars to get that dogged rocky look of suffering, perseverance, finally when you look closest, happy prim self-belief, with Western sideburns and big blue flirtatious eyes of an old maid and fluttering lashes; the small and muscular kind of fellow wearing usually a leather jacket and if it's a suit it's with a vest so he can prop his thick busy thumbs in place and smile the smile of his grandfathers; who walks as fast as he can go on the balls of his feet, talking excitedly and gesticulating; poor pitiful kid actually just out of reform school with no money, no mother, and if you saw him dead on the sidewalk with a cop standing over him you'd walk on in a hurry, in silence. Oh life, who is that? There are some young men you look at who seem completely safe, maybe just because of a

Scandinavian ski sweater, angelic, saved; on a Cody Pomeray it immediately becomes a dirty stolen sweater worn in wild sweats. Something about his tigerish out-jutted raw facebone could be given a woedown melancholy if only he wore a drooping mustache (a famous bop drummer who looked just like Cody at this time wore such a mustache and probably for those reasons). It is a face that's so suspicious, so energetically upward-looking like people in passport or police lineup photos, so rigidly itself, looking like it's about to do anything unspeakably enthusiastic, in fact so much the opposite of the rosy Coke-drinking boy in the Scandinavian ski sweater ad, that in front of a brick wall where it says *Post No Bills* and it's too dirty for a rosy boy ad you can imagine Cody standing there in the raw gray flesh manacled between sheriffs and Assistant D.A.'s and you wouldn't have to ask yourself who is the culprit and who is the law. He looked like that, and God bless him he looked like that Hollywood stunt man who is fist-fighting in place of the hero and has such a remote, furious, anonymous viciousness (one of the loneliest things in the world to see and we've all seen it a thousand times in a thousand B-movies) that everybody begins to be suspicious because they know the hero wouldn't act like that in real unreality. If you've been a boy and played on dumps you've seen Cody, all crazy, excited and full of glee-mad powers, giggling with the pimply girls in back of fenders and weeds till some vocational school swallows his ragged blisses and that strange American iron which later is used to mold the suffering manface is now employed to straighten and quell the long wavering spermy disorderliness of the boy. Nevertheless the face of a great hero——a face to remind you that the infant springs from the great Assyrian bush of a man, not from an eye, an ear or a forehead——the face of a Simón Bolívar, Robert E. Lee, young Whitman, young Melville, a statue in the park, rough and free.

The appearance of Cody Pomeray on the poolroom scene in Denver at a very early age was the lonely appearance of a boy on a stage which had been trampled smooth in a number of crowded decades, Curtis Street and also downtown; a scene that had been graced by the presence of champions, the Pensacola Kid, Willie Hoppe, Bat Masterson re-passing through town when he was a referee, Babe Ruth bending to a sidepocket shot on an October night in 1927, Old Bull Balloon who always tore greens and paid up, great newspapermen traveling from New York to San Francisco, even Jelly Roll Morton was known to have played pool in the Denver parlors for a living; and Theodore Dreiser for all we know upending an elbow in the cigarsmoke, but whether it was restaurateur kings in private billiard rooms of clubs or roustabouts with brown arms just in from the fall Dakota harvest shooting rotation for a nickel in Little Pete's, it was in any case the great serious American poolhall night and Cody arrived on the scene bearing his original and sepulchral mind with him to make the poolhall the headquarters of the vast excitement of the early Denver days of his life becoming after awhile, a permanent musing figure before the green velvet of table number one where the intricate and almost metaphysical click and play of billiard balls became the background for his thoughts; till later the sight of a beautifully reverse-Englished cueball leaping back in the air, after a cannonading shot at another ball belted straight in, bam, when it takes three soft bounces and settles back on the green, became more than just the background for daylong daydreams, plans and schemes but the unutterable realization of the great interior joyful knowledge of the world that he was beginning to discover in his soul. And at night, late, when poolhalls turn white and garish and eight tables are going fullblast with all the boys and businessmen milling with cues, Cody knew, he knew everything like mad, sitting as though he wasn't noticing anything and not thinking anything on the hard onlooker's bench and yet noticing the special excellence of any good shot within the aura of his eyeball and not only that, the peculiarities and pitiful typehood of every player whether some over-flamboyant kid with his eleventh or twelfth cigarette dangling from his mouth or some old potbellied rotation wizard who's left his lonely wife in a varnished studio room above a *Rooms* sign in the dark of Pearl Street, he knew it all.

The first to notice him was Tom Watson. Tom was a hunchbacked poolshark with the great moon blue eyes of a saint, an extremely sad character, one of the smartest well-known shots of the younger generation in the locality. Cody couldn't have been more than fifteen years old when he wandered in from the street. It was only that many years before, in 1927, that Cody was born, in Salt Lake City; at a time when for some

Godforsaken reason, some forgotten, pitiably American, restless reason his father and mother were driving in a jalopy from
Iowa to L.A. in search of something, maybe they figured to
start an orange grove or find a rich uncle, Cody himself never
found out, a reason long buried in the sad heap of the night,
a reason that nevertheless in 1927 caused them to fix their eyes
anxiously and with throat-choking hope over the sad swath of
brokendown headlamps shining brown on the road . . . the
road that sorrowed into the darkness and huge unbelievable
American nightland like an arrow. Cody was born in a charity
hospital. A few weeks later the jalopy clanked right on; so that
now there were three pairs of eyes watching the unspeakable
road roll in on Pa's radiator cap as it steadfastly penetrated the
night like the poor shield of themselves, the little Pomeray family, lost, the gaunt crazy father with the floppy slouched hat that
made him look like a brokendown Okie Shadow, the dreaming
mother in a cotton dress purchased on a happier afternoon in
some excited Saturday five-and-ten, the frightened infant. Poor
mother of Cody Pomeray, what were your thoughts in 1927?
Somehow or other, they soon came back to Denver over the
same raw road; somehow or other nothing worked out right
the way they wanted; without a doubt they had a thousand
unspecified troubles and knotted their fists in despair somewhere outside a house and under a tree where something went
wrong, grievously and eternally wrong, enough to kill people;
all the loneliness, remorse and chagrin in the world piled on
their heads like indignities from heaven. Oh mother of Cody
Pomeray, but was there secretly in you a lovely memory of a
Sunday afternoon back home when you were famous and beloved among friends and family, and young?——when maybe
you saw your father standing among the men, laughing, and
you crossed the celebrated human floor of the then-particular
beloved stage to him. Was it from lack of life, lack of haunted
pain and memories, lack of sons and trouble and humiliated
rage that you died, or was it from excess of death? She died
in Denver before Cody was old enough to talk to her. Cody
grew up with a childhood vision of her standing in the strange
antique light of 1929 (which is no different than the light of
today or the light when Xerxes' fleets confused the waves, or
Agamemnon wailed) in some kind of livingroom with beads

hanging from the door, apparently at a period in the life of old Pomeray when he was making good money at his barber trade and they had a good home. But after she died he became one of the most tottering bums of Larimer Street, making futile attempts to work and periodically leaving Cody with his wife's people to go to Texas to escape the Colorado winters, beginning a lifetime swirl of hoboing into which little Cody himself was sucked later on, when at intervals, childlike, he preferred leaving the security of his Ma's relatives which included sharing a bedroom with his stepbrother, going to school, and altar-boying at a local Catholic church, for going off to live with his father in flophouses. Nights long ago on the brawling sidewalks of Larimer Street when the Depression hobo was there by the thousands, sometimes in great sad lines black with soot in the rainy dark of Thirties newsreels, men with sober downturned mouths huddled in old coats waiting in line for misery, Cody used to stand in front of alleys begging for nickels while his father, red-eyed, in baggy pants, hid in the back with some old bum crony called Rex who was no king but just an American who had never outgrown the boyish desire to lie down on the sidewalk which he did the year round from coast to coast; the two of them hiding and sometimes having long excited conversations until the kid had enough nickels to make up a bottle of wine, when it was time to hit the liquor store and go down under ramps and railroad embankments and light a small fire with cardboard boxes and naily boards and sit on overturned buckets or oily old treestumps, the boy on the outer edges of the fire, the men in its momentous and legendary glow, and drink the wine. "Wheeoo! Hand me that damn bottle 'fore I knock somebody's head in!"

And this of course was just the chagrin of bums suddenly becoming wild joy, the switchover from all the poor lonely woe of the likes of Pomeray having to count pennies on streetcorners with the wind blowing his dirty hair over his snarling, puffy, disgruntled face, the revulsion of bums burping and scratching lonely crotches at flophouse sinks, their agony waking up on strange floors (if floors at all) with their mad minds reeling in a million disorderly images of damnation and strangulation in a world too unbearably disgusting to stand and yet so full of useless sweet and nameless moments that made them cry that they couldn't say no to it completely without committing some terrified sin, attacked repeatedly by every kind of horrible joy making them twitch and marvel and gasp as before visions of heart-wrenching hell penetrating up through life from unnumberable hullabalooing voices screaming in insanity below, with piteous memories, the sweet and nameless ones, that reached back to fleecy cradle days to make them sob, finally bound to sink to the floor of brokendown pisshouses to wrap around the bowl and maybe die——this misery with a bottle of wine was twisted around like a nerve in old man Pomeray's brain and the tremendous joy of the really powerful drunk filled the night with shouts and wild bulging power-mad eyes. On Larimer Street Cody's father was known as The Barber, occasionally working near the Greeley Hotel in a really terrible barbershop that was notable for its great unswept floor of bums' hair, and a shelf sagging under so many bottles of bay rum that you'd think the shop was on an oceangoing vessel and the boys had it stocked for a six months' siege. In this drunken tonsorial pissery called a barbershop because hair was cut off your head from the top of the ears down old Pomeray, with the same tender befuddlement with which he sometimes lifted garbage barrels to city disposal trucks during blizzards or passed wrenches in the most tragic, becluttered, greasedark auto body shop west of the Mississippi (Arapahoe Garage by name where they even hired him), tiptoed around a barber chair with scissor and comb, razor and mug to make sure not to stumble, and cut the hairs off blacknecked hoboes who had such vast lugubrious personalities that they sometimes sat stiffly at attention for this big event for a whole hour. Cody, Sr. was a fine gentleman.

"Well now say, Cody, how've been things in the hotel this summer; anybody I know kick the bucket or which, or seen Dan up at Chilean Jack's?"

"Can't talk right now Jim till I get the side of Bob's head done——hold on just a second whilst I raise up that shade."

And a great huge clock tocked these dim old hours away as young Cody sat in the stove corner (in cold weather) reading the comic pages, not only reading but examining for hours the face and paunch of Major Hoople, his fez, the poor funny easy chairs in his house, the sad sickening faces of his hecklers who always seemed to have just finished eating at the table, the whole pitiful interesting world in back of it including maybe a faint cloud in the distance, or a bird dreamed in a single wavy line over the boardfence, and the eternal mystery of the dialog balloon taking up whole sections of the visible world for speech; that and *Out Our Way*, the ragdoll rueful cowboys and factory workers who always seemed to be chewing wads of lumpy food and wrapping themselves miserably around fenceposts beneath the great sorrowful burdens of a joke; yet most blazing of all the clouds, the clouds that in the cartoon sky had all the nostalgia of sweet and haunted distance that pictures give them and yet were the same lost clouds that always called Cody's attention to his immortal destiny when suddenly seen from a window or through houses on a June afternoon, lamby clouds of babyhood and eternity, sometimes in back of tremendous redbrick smokestacks that were made to look like they were traveling and toppling on the first and last day of the world and its drowsy butterflies; making him think, "Poor world that has to have clouds for afternoons and the meadows I lost"; sometimes doing this or looking at the sad brown or green tint pictures of troubled lovers in sensual livingrooms of *True Confessions* magazine, his foretaste of days when he would grow up and spend useless hours looking at nudist magazines at the corner newsstand; sometimes, though, only fixing his eyes on the mosaic of the tiles on the barbershop floor where he'd long imagined each little square could be peeled back endlessly, tiny leaf by tiny leaf, revealing in little microcosmic encyclopedia the complete history of every person that ever lived as far back as the beginning, the whole thing a blinding sight when he raised his eyes from one tile and saw all the others like the dazzling crazy huge infinity of the world swimming. In warm weather he sat on the sidewalk on a box between the barbershop and a movie that was so completely beat that it could only be called a C- or a D-movie; the Capricio, with motes of dusty sunshine swimming down past the slats of the boxoffice in drowsical midafternoon, the lady of the tickets dreaming with nothing to do as from the dank maw of the movie, cool, dark, perfumed with seats, where bums slept and Mexican children stared, there roared the gunshots and hoofbeats of the great myth of the American West represented by baggy-eyed riders who drank too much in Encienega Boulevard bars galloping in the moonlight photographed from the back of a truck in California dirt roads, with a pathetic human plot you sometimes think is worked in to make everybody overlook who the riders really are. What disappointment little Cody felt never having a dime, or eleven cents to see the show; not even a penny sometimes to spend all the time he wanted selecting a chocolate candy from a lovely becluttered counter in a poor dim candy store run by an old Syrian woman in a shawl where also there were celluloid toys gathering dust as those same immortal clouds passed over the street outside; the same disappointment he felt on those nights when he sat amidst the haha-ing harsh yellings of those bums under the bridge with the bottle, when he knew that the men who were rich tonight were his brothers but they were brothers who had forgotten him; when he knew that all the excited actions of life which included even the pitiful getting of the night's wine by his father and Rex led to the grave, and when suddenly beyond the freightyards towards the mountain darkness inhabited by great stars, where nevertheless and amazingly in a last hung dusk a single flame of the sun now making long shadows in the Pacific lingered high on Berthoud's mighty wall as the world turned silently, he could hear the Denver & Rio Grande locomotive double-chugging at the base of a raw mountain gap to begin the train order climb to the dews, jackpines, arid windy heights of the mountain night, pulling the sad brown boxcars of the world to distant junctions where lonely men in mackinaws waited, to new towns of smoke and lunchcarts, for all he knew as he sat there with his ragged sneakers stuck in the oily yard and among the sooty irons of his fate, to the glittering San Francisco fogs and ships. Oh little Cody Pomeray if there had been some way to send a cry to you even when you were too little to know what utterances and cries are for in this dark sad earth, with your terrors in a world so malign and inhospitable, and all the insults from heaven ramming down to crown your head with anger, pain, disgrace, worst of all the crapulous poverty in and out of every splintered door of days, if someone could have said to you then, and made you perceive, "Fear life but don't die; you're alone, everybody's alone. Oh Cody Pomeray, you can't win, you can't lose, all is ephemeral, all is hurt."

Old Bull Balloon (speaking of loneliness and the diaphanous ghost of days) a singularly lonely man, and most ephemeral, along about one of these years went broke and became so poor that he went in on a ridiculous partnership with Pomeray. Old Bull Balloon who usually went around wearing a poker-wrinkled but respectable suit with a watch chain, straw hat, Racing Form, cigar and suppurated red nose (and of course the pint flask) and was now fallen so low, for you could never say that he could prosper while other men fell, that his usually supposititious half-clown appearance with the bulbous puff of beaten flesh for a face, and the twisted mouth, his utter lovelessness in the world alone among foolish people who didn't see a soul in a man, hounded old reprobate clown and drunkard of eternity, was now deteriorated down to tragic realities and shabbiness in a bread line, all the rich history of his soul crunching underfoot among the forlorn pebbles. His and old Pomeray's scheme was well nigh absurd; little Cody was taken along. They got together a handful of greasy quarters, bought wire, screen, cloth and sewing needles and made hundreds of flyswatters; then in Old Bull's 1927 Graham-Paige they headed for Nebraska to sell door to door. Huge prairie clouds massed and marched above the indescribable anxiety of the earth's surface where men lived as their car belittled itself in immensity, crawled eastward like a potato bug over roads that led to nothing. One bottle of whiskey, just one bottle of whiskey was all they needed; whereas little Cody who sat in the rattly back seat counting the lonely pole-by-pole throb of telegraph lines spanning sad America only wanted bread that you buy in a grocery store all fresh in a happy red wrapper that reminded him speechlessly of happy Saturday mornings with his mother long dead——bread like that and butter, that's all. They sold their pathetic flyswatters at the backdoors of farms where farmers' wives with lone Nebraska writ in the wrinkles around their dull bleak eyes accepted fate and paid a nickel. Out on the road outside Cheyenne Wells a great argument developed between Pomeray and Old Bull as to whether they were going to buy a little whiskey or a lot of wine, one being a wino, the other an alcoholic. Not having eaten for a long time, feverish, they leaped out of the car and started making brawling gestures at each other which were supposed to represent a fistfight between two men, so absurd that little Cody gaped and didn't cry. And the next moment they were embracing each other, old Pomeray tearfully, Old Bull raising his eyes with lonely sarcasm at the huge and indefatigable heavens above Colorado with the remark "Yass, wrangling around on the bottom of the hole." Because everybody was in a hole during the Depression, and felt it. They returned clonking up Larimer Street with about eighteen dollars which was promptly that night hurled downward flaming in the drain like the fallen angel——a vast drunk that lasted five days and was almost humorous as it described crazy circles around town from the car, which was parked on Larimer at 22nd, little Cody sleeping in it, to an old office over a garage in a leafy side street that Old Bull had once used as headquarters for a spot remover venture and where pinochle at a busted dusty rolltop desk consumed thirty-six hours of their fevered reprieve, to a farm outside town (now abandoned by some family and left to Old Bull) and where drinking was done in barns and ruined livingrooms or out in cold alfalfa rows, finally teetering back downtown, Pomeray migrating back to the railyards to collapse beneath Rex in a pool of urine beneath dripping ramps while Old Bull Balloon's huge pukey tortured bulk was finally reposed on a plank in the county jail, strawhat over nose. So when little Cody woke up in the car on a cold clear October morning and didn't know what to do, Gaga, the beggar without legs who clattered tragically on his rollerboard on Wazee Street, took him in, fed him, made him a bed on the floor like a bed of straw and spent the night thundering around in bulge-eyed sweat trying to catch him in a foul hairy embrace that would have succeeded if he'd had legs or Cody hadn't lowered himself out the transom.

Years of hopping around with his father like this and on freight trains all over the West and so many futilities everywhere that he'd never remember them all, and then Cody had a dream that changed his life entirely. It was in reform school, after the theft of his first car and when he hadn't seen his Pa for a year. He dreamed he lived in an immense cosmic flophouse dormitory with the old man and Rex and other bums, but that it was somehow located in the Denver High School auditorium; that one night he was walking across the street in an exhilarated state, carrying a mattress under his arm; all up and down the street with its October night lights glittering clear swarmed the bums, with his father off somewhere doing something busy, excited, feverish. In the dream Cody was thirty years older; he wore a T-shirt in the brisk weather; his beer belly bulged slightly over the belt. His arms were the muscular arms of an ex-boxer growing flabbier. His hair was combed slick but it was thinning back from bony frowns and Mephistophelean hairlines. His face was his own but it was strangely puffed, beaten, the nose in fact was almost broken, a tooth was missing. When he coughed it sounded harsh and hoarse and maniacally excited like his father. He was going somewhere to sell the mattress for wine money: his exhilaration was due to the fact that he was going to succeed and get the money. And suddenly his father wearing his old black baseball hat came stumbling up the street with a convulsive erection in his baggy pants, howling hoarsely "Hey Cody, Cody, did you sell the mattress yet? Huh, Cody, did you sell the mattress yet?"——and ran clutching after him with imploration and fear, a dream that Cody woke from with a repugnance that only he could understand. It was dawn; he lay on the hard reformatory bed and decided to start reading books in the library so he would never be a bum, no matter what he worked at to make a living, which was the decision of a great idealist.

At fifteen this child had the regimen of his life worked out in a confused and still and all pathetically practical way. He rose at 7 A.M. from Old Bull Balloon's rolltop desk (his current bed); if the office was filled with poker players he slept in the bathtub of the Greeley or other hotels. At 7:15 he rushed downtown, washed at barbershop sink, if it was not available he used the YMCA sink. Then he delivered his paper route. Around nine he went to the Smith residence, where he knew a near-idiot maid that he made love to on the cellar cot, after which she always fed him a big meal. If this friendship with idiot maid sometimes failed he ran to Big Cherry Lucy's at the Texas Lunch (ever since thirteen Cody was able to handle any woman and in fact had pushed his drunken father off Cherry Lucy Halloween night 1939 and taken over so much that they fist fought like rivals and Cody ran away with the five dollar stake). At ten he rushed to the library for the grand opening, read Schopenhauer and magazines (sometimes when he wasn't reading funnies as a child he'd get a real book off the old Greeley Hotel shelf and read down over the first words of every line Chinese style in childly thought, which is early philosophizing).

At eleven o'clock he asked to wash cars and sometimes asked to park cars at the Rocky Mountain Garage (already he could drive better than any attendant in Denver and in fact had stolen several other cars to try his skill since his time in the "joint" and parked them back on the same block intact except for change of position), noon hour he used a paper route friend's bike to ride five miles out to friends' families for big meals, then helped with chores till two. Back to library for afternoon reading, history, encyclopedias and the bloody sad amazing *Lives of the Saints*, and making use of the library toilet; four o'clock rest and meditation and connections in poolhall till closing time unless semipro twilight ballgame or other spectacles of interest sprung around town; eleven o'clock he stole nickels off newsstands for a Bowery beef stew and found the place to sleep.

IT WAS A SATURDAY AFTERNOON in Denver, October, 1942, when Tom Watson first saw pure-souled Cody sitting on that bench with his lower lip jutted up habitually in unconscious power that Watson thought was a gesture of profile power, a pose for somebody, when actually Cody was only dreaming there; wearing Levi dungarees, old shoes without socks, a khaki Army shirt and a big black turtleneck sweater covered with car grease, and carrying a brand new toy accordion in a box he had just found by the side of the road, perched among the usual great number of Saturday onlookers half of whom were waiting for tables and talking about everything that had happened during the week, the kind of things that made Cody feel like a sheepish fool with no news of his own and marveled to see them all curling their mouths in the derisive telling of interesting tales, even while Watson said to himself "Must be some young new punk." Cody sat there, stunned with personal excitement as whole groups of them shouted across the smoke to other fellows in a tremendous general anticipation of the rapidly approaching almost unbearably important Saturday night in just a few hours, right after supper when there would be long preparations before the mirror and then a sharped-up city-wide invasion of bars (which already at this moment had begun to roar from old afternoon drinkers who'd swallowed their bar egos long ago), thousands of young men of Denver hurrying from their homes with arrogant clack and tie-adjustments towards the brilliant center in an invasion haunted by sorrow because no guy whether he was a big drinker, big fighter or big cocksman could ever find the center of Saturday night in America, though the undone collar and the dumb stance on empty streetcorners on Sunday dawn was easy to find and in fact fifteen-year-old Cody could have best told them about it; the premonition of this oncoming night together with the dense excitement of everything around the tables in the shadowy hall nevertheless failing to hide certain hints of heartbreaking loss that filtered in with chinks of daylight from the street (October in the poolhall) and penetrated all their souls with the stricken memory not only of wild wind blowing coalsmoke and leaves across town, and football games somewhere, but of their wives and women right now, with feminine purposes, with that ravenous womany glee trotting around town buying boxes of soap, Jell-o, floorwax, Dutch Cleanser and all that kind and placing these on the bottom of their wagons, then working up to apples at the fruitstand, containers of milk, toilet paper, half crushable items like that, finally chops, steak, bacon pyramiding to eggs, cigarettes, the grocery slip all mixed up with new toys, new socks and housedresses and lightbulbs, eagering after every future need while their men-louts slammed around with balls and racks and sticks in the dimness of their own vice. And there in the middle of it stood melancholy Tom Watson, the habitué, the one always ready to take anybody on for a game, hunchbacked, meek, dreaming at his upright cue-stick as naturally as the sentry with his spear or the hull-bump of a destroyer that you see on the horizon with its spindly ghost of a foremast, a figure so familiar in the brownness of the room that after awhile you didn't see him any more like certain drinkers disappear the moment they put their foot on the brass rail (Old Bull Balloon, Julien Love, others), just for the most part standing there chalking his cue in the gesture of poolhall nonchalance he and all the others always used for quick look-sees, reassured. When he saw Cody he raised his eyebrow——he was interested in this wild-looking kid, but like an old woman rocking on a porch noting storm clouds before supper, placidly, dumbly surprised. Tom Watson on this lonely earth was a crippled boy who lived in unostentatious pain with his grandmother in a two-story house under great sidestreet trees, sat on the screened porch with her till

poolhall time, which was usually midafternoon; en route made
the rounds of downtown streets, mild, sincere, dropping a word
in the shoeshine parlor, another into the chili joint where his
boys worked, then a moment on the sidewalk with that watchful, spitting, proprietary air of all young men of American daytime sidewalks (there's more doubt of it at night); and then into
the poolroom like a man going to work, where you could best
judge his soul, as Cody did, seeing him standing stooped at his
cuestick with that unfathomable patience of an old janitor
awaiting a thousand more nights of the debris of rotation,
snookers and pinochle in the same brown meeting hall, his huge
round eyes once they were fixed on you persisting like a baby's
who's terrorstricken by life watching a stranger go by his part
of the sidewalk. Then again you saw that he prowled like a fox
in his atmospheres, a weirdy, a secret wise man, making his living at pool; if you looked closer you saw that he never missed
a difficult shot once he finally got down to it; that when he did
go down and propped his thin artistic hand with forefingertip
and thumb joined in a lean, architectural rest for cue's smooth
passage, unfolding his sculptured fingers below for ornament
and balance on the green, a gesture so sophisticated in America
that boys see it in their dreams as soon as they've seen it once,
at these times he was even less noticeable at work than when
standing loafing in bunchy balled-up gloom at the rickety pylon
of his cue-pole. Raggedy Cody sitting there watching this Tom
Watson was the enactment of the drama of an American boy for
the first time perceiving the existence of an American poet, this
Tom Watson so tragically interesting, so diseased and beautiful,
potent because he could beat anybody yet be so obscurely defeated as he slouched down in the press of the crowd, sometimes flashing a languid sad smile in answer to the shouts of
dishwashers and dryclean pressers but usually just enduring
eternity on the spot he occupied, his Pepsi-Cola unattended on
the ballrack, his eyes dreaming upon sorrows that must have
been as deep as an Assyrian King's and notwithstanding that
when Cody grew up learned they were nothing but the pure
dumb trances of a sweet crippled poolshark. At the moment
when this strange love for Tom Watson and the great American
Image of beautiful sadness which he represented was leaping in
Cody's imagination, and Watson himself understood from the

corner of his eye that this boy wasn't only interested in learning
pool from him but everything he knew and would use it for
purposes of his own which were so much vaster than anything
Watson had ever dreamed that he would have to plead for
Cody's guidance in the end, Cody immediately jumped up, ran
over and made the first great conman proposition of his life. It
had to be a fantastic proposition; the moment Watson looked
amazed and dropped his superior pose out of sheer perplexity,
in fact embarrassed pain because what was he expected to do
with a kid rushing up to him and saying "Do you want to learn
philosophy from me?" with a wag of the finger, sly eyes, neck
popping with muscles like a jackinthebox straining at the void
of the world for the first time with a vigorous evil spring, Cody,
his position established, leaped in. "Now further than that yet,
and of course omitting to discuss the fact because already almost understood, i.e., you teach me how to beat pool" (pointing at himself) "and I teach *you*" (socking Watson in the chest
with his forefinger and really hurting him) "I teach you further
into psychology and metaphysics" (Cody mispronounced it
"metafsicks" only because at this time he just hadn't carefully
looked at it yet and when he did several weeks later it caused
him tremendous private grief to remember this) "and further
beyond all that and in order to cement our relationship and in
fact——of course if you agree, and only if you agree, as I do——
in fact to establish a blood brother loyalty of our souls, if you
wish to use clitchay expressions at this time or any other, and
again just as you agree, *always as you agree*" (jabbing the iron
finger again but this time careful not to touch, just holding it
quivering powerfully within the tiniest fraction of an inch from
Watson's chest) "I propose *now* and without any further shilly-
shallying, though" (rubbing his hands busily, rocking back and
forth with one foot in front of the other, his head down but
watching Watson with an underlook that was very arrogant,
cocky, suddenly sarcastically suggestive, the rocking deliberate
not only like a boxer getting ready arranging his skip rope or a
pitcher on the mound rubbing up the ball with a half-sarcastic
expression on the catcher's preliminary sign but almost hyp-
notic in the way it attracted Watson who watched entranced
and just barely seemed to be wonderingly rocking with him)——
"though I can whip a car into a going condition even if it's

awful old tin and I know buddies for free greasejobs plus where
to steal cans of oil and even one tankful during the ballroom
dance at eleven tonight on Broadway when I go around the cars
parked in my boy's lot with my siphon and mouth-suck up into
cans on the average a half a gallon gas per car which is unnoticeable but awful hard work, etcetera on, I still *have to find the car*,
you see, huge troubles natcherly as I consider energy and every
and all contingency but listen carefully to me (and I will, no
fear, to compensate, find, or *steal* a car, any time you agree, or
say, whatever) if you want to go to the Notre Dame game this
Saturday in South Bend, Indiana and REALLY want to see it
and not just loafing the idea—stop a moment to understand!"
he commanded Watson who'd started to speak. "All week I
heard you and all the other fellows bettin, saying 'Well now I
sure would like to see that thar Notre Dame game by gawd' and
talking like people often do whose wish-plans never crystallize
see because of lazy blocks that multiply on the back road of old
delays yet I'm offering a *real ji-nu-ine chance* and I repeat if you
really want to see it I'll go get my Uncle Bull's old Graham-
Paige (!!!) if necessary" (this was such a tremendous concession
Cody showed a stagger) "see? Which he won't miss not only
because it doesn't run hor hor, but right now he's freezing his
assets in Montany ha ha ha hee hee hee" (staggering back with
a high silly-giggling laugh for what he thought in those days
was a tremendous joke and in fact bumping against others, one
of them a gloomy C.B.&Q. brakeman who was just then bending down for an easy straight shot and missed completely
on account of Cody in his foolish kid stupid excitement to be
noticed, a sentiment that the brakeman, chewing his gum as fast
as he could go while aiming now expressed by not removing
his cue from where it finger-rested but just turning to look at
Cody with his jaws chewing slowly) "and positively I can take
you to the game and back in record time through chill winters
and U. S. mails and all things and really blow the road wide
open so long as you provide your ticket of course, after all,
whoo!" (wiping himself in a parody of adroitness with a dirty
handkerchief) "see? Whereas you watch the game but I'll wait
outside either in the car or in a diner listening on the radio or
better try to see panoramic touchdowns from a roof or tree, or
even better I'll hustle around town while you're enjoying and

see if I can find some girls for us, money we can borrow with the promise we're cousins say from Oopla, Indiana next door and come in every Saturday to attend the fair you see and tell them we usually have a lot of money but not this time on account Pa's hard time with the hayin this fall and the pumpkins didn't sell etcetera and then we come back possible the girls coming with us far as Nebraska or someplace where maybe they get money from their aunt or cousins, anybody. See? All that and most of it simple except as I say omigosh a *ticket*, a ticket to the Notre Dame football game one thousand miles away, six million feet deep with telephones and luminaries I can't begin to even *imagine*, pity poor me and the big tickets to world stadiums, so I leave it to *you* . . . *you* . . . and also type of car, also anybody you want to bring. I be your chauffeur, you teach me pool, snookers, anything else comes in your mind, be my big brother, I be your helper. So it be! So it be! What say?"

It was too completely mad for flabbergasted dumb old Tom Watson, one of the kindest fellows in the world, who in any case could never be expected to even have the energy to face a thousand miles of deliberately absurd travel in a clonking old heap, no, Watson's first, real, and genuinely kind impulse was to quiet Cody down.

"My land," he said to himself, "he's practically crazy from being hungry I bet!"

He took him home that afternoon to his grandmother's house. They had a big snack from the icebox, Cody drinking two and a half quarts of milk in fear that he'd never see that much for several more years, and making sure not to tear the bread when he folded it over the butter, clutching his chest, actually clutching his chest when he realized Watson's grandmother was only standing over them to refill their glasses from a fresh bottle of milk, not pleased or displeased but just a nice old woman with a rosy moon face, glasses, white hair, wearing cotton stockings over her piano legs that supported her so firmly and unmovably in the halos of her bright linoleum and a housedress that in the course of tender chores around the house which was as comfortable as an old pillow, had taken on the kindly, almost dear shapelessness of her herself, the simplicity and sadness of her stolid motherlike repose at the poor hunchbacked boy's side as he bent to his supper, her grandson

whom she served and honored, enough to make Cody feel like
crying for his own mother whom he was positive now would
have been something like Watson's grandmother, just as calm,
plain, humble, like old women who run rickety grocery stores
in dumpy backyard neighborhoods of trees and woodfences. In
Watson's bedroom upstairs the boys spent a quiet hour facing
each other at a folding cardtable set near the window where the
lace curtains puffed in with the breeze and played over the flowery wallpaper and knickknacks of windowshelf, the mere sight
of this graceful drowsy phenomenon making Cody marvel and
enjoy life (always high at fifteen) to be in a real home that had
lace curtains and little feminine lonely frills in it to beat harsh
nature, as Watson, not realizing that Cody was thinking these
kinds of thoughts, proceeded in a thorough explanation of the
various first steps in cheating at cards.

"First off you see Cody you mark 'em best with your thumb-
nail like this, usin your own code if you like, to designate face
cards, acies and deucies."

"Yes!" cried Cody. "Yes indeed!"

From a closet next to a dark wood dresser with carved iron
grips that swung on little hinges in rich significant clicks, and
next to the right front bedpost of Watson's fourpost manorial
boxspring bed in which Cody imagined Watson slept like the
little boys in fleecy nightgowns in mattress advertisements of
the *Saturday Evening Post*, which he realized now he was confusing with a rubber tire ad that shows a little boy wandering
out of bed with a candle on New Year's Eve but expresses the
same tender comfort of angels and vision of American children
(ah poor Cody who'd seen this vision in those soaked magazines
that have been dried by the sun and stand on tattered edges
among weeds and cundrums of backlots), from that closet that
seemed too rich because it was next to these things and inside
had the luxuriant darkness of suits all flashing dim from starry
moth crystals (and their starry odor) and the faint gold of shoetrees, Watson pulled out a fairly good brown tweed suit and,
with a slight bow like a Viennese nobleman, like the Bela Lugosi
vampire Count bowing to the young hero at the door of the
rainy castle, he presented it to Cody to keep, Cody in turn offering his toy accordion as collateral anyway, with a smile and still
bowing Watson saying he'd keep it for him. It was Cody's first

suit: he bulged out of the new clean underwear; bulged out of the starched white shirt that was handed to him with a laundry cardboard brace in the collar that made him wonder if he had to fiddle with it like irascible millionaire husbands tugging before last minute mirrors in B-movies, he bulged out of the necktie that wound foursquare around the pillars of his neck, but out of the suit he exploded, the buttons were in danger of popping, the trouser creases were stretched flat out of sight on his thighs, the back seams of the coat showed connective spinal threads, the sleeves took the shape of his forearms that suddenly looked almost as big as Popeye's.

"Damn! Do I look sharp?"

He looked alright but strange. So awed by these new clothes that he could hardly turn his head when Watson talked to him, but only nodded up and down, his long hair bushy and uncombable, his thoughts all pompous sweaty astonishment like the cartoon characters they draw with bewildered perspirations raining from their heads, just as ludicrous as that, and yet as that bright afternoon that had shed its radiance unasked for so long now showed itself to be turned into old red afternoon when they stepped forth from the house, and piteous remorse among men, birds, and trees that had transpired while they were dressing still haunted the air with that hung silence that makes people ask themselves sadly "Oh what happened to the afternoon?" and later when the general autumn dying quietly like a brave soldier overwhelms them, "Oh what happened to the year?", Cody, very like an Episcopalian farmer boy going to church the Sunday morning before his wedding and with the same absent-minded ignorance of the wide surroundment brooding over him that characterizes all mortal persecuted breath beneath this hugeness, literally had to be led stupidly and stiffly down the street by Watson as they hurried back to the pool parlor to meet the entire gang. It was going to be a big night, suit and all. It didn't take long for Cody to quicken his steps with Watson's and soon they had pinpointed downstreet and were swinging around the corner to a big trolley line thoroughfare, hurrying for the big-traffic, ever-more-exciting, all-of-it-pouring into-town Saturday night, both of them with the same bright fresh gleam in their eyes that you see on the shiny fender of a new automobile when it turns in from the darkness

and outskirts of town and immediately reflects Saturday night
Main Street neons where before it just sat black in a dark garage
or else in the driveway collecting dim dressing lights from the
upstairs of the house, vanishing like a comedy team rightward in
a vision of ankles twinkling in the dusk with regardant bending
figures pointed downtown plunging through the same pocket
of excitement which was not only their point of sober discussion
but raised little fogs from their mouths as they yaketty-yakked
along (with lone envy Cody used to watch other guys cutting
along like this, sometimes from Mission reading-room windows
on nights when it was so cold he thought he could read what
the buddies said before their intense voluminous talking-fogs
whipped back to dissolve in wintry eternity); Cody finally forgetting he was wearing a suit, forgetting the high entrapment
of the collar and the woolly stifling around his armpits and the
unfamiliar scuffling cuffs out of which he soon in fact resumed
telling Watson further things and all things about himself, gesturing out of the shiny round starch his big grimy cracked hands
that were not at all the hands of an absorbed banker in the
street but more like a dirt farmer's at a funeral and worse like
horny toads in a basket of wash. "Now in Gaga's barbershop in
back and setting way up high behind the water heater I have a
bag of clothes, harkening to clothes, but to go and pick it up
involves terrible divisions with Gaga over money my old man
owed him even though it's just old pants and belts and polkadot
shirts, but further I have an extry pair of fairly good workshoes
settin way up high so nobody can notice on top of a locker in
the Y and my plan, actually and no lie, was getting down to
Colorado Springs or Raton or some such to freeze m'fingers off
in construction camps or whichever"——and so on as Watson
assured him he had plenty of clothes for him and not to worry.
Excitement of hurrying downtown on foot for the big night
reached a supreme peak when suddenly as they rushed arm-in-
arm and came to cross Broadway the light instantly changed for
them and they didn't have to wait but just hustled right straight
on across the street for the poolhall, that light that wouldn't
allow lulls in the rhythm of their joy holding up whole avenues
of traffic exactly for them to sweep along, profound, bowed,
bumping heads together; Cody so singing in his soul now that
he had to talk on several levels to express himself to Watson:

"Even though as you say there's just as much work around here and why even go to Fort Collins where it's so c-o-l-d (whee! zoom! look at that new Cadillac!) and I didn't further finish about earlier speaking of Gaga and all the things I want you to know——"; his arm around Watson, tight armpits or no tight armpits, he the only one who'd ever put his arm around the hump of Watson's sorrow; similarly in the moment, seeing, just as they reached the other curb, in the exciting shadows of a five-and-ten awning and to his deeper and simultaneously running amazement, a beautiful girl fixing on him from her casual one-leg-forward hand-on-hip position by the weighing machine waiting for the bus a cold arrogant look of sensuality done with misty eyes and something suggestive, impatient, almost too personal to understand, astonishing him in the realization that he was wearing a suit for the first time in his life and this was the first official sex-appeal look from a regular high-heeled downtown socialite honey (still finding room to yell "Watson watch that new Caddy beat the light now!") and reflecting: "So this is what these damn dames and big guys been doing, giving each other turble personal glances of angry snaky love that I didn't know about in my previous boy days beatin around the sidewalk with my eyes on the gutter looking for nickels and dimes wearin goldang cockin old pants. Damn! Lessgo!"

In the poolhall the hour was roaring. It was so crowded that spectators were standing obscuring everything from the street and somebody had the backdoor open simultaneously with the alley door of the Welton Street parlor so that you could see a solid city block of poolhall from the north side of Glenarm to the south side of Welton interrupted only by a little tragic alley of shadows with a garbage can, like looking down a hall of mirrors over a sea of angrily personalized heads and islands of green velvet, all in smoke. To Cody it was a vision, the moment of his arrival that everybody was waiting for, yet even though he stood in the door at the side of great cool Tom Watson the Virgil of this big Inferno, wearing not only his clothes but the same gorgeously sophisticated robe of their afternoon's adventure which was already undergoing a rich change to evening and the lazy explorations that were to come, a decadent refinement that all the dumb bastards in this dimness would have to struggle to understand to know anything hereafter even about pool, nobody made a move to notice or even gave much of a crap and Cody would have immediately felt drowned again except suddenly for the saving memory of a hunch he used to have in boyhood which was whenever he turned his back on the people who were involved with him and even others who happened to be standing nearby, perfect strangers sometimes, they immediately gathered with the speed of light at the nape of his neck to discuss him voicelessly, dancing, pointing, until, jerking his head around for a quick look or just slowly to check, it turned out they'd always twanged back in place with all-to-be-expected fiendish perfect hypocrisy and in exactly the same bland position as before. Remembering anyhow his father when in his cocky way of bums used to stagger happily into some place howling "Hallelujah I'm a bum, bum again" Cody as he came in, very carefully digging everything through shrewd half closed eyes so he could size up and savor the scene for everything it had, jazzing on the balls of his feet in that thing Americans do instead of pinching themselves, now repeated the song to himself, "Hallelujah I'm a bum, bum again," in a secret, sly, interested whisper of his own he always used to refer back to sad factors of the past. While Watson was busy looking around, Cody directed his attention to a spot on the floor near table number one where, after he had got tired looking at people on those long watchful nights, he used to spend stranger further hours on the onlookers' bench absentmindedly studying the reality and vying with the existence of cigarette butts and spit by estimating exactly how it got there on the floor, wondering why for instance a particular calm spit gleamed like it did even though it had been rejected like a person's rejected and spat out exactly (by the clock) two and a half minutes earlier by a bluejowled conductor who had to spit and wouldn't have spat otherwise but came apparently to think of something completely different at the button wire counting the score and scratching his chin (all as voices of the fellows reverberated around the walls of the hall and moaned in his absent not-listening ear), so that as far as the spot of this conductor's own spit was concerned it no longer existed for him, only for Cody; Cody then estimating exactly how he himself got there, not only the world but the bench, not only the bench but the part of the bench he filled out, not only that but how he got there to be aware of the saliva and the part of the bench his ass filled out, and so on in the way the mind has; at all of which now because it wasn't his best idea of what to do in a poolhall, in Watson's company he made his ceremonial sneer and official revenge, even in the roaring noise and even though among all these Saturday feet he couldn't quite see the exact spot he had studied, though he knew there were new cigarette butts and spit on that spot now, like little brothers and sisters following in the stead of others long ago studied and swept away, in any case doing all this so that the first full-fledged moment of his poolhall charactership would not be spoiled in fevers and forgetful excitement like running up to people to talk, but instead he would take advantage of his big chance to keep his attention disciplined on his good luck, and so do so in the roots of previous well-considered sorrow of October in the Poolhall.

"What are you doing Cody?" asked Watson when he noticed how pensive he was.

Oh ragged sailing heart!——it was far from time for Cody to be able to even want to explain his craziest secrets. "Actually and no lie, Tom, I was thinking to myself what a wonderful guy this Tom Watson fellow is really truly indeed."

Slim Buckle, Earl Johnson and Jim Evans were the nucleus of Tom Watson's gang at the time. They were grouped around a rear table in the usual ritual get-together game of rotation that they had every Saturday evening as a kind of preliminary tactical conference on the night's action and for starting and a Coke. The program tonight featured two girls who were baby-sitting for the weekend in a house up near the Wyoming line. But this night without knowing it they were grouped around with that hotheaded dumbness the purpose of which is always to be ig-norant of what's about to happen, the only sure thing you can remember when you look back to see what people were doing during an important historical moment, sore, sullen, sighing from the drag of time, inattentive as always, impatient not only with life but always exactly the life unfolding in the immediate vicinity, the miserable *here*, the lousy *now*, as though all the blame was on that, and yet the poor souls actually sitting in that mysterious godlike stuff that later makes them say, "Listen, I was there the night Tom Watson came in with Cody the day he *found* him, 1942, Autumn, they had the Army-Columbia game that day I bet on it and heard it on the radio too, we were all playing pool me and Slim Buckle who just got haircuts and Earl Johnson and Jackoff and I dunno who the hell else, Christ we all drove to Wyoming that night, sure, it was a *great mad* night!"

Cody was introduced around. "Here comes Tom Watson; who's that kid with him? What's that, your cousin? What happened to you and Jackoff Friday night? Cody is it? Hiya boy." And Cody with that strange little feeling of pleasedness that shivers deep in your chest and makes you want to hug yourself and explain everything to the man next to you, found himself standing at one table among all the others roaring with what he could now almost call his own gang as exciting shadows outdoors fell and they played eightball——Cody and Watson versus Buckle and Johnson with goodnatured Evans kibitizing. And everything they said——"That old Missouri twang Esmeralda swishin her butt around the Sandwich Shop I know her, if she had as many rods stickin out of her as she had in she'd look like a porcupine, yah, don't laugh I stole it from Tony"——and everything they did——one reaching up to slap over the score and another reaching down to carefully place his Coke and another looking horizontally along his cue to see if it was too curved——was all part of one great three-dimensional moil that was all around him now instead of just flat in front of his face like a canvas prop, he was up on the stage with the show now. So he stood there with his weatherbeaten face growing more excited and redder by the hour, his big raw hands gripped around a cue, looking bashfully at his new friends and planning deep in his mind from everything they said and did the positively best, in fact only way to begin completely, helplessly impressing everyone and winning over their favor so conclusively and including their souls that eventually of course they would all turn to him for love and advice; mad Cody who eventually did run the gang, who was now just being merely coy quiet knowing instinctively the best way to start despite the fact that he never knew a gang before and the only thing he'd done was grab some poor kid by the arm in the junkyard or a newsboy in the street or some of the bicyclists on the paper route and make long strange speeches to them like the great speech he made to Watson that afternoon but they were too young to understand and frightened. So he stood stiffly at attention at the table side, sweaty in his suit, or made stupid hilarious shots laying out his big hand flat and flaccid for a cue-rest as if a baby was trying to shoot pool, and the boys laughed but only because Cody was so seriously absent-minded in his hilarious dumbness (*trying to learn*, they thought) and not because he was inconsequential. Right away the biggest fellow in the gang took a liking to Cody, six-foot-four Slim Buckle all shiny handsome in his Saturday night suit, who was always looming over everybody with a long grave calm that was half comical because it seemed to come from the loneliness of his great height which prevented him from being on a level with other faces so that he dreamed up there his own special juvenile dreams all the less realistic because they were so far from his feet where the ground was, the others had to stare dumbly at his vest most of the time, a fate that he accepted with immense and tender satisfaction. This goodnatured long tall drink of water took a liking to Cody that soon became hero worship and later led to their rambling around the country, buddies——a thing that Earl Johnson noticed and resented from the start. He was almost instantly jealous and immediately proclaimed next day in Watson's ear (when it was too late) Cody wasn't everything he seemed to be. So when the gang gave up the precious table and let their empty Cokes plop in a floorbox with a "So long fellers" and left the hall to jump in the car, a '37 Ford belonging to Evans, for the ride north to Wyoming about eighty miles, the sun just then going down in vast unobserved event above the madding souls of people, and Cody above the objections of everyone else insisted on driving to show his skill, but then really fantastically wheeled the car right clear out of town with beautiful spot-shot neatness and speed, the guys who were prepared to criticize his driving and give pointers or stage false hysterical scenes forgot they were in a car and fell to gabbing happily about everything——Suddenly out on East Colfax Boulevard bound for Fort Collins Cody saw a football game going on among kids in a field, stopped the car, said "Watch" ran out leaping madly among kids (with noble seriousness there wearing those tragic lumps like the muscles of improvised strongmen in comedies), got the ball, told one blondhaired boy with helmet tucked underarm to run like hell, clear to the goalpost, which the kid did but Cody said "Further, further," and the kid halfway doubting to get the ball that far

edged on back and now he was seventy yards and Cody un-
leashed a tremendous soaring wobbling pass that dropped beyond the kid's most radical estimate, the pass being so high and
powerful the boy completely lost it in eyrieal spaces of heaven
and dusk and circled foolishly but screaming with glee——when
this happened everyone was amazed except Johnson, who
rushed out of the car in his sharp blue suit, leaped around frantically in a mixup of kids, got the ball (at one point fell flat
because of his new shiny-bottom shoes that had only a half
hour's poolroom dust on 'em) and commanded the same un-
complaining noble boy to run across the field and enragedly
unfurled a long pass but Cody appeared out of nowhere in the
mad lowering dusk and intercepted it with sudden frantic action
of a wildfaced maniac jumping into a roomful of old ladies;
spun, heaving a prodigious sky pass back over Johnson's head
that Johnson sneered at as he raced back, he'd never been out-
done by anybody ("Hey whee!" they yelled in the car); such a
tremendous pass it was bound to be carried by the wind, fall in
the road out on East Colfax, yet Johnson ran out there dodging
traffic as mad red clouds fired the horizon of the mountains, to
the west, and somewhere across the field littler tiny children
were burning meaningless fires and screaming and playing football with socks, some just meaninglessly tackling one another
all over in a great riot of October joy. Circling in the road,
almost being murdered by a car driven eighty miles per by Denver's hotshot (Biff Buferd, who tooted), Johnson made a sensational fingertip sprawling-on-knees catch instantly and breath-
takingly overshadowed by the fact that dramatic fantastic Cody
had actually gone chasing his own pass and was now in the road
yurking with outstretched hands from the agony that he was
barely going to miss, himself sprawling as terrorstricken motor-
ists swerved and screeched on all sides. This insane scene was
being beheld not only by Biff Buferd laughing like hell as it
receded eighty miles an hour out of his rearview window, but
across the wild field with its spastic fires and purple skies (actually an empty lot sitting between the zoom-swish of Colfax
traffic and some old homes, the goalposts just sticks the kids
"put up with believing crudeness of primitive Christians") was
propped all by itself there an old haunted house, dry gardens
of Autumn planted round it by nineteenth-century lady ghouls

long dead, from the weatherbeaten green latticed steps of which now descended Mr. behatted beheaded Justin G. Mannerly the mad schoolteacher with the little Hitler mustache, within months fated to be teaching Cody how to wash his ears, how to be impressive with highschool principals——Mannerly now stopped, utterly amazed, halfway down, the sight of Cody and Earl Johnson furying in the road (almost getting killed too), saying out loud "My goodness gracious what is *this?*"; same who in fact that afternoon, at the exact moment Cody was approaching Watson, sat in a grave of his own in his overcoat in an empty unheated Saturday classroom of West Denver High not a mile across town, his brow in his hand as blackboard dust swam across October fires in the corner where the window-opening pole was leaned, where it was still written in chalk from yesterday's class (in American Lit.) *When lilacs last in the dooryard bloom'd*, sat there in a pretense of thinking for the benefit of any teachers and even kids passing in the hall with some of whom just before he'd in fact been joking (threw a feeble lopsided pass across the afternoon lawn as he hustled from Studebaker to business), sat now moveless in a pretense of remembering, with severe precision, the exact date of something that was bottlenecking his entire day, left wrist raised for a quick look at how much time was left, frown of accompaniment already formed, drawer pulled with letterheaded memo paper ready to fly the instant he smacked the desk deciding, but actually choking over loss, choking over loss, thinking of the love, the love, the love he missed when his face was thin and fresh, hopes were pure. O growing old! O haggard ugly ghoul is life's decay! Started life a sweet child believing everything beneath his father's roof; went from that, immersed and fooled, to that mask of disgusted flesh called a face but not the face that love had hoped for and to that soul of a gruesome grieving ghost that now goes shuddering through nightmare life cluttering up the earth as it dies. Ah but well, Earl Johnson wanted to throw a pass to Cody and Cody challenged him and said "Run with the ball and let's see if I tackle you before you reach that Studebaker where the man's standing"; and Johnson laughed because he had been (absolutely) the outstanding runner everywhere (schools, camps, picnics), at fifteen could do the hundred in 10:9, track star speed; so took off not quite realizing what he'd done here giving Cody these psychological opportunities and looking back at him with taunts "Well come on, come on, what's the matter?" And so that Cody furiously, as if running for his life, not only caught up with him but even when Johnson increased his speed in wholehearted realizing race caught up with him easily, in his sheer excitement, with his tremendous unprecedented raw athletic power he could run the hundred in almost ten flat (actually and no lie), and a sad, remote tackle took place in the field, for a moment everybody saw Cody fly-ingtackling horizontally in the dark air with his neck bulled on to prove, his head down almost the way a dead man bows his head self-satisfied and life-accomplished but also as if he was chuckling up his coat sleeve at Johnson about-to-be-smeared, both arms outstretched, in a tackling clamp that as he hung suspended in that instantaneous fix of the eye were outstretched with a particular kind of unspeakable viciousness that's always so surprising when you see it leaping out of the decent suits of men in sudden sidewalk fights, the cosmopolitan horror of it, like movie magnates fighting, this savagery explosively leaping now out of Cody's new suit with the same rage of shoulderpads and puffy arms, yet arms that also were outstretched with an unspeakable mute prophesied and profound humility like that of a head-down Christ shot out of a cannon on a cross for noth-ing, agonized. Crash, Johnson was tackled; Justin G. Mannerly called out "Why didn't you try that in the road I have a shovel in the car" nobody noticing, even as he drove off; and Cody, like Johnson with his knees all bruised and pants torn, had es-tablished his first great position of leadership in Tom Watson's famous gang.

Long ago in the red sun——that wow-mad Cody, whose story this is, lookout.

A WHOLE BUNCH OF SAD and curious people and half morose kicked around the weeds in the ordinary city debris of a field off East Colfax Avenue, Denver, October 1942, with semi-disgruntled expressions that said "There's something here any-way." Crap in weeds was an old map, Cashmere Soap paper, bottom glass of a broken bottle, old used-out flashlight bat-tery, leaf, torn small pieces of newspaper (someone had saved a clipping and then torn it), nameless cardboards, nameless

mats of hay, light bulb cardboards, old Spearmint Gum wrapper, ice cream box cover, old paper bag, weeds with little
bunched lavender shoots and Rousseau-like but October rusted
leaves——old cellophane——old bus transfer ticket, the strange
corrugated cardboard from egg crates, a rock, pieces of brown
beerbottle glass, old Phillip Morris flattened pack——the roots
of weeds were purplish borscht color and left the matted filthy
earth like tormented dog cocks leave the sac——sticks——coffee
container——and an empty pint bottle of Five Star brand California Sherry drunk by an old wino of the road when things
were less grim.

What actually had happened a miscarriage was discovered by
some children in the field and reported to a cruising cop who'd
now sent his partner back to call up a morgue wagon. There
was something tremendously embarrassing about it because you
wanted to see it and yet if you did you had to be conspicuous,
had in fact to pick out the spot where it was supposed to be
and even if you found *that* had to crane over others and give
away the fact which is tremendously painful that you with your
personal embarrassed also disgruntled face want to see the red
horrible meat of a dead baby——have come snooping around
to see it——probably knowing all the time what it was——Cody
was embarrassed therefore till the other fellows (Tom Watson,
Slim Buckle, Earl Johnson) joined him from the car and then
it was easy to talk——But now: what a forlorn thing it is and
frightening that the nameless soul (the thing created by the
terribleness of a womb which when it does halfway work or
even complete work takes the melted marble of man's sperm
which is a kind of acceptable substance, say in a bottle, and
transforms it by means of the work of some heinous secret egg
into a large bulky piece of decayable meat——) that this nameless little would-have-been lay, spilling out of that grocer's bag,
grocer's wrapping, under a tree that by dry Autumn had been
turned almost the same shade of red, turned thus instead of by
wet and secret wombs——Girls are frightening when you see
them under these circumstances because there seems to be a
kind of insistence on their part to look you in the eye to find out
that personal thing about you which is probably the thing that
you expect and burn and kill to find *in them* when you think
of penetrating their thighs——that secret wetness of the woman

is as unknown to you as your eyes are to her when they're
confronted by a miscarried whatnot in a field under dark and
mortal skies——Thus Cody ponders. Whatever he says (in the
tragic dusk of this field, bareheaded), he says nothing now——

The roads that Cody Pomeray knew in the West and that I
rode with him later were all those tremendously frightening
two-lane bumpy roads with those ditches on both sides, that
poor fence, that rangefence next, maybe a sad cut of earth, a
hair head of grass on a lump of sand, then endless range leading
to mountains that belong to other states sometimes——but that
road always seems destined to bounce you in the ditch because
it humps over each way and the feeling is of the car rolling on a
side angle, inclined to a ditch, a bump in the road will bounce
it in——as a consequence of this Western roads are lonelier to
ride than any. Long hauls straight ahead and on a Saturday
night you can see maybe five cars in the next five miles coming
your way each headlight smaller and creating that illusion of
water on the road when they're so far the lights are absorbed
probably by the night mist entire or whatever it really is——the
mirage of night driving across great flat spaces——Cody like
everybody else to drive this has that elbow over the window and
he particularly with his thick muscular noble efficient (like necks
of great busdrivers) neck looks calm and relaxed and perfect at
the wheel as you look over his shoulder at that road which at
night only shows part of itself, the most conspicuous being the
five-mile headlights coming your way——coming into Denver
for Saturday night——and the swath, the side-wash swath of the
car lights catching the side ditches and a part of the range that
jacks over, inlaps the fence like a sea past a breakwater towards
the road showing forlorn tufts of bunchgrass on nobs of dry
dead earth flashing by in the night in swift blurrily fanning succession and just beyond you know there is, or are, ends of the
earth swinging out across the plain, thunderset, the desert, over
gopher holes, over brush, sticks, rocks, tiniest pebbles reflecting largest stars (which are in reality galaxies) till the inevitable
mesas that terminate Western horizons give some kind of indication that the world has contours and the flatness's got to
stop——this is flashing by, the stars are distant, if you put out the
lights of the car you would see what you sense——Cody drove
this that night eighty miles and drove it many other times too,

north, south, east, west, and was perfectly still at the wheel for
an entire hour and averaging an almost pure 80 m.p.h. in the
trafficless wilds except for a town while the fellows gabbled and
drank beer and sent cans banging after in the black abyss.

Now girls. The house was located on the Union Pacific railroad track under a watertank at the corner of a bunch of desolate looking buildings including one spare (the Anglo North
and its fool Norwegians have captured Moby Dick! captured
him a hundred years after!) vertical board church and a huge
heavengoing creamy white silo with the name of the junction
on it, a desolate place not even fit for a brakeman's piss when the
train's stopped and watering, re-coaling, tanks, coal chutes. The
house was somewhat sooty from railroad and therefore deliberately painted bright red window frames——brown sandpaper
shingles over walls and on roof, those on roof pale green——
weatherbeaten antique gray brick chimney protruding from
peaked roof——wooden porch made into an extension out front,
gray wood, full of bicycles, chairs, storm doors with lift hooks
not knobs——and behind with adjunct wings getting smaller
and beater in a graduating series, places to put overshoes, rubbers, umbrellas, addition-sheds, also gray wood but last little
outhouse one has cheap English lamp hanging——In yard an
old decrepit dresser facing house, shoved up against it with
bucket and upside down apple basket on it——boards leaning
on house——junk in yard, including an old water-heater tank in
high grass, pieces of sodden dog biscuit——and one old sunken
ancient car collapsed on timbers as if on display, decapitated,
emptied of all except flaps of leather, twang of seat springs, the
inner hay of seats, old red rust dials, a steering wheel cracked
so you can cut yourself on it, blind headlamps, a back trunk
where birds have nested and snow and spring combined to raise
a small green crop——old potatoes dumped from a sack rotting
next to the right front wheel hub——the kids' playplace——the
dog's pissery——the trough of moony cows in the summerrain.

It was a Saturday night and if a train happened to crash by
you would have to hold up everything you're doing to freeze
and wait. The two girls were not exactly the usual American
girl team of the pretty one and the ugly old one because in
this case the older one was extremely attractive herself only
you had to look twice or be an expert to tell that if passionate

fornication was what you wanted tonight, real gnashing passion in the black, this older one——who looked away resolutely from everybody as if she was a schoolteacher who had orders to do so but with exactly that kind of sternly imposed self-discipline that was so pathetic and so tight you knew it was bound to explode and when it did it would be good for a man to be there to catch the contents of the act——Now Cody although he was only fifteen at the time noticed this about her the first thing because it was his habit to make his judgments as immediately as possible so as not to waste preliminaries on ordinary hello how are you I'm Joe he's Bill hee hee ignorance——the moment he stepped off the dark curb of the car, stood in the muddy yard (it had rained in that part of Wyoming) and saw the two girls standing in the face of the onslaught they knew would come from such a carload he made his decision——simply, who's *best*. The younger girl called Marie was the epitome of the cute little sexy fleshpot of honey, gold and shiny hairs that you see in illustrations of Coca-Cola girls at fountains with equally pretty rosy boys and so much so, so startlingly what the guys wanted that immediately they were terrified to see it staring them in the face, the bird in the hand——with her pudgy arms that gave promise to the genuineness of two beautiful tits protruding from a deliciously soft cashmere sweater and her arched eyebrows and plump little foolish assy mouth. But I'll start again.

THEY GOT TO THE HOUSE where the girls were at nine o'clock sharp. It was located practically under a watertank of the U.P. railroad that passed right by and left that dark dirt which is like the concoction of an artist's palette after a short rain, the black color artists use to depict night, gloom, maybe evil—— and it had just rained when the boys pulled up and Cody cut off the motor in a kind of a driveway covered with this dark railroad snotground. A fitful moon was all that was left of that entire day's wild light (poolhall chinks of light, miscarriage field purples and iron file skies) and now nobody could see anything except the shape of the house, a few brown lights in it, and the hanging pendant globe of a streetlamp not across the street but across a whole plaza of dirt which might have represented a crossroad, a soccer field, a square, because at the other end of it just barely seeable was an old wood church with vertical boards

and gingerbread eaves, behind it even more vaguely in the lunar
underground a crazy huge uplifting wheat silo painted wild
aluminum and glowing like a June worm in the darkness of the
plains that seemed to begin behind it but actually surrounded
everything I've been talking about——house, clearing, watertank, tracks, lamp, and a few further indications of a townlet
beyond the road's lamp——in one hollow misty carrousel of wild
black space horses so close to one another that the only time
you could see between them was when a faroff light indicated
it, a railroad switch light or a roadlamp or an airport tower in
the other county or the topmost glimmer of an antenna in a
Cheyenne or whatever radio station.

Johnson who'd picked up one of the girls in Cheyenne a few
weeks before and *scored* tried the storm door first while all the
others stood around carrying the beers, the whiskey, the whatnot like altarbearers but with considerably more guilt and with
a stirring in their gut that you feel in a whorehouse when you're
told to wait for the girl and suddenly you hear high-heel steps
coming down the hall and envision the legs, the garters, the
thighs, the panties, the breasts, the throat, the face, the hair of
the woman coming——This was exactly the way they felt when
Johnson unhooked the storm door with that delicacy of thumb
and forefinger you need for such gadgets and as though he
was unfastening a brassiere from the bulge-back of the house.
Wild children opened the door; there was a lot of stumbling
over things on the porch floor but Cody never dreamed that
one of the crazy little giggling girls who had been sent by the
gals to open up while they brush up the last wave was Joanna
Dawson his future wife. In America it's always two girls and
one is always older and uglier than the other, except in this case
it was more accurate to say that one was younger and prettier
than the other because the older girl——Vivian, a sort of taut
redhead with fairly short hair, in dungarees, the chaperone of
the two and anybody looking at the younger girl could tell
she needed one——Vivian was really pretty and to Cody who
was only fifteen offered the most promise of passionate kicks
as he came in and sized up everything in one second (back)
"*you had to look twice*" or rather, here, again, he saw that she
was supposed to watch out for everything and because of that
and maybe had to that all her life was accustomed to acting

stern like a teacher among irresponsible elements that element year by year now becoming life in general so that he instinctively realized she was a plum to pick before the Puritanism sank in for good and she became an old Lesbic maid. Besides the dungarees Vivian was wearing moccasins and a blue man's workshirt washed and re-washed and now faded and made to look feminine only by the crucifix that dangled over a freckle in the little throat-hole at the base of her frightened neck: an outfit that showed she did a lot of chores around the house and yard all day and rode horseback somewhere but also on this night seemed to be a concession on her part to the wild necking party her younger cousin had arranged via Johnson. Marie, the younger, was a vivacious blond who habitually wore broad shiny leather belts, usually red, that emphasized the place where the finest part of her waist gave way to the swing of two white hips that must have looked like columns from there down to the toes if you could have looked under her skirt while the belt was on. Better than that, best of all, and for a reason that none of the guys knew or even tried to form in their minds, Marie wore glasses——dark rimmed glasses that gave her creamy white face and rosy natural lips with but just a tiny down of sideburn wisping down the cheekbone a price they could afford, without them she would have scared them off into the formal camps of complete ego-approach the kind American boys use for their Lana Turners in the rosy ballroom of the land, use for their idea of what it's like to make Lana Turner and Ava Gardner and such. The same kind of approach they use on the boss when they go out to find their first whitecollar job. Marie was a wild little thing who read books and Dostoevsky and enough of D. H. Lawrence to make her ten times more aggressive than any shambling shy boy she could meet in this forlorn district of the world whether they came driving from Denver or lived a couple of telephone poles away. These two girls were cousins; Vivian was the daughter of the thin countrified woman in glasses whose picture was on top of the player piano; Marie was staying for the month, visiting from Killdeer, N.D. One of the three kids was also visiting——little Joanna, from Denver, whose father, a cop in Santa Fe, was waiting for her annual visit from the general matriarchal Colorado. Big Slim Buckle sat on the couch among the others, Watson on one side, Johnson on the other, with a great beautiful sincerity that made Marie change her interior plans for the night, because it had been the prettiness of Johnson that attracted her and decided her to arrange this party no matter what happened, a prettiness that Buckle had in greater and tenderer proportions——

These imaginings lead me backwards to my one and original poipose.

DIRTY OLD VOYEURS. On Times Square all these dirty old men we all hate some of whom try to make boys as well as girls and are the ugliest old lechers, make you think of the Arabian proverb "A young woman flees an old man"——they wear hats, why all the time wear hats!——hang around subway entrances, little bookstores, library parks, chess arcades——prowl up and down——some so innocuous you don't notice what they are till they stop in front of you (say as you lean against building) trying to look casual but somehow with their dirty old hardpants pointed straight at you like a hex, a hoodoo pointed at the man goin down Dauphine Street to die——Nevertheless Cody and I have the same soul and we know what they do, we stood with them at dirty-picture windows from coast to coast——So here goes, all this was just defensive preamble, and I will add (at least my own) food kicks: (anchovies with capers in olive oil is so rich it stuffs the throat, so salty it chokes you, so strong it seems to permeate and flavor the tin of the can itself until the tin tastes saltier than any salt, a metallic salt, the salt of Armageddon)—— (this is a food example)——

Cody and I are continually interested in the pictures of women's legs——little black and white books nudged among many in a Times Square or Curtis Street bookstore window draw us to see the thing in lurid white, somehow interests us more than color, in black and white the thigh is all the whiter, the background all the darker and evil——

Cody used to say "Have this picture, I've used it." I have here a pix of Ruth Maytime (the famous Hollywood actress) and Ella Wynn and I love it——what tremendous lovely tits Ruth has, one shoulder strap of her suit is down, the other is flimsy, they reach very low because her breasts are low, heavy and way out thus stretching strap even further (ah me strap!)——her left breast occupies me for five nameless unconscious minutes on the sidewalk of Times Square and not her breast, just a pix of it, it is so vast, heavy, three-fifths concealed which is better than any other percentage, the nipple is in no danger of showing, what's in danger is the point at which the soft yearning bulge might plop up, almost out——Ella's is conventionally concealed, you can see the rich delicious soft living valley and then the bulge of the cloth following the holy contours we all know—— but Ruth's is as if Ella was a stripteaser who started the act and Ruth went next step——pulled cloth down but only one end so that instead of one-fourth upper left of a breast showing (with valley) now we see three-fifths full upper breast with valley expanding——Ah those gorgeous breasts——I stand here among the religious dirty old men of the world, chewing gum, like them, with a horrible beating heart——I can hardly think or control myself——I even know this is infinitely more delicious than touching Ruth's breast itself (though I'd do anything for the chance)——But more, more about the breast itself——all my life I've dreamed on breasts (and of course thighs, but now we're talking of breasts, hold your Venus, we're talking about Mars, and your water, we're talking about milk)——the dirty magazines of boyhood become the religious publications of manhood——to stop joking——one pull on that cloth and a great breast plops out, that's the thing that is holding me here and all these lechers, some of them ninety, holding us captive and especially because we know it'll never happen, it's only a pic- ture, but IF IT DID!——If so, a magnificent bouncing jelly-like white-as-snow warm strange Ruth-personal breast with a name- less but revealing nipple which would tell us everything we need to know (the exact nipple will tell us more than Ruth's entire life story, "Around the beauty parlors of Brooklyn during World War II a strange energetic young lady began to be noticeable to the characters who frequented the places afternoon and night and even to the casual visitors . . ."——the first glimpse of it and we've finally seen her soul, its perfection and its imperfection, its confession, its secret girlish shame, which is best of all what we want) and everything we've all our lives wondered about Ruth speaking of Ruth as a woman who's come across our attention only through her fame, pixes, husbands, and if she complains it's her fault, I didn't ask her to have three-fifths of her living breast that I want to nudge between my lips photographed, she offered it herself and I'm sure God will reward her for doing it——Ah that breast! it is such a casual breast, it just went swimming with her, her hair's wet, she's cutting a cake on Orrin Wynn's yacht, Edgar Bones the idiot is husbanding cutely at her side——her mouth is done up into what is supposed to be a smile but is really a great bit of desire and shuddering sensual bitterness (she's really *cutting* the cake) and her teeth are like my teeth when I bring a little kitty's nose next to mine——This pix is black and white, this breast is gray——there is more reality in gray for me (and for Cody too) because I was brought up in the balconies of B-movie theaters. Ah the holy contours all we men know——Now, not to leave that, but let's turn to knees. Ella's knees are showing——Ruth's are under a towel. Now all we lechers turn our vast, rumbling attentions in a body but with no military music and no salute and no flag except the Cross and Bones to the knees of Ella Wynn——they're crossed, which would be unfortunate except by so being a little lovely dimple was formed on the back of the uppermost knee——I mean under the leg (sweet smooth underleg like the belly of a warmblooded fish but much better). This dimple, which is just a crease between some back knee flesh and the inner bottom thigh smoothness is especially notable because it emphasizes as nothing else could the main feature which is the lowermost knee, the knee that's crossed on——the great thing about that knee is the glossiness, indicative of the texture of that gal's flesh and of the further textures inward from the glossiness (my heart beats again!) to the thigh areas, deeper, more dazzling, dizzier, like climbing a mountain, till the gardens of her soul are within earshot and you are eligible to look for her face along and among the mountains to see what expression it wears alongside the long beautiful hair in a big ribbon——we lechers by now really raping the poor girl whereas tough Ruthy didn't give us half that chance and subdued us and we jumped on her friend in cowardly revenge. We glance at Orrin Wynn as though we'd known him forever and recognize him with a smile, that is, recognize that his eye is on the sparrow, i.e., Ruth's tit, not on Edgar as you might think if you don't look close and Ella unsuspecting of this is smiling at the cake knife although that in itself is strange and perhaps infinitely more sadistic than Ruth and her gritting teeth——but Ella generally is a sweet little thing

and although we've all just raped her, at least threatened to do
so, we don't want to harm her. We also wonder if there have
been orgies and switchovers in this foursome and earnestly hope
so as we might hope, as an example, for World Peace.

The lurid big pictures of immense-thighed burlesk gals
on corner newsstands make us hold up sidewalk traffic day
and night. My next stop must be France (postcards on the
boulevard?)——but further and later.

SO IT WAS AS THOUGH CODY POMERAY'S early life was haunted
by the sooty girders and worn old black planks of railroad
bridges behind warehouses, by cinder yards where great con-
centrations of cardboard crates that were a nuisance to foremen
of factories became the sly opportunity of bums——the back-
places of what we call downtown, the nameless tunnels, alleys,
sidings, platforms, ramps, ash heaps, miniature dumps, unofficial parking lots fit for murders, the filthy covered-with-rags
plazas that you see at the foot of great redbrick chimneys——the
same chimney that had bemused Cody on many a dreaming
afternoon when he looked at it toppling forward as clouds up-
swept the air in readiness for the big disaster——it was as though
these things had been the——(and of course many more, why
list any further, and besides we shall come back on other levels
and more exhaustively)——these things had been the necessary
parts of his first universe, its furniture, just as the little rich boy
in a blue playsuit in some swank suburb outside St. Louis
stands, in November, beneath the bleak black branches, staring
at a universe which is necessarily and unalterably furnished with
things like half-timbered English style housefronts, circular
wooded drives for avenue blocks, forests of birch, the wire fenc-
ing in back of Tudor garages, boxer dogs, bicycles, sleek autos
reposant at dusk before the warm lights that shine behind the
drapes of a Spanish style house worth twenty-eight thousand
dollars bought by an insurance broker who cuts along the narrow redbrick downtown streets of St. Louis near the markets
by day, where you can see the river between box factories, earning his living among the trappings of the poor and of bums of
all kinds but is incapable of stretching his home bones anywhere
twenty miles away, inland from the river and the unclean city in
private parks, quiet neighborhoods——Cody's life, with the

coming of the suit and consequently the beginning of some
kind of different adult existence that for instance reached its
own maturity when he also acquired a winter topcoat from
Watson or one of the others in the gang and that nameless
gesture that men have, became his, when they reach for something in their pants pockets and flapshroud the coat away,
elbows bent, head to one side, like a theater manager coming
out at midnight in a hurry checking to see if the keys are all
there. With the coming of the suit and this adult gesture, Cody's
life in Denver entered a second phase and this one had for its
background, its prime focal goal, the place to which he was
forever rushing, the place his father had only known as a bum
in meek stumbling uplooking approach or had more vigorously
known in his youth but that was Des Moines and long ago,
nothing less and nothing more than the redbrick wall behind
the red neons: it was everywhere in Denver where he went and
everywhere in America all his life where he was. It was in the
secret dusty place around the corner of the frontwall of the
poolhall, up near the second-story beauty parlor windows there,
actually in the alley or area between buildings no more than a
foot wide or floored by anything but the most darkened debris
of the city but it was illuminated by a nearby red neon and some
from the poolhall below, it showed every furrow of the brick,
it clicked sadly on and off with the lights——in the beauty parlor
itself you could see the interior with its fathead shapes haunted
by red and empty now, see through it in through the around-
the-corner window that, like the wall, hid, as so many things in
America on Main Streets and now even on bleak suburban
streets that have chiropodists' and lawyers' offices near rectories
and old houses with hooks over a defunct second-story door
without stairs which is the old hayloft door and maybe a man
in a roundpeak nineteenth-century hat was hanged from that
hook, these things also hid behind the red neons of our front-
ward noticeable desperately advertised life. The new loneliness
that came to Cody with the coming of a suit and a topcoat was
the difference between sitting on an upturned bucket in the
smoky exciting dumps of Saturday morning on Sante Fe Drive,
near the unbelievably exciting crossing of the D. & R.G. railroad tracks that nudged a long smooth corridor through the
lean and ricket of dumpbacks, junkpiles and hangbrowed fences

for a solid mile, a place at least of wild playful promise where all
you had to do was wear overalls (like the can jungle place *My
Man Godfrey* wanted to go back to after he got his fill of Park
Avenue in a tremendously Hollywoodian naïve Depression
movie that was nevertheless naïvely true, the unspeakable visions of the individual), the railroad track that swooped from
the smear of dumpsmokes in the blue morning air cleanly and
swiftly to the mountains of the mist, the green banks of another
El Dorado, another Colorado, which was a loneliness that could
be diverted by the actions of one hundred interesting grimy
junkmen laboring with tragic heavy importance among the
skewered wrecks and rustpiles——the difference between this
and standing in the middle of the winter night on a sidewalk
that is not your home beneath cold red neons glowing as softly
as if it was still summer but now on a redbrick wall which es-
chews a humid and perforated iciness of its own, corrupted,
dank with winter, not the place to lean a lonely back and in spite
of all this grimness inherent in it suggesting more than it ever
could suggest in the summer and with infinite greater adult
excitement than the dump a joy, but a joy so much stronger
than the joy of the dump that it was like the man's need for
whiskey supplanting the boy thirst for orange soda and took as
much trouble and years to develop, the joy of the downtown
city night. Great sign posters set on top of low graveled roofs of
bowling alleys and shining fiercely against the bare bald backs
of windowless warehouses, or maybe filling the windowed eyes
of a hotel with their sheens, the glitter and yet the hidden be-
yondish gloom of this drove Cody in his secretest mind as it has
myself and most others to further penetrations into the interior
streets, the canyons, the ways, so much like the direction music
takes in the mind or even the undiscoverable flow of dream
images that make dreaming a tragic mystery; and so seeking
rushing all dreams into the heart of it, always the redbrick wall
behind red neons, waiting. Something was there that Cody and
I saw together in an alley in Chicago years later, when we parked
a Cadillac limousine in an unobtrusive black corner, pointed it
to the street; that Cody saw a thousand times in the walls of
towns of Iowa, Virginia, or the San Joaquin Valley; something,
too, that was namelessly related in his poor tortured consciousness to the part of the redbrick wall he had always seen from

the smooth old waitingroom bench of the County Jail when his
father had been arrested for drunkenness on Larimer Street
probably with five or six others taken en masse from a warehouse ramp, waiting for his appearance before the judge to
appeal to the court for some mete of mercy for his father, swearing he hadn't drunk for a month before and soon making great
childly speeches that sometimes astonished people and later was
brought to the attention of juvenile authorities who come looking to aid Cody like the Beast to aid the Beauty: the brickwall,
always dully glowing from dark red to gray bleak red as a neon
somewhere flashed, seen through a little barred window on the
inside wall and where calendars depicting Indian maids in the
moonlight with beads and exposed breasts drove Cody to wonder about the world that spoke of beautiful piney islands and
Indian love calls and Jeannette MacDonald yet had nothing to
show for it but jailhouses, arrested fathers, distant moanings,
clocks tocking, and the one spike-driven sorrow of that red wall
besmirched with lights that were intended for the streets for
official passersby, but hid something behind for some sad and
dishonest reason faintly related to what his father sometimes
complained about; and yet had the ability like any old brickwall
of a factory if you put a white unloading light on it instead of
red of shining as forlorn as brown snow.

Reaching into his pocket with that gesture, the topcoat flying
behind him, see Cody hurrying into the heart of Denver with
the same gleam in his eye you see on the fenders of shiny new
automobiles just dusted out of that old house-light reflecting
garage but now wink to the wild neon of Main Street; see him,
sometimes in such a big hurry that it seemed the traffic light
clicked green just for him and whichever buddy arm-in-arm
with heads knocking in talk he sweeps along with, twinkling
'round-corner in a vanish of heels, so they don't have to stop
at all but cut right along to the poolhall, levels of conversation to match the exciting joy, wham, bam, those voluminous
talking-fogs whipping back like dialog balloons dissolving in
wintry air, a sight (again) little Cody oft dug from that lonely
Skylark winter window of his poor bumfather's creaking in old
chairs behind his watchpost dusty glass; maybe as he rushes a
bus-waiting girl, (again), legs akimbo, watching him suddenly
with that snaky sexy lovelike look and the kid's saying to himself

"So that's what they been doin all this time the big guys and girls (damn, damn, look at that Cadillac beat the light!)," the girl standing under candy-striped late Saturday afternoon October five-and-ten awnings, with dark glasses, a regular highheel downtown Denver broad; see Cody Pomeray trying to hurry into the heart of the great Denver evening that to him will find its obvious focus in the poolhall where sometimes the hour is so roaring that with the Tremont parlor backdoor open you can see a solid block of poolhall through the two joints like looking down an endless mirror all cuesticks, smoke, green; hustling to stab the heart of the night or be stabbed but always missing because it is not in the poolhall, or downtown further where the redbrick walls lead further, glowing from blackracked neons into unspeakable secret glittering centers where everything must be happening or at least give modified indication of where to go for it, show down what long dark lane and boulevard with its nameless forlorn corner (the Fox and Hunt Bar!) where a neon light hidden behind further buildings is sending an aura of invitation and calling men to come and make their mothlike approach (like the heroes of Dreiser whom he has hurtling like beetles against summer screendoors, against sad refinements and excitements in the huge dark of America, umalum, umalum), and instead the whole night and everything it'll ever give anybody besides death and absolute loss is to be found twelve, thirteen feet above Cody's head as he rushes all eyes into the poolhall, either with Watson the big Virgil of the Poolhall Night with whom he shares the same robe of refined dissipated excitement everyone else's dumb about, the shark and his boy, the stars of loungey interviews at midnight, like Miles and Lee Konitz cutting into a bar together, or, say, Ike and Harry Truman, or me and my boy into the union hall three thousand miles from home, or alone hankering; twelve, thirteen feet up the redbrick wall and barely around the corner into the between-buildings alley, so tragic and hidden from the city, right there, the vision, what you get, what there is.

To emphasize that it's Saturday night some people bring boxes of chocolate that they buy in poor beat drugstores that have bedpans and jockstraps in the window, thinking the ribbon, and the moonlit Indian maid with beads but this time (because dealing with ladies' tastes and palates, not rough crotches of cops) no breast, makes it Saturday night truly; Saturday night, which makes it entirely different that, as you walk by a drugstore with nothing to do and maybe a glum lack of interest, you see an ad for chocolate candy in the window——those selfsame boxes that used to have even more ornate Indians on them and women with longer beads framed in silverer moonlight——even the names are Saturday night sad, "Page and Shaw," "Schrafft," etcetera and all this is as connected to the meaning of Saturday night as those old syphilis movies of the Twenties showing a couple all dolled in evening clothes rushing uptown in a mad glitter of lights to a party (where they get the clap or the syph and later, after Saturday night is over, they have a suicide pact in ordinary weeknight clothes——) (this was an actual pix I saw and it wasn't a Thirties film because I saw it in the Thirties and even then, aged twelve, wondered about the oldness of the film). Candy in fancy boxes, chocolate, it's the only thing a drugstore that sells nothing else to eat will sell, the serious drugstores without sodafountains sell chocolate candy; ice cream sodafountains, the fancy kinds that make their own ice cream and candy and have tile floor and jars of hard candy all spick and span and intricate like you might imagine old Vienna looked, they also sell boxed candy, have big displays of it, all brands and the boxes with their golden arrangement and ribbons and fancy lettering catch at my heart as I say with this unspeakable realization that it's Saturday night——not only because the beau might tip his cap at the dismal door and present such a box, or because in a drugstore window otherwise made up of pans and rubber a lavender candy box sits humanly, sweetly, God-knows-whatly, *dearly*, *dismally* and the only person who's aware of drugstores on Saturday night is necessarily alone and lonely, but because in the Saturday night darkness and glitter (the special kind that makes iron fire escapes of the sides of theaters particularly bleak) boxes of chocolate candy signify staying at home in spite of festivities everywhere so-called, signify the speechless yearning to reach a hand across the abyss and in gentle self indulgence like that of the opium man across town behind drawn shades plop rich chocolates one by one into the mouth, listening, I'd say, not to the Hit Parade but the Saturday night dance parade remote band-broadcasts most networks have (while the woman of the house is ironing

the fresh fragrant wash), in your bathrobe and slippers, preferably Chinese style, with the funnies. But Saturday night is to
be best found in the redbrick wall behind the neons, it's now
infinitely bleaker than ever, like the iron fire escapes at the blind
wallsides of those great fat movie auditoriums that squat like
frogs in businesslike real estate are so much bleaker on Saturday
nights, they cast more hopeless shadows. Saturday night is when
those things that haunt us beyond our speech and the formations of our thoughts suddenly wear a sad aspect that is crying
to be seen and noticed all around and we can't do anything
about it and neither could Cody; and to this day he, older and
after all this time, goes now haunted in the streets of Saturday
night in the American city with his eyes torn out like Oedipus
who sees all and sees nothing from the agony of having lived
and lived and lived and still not knowing how to conjure from
the pitiful world and the folks around some word of praise for
something that makes him grateful and makes him cry but remains invisible, aloof, delinquent, complacent, not unkind but
just dumb, the streets themselves, the things themselves of life
and of American life, and the faces and hopes and attempts of
the people themselves who with him in gnashing map of earth
pronounce vowels and consonants around a nothing, they bite
the air, there's nothing to say because you can't say what you
know, it's a void, a Demosthenes pebble would have to drop
way long down to hit that kind of bottom. Sometimes way out
of town, say miles out on East Colfax, Cody, waiting for a bus,
or a ride, would see the distant rust glow of downtown neons
and be so impatient to get there at once that with his chin
lifted to his goal he would walk fast in such intense get-there
preoccupation (in his topcoat pockets his fists pressed against
his thighs for speed) he'd be like a man riding a wheel, a flat
wood doll you hold in your hand and give the legs a blurry
spin because miles from downtown was like the sudden tragedy
I felt one Thanksgiving in Lowell when the family decided to
go to the movies and though it was the biggest event that I
could've wished for I said I'd stick to my regular Thursday
night YMCA exercise gymn class and yet when I got to the Y
steps, even before my father's old Plymouth was vanishing in
a wink of red light as exciting as the red neons up against the
Kearney Square buildings and Chin Lee Restaurant five blocks

down and around the corner of which wildly I knew the theater was glittering, I realized it was Thanksgiving and there was no gym class (and so ran through shortcut railroad canal bridges among cardboard crates and mountains of millrags blue with dye, straight for the red walls of movie street as though, clutching my throat, only there I could ease the horror which had suddenly lifted me in the air in a dreamy realization that I was going to die), Cody feeling that way on lesser impulses most likely and maybe wasting his, dissipating his last dime on a wild promiscuous trolley ride that plummeted him in, and he ran to the poolhall, and nobody was there, it was closed for repairs or Thanksgiving, and always as he stood there on the sidewalk beneath the redbrick neon wall, thinking, unthinking, a cop cruiser came around the corner in a flash of evil two-toned black and white with shiny antenna and the growl of the radio and he turned away, he moved along, he had hurried for this and always for nothing more than this.

His father had never done anything but stare dumbly in alleys beneath windows of hotels that had red neons, in fact with that same grave careful floppyhat adventurous sorrow beneath the redbrick glow wall looking straight ahead with his eyes moist in the moon, but Cody was ambitious to conquer the world of men that existed up there in the shadows behind the swarming gloom in back of the neons that spread like brickdust softly exploding red and then dark again . . . and somewhere on the main drag a man hurrying across the street to serious business. When on rainy nights Cody happened to have fifteen cents for a bowl of noodle soup with rye bread and one pat of butter in some diner downtown, and sat there by the window with a stolen newspaper, and saw, through mediums and worlds of dark steel, concrete, and wetsplashed tar, through populations of parked cars beaded silver in the light from the diner and passing buses and Railway Express trucks and iron fences, through arches of nameless overpasses that for all he knew through the diner's silver reflecting window were the overpasses of darkness and the night itself, when through all this, as in a dream suddenly fished from loving infancy, he saw, barely saw, two blocks away, the deep bloodred neons of some bar and restaurant winking against the distant brownbrick of its building with subsidiary blue moons of neons that said *Sea Food, Steaks, Chops,* saw the thing agitating in otherwise gloomy city darkness more like the darkness he knew in the backass bridges and meatpacking porches of Wazee and the railroad tracks and agitating with a comfortable little message of joy to anybody who had the money or knew the people there to come on in and enjoy the shelter, the sea food, music, the waitresses, the hot hissing radiators, he wanted to go and be with it and go gabbling among humanities and not just meander in a blind chagrin like his Pa. It was like he wanted to penetrate and know the poolhall. Leaning his head on his hand at two o'clock of Monday morning in that diner and staring that neon, he thought, "And now, unlike Satnite when I came here with sixty-eight cents and had the wheatcake with sausages at thirty-five, and the fried onions with order at five, then the cream cheese sandwich at fifteen, and that gal with the marcelled hair in the green coat was making googoo eyes at me and I thought by gawrsh it was going to be one big dinger of a night and so and so but now, now, now, now and time has flown and rolled ah me and this pair of rubbers developed a hole sinst, now it's Sunday night or should I say Monday morning (yawn) and now for me to cut over there and eat the blue chops only the *ops* of which I can see in blue thar with the gaspump hiding the *ch* and my rubbers leaking I go over that pattering shiny rain that ain't interested in my mother or me and never has to do with anything but where it falls and maybe I slide in oilslick and go off that high curb, jump over the puddle as only I can, on tiptoe, zoom across the middle island, zoom to the dry sidewalk along the gray wall with the bulbs and down through that part that I can't see to that bar that starts town with a bloody light separatin this edge from general restaurants and bars of Denver as I go along, but here really if I'm going to die why do I get to feel so good and how come I feel so good so often anyhow, I don't even figure with any exactness what my next shoes will be bought out of, it's all fine and good to sit in a diner and enjoy soup and papers and looking out the window but sonofabitch goddamn if that coat hadn't been given me I'd be freezin this winter and where the hell have they put my father with all their lousy systems of lopping and laying away people, I've got a long long ways to go before I get to that hard bed in Johnson's buddy's attic, and a climb to boot, and in the rain, and my eyes are hot, and

I ain't got a belt, and finished my soup and would like to eat sea food, steaks and shops of chops *right now*. What is all that brownness of light in the railroad station damn damn damn. There's Denver, I always told Pa I wanted——he didn't believe me when we had that friend with the printing shop and let us sleep on the cots and I seen those beautiful views of the city with lights shining full of movies and plays and lobsters flown in from New York, and pretty women with silk stockings tied by garters to their cunt hooks where I gotta go with my hand tomorrow night, he didn't believe me when I predicted I'd be a big dispatching agent someday with a wife waiting for me where they have lit-up foyers and potted palm trees by the desk and upstairs you look out the window and there she is, the red light that says *RESTAURANT*, and the brick wall in back of it, and in blue *SEAFOOD, STEAKS, CHOPS*, and it's raining and I got a wife and car and Watson is with me in a tuxedo because he just won the World's title at billiards beating Willy Hoppe and we're gonna go push that car and make tire tracks in the rain to the middle of town and eat all we want, talking to the Mayor in the lobby, passing by the boxoffice with a pass, sitting in the box of the theater the three of us like in Vienna, us leaning forward and her hanging back with a wrap and everything dark and great and after the curtain goes down they yell 'Author! Author!' I guess I'm the author, did that whole thing while selling in Chicago, I bow then I go out for a smoke on the iron balcony overlooking Denver and I see the whole town and all the red lights blue lights below me and I even see that place where me and Pa slept on the cots and I teold him I sure did tyell him but all he thyought about was other things."

THEN ON THOSE MAD MYSTERIOUS gray afternoons when all of a sudden it was as though the Atlantic Ocean had swept its clouds over town and they had been further torn and tattered on the mountains and were swooping in a raw chill universe from all directions, screeching birds diving to see, occasional splutters of soft rain blowing upon the faces of people who stood at bus stops hugging their coats and packages to their bellies and not seeing their reflections in ruffled puddles at the curb——that kind of day, that'll only know a rosy cloud at sundown when the sun will find its tortured way through masses

and battles of fevered darkening matter——raw, dank, the wind
going like a gong through your coat and also through your
body——the wild woolly clouds hurrying no faster in the heavens above than the steam from the railyards hurrying over the
fence and up the street and into town——fantastic, noisy, the
kind of insanely excited day when suddenly at 2 P.M. you notice
some places (say, nothing more than Haggerty's washing machine distributor) have turned on their neons in the gray dark
and men in topcoats and hats go rushing towards the redbrick
walls and the Rathskellers of late dark-days, on those days Cody
too was rushing, looking around to see where to rush, everything was hankering, pointing, leaping, arrowing towards some
place in the mute gray mist of the wild city where, though the
premature red neons of the afternoon were already turned on
by busy absorbed office girls——Haggerty was standing there in
his store with one hand holding the front of his coat down, the
other reaching around and inside shroud of coat to pockets and
down deep there, for money or keys, saying to them "Say wait,
Sue——did I leave that box of samples in the Club McCoy last
night or in the back of the car?"——outside his windows, which
are gleaming red in the mad Denver afternoon, young assistants
of state senators and pretty mink secretaries of 17th Street are
rushing by and suddenly one pitiful raw ranch hand, to some
nameless point that all the whole city twenty square miles of
it squeezes and contracts in one speechless huge star-shaped
bat-ribbed air nerve to locate and centralize——there, and there
alone, we'll find our chops and smoky talk of the most important dinnertime in Denver——but not only the most important,
the one most reminding of the joy of the crib, the answer to all
the countrified American crying in the wilds. "Yes, yes, oh yes
indeed, yes siree, yes, yes." Maybe poor Cody, collar up, feet a
little damp because of the hole in his rubbers at the toe-end,
would be walking along a block-long wire fence of a factory, the
traffic bowling in the street all in the same direction, and ahead
in the flying mist through steams and soots he saw the huge
wonderful neon of a major hotel rising——this for the son of a
man who'd been born in a little impoverished junction town
in Missouri represented the thrilling unspeakable answer to all
the wants of life, no more the log fence in the gray fog and the
mountain of used cars——and he would think "Oh damn how

delightful it'll all be in a minute as soon as——say wait——" and he too reaching in that pocket——So now, a minute before gray becoming dusk, Cody stands in the doorway of the poolhall waiting for Watson, Buckle, Johnson, Evans, Jackoff, anything to come and unfold themselves, and he does not know, does not know, cannot know, even I don't really know, and that thing twelve, thirteen feet over his head, that spot haunted red wall, what it is that makes the approaching night so exciting, so shivering, so all-fired what-where, so deep. It was years later before he found the answer in the little nameless second when, after meeting Joanna in a sodafountain and taking her to the Ouray Hotel, Tremont corner fifth floor room, and turning from his pants on the chair to go on with what he was saying to her his future wife as she spread her thighs experimentally on the faded pink bedcover, a beauteous creature of the first order with long ringlets and curls and only incidentally fifteen at this time he saw in the act of swinging his eyes from chair to bed a nameless red tint fading and flashing on the redbrick wall just outside the window, saw this in a fraction through the little dirty thin muslin curtain that billowed in the drafts of steam from the silver radiator which was also slightly roseate from the neon, the dirty sooty sill also almost rusty lit from the glow, a scrap of paper one hundred feet off the snowy ground suddenly swirling past in the January nightwind, the whole big flat window rattling, the neon coming and going on the brick, the poor hidden brick of America, the actual place that you must go if you must bang your head to bang it at all, the center of the grief and what Cody now saw and realized from all that time the center of the ecstasy.

SLIM BUCKLE WAS A GREAT BIG figure going down those Denver alleys between the rickety backs of houses that were completely suburban and respectable out front with lawns and sprinklers because the heat of the plains sun turns the grass brown, striding with bowed head in some kind of tremendous concentration of his own among the smoking incinerators, the brick ovens of Denver backyards that once you've seen them you wonder why they didn't have them in your neighborhood they're so exactly like home, they remind you of Saturday mornings when you were six and knew the day was young and blue just by looking over the fence through pale smokes of whoever it is is always burning something on Saturday morning (and hammering on nails in the afternoon). In fact Buckle went through these alleys (en route to the poolhall) with his hands in his pockets like Sad Sack but whistling like Genet's Alberto at his gayest, a way of walking and whistling when he was a little kid and scrabbled after others in a calm universe of his own that he carried around to wherever they wanted to go, spitting silently through his teeth and probably like Lousy over the waving grasses of afternoon in some occasion when the gang had fainted under a tree and was too lazy to play jackknife or call others over beyond the fence. Trotting along like this, calm, lovely, bemused, he approached the grownup gang as though he wasn't six-foot-four at all.

FRISCO DREAMS, the most huge beautiful hill in the world with a broad Main Street with trolleys and activity on both sidewalks, a mighty swoop——as though Frisco was suddenly as big as New York, as though it had hills like Amsterdam from 125th to 140th but steeper and so white——

It had elements of a strange Chicago I've known, God knows pourquoi Chicago, mais now to facts——Pop lived on that greatest white hill——at top it overlooks sea and even junction of Alameda and Frisco road near the sea to which one arrives after the rollies of Iowa and world-views of Colorado——

A lot of Fillmore in that big hill——Like heaven going up the thing on foot——the Chicagoan thing is the ferry to Oakland ——Though I never took it and no ferries in Chi, it is the water——The new, latest Frisco hill was more downtown (that's great joy of bighill, out, like N's Robinson Street, in the white jewelry sunshiney part of town) new part had more bigcity gray and redbrick in it, there was an enormous dormitory-mine with a gymn on main level, like Orson Welles hall of mirrors in Frisco Park (*Lady From Shanghai*) and I walked, there was something over my head, balloon or pigeon, a vastened downtown Frisco and the one I in real life dug back of Embarcadero, old western warehouse firms——Why doth the Lord make me wonder in those places?——

A woman in a beat car on that gray hill——an infant—— cobbles——it's other side of town than Cody's and my Pop's white hill——unjoyous——connected with those salt mines——as though it was her, the baby, and jail for me——but much more than that because to the side were some of those doorstoops of Montreal and Brooklyn and some of my old relatives, Aunt Marie, Lynn, potted plants and everything's waiting for me to understand it.

L's BAR——I WAS OF COURSE so stoned I thought I was in Mexico in all those marvelous marijuana hallucinated nights when I didn't even know where I was without some tremendous effort and sometimes actually didn't as in case of *Battleground* movie house to which we arrived in a trance from a taxi wherein apparently some interest had absorbed us a million miles from either Mexico City or the movie——and incidentally activity that directly contributes to my Mexico City dreams, there were imageries, exactly in that neighborhood, a side street running parallel to Juárez but to the south and to the side, a place I walked in a dream but never really walked except nearby (or that is symbolically nearby) with Ike and Dave the night of the weed adventure——I believe an image which later became the bulwark of one of them of my dreams of MexCity was actually formed while riding, high, to *Battleground* in that taxi——

All this whole consciousness of cities as bigger versions of Lowell kicks as my father must have experienced them in his own raggly day began with Mexico——and it was because it so wondrously reminded me (in its simplicity, straightness) of Lowell (and French-Canadians). At Danny's I got hi true, but just so as to say "Time hasn't moved though of course I know it has"——and actually it *was* ten o'clock before I knew it. Walking forth from D's the real high began——now let's *talk* about high till daylight——after all, I'd not smoked for so long, or got hi, I was pure and not a dissipate——The highness first manifested itself in an exaggerated sense of the importance (mind you *not* the significance) of what I recounted——utter contempt for ordinary connectives, so that Danny wanted to have explanations to be conversive——I plunged into the bottom of my subject which was the origin of young guys who drink in Bowery at twenty and lose teeth but not muscles at twenty-five——origin was Lowell dump, where in North Carolina tea-dreams I also saw Cody and tried to write a "story" about it——and as I told everything swam in front of me, all the Centralville Lakeview dreams of the dump and along the dump and the brown nights and my father ignoring me again as I now ignore my own boy——and have to, as *he* had to——but when I was alone I met that man in hall with garbage, rode in dumb silence after "Gettin cold out!" but everything seemed self explanatory when he didn't get off in lobby but continued to basement and I said "Oh, you're going to the *basement*" and in that high "cheapness" I've noticed assuming that his silence had only been a menial form of humbling himself as though he was the janitor, not on speaking terms with guests where at first I'd dug him as snooty citizen. Assured by the basement I went out into cold night and cut (deep in thought of something till I crossed Seventh Avenue) then, as usual, turned to look at Danny's window and imagined everybody in apartment which is so *eternal*, we've all seen it so many million times in death, everybody watching me, curling their lips "There he goes now, I've seen that one before, he always leaves drunk and stupid." Up Greenwich Avenue I then go to meet Irwin and Josephine at San Remo's, digging people in streets, stores, women's jail, the *coolness* of the world in general as though it wasn't *l'Enfer* at all, losing stretches of this in myself, popping back at Sixth Avenue to decide a glance at Waldorf then up Eighth Street and for this circling far to the right of my course and because of that and that only running smack into Irwin and Jo who didn't seem pleased and nobody's pleased with me any more, I'm going to Hongkong, fuck 'em all.

In fact I felt the utter horror of having to be with them in my high, because they are evil, both of 'em.

We somehow got to L's bar and I didn't know where it was—— I asked twice, they said Thompson Street, it meant nothing to me except with tremendous effort trying to recall Josh Hay (who'd lived on Thompson) in another city a million miles away just as the "me" that slept behind the outdoor ad sign in Asbury Park in 1943 and many others before and after have no relation to the "me" of now; so L's bar was located in heaven, or anyway in the world and madly——on a blue street in fact, powerfully reminiscent of the location of Las Brujas nightclub in MexCity on its sidestreet off Letran and with the same Eternity. This location is like seeing, for the first time, a great and beautiful inevitable face, a face that couldn't have failed to exist. It was a Les bar and not only that the coolest and best in New York——Irwin said "They're all *kind* in here, it's not a wild dike fight hole"——and it was so, quiet, cocktailish, the jukebox blowing the finest softest tenderest records (Frank Sinatra's "April in Paris," Tony Bennett's "Blue Velvet") for these little gals some of them gorgeous had refined taste and because women love love, women who love with women if only for a fling are the most (though this still depends on spirituality) loving and understanding of love and hungup on love in all creation——bah.

IN PUEBLO, COLORADO in the middle of the winter Cody sat in a lunchcart at three o'clock in the morning in the middle of the poor unhappy thing it is to be wanted by the police in America or at least in the night (slapping dime down on counter like killing a fly with hand)——America, the word, the sound is the sound of my unhappiness, the pronunciation of my beat and stupid grief——my happiness has no such name as America, it has a more personal smaller more tittering secret name——America is being wanted by the police, pursued across Kentucky and Ohio, sleeping with the stockyard rats and howling tin shingles of gloomy hideaway silos, is the picture of an axe in *True Detective Magazine*, is the impersonal nighttime at crossings and junctions where everybody looks both ways, four ways, nobody cares——America is where you're not even allowed to cry for yourself——It's where Greeks try hard to be accepted and sometimes they're Maltese or from Cyprus——America is what laid on Cody Pomeray's soul the onus and the stigma——that in the form of a big plainclothesman beat the shit out of him in a backroom till he talked about something which isn't even important any more——America (TEENAGE DOPE SEX CAR RING!!) is also the red neon and the thighs in the cheap motel——It's where at night the staggering drunks began to appear like cockroaches when the bars close——It is where people, people, people are weeping and chewing their lips in bars as well as lone beds and masturbating in a million ways in every hiding hole you can find in the dark——It has evil roads behind gas tanks where murderous dogs snarl from behind wire fences and cruisers suddenly leap out like getaway cars but from a crime more secret, more baneful than words can tell——It is where

Cody Pomeray learned that people aren't good, they want to be bad——where he learned they want to cringe and beat, and snarl is the name of their lovemaking——America made bones of a young boy's face and took dark paints and made hollows around his eyes, and made his cheeks sink in pallid paste and grew furrows on a marble front and transformed the eager wishfulness into the thicklipped silent wisdom of saying nothing, not even to yourself in the middle of the goddamn night—— the click of coffee saucers in the poor poor night——Someone's gurgling work at a lunchcart dishpan (in bleakhowl Colorado voids for nothing)——Ah and nobody cares but the heart in the middle of US that will reappear when the salesmen all die. America's a lonely crockashit.

It's where the miserable fat corner newsstand midget sleeps in the lunchcart with a face that looks as if it had been repeatedly beaten on the sidewalk whereon he works——Where ferret-faced hipsters who may be part-time ushers are also lushworkers and half queer and hang around undetermined——Where people wait, wait, poor married couples sleep on each other's shoulders on worn brown benches while the nameless blowers and air conditioners and motors of America rumble in the dead night——Where Negroes, so drunk, so raw, so tired, lean black cheeks on the hard arms of benches and sleep with pendant brown hands and pouting lips the same as they were in some moonlit Alabama shack when they were little like Pic or some Jamaica, New York nigger cottage with pickaninny ricket fence and sheepdogs and Satnite busy-cars street of lights and around-the-corner glitter and suggestion of good times in tall well-dressed black men walking gravely thither——Where the young worker in brown corduroys, old Army shoes, gas station cap and two-toned "gang" jacket of a decade ago now the faded brown of a nightshift worker dozes head down at the trolley stop with his right hand palm-up as if to receive from the night——the other hand hanging, strong, firm, like Mike, pathetic, made tragic by unavoidable circumstance——the hand like a beggar's upheld, with the fingers forming a suggestion of what he deserves and desires to receive, shaping the alms, thumb almost touching fingertips, as though on the tip of the tongue he's about to say in sleep and with that gesture what he couldn't say awake "Why have you taken this away from me, that I can't draw my breath in the peace and sweetness of my own bed but here in these dull and nameless rags on this humbling shelf I have to sit waiting for the wheels to roll" and further——"I don't want to show my hand but in sleep I'm helpless to straighten it up, yet take this opportunity to see my plea, I'm alone, I'm sick, I'm dying" (a groan from another sleeper and one that has so little to do with a waiting room, rather with a dying room, sickroom, operating room, battlefield, doom's gate)——"see my hand uptipped, learn the secret of my heart, give me the thing, give me your hand, take me to the safe place, be kind, be nice, smile; I'm too tired now of everything else, I've had enough, I give up, I quit, I want to go home, take me home O brother in the night, take me home, lock me in safe——take me to where there is no home, all is peace and amity, to the place that never should have been or known about, to the family of life——My mother, my father, my sister, my wife and you my brother and you my friend——take me to the family which is not——but no hope, no hope, no hope, I wake up and I'd give a million dollars to be in my bed, O Lord save me." There's nothing in this speculation and delirious sleep——I hear the click of a newcomer's heels, the litany of voices, the doors squeeking——

NOW THAT IT'S ACTUALLY TIME to leave home and go to the last coast——across the mist and cold——I'm packing——it's only at this very moment as I sit to mourn this terrible night in my life whether I'm Duluoz or whoever I am that I realize why Cody didn't write in answer to that foolish letter, it was because I mentioned Josephine for his couch on the same page that I scribbled a letter to his wife, why last summer he'd worked out an elaborate code for talking about Josephine, it was at the head of the letter *Dear Cody* (she was coming) or just *Cody* (she wasn't). But do they suppose that I'm evil or mean to do harm? I've finally become so distracted that it's going to be only with the greatest struggle that I'll be able to find out who I am in the coming months in the hell and gone of the world at the risk of losing my mind forever. Who would ever have thought that Duluoz, poor Duluoz who was after all just a nineteen-year-old kid with a sense of exile when most other guys are simply brooding in early bars, that Duluoz would come to lose his mind. No, I've got to live——and Metkovich today said his father was joyful at seventy-five and *his* own father had lived to one-o-nine, 109, because of an earthy Yugoslavian *will to live* and if, he said, we didn't hustle to understand what that meant we were liable to die——of emotional congestion, poor American folly, fear and self-horror. Many many times tonight I cry in my wandering soul "Oh why didn't my father live?" I look at the galleys of *H from the C* I threw away in the poor football pennant basket my mother bought me for the gay October afternoons of 1950 upstairs (don't you realize what upstairs means, I'm exiled and she's exiled to this horrible downstairs because of my own stupidity that the ghost of my father never warned or curbed, we have half the room we used to have, same rent, more problems, have to listen to the sounds of the new tenants upstairs as if in hell listening to the upper sounds of heaven, they are a middleaged particularly materialistic complaining New York couple, one time the lady had me help park her car when she got stuck on the big tree out front that figures in the drama of my stupidity because it was my lovely summertree of 1950 T-reveries which led to fear, to her, to not refusing to move from upstairs with her leaving my mother alone and subsequently weeping to move to South, to Nin's, O when will the troubles of this *cursed* family end, why were we all made to totter in the dark like slaves while other lesser families shit in the light and moon over their own dumb asshole ignorant emptiness, why were the wild dark Duluozes cursed and especially the ones like Emil and Michel?——that tree——that couple upstairs——and having finally reconciled myself to downstairs after the horrors and pains of late September after her first insult, working and earning a few bucks and getting a bed into this room and oiling my machine and yet suddenly inexplicably getting drunk too often and abandoning Rachel and Janie Thaw for that bully Josephine, it all began October 25 which was also the great moment of discovering my soul, yet reconciled to downstairs as a cute cozy place only now to find myself hounded to the end and have to pack and leave and head for the hell and gone even from the desk I only finished repairing three days ago and which was going to be the scene of studies and the whole vast ordered universe of my life which I loved, I have to, go, like a fugitive, staggering again in the dark just like that dream of me and Pa and Ma, never Nin, staggering with few belongings on a dark road from New Haven back to home and our cats following us about to be run over by cars with their blinding headlights coming at us on the highway, I have to pack, clear completely so as to comply with evil hidden wishes of this world, have nowhere to go except the water, the terrible terrible dark sea water leaving behind the fields of life and my mother the great and final protector of my life and soul who sleeps or maybe doesn't in the next room right now, O who can I pray to for mercy, I prayed to my Pop to make her happy and that's a futile thing to ask——there she lies, when I go for coffee I hear her waking, it's a bad night for her too, for this is the night I came home and said "I'd better leave once and for all, it's the only way to save trouble all around," and so in effect, "This is my last night in your house, mother, that you so lovingly prepared for me yet how could you foresee or even prevent my evil which precipitated its own evils, and the first evil was not putting her down when I first realized I didn't love or like her at all eight days before our marriage"——O dull clown. And now to make up for the botch of my days I think I can create a great universe and of course I can——) as I say, I look at the *H from the C* galleys in the basket and I remember my Pop the printer and how he'd have treasured them and never allowed me to throw them away. Maybe I'm throwing away my life there but I swear I'm not——This night is so tortured it's unthinkable——I'll come back and catch it all on sober gray mornings of the sea, of Alaska, of South America, of Javanese cities. I'm in love with my life and I'm sticking to it——I mean the belief in it. I may be a distracted wretch but I am still a man and I know how to fight and survive, I have before. Gods, if not help me, if instead barb me, be careful of me, I can catch thunderbolts and pull you down and have done it before. Adieu!

AND NOW LOOK, IN 1943 I dug the meaning of the sea when I called it my brother, the sea is my brother——Now it's up to tomorrow if I go at once——on the great ship, Den's round-the-world cargo ship, my destiny——I want to watch along the Nile and the Ganges——In any case now I am alone. Sin is sinking in my bones and making me older and wiser. But I'm only wiser to the wise men——my children grieve for me. Weep for me, weep for anybody, weep for the poor dumbfucks of this

world——weep for the waves——weep, weep——now my eyes
begin a voyage from which I am going to return resurrected
and huge and silent. So I packed all night, just desk papers, and
that's the horrible sad thing——my dark glasses of the hospital,
okay (given to me by jovial veterans' committees); my reading glasses twelve dollars when I sold my book; my machine
shrouded now for good, I can't take it with me, I remember the
day it came home on Sarah Avenue when Pop lost his business
and I started right in with stories about Bob Chase owner of
the New York Chevies and typed up the summer league (Gulf,
Tydol, those namelessly sunlit names on purpose, Texaco, refinements of sunlight in each one, *dissipating* in the refinement
of sunlight in the entire operation of the league); that machine,
that the poor spastic flayed, and now everybody knows it from
H from the C, that machine my father himself wrote on, editori-
als, letters (the trouble with life is that it has its own laws and
controls the souls of men without regard for their least wish,
and this is slavery); my Harcourt ad that Deni Bleu proudly
wants and will see tomorrow (and how will Deni receive me
now?); my little erasers, the round one which I'll bring, the soft
straight one which I'll leave, all this matters to me like State,
it's vaster than Assemblies; the poor pipe (Pop's) and pipe rack
I can never use again, which is reminder of change (no more
smokes) more than anything else in my tragic coffin of a desk
tonight: O the child of the Phebe livingroom with his first vision
of the marbles, did he come to live just to be buried? (this desk
actually an old Faulknerian desk from a Southern mansion, Nin
and Luke birthday gift 1950, when birthdays were birthdays
and not anniversaries of guilt and culpritude); the sales slip,
Ma had just bought me new crepesole shoes for home here
and now I have to lay them down on foreign ground when she
had intended them for Radio City or her first pitiful sight of
U.N. building; Lord please protect your tender lambs! if you
can't do that then bless them, bless them——my blue Eversharp
pencil also from hospital, with which I started that great diary
that temporarily saved me and started the international spectral
and now lost Duluoz of the Dolours; a bundle of recent letters,
tied, with pathetic messages from the good hearts of the world
including June and it's as though I was battling black evil birds
tonight and not anything human, something that the Devil

sends, not the world, and the great black bird broods outside
my window in the high dark night waiting to enfold me when
I leave the house tomorrow only I'm going to dodge it successfully by sheer animalism and ability and even exhilaration,
so goodnight——

And to go on and I meant to tell everything about my departure, only way to do it one by one the haunting things of
this breathing life——Roy Redman of Clyde Lines, who is a
curly colored guy working as attendant at Kingsbridge V.A.
Hospital and reminds me not powerfully etc. but *exactly* of my
sister in his every bemused method of, say, watching television, forgetting what you just said, the same lips too (nothing
feminine 'bout him at all and especially nothing Uncle Tom
Negro) and who was one of the hardtime organizers of the
N.M.U. back in the Depression when seamen were bums to be
attacked by cops on old inky waterfronts of early Pathé Newsreels and you saw clubs flying, well you saw this Roy Redman,
he signs his name "Red" with quotes, and in parenthesis, like
this, (Clyde Line)——he wrote me a letter of introduction to
the VP-president of N.M.U., beginning "This will serve to introduce to you a very good friend of mine, Jack L. Duluoz.
I will consider it a personal favor to me if you can see your
way clear to extend any courtesy or consideration within your
power to him. Please accept my good wishes and in memory
of old times together, thank you, Yrs. very truly 'Red' Redman
(Clyde Line)"——this courtly letter which is one of my greatest
possessions may breeze me through the N.M.U. at a crucial
moment tomorrow or Thursday——and it rings exactly the way
he talks, slow, grave, certain, bemused, gum chewing. Everybody believed and trusted in Red at the hospital, just to see him
sometimes you'd shiver joyfully in your chest especially if it was
night and the fights were coming on in Television and everybody sat around, with Red, only for a moment off work, saying,
"Who's oan tab to-night?" with that very nameless drawl that
he developed and took with him probably round the world
ten times in the great night of ships and men that I will love
if it's full of Reds——and one dewy morning I observed him
in a new light from the window of my ward by watching not
him but other colored men coming in to work where they lost
their Negro street personalities and became attendants, trying

to imagine Red on the street in Harlem or wherever or even
in Ralph Cooper's hip nightclub, how he would carry himself
in that great challenging parade which is the American Negro
Sidewalk of the World. So there's that letter of intro——and
I'm taking with me the little tiny handsized Bible I stole from
that Fourth Avenue bookstore in the used religious book section at the back because I thought the guy was a cheat in his
bargainings with me over the exchange of new textbooks for
used books, the Bible that I read only once or twice the print is
so small and the big occasion was in Mexico City when in the
incredibly warm glow of my lovely checker-cloth beside the soft
goof lovely bed, well fed with midnight cheeseburgers from the
Insurgentes lunchroom or just newly high, sitting on the edge
of the bed for a moment before the sleeps that in MexCity on
T were never equaled in sheer sweetness and LOVE except on
sleeping pills recently at Kingsbridge (in fact I dug Red Redman on goofballs, that is, just watched his face, many anight
before I fell asleep in fleece), I was on that bed-edge maybe
with a smidgin of sweet vermouth, maybe Sherman was high in
his room or gone, but I happened to pick up this midget New
Testament Bible and in my huge-hearted state of high love I
saw the great words (at eight thousand feet above sea level!)
and was so amazed with almost every sentence or that is line I
saw that I felt *attacked* by words, overtaken by great blows of
consciousness I should have absorbed a long time ago, realizations of Jesus I'd never dared before, Jesus as a prophet and
his political necessities and positions as a prophet, including
charmed and awed interpenetrations of the mystery of the Bible
and especially of ancient Jewish need in rote, till I fell asleep,
in balms, as I can no longer do for I'm now a man of the wide
wide water and of strife, but then I thought about the fleecy
lulls of the Eternal Lamb and so perhaps one stormy night in
the Indian Ocean that I read about in old *Argosy* magazines
of 1933 when I thought the sea had shrouds and heroes only,
I'll look at my little hand Bible, holding it over my face on the
bunk, and a newer further diving into the awfulness and beauty
of the Great Bible will happen to me——(Behold, your house is
left unto you desolate)——Oh so!——I'm taking that with me,
and the little tattered red French dictionary sitting under it in
my poor rolltop cubbyholes, I'll need it in Marseilles and Le

Havre and Algiers and to read Genet——What kind of journey is the life of a human being that it has a beginning but not an end?——and that it gets worse and worse and darker all the time till time disappears?

And for Den I have a surprise, his white silk scarf that he forgot at Lionel's that night last Spring when Lionel and I imitated Alastair Sim for the girls from the office, Janie, Alice, Lola, and the great young kid Sid, and Den showed up with that sour seaman whom I am going to see tomorrow and in fact called three times in the past two days always fearful of what he really thinks of me and actually what I've got to do is not care what he thinks and indicate that to him somehow or he will undoubtedly try to hip Deni wrong to me, though because my lot is now Deni's if we sail together or even later the seaman his friend is a friend of mine, "any friend" etc. I'm going to present Den his scarf. O reader just follow me blindly into the hell and gone! And for blazing sea days I'm bringing my new dark glasses in their white plastic case, the glasses I won at the hospital in the carnival where you couldn't lose and I haven't used them much yet and still feel almost guilty (everything belongs to me because I am poor) when I consider that I flubbed off since the hospital when I didn't have to as the calm immortal presence of those glasses indicate, glasses put together by careful workmen using parts gravely manufactured, and why does it reach *my* destructive hands?, I'm not taking my brown writingboard that I found in a waste can here in Richmond last year on a walk——nor my briefcase, what do I need now with a *briefcase*!!!

EN ROUTE TO STATEN ISLAND in the rainy dawn I walk rapidly on balls of my feet like a Cody heading for work and remembering Washington 1942 and other dawns when workmen stand in doorways, nothing else could have reminded me of a special series of going to work hot-eyes dawn and general strange manly sensation——passed Crossbay Boulevard a rainy green alley towards the sea, only saw it last minute looking up from *Daily News*, Ah me——Oh Lord——Now the gray rooftops of Brooklyn as I head for the ship that has been flying towards me in the night all night——Dawn lights in the kitchens of raw rickety outer Brooklyn——We make the same big famous curve (on El) that I first made June 1943 at a time when, twenty-one,

I should have kept on going to sea, at a time when I thought I was old and had syphilis (warts)——When Pop was alive and would have been proud of my manly seagoing which only now almost nine terrible years later I acknowledge to his grave which is also under this great rain that extends in mist to the tragic rainfields of Nashua where my brother's lost wails sleep and new autos roll in the slick road that I saw the day of his funeral 1926, year of Cody's birth——The big ship at eight is due to be warped in at Pier 12 Army Base, the *Pres. Adams*——Tall, French, sad, whooping Deni Bleu will be standing among tangles of wires in the engine room when they inform him that chagrined J. D. waits outside four years too late after our agreements of 1947 in the fog and dark of Marin County that I'll never forget and haven't even begun to penetrate——(that's for memory)—— Brooklyn——a few scuddy clouds from the sea, a whip of rain, a smoke and all the beauteous, bottom-of-the-tank feeling of real life to which I now return amen.

STATEN ISLAND, six million things inundating my brain—— Sitting in the little diner outside Army Base, watching sharp Negro cats with suitcases, and Puerto Ricans with coats, taking quick shot drinks at bar, who're cutting off the ship for kicks, maybe the *Adams*——a gray exciting Atlantic day again but now a wild one connecting me namelessly with Oakland and the time I went there on Bay Bridge train for a reason I can't remember——also when I was with Den, at Golden Gate track, back across the land to here, Staten Island, to which I just arrived in the wild ferry where I chatted with a tanker seaman and dug planks and flotsam in water remembering the danger I faced foolishly in summer 1943 when I dove off the stern of the *George S. Weems* to keep cool——the same waters where corpses floated——a ferry in the grayness making you realize what a mad mind Jack London had (strictly as a guy)——sitting in the window of diner across gate to make sure Den doesn't slip into New York——the Puerto Rican left, headed for two days of kicks in East Harlem fucking gone girls on Oriental bedcovers and eating yellow rice and beans *con pollo*, the colored guy he'll whoop at the Palm Café, these guys the sharpest workers in the world, more, say, than Cody, because traveling, and I am here in same moodway as Cody, fast, talk to everybody, no "dignity," speed, kicks (I only know, that is, I *strictly* know what I know and that's why sketching is not for my secret thoughts——my own complete life, an endless contemplation, is so interesting, I love it so, it is vast, goes everywhere——) And this gray day as I wait and pray for that world ship is the same that gloomily unfolded in Ozone Park and Brooklyn as I came over——but now it has gulls, wild hungers, voices of workers, figures crossing rainy supply dumps with umbrellas, black wires, poles, masts of ships, black forms of all kinds, a call from across the world and from the great gray mist of America and American things and wild smoke of boy headed for prepschool but so much more.

BROWN HALLS OF MEN——now by God many hours and events later I am finally entrenched in the vision that I re-discovered my soul with, the "crowded events of men" only now it's me, myself smack in it——at the moment, flush because I'm going to start earning within a matter of hours I'm having a huge fifteen cent beer in a bar off the waterfront but a brown businessman's bar and at the hem of the financial district with Emil-like fathers and men drinking at long bar——I say "brown" bar not in jest, red neons or pink ones too shine in the smoke and reflect off dark browned panels, the beer is brown, tabletops, the lights are white but embrowned, the tile floor too (same mosaics as the barbershop in which I had visions of Cody staring). Now what I'm going to do is this——think things over one by one, blowing on the visions of them and *also* excitedly discussing them as if with friends as I did last night joyously drunk in the West End (see actually I'm not old and sick at all but the maddest *liver* in the world right now as well as the best watcher and that's no sneezing thing)——signs for Guinness Stout are namelessly brown——I'm sitting in the backroom so as to think but I'm in the whole brown bar and one of the men——All day I've been amazed by the fact that I'm a man and have the right to work for a living and spend my money as I see fit——I guess I'm finally growing up——amazed with for instance the union meeting in the brown hall of Marine Cooks and Stewards especially the big mad colored cat cook who got up and blew a crazy speech that was like a tenor horn in its wild jump and pitches but of course compared to other speeches infinitely more real and joyous especially when he kept saying "Frisco, Frisco" and that is my

mad dream, I want (I'll do anything) to be on a ship that sails
out of Frisco that supra-marvelous city of brown bars and smoke
and men and S.I.U. white-capped seamen's halls and Cody
and Buckle, the principals of the Denver poolhall, and Frisco
poolhalls themselves, the whole wild world of men in crazy
smoky places including the M.C.S. Puerto Ricans who take us
back past Adam and Eve to meetingplaces of the great *Latin
night* that I dug in MexCity——Now, I'm going to be interested
in these things all my life but in order to really involve myself
as a man on the other level of man-to-man communication I'm
also going to talk about these things with people if I can, like
for instance Deni's beautiful story last night about the assistant
electrician who got off the *Adams* and is now replaced by wonderful goodnatured simple Joe-like guy (a few beers gives a man
the *power* to think like I'm doing but too many robs you of the
rest)——I'm going to talk about these things with guys but the
main thing I suppose will be this lifelong monologue which is
begun in my mind——lifelong complete contemplation——what
else on earth do I *really* know unless I'm depriving myself of
kinds of knowledge that would bring out those qualities in me
which are most valuable to others; not me, although I keep
thinking what's good for me is equally good for any of my
intelligent friends——Last night in the West End Bar was mad,
(I can't think fast enough) (*do* need a recorder, *will* buy one at
once when the *Adams* hits New York next March then I could
keep the most complete record in the world which in itself
could be divided into twenty massive and pretty interesting
volumes of tapes describing activities everywhere and excitements and thoughts of mad valuable me and it would really
have a shape but a crazy big shape yet just as logical as a novel
by Proust because I *do* keep harkening back though I might
be nervous on the mike and even tell too much). These two
days——well first, Deni did come out to meet me (after those
last thoughts in the lunchcart across the wire fence, recall?)
(now hear this Jack: the *S.S. Pres. Adams* has *red* lifesavers on
a *white* rail, at night the water is dark behind them as you look
from an eventful cabin of smoke, drink and talk through the
porthole, and the lifesavers say *San Francisco* against these dark
piers of the world, for Frisco and as I say about that Negro

cook, is really the *port* of *ports* and for this therefore I'm almost
ready to decide to sail at least one four-month run on deck,
as ordinary seaman, though I have a job waiting for me in
the morning as bedroom steward on another ship, West Coast
company but bound for France)——Now events of this moment
are *so mad* that of course I can't keep up but worse they're as
though they were fond memories that from my peaceful haci-
enda or Proust-bed I was trying to recall in toto but couldn't
because like the real world so vast, so delugingly vast, I wish
God had made me vaster myself——I wish I had ten personalities, one hundred golden brains, far more ports than are ports,
more energy than the river, but I must struggle to live it all,
and *on foot*, and in these little crepesole shoes, ALL of it, or
give up completely. Now, outside this bar is a little park, I shall
sit there, high (on myself) watching the last of the Wall Street
blue lights in high windows, remembering the dream of me as
a seaman walking right by these nameless lights where a man
bends over a blueprint to visit a girl that I fuck, and actually I
did that exact thing in 1944 when getting my Coast Guard pass
for the run to Italy on the *Holt Johnson* and was embedding
my beautiful prick in the beautiful soft, wet between-legs slam
of Cecily Wayne and coming with a bulging head. Now life is
great and tremendous and beautiful; here at twenty-nine I feel
like an old sick man; but time has come for me to build myself
up again; and I will; and I am happy for the first time in a long
time. Picked up my last sixteen dollars at work today, phooey.
I can make one run round the world on the *Adams* as O.S.
deck (the same dark ship that to me came flying in the night
like Blake's worm) and then somehow, in Frisco port, switch to
messman if I can, if not, switch to mess on another ship. The
true story of merchant seamen is not only their drunks in ports,
and adventures, and their work, but the huge universe of their
complicated conversations in Union Halls about ships in, ships
out, papers, ferries, validations, dues, wives, beefs, passes, tricks,
being late, being early, *you* know. (more later on that)——

But HOW am I going to keep my mind filled like this and
incidentally also talk about everything with everybody first of
which is Deni——by sober energies in the gray morning off gray
Seattle.

O BROOKLYN, Brooklyn
where I have lived
all these years
Did they build a bridge
straight into your heart
And past that spectral
stupid Squibb
Raise airs of rosy night
all for nothing?

but now to Brooklyn, this is like the night I watched Boston
Harbor, same situation, and same distant lights but New York,
vaster, seaward, with spectral rosy Brooklyn across the way but
now I'm stuttering like Tony——

O sad night——O waterfront!

PIER 9, the *Pres. Adams* is my ship of destiny, it must be, I keep
knowing everything about it ahead of time——I'm waiting here
in New Jersey before it's even arrived and I know that a mountain of Four Roses whiskey is going on the *Pres. A.* to Yoko-
hama and glassware to Hong Kong and machinery to Frisco
and other things to Singapore, Kobe, Manila where I suppose
further is to be picked up for the Venices and Triestes of the
return swing round the world——but more of this later, i.e.,
the cargo, the shed at Pier 9, the enormous Erie railyard of the
world, the truck ramps. Just now, in the Erie railroad waiting
room (same railroad that had such a rainy wilderness sound
when that Old Ghost of the Susquehanna listed it among all the
others in Harrisburg Peeay and the actual stops of which the
announcer with a W. C. Fields lilt is now announcing but all
the little New Jersey stops with names like Arlington and Mont-
clair, not interesting wild names like Erie itself)——here in the
station on a bench with arms I suppose to prevent bums from
stretching out, I took a nap after calling Blackie, but of Blackie
in a second. In my nap-waking I suddenly remembered that
beautiful whore from Washington Mildred who stayed at Danny's with sixty-year-old Madame Eileen that I screwed all night,
and the morning Mildred came back from a night of hotel
fucking with the rich strange millionaire guy from Vermont and
took off her clothes, sat in the chair in her slip as I watched from

Eileen's couch (smoking and just having had a morning marijuana forced on me by Danny) lifted up the slip, which was
black, grabbed her own cunt which Danny says is the greatest
in the world because it squeezes your cock like a soft fist, and
said "Old raunce need a ride." If it hadn't been for that T which
only allowed me to goof and stare I would have done either of
two things as I look back on it from my bench here in the Erie
Railroad waiting for the Singapore-bound *President Adams* and
my meet with Blackie the Bosun for my last chance to get on
board the dark ship of destiny——I would have said to Eileen
who's her madame and old buddy, "Eileen fix me up with Mildred," loud, with their peals of laffter rising, or I would have
kneeled at Mildred's feet and said "If you stroke that pussy too
much it'll start purring." Now why in the fuck didn't I do
that!——how could I have passed up such a piece of ass!——what
effeminacy, what narcolepsy has come over me from overstaying
my "leave in Manhattan" from 1943 or even 1944 or worse
1939——a cunt like that and then we would have fucked sweetly
in Danny's red bedroom, I would have said "O my God what
a perfect saddle" and she'd have said "Iffff, oooo, drive it in
daddy" and don't you think I would?——with old sinister Eileen,
naked, sixty, white all over, tall, bellied but well breasted, watching closely every movement of interlocked limbs and with a
look like that look of madames in dirty books (in fact we'd been
lookin at dirty books all morning, photos of Paris 1910 the best
one being a guy in spats and hat ramming his finger into a
woman's cunt as he bends her back, dress up, over an ironing
board), that careful heavy-lidded halfsmiling half snaky look of
lecherous voyeurs in rooms so sensual you can come just by
looking at them. So I vow to hit Washington next go round the
world (if I get on the *Adams* and if I don't all this waiting will
have ironic uselessness although I will be managing to get
round the world in a less direct way, ship by ship willynilly) and
look up Eileen and Mildred, dig gone whorehouses of congressmen, fuck, eat, drink and see my former landlord and maybe
even introduce Mildred to him just for kicks and as if I was
pimping so as to surprise him and make him think that's how I
get my dough because he would tell *her* whatever he knew
about me. These were my thoughts as I woke from this refreshing little nap and I needed it. Last night at home I talked with

Ma, promised to take her to a show and dinner (I pick Sweets for this) before I leave (if I can) and hit sack at eleven, woke up at four restlessly, hurried to Jersey City in a long foolish ride on the E train with those miserable whitecollar Queens commuters who swoon in stuffy trains not only going but *coming* from work, five days a week, all for comfort and habit while I endure it only once (it was my very first morning ride on the citybound E, and this after two and half years in Richmond Hill) for the sake of Singapore——then, at Chambers Street, I dashed out to hit the nine o'clock call in Marine Cooks & Stewards and there was no *Adams* job so I dashed back, hit the Tube, got off at Exchange Place, mistake, re-routed in a complication of tokens and refunds with refund slips, elevators, ramps, got off at Erie Station, followed signs through the waiting room halls to the footbridge that's just like the one in *This Gun For Hire* with Alan Ladd (a pix incidentally that I saw the afternoon before I signed on for Arctic Greenland in 1942, when I lay in the grass of Boston Common thinking of death because then it was torpedoes and war and certainly no Singapore except that Duluoz that same year earlier made mention of it in his smoky newspaper office), a footbridge over a solid half mile of (almost) tracks with boxcars that Alan Ladd jumped into and are from all over the raw American land lined up facing North River with all its barges, tugs, piers, smoke and ships and the one huge green shed of the American President Lines that says "Far East" on it, boxcars that say "Route of the Phoebe Snow" and "Canadian Pacific" and remind me of Cody, his old man, Nebraska, gray day in Denver right now and raw men with big hands standing under foggy trees right now in the Far West or just soogeeing Railway Express cars in the railyards of Portland, Oregon or Kansas (as I think this, to my left is a big sign the kind that advertises plays and Radio City in railroad stations clear to Boston and Lowell, and this one tells of AFFAIRS OF STATE with June Havoc, written by none other than Louis Verneuil, the same I met at age eighteen when secretary for Professor Schiller at Columbia, N.Y.A. job, shortly before I worked for New York Central R.R. dragging mailbags across *le grand plancher sale* . . . the big dirty floor . . . and French is so simple, a job I remembered so vividly last spring when we left Ma alone and I began reviewing all the jobs I ever had in this earth of labor and sorrow, thinking to myself "*The night is my woman*," the same Verneuil who was in his dressing gown, had dark rim glasses and apparently since then has been going along successfully for they call it a "comedy smash!" (according to Garland of *Journal American*, the same I read during hamburg-sizzling suppers of home in New York that are now no more) and so while I struggle in the dark with the enormity of my soul, trying desperately to be a great rememberer redeeming life from darkness, he calmly goes along filling in forms like plays and making name and money and with same Gallic cool-ness he displayed when I delivered that envelope to his apart-ment with the glittering Gershwin Manhattan view that was the sudden realization of my dream of New York which flared briefly then and also at Marshell's party in a penthouse on Cen-tral Park West near Winchell's but never to flare up again) (and Marshell being that New York hero who takes two girls to the nightclub with "Daoulas" in the abortive attempt to resume the writing of the *Vanity of Daoulas* back in the city of desires) and since then banking down a flame of dreams into this bottom-dark night from which at the last possible minute I now make my *EXCAPE* back to the sun of decks and the dewy mornings under Guam trees like the trees of the Marine base in Ports-mouth, New Hampshire with Joe and the French-Canadians building a fence, back to the sense of life I had as a child un-complainingly getting up at seven in the morn to go to school and on Saturdays joyously to go play, back to the open air of the world, out from dark *enfer* New York where, if a pine tree stood it would only stand in Rockefeller Plaza with bulbs, where there's now freshwind blowing through window of kitchen or galley from rosy morn or from piney dews. The footbridge overlooks miles of railyard and some of it is overgrown with brown weeds, unused tracks, nameless smoke-puffings far off at the other side, sooty mudground, views of New York across the Hudson, then the Pier and the place where the stevedores are waiting by the adjustable gangway one hundred feet spectrally over the water of the slip for the *President Adams* to come in at one, as soon as barges are gone, a platform I leaned out of to check the river to see if *P. A.* was coming but found out, calling ship at Staten, it wasn't even shifted yet, a platform like some-thing I dreamed and I kept thinking of diving off, continually, till at one point (all the time positive I could handle the dive and live, easily) I thought the frantic secret thought over a barge and as I pictured myself falling through the air I tried to fight the air, squirm, so as to fly off and move over to hit the water not the barge, and the futility of that!, this platform reminding me I dunno why of the dream of the enormous apartments in the Paramount Building, I guess the hugeness of it, who ever heard of a warehouse platform one hundred foot off water and of a shed a quartermile long. It took me ten minutes to penetrate the shed; lines of trucks were winding up the ramp and going in, some of them the huge trailer trucks of Georgia, one said "Ruby S.C. and Atlanta" and I said "South Calina aa-haa!!" Big crates everywhere, for instance veritable mountains of Chianti crates (just got in)——and most of the crates, barrels, boxes, bags, rolls, etc. said *Pres. Adams* on them with the destinations, and they were as I say, "S.F., Yoko, Kobe, Manila, one Malayan port I can't even pronounce or recall, Hong Kong, Singapore" and that's all, no sign of further ports like Karachi or Suez, *which we also hit!* So I've just *got* to get on and if as deckhand, well, I'll keep thinking of William Faulkner, make myself a man, like him the boiler factory, work the lard off my belly and lines off my pasty cheek. If I don't make it, goodby Singapore and Den and the red lifesavers, the same lifesavers that struck me so deeply like a dream that only they alone now seem to be assurance from my psychic future-sense that I *will* get on! Blackie sounded like a real friendly intelligent guy on the phone, he's bosun or carpenter, the delegate on the ship, S.I.U., I will make friends, work hard, I meet him, or that is yell for him from the gangway at one o'clock in the huge green pier over the footbridge from here . . . the pier of the world, at the foot of the railyard of the world, across the great Wolfean river from the World City, and huge spectral awe in the early morning air and workmen who don't give a shit talking and smoking on all sides in their lovely conspiracy to enjoy life as much as they can. En route I'll watch from the footbridge: (but further *events*).

MISSED IN NEW YORK, I missed the boat, the O.S. and the B.R. jobs were both snapped up by bookmen and I stood there in the pier watching the *Adams* warp in with a feeling that I'd miss. So now Deni says I must stick it out and follow the

President Adams overland to San Pedro, Calif. where it arrives Christmas Eve and the Chief Cook Antonio writes me a letter to the union agent so I can snap up the fireman's mess or anything else in steward's department——and so the plot thickens for now I'm going to *follow* the dark destiny ship and do so ON THE ROAD——

Thinking this on cardboard boxes that are stenciled for Hong Kong. A longshore truck roars by sending blue fumes over me——There's the drowsy racket all over of hundreds of men working——immortal lazy clouds gave way to gray afternoon—— a red Clark truck sends hot exhaust in my face. Out of a huge house of a truck they're unloading wooden crates——There's ammo in the hold and a special locker is full of some priceless cargo bound for Penang, probably champagne——There are rowboats or skiffs, crated, for Singapore——Valentine's Meat Juice from Richmond, Va. is also bound for Singapore in crates——barrels for L.A.——the complicated and tangled rigging is working, they're loading on and I, a poor ghost, have to run on land like I used to do in imagination along the car——If I don't make it on the Coast I shall have committed a frantic foolish blunder but Deni says "You are a frantic fellow, it will not be unusual for you." The drowsy shed, the racket of winches, the smell of cinnamon and oil, the whine of trucks, the smell of coffee beans (a mad longshore truck going backward among cities of produce thirty miles an hour)——Almost four, everybody's knockin off and I've missed the last four o'clock call at Marine Cooks & Stewards and am sunk, doomed again for the goddamn road, Den will lend, I go to Cody's——

On footbridge, and now the sun's going down on another mad day of mine at the hem of the *Adams*, going down in a big red ball that blinds over the boxcars (Boston & Albany, M.D.T., a faded khaki wood car, Chesapeake and Ohio, El Capitan), over hundreds of boxcars on tracks extending from the impossible smokes of intown Jersey City where I can see a big white neon frame *Davis Baking Powder* to where the sun is setting over black grimes and further entanglements and gatherings of steel that are lost in a rosy distance behind the sun, including one faint crazy smoke-begrimed-from-sight steeple——white smoke, black smoke, hundreds of cars of workers everywhere parked, the huge scene of Erie, the old buswagon hotdog trucks, two of 'em, below, men with grimy caps coming up the footbridge steps, the footbridge extends along the waterfront, the actual oily wet waters which connect us to Penang, towards the station where I dozed and beyond which I am now going in this mad immense dusk to get two cases of Budweiser in cans to be drunk tonight in Den's cabin with cook, first engineer, etc. The light deepens and so the smoke seems to increase——and at last far off at the termination of a pinpointy track I see red signal lights that without knowing it are preceding the neon night of Jersey City——so next I watch the whole land.

SAILING DAY OF *ADAMS* FROM NEW YORK——Quarahambo and Quarhica, savage tribes at the headwaters of the Orinoco River in the Venezuelan wilds, along the Ventuari River that has great rapids roaring in the South American jungle——I could hear the roar of wild hard waters over ancestral rock in the completely unoccupied middle of great huge South America continent, just by reading above words in Hudson Tube and pretty soon I could hear *drums* of the Quarhica who undoubtedly blast the Quarahambo in traditional war, the thought that *savages* still exist (after all our complexities and Washington mink coats) making me stare into the darkness——Today, December 10, I feel sad, in a quandary, "as before," no-good. Spent the night mourning and slowly packing——But it all goes back to the setting sun over the Erie Yards Friday evening. I went for the beer along the most dismal the most tragic the most begrimed dark Slavic street I've ever seen anywhere (this mad Jersey City!) and the name of it, perfect, is PAVONIA AVENUE with fat sad short men in cloth caps and black gloves, everything black, drinking at wild hollow bare-plank dim bars or trudging across the railroad tracks with hands muffled in coat——as always overhead the great sootclouds roll in darkness and suddenly you pass the open backdoor of a locomotive roundhouse, a great loco is standing there like a supercharged supersized but terrible——

All my boyhood in America, though, in the little blond refugee with his mother in this Erie Station lunchroom——his little sister won't eat anything but cake——the boy is amazed by everything, the old Erie conductor having coffee and cruller (glazed), all——The mother ordered five roast beef sandwiches, she'll be surprised at price——it will be a big story——Little girl gulps the cruller, both hands——her poor little East German palate learning things (Public Address man calls stops, including Irwin's RIVER STREET, Paterson)——Meanwhile the *Adams* is pulling out without me, behind me and all those tracks on this cold whipping sea-day with the cruel towers of Manhattan flashing in the winter sun like they do where rich men live in East Fifties apartments and a Negro is slamming a garbage barrel on the sidewalk (as once, incidentally, my first view of Frisco, a colored guy banged a barrel in a foggy dawn). The mother is so hungry she ate the little girl's beef too——the old one that is, there's a young mother and she just smiles and doesn't want to sit down she's so excited. On Pavonia Avenue, meanwhile, I walked along, hit a bar, they didn't have Den's specific Budweiser so I had a beer and moved along in the murk——went halfmile, in a bar a Budweiser man, driver, who was real dumb and gawking in the street wanted to talk about something after giving me directions to a delicatessen but had no words so I got to delicatessen, bought two cold cases, chatted with young prop. and staggered out in the smoky slum streets that here bisected Pavonia at the railyard hell's limit——I found a beautiful young girl in an Aiken-Street-like door looking blushy at things——found cab, rode back along hem of Holland Tunnel bound traffic, pass't yards, saw yardlights disembodied in smoky night sending smoke halo stabs down on clutters and rails—— staggered along great length of pier to gangway. Now it was evening, party was in order, but actually everybody went ashore into all these mad areas and irons of Jersey City.

——*Later:* And now I'm in Danny's music store, in a booth, just took dexy, am blowing some Allen Eager and Gerry Mulligan bop——Have fifty-five dollars with which to hitch to Frisco starting *matin*——no bus——okay——and fifteen dexies, five bennies——till Cody——then all straight——till I then run down to Pedro, it's Pedro, meet you in Pedro, yes it's Pedro (home of Ray the wiper, whose job I may get)——Trying to borrow $ for bus ride to Frisco but nobody has——Here are the mad complexities: and to return: everybody went ashore, only the first assistant engineer drank with us, a big Thomas Mitchell who the night after, night of Lacoucci's party, dug my Ma——also Mr. Smith the fat alcoholic sicksad beastly wiper had a drink——and

crazy Ray——but I got stoned, yakked in poor Deni's ear about
nothing, went to sleep in cadets' stateroom——in morn had coffee, felt guilty (for deciding to follow *Adams* to Frisco instead
of shipping out from here pronto with mucho loot), had chat
with our wonderful chief cook Frederico who's my friend and
is going to teach me cooking if I get on *Adams* (I've become
the great mad Cook of THE ROAD)——of ROAD, where goest
thou now?——I came home Saturday morning——but later——
AND AT THIS VERY MOMENT AS I SIT HERE THE *S.S.
PRESIDENT ADAMS* IS FLYING SOUTHWARD OFF THE
JERSEY COAST.

Just as in 1942 when I shipped out for Arctic Greenland I'm
now going through all kinds of mad complications, like, in
Pedro I'm getting a letter from the cook written in Spanish to
the Agent of M.C.S. at Frisco; already I've got a letter to Wilmington, Calif. agent——also I have to look up his Friend Joe
in Frisco to tell him that the gabardine from Italy is ready and
if *Adams*, because late in schedule, doesn't dock in Frisco Antonio will mail from L.A.——I also have to look up the GUIDE
to see where the *S.S. Lurline* is at, to locate Jimmy Low to
check on Deni's deadly enemies Matthew Peters and especially
Paul Lyman (Matthew is a hipster, Jimmy a little guy, Lyman a
gunman)——also, I look up a woman in Hollywood, my same
1947 Hollywood and soon. And I've decided to hitch-hike with
my seventy dollars and hit all the bars in the snow of the great
land between here and Frisco——if I freeze to death it won't
be from lack of beer and *food* (!)——straight for the Coast so's
to save 1000 miles of South and should be watching the roof
of Cody's house on Monday December 17 I hope, then leave
around 23rd for Pedro preferably with Cody in car and kicks, so
I have loot for kicks. I just saw Jody Mifflin (after long Duluoz
walk along park in gray nippy day, Central Park South) and
borrowed thirty dollars from her, but bus, I find, is sixty-five
dollars so fuckit. Last night got hi with Danny, bought plenty
dexies, bennies, all set to go. The last thing is actually putting
clothes in bag and saying goodbye to Ma, dammit——but I
gotta go to those brown union halls of the gray West Coast and
make my way, and find my work on the run. Jody and I had
long talk——perhaps she'd disapprove of these ideas of mine——I
must write down *books* too, story-novels, and communicate to

people instead of just appeasing my lone soul with a record of it——but this record is my joy. Now, Saturday morning I wrote, typed a letter to the agent in Wilmington, Calif. where I'm to meet ship and renew old strange haunting acquaintance with that L.A. that's made me dream since, the actual ORIGIN of the B-movie and the center of the California Night, find how to reach Pedro etc. by myself on those humming sidewalks in the mild wild night (hit colored bars from here to there! blow jukes, talk up with cats!) (buy a whore or two!), the same L.A. I travailed and was hallowed by with Mexican girl 1947 when we cut along together in the unbeatable sweetness of man and woman. Let me tell a story: I'd met her on a bus and all that, and we'd decided to hitch to New York over Route 66, were out there——but wait till *tape recorder!* (for this particular past story). I want to start hitching tonight from in front of Lincoln Tunnel, why wait? So I will. And buy further sleeves for my heart.

ON THE ROAD, HARRISBURG, PA.——4 A.M., just took jog in cold narrow street——bus to Frisco——all closed in New York——thinking——fast bus——*Pittsburgh*——Jogged across my bridge——sternwheelers of old used as tugs pushing barges in freezing Ohio River——same that will transfer its waters to the warmths of New Orleans——Long lines of freights snaking along cliffbottoms——ancient blackstone monument of some kind——I ran to P. & L.E.R.R. waiting room so ornate and dignified (the terrible name of Lehigh, the terrible name of Lackawanna, they make me think of that seven-mile hike in the misty night among the bushy crags of the horrible Susquehanna flowing in her October with flare-fires of grim locomotives across the water-bed, me and the Ghost of the Susquehanna walking, walking for the bridge that was never there Ah me) I no go in with dungarees blackjacket——new visions of Pittsburgh, old orange trolleys——skyscraper Ward Morehouse office buildings rising in the joyous winter morning——boys in a parkinglot plotting jazz——

Dug DEERTRAIL, OHIO——Long walk——hot cocoa in truck diner——

OUTSIDE CLEVELAND——A graveyard of Thirties wrecks covered with snow, like Old Cody Pomeray dead——

CLEVELAND——Blizzard——white——ricketiness——*Kitchen Maid Meats*, a butcher store, with Xmas garlands——SOHIO gas station with old cars and trucks in the snow——*Leader Department Store* with hat, sport shirts and blankets (and Xmas Tinsel) in the window——Dark shiny plastic drugstore—— *Olympic Confectionery* candy store——Old picketer in white and green hunting cap picketing sign says "These clothes are not union made" in snow——*Andy's Coney Island Hotdogs* on trolley sidestreet with four women waiting for bus in doorway—— Main leading-in street snowy, dark, mad, white-lined, American, meaningless——iron fences, porticoed mansions that are now funeral homes——puke-yellow furniture stores with bargains in big print——a huddled pedestrian in a yellow and black check hunting coat and brown felt hat walking and trying to read order slips on blizzardy sidewalk——great empty lot with snowy stones and hints of crumbled ashy timbers in the whiteness——Sunoco station, attendant bending dismally to tank, gloved——Beat-up sooty old brown-shingled Main Street house——huge smokestacks in swirling shroudy snow across the city plains——bridge over railyard with snow-covered oil cars, tanks, Xmas billboards, Pennsy coal cars, Nickel Plate coal cars, distant nameless bridges in black iron, red wood warehouses, mysterious refineries, rooftops of Cleveland Man finally——old redracked wood trailer trucks——a horse drawing a flaring stanchioned junk wagon on glistening wet paving——brownbrick truckage buildings in the storm——*Allied Florist Exchange*, purple brick, snowpiles, dusty front windowpanes——downtown people huddled in rainy snow under the everlasting red neon.

IOWA, Chicago Great Western (boxcar)——Inscription on shithouse wall Grand Island, Nebr. "I was in a suck party one nite with 4 fellows we sucked cocks and fucked each other in the ass hole at the Olds Hotel one salesman come 8 times." I want to suck 2 cocks while my cock is being sucked too" etc.—— all like that, land of Bill Cody.

WYOMING——Shrouded windswept snowridge in the blue——marshmallow humps——a whiteness riddled with brown sage——lonely cluster of shacks——my window is clouding and icing again. Dug backalleys of Rock Springs, Wyo.——a bench along a shackwall, sign painted on wall "Don't sit on Whitey's bench"——cowboy with ruddy lean features walking beanpole from the bank along the railroad street of cafés and stores—— Pretty Wyo. cunt in car, a rich rancher's daughter. . . . Sunny valleys of snow in the great rock waste——reddish buttes——far off ravines of the world——Last night I dug the snow swept road in front, to North Platte where had three beers.

SACRAMENTO——The myth of the gray day in Sacramento ——intersection, with Shell station (tan and red) on one corner, a distant palm visible in the fog over the creamy California roof——Nameless young Jap cats of California cutting by—— Much traffic, a few old trees of Sacramento——*Colonial Arms* a brokendown wood structure——then *Sacramento Public Parking Inc.*, a big lot with namelessly bleak two-story redbrick apartment beyond——then the people——I'm exhausted.

THIS TRIP IN DEPTH, THEN, beginning, New York, colored queer cat with radio no battery——pull out fast——at New Brunswick wild Air Force gang in Levis get on with satchels of whiskey, wine and jewelry for wives in Colorado Springs . . . the leader is big handsome Ben from San Antone, his buddy is crazy snap-knife Doug with blond hair——others——Ben says he was knifed in Amarillo, an X in his back, got a buddy to hold the gang at bay with shotgun and *stomped* all four one by one, stomped one's tongue out accidentally——They call their cocks "hammers," cunt's a "gash" and do the up-your-ass fingersign slapping finger down into palm, wham——Bus went through pretty Princeton, made me homesick for oldfashioned Eastern Xmas dammit and especially now as I sit here in Ross Hotel in sunny dull L.A.——then into Pennsylvania and hit the mountains and first snow swirls at ridge top immense truckstop——in Harrisburg I jogged in eighteenth-century streets remembering the Ghost and also it's like Lowell——Turnpike in snow to Pittsburgh——I on dexies feel relaxed, moveless but time is long——in Pittsburgh as I say I run across Ohio River Bridge—— eat my first two ham sandwiches on bus locker outdoors while Negro cleans out bus and others eat ham and eggs inside——At Deerfield I walk up and down highway in intense sunny cold of old Ohio——Then Cleveland, and bought a pint of whiskey cheap——Cream of Kentucky——Airforce boys plying me plenty good whiskey——we talk——I dog everybody straight, no more brooding or paranoia or nothing, preparing for world——(but I've *known* the world, it's all happened before, why do I kid myself with these artificial *newnesses*)——from Cleveland, to Toledo (ate sandwiches) in cold downtown red neon night, I walked, ran, froze, had just hot cocoa, dug a Cody Pomeray Toledo——Then across to Indiana and the lights of Xmas trees of supper evening coming on in little towns like LaGrange and Angola (remember Fred MacMurray and Barbara Stanwyck going home to Indiana at Xmas?)——at South Bend I run, get a drink in mad little bar with young beefy sad organist up in portico and characters, old man who changes a ten for every beer——Then into Chicago and the fantastic big red neon of ITS night——around midnight——the great glitter in the cold lakeshore night (Dreiser should have seen, but he *did*!)——I ran for beans, coffee, bread——very, very cold on the Loop——I saw no bop, hurried——saw North Clark trucks with girlieshow flaps——Across Illinois to Davenport, where I woke up just before dawn, dug the Mississippi again, the ninth time, now flowing in winter, walked in cold dawn near oldman bar's street where I slaked my hot thirst in summer 'forty-seven——thought "This night has names" outside Rock Island——for a letter to Wilson——nonsense half forgotten, thing to do is GO ON—— Cut along the river we did as russet East flared over frost fields to Muscatine, Keota (the Golden Buckle of the Corn Belt), Sigourney where I walked in freezing morn while others ate joyous breakfasts——in Knoxville, Ia. Negro mine operator told me his life, looked like Pa——Drank with boys——at Council Bluffs everything was gray and Western and inevitable, even rollercoasters——bam, in Omaha it's snowing——a blizzard—— dirty old scabrous shithouse character watches me shit, another sells me comb for dime, I eat sandwiches (now down to bread and boiled eggs) in Omaha doorway facing Missouri River Street down by warehouses in huge blizzard, I look real handsome passing plate glasses, like new cowboy, old scabrous finds me, wants sandwich or dime, I say "Get money from the rich!" and I'm mad but guilty, recalling Dostoevsky's sayings——Bus slowed down plows along to Columbus and Grand Island where, while others sup, I cut around, in toilet read, take dexy——storm is thick, I dig from front window, and old men, old Nebraskans, two, one an usher now in Frisco Mission Street

B-movie and knew Buffalo Bill, the other a farmer goin to
Frisco or such, North Platte was where Ben threw a snowball
through a small hole in wall and everybody so exuberant sailor
puts arm around me as we go in bar for three beers——which
start me and send me buzzing, also dexy, so from North Platte
to Cheyenne the route of my great 1947 flat-truck rotgut whiskey ride with Mississippi Gene and the boys I am DRUNK and
finish all the whiskey, talking to everybody, seat jumping, running out with old man to piss at Chappell, busdriver says "I
know there's a bottle on this bus——if anybody needs a rest stop
speak up"——and I say "This gentleman needs to go to the
restroom"——bravado at height, like I'll use in Paree some
day——next year——the Handsome Stranger that I dug first in
Omaha lunchroom watching waitresses dig him, unconscious
slouch hat, mustache thin, great angular Indian face, dark ma-
roon skin texture (from cold winters, he no look like farmer but
is), dug him in the bus chewing slowly under his personal reading light with twenty-five-cent book and little girl digging him
and calling her mother's attention to it across the aisle——so
drunk that I told him all this before he got off at Chappell or
Sidney, Nebr. or wherever to go to his farm where he *lives
alone* (!) and screws all surrounding countryside women——Till
at Cheyenne I was stone cold out when they woke us up to
change buses because heating system no good in New York
coach——So now here I am waking up somewhere in Wyoming
as great sage-snow-eternities spread everywhichway (Denver
one hundred miles underneath, my poor Cody Denver)——at
Rock Springs I walked and decided to splurge on big eggs and
potato breakfast (at the last minute as driver called), great——
next stop (went through Fort Bridger in his great land discovery country) wonderful drowsy winter afternoon Mormon
town with steaming cows in corrals and silence of mountains at
I believe Wasatch (dunno)——walked, dug old *small* covered
wagons families keep in backyard, as relics of past like Lowell
people keep daguerrotypes——then Ogden, which I dug, Jap
hipsters, crazy bum street with Kokomo Bar at foot of which
white-capped mountains rise——a town I'd heard about some,
I can see it's something——then I from window dug Farmington
a little hem-of-the-mountain settlement——then at Salt Lake a
major four-hour wait because of strike of drivers, which I make

partly by myself walking and digging Jap pool parlor and hanging round station with the Frisco-bound sailors——and good
old Airforce boys whose whiskey I'd all drunk up ere Cheyenne
got off Ogden——also two old seamen bound for N.M.U. Seattle, one of 'em knew Nebraska and Wyoming years ago as
circus man!——but old asshole bores like North Atlantic A.B.'s
1943——Left Salt Lake after I took *three* walks, long ones, at
nine or so, crossed flats, began stopping every literally ten miles
in Nevada for passengers to throw money on slotmachines,
chief sucker my sailor pal——Wendover, Wells, Elko,
Winnemucca, Lovelock, stopping all the time and I walk and
dig all over, and it's deathly cold in Nevady——Finally I get to
dig that crazy Reno high on dexy at 6:30 A.M. booming with
roulette and house girls and me three beers and almost miss
bus, and tic-kid with money so handsome and tragic at faro
table, three fags watching, and soldier asking for girl at bar and
Jewish New York handsome gambler with girls, and foggy
streets, and those *cunts* it's a sin that town——then the new fag
driver with ONE glove (and the young Skippy soldier in front
of me with his queer chin tweaker and lover)——up the mountain and home in Truckee, just like Lowell, gingerbread houses
and five-foot snow, I took walk, my nose dried up——over Donner Pass, and down to fogs of California, Colfax, Auburn, Rose-
ville, old loud talking W. C. Fields Sacramento lawyer with cane,
and kid, my bleakness in Sacry, and over to Frisco which
couldn't be seen from the Bay Bridge though en route I tried
to dig Frisco kicks in little character with cloth hat in front of
me and scenes outside——Called Buckle, waited for him in
saloon at Mission and Sixth——all Buckle's till Cody showed up
with ONE precious stick that rode us high-crazy-yelling-wild
clear into the Little Harlem Satnite where they told us Buddy'd
slashed his woman and for want of money I gave away my
MexCity wallet to gal who, Five Guys Named Moe in the crazy
drizzling Negress morning I screwed forty-eight hours later——
Oh mad!

NOW DOWN IN L.A. TO MEET DENI'S SHIP——L.A. XMAS, the
Great American Saturday afternoon but in L.A. and at Xmas
shopping peak——just like Lowell is South Broadway but in a

warm strange sun——Little Mexican girls in pink blouses cutting along with their mothers, shopping bag over the shoulder flung——sharp characters by the thousands in every kind
of jacket, shirt, shoe, sometimes half sharp on top with wino
pants below——And cunts! Purple bandana, red velvet skirt,
long legs——Beauteous Mexican girls with those full tits, lips
and cougar eyes——Colored cats in black shirts with light hats
and checked coats——Girls in floppy sharp jacket-coats over
loose slacks, looking doll-like just like Evelyn in her shirt and
dungarees——it's a California dolliness——whole families eating
in Clifton's celebrating the shopping——Just like Queen Street
must be right now in Kinston, North Carolina and Ma and Nin
are cutting along——A carful of Negro sharpies——sailors——
crazy trolleys——the people different and crazier than New York
and refined to the sun in clothes and feel——Pouring pouring,
this poor mind can't compete or even these eyes——Girls in
short tight skirts, barelegged, in sandals, long hair, I die.

L.A. PLAYLAND, but there's something inexpressibly sad right
now——in this beat old Playland, at the coffee counter, Bing's
"White Christmas" on juke, some sadness that draws my mind
apart and makes me want to moan——I remember how Irwin
years ago used to dig these joints from New York to Denver
to Houston and back and how it took me so long to follow
suit——but without selection for he chose his monkey image in
this maze and applied it to the interests of that day and all I do
is roll along anyhow——from across South Main Street it's like
looking at a realistic American painting——PLAYLAND, the
great square stage, and racing tip sheets tacked up on right——a
family, mother with long tumbly hair in overalls and black jacket
fiddles pennies into weighing machine with the kids, the old
man in yachting cap with anchor and wino pants and who brings
his family to South Main Street on the big pre-Christmas Saturday afternoon only because it's the street of his own hangup
just as old Cody must have brought him and Ma Pomeray in
her mad tubercular Okie overalls to Larimer on this day or in
Lowell the poor sepulchral farmer comes not to Central Street
but to the brokendown stores of Bridge Street (though not
really comparable)——the little kid therefore remembering his

Pa in his own appropriate sad setting——Sailors and Marines, one Airforcer studying those nude magazines, I see him poring over two crazy cunts reclining in the sun together bellyup, legs closed, "health-y," and "Europe-Nude Impressions of Europe (!)"——the incredibly beat fortune machines, a gypsy woman plaster head with plaster wart——the antique pistol machines—— a great amateur canvas depicting destroyer on blue sea, now torn at one end to show dusty electric fixtures in back——a hole in the floor, cubbyholes of tools down in it to repair crazy kick-machines——hootchy movies with actual flapping white electric dolls that Jap and Mex kids dig (those kids who comb their hair sleek and horizontal at back and vertical up front like movie stars, they have no loins, just a Levi belt and presumably a cock although there seems to be no room even for an ass, they float disembodied or that is dis-hipped, dis-loined over the sidewalk like spindly sexless ghosts, either that or they slouch loose in huge sharp suits with those L.A. sportshirts that are the mad-dest for this is home of sportshirts)——Saturday afternoon in Playland, some of the families I dug 1947 who drive from the Zorro night to Hollywood and Vine to see stars filtered in here now (I saw the Pacific feathering the night shore south of Obispo, wow). All the machines, muscle machines, photos, ordinary bowling, etc. and the juke blowing Ella, Mr. B., Bing, and blues and across the street down a ways my shoeshine friend who goes falsetto squeal while shining shoes, keeps digging street first over one shoulder then other, jumps, yells Blow!, spends all his money on juke in shack, wears plaid bop cap, says "I *love* money I dunno what's the matter with me" and in course of talking and jumping (played "Illinois" on trombone and Lester and Hawk together records) tried to hook me with $1.25 "dye" shine but I got off, in genuine disappointment in him, with thirty cents, but I blame it on his morose boss Negro that when he showed up the saint stopped jumping and digging street, a big hype——South Main mad and L.A. too, more than ever——The "Optic" B-movie right across Playland here with fiddly little marquee and "open-all-night" boxoffice, colored cats digging pixes in front ("Little Egypt")——Now a Negro family comes to Playland from hotsun street——Now I'm being swept away by a broom!

SOUTH MAIN STREET, bums with bloody foreheads——
Indians——buddies of Marines in bloodred sport shirts——
Indians in hip blue serge suits——Prado's Mambo coming from
Over the Top Bar——*Gayety* another B-movie——Negro kid in
dungarees, black suede shoes and old red sport shirt——Every
cocktail bar has inviting B-girl on first stool and blue interiors
waiting——Old Indian worker (or Mexican) in brown leather
jacket but regular felt hat though somewhat Western——A family: a Mex lil hunchback Pop, wife, cute, and cute little dotter
five with present——he wears farmer coveralls——white shirted
Mex goes by with dark tragic mouth——

WILMINGTON, ATE TERRIFIC MEAL in Jack's Star Cafe——short
ribs of beef, sweet candied yam, buttered beets, was full for
first time since Evelyn Pomeray's mother's wonderful hickory
smoked ham at Cody's filled me (ham feast). I was weak with
hunger from walk——Catholic Marine Club to Berth 154, a one-
and-a-half-mile walk in cold raw California winter night which
earlier at work in Frisco gave me this terrible cold that literally
prevented me from *seeing* out the Zipper caboose window and
which I personally checked with twenty-four hours in bed, a
pint of bourbon, lemon juice and Anacin——a ten-dollar treat-
ment (including a turkey dinner in L.A. bum cafeteria). Meal
earlier today at Clifton's, lamb rib, was too small and not half
as good as this Wilmington Jack right by Pacific Redcar tracks.
The ride down phenomenal——after Compton the bourgeois
town and rickety wild L.A. suburbs of garages, cottages next to
tire mountains, green stucco box houses, nigra coal and coke
shacks, there arose on the plain whole metropolises of oil drills
and then refineries, all sides, pumping, smoking, mad——And
the *S.S. President Adams* is now turning in at Berth 154 and
I've come overland to meet her——Suspicious characters around
dock, Matthew Peters? Paul Lyman? I have to be alert for Den's
safety, really. Same shiny waters that connect Penang and Jersey
City are here too.

Four days of hard work at railroad baggage department Frisco
heaving mailsacks, $10.40 clear a day; spent ten-dollars on kicks
and Marie——came to L.A. in Zipper freight caboose Cody put
me on, with thirty-dollars——half dead with virus pneumonia,
three different conductors forced me to retire into sleep or I get

questioned——walk two miles in bleary sorrow with burden bag
from L.A. railyards clear to South Main and Fifth and lifesaving
hotel and lemon and bourbon. This is records. Lonesome for
Ma, Nin, Luke and Kinston today——I'm going to go over the
entire Tragedy No. One of my early life on my ship whichever
it may well be. Hope it's *Adams*, old dark *Adams* now in the
vast Pedro night reaching to touch me.

YES, TO RECALL, MARIE, DUG HER, SHE DUG ME, in Little
Harlem at Third in Frisco——gave her hincty Mex wallet, got
rid of that though worried——on a cold rainy morning at 7:30
they told us to come in work at 6 P.M. so Cody and I'd rattled in his old green heap to housing shacks across tracks and
beyond junkyards at five-mile house——woke up Marie with
pint of bourbon and split bottle (poorboy) tokay——her sister
asleep with her dotter (seven) in bed, white sailor in bedroom,
but records right off (Five Games Named Moe, Little Moe,
No Moe, Half a Moe, Big Moe, Never Moe etc.) and then
breakfast and brother-in-law and we bang in bedroom, talk of
her $4600 inheritance, Cadillac or goose farm——Slim Buckle
came with fifth burgundy——drove around Third Street for T,
none, characters in and out——Old Jabbo——then home to sleep
two hours in afternoon, Evelyn had fits, wow!——And in L.A.
I never got that ship!

THAT WAS IN FRISCO when I was still sure I could get the
Adams but now it's the San Pedro blues, walking back from Joe
Wilkinson's M.C.S., Xmas Eve, missed the ship, along the tracks
stumbling in a universe of burning rubber and oil refineries in
the hot dumb sun, loss, loss, my charade, tirade——worst of all
meeting sexy box juicycunt Rickey in Long Beach at Stardust
——after that mad day in Hollywood and Santa Monica walking
with Deni drinking champagne and spending one hundred dollars on all kinds of nonsense (Larue's, five-dollar taxi rides with
no destination, case of beer for girls that put us out the door,
etc. Lola, Anne, Monroe Starr by swimmingpool).
    NUTHOUSE bar, after Xmas Eve of Cruiser at 4 A.M. silent
with star and stem-to-stern lightbulbs——trudging in dark tracks
with Mr. Leonard and his bop cap——Xmas dinner of turkey
and Danish beer on *Adams* with uproarious cussing laughing

crew——hot sunny Xmas afternoon in NUTHOUSE bar Wilmington, Rickey no go, crazy fistfight between Okie lovers,
I'm hot and unfucked, drowse, beer, shit on it. Where's wife?

At LaCienega joint the pretty couple (Encore Bar)——the
fireplace, the L.A. night——again later at Sunset Strip bar
with Lezes——My vision of men enslaved to cunts, to women
who at or near thirty become lost in a dream of maternity as
men die in the night with slavering thirst for the eternal food,
the inexpressible security of a conscious caress (or dreamy
unconscious)——poor Mac, Cody, broken by their cunts——but
not me——the son of the Nuthouse proprietor riding a foolish
singlewheel in the afternoon horizoned by pumps, tanks and
towers——issempassem——Den's many expressions——What do
I love? Den says my own skin. I have $14.50.

Sitting on a stool facing blinding open door——parking lot
beyond little porch of concrete——post——then brown fields,
wire fences, oil cranes, blue haze, telegraph wires, shapeless
black steels, hills, trees, houses, Pacific Sky over Pedro and then
ocean.

3

Frisco: The Tape

JACK. ——and during the night he said "I'm an artist!"

CODY. Oh no! he he ha ha ha, he did huh?

JACK. Yah

CODY. Well, you know, ah, Bull . . . all Bull does is sit there and read all day, and so I just happened to pick up this *Really the Blues* and I read the whole thing through in a day or two, you know, just sitting there high, and readin. I'd sit opposite him, see I wouldn't do any work either. Huck and June doin all the work and there's Bull and me sitting there readin all day. You know this *Inside U.S.A.* of twelve hundred pages?——and I read every WORD of that, of that motherfuckin thing

JACK. Just facing Bull?

CODY. Yeah, just as we . . . read a book. I read that book and I read *Really the Blues* and a few others. And that's all we're doing, we're just sitting there all day readin, high, see, him and me, and so what I'm sayin is——he's——after I was all done——

JACK. Oh you'd read to one another?

CODY. No, no, no, silence

JACK. Silence?

CODY. Yeah, silence, yeah, he'd be reading and I'd be reading, the rest them in there workin, that's right, and so then he said "What do you think of that *Really the Blues?*" "Oh it's alright I guess." He said: "That guy's nowhere," he says, "I read that goddamn thing" . . . you know how Bull viciously——you'll see him attack something——doesn't mean anything one way or another but he's always saying "Well I don't know, that's no good." You know how he'd always do——THINK of him! Lots of times I've been amazed and looked sharp, when I was younger I used to look at him as though to *take* him seriously, you're not supposed to take him seriously, you don't know what he's saying about——and he'll say these horrible things "Ah Jack that's no good, that fuckin shit's no good, I'm gonna build a house last thousands of years," 'cause he don't know, he's sayin "Well, well . . ."——well man what I'm sayin is, "That poor sonofabitch," he says, "I read that fuckin book," he says, "the goddamn thing was"——you know——he says——Jesus I can't think of it, "The

145

guy's just nowhere," you know what he's saying, "this Mezzrow character"——Oh no! then he said: "Sure a nigger lover ain't he?" You know, he he he, just like that, you know how he acts with that Jimmy Low, that Louisiana——have you heard that story of his that he'd come and he'd say "Oh man it's FRAN-TIC," you'd get high man, and he'd say "And so we got in the schoolbus with the bunch of them young girls," he says, "Old Jimmy went w-i-l-d, completely wild, he raped all the young women and the thirteen-year-old g-i-r-l-s," he was the school-bus driver, see, trying to get himself——man the whole thing, it goes on for an hour like that, Jesus, that sonofabitch

JACK. Is that what his job was?

CODY. Yeah Jimmy Low

JACK. His job was driving the schoolbus——

CODY. No . . . no, he just invented that, y'know, Old Bull, he just gets high and invents that story. No, Jimmy Low was the guy that——

JACK. Farmer huh?

CODY. ——yeah, that owned that store down the road, the country store, yeah, Bull would go down there to this country store and dig this Jimmy Low

JACK. And Jimmy Low was supposed to have these Little Orphan Annie eyes, like buttons?

CODY. Is that what he said, that? I never heard that one

JACK. That's what Irwin says

CODY. Oh yeah

JACK. Garden

CODY. Oh yeah, yeah, yeah, yeah I remember Irwin, he was there too, when . . . (*mumble*)

JACK. He says that one day you were all high in the living-room, and all high, goofing off real high, and in the door suddenly Jimmy Low was standing, with his Little Orphan Annie eyes fixed on space

CODY. Gee

JACK. Not saying a word——

CODY. Yeah . . . those old eyes

JACK. He's just comin in to say hello, that's what he's doin in the door, he's such a country farmer——

CODY. Yeah (*laughing*)

JACK. Well, he's a real hoodoo . . . June said——

CODY. Yeah, I guess he is . . . man

JACK. Bull goes up to him and he says "Say, ah, how does that divining rod work?" And Jimmy Low says "It ain't exactly a divining rod, it's a divining twig that I balance on my fingertips." Bull says "How does that work?" "Well, all depends on instinct."

CODY. On instinct

JACK. To find water, see?

CODY. Yeah, that's right, hee hee hee

JACK. Jesus

CODY. Hee hee hee hee all depends on instinct

JACK. You find water there, it'll balance off your fingertip when there's water

CODY. Yeah, by instinct he does it

JACK. He actually DOES find water

CODY. Yeah, that thing works, yeah

JACK. So, ah, and one day somebody came up to——somebody was sittin there——and it's started RAINING . . . THAT'S WHAT IT IS! When he came in the room, and everybody was high, and he's staring into space? It started to rain and thunder

CODY. Oh y-e-s, phew!

JACK. Thunder crashed outdoors?

CODY. Man, instinct

JACK. He said "Wal, I guess I brought the rain with me."

CODY. Oh man, like that guy in "Lil Abner," Gloom, goes around, with the rain comin down on him? Irwin told you about that? about an actual happening?

JACK. That's the story he told me

CODY. I never could remember it at all

JACK. He said June told him this

CODY. Oh yes, "I guess I brought the rain with me. . . ."

JACK. The type June would have remembered, see? And I remembered the other story about a horse? And old Bull was practicing with a shotgun?——

CODY. Yeah, I was there

JACK. "Hey, the redcoats are comin!"——and he sticks his gun out the window and shoots

CODY. Yeah, I was there, yeah

JACK. Why——why did he shoot?

CODY. He didn't stick it out the window, we was all sittin on

the porch, Huck is playin his Billie Holliday, see, right here, and
Bull's sittin there on the porch with his rifle 'cross his knees, see,
sittin there like this, and we're——I'm sittin there, and that's——
so when he says . . . somethin like that, he didn't say that at
all, what he does, I don't remember that, he might have said
somethin, but, the horses, I'm sittin there stoned, and I look
up, and here's Bull, C-R-O-W-S-H, at a dead treetrunk, which
he thought see, for kicks, he'd shoot the treetrunk, see, there
was a big treetrunk, it was about a hundred yards away, fifty
yards, seventy, about fifty yards, yeah, seventy, sixty yards, and,
ah, it was rotten, see the treetrunk was rotten, you know the
rest of the story, you know, the ball went through the treetrunk,
it was rotten like paper (*baby cries*)
JACK. Yeah
CODY. See, it hit the treetrunk alright, but the horse passed
right behind it at that time. Of course Bull can't SEE, what
really happened the horses were fifty yards away, you know
by now, when the report sounded, but Bull can't see and he
thought he hit the horse, or he knew he came damn close you
see with this aimin at this trunk, so he goes "Hey I hit the
horse!" and he jumps up, you know, says "Oaiy!" and he jumps
off the porch, hee hee, the horses are trottin right along, he
hasn't touched nothin see. . . . Here's this Bull, he's so high,
he's just sittin there with his bad order high, see he can't see
a hundred yards, y'know, that sonofabitch, no wonder he hit
June and killed her, imagine, no shit, he can't see with them
glasses. . . . Why we drove to New York, it was so awful, a truck
or anything would be anywhere near him, within fifty feet of
him, see, and he'd put on the brakes like this see and pull over
to the right hand side of the road, just like an old woman, not
because he can't drive or nothing——but he can't SEE, no kidding! I dug that! So we made an agreement that I'd drive all
night and everything and if he ever wanted to drive or anything
why sometimes he'd drive in the afternoon an hour or two . . .
so . . . that's what he did . . . but, he's, ah, crazy, man, that Bull,
hee hee hee. . . . Phew! naw, but man, what I'd tell you is, I
didn't know that I'd appreciate remembering these things more,
so therefore when I was there I didn't pay much attention to
any of this, I was hung up on something else, you know, so I
can't remember, say, like for example, I can remember NOW

for example, but now that I CAN remember it doesn't do any good, because . . . man . . . I can't get it down. You know . . . I just remember it, I can remember it well, what happened 'cause I'M not doing nothin, see?

JACK. You don't have to get it down

CODY. (*demurely downward look*) But I can't remember what happened there, man, except I remember certain things. . . . But I'm sayin like Huck, me and Irwin goin out in the middle of the Louisiana bayou on a particular New York kick——now this is one time, now I'm really——Huck, you remember how he is . . . so Huck's sayin "Come on, man, I want to show you something"——he'd——and Irwin——he and Irwin were that way a great deal, Irwin would say "You've got to see this piece of cloth," and Huck's sayin "Man you've got to see something, ever since you been down here I been telling you about it, now you've got to see it." Because what had happened, Huck . . . had gotten high one day and we were cuttin through this forest vine place, it's only about oh a half-mile behind the house, really, about a mile, no one ever goes over there you see, and it was an impassable bayou that he'd dug the flowers and the gone colors and he was so high, see, jungle stream, and everythin comin down, and crocodiles and everything in this goddamn swamp that's right beside. So he's going to take Irwin over there, so we go on over there, and we lit up, you know, to make it just like we'd do, we'd be sittin there, "Come on, I'm gonna show you this now," you know . . . "Well alright." And so we all blasted and we went there and we sat there, so what happened, you know, as far as happenings go, but I remember that, Old Huck wanted to see those——he wanted Irwin to get hungup on those bayous, whereas, really it was about fifty yards from where we'd bathed every day. And we did see a corner of the thing, whatever he was talking about, anyhow, every day . . . we'd go down and bathe. One day June said "Well come on if you'll take us down to bathe," Bull sittin there and he looks up over his glasses, you know, the way Bull looks up to June. Man, relationship completely a stone wall between me and June, as far as that goes, see, although I don't want to be that way, naturally, but I mean I'm not, ah——so like a young schoolkid I say "Well now, I'll leave you down there, then I'll come back, say, then I'll go down and pick you up say in twenty minutes or something," like a stoop see but man there's nothing I can do, and June didn't say yes, or no, or anything. Then we got there, why we sat and talked for a few minutes, and I say "Well I guess I'd better get back," why, 'cause she's startin to go down and get undressed there, in the pond, you know, and the pond is right there every day, you lay up there in the pond with the fishes hittin you in the ass, y'know, man they're a terrible feelin when you're high, you gotta get in this muddy old swamp water, see, and you got that little embankment there, see, but there that mud on the bottom in some places there, it's pretty bad you know, and so you're trying to relax, you know, set yourself down a little bit, and you just about get halfway settled, you know how sensitive you are, and here these fishes start biting at you, little fishes, man, just little things, you can see 'em, sometimes you can't 'cause you kick up the mud, see, but man, it's a sonofabitch, we've all got bites all over——

JACK. Who's goin in there with you?

CODY. Oh me and Irwin, every day, we'd goof off——

JACK. What'd Irwin——do——what'd HE say about the fishes?

CODY. Oh he's just sitting there squatting, he's sitting there talking all the time

JACK. He doesn't notice those things——

CODY. Yeah, and I'm trying to lay down, you know, and so, Jesus Christ man, that's a fuckin high place, that Texas, that's high, you know, it's not low, down there, sonumbitch, phew! Ah man, Old Bull I said to him, "Well Bull" I said "maybe I better go out and get a job here," you know, imagine, there's no jobs, you have to work in the fields like a nigger, man, with the heat so hot, man, that, phew, and he says "No that's alright Cody, you don't have to go to work," so, I'm there, that's wonderful, I say to him "That's fine, I won't go to work."

JACK. Jesus Bull's wonderful, huh?

CODY. Yeah, shit, sonofabitch he——he don't do that no more, I don't know what's the matter with that guy, man, every day we'd have to drink one case at least of Coke, half a case or more of Seven-Up, and about a half dozen bottles of various little punches, sodas, see . . . June was drinking all the time . . . like that, and Huck, June and Huck both (*swinging drinks in*)

JACK. Really blasting it, huh?

CODY. Yeah, blast punches, that's right, and, of course, every day speaking about other things, that wasn't what I was going to talk about but I've forgotten about what else there was so I was——we'd got all the gin out of the local stores so we had to go into another town to the BIG drug store and liquor store to buy . . . the gin and the rum and all that stuff that Bull drank

JACK. And tequila

CODY. (*temporarily hearing "Nakatila"*) No . . . Oh, yeah, terrible!——that guy, he'd——phew!——just sit there and drink (*both laughing, high*), man . . . he wouldn't do NOTHING

JACK. Why that sonofabitch, he was in *Berlin* once!

CODY. About ten-thirty A.M., man, he'd show up out of his room, see he'd retire early about eight-thirty, then about ten-thirty A.M. he'd come out of his room all dressed complete with tie and everything, he'd come and he'd sit down, "Good morning, any mail yet Cody?" and I'd say "No I didn't go for the mail yet," and so, and he'd say "Well," and he'd sit right down in his chair, man, right there a minute and he'd start reading his mail, first thing in the morning, reading a newspaper or something, and if he felt good why he'd be talking to June "Well I see Peaches Browning got another divorce here," and June'd be "Yeah yeah" in the kitchen, you know, right over the embankment is what it was, see the kitchen's there and there was just a little half wall, so they'd be lookin at each other, and, but if he wasn't feeling so good he'd just sit there——

JACK. And he wouldn't say nothing!

CODY. In the meantime Old Huck, he's been out gathering firewood cause he's used all the firewood everywhere around so he's packing it, man, from a quarter half-mile away, here he is, Old Huck, Bull would——building himself up, see, and he's got this terrible disease of his skin, man, what a horrible disease, great boils on his legs and everything, and holes everywhere, no one knew what it was, even the doctors didn't know, he'd been to a doctor twice and they didn't know what it was, some kind of skin disease, never heard of, but, imagine, so everybody's leery of Huck, see, poor Huck, nobody'll go NEAR him and he'd go bathe by himself down in the crick 'n' everything. But I don't know if that's the case but it seems to me, it doesn't seem like it's usually been now as I remember because I wasn't thinking about those things, I certainly wasn't hungup on that, but it seemed to me June was the instigator of all this, "Better watch out for Huck," you know . . .

JACK. Yes

CODY. "He'll give you that fungus bungus you know," it's a fucking thing, but what I'm saying is that Huck he'd have the firewood because he had to cook the steaks, as soon as it was getting dark, you know, he had to have plenty of firewood to get good and hot, oh he was always hungup on his firewood you know, he was always talking about firewood——

JACK. Huck?

CODY. Huck was

JACK. What it LOOKED like?

CODY. No, he was always TALKING about it, "Oh gotta go git some firewood," complaining about it, you know

JACK. Just had the word *firewood*

CODY. Well yeah, you know, he had to get all this damn wood . . . what I'm saying, that, I can remember him several times distinctly walking a long distance under his wood . . . and also complaining about it . . . and also feeling a big release and relief when he got to go into Houston and I got to drive him in. That's sixty miles

JACK. Hmm

CODY. Man, and he'd sit down and he'd be talking about this and that, man, he'd be happy as a little kid, he's goin into Houston to pick up the benny, 'cause we had stripped all the Benzedrine out of every store everywhere around including Huntsville the state pen and everywhere, you know man, and so we had to go, we finally got a place in Houston, drugstore where we'd get a gross of it, a hundred and forty-four Benzedrine tubes, so we had to do that every two weeks, go into Houston and get a gross of benny for June, man. Oh Jesus Christ what a trip. . . . And pick up some Nembutals, man, that's what that Huck was hungup on then, he was vicious too on that stuff——

JACK. What he do?

CODY. Oh he was, ah, ah, how would you say it?——vililifying everybody; you know he was, ah——well him and June really were in the heights of a great feud, no shit, I really think so, because June was always "That Huck"——In fact it got so bad,

I can remember, you can ask Irwin, the incidents like at the supper table Huck would get hysterical, you know that never happens, and he'd throw up his dish and go away, and Bull, he'd "Ah, Huck," you know. . . . But I'm not digging any of this so much, I'm on other things somewhere. . .

JACK. What were you doing?

CODY. Oh I don't know what I was doing, I can't remember man, it's a terrible feeling not being able to remember what *I* was doing (*laughing*). . . Jesus was I there, I don't remember where I am but I think I was there, sh——one time or another, damn that, Oh Christ, mmm. . . . That's an interesting question, what WAS I doing? (*laugh*) What I was doing I think—— the reason I don't remember too well——

JACK. All I know is what Irwin told me

CODY. What's that?

JACK. About what you were doing

CODY. What was I doing man?

JACK. What Irwin told me?

CODY. I'm trying to remember, yeah

JACK. Oh, hitch-hiked, from Denver

CODY. Yeah

JACK. He said you kneeled on the road in Texas at night—— swore, or something——

CODY. No kidding

JACK. Yeah, facing each other, he said you kneeled in the road——

CODY. Oh I remember now, but that's not what it was, except some understanding

JACK. Some understanding . . .

CODY. Yeah

JACK. To understand . . . some understanding to understand

CODY. Yah. We WERE very high. Yeah. Ah, yeah

JACK. Well why did he shoot, why did he let go a blast of the shotgun at all?

CODY. I dunno

JACK. You don't know why, you just looked up and he was ba-lasting away

CODY. He didn't care, yeah

JACK. But he's sitting on the porch and then he suddenly . . . shot the gun

CODY. Yeah——but he shot it, a time or two before . . .

JACK. Oh I see

CODY. He'd shoot an armadillo, you know, just something to play with (*to baby*): Hey kid aren't you ever going to bed? . . . it's past your bedtime man, you been sitting there staring at that light for three hours! I wonder what you——hey he hasn't done nothing but stare at that light for three hours——what are YOU thinking about man?

JACK. Why he's high

CODY. He just lays there . . . what's the matter with you son? That's all he wants to do is look at that light. Ain't that crazy? Look at that fuckin light man, every time I look at it it just looks like this to me (*covering up*) . . . it's too *strong*. Look right into that light like he does, Jee-sus

JACK. I *could* look at it all night

CODY. It's *terrible*

JACK. Well after awhile that would really——be a lot of fun——

CODY. Yeah. YEAH I'll say, look at that. Man!

JACK. Just do that all night, looking into the light

CODY. And he's relaxed, see, and he's just looking at it

JACK. See, it isn't strong . . . it just opens up your eyes further, your irises

CODY. Yeah that's right . . . that's right, yeah

JACK. But he looks away from it once in a while doesn't he?

CODY. He doesn't seem to——wal, I guess he is

JACK. Well, that's harder than staring into it all the time, you know, it's . . . refocus and focus . . .

CODY. He's getting his eye exercises see

JACK. He knows what he's doin

CODY. Goddamn right. Well lookit man, I'm gonna change your pants and put you to bed, right? He is a weird kid, weirdest kid I ever seen. What the hell did I do with my——Oh damn it, where'd I put it boy? You see I'm high!

JACK. Diaper? Wh——?

CODY. The——the pin

JACK. Hey there it is!

CODY. Ah here it is——yet, there was two pins. Here it is . . . (*mumble*). Well, what are you saying?

JACK. I said YOU never told me what you did in Texas

CODY. No

JACK. See. All I know is what Irwin said

CODY. Yeah. Goddammit what *did* he say?

JACK. He said that when you were driving . . . across Houston you told some . . . (*pause*). That's one thing I don't know what the hell

CODY. Yeah. Well I'll tell you man, the interesting thing about this stuff is I think the both of us are going around containing ourselves, you know what I mean, what I'm saying is, ah, we're still aware of ourselves, even when we're high

JACK. Well I feel like an old fool

CODY. Is that it? Yeah . . . yeah. That's very good . . . I feel, ah, man, what do I feel? I . . . yeah . . . I feel very foolish

JACK. Hee hee feel foolish . . . but you still feel like a YOUNG fool

CODY. Well . . . I've been an old man, Jack, in Watsonville, and my eyes going bad, and my . . . yeah . . . Well I feel like a middleaged fool

JACK. You do?

CODY. Yeah. But I know I'm very young kid——type——in fact sometimes it might even occur to me to worry about it——but I haven't ever yet. You know. Man, I kinda dig you as a young kid type too you know

JACK. What?

CODY. I kinda dig you as a young kid type, like myself. But anybody else digging us thinks we're young kids but not you so much 'cause you're dark but I'm light complexioned so I look like a young kid all the time. But I never thought of that as——anything to worry about . . . (*pause*). Well I'll tell you this, I don't feel very intelligent . . . any more, at times, for a long time. . . . When I get high I feel——

JACK. That has two meanings

CODY. Yeah? Well——

JACK. I mean intelligent

CODY. I don't feel able, capable of the work, the effort, not the effort itself, I go through a lot of effort, you've seen me man, I've been on my feet here for sixteen hours. I——

JACK. You can't keep something up

CODY. I can't write it, I can't say, I can't, ah, you know, I mean, I'm——I can't get anything personally done like that

JACK. Yeah

CODY. I can't even get arr——. . . and when I'm high, shoo, I realize, that it doesn't have to matter——now you drank water, see, you RUINED that——our mouth is so dry and so——aren't they——that you ruined it with some water and I didn't catch you till just now. And here's what I'm gonna do, see, I was going to open this up, see? 'Cause our mouths is so dry

JACK. Oh gee. Well isn't there a roach? (*pause*) Go ahead

CODY. Well that's a——that's a——how many did we smoke man? how many you think?

JACK. I shouldn't have drank that water, that's all

CODY. That's the only thing, that's right. Well we'll smoke some more in a minute here but I gotta put this kid to bed, see, I've been hungup an hour, I'll be RIGHT down in two minutes, or less than that possibly

(THE END)

JIMMY. (*coming over telephone*) You know where that's at?

JACK. Wait a minute. (*to Cody, blanking mouthpiece*) He wants you to pick him up there

CODY. Yeah?

JACK. Course not right away, really

CODY. Yeah? Tell him, what——

JACK. Hello?

JIMMY. Yeah!

JACK. Now, we'll try to give it to Cody now, Forty-three——

JIMMY. Forty-SIX

JACK. Forty-six

JIMMY. Eighty-three

JACK. Wah?

JIMMY. Forty-six eighty-three . . . Seventeenth Street

JACK. Forty-six A?

JIMMY. No forty-six——alright now, four . . . six . . . eight . . . three . . .

JACK. Yeah

JIMMY. Forty-six eighty-three Seventeenth Street . . .

JACK. Four six eight three Seventeenth Street (*to Cody*)

CODY. What time?

JACK. What time, Jimmy?

JIMMY. Well, what time——what time is it convenient for YOU?

JACK. Oh I dunno, I guess any time. Immediately? Or you want to wait?

JIMMY. Make it easy on yourself, man, you know, easy does it

JACK. Well, what are you doing there?

JIMMY. I'm . . . visiting my daughter, you know, I'm——I have a lot of fun here

JACK. Oh you're having a lot of fun?

JIMMY. Oh with my kiddie, sure

JACK. Oh we might as well wait a while, huh?

CODY. Yeah. Ah, we'll be up there within an hour

JACK. Within the hour we'll be up there

JIMMY. Within the hour

JACK. Is that alright?

JIMMY. Oh sure, I could meet you somewhere more convenient, if you want

JACK. No, no, that's the place

JIMMY. Okay. Well, if you get lost, ah, call Butterhill one eight six four-o

JACK. Butterworld——Butterhill one eight five four-o. Hee hee hee hee

JIMMY. Yeah in case you get lost, then ask for Jimmy Low, right?

JACK. Okay Jimmy

JIMMY. Okay Jack, ah, easy does it heh?

JACK. Yeah

JIMMY. Righto

JACK. Easy does it

JIMMY. ——'tsa deal

JACK. Bye (*hangs up*) Er ah ear ah, well . . . well that's the thing, you're cuttin the thing

CODY. Goddamn it . . . this evening . . . and it's fat, man, and best of all it's loaded with a lot of great shit. This isn't any old stick of tea, man, when you get this down your gullet gonna have to give me a match (hee hee hee hee *as J. goofs*). Forty-six eighty-three Seventeenth Street, where the god's hell we ever gonna get out there. We're gonna have to do that, immediately! Ha! Humph! If this doesn't get you high man, nothin will. Here take this (*as J. seeks a roach*). Hmm (*exhale*)

JACK. But did you dig this? (*indicating typewritten sheet*)

CODY. Yah, that's what I've been in the process of doing here

JACK. Boy that's really somethin. . . . You don't want to dig it now, do you?

CODY. Do whatever you say (*disposable*). Get high, get h-i-g-h. . . . See . . . I know you got the recorder on, if I . . . ah, even if I . . . (*laughing*) damn him

JACK. Huh?

CODY. No, that's awright, man, that makes it alright, I just didn't want to have you under any false impressions, you know, YOU know what I'm saying, you know because like if I acted as if I didn't know it was on, why then, there'd be an ambiguity of . . . of, ah, ulterial motives, drooning, you know, 'cause you'd be in the process of getting me around under the machine and I'd be in the process of, ah, saying, like for examply, the reading of the manuscript, see, wal, hmm, wait a minute——I lost it (*laughing*)

JACK. Oh *that*

CODY. No——that's just pencil——Hee hee hee, damn

JACK. See, did you dig this here? I didn't notice that till I played it back

CODY. (*after long silence*) . . . (*laughing*) . . . It's like last night——ah damn thing

JACK. Hmm boy that was good. That was a good one wasn't it?

CODY. Phew!

JACK. Hmm . . . "And I remembered June's story about the horse" question mark? (*reading*) Yoohee, it's like a line of poetry. Is that what you said, "bad order high"?

CODY. Yeah, meaning, no good

JACK. I put that in

CODY. Yeah

JACK. But I didn't know that when I put it in

CODY. Yeah

JACK. Now go on

CODY. Bad order, with his bad order not *high* but *eyes* . . . see, he's got bad order eyes, he can't see, that's what I'm telling you, see

JACK. Oh yeah?

CODY. I say . . . "he can't SEE"

JACK. Oh bad order high——

CODY. Bad order——

JACK. Eyes

CODY. ——eyes, yeah

JACK. Aaaah

CODY. His eyes are no good, see

JACK. I thought you were saying he was bad order high

CODY. Yeah

JACK. Okay

CODY. Same thing though, it *is* here

JACK. That son of a bitch. (*Cody laughs*) Look at that son-ofabitch

CODY. Yeah

JACK. Then I remembered this, "demurely downward look"

CODY. I seem to remember that myself

JACK. Although it wasn't really

CODY. No

JACK. It was *my* idea

CODY. Yeah

JACK. About the look you had

CODY. Well yeah . . . it was kinda of a——

JACK. But it apparently wasn't . . . what you were really doing . . .

CODY. That's what it really amounts to, though

JACK. Why, because lookit . . . the talk is far way from demure . . .

CODY. Well, the reason for the *demure* is . . . any approach to the words like, as I remember like what I said . . . here, ah, "I can't get it down, for example, you know, "I can't get it down"——Well, I approached that very terribly, I was talking you know about something you know, that——it's goin on—— You know what I'm trying to say?

JACK. Hey? (*suspiciously*)

CODY. See? Here's what I'm saying, for example, I say, now man, "can't get it down," you know, and even as I say it it sounds awful, then also it sounds like struggling to get it down, and also sounds like whatever approach a young kid would, ah, approach with definite talk of getting it down, or in other words it might be an idealist who is no longer idealistic, and so he no longer wants to talk about ideals, y'know, and he doesn't want to, you understand what I'm *sayin* though don't you. . . . And, so——that's what I say when I say "I can't get it down," and then . . . "two minutes"——but you picked up on that, of all the different things I was sayin, and so you said, "But you don't *have* to get it down," you know, that's what you said . . . and so the demure downward look . . . was simply in the same tone and the same fashion . . . as my reaction and feeling was when I said the words "but you can't get it down" you know

JACK. Ah . . . you *were* demure when you were saying those words

CODY. No, I said this——

JACK. I don't know why you were demure if you *were* demure

CODY. I was demure simply because of the same reaction of those words, 'cause you chose "I can't get it down," and I approached it with a hesitancy, you understand what I'm sayin? What I'm saying is——

JACK. I thought you were bein demure because when I said "You don't have to get it down" . . .

CODY. Yah?

JACK. . . . you thought it meant, ah, that I was saying . . . ah, you don't have to write, see, *I'll* write. You looked away demurely, guy's saying "I got bigger muscles than you have"

CODY. Yeah yeah, that's right, yeah. Well it wasn't——and I didn't dig it personally, I dug it, as a, like I say . . . ah, a remembrance of my own past, my own, you understand——it was all an inward thing——not outward, you understand. . . . So when I looked down demurely it was the same way as . . . ah——in my own self . . . I approached a word, just like when you hear a bad word, or see a poor word, or dislike some particular phrase . . . like some guys are hungup on disliking phrases . . . you know, like for example I can remember, the Okies, in this country, especially out here in California when they say something, like instead of saying it's either one or the other, or something like that, they'll say "Man (*cough*) I was either gonna shoot that guy, or beat him up, *one*!" See, they use the word "one," one or the other they mean, see, I was either gonna do this or that . . . one way or the other but they always say "Man I'm gonna hit him this or do that, *one*!"

JACK. So?

CODY. Well I'm sayin, like when you come to dislike that phrase, the same way here, I come to dislike any concern about talking with the facts of "I can't get it down"——meaning . . . generally, writing . . . or, whatever it is the object that——

JACK. You don't like the phrase?

CODY. Not only the phrase in terms of phrase, but I mean the——in my own self when I approach the word . . . or I've come to dislike the phrase only 'cause it's associated with the fact that . . . I'm talking about something I no longer want to approach, or am approaching properly . . . or, what I'm saying is, you know . . . you have certain things inside your mind . . . when you catch yourself talking some other way from . . . what the way you want to be . . . caught talking

JACK. Yeah yeah yeah!

CODY. Well that's what I'm meaning to say that when I say a word like that, or a phrase of that particular nature, so therefore when you picked up on that and said "But you don't have to get it down," half consolingly . . . and also, still it's kicks enough in itself . . . and so on . . . that's MY interpretation . . . at the moment of when you said that, what you meant . . . and so when I demurely look down there . . . the concern (*cough*) was the remembrance of the reaction, ah, the thing that I had, ah, the same feeling that I had in me when I said the words "I can't get it down" came out in the downward look of half disgustingly . . . really having to approach a problem, or a concern——or something, that is that you haven't lately been in the habit of doing, and also that you're not sure is exactly——in other words you know you're a long way away from the problem, that's what I'm trying to say. . . . You know you're out there someplace else where you really don't want to be . . . you feel half disgusted at having to be out there . . . at the same time the demureness that comes into your expression is the——you know, it's too——you just feel very——ah strangled, do you know what I'm sayin, you feel very——

JACK. Are you sure? (*joking*)

CODY. You know what I mean, you're a long way out and . . . the demureness is the, ah——

JACK. (*imitating Lionel*) How can you be so suah?

CODY. ——is the opposite side of, ah——the demureness is the opposite side of, and the reverse feeling from, ah, and anger, demureness is a kindliness cast as a cloak over anger, or, ah, it is a shielding, or a shell for the inward frustration . . . which the anger is, you see, the anger is the internal anger, and the weariness that comes into the heart, unless you know that Jesus is always on your side. Now remember that (*paternally*)

JACK. (*laughing*) I was trying to find Billie Holiday's record of "Body and Soul" and put it on that jukebox there, plugged in——

CODY. Damn thing, couldn't find it

JACK. Couldn't find it

CODY. Well you just played it an hour ago, two hours ago, three hours ago (*inhale*)

JACK. Yeah, but purpose . . . of playing it at this moment was to evoke the musical sound——

CODY. Oh yes . . .

JACK. ——of the *Texas* that we were talking about last night

CODY. Texas, why——

JACK. See, that's what I was doing over there

CODY. Yeah man, I know you were, you've been——see, all the time I've been talking, every minute I've been speaking here about this subject, why you've been picking up and putting down those records and you went through the entire case of fifty . . . three times! So that means looking on both (*laughing with Jack*) sides of the record . . . three times would be a hundred and fifty times two, is three hundred times you moved your arm up and down and cast your glance up and back to manufacture something by finding——what if you have to do that all day, countless-ly twelve hours a day sun-up until sundown with children that is with objects which have to be taken care of, see, automatic, and so you have to go up and down three hundred times like that you know . . . every minute 'cause you're always supposed to be doing something——

JACK. (*interrupting*) Oh if I really wanted to find it I'd take them all out and stack 'em up

CODY. Yeah?

JACK. No, I'd go one by one but it's not there

CODY. Yeah

JACK. Where is it?

CODY. What did you do with it, you played it three hours ago, remember? Hee hee. So it's a mysh-tery . . . where could it have gone? You wouldn't have unconsciously put it in an album? But since you've nevertheless——

JACK. No I didn't do that

CODY. None the less I'll do something like this, watch, I'll just pull one out and I bet it's Billie Holiday just to be vain, see?

Now I haven't looked at it you can tell, have I——and certainly I don't intend to look at it, I'm just trying to put this plug in, see, I've been watching with my eyes, so you can see I'm not cheatin and lookin. Awright. See . . . damn thing . . . ah I know, it's too loose. Now I hope I——I hope it's Billie Holiday (*both laughing*) Huh? After you made three hundred motions . . .

JACK. You don't even know what it is

CODY. No . . . ready? Wait till the volume gets a little loud. Because the best part about Holiday records——for example you know that "Them There Eyes"(*sings it, the riff intro, with little Texas upflip*) And then, you know after they do that twice, three times really, why then she starts singing . . . but you know that opening? Remember the opening? The first eight bars? Ready? Billie Holiday . . . (MUSIC *starts*). I don't know the name of it

JACK. "Good Morning Heartaches"

CODY. "Good Morning Heartaches," yeah. (*laughing*) Good morning heartaches!

BILLIE SINGING: Good morning heartaches . . .

JACK. What do you think of *that*?

BILLIE SINGING: . . . you old gloomy sight . . .

CODY. Man, she just sits there . . .

BILLIE SINGING: . . . good morning heartaches . . .

JACK. Wow

BILLIE SINGING: . . . thought we said goodbye last night . . .

JACK. This thing here when Bull is sittin on the porch with his rifle across his knees? Now where is that?

CODY. Yeah, yeah, well it's back there . . .

JACK. Wherever it is——'course I know where it is——at that moment——hmm

CODY. What are you doing? I know where it is——I say here——

JACK. Where is it?

CODY. Right here, "settin with his rifle 'cross his knees" . . .

JACK. Yah. Now see these big questions . . . "yeah, I was there, yeah"——I say "Why did he shoot?" Cody——"He didn't stick it out the window, we was all sitting on the porch"——the moment you said that I feel the outdoors of Texas

CODY. Yah

JACK. Huck is playing his Billie Holiday, see, right here, naturally the guy's pointing to that part of the porch, and that Huck plays Billie Holiday outdoors in the middle of Texas is——see, "And Bull's sittin there on the porch with his rifle 'cross his knees" . . . as *that* is playing in Texas

CODY. Yeah, yeah, now you're talking

JACK. Sittin there like this, and where "I'm sittin there," and that's the way it——see, then "C-R-O-W-S-H!"

CODY. Yah that was crazy

JACK. "A dead tree strunk, he thought, see, for kicks, he'd shoot the treetrunk see?" (*reading on to* "baby cries")

CODY. (*laughing*) See, "it hit the treetrunk awright" . . .

JACK. See, "Billie Holiday——"

CODY. Oh. Yeah man. . . . Now here's somethin you won't believe. Now here's somethin——*I'm* gonna tell you somethin you really won't believe, now I'm gonna lay something down to you and you've got to really think about it in the same sense like we talked about "I can't get it down" or somethin, see? But not about that subject, but you got to understand the meaning of the words and so on. Just as I can talk there for twenty minutes about the reaction that made me give the demure downward look or the feeling of the "I can't get it down" you understand, in the same sense of those phrases you must understand that at the moment that I said these words "sitting on the porch" I chose those and thought of those be*cause* I had the same reaction of the outdoors of feeling like the *outdoors*, that was the very *word*——in fact it was the very reason that I began to speak . . . because you said——you know often, I don't even answer . . . (*blurred tape, talking about Jack saying Bull Hubbard shot "out the window"*) . . . and then I said "Yeah, I was there" and I just lifted my mind up and said that——I had to say that for another reason, which I don't want to tell you, man——what I'm sayin, is the reason I don't want to tell you is 'cause it was a reason which——what I'M sayin, what it really was, *was*, with the tape record, you know, well I said "Yeah I was there," ordinarily (*Jack laughs*) I wouldn't have picked up on that and talked about it see, you know, but the fact that we *are* recording . . . so it was a kind of a lifting yourself up to say "Yah I was there." Now then, ah, on about two three seconds later and when you said they were inside the window immediately my mind visualized that window as impossible, you know, it was, window, he couldn't have shot out a window unless he was trying to sniper, you know, it was like this, the windows were all——you know what I'm sayin, and, so, but . . . sitting on the porch so, because we *were* always sittin on the porch and the porch where we were sitting it's all an open front porch long and everything, and that, and while I *said* "sitting on the porch" I thought that would *show* that it was outdoors . . . just like you say . . . and then, ah, but instead, my mind then got hungup on the fact that he couldn't shoot through the . . . porch . . . because it was screened in, so Bull actually was sitting on the front steps is where he was sitting! Because the whole thing was screened except the door, yeah, and he's sittin down there on the front steps——but it seems to me he was in a chair . . .

JACK. Where's this thing play, inside the screen?

CODY. Off in the corner——yeah inside the screen, yeah

JACK. On the porch or in the house?

CODY. Yeah and I'm sittin, on a bench——I'm sitting on a Somerset T-type bench all by myself, and Huck's——

JACK. Yeah. Where were the washtubs?

CODY. The washtubs were on the other side of the porch—— where June is, she's over there in the washtubs. And Huck's kneelin down and sittin on a small chair by the phonograph record to keep the music goin all the time

JACK. What's he sayin?

CODY. Yeah. Nothin. He's just sittin there (*laughing*), he was there blastin, that's all . . . he'll pass it to me and I'll pass it to him, and we're just sittin there like that, we weren't talking about nothing ever hardly . . . but I mean he was, once in a while he'd talk, you know, when we were alone driving together we'd talk, just about like we are now see. But Huck at that time was very worried and hungup kind of guy, you know, he was living under a lot of pressure, he really was, see, you understand, and, but he and I dug each other all the time real fine, every-thing real smooth. But——

JACK. What would Irwin be doing?

CODY. Oh he left, he was only there three days, I never told you the great story of the bed, about——you must have heard about it though, the bed, the symbolic bed? that Irwin and I were gonna build man? I didn't tell you about that story? man I got to tell you about that story. You mean you——we've only played this once? (*at phonograph*)

JACK. No, you played it twice
CODY. "You played it twice" (*repeating*)
JACK. Yeah
CODY. Twice
JACK. Yeah. Well. Play a little——little blue eyes there——dem
there eyes
CODY. This isn't *blue* eyes
JACK. Dem dere eyes (swiftly)

(MUSIC STARTS)

CODY. Hee hee hee. And the needle. This is the way it was
in Texas, the needle's ruined, see, and this kinda music, and
of course *Bull* would say "Play some Viennese waltzes" and
Huck'd have to play 'em, Bull was deadly serious man . . .
JACK. About the Viennese waltzes?
CODY. Yes! 'cause Huck'd say "Aw man, you don't wanta hear
Viennese waltzes," and he'd say, "Oh, I really do"——and he
wasn't just making an issue one afternoon. . . . But Huck told
me a long time before that had begun, and Huck said "Naturally I thought the guy was just kiddin," but he really meant it,
and he asked it, so every afternoon he'd play Viennese waltzes
for Bull, see
JACK. Of course Bull insisted
CODY. And here——I don't know——and here, with an awful
needle like this and a poor machine but very loud, the music
was coming out b-r-r-r, scratchy, and it was Viennese waltzes
comin out real awful, you know like a tinny phonograph, and
here in this——and it was sunlight, and hot man, out in the——
this outdoors, just like we was saying man, it was——you understand, that music was comin out there, like I'd go outside
and take a piss or something and I could just hear a little bit of
this noise you know, comin off this porch, see, way down in this
Texas place (*all laughing*), real crazy . . . 'Cause it was so *hot* all
the time, it really wasn't . . . outdoors or anything——but what
I'm tryin to say is that Irwin got . . . after——now the understanding that Irwin and I had was not any——coming back to
understanding about anything, but we were just——we'd been
high together all of three days, see we'd been together and we
both were still young enough that we would talk and talk and
talk every minute see and naturally it builds up a big lot of

structure that's private that you build on the way down, and is just an interchange of different ideas that you have and different feelings but not about concretely or anything, but just, you understand what the person means 'cause he said that before or somethin——something like he'll say "Like what I'm sayin so and so what I really mean is *this*" and so the guy'll understand either because you tell him or either because he picks up on the way that what you meant about——something when you tell it be*fore* like that something-or-other, why, he'll keep building up so then (*laughing*) around a pyramid. And so we was real high just before we got there 'cause we made a long twelve-hundred, thirteen-hundred-mile trip pretty successfully see, we could have been hungup, we were hungup one more day just going nowhere, but at any rate now I'm sayin——so we're gonna have this great big bed, see? that we were going to——but it was gone, I haven't even told you about it——

JACK. Yes, with cots or somethin

CODY. Listen to this, I'd never seen Bull or nothing, see, I never had met any of these people, see, so Bull's puttin on a big show, you know, gettin *his* kicks you know, and Huck is saying "Glad to meet you and everything man," you understand, think of that now, see. And so . . . so we're out on porch the first day and Irwin his only concern was building this bed for where we was gonna sleep that night . . . and there was two cots, see, and that was what we were going to sleep on, but Huck and Irwin had the big idea to join the two cots, and that entitled a great deal of work, you see they were Army cots securely stapled together, and had to break all that, and pull all the front whole side of both of the cots, and then put them together . . . by—— terrible, *hard*, see. . . . Well for *three days* he and Huck worked on that . . . in the front yard, you understand see? And . . . Huck was very queer about the whole thing, see, he was happy and queer . . . you know what I'm sayin, he was eggin Irwin on, and Irwin asked me seriously, and I said "I don't care, brrp, brrp" you know (*laughing*), when——and that was the reason that he went to Dakar, see, because the bed was not a success (*laughter*). Yes. Soon as we got in bed together——Oh it never did get built and so finally we had to just what we did, 'cause we couldn't get it together, we collapsed the other end of both of the cots and just slept on the floor (*laughing*), two cots on the floor, with scorpions, man, so it scared the hell out of you, see, you're only that far off the floor, and, ah, man, that was kinda of a drag, so, what I'm saying——but no kidding Jack, now this is of course, now you know I'm no——I'm usually not talking about——you understand that I'm not——I'm not even lookin, at what it was . . .

JACK. Oh yeah yeah

CODY. See? I started to look but I didn't, in the same sense of kicks, see, I don't know what it is, see, so, here we go (*Jack laughs*)

(MUSIC STARTS)

JACK. Viennese waltzes!
CODY. (*laughs*) Yeah
JACK. *That's* what Bull insisted on, huh?
CODY. Yes

(MUSIC: "Stay With the Happy People")

CODY. That's right! (*like Frank Morgan, enthusiasm*) (*laughing*) Now what I'm saying is (*laughing*) . . . The bed didn't work, but what I'm saying, is just a——continue the continuity, I got so I couldn't stand Irwin to even touch me, you know, see, only touch me, it was terrible. And man, I'd never been that way, you know, but, man he was all opening up and I was all——but what I'm sayin is that, ah——so he was going to take a ship, in Houston, and I got high on Nembutals, so I go out, I pick up a girl, in the jeep, while Huck's down digging the cats in the corner saloon with his stuff, see, and Irwin's waiting up in the room, so I come back with the girl . . . and a quarter-of-a-block, no a half-a-block but quarter-block away I was perfectly in . . . capacity of my senses driving along and . . . within a quarter-block, and I was just approaching the hotel, and the Nembutals hit me! Bam! Man they hit me just like that, and I couldn't quite reach the curb, I was completely (*laughing*) in norm——control, but right in front of the hotel see, and I've just swung a right-hand turn around the corner——and it hit me man . . . and it was all I could do to hit the curb, and I looked at the curb, and I banged into it, really, I parked too close is what I did, scraped——but I managed to——but I was in a no-parking zone right in front of the hotel see 'cause ordinarily I wouldn't do that you know, I would have parked it someplace else, but, and I conked out like that, see, but I was still kinda, little bit, 'cause I——so I, seems to me that we sat there . . . the girl was an idiot . . .

JACK. Yeah

CODY. She was, she . . . told me that she was an idiot, and since she had been——they picked her up the next morning—— Yeah, she'd be in an institution, and, ah, they picked her up periodically every three or four months, and put her away, she'd get out after awhile, because she was harmless. But what I'm saying is that, she drug me up the stairs, to Irwin's room, and we got——and she went in bed with me and I tried to screw her and everything and I managed to finally even though I was so high . . . man and everything . . . but nothing else happened 'cause Irwin kicked her out, see, and, so then I——(*laughing*) . . . owf

JACK. You wrote . . . me about this or somebody did

CODY. No kidding (*stops music at phonograph*). Now. Pardon me son, I don't want to——you see I've different things that I've got on MY mind you know what I'm trying to say to you is, I'm gonna tell you somethin, although there might be other things that I'm hungup on, ah——the only reason that I'm playing this record is 'cause now you're high and you're gonna hear see . . . so now I'm gonna relax it and listen to it, you're gonna hear the *different* things they play. (MUSIC: *Coleman Hawkins' "Crazy Rhythm"*) (*and demonstrates ideas with hands*) I don't choose this record for any reason except that we played it three or four times see, so, that's why you know——even though it's not really——but listen to the man play the horn, that's all (*they listen to ensemble beginning work*). Ah man I'm gonna try to change that needle (*after stopping music, and Jack riffs on*). Did you hear that riff? (*puts music back, on alto solo*) when they begin—— listen to here (*off, on again*)

JACK. That's the old style . . . Chu Berry used to blow like that

CODY. Who?

JACK. Chu Berry

CODY. Yeah Chu Berry

JACK. *Man*, he used to blow like that *all* the time. That's where Hawk learned . . . they all learned from Chu those old swing men

CODY. Yeah

JACK. Lionel was very close to Chu

CODY. That's what he said, before he died he played a couple of his records that knocked me out. *You* remember that

JACK. Yeah that's right

CODY. Shit . . . yeah (*laughs*)

JACK. Who's playing now, is it the Hawk on tenor?

CODY. No, that's the guy who blows so sweet I told you

JACK. That Benny-what's-his-name

CODY. Yeah

JACK. That's Benny Carter!

CODY. Let's see in a minute

JACK. Playing alto!

CODY. Yeah

JACK. Benny Carter

CODY. Now Coleman comes in . . . listen to Coleman. (*Coleman comes in low toned, fast*) Hee hee hee way down there (*gesturing low at waist*)

JACK. Yeah

CODY. Hear it? (*they laugh and gloat*) See? he keeps blowin. Now here comes Benny, Benny plays like he did first only he backs off more, listen . . . hear it? Hear? He's going up, and—— he's not rockin, listen. (*they listen*) Hear him come down on a riff?

JACK. Yap

CODY. He really got that riff didn't he? (*laughing hungrily*) Stayin up there, see, and here comes Coleman (*low again*)

JACK. Ooo-*hoo*! Hey, yes

CODY. He keeps drivin see?

JACK. Yeah, drivin

CODY. (*laughing ecstatically*) Blows that sonumbitch does. Of course (*changing his tone*) near the ending he falls apart here. Poor man. (*Jack laughing*) He doesn't——it's just, you know, record . . . the ending. (*bassplayer on record calls to Hawk:* "Go on, go on.") (*Hawk blows aside complex what's this? riff*) What do you mean falling apart?

JACK. Yeah (*laughing and riffing*) Say you know what Danny Richman does?

CODY. What?

JACK. He plays me his Charlie Christian thing which lasts two hours? and he'll go . . . (*gesturing*) . . . up to this you know . . . according to the guitar. He'll do signs like that all night

CODY. That's what he did to me the first night I walked in there

JACK. His whole idea is for you to go and watch him do that

CODY. Yeah, that's right

JACK. Think how crazy he is . . . and you know what . . . then, when he sees that you're digging him . . . digging Charlie Christian . . . with all these things . . . you begin laughin! then he turns on his serious music there, that Scho-enn-berg and everything, (CODY, *yeah!*) he starts makin——

(MUSIC STARTS: *Perez Prado Mexican mambo*)

. . . . he doesn't like that shit

CODY. He doesn't

JACK. He doesn't listen to it

CODY. Yeah. Yeah.

JACK. Play it man play it! (*drums*) Oooh! Ha!

CODY. Here's where we are

JACK. Mexico!

CODY. "Demurely downward," see? I haven't read past there, I been savin see waitin . . . for this big thing here

JACK. Wow

CODY. But I can't remember what happened there man . . . except I, "Except that I remember certain things" (*reading from manuscript*) see, I do remember what that meant but I do, "Except that I do remember certain things"——which means only obviously, see 'cause after all this is me talking

JACK. Yeah

CODY. So I'm gonna tell you (*laughing both*) . . . you understand, see, but you know it just meant . . . that I remember . . . you know I have ordinary little ideas, things I do remember, like, like that bed for example, you know, things that are—— that's what I meant . . . see? . . . and that's the way it sounds (*pointing to words on manuscript*), and that's exactly what it is, right? Huh? Like everyone out there of course I do remember certain things, you know, just as normal . . . see, but I'm saying, like "Huck me and Irwin going out in the middle of the Louisiana bayou on a particular New York kick," you know how Huck and Irwin were . . .

JACK. New York kick . . .

CODY. Now this is one time, now, see at——exactly, all this I
told you which was really nowhere or nothin, just like the bed,
see, just the, the thing, that is just because I said these words "I
remember certain things" . . . so I decided to *tell* you about one
of 'em, and it just came into my mind, see . . . about *this*, see,
awright? Awright? And now look, see, it's never been, there's
no meaning here——now I mean it's a, a——

JACK. You know what you're doing there don't you?

CODY. The continuity——Oh I know it's——

JACK. Now, er really?

CODY. Ah hum, I know exactly what I'm doing man . . . I——
it's just like askin a man if he knows how to blow the horn see,
you know, like if Slim was blowin somethin I recognize that
Slim thinks that *I* was blowin man you know, and I always blow
like that see . . . and everything. . . . Now when a man does
somethin on a horn he wonders if someone else really hears
him, like oft times I used to think about, "Did Jack hear that?"
or ah, somethin about a particular record a long time ago or
somethin like that see. . . . But what I'm sayin is that, I say, well
of course he does man, he knows more about it than I do, he
knows about that, you know, he knows about, you know, see,
(*laughing*) and so that's the same way that what I'm sayin, I
know——but, so I have to tell him, I'm just sayin, those words,
remember certain things led me to think of all this, here, which
wasn't anywhere, as I said, it's just like even now, as I told in
the story about the bed . . . I didn't really feel it was anywhere
but it wasn't *any*-thing. In fact it was——what it actually was,
was a recalling right now on my part, a recalling of me having
either told about or thought about the bed concretely before,
see, so therefore I, all I did now was re——go back to that
memory and bring up a little rehash of, ah, pertinent things,
as far as I can remember, in little structure line, a skeletonized
thing of the——what I thought earlier, and that's what one does
you know, you know when you go back and remember about
a thing that you clearly thought out and went around before,
you know what I'm sayin, the second or third or fourth time
you tell about it or say anything like that why it comes out
different and it becomes more and more modified until it becomes any little thing that you say, see, like for example, I can

remember walking home from school when I was seven years old, you understand, and I'd already had such a long sex life and it was so involved that all one semester, every day, me and this little Mexican kid didn't talk about anything else and I simply told him all about what had happened to me since I was old enough to remember, see, and it took me all semester, and we walked a *long* way, man, from Larimer Street clear up . . . see. Terrible business. See now the only——see Jack I wouldn't have said any of *those* things, I'd have continued reading, I wouldn't have talked, except you looked at me to . . . so . . . I thought I'd better, so I wouldn't get hungup like I used to on tea, see, get hungup and not remember what I was going to say next, or not even finish the sentence because the effort to go back and remember in detail all those things that I've thought about earlier, is such a task, and unworthy, and it wasn't exhilaration, for the thing to do——it——like you go into something the first time you see after a certain period of time, roughly, about four, five years ago after I got hungup with Joanna, why, since then there's no more spontaneous, there's no more, . . . first happenings any more, you know what I'm sayin, which are things that are to be thought about, or things that are, you know, there's no more opening (*laughing*). . . . You understand anyway, yeah I mean you're just, ah, going along, see, and so, it's hardly worth it (*laughs*)

JACK. What's worth it?

CODY. Used to not feel couple of years ago hardly worth it to complete the sentence and then it got so try as I might I couldn't and it developed into something that way, see, so now in place of that I just complete the thought whatever I've learned, you know, like I see it complete whatever thought comes, see, instead of trying to make myself hurry back to where I should be here, and also . . . and only indications that lead me to go on this way like, you're looking at me to say that, only you didn't say anything, but you looked at me and so that I go on talking *about* these things, thinking about things, and memory, 'cause we're both concerned about, ah, memory, and just relax like Proust and everything. So I talk on about that as the mind and remembers and thinks and that's why it's difficult for, to keep, ah, a balance, you know, that's, but it's not really a concern because you can get hungup if you don't know when sharply to cut the knife, see, and switch back to something, you know, or something, because it becomes a hangup or just meaningless talk, you know what I'm sayin, see, so that that's hard, you know, as I continue, see, because really I don't *like* this! The same feeling, right here, see, as I remember telling that last night . . . I don't like it, same feeling that I had with "It gets you down," not that I had the feeling when I read it, but on the contrary that's the words that produced it, you understand, like I went through earlier, on previous. . . . Same way here I keep having difficulty going back to this because I'm not . . . I don't, you understand (*laughs*), feel it, proud of it, or anything, you understand, see, and so it's hard, it's hard to come back to this particular, see, so I've been postponing it really, see? (*both laughing*) Turrible thing. Now this one time, really, that's what I mean here, see, same thing, "Huck, you remember how he is," you see, "New York kick," so, "Huck said 'Come on man I want to show you something' he"——and Irwin, "he and Irwin were that way a great deal, Irwin would say 'You've got to see that piece of cloth,' Huck was sayin"——(*reading haltingly*) . . . because see that's what happened, see, and I'm describin now, see, now here I'm going through the process of telling *you*, and you're the one who *wrote* it down, see, so I'm saying, you know, you know more about it than *I* do——

JACK. I didn't punctuate it

CODY. No, you know more about it than I do . . . no——well, it *was* unpunctuated talk anyhow. What I'm sayin——you know what *I'm* sayin, so the reason I'm hangin up right now, talkin this way is just in the same sense that I want to tell you that rememberin certain things led into this see, and I've already said that, by telling you about this and saying I don't want to go back to it because of that, so now I'm . . . I'm ah . . . going on with the reading and still using the same process, I'm saying . . . so that means that up here Jack. Well that's not necessary now, we passed through that, because now we're talking just about the very thing that *I* thought about which was as I said earlier a mo-difi-cation, a skeletonized form of one of the things I happened to remember down in Texas you know. . . . And so . . . yeah well pick out a new needle, man, something you might find that would be——now listen I want to tell YOU something! You know I looked at the clock when Jimmy Low called at nine o'clock . . . now it's quarter to ten, he said within the hour, see, and also time and everything, and, we went through here for a minute, haven't we——

JACK. Yeah

CODY. ——you know. We've got to break loose *out* of that man (*meaning recorder*)

JACK. Out of what! Out of this?

CODY. Yeah. I got to go, out there

JACK. Working for nothin! (*going to machine*)

CODY. Whoa (*holding him off*), fatal . . . fatal. But what I'm sayin is, I got to get hungup on *my*-self goin out there, and you gotta get hungup by *your*-self here and that's a kind of a drag, man, you understand. I felt like Lionel when I said that, "That's a kind of a drag man," you know how, how Li's always sayin "Oh that's a drag man," you know how he's always sayin that, y'know, sympathizin with you, you tell him something, he says "Man that must have been a drag!" man, or else he'll say—— and it is a drag for when he's describin it himself——but——so I got to do that man, I'm sorry, but we gotta get a renewal of the supply of the material which makes it possible for us to *be* this way

JACK. We'll save the rest for Jimmy

CODY. Yeah!

THE HANGING (*Same Night*)

(*everybody laughing. Cody dancing to classical music.*)

JACK. Imagine a ballet dancer doing that, on a stage, in a ballet, a guy——

JIMMY. Wouldn't he be terrific if he was dancing with skin tights? Wouldn't it be terrific?

CODY. No (*choking on smoke*)

JACK. No, no, dressed just like that!

JIMMY. Come on man, get with it (*laughing heartily:* ho ho ho)

CODY. (*blasting*) That's a ballet, see? One of those mechanical modern dances. Now *he's* got it . . . see I couldn't drag myself away from it. (*laughing*) Sweet and lovely isn't it. . . . Careful, this is the last roach, men. (*blasting furiously*) (*gagging, groaning*) This roach, this immortal roach, this tremendous. . . . Which one is the tokay? All three. This is the one you gave to me, hey? The fullest one, obviously, I've not touched it. Now this roach, this immortal roach like a beautiful soul of some dead blossom of a rose will plop into the muscatel, only it's tokay, flame tokay, and I shall drink it (*laughing*) in liquid form, a concoction of, ah, doubtful, ah, qualities, 'cause you know, not being a lush type . . .

JACK. (*up on chair*) Rub off the dream here a bit (*flakes of blue paint on kitchen bulb*)

CODY. Oooh my goodness yass, (*imitating old man*) that blue light I've seen it every day since I been in this house, used to be all covered with all blue and everyone looked all sick in face you know, but gradually time has, ah, wrought its wreath (*goofing words*) and I shall rip with my initials, (*drunk*), same empty fiver, let it underline, my god (*all laughing*)

JIMMY. How weird

CODY. (*all laughing*) That's not good tea huh. . . . Here we go men

JIMMY. Hey the dog ain't underneath here is he? Can I crawl under if the dog ain't underneath there . . . is there? I'd like to crawl under there

CODY. (*blasting*) Dog no, there's no dog on the premises. Yeah man, it's perfectly permissible. . . . You park the chair Jimmy. Right. This is a hangman knot with seven threads. (*Jack now standing on chair by cord*) Seven threads, I have here, I have illegally concealed a spring in the trap so that instead of breaking his neck, pacaah! and killing him, he shall slowly strangle to death and take him forty-five minutes 'cause the spring will *give*, see

JIMMY. Let me help you, alright?

JACK. Why didn't you tell me sooner?

CODY. This is a formal hanging but nonetheless it'll have that interesting byplay the twi-tiching, you know, the old muscles (*gagging in hands*) stiff and jerk——oak (*chokes*). Sit down, have a seat (*to Jimmy*) AH! (*all laughing*) My first job as executioner

JIMMY. Hey can we have a knife so we can cut his ton—— testicles while he's hanging?

CODY. No, no, n——wait . . . we'll desecrate the body after. . . . After ha ha

JIMMY. I mean let's, let's hang him up and put him over on top a pawnshop, I mean . . . ah . . .

CODY. Yeah. The best part is to catch him unaware. Unaware! You catch him unaware (*to be heard*)

JIMMY. This is free

CODY. Which way will I pull it Jimmy, that's all, the only thing that worries *me*

JIMMY. Ah we gotta have a knife to cut him down in case he slips, y'know, huh? (*hard laughter*) We'll make a slit, I mean

CODY. Ah no . . .

JACK. (*with rope around his neck*) Continued next week

CODY. We'll catch this . . . villain, if we'll hang him from the nearest yardarm, ah. (*crash! tittering laughs! crashes!*) Hee hee hee hee hee. The sonumbitch's got such a strong head he broke the trap! He broke my favorite trap! Down! c-c-c-c!

JIMMY. ——very mad. Go now——

CODY. Distill the precious liquor! (*laughs*) (*drinks*) I had it cleverly concealed but he, the villain, he was on to me, this Hopalong Cassidy serial is just a little bit too, goddamn, I'll get even with him next time, I've got a knife outside, he ain't no—— he'll learn when they——when they start knivin 'em out west, hey Jimmy? These Easterners. (*laughter*) I knew that spring would come down, Evelyn said it was about to. Now be careful where you sit, there boy, you better watch along——Now it's almost five o'clock so we almost have some music, it's——he turned it down——(*Jimmy laughing, radio starting*) The radio announcement, the Chinese silverman gold ren-fer trouble, trupple, triple, that's been publicized, analyzed. (*whoop*) (*dropping ashtray*) Hey! (*laughs*) (*music starts*) (*swing*) A drunken carrasal! . . . see you got my roach

JACK. (*laughing*) I didn't know. (*imitating W. C. Fields as he drinks roach*) Too many maraschino cherries in the Manhattans makes me sick

CODY. (*drinking*) Ugh. I never tasted the stuff before myself (*piccolo*) Take a good slug of it, and no more

JACK. Yeah? You lush!

CODY. Man it'll hit your belly, instead of sipping wine take a gulp and that's all. (*piccolo and blasting*) (*Glenn Miller "Moonlight Serenade" on*) It's Jimmy and Glenn Miller

JIMMY. Oh high!

CODY. What we've got to have is another piccolo. Now wait a minute

JIMMY. I got one here

CODY. Well you've got one, new here's——we're gonna have a trio, did I ever tell you that one about the——"There once was a man from Canute, had warts on his cheroot, he poured acid on these, and now when he pees, he fingers his cheroot like a flute?" D'I ever tell you that? You never heard that one! We gotta——also we can hear the trio, and we'll trade off. (*as classical music begins*) You'll play the white piccolo, and you play the black piccolo, I'll play the sweetpotato, for two minutes, and then you'll take the sweetpotato, we'll pass it around in rotation see so we don't get on any bum kicks because of the poor instrument. Sit down! we're gonna sit down to the quartet, the Beethov——come on, str——string quartet man . . . well this is a clarinet trio, you understand

JIMMY. Who's gonna pass on this ability here

CODY. On ability the machine itself will pass on

JIMMY. Is it stopped?

CODY. No . . . we don't, no we just wanta a three-way here——

JIMMY. A little cooperation here——(*experimental flutings*) (*as Jack dials*)

CODY. Listen, for real tea-head goof kicks man, we can't have any——we gotta be like a string quartet, no beat and syncopation whatsoever, see, and we'll just goof you understand, like a string quartet, you understand, but he'll play his solo there, you know like he just did, see——Let's make sure we're getting everything here. (*adjusts mike*) (*first notes, challenges*) Hey man, hey, the guy who has the soft one must be sure and get his thing to hear close enough so it can be heard

JIMMY. I can't hear my thing——

CODY. No yours can be heard, yours is the loudest, you sit like this, and Jack's about right, he might turn that way a little, but I have to keep going this way until it's your turn then you have to keep turning that way——Now let's goof again, let's goof again (*laughing*), I didn't mean to interrupt and all this 'cause you guys——

JIMMY. (*was saying*)——I turn this thing on my leg——(*now laughs*) Hey I got to get a girl to get me incentive——to reach that damn thing——

CODY. That was, ah, that was amazing, I began to think of snake charmers and then I began to think of the, toot toot toot, and so therefore I had to cut you all a great mighty solo . . . my mighty solo was about to come in there . . .

JIMMY. Oh the rape charmers

CODY. Ready? (*announcing*) The rape charmers of the Indian plantation system

   (*they play*)
      clarity of tone . . .

JIMMY. Ah!

CODY. . . . an attribute

JIMMY. Yes sahib

   (*they play*)

CODY. Slowly, children, slowly. (*they play a long while*) Now we trade, now we trade

JIMMY. Hey!

CODY. We gotta get accustomed to all the instruments

JIMMY. (*protests*) Jesus Christ, hey, wh——

CODY. No, like we . . . hee hee, come on go on, music! there you are

   (*handing*)

JIMMY. What is the ho——here?

CODY. That's it see

JIMMY. Hey what's this little tiny hole here? That isn't a piss hole is it?

CODY. Never seen a hole that small before

JIMMY. Is this the piss hole?

CODY. It's the piss hole, the mighty seven epistles. (*Jimmy blows*) All wind . . . (*laughs*) . . . all hollow blowing. The hole's up here . . . there you are

   THIRD NIGHT

CODY. (*singing at table*) No more women . . .

JACK. . . . in the crank

CODY. I been spanked. . . . What to do about it

   (*singing*)

JACK. Chapter one (*flutes on piccolo*)

CODY. . . . Let's put out the lights and go to sleep (*singing*)

JACK. First sentence of the book (*reads*) I TAKE MY FRIENDS TOO SERIOUSLY

CODY. Great, great, great

JACK. Why, why, why is it so great?

CODY. Man that's just the kind of a tone of a book that I'm trying to write man, that's the tone, you got the tone right there

JACK. (*flutes*) Awright. Second sentence. (*reads*) EITHER THAT OR I DON'T LIKE LIFE ANY MORE

CODY. Man! Now you're getting profoondified, now that's exactly——that's beautiful. G-r-eat shit. Now that's the greatest stuff you've written since you've been in this house. (JACK (*laughs*) *Yeah?*) That's the kind, that's the way, I'm thinkin all the time, that's the kind of things, that's what I'M tryin to write, it's what I'M thinkin about, exactly right

JACK. Well I think like this all the time but I never write this

CODY. Man . . . that's the way to write

JACK. (*reading*) I MEAN *MY* LIFE OF COURSE

CODY. That's right. That's your third sentence

JACK. Third sentence (*flutes*) IT'S TOO GUILTY NOW TO HAVE FUN . . . (*waits, flutes, no reaction*) IF I HAVE TO MAKE A MATURE ADJUSTMENT TO A FUNLESS LIFE I THINK I'D RATHER COMMIT SUICIDE

CODY. Jesus Christ, whoo!

JACK. But instead of getting hungup there you notice I went on playin the flute

CODY. Yeah

JACK. The next sentence is this: and it's better than what I was goin to say: CHURCH MUSIC, THAT'S BEST, JUST LIKE ARTIE SHAW SAID. We were playing church music on the flute . . .

CODY. Ah huh

JACK. . . . Artie Shaw, Billie Holliday record, "Gloomy Sunday," the suicide record of the Thirties . . .

CODY. Yeah

JACK. . . . you didn't, did you, know that? about the record?

CODY. Ah huh

JACK. Did you connect Artie Shaw with it?

CODY. NO!

JACK. Is it interesting to connect Artie Shaw with that record?

CODY. Yes

JACK. Why?

CODY. Well man you don't expect him to have that inside of him . . . with all them cunts a man——listen, a man that has as many cunts shouldn't have anything else on his mind

JACK. About what, cunt?

CODY. No, not thinking about cunt, he shouldn't be granted the right . . . to have any *other* kind of a thought except what lies between them little gals' legs. . . . So if he'd say a whole kind of stuff like that why, he'd get scrupefied. Very interesting

JACK. That's what Artie *Shaw* said (*reads, flutes*) I KEEP FEELING THAT EVERYBODY KEEPS PICKING ON ME (*Cody laughs*) NOT ONLY CODY AND EVELYN BUT YOU TOO

CODY. Hee Hee, "you too" huh?

JACK. I'M TRYING TO FIND SOME WAY TO END IT ALL

CODY. (*laughs*) That's good, boy, that's damn good. (*Jack flutes*) Very good. Geez if you could write like that . . . for a thousand pages (*flute*)

JACK. Yeah, well it's not a story. (*flutes*) It's a kind of story?

CODY. (*eating at table*) Shua . . . kinda story I wanta write about

JACK. (*reads on*) I'M VERY DECENT IN FACT TODAY I PUT ON FRESH CLOTHES TO GO TO WORK IN BE-CAUSE I HAD TO HAVE A PHYSICAL EXAMINATION FROM THE DOCTOR FIRST AND I THOUGHT OF THE POOR BASTARD HAVING TO TELL MEN TO STRIP TO THE WAIST FIFTY TIMES ALL DAY ALTHOUGH BY NOW HE'S USED TO IT OF COURSE, THE POINT BEING I'M NOT, IN OTHER WORDS THE UPSHOT IS I'M CRAZY AND SHOULD BE IN A COMFORTABLE MADHOUSE AND I DON'T LIKE THE IDEA OF GIV-ING BLOOD

CODY. (*laughing*) That's great . . . great shit. Now you're really talkin. (*Jack flutes*) All that tea has finally produced somethin

JACK. It has, hey?

CODY. Goddamn right. We'll have to get some more of that stuff

JACK. You know what that sounds like though . . .

CODY. What?

JACK. It sounds like . . . the way that Dostoevsky started the, ah, *Underground, Notes From the Underground*, Jesus, that's

what, he started it by saying, ah, (*flute*) "I don't like you . . .
reader," somethin like that . . . "reader, you're picking on me."
(*plays "Them There Eyes" upflip on flute*) (*and then a long solo*)
I will write the next sentence now. (*flutes faintly, then wavery,
then types, wham, wham*)

CODY. Well for crissakes, Jack, can't you make your piecrust a
little harder? (*W. C. Fields-ing*) (*laughs alone as Jack types*) Jesus
Christ! See I thought of that line before I said the first one . . .
that's why I said "for crissakes," I thought of the . . . catchline,
see?——I gave it plenty of weight, weighed it see then after I
said it I thought "Gee, I waited too long, he might think I had
to think of that last line." (*Jack flutes*) I thought of the first line
first, I mean the——yes I guess I did after all, but the second
line I had before I finished the first three words of the first line,
I just . . . waited too long . . .

JACK. That's it, boy, you come over here and tell me now

CODY. (*laughs*) I'll tell you Jack, here's how I'll tell you——I
think what you should do is ask questions, like for example——
phew! man I had it a minute ago, why didn't I blurt it out——
Shit! The reason I didn't blurt it out 'cause you said "Now I'm
gonna write my next sentence," so I sat down thinking about
you writing your next sentence, and I thought to myself "Now
if he can ask himself questions . . . that, that, ah, he'll know
instinctly, what it is about him that's that way," why then you
can make a statement about it, like, "I'm very decent," only on
a much better level, like if he——Jesus Christ I'm trying to think
of what it was I thought of . . . I didn't . . . damn! . . . let's see . . .
(*Jack flutes and waits*) . . . (*Jack types*) . . . (*for sixty seconds*)

JACK. Go on Cody

CODY. Man, I'm thinkin. I've just spent the last minute thinking and I had a complete block

JACK. Well speaking of that, look at this sentence. (*flute*)
Now. Concerning . . . THE TAPE RECORDER IS TURN-
ING, THE TYPEWRITER IS WAITING, AND I SIT HERE
WITH A FLUTE IN MY MOUTH. And so you're just sittin
there thinking while it's playing (*plays flitty flute*)

CODY. That's just what I've been doin but I couldn't think of
the thought. And I guess the reason I can't think of it and why
I'm blocked is because I didn't formalize it or I didn't think
about it long enough, soon as the thought hit me, why, I didn't

think it out, because I was gonna blurt it out. Damn, if I'd have just spoken——(*Cody running water at sink, flute blowing, watery flute*) Your coffee's gettin cold. *I'll* bring it over but I don't know which one it is (*really meant, he says, he didn't know whether I wanted cream or sugar or what*)

JACK. See how terrible it is when no one listens

CODY. Oh man, yeah, I *know* how terrible it is. Christ yes

JACK. Why that's——I'm going mad now, see every time I start something I go crazy. That's my next sentence. (*pantomimes collapse at typewriter, falls on floor*) See? What was it? About——

CODY. "Every time I start something I go crazy" . . .

JACK. Ah. . . . (*types*) No, no, no, I didn't say that! What was I sayin? About the coffee?

CODY. "See how it is when nobody listens?"

JACK. Yeah, that's what I was sayin. That's not what I wanted to write

CODY. No

JACK. No. . . . When you answer you're goofed. Don't goof here

CODY. Ah huh

JACK. Although that would be good to write wouldn't it now

CODY. What

JACK. What would be good to say, to write that, I suppose, you can write anything in there

CODY. Yeah

JACK. . . . something like that, that's the trouble with that

CODY. Yeah that's the trouble

JACK. But in fact that's what's good about it, you can write anything in there. Huh?

CODY. That's right. Has to be damn sharp though. Celine does a lot of that

JACK. What does he do?

CODY. Ah you know how he writes . . .

JACK. He does a lot of, ah, that, yeah. . . . It has to be damn sharp

CODY. Yeah, damn right

JACK. How can I be eating on Benzedrine? (*eating at table*)

CODY. (*laughs*) That tea'll overcome anything. (*pause*) . . . Why don't you let me read John's letter? (*playing whiny little boy*)

JACK. Didn't you read it? . . .

CODY. Now see, you know four times I asked you and four times you didn't answer me see, so at this time I said "Well——" although I've hesitated asking it several times, I thought "I'll make Jack say 'Nah don't read it'" you know, and . . . 'cause you never did say it, see. I kept asking and asking and you never answered. . . . You always give some ambiguous statement or you never say anything at all like you just now said "Didn't you *read* it?" 'S' if it was perfectly alright (*laughing*) . . . I would have read it long ago if I'd known I could have read it

JACK. Oh. (*Cody laughs*) Well . . . the first page was written before I got high

CODY. Oh I know that, I remember exactly where you got high

JACK. And I feel very guilty about it

CODY. Oh I see, uh huh

JACK. Well read it. (*pause*) . . . I feel that I'm assailed from all sides. . . . I'm being flailed from all sides

CODY. Jesus Christ, man, that's a terrible feeling . . . Jesus

JACK. But there's no time for feeling, huh?

CODY. Well there's time for feeling, it's just how much——first thing you would do with it you know, I mean, ah, I can't, ah. . . . It's very hard, in the end we're all by ourselves. . . . So, got to figure out ourselves. . . . But the thing is, what I don't know, I think your mind is too much on the writing so that you really don't have time to really sit down and go into whatever this is that's flailing you, all these people flailing you, and so that you're not really hungup on that, it's just a feeling that you don't deal with, and so you, you know 'cause you've got too many other things on your mind. What it is with me would be a change in personality . . . I mean a change in values, change in——

JACK. In what way?

CODY. Well you know, a change in your concerns, what you're concerned *about*. See you're not really concerned about that or else you'd think about it more and be hungup on it. You're hungup on it alright.

JACK. On . . . *writing* about it!

CODY. Yes, it's just because you're writing, see, you're really only concerned about the writing . . .

(*tape goes blank for four minutes while they go on talking, about fame, not wanting to be destroyed, status, career, control, both of them extremely sad and close*)

(CONTINUATION OF TAPE)

. . . that'll make some difference, but ah, I got a little better control than I used to have but it's still not the right kind I guess

JACK. Well you're, you're a family man now. . . . You know, James Joyce had a big family but, ah, well, I don't know how he got to write so much; he lived in Switzerland, France; he had his study, you know, he was a man of serious solemn habits, that's all, took walks in the morning, and wrote, had a job as a teacher. He had a lot of children but I don't think he spent any time taking care of them, see, except once in a while, an hour or so a day . . .

CODY. You're not gonna get hardly any of this recorded you know

JACK. Well, that's the sadness of it all

THE PARTY

PAT. (*after hubbub*) But that's the one of "Leave Us Leap"——I got hungup on that one one night at Jimmy's place and I must have played it twenty times

CODY. Yeah . . . ah . . .

PAT. That "Leave Us Leap," Gene Krupa's "Leave Us Leap," (*"Them There Eyes" begins on phonograph*) Boy it's got everything, it's got, oh man, you got——piano passage in it that's *terrific*. . . . Everything, everything in the thing is good. Did you——did you hear that "Charmaine" by Billie——Billie——

JACK. I can't remember "Leave Us Leap"

PAT. "Leave Us Leap"? Oh man it's sensational

JACK. Roy Eldridge on it?

PAT. ——one of the best numbers I ever heard. Doesn't tell you. Must be

JACK. Well he had quite a band, sure

PAT. (*as Cody talks far in background saying:* I saw . . .) But man that "Leave Us Leap," it's just . . . it's almost like "I Want to Be Happy" with Glenn Miller, you know? You know how he——before that, drivin all the time you know? Sounds like there's a tension. . . . (*as Jack sings "I Want to Be Happy" in* *harmony with "Them There Eyes"*) No . . . ten times as fast as that

JACK. That's fast though . . . that's the tune

PAT. That's what it said on the label but you'd never know. (*Jack laughs*) The tension and drive all the way through

JACK. (*bemused at phonograph*) Ooh . . . we'll play the Dizzy

PAT. (*still reading cookbook*) Huh?

JIMMY. (*playing with toy telephone*) Can you tell me why the manufacturer forgot to put a hole in the——the part where you hear through?

PAT. So it's so you can call your wife

JIMMY. Ah . . . I was——

CODY. (*laughing*) So you can call your wife . . .

JIMMY. It doesn't fit on here . . . sounds better (*squeaking it*) that way

CODY. (*entering now*) Man . . . aww . . . Jimmy . . . is this different pot than what——

JIMMY. No . . . there's only one difference, there's about ten roaches mixed up, you know?

CODY. Yeah! Boy! (*Jimmy laughs and says something inaudible*) (*Cody watches Pat*) He blasts like Louis Armstrong! Zoom! It's gone in two roaches . . . it makes a roach out of a joint in two puffs. (*everybody laughing*) That sonumbitch is high, man. . . . No, he's going, ffff, sss, man he just keeps going up, up, up, and I'm watching down, down, down. . . . Now. (*laughs*) Ah look at him! (*much blasting . . . Lester Young starts*) (*groaning and blasting*) No, what? (*Evelyn speaks faintly from way back*) Oh yeah? Hey Jack

JACK. Huh?

CODY. She's reading along here on a page and she says "You and Jack had this exact same conversation tonight" . . . the same paragraph . . . of Billie Holiday

JACK. Yeah

EVELYN. (*reads*) "Good morning heartaches"——"Good morning heartaches"——"yeah" . . .

PAT. (*discussing something briefly with Jimmy and laughing as Evelyn reads*) . . . did you hear that record "Charmaine" by Billy May? (*to Jack*) Boy, you know . . . oh man, I was gonna go in the store the other day and buy it and bring it up to Jimmy's, and I thought "It'll probably cost me a buck, I don't——

I don't——" ah, boy it's really fine, one of the finest records I ever heard

CODY. (*whistling strangely*) Here you are Jimmy, watch out you don't lose a finger there——

JIMMY. Hey! (*burning on roach*)

CODY. (*laughter*) Watch out . . . YOU don't lose a finger (*to Pat*). We barely made it man, the transfer. She's burned his finger, and I'm goofing off here this way

PAT. Burnt my lip awhile ago

CODY. Yeah, yeah . . . yeah. (*Evelyn speaks*) Yeah, you're not the roach type hey? I'll get down and suck on it anytime. Hmm, it's not down yet. (*losing roach in mouth*) Burnt your lip hey? (*to Pat*) (*laughs and Dizzy starts*) Oh *well*, now wait a second . . .

JIMMY. We've smoked this to the last, I swear the last——

PAT. *Did* you ever hear that record by Billy May of "Charmaine"?

CODY. Here you are, here you are! Yes! Jack has . . . 'cause, remember "Charmaine" on the . . . "Sepia Serenade"? You may not remember just the name "Charmaine"

JACK. No I don't remember that

CODY. Guy named Billy May?

JACK. Billy May . . .

PAT. Boy, what, listen, it sounds better than Glenn Miller ever used to, well not better, but you know, almost, as——

JACK. (*as Cody laughs*) What is it, a big band?

CODY. No, colored

PAT. No, real drive colored swing outfit

CODY. (*to Jack*) Can't get it? Ooh man, it's flaming

JACK. Oh . . . there was nothing there

CODY. No, there's nothing there . . . was a little flame . . . one little nothing that was there was going but you couldn't feel of it because it was so . . . small

PAT. You got it? It was out on transfer

JACK. What kind of band is it? a colored big band? Jive——

PAT. Yes, about set up like, ah, Miller used to have . . . just about the same setup and everything

JACK. I'd rather hear the colored guys play bop

PAT. Oh man, if you hear this "Charmaine," boy, you'll say it's terrific

JACK. I'll bet they blow sweet at that

CODY. What I said was, Jimmy, ah, I was going to say, thank you for getting me from halfway up to all the way up there . . . over the hill, there, you know what I was sayin, you understand (*laughs*), you know what I mean. . . . Phew!

JIMMY. You're now a profound thinker

CODY. Man, no, I'm just——

JIMMY. You're just found

CODY. ——trying to remember what transpired before the beginning of that there cigarette

JACK. Dizzy (*as Dizzy plays wild trumpet softly*)

CODY. (*after listening to Evelyn*) Yeah? Yeah, all we talk about's Bull and his shotgun. Yeah. That's right. Of course. That's right. (*hubbub*) That's what I told *him* here, all we talk about is Bull. Yeah

JACK. (*whistling with "Bebop" end-riff*) All one breath! Man, what . . . big chests!

CODY. Good or bad . . . why not? (*talking with Evelyn about too much T or not*)

EVELYN. (*laughing*) Well, I don't know why (*Charlie Parker's "Lover Man" starts*)

(MUSIC *drowns out mumbles, hubbub, Cody and Evelyn softly*)

JIMMY. What are you reading that's so interesting?

CODY. More of the——more of the——

JIMMY. What *is* it? (*Evelyn explains softly*)

JACK. Listen to Charlie

CODY. Yeah

JACK. You gotta stare, I guess . . . to really listen

CODY. Oh yeah

JACK. What were you going to say? What'd you come over here to say?——(*then meaning Pat*) Still reading the cookbook!

CODY. (*laughing*) Man, yeah. I tell you, nothing like putting into practice the good words put upon a printed page

PAT. Hmm? I can read these things, like some people do novels——

CODY. (*laughing*) That's great——I was thinking have they got a good apple pie recipe in there? (*laughing again*) Jack's been hungup making apple pies. He's made three apple pies in two days, or vice versa, 'cause I got a whole bunch of apples, see, every day we'll buy one of the——so tonight he finally gave out, see, I said "Well where's the pie?" "Well, ah, we won't eat it till tomorrow so I'll make it tomorrow" he says you know——(*Evelyn and Jimmy chuckling over manuscript*) What's happening over there? Ooo, Jesus . . .

PAT. Man, I'm sure gettin a goofy kick this time, I don't know what's floatin (*laughing heartily*)

CODY. Who's, hey, wait, I, I missed that one, hey I *missed* that one, he's getting a——

JIMMY. He's gettin a kick off that recipe

CODY. He is? Well let me see it

PAT. I'm reading a . . . alligator pear salad

CODY. Alligator pear salad

PAT. Says here a big outfit——I'll read——

CODY. Great

PAT. . . . reading the cookbook and one thing——

JIMMY. My oh my, that's great, always——

PAT. What the hell am I doing in here? . . .

CODY. WHAT pears?

JACK. Brrrp,

PAT. . . . avocado . . . geez. . . . I know but I couldn't remember when I got down there . . . you know, you feel like slamming your hat down and jumping over it . . .

CODY. (*laughing, new music, hubbub*) You gotta concentrate——

(MUSIC *now Flip Phillips*)

PAT. (*still talking about same thing*) . . . Chinese . . . hiccups . . .

CODY. Chinese

PAT. Chinese

CODY. Yeah

PAT. Chi-*nese*, though, I kept going up and down fast . . . cheese looked like Chinese

CODY. Oh, yeah

PAT. Cheese . . .

CODY. Hey. . . . Ah . . . how to cook game, huh? Hoooeee! (*to music*) (*Jack is whistling, swinging*)

PAT. That stuff was alright wasn't it?

CODY. Oh *was* it alright! . . . Just a moment . . . just a moment please . . . just a moment. (*turns off music*) Just a moment please. (*as Jack goes on whistling to gone-off record*) Just a *moment* please. . . . Just listen to the piano. (*starts same record again*) Just listen to it

JACK. (*laughing*) No flutes!

CODY. (*blowing jazz flute*) Listen . . . (*Jack joins him on black piccolo*)

JACK. You told him. . . . He blows though——(*clapping beat for Cody, then laughing and retiring*) (*to Jimmy*) Flip Phillips see? (*Cody playing and watching Jack*)

JIMMY. Yeah

JACK. (*laughing at Cody's swing*) All hollow blowing . . . all wind

CODY. (*laughing in mi mi mi mi mi notes, ha ha ha going up*) (*elaborately, and later said he didn't know he was an opera singer, that is, doing this*)

JACK. Well, ah . . .

PAT. Someone's been trying these sauces already, huh?

JACK. Here's a big roach for me (*laughing at discovery on the floor*)

CODY. Boy you sure tricked him that time. . . . Did he look up when you said that?

JIMMY. Who?

CODY. He said "Here's a big roach for ye"——Don't think I didn't overhear that

JACK. Where did the, ah, tweezers go?

EVELYN. Oh (*explaining where softly*)

CODY. Man, somebody's made away with my record

JACK. What did you do with the——

CODY. What's happening. . . . Oh no wonder, he's got it all propped up here

JACK. Where'd you put your tweezers?

CODY. Aw they——they're up on top, man, in the bowl, where everything belongs

JACK. Oh yeah, there they are, sticking up. See I knew Cody is systematic

CODY. (*starting "Honeysuckle Rose"*) Wait a minute! (*stops it*) What's happening here? What's happening in this household? What's going on in the vicinity of this place? What's happening?

EVELYN. (*talking far back*) . . . parts that weren't there . . . next time . . . you go on with the story . . . the part about Bull shooting out the window . . .

(MUSIC: *loud revelry interrupts Cody loud on flute*)

PAT. That stuff must be good, I'm tellin you

CODY. (*laughing happily*) Hear that Jack? He says "That stuff must be——" (*resumes flute*)

PAT. This is a good number, what the devil is that?

JIMMY. . . . drums on toy bongos

CODY. (*as Jack and Evelyn ask him a question about what he meant by* "Somerset T-type bench") Ah, I'll tell you in one second . . . I'll tell you in one second. (*resumes flute*) Ah ha ha ha. . . . Now. We'll pick up the beat a little bit here, play that old standard classic. This record was made twenty years ago, I want you to hear their saxophones. Listen to this. (*starts "Crazy Rhythm"*) (*flutes*)

PAT. Dig the drum here. You know that one. You don't believe it, you know

CODY. Listen to this *sax*, alto, listen. Listen. . . . Listen. . . . Listen . . . to Coleman Hawkins, listen . . .

PAT. Ralph Parker's the guy he was trying to think about in Australia

CODY. Here he comes

JIMMY. Ralph Parker's the guy he was trying to think about in Australia? (*laughing*) An *hour* later!!

CODY. He remembers! Listen to Coleman, real open tone. Here comes the alto again, now listen to the alto, here he comes. . . . Hear him? . . . real sweet but he rocks. . . . He'll play the same phrase again, he'll play it again, real sweet. Watch him hang on it. . . . Here comes Coleman real low

PAT. Man, that's fine. . . . He blows

CODY. Bassplayer says "Come on man, come on!" He goes "Prrrr. . . ." Listen——He says "Come on——"

JIMMY. "Blow me an extra one," huh?

CODY. Yeah. He says "No, no, no, the hell with you," you hear him? He says "Prrrr. . . ." He'll play anything. You like that?

PAT. Yeah

CODY. Play it again huh? Right away or do you want something in between? Right away?

PAT. Let's——let's go right on with it . . .

CODY. Alright now that's great, now you're talking. Sit down and listen to that alto first . . . first they play together . . . this was their band in France in 1920 right after the war——

PAT. What was this?

CODY. Coleman Hawkins and "After You've Gone." I mean ah——

PAT. In 1920?

CODY. Yeah, listen to it, sure . . . that's the way they blew those old alto men. . . . Boy they're swell . . . listen to 'em swing! (*flutes*) Listen to the alto, see?

PAT. They played like that in 1920?

JIMMY. Some of 'em were terrific. People knew what the hell it was, in New Orleans . . .

PAT. Bet my old man knew, though . . .

JIMMY. Yeah he was always talkin, so,——

CODY. Here comes Coleman, first time, here's Coleman . . . listen to him, real *low*. Listen to him walk in, hear it, hear him come in there? Whooo! He blows. Now here comes the alto again, he plays the same way he did before only slower man and way up, listen, here he comes slow, he's very slow, wow, he'll play it, now listen, hear him blow that phrase? Whoo! But old Coleman he's got——dig him! (*Jimmy's drumming*) That's Coleman, remember how he sounds? (*tape runs blank, five seconds, then when it comes on again Cody is saying:*) . . . same thing . . . here's the way he plays that same song today. Real different, dig this . . . see how subtle he is? Here he is, listen . . . he's changed, he's twenty years older, playing the same song. Hear him? different

JIMMY. Can *you* change the needle?

CODY. But I haven't got any needle. . . . That's the trouble man, my needles are all shot. (*pulls record off to change needle*) Don't have any

JIMMY. Let's find a needle (*sepulchrally*)

CODY. (*music re-starts*) That's better!

PAT. Gee this is a swell number isn't it huh? Is it a reprint?

CODY. May-be . . . we were discussing that last night. (*after music*) Here he comes . . .

JIMMY. Yeah

CODY. Piano

JIMMY. All bass

CODY. Yeah bass

PAT. I think this is an original

CODY. Might be, it's what he says, 'cause it doesn't say reissue (*after long listen to music*). . . . Now he really goes, he's been playing here for five minutes and he still hasn't got it——ah, hear him blowin in there? (*machine stops there, then re-starts*)

EVELYN. Cody remembered a whole lot of this conversation on the way down there (*talking with Jack about the missing parts of Third Night*)

CODY. (*after singing with Josh White record of "Bad Housing Blues" and goofing*) Hey man. . . . W.P.A. kicks. . . . Hey Jack, here's an unbelievable thing!

JACK. Oh . . . what?

EVELYN. (*seeing joint*) Oh my God

CODY. He decided to cap it——to cap it off, you see

JIMMY. He turns around like I was doing the striptease or something

EVELYN. . . . real high, I should have known

CODY. Man . . . you know . . . ——no, it's the Dexedrine darling, the Benz——the Italian Benzedrine

JIMMY. Eh, ah, oh that Deni gave you! (CODY, *Yeah*) Oh man that must be frantic, he told me about 'em

CODY. I been on 'em since about seven o'clock this morning

JIMMY. I was on——on two——two of the regulars tonight and I'm feelin . . . quite mellow

CODY. (*laughs*) That keeps everything real cool. . . . Still have a little energy left. . . . (*imitating W. C. Fields*) I'll show you the . . . I used to be . . . I used to be an acrobat in a circus, Jimmy, you know that? (*while others are talking*)

EVELYN. Oh boy

PAT. Do you——do you——break easily?

CODY. (*laughing*) See, he doubts the ability——I do it better with m'shoes off . . . because of the confines I hope——I gotta have a little music though

PAT. Don't, ah, knock your skull there or nothin

CODY. Oh yeah, well I won't go up I'll go down, I mean . . .

JIMMY. You gotta have music for this little act?

CODY. Hmm . . . gotta relax the muscles and the nerves. Threw the cigarette out so that, ah, the throat would not be ah, er——

EVELYN. (*seeing he's looking for something*) Have you got something in mind?

CODY. (*coughs*) There it is, there it is, I see it, on yon horizon

JACK. Yon eastern hill

CODY. Hmm. (*mambo comes on*) (*blasting*) I got smoke in my eye, I didn't get it. (*taking three, four more puffs than he ought to*) (*Jimmy laughing*) (*Evelyn laughs also*) See, when I get *her* high man, sh——one night——we just got one stick between us, that's all I'd managed to salvage, scalvage around town and scravenger up, so we're in a vile mood and we sit down there and in five minutes after we blasted she gets up and walks to the stove and she falls *flat* on her ass, right in the middle of the floor from thinking she saw something, or something

EVELYN. Oh, you know better, you know that it's all wrong

CODY. ——just the same tonight . . .

EVELYN. Hah! you didn't finish the sentence, then you came over to pick me up then fall flat on *your* face

CODY. I (*among laughs, hubbub*) guess that's the quick approach, is all, ahem . . . no——

EVELYN. I tripped over a wire

JIMMY. ——instead of helping a lady up you get down right there with her

CODY. You got the right idee

EVELYN. Really was funny though wasn't it, everybody falling down . . .

JACK. I didn't have mine yet did you? Did you s——who started it? Let's get the circle going . . .

JIMMY. Evelyn did

EVELYN. I did

PAT. Hey! hey! hey! (*calling for roach*)

EVELYN. ——"here we go round the mulberry bush, the mulberry bush" (*laughing*)

CODY. Now, I'm really relaxed. . . . Phew!

PAT. Didn't you get it second? (*to Jack*)

JACK. No

PAT. Oh

CODY. I remember one time in Louisiana, Jack——we went

out and we did a standing high jump, and kept raising the stick up and up, this high

PAT. The better the tea the higher you go

JACK. ——Buckle and I held an iron bar and Cody was going f-w-i-t! (*Cody goes* Ha ha ha!) I can do about this much. . . . You do this (*holding hand to higher level*). I can't do that. . . . (CODY, *Yeah*) Nup, I can't do that

EVELYN. What kind of a jump?

CODY. Standing . . . broad jump

JACK. Standing *high* jump

CODY. I do a backflip up . . . the stairs

JACK. Broad jump is going that way (*demonstrating*, CODY, *Yeah, oh yeah*) You know, off of the board?

CODY. Oh I——man, I'm gone on the standing broad——now wait a minute

JACK. (*amid laughter*) He can do it——he can do over nine feet

EVELYN. When did you do all this?

JACK. In the street, in the street . . .

EVELYN. I say *when*?

CODY. Why man, a standing broad is crazy——any broad that's standing is crazy——this is standing broad——now come here——

EVELYN. When did you and Slim and Cody all get together

JACK. Oh, New Orleans

CODY. Now look, put your feet against the back here, so, you know, you got——well——

JACK. . . . you'll hit the stove . . . alright! (*moving over*)

JIMMY. Oh you mean, s'frum, s'frum, from *standing* position?

CODY. Yeah

JIMMY. Oh, no kiddin

CODY. Go ahead, jump

JIMMY. How——how many feet?

CODY. How far?

JIMMY. Hey, ah, how, what do you call that, what kinda jump you call that?

CODY. Standing broad jump

JIMMY. Hey Pat

PAT. Huh? (*looking up from cookbook*)

JIMMY. When you stand perfectly still to make a jump . . . now wait a minute, how about——how about when you're running, and *then* leap!

CODY. (*laughing*) Man . . . never done nothin . . .

PAT. That's the *running* broad jump, that's the *running* broad jump!

CODY. Just discussed that, see (*laughing*)

JIMMY. Oh what I'm tryin to say, how many feet can you do?

CODY. Oh darling I'm sorry! (*accident with roach*)

EVELYN. No *I've* got it

CODY. Did you get it?

JIMMY. Hey, hey——how many, howmany, howmany feet?

CODY. Ah (*choking*) (*holding breath*) you got that one. . . . Here's what I always say Jimmy, it's not how many feet you *could* do, it's how many feet can you do now? Right?

JIMMY. Ah ha, what a conniver, what a——

CODY. Yes s'what I mean——see he didn't even think I heard him, see——

JIMMY. I know, I know, I'm hungup, I'm hungup, two ways, man (*laughs*)

CODY. Man he's hungup *three* ways, I dug every way he was hungup that time, everywhichway he was hung . . . three, right? (*blasts*) What am *I* doing with this?

PAT. You——I don't want any, Jimmy, you can take it . . .

CODY. I'll get the crutch, men . . .

JACK. I'm in on this one, on this kill——

CODY. This is a three-way job, girls, sorry

JACK. Awright, I'm out

CODY. Come here! (*then to Pat*) Go ahead, man, go ahead!

PAT. By the way——oh, ah, I got enough

CODY. Come on here, just——at tat tat——there you go——

JACK. Take it easy boy

CODY. W-w-ah . . . (*coughing*) I got the paper-aher-AHER (*crying* boohoo) . . . paper . . .

PAT. (*still reading*) Man, there's——

EVELYN. You got all the middle of it——

PAT. ——squabs in here and——

CODY. Yeah I did at that, come to think of it, yeah, well . . .

PAT. ——frog legs, boy oh boy, roast pheasant——

CODY. ——feel better, don't you

EVELYN. Hm-hm, don't *remind* me, or I'll start all over again . . .

CODY. MORE?!!! Pardon me I was about to perform an

exercise, get out of the way, sit down will ya? one at a time, here, one at a time! (*smash*) Oh the standing broad jump——

JACK. Yeah that's right, that's right, the standing broad jump

CODY. Now here's the approach . . . assuming you come tripping out on the athletic field in the Olympics, you know, why you've got to have sensational approach, you just don't step up to the line, there's the line see, and we're all cuttin up like the horses, racetrack, so I come leaping in, with my roach, (*laughter*). . . . Man

JIMMY. No the roach *is* gone

CODY. Well, man

JIMMY. Drop it in the fly catch

CODY. What happened to the flutes? They're much more peaceful! (*clink of glasses*) (*laughter*) What's so acti-actilivity? That's the sidewise——(*laughter*) . . . See . . . you know . . . you know. . . . (*he and Evelyn laughing and talking*) . . . Oh I did, yeh? . . . Dig th——you're really figuring on——listen——I know, I know, I know . . . I really dig you! . . .

EVELYN. Oh yeah (*laughing*)

CODY. (*laughing*) Yeah, I understand what you're sayin, she's, she's, picking up here man . . . Evelyn's picking up, I feel real fine . . . . Hoo! . . . well, I'm ready for any change, I was just telling her it's a momentary, just a momentary diversion, you know, anything else is perfectly alright, you know what I'm *sayin* Jimmy. (*Evelyn laughing*) You understand, Jimmy

JIMMY. I know, I know that you're high, kid, I can see that

CODY. I'm high, goddamn, I'm really high, real high

JIMMY. . . . . real high . . .

CODY. Phew!

EVELYN. (*coughs*) Oo, I've got a nice cough now

CODY. Yeah, just, just feels good doesn't it?

EVELYN. Loose

CODY. Loose, yeah. (*"I've Got a Love-ely Bunch of Coconuts" starts*) Oh let's change the needle! That's such a lovely song we can't——

EVELYN. (*to Cody*) You've spoiled it

JIMMY. Ruined the tenor

CODY. Alright so I'm sorry I cut you, Jack, I'm sorry to cut you man, sorry, man, to cut you, you dig me

JACK. Yeah, yeah, I won't remember till tomorrow

CODY. (*laughing*) Hear him, see? but you don't know somethin Jimmy, but we're recording . . . all this

JIMMY. Oh y'are

CODY. Man you don't believe it?

JIMMY. I kinda figured when I saw that thing going around, that something was doin——oh, you know I was over there hungup on the telephone, first of all that I discovered that the——this thing was off, laying on the thing (*meaning phone receiver and cradle*), and I said "What the hell, supposin somebody's tuned in and hearing all this talk . . ."

CODY. ——that needle is——hey Jack——that needle is *worse*, that needle is worse, that needle is WORSE! (JACK, *Oh yeah?*) As far as I——see I'm hungup, I'm runnin out of needles——

JACK. Where are the needles?

JIMMY. . . . that thing goin around and I thought "Well how the hell!" and then I figured——he forgot about it when he reminded of——where's the profit to hang up that way? . . .

CODY. I've used these same needles for fifteen years, I've only got five of 'em and I keep turnin 'em and——

EVELYN. . . . yeah . . . telephone . . .

CODY. ——wait a minute, wait a minute, the perfesser told me never to give in to you guys, and if you belong to the wrong union, why, there's just no reason to get your props elsewhere . . . I don't know any prop that, is, worthy, of, of that——listen you're interrupting . . . the music! (*laughter*) What I want to call your attention here (*aside to Jack*) You've got to turn it over in a sec——

JACK. Who, me?

CODY. ——that's the prop, man, that's the prop——well who's gonna handle——who's gonna handle the prop?——go ahead, take it, I don't care . . . it's yours. . . . You come in without a prop, you got a prop (*Jack laughs*) (*because Cody imitating an Italian*)

JACK. You're the Italian, see, who's sellin the coconuts

CODY. Well if I'm not gonna smoke any Prisno beach I shall return . . . to my shoes——Phew! I was missin you round Akron, trying to catch a glimpse of your eyes. Some as big as your head, Jimmy!

JIMMY. Yeah?

JACK. Where's me wine? . . . oh there it is! (*Evelyn has it*)

CODY. He's drunk. . . . The wine of contention has become the wine of mellowment and merriness

JACK. Oh the wine of mellowment! And *what?* . . .

CODY. And merriment! No I said melliment, mellimist——

PAT. ——I thought you said merriness——

CODY. . . . sepurious . . .

PAT. What, su*per*fluous

CODY. Superflous, that's it . . . wine has become superflous

PAT. Superious

CODY. Sup*eer*ious, that's the word

EVERYBODY. What word?

CODY. Spoorious . . . spurious

> (*Party Continues on other side of reel*)
> (*Stan Kenton band playing "Artistry in Boogie"*) (*very loud*)

CODY. (*half drowned out*) Now——ah, standing in position like this (*laughs*) . . . you know. . . . There! . . . (*in answer to Evelyn*) Yes! that's right! . . . (*Evelyn laughing*) I knew this——(*music ends, laughter all over*)

EVELYN. Oh no you didn't!

JIMMY. I got him that time! I got him that time!

CODY. Anguish . . . anguish . . . anguish registers on my features. Just——(*as everybody talks and laughs*)——just a moment . . . see? Shit, you've been pullin all day——

JIMMY. . . . three times . . .

CODY. See? he can go all day (*crash!*). . . . There! . . . (*The party goes on into the night . . .*)

FOURTH NIGHT

CODY. (*reading*) "Very good luck to you, I appreciate hearing from you, I will try to send news about your grandson from time to time, I have a very nice——" listen to this——"a very nice picture of him, my grandson, will be appearing in newspapers all across the country——perhaps I will be able to send you a copy" . . .

JACK. Why? Why the picture?

CODY. It doesn't say. She writes to me, she says, "Cody, the enclosed letter from your father speaks for itself"——"I'm also enclosing a carbon copy of my reply, hope it's alright"——"He sounds really lonely and homeless and wants to be with you, I bet he could be a big help to you and Evelyn!!!" ——"you might even want to try him on on taking care of the kids so Evelyn can get her chance to work, and not be tied down. . . . Anyway he needs a home. . . . Note stamp that he enclosed for a reply. He can't come here even if he wanted to under the circumstances . . . because my family would jail him, after all in New York State he's next in line for Curt's support . . . and would have to post a bond or some such. I hope you can send me January money very soon, I'm very poor and I've been waiting and waiting, in fact for the past week I've been living on cheese sandwiches and coffee in order to pay doctor bills, my cold and Curt's hangs on and feel real dizzy when I set at work, D." But those are *her* letters, you see, to explain his——

JACK. Let's hear his——because his——

CODY. Yeah but I want you to *read* it. Yeah that's what I'm tryin to say . . . it's real crazy. . . . See, here's the way he writes. You can always——he can't write on a straight line, see, and he's very slowly, carefully like a child, see . . .

JACK. (*reading*) Diana Pomeray

CODY. Lookit. . . . D. O. Arlington . . . *a-i-r*——

JACK. What does *D. O.* mean?

CODY. I don't know

JACK. Do?

CODY. Lookit, Airlington, see, it's really north but he doesn't know, see

JACK. How to write an *n*?

CODY. I guess *n*——well, he does that but he might have, misunderstood, but here Airlington, *a-i-r-l-i-n-g*. . . . Airlington

JACK. Nappan who's that? That's the——

CODY. That's their name, yeah, care of Cody Pomeray, that's his address for the last fifteen years, it's Green on Market, see——

JACK. Market Street Denver? (*because of Frisco*)

CODY. Yeah. . . . this letter. He usually only writes one page, he never puts any date or anything, see? "My dear"——see how he does it? (*laughing*) . . . "son and daurter" . . . *d-a-u-r-t-e-r*——

JACK. Daurter

CODY. "Received——"

JACK. *R-e-c-d*!!

CODY. Yeah, he does that right. "Your most welcome" without an *e* (*laughs*) "and was . . . your most welcome . . . and was" (*laughs*) dig him, see?, that's formal, see, according to *him*. He's writing a nice, you know, literary——(*both laughing*) You understand, right? You know, it's just like "Yours of the Twelfth?" you know, that's where he's got the idea, right? Isn't it! Isn't it! Huh?

JACK. Yeah

CODY. "Received your most welcome and, was, sure glad to hear, from"——

JACK. But he has a *y* instead of an *f*

CODY. That's right! Hasn't he, yes! Maybe that *D. O.* is really supposed to be an *N.*! See I dunno! "You, from you," period, "*and*"——see his style, you know, "and . . . often . . . wandered——"

JACK. Instead of "wondered"

CODY. Yeah . . . "where you . . . and Cody . . . was at"——Of course the——the mistake of saying——

JACK. ——"you and Cody was at"——

CODY. That's right, instead of saying "was"——"he . . . sure . . . is a nice looking boy,"——he sure is a nice looking boy, that's alright, "you have"——

JACK. ——"you have"——

CODY. ——"you have"——haven't . . . *l*, have, period, "*and*," same thing see? "have, and, he sure——" He always says sure, sure glad, sure is, sure, "looks healthy" . . . *h-e-l-t* . . . that's pretty close, he needs an *a*, that's all. . . . "Thank you . . . for the picture"——that's alright, it's *e* and there's "picture" . . . "you sent me and I'll sure——" see? another "sure,"——"and I,"——here it is!——"I'll sure will take——" remember what I told you?

JACK. Yeah, yeah

CODY. "I'll——"

JACK. "——sure will——"

CODY. "——take care of it . . . would like to see you and Cody and your son also, tell Cody I took a trip back home last summar . . ." *Summar*, see, *summar*, he hasn't done that since 1930 see, he must really be hungup, "summar," no comma or nothing, "I enjoyed my trip"——see he says *trip*, up here, "trip . . . very much but . . . most of my sisters are dead . . ."

JACK. Just like . . . my folks . . .

CODY. "Only two," I guess that is, right?——"of my sisters were living, Sister Eva"——that's the one *I* know, and I don't know this one——

JACK. Emma!

CODY. I don't know her. "Would . . . like to see you . . . and Cody very much." That's just what he says up here!

JACK. Imagine Diana goin to Missouri

CODY. Yeah, wouldn't that be crazy! *Wouldn't* that be crazy! I'd like to do a hundred things like that, you know, you get a——but up here he says "Would like to see you very much," see? . . . "sure like to see you and Cody very much," remember? Very much, period. "Might make a trip . . . back sometime," he always says "back," see it's "back home," "trip back," meaning a trip back to New York, "back sometime . . . Cody will tell you we both took a boxcar"——phew!——"farther?"

JACK. "——farther on——"

CODY. ". . . farther on . . . that . . . where . . ."

JACK. "——he was——"

CODY. "——he was twelve years old . . . twelve years of D——"

JACK. "Farther than——" What is he talking about?

CODY. We went fourteen thousand miles accordin to what he tells me, but I can't see it myself, 'cause I can only remember I went back East, and I went to Salt Lake and I came here to Oakland and I went down to L.A. and I went back with him, as far as I know that's it, 'cause I never——fourteen thousand . . .

JACK. Oh you didn't——you never went——back to Missouri or anything

CODY. Yeah I did! Went back East first, with him, when I was six, then when I was seven I came out here . . . did the same thing next summer

JACK. In 1930?

CODY. Yeah 'thirty-one . . . 'thirty-two . . . no, no . . . 'thirty-three, 'thirty-three, 'cause I was . . . yeah, 'thirty-three . . .

JACK. Did you see . . . Eva . . . and Emma?

CODY. Yeah, Eva, I remember Eva, and her sister see, and her, and her daughters you know, and so on see. No it's just the piccolo in your pocket see (*as Jack sits and Cody warns with gesture*) and it was hittin here. Now here——I knew you saw it (*meaning obstruction couch*)——but here he says, lookit here, ". . . Might make a trip back," see, but here, twelve! I was *twelve*——I was living with Jack from the time I was ten until I was thirteen, every minute. And I was living with my mother from the time I was nine on . . . and I did all this with him when I was six and seven and eight, see?

JACK. But he thinks you were twelve

CODY. Yeah! thinks I was twelve (*Jack flutes*) So now. . . . But here, further on, that's right, ". . . tell Cody they all ask about him . . . and wanted very much to see him. . . . I told them that he was married and where he was at"——*when* he was at, see, he's all mixed up, he said "where" for "when" and "when" for "where", didn't he

JACK. Yeah

CODY. Didn't he? "where he was twelve . . ."

JACK. He sure did, he sure did

CODY. He sure did. He was at . . . P.S., that's P.S. ——

JACK. B.S. man!

CODY. I know it but that's what it means though

JACK. "Bull shit . . ."

CODY. Yeah. ". . . tell Cody I haven't heard from Shirley Jean so I don't know where his sister . . . is . . ."

JACK. *When*!

CODY. (*laughing*) Yeah!

JACK. "Where his sister is at . . ."

CODY. But it's really "where" without the *e*

JACK. Yeah

CODY. "Where"

JACK. Yeah

CODY. ". . . his sister at . . ." Ah (*Jack flutes*) . . . "think she is married now . . ." See, "think she IS . . . married now," alright, but usually he just writes——see he thought he was done, see, he always writes one page no matter what, or anything, even if he doesn't tell what he wants to tell, see, and so he started to, see, and he——but he *still* had to go on, see, so he did . . . "my mother's name"——he forgot, that he had to write to Diana, see, so here's he's writing, "My mother's——"

JACK. ". . . My mother name . . ."

CODY. Mother *nance . . . n-a-n*——but it's really name, though, *m*, yeah, "was," "Mildred,"——see I don't know this——"Mule . . . en . . . ex . . ."

JACK. Mullinex!

CODY. Yes! That's French isn't it? with an *x*? . . . ending?

JACK. No . . . impossible name! Mullinex!

CODY. That's what it is

JACK. Couldn't be

CODY. No? French don't use that——I've looked——looked up that——

JACK. No they don't use that, never

CODY. See, he made some kind of mistake or something. Diana——

JACK. Well his mother . . . his mother was. . . . Oh his mother was——

CODY. Yeah he——she wants to know all these things, see. . . . She's very hungup on the family tree stuff. . . . "Diana, my father," father, see without the——yeah——"was Samuel, no middle name; Mother named Mildred". . . . Now here he's got, quote, "no middle name," meaning, yeah, "Mildred, no middle name," right? ". . . How are you getting along?" . . . see nothing (*laughing*) . . . "How are you getting along . . ." Listen!——this is crazy here!——"Please write and tell me how . . . you're getting along" . . . see, he just said it, didn't he? (*both laugh*)

JACK. He just said that

CODY. Yeah! "How are you getting along——please," ah, "tell me how you are . . . are . . . are. . . ." He says "You . . . are . . . all"——that's it, "all . . . are,"——no here it is, "You are," he means "*you're*," and he says, "You are . . . all . . . are," see he puts it in there, "getting," that's getging, although it's *g*'s, you know, but it *is* getting, "along," right?, "would . . . sure . . . like to hear"——sure again, see? . . . "Like to hear from you," he always says that, "would sure," "like to hear from you," sure like to hear from you, "and . . . about . . . you . . . and how you are getting along." (*laughing both excitedly*) Is that crazy?

JACK. Yes

CODY. That's the gonest. It reminded me of, so many, like the way we talk, in this thing or anything, and think——that's the gonest thing, you know, and, and, he interrupts here to say "How are you getting along, please write and tell me how you all are all getting along"——"Would sure like to hear from you and about you and how you are . . . getting along." . . . See? that's how his mind is, he's, ah——now wait a minute now, "And about"——he's still continuing, lookit, "getting along . . . and

. . . about Cody"——he's continuing——"and what he is doing now." Then he puts a question mark, "If you . . . write and tell me . . . all the news . . . and if *your* folks," see, but "YOU——"

JACK. "You folke . . ."

CODY. "Folkee . . . would like to see me I would make a trip back there" (*laughing*) . . . "I am not too old"——now here he jokes, this is very pitiful, 'cause he never joked ever, as far as I know, and he's never, here, "I am not too old . . . can still ride that old boxcar . . . yet," see, he's gettin, see, "Tell Cody I haven't come to that second childhood yet," quotes here, see

JACK. When you can't ride an old boxcar . . .

CODY. "So I am still in my prime, Ha, Ha," dig him——But he's makin a joke, he's feelin good, see, and he's "Ha-ha, only fifty-nine this year. . . . Well, sure——"

JACK. That's really young, much younger than *my* old man——

CODY. Yeah. *Sure* again . . . "Well, sure was glad to hear from you"——*From* again

JACK. "——and write——"

CODY. "——and write often, yours truly, Cody Pomeray, care of——"

JACK. Cody Pomeray! That's your name!

CODY. Yes. Nineteen twenty-three Market——

JACK. Care of J. J. Green Company——Green——

CODY. Yeah, it's Green, I know that——

JACK. Nineteen twenty-three Market Street——

CODY. Yeah I've got——or, Gaga Barbershop

JACK. Still care of! Well *man* I should have gone to Denver this time. That's what I was headin for

CODY. What for?

JACK. To look him up

CODY. Yeah?

JACK. See I went to Cheyenne . . .

CODY. We oughta bring him out here. Oh, you shoulda went through Denver huh? . . . whenever you want to find him——

JACK. I went through Cheyenne . . . I thought of getting off the bus at Cheyenne

CODY. No kidding

JACK. And I would have gone right straight to Gaga

CODY. Would you? You know about the Gaga

JACK. Course I know about the Gaga . . .

CODY. That's a crazy letter huh? Jesus Christ, I got a couple others upstairs——

JACK. Where did he write it from?

CODY. Denver, January fifth

JACK. Where? Where did he write the letter *at*?

CODY. Oh, a flophouse, see, he got hold of a pencil, or a stub, pencil——

JACK. Huh? Yeah, but I mean, ah, what is he doing now, see you used to share his problems——

CODY. Well I'm hard——what he's doing is, ah, he's, ah, he's ah working with for J. J. Green, still . . . see, periodically, see he works as a, either a, ah, he's a swamper, you know, he's a, ah, dishes, he cleans the dishes, and cleans up 'n' everything, for the *section* hands——

JACK. OH?

CODY. Well I don't know. I just happened to remember that. I think that's what he called it . . .

JACK. Railroad?

CODY. Railroad sec——you know how they're the lowest of the low! You remember that. You know, the Mexicans, they're treated with such great contempt and everything, but I mean they really ARE nowhere, you know . . . they're just, guys who can't talk English and everything, you know, the section hands, that do this menial labor——and he cleans up for them, and sets their breakfast for them, and all that, see, 'cause this J. J. Green is a commissary, he's a c——gets a commission, say, from railroad to say, they pay . . . him ten thousand dollars for——to take care of a hundred men for a year, see, and so Green on his own hires several men, like my father, to go out there, and dish out the grub, and——

JACK. You know what I had? In my thoughts I had, I thought, "Old Cody works as a railroad . . . scullion . . . cookshack . . . railroad cookshack" . . .

CODY. Well that's what he is, exactly what he is . . . except he's not a cook, see, he's not a cook

JACK. He's just a scullion

CODY. He's just a scullion. Yeah, that's right (*Jack flutes*) That's what he does and so . . . peri——that's only periodically, see, he'll go out on a job for a couple months, see, and he'll make say a hundred dollars or something, he'll come home, he'll come into Denver and he'll spend it all, drinking, you know, and laying up in the——until he's completely broke and on his ass, and that'll take a month, or six weeks, or something like that, and if he's not arrested, thrown in jail like he was the last letter I got from him, see, about a year ago, he was in jail, so had to write to him there, County Jail——

JACK. Was it the letter when you . . . were living on East Forty-First?

CODY. Yeah! that's right!

JACK. The letter spelt baby "babby"

CODY. Yeah, that's it, yeah, that's, that's it. . . . Well, ah . . . so now, so he'll be in town here for about a month, or six weeks, mebbe all winter, see

JACK. What, Denver?

CODY. Yeah. And then they'll have another commission, another contract, see, and he'll go out with Green again, you understand. And he's been with them for about, oh, almost eight, ten years now, that way probably, and, not really that long, I'd say about seven, at the *most*, really about five . . . but, ah, so, that's him, see, but now he's hungup, he probably has got all winter free, open, see——

JACK. I always thought he went to Texas in the the——Texas——

CODY. He does. He does go down to Texas and he goes other places——

JACK. In the winter, came back to Denver in the summers . . .

CODY. Oh, I——yeah. . . . No, he does that only for jobs down there, he's——he's very ah, he's dependent only on wine, he's not——he doesn't, he's nowhere of course——he's not independent at all, he has to do——

JACK. You should have seen what in imagination, man, I wrote a thing about you and him and Old Bull Lewis, Old Bull Balloon, and I changed his name to Old Bull Lewis because he was supposed to be a farmer, had a farm, outside of town, Alameda there, and I said "The three of them got in the car for some unknown——well they got a lot of, ah, wire together and, and screen, they got together, and they got a——they went out to Nebraska to sell these flyswatters, made these little flyswatters . . . the car like a potato bug crawled eastward for no reason under the huge skies"——all that kind of shit?

CODY. And it's just what happened, see, I remember that trip
JACK. Carl Rappaport was all hungup on the way that I had
picked up on the images, of what you told me about yourself,
and projected them on the wall, all ballooned up——
CODY. Enlarged, yeah
JACK. . . . and cracked, crazy, (*Cody laughing*) Old Bull Balloon, see? Who was actually the guy? . . . that went with you . . .
CODY. Well, he was a guy either named Blackie or, ah, something like that, but he was a tough, muscular——
JACK. Listen . . . I had a guy called Rex . . . a bum, he was a
buddy of your father's, but I know there was no guy called Rex
but do you know why I called him Rex?
CODY. No
JACK. I said "Because he was no king, he was a guy who never
wanted to grow up and so an American who, ah, never, ah,
outlived the desire to grow up and so lay on the sidewalk"——
you know, like we all want to lie down on the grass on the
sidewalk, and there's a——at one point your father, Cody, see,
Old Cody's——he's lying under a pool of piss under old Rex,
something, under the *ramps* . . .
CODY. (*laughing bemused*) I've seen him lying in many a place
like that, but this guy going to Nebraska was like I say tanned
and muscular and . . . very eminent, he wasn't in the depths of
alcohol like my father although he was a complete wino and
drank all day and everything, but he was young, he was only
about thirty or so, see——
JACK. Oh yeah?
CODY. And——yeah, he was a younger man——and he's the one
who owned the car, in fact my father could barely drive, see,
Model T, an old Model T, which was old at that time, see——
JACK. What year was that?
CODY. I was nine years old, so that's——makes it 1935
JACK. What year was it?
CODY. Model T, the last one was built 1927, so that'd be ear-
lier than 1927 . . .
JACK. Oh my father had one, Model T Ford
CODY. Yeah
JACK. Square
CODY. Yeah, that's right, and, ah, so we went, and I remem-
ber all about the trip and everything, but about this man I

remember only that he——I didn't admire him in fact, of course I was with my father wholeheartedly, and everything you know, of course, so I really didn't like the guy and of course finally the reason my father came to dislike him, because the guy was really too——well he knew he had the upper hand, as far as that goes, you know, because he was, ah, independent young guy and everything, and but ah, I do remember one time on the trip, I remember lots of things about the trip but I just want to mention about this one guy, speaking of other things . . . I remember one day I caught him taking a piss behind the car or something, see, and he'd just woke up in the morning, you know, and he had a big piss hard-on you know, and I was stupefied and knocked out by the size of his cock, you know, see, 'cause I was only nine, of course, and noticing those things I guess more or less then but not in——any way, but, just——I remember now distinctly in my mind what an enormous penis he had, you see, and then the——

JACK. There's a——yeah, it frightened me——

CODY. Yeah. It wasn't——it was——I was——I felt a great deal of envy, just like in this *Neurotica* that I just read here, castration complex, see . . . the whole thing is devoted to that and this and that

JACK. In the *new* one?

CODY. Yeah, it just got here, I didn't——I got it——Evelyn subscribes . . . it's upstairs . . . you don't subscribe do you?

JACK. No!

CODY. ——well I don't either, of course, but Evelyn did a year ago and this is the last issue, just out now, winter of 1952, just came

JACK. You know, I know 'em all . . .

CODY. Oh yeah. But they're all hungup on this and they're talking about it

JACK. They wanted me to write a whole issue——

CODY. No kidding——Jesus——that would be gone, wouldn't it . . .

JACK. ——by myself, about bop, so Chapman says "The thing to do, now we gotta get together on this——"

CODY. (*laughing*) They got things——

JACK. ——but no money

CODY. It has a progress report, you know, and it says things about "That Jay Chapman is great, great!" and then Alfred Citee, you know, Wilson? one of 'em is, real crazy, see, they sent out cards to the subscribers, said, "Please write in and tell us, ah, do we fulfill a need? are you interested? would you continue? how is past and how is our present and so on . . . what do you like about it . . ."

JACK. You know who's running it now?

CODY. Yeah, this other guy, you told me, Pratman——which is he——he's an older——and, you told me something about him, he's an older man, he's hungup on——

JACK. Oh he's infinitely . . . madder

CODY. Madder!

JACK. He's greater

CODY. He's greater too, yeah, yeah well Jay's just a young kid, he's nowhere

JACK. Just a young playboy

CODY. That's all he is

JACK. He went back to St. Louis to sell antiques for his old man

CODY. Yeah

JACK. But he has a beautiful wife

CODY. But one of those things said ah, said ah, "Alfred Citee is the greatest." (*Jack flutes*) "Your . . . past Alfred Citee, your future Alfred Citee . . . and so on," signed, "a Citee admirer" . . .

JACK. R——Carl *told* us who Alfred Citee is

CODY. Who?

JACK. Well at first it was John Watson, and then it was——

CODY. ——a collection of writers . . . it says in there . . .

JACK. No, there's a name, ah, can't remember the fucking name

CODY. Oh I see

JACK. No! there *is* a name, man, no shit . . .

CODY. Well what are you looking for, the . . . *Neurotica*, or the name?

JACK. No the name, there's a name, Spanish kid . . .

CODY. Oh he told us in the letter!

JACK. Puerto Rican kid

CODY. Oh is that what he's sayin!

JACK. About Alfred Citee *now*

CODY. Oh I see

JACK. But that's all a lot of bullshit

CODY. Yeah. . . . Oh yeah, yeah

JACK. It must be in ah, Carl's big letter, I don't know where that is, where is that?

CODY. Oh I've got it somewhere, I think it's upstairs

JACK. Fuckit anyway

CODY. Yeah I think it's upstairs . . .

JACK. I'll go take a piss, huh?

CODY. Yeah. Just did, didn't you?

JACK. Yeah I did

CODY. Geez. Benny affects me, yeah, the same way. . . . (*now alone in the kitchen, coughs*) . . . Eleven o'clock! I just don't——

JACK. (*offstage far*) Take it easy, boy!

CODY. Yah. (*laughs when Jack says something about the machine from the yard porch outside*) Amazing instrument . . . m'a'zing! Well, I don't know what's happenin though . . .

JACK. (*returning*) Doesn't——I wanta——I wanta prove something to you

CODY. Alright

JACK. See you say it's fatal but it *isn't* fatal (*cuts off machine*)

(MACHINE RESUMES)

JACK. See the reason——'cause there's a——ah, we imitate W. C. Fields, and we imitate Bull——

CODY. Yup

JACK. ——"Hey J-u-n-e," and we imitate your father, "Hey man, Red, ab——bring up the wine!" There's a connection between Bull, W. C. Fields and your father so I'm gonna tell you about the original Bull

CODY. Oh yeah

JACK. The first time that I saw Bull, 1944——what were you doing in 1944?

CODY. Yeah I was in jail, most of the time, the latter half of the year, the first half of the year I was——

JACK. California?

CODY. ——the latter half of the year I was . . . coming *from* California; I know 'forty-four backwards and forwards

JACK. Let's see, I was twenty-two, and you were . . . eighteen, seventeen

CODY. (*figuring*) Eighteen . . . just turned eighteen February

JACK. And Irwin was there and he was eighteen too

CODY. Oh yeah, he's the same year as I am three months younger

JACK. But this was even before Irwin showed up

CODY. Ah huh (*waking*) Oh yeah? I didn't know that, see, I thought Irwin knew Bull before you did

JACK. We're sitting in Bull's room one night——

CODY. Now wait a minute, you gotta begin at the beginning with Bull

JACK. Oh the beginning? Well I told you about the beginning——

CODY. No!

JACK. ——coupla weeks ago

CODY. Where'd you first meet him?

JACK. Alright, now let's see, now I was——

CODY. I mean you don't have to get involved, but I mean, just——

JACK. Yeah. But in those days I was living with Elly and all I did was hang around with a towel around my waist. Bare, naked . . . because I was always taking showers in the hot summer and I didn't give a shit about anything but being comfortable . . .

CODY. You lived up round Columbia and you'd just gotten out of, finished college, quit, or began, or it was——

JACK. Oh no no! it isn't that simple (*laughing*)

CODY. No I see, no, course not, but I'm just trying to get, ah, connected, like I know 1944 in three movements

JACK. I had just taken two big trips in the merchant marine, and been hungup and everything, and I had, ah, oo, you know, wah, but I was now rebelling against working in the merchant marine and shit and sailing and being a big this and that, and I was fartin around being a big Bohemian, living with Elly. Naturally all the cats, all the kids, the Bohemian kids from the neighborhood came up, but, I didn't even think about that—— because all I thought about then was eating and fucking, see, as I should, as all men should all the time

CODY. That's right

JACK. So that when Bull came in, see, I was in——*Julien* had come around, and Dave had come around——

CODY. Where'd you meet Julien? See I don't know where any of this began

JACK. Well, while I was in Liverpool on the . . . merchant marine, on a ship, Elly . . . run around the bars, with June, see she was June's roommate!

CODY. Oh I see . . . see, now, I don't know any of that!

JACK. They lived together. When I left to go to Liverpool they were living on Nineteenth Street . . . One hundred and nineteenth Street . . . I said "I'll be back." When I got back they were living on One hundred and eighteenth Street, they'd moved around the corner, and in that interim, while moving around the corner, they went to my house in Ozone Park and got all my records, I told 'em "Go to my house and get all my records!" My mother and my father said "Who are you?" Elly, June, they never met, see. They said "Jack told us to come over and get the records,"——so my mother said, my father said "Well alright but we don't even know who you are." But they got the records, came back, long trip——I came back from Liverpool . . . it was raining? I came to the door, I knocked on it, Elly came to the door in her shorts, she said "Ao! I never thought I'd see you again!" y'know. And then, she melted right away you know, and I said "The first thing I'm going to do Elly——" and June was there, I said "Hello June," see, I said, ah, and June said "Ah ho, ah ho, Elly's gonna get . . . screwed tonight," you know, and I said "Yeah, that's right" and I go out on the phone, I call up Lionel——

CODY. Oh Lionel

JACK. And I say, ta ta ra ta ta ra ta ta (*riffing "Crazy Rhythm"*) You know what I actually did? What did I actually say! Over the phone I actually riffed something, see? De te re, somethin like that, and Lionel said "Yeah man, Ja——it's Jack!" I said "That's right, it's Jack." He came running over and we talked awhile and he went back and that night was the first night that Elly blew me, you see, cause June had told her "*Blow* Jack"

CODY. Great, great, great

JACK. So here we are fartin around, and, ah, she had been in the West End and met Julien——"Who's Julien?" He's th—— sittin, standin at the bar, or sitting at some table with five, six, seven, eight guys or maybe blonds with him. . . . Aaaaa (*nasal imitation*) see, he's talkin like Rimbaud, the way——he was really magnificent in those days

CODY. I guess he was yeah

JACK. And then, Stroheim showed up and I said "Who's this Stroheim?" I go in the bar and I meet——the first night I met Julien was——and, Elly says "Here's Julien," I says: "Well—— there he is" and I——I feel like Jean Gabin, see, I'm runnin around there, I'm lookin around, and there's Julien, he looks around, and, we're both talking to each other, see, (*laughing*) What's the meaning of this? What's that?

CODY. (*whispering*) That's the machine

JACK. Yeah . . . yeah (*both listen*)

CODY. Really is you know! If you turn it on——

JACK. It bugs me, you know? . . . My first impression of Julien was, he was a mis——mischievous——

CODY. Oh yes

JACK. ——horseshit

CODY. Yeah

JACK. You know, character, you know, and I said, "Who the fuck, is this the big Julien Love?" And he come around and he had, ah, yellow hair hanging over his eyes, and lookin around and real coy, you know——I didn't think of——*anything* of him! Then one night I come in the West End, he's sitting in a booth with a guy with a great big red beard who's just like——and he said "Jack, doesn't this guy look just like Swinburne?" I said "He sure does." He says "This is Dave Stroheim, the guy I told you about from St. Louis . . . the guy that's been following me, all over the country." "Hiya Dave." "How are you, hello Jack." See? And then finally one day Dave, came around a couple times, and he always talked, do you know how he talked to me?

CODY. Huh-hm

JACK. He would talk in graduating tones until finally you couldn't hear him any more . . . except when he talked to Julien, then he talked always on the same level, but anybody else, it didn't matter whether it was a man or a woman, he just didn't really want to talk and he sort of faded away

CODY. Amazing. I——

JACK. So he came around, he had a, a pair of seersucker trousers, but Hubbard had the seersucker trousers and the coat and the hat——

CODY. Oh yeah

JACK. . . . or some kind of hat . . .

CODY. A black hat! just like that (*pointing at black brakeman slouch hat*)

JACK. Yeah, that's the kind he wears, slouch hat. Only it isn't so slouchy, beautiful! And there was some kind of——when he came in he said "Jack, I finally brought Hubbard around,"——I had already heard about Hubbard, my impression of Hubbard was of a short, squat . . . *tough* guy . . . I . . . hearin, you know, you hear a guy, you hear about a guy continually——

CODY. Yeah, Yeah, that's right

JACK. ——and you say "That guy must be a tough guy"

CODY. Yeah, you think he's got somethin

JACK. Big tall, lank, sort of shy, meaningless, unimportant little guy, but thin, and tall, comes up to me and says "Well, ah"——so, I sat on a hassock, in the middle of the room, see Elly was sleeping, it was the middle of the afternoon, I had just fucked her and——and I had got up, took a shower and they rang the doorbell as I was coming out of the shower, with a towel around me. So I opened the door, and I put on my wino pants, chino pants, and they came in, and I sat on the hassock and they sat on the couch. The sun was always shining, it was always hot, into this room, the top floor of a pad, see, One hundred and eighteenth Street, and I said "Well, shipping's pretty good, Bull you can go out there, and you can get papers, and I'll——"

CODY. Oh, Bull shipped to sea

JACK. No, no, he was just asking questions, he was . . . making friends with me

CODY. I see

JACK. See? He said "Well, I have seaman's papers and I've . . . thought of going to sea several times when I was down . . . so and so . . . Philadelphia and so and so . . . but I'm not really——right now I'm serving summons, and so on, I'm a bartender——"

CODY. (*snorting, sniffing*) That's——that's him snortin . . . I can't snort like he does 'cause I have a bad nose

JACK. I dug Hubbard at——

CODY. Let's see you snort. . . . (*Jack snorts*) Well . . . that's it, yeah that's it, it's in the throat——

JACK. Well he didn't——

CODY. It's in the throat——he didn't then?

JACK. No

CODY. He didn't then

JACK. He went . . . he went through a *long* process to come to that, man

CODY. I see, I see, oh I *know*——but I thought it was in——

JACK. ——it involved Val . . . Hayes? . . . it involved everybody

CODY. Well he was pretty normal

JACK. Of course, at that moment when he came in, with that seersucker suit, June . . . June wasn't there, she was in the hospital . . . having her baby, Julie . . .

CODY. Oh. *Je*-sus Christ, ah-huh

JACK. See? from that month on . . . on into August, and in between June and August everything happened, the murder took place

CODY. No kidding, while June was having Julie, *I* see!

JACK. So that when June came back with, *with* Julie, ah, everybody was in jail, everybody was gone, and she just merely got a new pad on a Hundred and ah——

CODY. By herself? Yeah . . . she was, because . . . I remember

JACK. Yeah, she was, because well I——yeah. But . . . you know the first time I met June?

CODY. No

JACK. It goes even further back . . . 1943. I came out of the Navy nuthouse (*Cody laughing, Jack confidential*) . . . and I came, and I took a Elevated ride to my new house where my mother and father lived, and wondered about it, you know, I mean that fucking Elevated was——

CODY. Where was it?

JACK. ——taking a big curve, Ozone Park where you used to stay with me see? You know where the Elevated takes a curve?

CODY. Jeez, you've lived there since 'forty-three? the same place? on the second floor?

JACK. Yeah, yeah. Remember where it takes a big curve and you think you're gonna fall?

CODY. (*whistling*) Yeah!

JACK. I said "Jesus Christ! I'm gonna do this——"

CODY. Yeah

JACK. Er, I got out there, it was early morning, I walked there——My mother and father were there, the *piano*!!! fucking goddamn ten-dollar piano they carried, they spent twenty-five dollars to ship it from Lowell!

CODY. Yeah, at least——

JACK. ——was there, everything was there, all the things of my family, except my sister was in the WAC now, WACS?

CODY. Oh yeah, WAC. I'll be damned, I didn't know that, you know. Go ahead

JACK. Yeah. So . . . so we went——and, ah, at that time, I had begun to grow warts on my cock——

CODY. Amazing! That's . . . supposed to be great you know

JACK. ——I used to sit in the toilet and look at the warts all over my cock

CODY. Amazing!

JACK. I said "Jesus Christ, my end has come, I'm doomed"—— (*laughs*)

CODY. No . . . I would feel real great——

JACK. Twenty-one years old! Think of it, how young!

CODY. Jesus, yeah. I'd feel great if that happened to me, you know——

JACK. I said "I gotta go find Elly"

CODY. No kidding

JACK. Where was she? Asbury Park. I hitch-hiked to Asbury Park . . . when I got there, I was exhausted——

CODY. How'd you meet Elly? After you tell me how you——

JACK. Man, I had met Elly in 194-2! (*Cody laughing*) It all goes back to 1942!!

CODY. That's where it begins

JACK. ——when I came back from Greenland!

CODY. Je-sus Christ

JACK. ——with a eight hundred dollar payoff in my pocket——

CODY. Oh, no wonder

JACK. ——gave me mother about, say, three hundred?——five hundred I said "send it to me, send it to me," she kept sending it to me, I was at Columbia, I went back to Columbia University to play football for a couple of weeks, see, quit the team, because I heard *Beethoven*

CODY. No shit

JACK. One afternoon it started to snow, Beethoven came on, it was time for me to go to scrimmage . . . the snow was falling . . . ta ta ta taaa! (*Beethoven theme*) ta ta ta taaa (*each time Cody says* Yeah *solemnly listening*) (*as Jack solemnly sings*) I said to myself "Scrimmage my ass . . . I'm gonna sit here in this room and dig Beethoven, I'm gonna write noble words," *you* know——that's the way I quit football (*laughing*) nothing more logical or less . . . logical

CODY. When was you in Hartford? Remember when you told me about Hartford? What year was that?

JACK. 'Forty-one

CODY. 'Forty-one, ha ha, I got you goin back. . . . Tell me 'bout June

JACK. June?

CODY. You met June, you went to Asbury Park, you're tellin me how you met her

JACK. To find Elly! And I found her, and she had a big sunburn, and she said "You . . . you . . . you don't wanna come back to me," I said: "Yeah, yeah"——And we took a walk along the boardwalk and I went in the drugstore and bought a rubber, and she said, and she said "What'd you go in there for?" I said "Oh I bought some aspirins," I said——actually I bought some sunburn lotion——and I *did* also, Noxzema. . . . We went up to her . . . MY room, and I said "Lemme put this . . . lotion on you," see? over her red skin, see? (*Cody whistling*) We sat all afternoon on the beach and I had her necklaces on, on the beach, and some girls passed by, such beautiful cunts passed by, said "What is this, *pagan?* What is this boy here, a gypsy?" And here I was with these fucking——and I thought I was——

CODY. *Earrings* you mean

JACK. ——and I thought I was dying because I had these . . . things on my cock, see? these . . . staples on my cock . . .

CODY. The staples, yeah

JACK. Man! And so I said "I'm an old man, I'm going to get *fucked!*" And I . . . rubbed this lotion all over her all the way to her thighs, and, ah, then I had a hard-on, and I simply (*clapping hands*) . . . fucked her, see? And she said "I knew this would happen." Then everything started up again! And in the morning, see? at night after I fucked her I passed out, cause I had a sunburn, she went across the street to her grandmother's house, and in the morning she woke up, I went over there to pay my respects to grandmother, her sister——Elly came down the stairs all her face puffed up, from the sun, she had a real serious burn!

CODY. (*listening*) Oh yeah . . . (RECORD ENDS)

CONTINUATION OF SAME NIGHT

CODY. . . . and, ah, well she leaned over like this, see, and I'm sittin in the chair, and then she suddenly realized that it was showing, see, from the rear, you know, see, and I kept trying——

JACK. No, no, I can't picture this

CODY. Can't you?

JACK. No——where is this?

CODY. She's bending over the kid, see, the thing comes to about here so it's safe . . . ordinarily——

JACK. What thing?

CODY. This kind of a T-shirt type thing, she's wearin, with no pants on, but she wore that all the time in the house——

JACK. I got a big story like that

CODY. ——yeah, tell me about it

JACK. Same thing!

CODY. Yeah. The moment she realized it she straightened up, she . . . looked over her shoulder, see if I was watchin her——

JACK. Man!

CODY. ——course I was watching intently but I averted my eyes just in time; but still she knew I saw it, see, and——but that's all, I mean there was no, like I say I was very careful——

JACK. Wa wa, what I was goin to say was, around 1945, or 19– no, wa, I dunno what year, 1946 when everything blew up, when Bull went to jail for . . . possession, and she took up with these hoo——hoodlums from Times Square . . . Blackie? a couple of other guys like that? (CODY, *Oh yeah*) Huck . . . introduced her to Blackie . . . she had to have somebody to pay the rent, so Huck went down to Times Square and picked, and got a bunch of guys that he already knew to pay the rent, see, not *Phil* Blackman, this is *Blackie*, this is, in fact, probably Willie's——

CODY. Oh yes, that's right, yeah——I remember that

JACK. See? And, ah, I wandered in there from Val Hayes, from, ah, that kind of jive, from the West End and all that horseshit, to see what was going on over there. And, ah, she was out of——out of her fucking mind on Benzedrine, and she came in, and she immediately stripped. I said "June what are you doing?" She said "Who are you you strange man, get out of this house." Standing there . . . she didn't strip . . . she, ah——Yes! (*snapping fingers*) Man she *stripped!* I was sayin "I'm not a strange man June, I'm Jack." Huck was sleeping in what used to be Val Hayes' bedroom, she went in there, knocked on the door, he said "Uuuh," and she goes, she says "Jack is trying to rape me, Jack is . . . bothering me, Jack is annoying me"——Huck says "Well ba-by, I don't know what to *do*." She said "Well you've *got* to do something *about* him." Finally she closed the door behind her and went in to talk to Huck about it, apparently though standing in the middle of the room, you know, and Huck's in the bed saying "Well I'm all hungup baby I——"——I'm standing out there, I've had a glimpse of her *ass* . . . but a year before that I screwed her, ah you know what I mean. That's the way it always was

CODY. Hmm. How'd you meet Huck? Where'd *he* come in? How'd *he* start? He was, how'd——he must have known June and them before

JACK. Oh man, how I met Huck! . . . See, here I am with Bull sittin on a park bench, I'm sayin to him, I'm sittin in Washington Square, saying, "Bull," I'm saying, "Jesus Christ, people die don't they, I mean, what happens when you die? What happens after you're dead? what goes on?" Bull says, "Well, when you die you're dead, that's all," he says, "they just don't . . . do anything but d-i-i-i-i-e. . . . (*extending* die *for two seconds*) So, you see, it's always like that, see, but, always going up and down Eighth Avenue the two of us. We preferred, don't know what for, Eighth Avenue; we used to go up, there was a bar there called Kieran and Dinneen's——

CODY. Yeah, that's on ah——by Forty-second Street

JACK. Yeah. I'd say to Bull "Well shall we go in there?" He'd say "Wal, it's actually, it's just a goddamn bookie's bar——"

CODY. That's the first bar Bull took *me* into when we hit town——

JACK. So!——I'd say "Yeah" and I'd say "What about this bar?" He'd say "Well, ah, it's an old man's bar. . . . This is a *queer* bar," so I'd say: "Where do we go?" We'd go to Kieran and Dinneen's because the bookies are sharp, cool characters, we go into Kieran and Dinneen's we see all these bookies . . . standing at the bar, drinking see? Bull and I were there, we're talking about Berlin . . . Bill Fillmore . . . Africa . . . um (*snaps fingers*) So! so one night he said "I know a guy, I met a guy called," ah, what the hell was that guy's name, he killed——he died recently, big . . . fatty, he used to work as an attendant in a

Turkish bath, he was a big swishing fag, and he lived at the foot of the Manhattan Street Bridge with Huck (*Cody laughs*), and several other people like *that*, so . . . this is long before you ever even *heard* of Huck man! even before *Bull* knew Huck . . . this big fag who died last year, killed himself, in other words Phil *Blackman* committed suicide last year and *so* did this big fag

CODY. Did he? Phil Blackman? I didn't know that

JACK. Phil Blackman committed suicide in the Tombs last year

CODY. I didn't know that

JACK. See he was picked up for possession (*Cody whistles*), the cops grilled him, put the light on him, made him tell, on *some*-body, and you know Phil Blackman hurt——killed a few guys, too

CODY. I didn't know——

JACK. I don't know about——I don't know whether . . . it was anything to do with *that*, 'cause I *know* that Huck was told by Phil Blackman . . . who he killed, what store, what street——Phil Blackman was a holdup man . . . and he was . . . Bull's big hero, the guy that got Bull going on junk

CODY. I see

JACK. So he told Huck, and Huck told me, confessed to me, and I confessed to Irwin, see everybody knew about it finally?——but Phil Blackman finally hung himself in the . . . Tombs, last year (CODY, *Geez*) Kay Blackman was his wife——

CODY. Yeah, that's the one——

JACK. I used to want to fuck her——big fat woman like Jerry Fust

CODY. Yeah——she's the one who had a dildo, you know, and Bull and Huck, for all across the state of Virginia and that's a long way in a jeep at thirty-five miles an hour, why we talked about Phil Blackman and Kay Blackman, Blackman, and how . . . Bull said "Why I used to go up there and Kay'd say 'Bull you've got to do something about Phil (*imitating woman,*) he's been taking this——this junk you know and he can't do any good now and a ma——woman's got to have her tail and all that, and,'" ah——

JACK. Yeah, she used to love it, man

CODY. Yeah. And Bull said "Wal I can't do nothin," you know (*laughing at his whining imitation*) and he went through all that, he must have felt very good that afternoon because he talked about it for hours all the time, see, connections that way 'n' everything, *I* remember that, Phil Blackman, I was just wondering if that was the same guy

JACK. See Phil . . . when Bull got this apartment on Henry Street, I say apartment, it's this fucking coldwater flat, Huck lived in it, took care of it, Bull came there occasionally . . . it was actually owned by Dick Clancy, the guy who picked up Joanna by the cunt——

CODY. I remember him, yah, I remember him

JACK. See? Now the——the only guy who had enough nerve to stay there most of the time, was Huck; half the time, was me; and of course Irwin . . . came there on Saturday afternoons and played Stravinsky, and he played, ah, Prokofiev, eh, you know that's, ah, "Nevsky Suite" . . .

CODY. Yeah I remember that

JACK. Ta ra ta ta! And we'd go out——with Phil Blackman, Kay Blackman, Bull, Huck, me, and June, and Elly, would go down the street and eat in Chinatown, which is right around the corner

CODY. I see

JACK. Phil Blackman had the *bottom* floor pad, for *one* week,——ah of course we all knew each other very well, and I often looked at Kay Blackman and thought of fucking her see, and everything——where was I? How I first met, ah, Huck, Huck, so!——Yeah——so Bull and I went down to Henry Street to look up ah, Huck! we went to his pad, fifth floor of a pad underneath the Manhattan Bridge, knocked on the door, who opened the door? Who opened the door?

CODY. Who did?

JACK. Vicki

CODY. VICKI?

JACK. Vicki . . . young Vicki

CODY. I'll be dog——when she was young, eh, she must have been *very* young

JACK. Yeah, she was, she was——

CODY. I'll be danged

JACK. And she said "Yes?" and we said, ah, "Huck here?" She said "No who are you?" Bull said "I'm, ah, Bull Hubbard; I, ah, was sittin with him on One hundred and third Street and Broadway on a park bench, we were, ah, talkin about junk, thought we might pick up a little junk." See Bull was naïve in those days, see, saying *junk*, and Vicki of course "Looka him," dug him right away, then she looked at me and dug *me*, physically, you know, because I say, the next forty-eight hours I fucked her solid

CODY. Yeah, on Benzedrine

JACK. She dug all that, she said "Come *in!*" She says——she got us in the door——she says "The first thing I always do I always gauge who's at the door, if it's——if it's a . . . guy who wants to collect a bill, I tell him 'Look behind me at all these hanging . . . ah stockings, and clothes, and this dirty old washtub, I'm beset on all sides, I'm a poor housewife, can't do it'"——she says, "If it's friends I get 'em right straight through this little kitchen into this little black pad," and there's the pad, you know, the thing that Hindenburg——course Hindenburg was there then, Little Zagg's——

CODY. Geez . . . Little Zagg *then*?

JACK. Little Zagg had just gone to the can for a Washington, D.C. safe robbery in which the guys stole a safe, and they went riding along in a car where they thought that the cops were suspicious, and somehow or other they stopped somewhere and got the c——the fucking safe out of the car, and as they were struggling out of the car with the safe they dropped it through a manhole, or, they dropped it down the goddamn stairway—— Oh and another time they stole a safe out of a theater, and they were getting it down off the second floor down those long car-peted stairs, you know? and the fucking thing started tumbling down the stairs (*laughing*)

CODY. OO-whee, the law——that——that must have been crazy

JACK. 'Sall that kinda——see, so Little Zagg was in jail, see—— so Vicki, she, all she had then was Normie, Krall, who was at that time in the *Navy*

CODY. No kiddin

JACK. She says to me "I have a boy in the Navy," I said, I said: "So it makes no difference," (*bangs his head three times on wall*) see, and I'm bangin my head on the wall, like that——she gives in. But that's after forty-eight hours, it's a long, long story . . .

CODY. Hmm, yah, you told me portions of it, I recall

JACK. Well she said "Alright man, we'll pick up." I says "Do you pick up jazz baby?" she says: "I pick up with Charlie

Ventura"——1946, see?——so we got in the cab, we got on . . .
subway, Times Square, no it was in the *cab*, go around Times
Square, we go up to Pickarib, Benny Goodman's Pickarib,
where she pulled out this Benzedrine tube, two or three of
them, she said "You take this one, you take this one; break it
open, eat everything in there." Bull and I each ate a whole tube
CODY. Phew! Jesus
JACK. But man! . . . three hours later, we're with her back,
not in *her* pad, but Bull's, Dick Clancy's, pad, another block up
(CODY, *Wow*) and she breaks open two more, crack, crack, "eat
one, eat one, eat one." Man did we get high!——boy oh boy——
CODY. Man, I could never do that. Val Hayes broke *me* in on
benny you know. Yeah. Val Hayes, in Denver, yeah
JACK. I've really got to piss
CODY. Yeah (*shutting off machine temporarily*) (*machine resumes*) We're in a——we went down to the poolhall, no, no,
no, by golly, that's not the case, actually it was at his house or
up a——wasn't at his house, it was on a——it was in a restaurant
on Twentieth Avenue, there, by the Crest Hotel, but, I think
that was the night before——the fact of the matter is I can't
remember exactly the locale. But at any rate, ah, gee whiz, very
quietly, it seems, he said something about Benzedrine, or, ah,
the . . . fellas back East take this Benzedrine or whatever it is,
why he's, ah, that's what it was, he just mentioned it, that they
took Benzedrine, and I said "What's *that?*" He said——he said
"Oh that's——you buy it in a drugstore, you go down, ask for a
tube of Benzedrine——" and I said, like I always do about directions and everything, I said "What's that now, ah, Benzedrine
inhaler?" ah, you know, and got all the . . . information straight,
see, and he said——
JACK. (*looking at clock*) Ten?
CODY. Yeah——oh yeah, so "Go ahead and try it" he said,
"but don't take more than half a strip or at the most one strip,
but don't take a half a strip, especially at the beginning and
everything"
JACK. What year is this?
CODY. And so——this was in 'forty . . . s-s-s-s-s . . .-ix, spring
of, ah, he'd just come back from school, summer of 'forty-six,
we were together all summer, he and I. . . . No! 'forty f-f-f- . . .
-ive, 'forty-FIVE, yes, 'forty-five! summer of 'forty-five. And he

told me about Irwin, and he told me also about you but no "*about* you," he might——he mentioned——yes he mentioned you, of course but not . . . really a lot, ah he seemed to be more . . . mentioned Irwin, or at least Irwin stuck in my mind more for some reason or something of that nature, but I remember *you*, but at any rate, he, ah, so that day I did . . . buy the tube of Benzedrine, and I remember, I was very . . . oh not frightened exactly or anything like that but I *was* a little bit wary, but not because of fear, or not because what would happen to me, but——actually I'll tell you what it was, it was an excitement, it was an anticipatory . . . sense of I was going to try something new, that's what it was, see, so I postponed it and stood around on the——actually I was sitting on the poolhall bench, that's where I took it, in the poolhall, see——

JACK. One more half hour we'll be high

CODY. Yeah (*laughing*) That is so, I hope so! And so we, ah, so I sat in the poolhall bench there and I . . . took it out, ah, half a strip, and rolled it up in a ball, a little ball you know, and held it there and held it there, and I told Watson or somebody what I was doing and everything, and so they wanted to try it too of course, and so then I went back to the fountain in back of the poolhall to get a drink of water (*sounds of wine pouring*) and put it in my mouth, and took it. And I got high, and after that I took it regularly, not regularly, no——ah, I, after that I, say, three or four times that summer, but never in great quantity or anything——

JACK. You sure this is the summer of 'forty-five?

CODY. Well, now I've really got to think. See the reason I don't stop to think is because I'm aware of the machine, so I can't stop to think——

JACK. No, I know——fuck the machine, man!——I didn't meet Val until the summer of 'forty-five

CODY. Yeah, well he, it was——I'll tell you exactly . . . I went to jail in July 'forty-four, got out in June of 'forty-five, and I that s——yes, it was summer of 'forty-five——absolutely because ah, because 'forty-six I was doing other things. It was the summer of 'forty-five; summer? 'forty-five, that's right!

JACK. Fuck the machine, man

CODY. That's right, summer of 'forty-five

JACK. Now I gotta tell you about Vicki though

CODY. Yeah, you were

JACK. I mean I *gotta* tell you about Vicki

CODY. Tell me about her

JACK. I *did* tell you about her already

CODY. Well you did portions of, thereof——

JACK. Yeah, but ah . . . wa——as I say, I got so high, with her, on Benzedrine, that I didn't know where I was, and I said "Are we in St. Petersburg, Russia?"

CODY. Oh yeah that's right, yeah

JACK. Remember that? and really thinking all the time, really and truly, not knowing at all, that "Are we in Petersburg, Russia?" and then suddenly snapping back and saying, "Why, ah, wa, no use talking nonsense my boy," and I said, "Are we in *Chicago!*" (*Cody laughs*) See? and I'd never been to Chicago, or Petersburg, Russia

CODY. Ha ha, man, I do remember that

JACK. But did I tell you, did I tell you about——well, see, well here's what happened, see, uh, and we had that, we ate those strips of benny, and we got in a cab, Bull paid all the fares, and she said she was going to pick up on some tea——at that time Bull was interested in paying cab fares to pick on tea!——because he wasn't on junk yet. So we're riding up and down Times Square, and she's jumping out of the cab!——

CODY. Man!

JACK. ——and running out in the street and saying "Hey Red," "Hey Mac," and saying "Stop" and say "Hey ba-by!" you know? and they'd stop talkin on the sidewalk, she says, and she says "Anything man?" they say "Nothing ba-by!" and she'd jump back in the cab and say "Drive on" and somethin, jump out again, finally, we ended up on the Forty-second Street subway, and we got in the subway train, and of course, now I'm completely buzzing, and I'm sayin to Vicki I say "Hey," I said "my ear's ringing, I don't know where I am"——She says: "You're *buzzing* ba-by!" We get in the train, and all the way down to . . . East Broadway, which is the stop, you get off at Henry Street, in other words you take the goddamn——

CODY. Uh-huh . . . S-s-s-s-s . . . goes down Sixth Avenue and cuts across . . .

JACK. At Washington Square you change for an F train—— while we're riding down there, and we're all standing, holding onto the straps, and *talking* and you know we're all buzzing and she's explaining to us what it is to be high and all the time we're digging everybody in the car, with all those bright lights, and she's telling us *how* to dig them? and for the first time Bull and I are together! See after I dug him as a——comin into an African compound, all that shit, he came in——when he came in my pad, see, with Elly, now I'm digging him and he's digging me as really being put on for the first time, by a real . . . (*laughs*) . . . person, see

CODY. Crazy. Huh!

JACK. We got off at our appointed station, which at that time to me in my naïveté, was an evil . . . station, see, East Broadway, and who's standing on the platform? dusty platform . . . is standing Huck

CODY. No

JACK. A little short dark guy . . . and at that time he sported a fucking zoot hat, he had a zoot hat, man, and I dug him as an . . . ordinary zoot suiter

CODY. No kidding. Wow! Hat changes. . . . Yeah I dig him, yeah

JACK. With him was a great big huge bulky guy called *Big* Blackie——he's the Big Blackie who knifed a guy in the back in, ah, the bar there, Ross's? that Bull writes about in his novel? you know about it . . . he actually knifed a guy, see——One night Bull was in the bar with Huck and Phil Blackman, Ross's, Blackie was there, he was grumbling

CODY. Uh huh, I know where, Forty-second Street . . .

JACK. See, always grumbling, see, a whole bunch of guys were lined up along the bar, Blackie was goin up along the bar asking for drinks, they say "We don't have any money Blackie, fuck you man." He pulled out a knife and haphazardly jabbed it into one guy's back. Everybody just flew out of the bar, see, and one guy stayed, his name I don't remember, but he supported him out on the street, this guy that got knifed, and they went to Polyclinic, just like in Damon Runyon, they go to Polyclinic which is right nearby Times Square . . . where he was treated, but that's Blackie, Big Blackie. And already Vicki is saying, and we're walking up to them, she's saying "Ah that Big Blackie, don't, don't——he's——he's nowhere, be lookout, be on the lookout for him," she says: "*Huck*, he's my father, he's my *mo*-ther," *you* know, he's her mother, (*Cody laughs*) and I say "He's your *mother!* . . . how——what's the meaning of all this?" And here's Huck see, with his big zoot hat, real level, and——he's looking at me and he's saying——

CODY. It must have changed him entirely to wear his hat——

JACK. ——he's looking up——

CODY. ——under a big hat, see, complexity——

JACK. ——oh he looks just like a zoot suiter! He's saying to Vicki, saying "Where you cuttin out now?" She's sayin "Well we're cuttin over to . . . Bull, here, this is Bull, has a pad a block away from where we live." Huck says "Really?" and, ah, Bull says, ah, nothing, see, and I'm looking at Huck, because I been told who to look at, and Huck's looking at me, see, and he's saying "Well, what are we gonna do tonight?" Vicki says: "Well we're just gonna——blasting benny, and we're gonna talk all night, see, and we're gonna do this and that, and I'll see you tomorrow night, at the pad," where she's living with Huck, Hindenburg, Phil Blackman, and some other guy, the other guy being a guy that while . . . Bull and I first met Vicki in that kitchen she told us to go in? . . . he came in, sick——you know, I don't know!

CODY. Oh I see

JACK. With a stamp machine

CODY. No, I didn't hear at all about this

JACK. No he——he——he——he——ripped the stamp machine . . .

CODY. Never heard of it——

JACK. ——of the, ah, drugstore, carried the stamp machine——

CODY. Yeah, up home, yeah

JACK. And in the street he knocked out the money from it, somehow or other and for *some* odd reason carried the stamp machine up to the room and he gave it to us "Stash it," see, and went to sleep, sick, see, when we——we went out and we stashed it, see. . . . Wa——that's Huck . . . I——and so as you know . . . did I ever tell you about my paranoia? No, see, we went over there, to Bull's pad, and for the first twenty-four hours Bull and . . . ah, Vicki . . . talked, about general things, principally, her one hundred dollar a night whorings . . . see, and how a guy——one particular guy once had a leopard skin——you heard all this though!

CODY. No man! I didn't hear that, I seem to remember Vicki——

JACK. ——one guy once had leopard skin on, he wants to grovel in a corner in leopard skins, on hands and knees, g-r-r-r-r, he wants Vicki to come over and say "G-r-r-r," and they go at each other and they bite at each other, and somethin happens, and a hundred dollars!——and she's saying all this and Bull is saying, "Why——", and she's saying "All these guys are *Johns!*" That moment on, Bull is not a John any more! see. . . . Then . . . but do you know, ah, remember when you and Joanna lived at Markan's in Espan Harlem? (CODY, *Yeah*) Well after you left there came the, ah, New Year's Eve of 1946 entering 1947. That night I, in there, had Vicki and Julien Love meet me——after you'd gone back to Denver——then, ah, the three of us went out——hit . . . parties all over town, which were being thrown by my ex- . . . millionaire friends from prep school . . .

CODY. Ah yes

JACK. . . . Jewish millionaire friends, throwing luscious parties in duplex apartments with . . . socialites, like Gloria Vanderbilt, and all that stuff, then we went around, in our ordinary clothes, with Vicki, Julien and I, so that every party we hit we'd always invariably sit under the piano with the drinks, leaning against the piano legs, talking, see, until finally late at night, Vicki stole a couple hats, and purses, and everything you know, (*Cody laughs*) (*has been for five minutes laughing*), and Julien laughed, and we woke up in the morning in that pad, that Markan had, and Vicki is saying——

CODY. On that little thin bed——

JACK. ——Vicki . . . has started throwing up off the bed, and she said "Daddy I'm no good; go over there and sleep with Julien, I can't do you any good," and Julien is saying, "*That's right man!*" (*shriek imitation of Julien being shriekfiendish St. Louis*), you know, but he's not really saying that, you know, but, that's the way it was

CODY. Yeah I remember that

JACK. That's New Year's Eve of 1947, Vicki and Julien

CODY. Hmm. That's funny 'cause, ah, hmm . . . time element . . . seems to me I didn't leave there until the coming spring, of 'forty-seven, but that's——ah, I mean, I'm not, I'm not even thinking of that

JACK. Oh you were still there, yeah——where were you that night?

CODY. Well I must have been somewheres else

JACK. Oh yeah

CODY. I was working, that's right, that's right, New Year's Eve, I was working, on the parking lot, that's right . . . we had moved to Bayonne——

JACK. New Yorker?

CODY. Bayonne, New Jersey

JACK. Oh! I'd forgotten all about you!

CODY. Yeah, that's right, yeah. See I hadn't——no, I haven't—— (*arguing*)——I hadn't met you yet, that's it!

JACK. Yes you *had*——*man!*

CODY. Wait a minute . . . I'd met you for a day or two, remember? but I didn't come out to your house or anything of *that* nature, till after she went back to Denver, remember?

JACK. The night I met you——

CODY. Yeah? I remember that night. But after that where did——just stop and think——after that when did we see each other?

JACK. ——Joanna wanted to sing in a band, so Calabrese and I took her to the . . . Livingston, ah, Hartley Hall, she sang, and you were there with us . . .

CODY. . . . for a night or two . . .

JACK. We all ate that night, and it was October, October 1946——

CODY. Yeah. But after that, man, we didn't see each other hardly at *all*, 'member?

JACK. No, not for a *long* time

CODY. That's right, that's right, until after she left——

JACK. ——but I had *not* remembered that (*interrupting Cody*) that we didn't see each other for a long time——

CODY. Yeah——

JACK. And now you occupy my thoughts *all* the time! (*Cody laughs*) In those days you didn't, for long spaces . . .

CODY. Yeah. Not until we got together, out, ah, my routine, you know, you remember what I used to do, remember? I'd stay at your house . . . one night a week, or two, I'd stay at Markan's one night a week or two, and stay at Irwin's one night a week or two

JACK. Then Irwin's——yup

CODY. You were about to begin when we began this reel, not this one but the other side of it, you were about to tell me about how one night you were sitting up at Bull Hubbard's and Irwin . . . came in, and, ah, you remember that? I said to you, I said, ah, "I thought Bull knew Irwin before he knew you," and you said "No, Irwin . . . I knew, Bull first" and you started to tell me something, you remember?

JACK. Ah . . .

CODY. Now from what——just, in other words you started to say at the beginning of this, I can verify it by the reel, the other side, where you started to say "Well one night we were sittin up at, ah, Bull's pad, and Irwin came in," what——and I think you were beginning, you began to tell me about——

(TAPE GOES BLANK *for four minutes*)
(TAPE RESUMES)

JACK. . . . went to the, ah, one of the halls on the Columbia campus to look up John Macy

CODY. Yeah, upstairs over a hundred——

JACK. He told me he ran upstairs, it was a snowy night, snowing

CODY. I seem to remember somethin——

JACK. ——and he knocked on the door which he thought was John Macy's, and ah, Julien opened the door——

CODY. That's right, that's right

JACK. And Julien was playing . . . Brahms

CODY. Yeah, that's right, that's right, they——and he went upstairs or something and then an hour later or something——

JACK. ——came back

CODY. That's right, I remember that. Yeah

JACK. "I'm quite amazed that you were playing Brahms!"—— see, an hour later he said Julien insisted "Come right in!" He said, er, "Swinburne will be here in a minute," in a minute Stroheim came in with his big red beard, see, so, a few nights later they went down, Julien and Irwin, to Stroheim's pad down in the Village, which is down on Sixty Morton Street two . . . numbers . . . from . . . Fifty, Sixty——which is the pad where a big fag now lives that Deni Bleu stays with when he hits New York——

CODY. No kiddin

JACK. ——but not as a fag, you know, he just doesn't know that guy is a fag, see, he doesn't know the . . . heinousness of that neighborhood

CODY. I see, I know, yeah, I know most of th——

JACK. So Irwin went down there, and at that time he was reading *Anna Karenina*, did he tell you that?

CODY. No . . . but I knew about——

JACK. He went into Stroheim's pad with Julien; Hubbard was there! . . . and he heard, he'd never heard such . . . diabolical st——talk; and also there was a guy called Dick Frankenstein, was there that night, and he was an old buddy of Jay Chapman's, from St. Louis——

CODY. I'll be darned . . . no kidding

JACK. He writes for *Neurotica* now, under an assumed name, and he was trying to start a fight with somebody or other, and Julien bit his ear off, or some goddamn thing——Julien threw him off the balcony, and there just happened to be no balcony, he just threw him two floors down; and they cowered under automobiles, and fought, and some kind——somebody pissed, and, everything happened, you know, see, I don't know exactly, but Irwin was quite amazed; came back, uptown, and at that time, you see, I had told Elly that I was . . . on a ship, bound for the South Pacific, it's what I told my mother and father, it's what I——

CODY. You *were* shipping

JACK. Well everybody thought I was, including the merchant marine, and the F.B.I. which was looking for——to draft me, and all I did was sit——jumped the ship . . . in Norfolk, and come back up to New York and get after Julien's old cunt, there, Cecily; I was fuckin her regu-lar

CODY. No kidding

JACK. ——but now I'm talking about a year later, I guess . . .

CODY. I remember that Cecily, yeah

JACK. And I wasn't really fuckin her regular, because I only fucked her once, but, ah——

CODY. You wrote about this in a novel, about the death you know, about, when you . . . and Julien was gonna ship out? remember? and all that, and you never did . . .

JACK. *What* novel?

CODY. Man, that hunnerd . . . page novel that you wrote, that you were gonna write about——

JACK. Yeh, the *Julien* novel, yeh

CODY. Yeah, yeah, right? That's the period . . . that you was—— I mean, that the——before you was gonna ship out, and . . . didn't, see

JACK. All that is extremely interesting but I think that now is more interesting because now you got the whole thing fuckingwell summed up, see, now if *Julien* was here he wouldn't know——Julien, I dig him, I always will . . . in fact, you know, what he has done, and so on, so . . .

CODY. Yeah, oh yeah, sure

JACK. And Jim's married, he got married New Year's Eve

CODY. To that girl? Elizabeth?

JACK. The night we did the Shakespeare?

CODY. Oh, yeah

JACK. He got married

CODY. What just now? to that Elizabeth

JACK. No, no——*Bessy*

CODY. But that *one*, that one that I just saw up there, she was feeding drinks up there, at Josephine's pad? that one he came in with. Just for that one second that one night. Yeah he came in for a few minutes and sat on the couch. Jesus, a new one huh? Where does he meet all these women? (*Jack murmurs something*) Oh yeah?

JACK. Shh. (*Cody laughs*) Don't tell anybody

CODY. I'll be damned . . . and he knows that of course, and he's married now, if there's something——huh? I think that's——

JACK. No, ah, he——first place he claims she's a sex fiend nymph; second place, she's the daughter of the editor of some magazine; third place, see——Third place she's been to all the schools Jim's been to, you know like, she's been to Black Mountain, and he was, while at Princeton, while at so-and-so, he went around, fucking around with Black Mountain girls——she's his class, his type, his life; really, the good girl for him, and I like her, she's very fine, but she's *funnylooking*! Man is she——hishh . . . but amazing. At the same time she has a beautiful body, and a beautiful cunt——and all that, you know——

CODY. Ah yeh, well that's great——I *know* (*laughing*)

JACK. ——but her face is sort of masculine, very masculine——in fact she looks like you. . . . (*both laughing*) She looks just like you!

CODY. Jesus . . . terrible

JACK. You know, ah, but I mean by that——

CODY. I know what you mean, yeah

JACK. ——she has a real . . . un . . . ah . . .

CODY. Pronounced!

JACK. ——a real pronounced masculine face

CODY. Well see, here's what I'd like to do, is summarize about——I think that's water I'm afraid, I'm not sure though, but I think it is, I'd like to summarize ah, what's gonna happen and what has already happened to everybody, like for example we know what's happened to Finistra, see, and we know what's happened to June, you understand, what I'm sayin?

JACK. And June was an accident

CODY. Yeah, well let's see what's happenin . . . and *must* happen . . . see?

JACK. Finistra heh?

CODY. Well, we can start with those two, that we know of, anyhow, see——

JACK. Alright

CODY. ——but just a-sayin, like I don't know Finistra well, what do *you* say about Finistra

JACK. Let's talk about it

CODY. That's right

JACK. Let's talk about . . . what we know about the two of them

CODY. Yeah, and then after them about everybody else, and what's gonna happen to everybody else, see?

JACK. Yeah

CODY. See what I mean?

JACK. Alright (CODY: *Yeah*) Is that the second half of that reel?

CODY. Yeah, I gotta put a new reel in——

JACK. We'll start a new one . . .

CODY. Yeah

JACK. Okay. Listen, no more wine?

CODY. No, uh-huh. We have to get some more huh?

JACK. Oh——another ten minutes and I'll be high

CODY. Yeah? with-*out* the wine?

JACK. On benny

CODY. Yeah but with-*out* the wine . . . you don't want to get another one

JACK. No

CODY. Alright?

JACK. I *do*, but I mean, ah——we don't have any money

CODY. Well I know, but it's not that drastic, you know . . . I mean it doesn't really *matter*, as far as *that* goes I can go down and get another one. May as well have it in the house, huh?

JACK. O-kay

CODY. Yeah, I'll put on my shoes, it's the end of the reel anyhow, see, give the matcheen, machine a chance to rest

JACK. Yeah

CODY. Alright, see? won't it——(*machine stops discussion*)

EVELYN. (*speaking from New Year's Eve tape of "Hamlet"*): ". . . which is the might . . ."

(*click*)

CODY. (*resuming tape, he's shut it off while Jack pissed again on porch*) . . . whole cabinet so crazy, that I thought it was, ah, the beginning of that, ah, German picture I told you about one time . . . very frantic——

JACK. (*way back*) . . . man, very cool . . .

CODY. See the whole screen vibrated and shook

JACK. I'm getting to be a drunkard Cody (*from porch*)

CODY. Yeah, I can see that——

JACK. You know that?

CODY. Ah . . . you weren't a year ago; although you really were I g——suppose but you were not, ah, well I'll tell you of course, you gotta remember this Jack, you're living under an artificial, ah, ah, excitement, or an artificial . . . environment, you know. See th——I mean the primary purpose, it's just as though I was living at your house, or I was, or as though, ah, you understand what I'm saying or do you? (*no answer, door just opening*) You know what I mean to say? (*no answer, door just closing*) Here's what I mean . . . if you were home or something, why you wouldn't be, ah, exactly like this, you're under, see, you're in a——you're at the, ah,——how do you say the word? culminating, kewlminating, you know, culminating, ah, point, in a lot of your, for the last year what you've been thinking about and working on, and doing about, and everything, see, (*sniff*) so you're in this town and you're in this house, see, and so you're under a, ah, under a ah, ah, like I said earlier, excitement, well what I mean to say here an ar——an artificial position, the *main* idea what I'm trying to say, is, the idea is kicks not . . . like, ah, having fun . . . (REEL ENDS)

(MACHINE RESUMES)

CODY. (*speaking from last month on unerased tape*) . . . just stays home, and——
JACK. ——and goes to school——
CODY. Yeah goes to school, and an average sort of guy, he's—— in fact you just think he's a big average American GI type, see, but here he knows where to get the peyotl and everything, see, he knows, you know what I'm tryin to say? (*end of last month's tape*)

(MACHINE RESUMES)

CODY. (*amid mumbles*) Now see it's working, see? look, see, whoop, there, see——
JACK. Man, that's great, alright. . . . We'll get high at twelve-thirty. (*snickers*) We don't have another roll do we?
CODY. No, that's all; well you know we've only got part of that one-hour, that's all you got, yeah, you got an hour. So Finistra . . . killed himself, he didn't do it deliberately, but at the same time, he was pushin himself that way wasn't he, you know he was hungup with the idea, countless . . . times he has been, you can just imagine the number of times he thought about killing himself can't you, but at the same time when it came down to the fact of doin it, he never did——
JACK. He didn't mean to kill himself
CODY. ——and when he finally did he did, yeah, so that shows the, what's it called, ah, you know, like the humorous tragedy of it or the coincidence or the, you know, fact that a man was trying to kill himself all of his life——sounded like a radio program, the guy tries to kill himself and tries to and tries to and can't quite, and doesn't, and when he finally does, why, it's accidental, he doesn't intend to . . . but he does, because somehow he's been preparing himself for it, just like this, these stories of people, certain people being accident prone, you know the

type of shit and all that, right? You know, some workers are always cuttin off their fingers, or something, and others never have any trouble, same type of thing, I *s'pose* . . . it really isn't too important, June's more interesting, especially since I don't know Finistra, really, you know, except for what he stood for sort of, yeah. . . . As far as June that's another thing, I wonder what, rather than speculatin what *did* happen to her, but of course you can but, what *would* have become of her, that's what I'm thinkin of

JACK. That's the point

CODY. That's 'cause——

JACK. (*imitating drunken tragedian*) Especially . . . in this dire hour . . .

CODY. (*coughs*) Because from what *you* were saying when I was reading Irwin's letter and you said "Here let *me* read this" and you read a line and you'd say "Well now here's what *really* happened" and you described about June and Julien and everything, and I saw a lot of things in there that ah, she was getting more ah, you know, ah, I mean not that she could I guess become more extreme but I mean she was just more . . . capable of practically anything, huh? wasn't she. So, ah, and but the way she was letting herself go, you see, with her black teeth, and with her uncombed hair, all those things, huh? . . . huh? Well, what I'm saying, if those things happen, why, maybe she probably would have died of some, just a . . . ordinary disease, see, that would catch her, or maybe alcoholism of the liver or something, you know, that kind of death like my sister died of, May, she was twenty-four, see, and, drank and killed herself, in 'forty ah, 'forty ah, 'fory ah, -four, 'forty . . . -three actually, in 'forty-three it started and 'forty-four——she died in January, I went out there. It was because of her again that I——

JACK. Out where?

CODY. L.A. From Denver

JACK. How?

CODY. Ah, oh, well I'll tell you how, I ran into my father accidentally on Larimer Street and he said "Come on boy, let's go together and batch together again like we used to," and all that, I said "Well——"

JACK. Where had you been before that?

CODY. ——'forty-three I was——I was, ah, well this is the Fall of 'forty-three, I was, I'd just gotten through a long period of working two different jobs and going to school at the same time, sleep five hours a day, go to school from eight until two-thirty and run a service station me and another fellow at *least* owned . . . jointly

JACK. In what school?

CODY. ——ah East High, and ah, and ah, I ah, used to run the service station from two-thirty till seven and then the other partner came on, ran it five hours while I slept

JACK. What kind of gas?

CODY. Oh, ah, man, some off brand, ah, see some off brand (*Jack laughs*) ah, and then from midnight till eight we worked recappin tires at Firestone, see, and I lived with Kriloff the Bulgarian at that time, but instead of sleeping from seven to midnight, from seven at night till midnight, five hours, why I had a girl, couple girls, and so I was going out with girls instead, see, so I never got my rest so after six weeks I fell . . . apart completely, and gave up the gas station, and had to quit my job at Firestone, and quit school, and laid around doin something or other, but I never laid in the sense that . . . we'd lay around or, people in New York lay around, I was doing something all the time, I never laid around until after the poolhall, which was——

JACK. One of these days tell me about the poolhall——

CODY. The poolhall was much different. I really can't approach that yet, 'cause I don't know anything about it . . .

JACK. So you met your father on Larimer Street

CODY. He said, ah, "Come on let's batch together" I said: "What you got in mind?" he said "Well, ah, they're building a construction camp, they're building a great steel mill, Columbia Steel Mill, Provo, Utah, and ah, so they're startin to build it and we can go to work up there." So he had some money, for a change, forty, fifty dollars so I said "Alright I'll go with you." Provo, Utah, yeah, that's a big steel mill; very dead of winter, so we went up there, it was just about Christmas time, and ah, so we went to Provo, and ah he got his job of course and we got all ironed out, took us a day or two, so I was all hired and everything except inadvertently I said I was seventeen, would be eighteen in a month, see, February eighth, you know, my birthday, the guy said "I'm sorry, can't work until you're eighteen," so, that was a hangup; but, at the same time, we went through a lot of other difficulties like, ah, well the inability to get liquor there, and I, I saw that I'd just be making runs for my father all the time, and things like that, see you got——they give you a ration card, a permit in Utah, like in other states similar to that, I think Oregon is one of 'em, but at any rate, so, why, ah, at the same time by the time we got to Provo I was all hot nuts to get to L.A., see, 'cause L.A. was my mecca then, and I'd already been out several times before, and so I couldn't resist you know what I mean? So, semi-against his wishes and partially not, why, I told him that I was going to go to L.A., and ah, managed to have just enough money——now that he had his job he wasn't——so he gave me all his money, and I got a bus and went to L.A. from Provo on

JACK. He gave you all his money

CODY. Yeah, well he had capital, I mean it wasn't froze, so, as far as that goes——

JACK. What, wa, what was your——what happened?

CODY. Well when I got to L.A.——previously I——had been in trouble there a couple times before, I'd get all involved talking about that and . . . so——

JACK. No I mean what happened when——with you and your father, personally? . . . going from Denver to Provo——

CODY. Well I can't remember much, it seems to me we'd sit and talk on the bus, I was embarrassed by his stupidity and that people could dig, you know, and perhaps by his appearance, and I remember it was very cold and everything was awful because one of the buses broke down——

JACK. He wrote in his letter about it

CODY. . . . Yeah, but, ah, at the same time already I was reminiscing about him and thinking about him or concerned about him but I wasn't——ah, really considerate and careful or anything of that nature, but at the same time there was no outward, ah, there was no rupture ever or anything of that nature, we'd never argued except, ah, over women that I was screwing and he was screwing, like Mrs. Blood, but, but there's no, ah, difficulty that way, except that it was a drag to me, personally, see, because he's content just to lay up in a hotel room and get drunk and then go to work those eight hours a day he has to. . . . It wasn't really anything that I can talk about because ah, it was just a bus trip, I 'member him reminiscing himself ab——a little bit about the past, but he's always doing it now, whenever he's with me, he says "You remember the time boy that we did this, or that?" and I usually don't

JACK. You usually don't!?

CODY. No I usually don't. . . . See, that's why I say, instead of sending this to Carl what I should do, see, 'cause this prologue is all nothing I *know* anyhow and it's not necessary or anything to begin with . . . what I'm saying, if I could get him *out* here he could sit down, he could *tell* me, he could tell me, on this recorder he could tell me, see? all the different things that I don't know and have no idea of——

JACK. But the things you remember *he* doesn't

CODY. Perhaps . . . yeah, oh——course now his mind probably is so bad *he* . . . won't even remember

JACK. We'll get him out here

CODY. I'd *like* to, of course Evelyn . . . won't, but one, while——

JACK. Imagine, it's like getting *my* father out here! (*cackling*)

CODY. Yeah, that's what I say, goddammit, that's what I say we've got to do that, a while back——

JACK. While he's still alive——

CODY. Yeah, that's what I say; so finally she consented to say that, "Well we could have him for a visit at least . . . or something," so, that's alright, so, we'll do it, that way, but ah, what worries me is the transportation *plus* the fact——here is the point: Buckle's in Denver now, right? Buckle is there, he has a pass in his pocket that he's not using, remember that hangup he's talking about the pass Henry Wunderdahl gave him?——over different railroads?——and so here he's got this pass that my old man could use, see, and at the same time even if he *didn't* use the pass Buckle could bring him back with him, see? he could come back with Buckle, even if it means layin out some cash somehow see, but instead of that I asked Evelyn today what Buckle's address is and where he is there, course *I* didn't ask him like a dope, and she didn't know either of course so there we are, we don't know where Buckle is

JACK. We're gonna be high in another ten minutes . . . ten more minutes kid

CODY. Oh it's funny——does this hit you, or not?

JACK. (*mumbling*) Yeah, it . . . sure . . .

CODY. ——but at any rate——

JACK. ——four grains of benny——

CODY. ——that's the problem, how you gonna——how you gonna get him out here, that's the problem, we haven't got—— unless the obvious way to do it, how are you going to find Buckle? see? and tell——

JACK. See when we're *all* working . . . (CODY, *Yeah*) . . . we can very well support that old guy!!

CODY. Yeah and he can take care of the children, but of course Evelyn is worried about the kid——because——

JACK. He can't because he's too drunk . . .

CODY. Yeah, well that's what I say . . . I *know* that but here's what I'm sayin . . . Evelyn won't have him in the house if he's drunk, see . . . well that's what I want to know, if he could control himself for awhile, we'd have to see, we could *get* him a little place . . .

JACK. Get him to Frisco

CODY. Get him to Frisco, that's right, get him a little place down on Third Street——

JACK. That's right——

CODY. ——that's the thing to do, *exactly* the thing to do. . . . Alright, well we've got to——

JACK. Or a room, on Mission Street——

CODY. Alright, how are we going to get him out here? we've got to get in contact with Buckle, write to Buckle; now, we don't know where Buckle is, right? Okay, so——

JACK. I know where Buckle is!

CODY. Where? In Denver? no you don't

JACK. Yes I do

CODY. He's given you his address? Given you his phone number?

JACK. Well, he's at his sister's

CODY. Which sister, though——he's got several

JACK. Jo . . . Josephine

CODY. Josephine. Alright, where does she live?——I, I know where she lives geographically, she lives in a school——across the street from a school in south Denver, but I don't know where——but if that fails, I——it seems to me we got a letter recently, from——a postcard it was, or a Christmas card, from, from Earl Johnson see, so that'll have Earl Johnson's address——

JACK. Is he back?

CODY. Yeah he's in Denver now . . . so we've got to write to Earl Johnson to look up Slim Buckle, see?

JACK. (*showing address book*) Yeah (*nonchalant*)

CODY. Where is it? That's it by God!

JACK. Three fifty-four West Third Street

CODY. That's it!——that's Denver, doesn't that say city Denver? it does doesn't it! That's the number, we can call him up right now . . . Race six two seven-o, there you go . . .

JACK. See? That's me

CODY. That's it, Three fifty-four West Third Avenue, that's what I told you, in south Denver, see, that's——West *Third* Avenue? No, it should be west of Alameda, south of——I think that's the wrong one——

JACK. That's where he lived with Helen

CODY. Oh, well that's not it, oh no, see that's not it (*snapping fingers*) Damn! No it's a——see, Third I confused with Alameda 'cause Alameda's three hundred south, that's Third Street only it's just six blocks' difference between 'em, 'cause zero, see, three and down to zero and then three hundred south six blocks——but that's alright we can take care of that, if ah, we're going to do it, and that's the thing I think that's necessary to do, especially since——

JACK. Oh God, you know what, we know what to do!——we'd write a letter to Justin Mannerly——

CODY. No, no

JACK. Call——*I'll* write a letter to him

CODY. ——No I'll write——simpler, it's simpler——

JACK. "——Call up Slim Buckle immediately at Josephine Buckle's house, his sister's"——

CODY. No. Yeah. No wait a minute——

JACK. ——"find out where his sister lives, what her number is, tell him that Jack and Cody said to Val, to Slim, to go down to Gaga's barbershop——"

CODY. No here's what we're gonna do——I've got, I'm going to write——

JACK. 'Cause I mean, you know, Mannerly, boy, he's my boy——

CODY. Yeah I know but Mannerly's not——doesn't have to

be brought into this, because ah, what I'm sayin is, besides he doesn't know Slim or anything . . .

JACK. Yes he does

CODY. He knows Slim, he knows how everybody is like "Who's that big guy?" or somethin see

JACK. Well I introduced them to each other

CODY. Yeah. What I'm sayin what we've got to do is write to Earl Johnson——

JACK. Earl Johnson? Where *is* he?

CODY. He's in *Denver*

JACK. Same address?

CODY. (*annoyed*) No, we've got his recent address, we've got it here, he sent us a postc——a Christmas card, see, so we got his address, I've got to find it though . . . write to Earl Johnson——

JACK. Listen . . . could Earl Johnson beat you running?

CODY. N-o-o-o-o!

JACK. He said he could

CODY. He said that hunnerd times, a hunnerd times a night I'd prove it to him, he doesn't even know what he's talking about, 'cause I could beat him in everything

JACK. I bet I can beat *him* running

CODY. ——sure, see, but what I'm sayin is Earl . . . is workin for his father there, see, that, ah, distributor for Old Forester whiskies or something, lots of money, see?

JACK. In *Denver*?

CODY. Yah and so Earl——Oh he's been there for years, yes—— stepfather has loads of money, they live in that ritzy joint out there, Twelve fifty-four Fairfax, I already remember his *parents'* address, just like that

JACK. By God . . . Ed Gray's a——address, Fairfax Manor . . .

CODY. Yeah, Fairfax Manor, that's right, yeah, that's what it's from——

JACK. Where Minko and I stayed in Ed Gray's . . . pad, for the summer——

CODY. Yeh that was across the street sort of but down the road awhile, but that wasn't where it is——I remember Minko's pad, yeah, I remember Minko, I remember Ed . . .

JACK. You know Ed Gray is really great?

CODY. Oh, ar, I——

JACK. He came to New York and I didn't——man, I was so busy, and so drunk, and so hungup on the few cunts I had, and so many things to do, that I didn't even spend enough——half enough time . . . with Ed Gray . . .

CODY. Hm hm, yeah, Oh he's great

JACK. I know that he's very sad about that

CODY. Yeah

JACK. I know that *I* am very sad about that

CODY. Yeah. . . . . Ed's, ah——

JACK. Ed is one of the greatest . . . men that ever lived

CODY. Yeah, that's . . . right, that's right——at the same time the reason he'll knock you out so is that he's completely normal, completely——I mean he's, well *you* know——isn't he? He's not, you'll never catch *him* goin off on some, ah, hangup, or saying——you know what I mean, you know, he——that's the amazing part of him, in fact, he's so, ah, relaxed and normal that . . . he can be a drag, you know what I mean?

JACK. (*laughing*) Yeah

CODY. Just because——like if you got suddenly excited or somethin, see, well he'd go along with you and all that, see, but he'll never manufacture the excitement himself, or feel it himself, you know, like s'far as . . . comin out, right?

JACK. (*singing "Them There Eyes" upflip riff*) How does it go? (*repeats*) Sing it——sing it elaborately——

CODY. Hm hm. That's right. . . . I *can't* though——alright (*but sings it*)

JACK. It didn't go like that!

CODY. That's the way it goes though

JACK. (*sings it again, as Cody chuckles*) Now sing it!

CODY. That's right

JACK. Sing it. . . . (*Cody sings it*) No! you gotta go way up there!

CODY. (*laughing, as Jack demonstrates*) Oh I see. Yeah, that's right . . .

JACK. (*singing words now*) "I fell in love with you, the first time I looked into, them there eyes . . . They make me feel so happy——" Okay, I'll play some record while you talk

CODY. (*chuckling*) Or else you could turn on KWBR——

JACK. Them there eyes!——

CODY. ——he's real crazy; he never talks, you know, that

KWBR . . . thirteen-ten . . . except, dammit, we might get a little buzz out of it——

JACK. You don't realize how I'm feeling real drunk

CODY. Are you really? (*laughs*) Geez I'm not. You remind me of some——some——ah——

JACK. See? where in the middle there, talking, now you tell me about what *you* did with Vicki, 'cause that's a . . . world-shaking cunt

CODY. Well you know I never dug her, like the first night I told you——

JACK. You dug her as a worldshaking cunt——

CODY. No, you and me both dug her as a big sloppy gal, you remember that talk, you remember, man, she's all very hep and very fine and everything, but talking about appeal, attraction, *you* know, she, you know, she——you don't keep gettin . . . creamed over her——

JACK. Oh yeah . . . Oh no. . . . Yeah

CODY. ——'cause you know her completely, see, she's just a big woman, right? you remember our conversations about Vicki, you know, so for that very reason I never was, ah, really. . . . No I think you got——no, that, he would never play that, see?, now watch, that's KW——that's KYA, twelve-sixty, see we gotta go to fifteen-ten, watch (*dials radio*)

JACK. There it is!

CODY. No——that's KWBO

(*"Just One of Those Things" plays on air, Jack sings, hums idly to it*)

CODY. I got it soft enough so we can hear even our smallest monosyllable, at the same time you and me personally can hear it, see, right? (*Jack sings*) . . . What are your good reasons for being lush? You know the only reason I'm not a lush?

JACK. Hmm?

CODY. You know the only reason I'm not a lush?

JACK. Why?

CODY. Because I really don't enjoy the . . . ah, the——if, you know, I mean I——to, you know——it doesn't, ah, of course I've got drunk quite a while . . . and I've been *very* drunk . . . see I'll bet I've been drunk six months straight, see, with Watson? see . . .

JACK. Tom Watson?

CODY. Oh yeah I spent——he had a, he made a great killing in poker, and also an insurance check or something and he had over five hundred dollars? and so, ah, we, it took us six months to spend it, ten dollars a night, we'd sit and drink, he spent it all on me like that, see——

JACK. Where?

CODY. In Lloyd's of Denver, a bar . . . it's a kinda fag bar now, in fact it always has been, really, but it's more fag, you know usually just a bar with a few fags, but now it's faggish

JACK. Yeah?

CODY. But——yeah——we sat there every night, and played things like, oh Maurice Rocco, stuff like that see . . . Charley Spivak

JACK. The guy that stands up——

CODY. Charley Spivak, which I really don't——'cause there was nothing else . . . at that time we both liked the trumpet instead of the saxophone, and everything . . . in fact we were very young, in fact at that time——

JACK. I went into, ah, MacDougal's Cafe . . . but . . . go on, "in fact at that time" . . .

CODY. ——I was talking all the time continuously, philosophically, questionings and reasonings about certain things, statements about everything, which I've *completely* forgotten now and yet the words I said probably——a *million* words, more, more than that, for three years straight but I mean that was the end of it, there . . . but finally, I remember, finally, near the end I can remember a certain thing, like, like I'd talk for two hours and I was, ah, and everything was *real* crazy, real gone, and finally the guy——one of the guys I was talking to, the cab-driver, he said "Well that's all real good, and real fine, and real great, Cody, but ah, but ah, you don't have any MONEY," or somethin like that, he showed that everything I said was just nothing, just wasn't right, but, that wasn't the point. That's one thing I'll never be able to recall, all the things I said, all the things I speculated about, which were so——the way I did it, or, the voice, or something, or at any rate——so that, like I told you earlier probably, why, these friends of mine like, like Tom Watson, and other guys around there, other guys——guys I've never . . . told you about, a kid named Joe, ah, Joe——Gooley or

somethin like that, not Gooley 'cause there's another kid named
Gooley, but Joe somethin, but at any rate, the other boys they'd
bring down whenever they'd meet a strange girl, or couldn't
make it, they'd bring her down to my house so I'd lay there and
talk to them all night . . . get her on top . . . so they could screw
her and all that . . . but I can't remember——see talkin about——
JACK. Talk about what?
CODY. Make as if he owned her!
JACK. Would that make the girls hot?
CODY. No!——because it was very . . . pedantic and, ah, very,
ah, speculative but I was——you know, I'd just stay there and
talk about . . . well now for example, we know that I——
JACK. You had no cunt yourself?
CODY. Oh yeah, I usually always *did* have a cunt, always have,
yeah, in fact, *always* have, always *have* had . . . yeah . . . but, ah,
those weren't the things I was meaning to talk about, but I do
recall at that time that was the end of it, I finally got so sick of it,
not that I was doing it artificially or nothing, *you* know, in fact
I was completely hungup on it, but——well I'll tell you exactly,
you know what ended me? from that whole period? From the
time that I was fifteen till I was eighteen, or, nineteen even,
well, and I was hung in there completely, and I mean some real
crazy way, why, ah, and I mean things to be proud of too, in
fact things that I see guys now hungup on that——which I have
told you about sometime, a guy that's, see, who's, but at any
rate, I won't now, but he's a brakeman that lost his job after
two, three days because he——he used to stand up on top of
the boxcar, but that's not the reason he had an accident, but
that's not the point either . . . what happened is, that, ah, one
day I was——and I had just got out of jail, I'd been in jail eleven
months and ten days, and ah, Justin still loved me enough so
that he got me a job, a good job recapping tires, a trade that I
had learned earlier, three years earlier under his auspices, and,
workin at night and goin to school daytime and so on, so I
had a good job, and a . . . great cunt, and I had everything all
lined up, I was living . . . real fine, in fact, I was living *real* fine,
see, and so I was the boss of the joint after five o'clock because
everyone went home and I was alone so that every night the
boys would come down with their girls and we'd have a big beer
bust and a ball, and Benzedrine too, but any rate, so ah, one

day about five o'clock just when the place was closing, they have tire changes, you know, four or five of 'em, three or four of 'em changing tires all the time, course I didn't do that, I let them cap the tires themselves, which is different, but at any rate, this blondheaded kid there, he was bendin over changin tires, and finally he got up, and I happened to be standin there watchin him for a second or somethin, and he said, "Say," he said, "isn't your name, ah, Cody Pomer——" I said "Yes." He said "Well my name is Val Hayes, and ah, and ah, Justin Mannerly, I think we have mutual friends, Justin Mannerly." I said "OH! Val Hayes!! Yeah I heard about you, yeah, you've got such a great brain and everything" and he said "Well," and all that, and he came on very . . . cool; at any rate but I popped right on him right away and hung to him, so much so in fact that he came back——

JACK. You *what* to him?

CODY. *Hung* to him, you know, so, so much so that he came back after he went home to eat supper——but Val has always been, as he still is now, only of course more so, so that we never see him or hear from him, he's always been very "Well now I, I'm sorry but I've got to go do this, and go do that, and so I can't,"——but, ah, that night, that first night of meeting he said, ah "Well I do have to go home and eat supper, however I'll come back around seven, seven thirty or eight, see I'll g——and we'll talk," I said "Fine," so he went and he came back, and, so I closed up shop, and we went over and ate, to eat supper——usually I ate my lunch or something but I closed up the joint and we went over to a café and sat there and talked and everything, and ah, so, that very first night if I'm not mistaken or very close to the first time I ever met him why, ah, I was startin to come on one way or another and like I said "Well Val, course I think the most important men in the world, the most important *thing* in the world of course and the thing that really counts of course is philosophy," and he said: "Oh, why no, it's, ah, to me I should think that the . . . poet is much more important than the philosopher." I said "What?" and I was so stupefied and astounded and nullified and disturbed that anyone could honestly believe that, that I, well I——*you* know, I really was, ah, upset about it, and ah, went into it——but of course by this time I had rehashed all my thoughts completely and extended the limits of my thoughts in every direction so

much so that everything as I was telling you ab——ah, last night
when I was telling you about the skeletonized form? and about
. . . the remembrance, see? like if you tell mey——ah, *or* have
gone through a thing completely in your own mind yourself,
ah, and so that you've got it all formulated, and so that sometime a guy'll say "Hey, when's the first time you met Val?" well
you say "Oh well I was walking down the street and that's how
it happened," well, and so you say it three or four times, so
pretty soon, especially if it's a thought, not a happening, but
a thought, so if you have to go through a thought again and
again pretty soon it becomes an abstraction of the thought and
you still follow the form and structure of it but you just say
"Well so this happened and *that* happened," and it becomes just
a dry, drab nothing, you see? It's not like it was at first. So at
any rate, ah, I had that disadvantage you see, 'cause I was right
at the tail end of my whole . . . school of all that, and the whole
system that I was concerned about and everything that was
my-self and so completely wrapped up *in*-to that that I really
had nothing with which to answer him because everything I
said——course I could think of a thousand things and come up
with 'em all the time but, but it was just . . . statements, period,
this and that you see, without the——without all the things that
are between that build it up into a solid building, like you can't
make it out of just bricks, but, so, at any rate, after Val said *that*
and, ah, what, by golly after, ah, three four days and also——
probably, I don't really want——care to speculate to say *why*,
that the reason came about, but suddenly I realized that the
philosopher was not——that the poet *was* more important than
the philosopher, you see——
JACK. Course!
CODY. ——and ah——well of course *now*! (*and laughs*)——that
I understood immediately and completely, but you see, actually what it means then that I must have lived in a very——well
I did of course live in a very strange, frantic world th——I, ah,
I'd go sit in the library and get all hungup on those things, just
completely involved trying to find what it was, or whatever it
happened to be, but at any rate that was . . . my whole life and
everything, ah, so much so that I developed a great smugness
and complacency and a, ah——'course I was never a snob or
anything of that nature, really, except perhaps the way that I

happened, or might be, not that it concerns me at all but I'm
just saying that——that's how I met Val . . . and that summer
was real great because, about three or four days later why I
happened to remem——see I don't remember now of course
absolutely this or that happening or this or that happening,
but I do remember is . . . all——days that we had together, and
other nights, and——but I would just . . . briefly without going
into a lot of things like, ah, like ah, well like one morning, see,
he would do things that he wouldn't ordinarily do, *now*, I see
he wouldn't, you see, so that I got him up at five A.M., ah, got
this girl for him, who was *my* girl you see, but of course she
was so great and so gone and everything, besides at that time
I'd never known what such a thing ima——I couldn't possible
imagine such a thing as jealousy, or anything, couldn't *possibly*
be concerned with the fact that, ah, anything of that na——like
I say, but, so, therefore naturally I was always making a girl and
turning 'em over to my other boyfriends, I did that with several
girls but all this is all nothing but what, wa, what a lot of other
fellows have also done that doesn't mean anything, but what
I'm saying is, so, *for* those reasons and everything why, I said,
"Come on Val, I've got this great girl," and which was my . . .
girl, and at the same time I'll pick up on somethin else that
I ran into the other day, a fifteen-year-old girl, so ah, he said
"Fine" so I said "Alright I'll come around your house about five
o'clock in the morning," this girl has to get out early 'cause for
. . . some reason or other so I picked her up, went to his house,
and at that time I'd——rent trucks from Hertz system, it only
cost two bucks a day, see, and I'd disconnect the speedometer,
that's why——
JACK. From who?
CODY. Hertz . . . system, drive yourself system, trucks, and,
ah, Hertz, yeah, yeah, *H-e-r-t-e-s*, ah, *z*, and, ah, so I'd get a
panel truck, panel, you know enclosed? . . . small . . . drive . . .
pickup, only it's not a pickup it's a panel, but I put a mattress
in the back, see, Kriloff's mattress, see, I'd take off the, ah, and
throw blankets in there, see, so then I'd pick up the people and
we'd take off to the mountains, where I had a cabin up there
who was a . . . friend of, well the cabin belonged to a friend of
Jim Evans but, at *any* rate, so, we——
JACK. I knew Jim Evans

CODY. Yeah I know that you do know . . . him, that's why I mentioned it, but, ah, so we went up there, and we had our kicks all day man, and I mean my . . . kicks then were driving kicks, see my——here's, here're what I'd do, I'd go pick up two or three or whatever I had, a couple or, one, or one person or no persons, and drive 'em up to the cabin, then I'd . . . take right off and go back to town, pick up some more, by that time somebody else had to go home from the cabin so I'd take *them* home, that's what I'd do, see, thirty-five miles, just back and forth, back and forth, gettin my gun off *that* way, see?——at the same time bangin and everything (*socking palms*) and having my kicks, but, so I did that that day of course, see, and finally it got so involved that, that Val had to go home by himself, so I stayed there for another reason and, and so ah, he didn't get back till after midnight, see, and we spent the night up there just he and I layin there talkin and everything, and then at any rate, ah, it finally became so that, ah, I would meet him, ah, every . . . night around suppertime, er, no, I would meet him whenever he was free, like say Saturday noon or something, and we'd go to the . . . bar, directly across the street, fifty yards, ah, from his house, we would sit there and drink beer——*you* know that little bar, the Marion Inn——

JACK. Marion Street

CODY. Yeah Marion, that's right, the little bar up there at Park, Seventeenth and Marion, Park Avenue also, it's a three-way intersection

JACK. I know that bar

CODY. Yeah, and, so we sat——well that bar also has a lot of other happenings and meanings to me which I won't go into now, I mean 'cause they're more a——ah, different type of thing, but at any rate——

JACK. I got unconnectedly drunk in there one time (*a lie*)

CODY. Yeah. Well I did too——I got so drunk in there that . . . Val would have to go home and I'd lay in the grass, beside the bar there, and I couldn't get up or anything see, and he said "Well, I'm sorry to leave you Cody but I've got to go home and eat supper and," so on, and he'd go on about his business see

JACK. You'd lay in the grass real drunk

CODY. ——I'd——so drunk I couldn't stand up man, I was a drunkard boy! I'm telling you I was——all the time I was drunk!

man I was never——'cause that's all I had, see? and ah, so ah, but at any rate, that's what I'd do, Benzedrine 'n' everything, but what I'm saying, I can recall our conversations *now*, more, like he'd say "Well now take for example if you would, ah, well what for instance, say, if we *didn't* have an army? what would happen if we didn't have an army, what if we didn't have any kind of defense? I say let's not have any and so on and so forth, nothing could happen, so we get taken over, so that doesn't matter——" and all that kind of stuff, see, at that time he was hungup because he thought the Army had almost ruined him, see, and things like that, see——

JACK. Yeah . . . he did . . .

CODY. And other things, ah——er there were a lot of other things that bothered him . . . but at any rate gradually it dwindled off, toward the end of the summer, as he, as he began to ap- proach going back to school I bet, so——you know——so I said "Well I'll see you," and everything and "I'll write to you and everything;" so we *did* write some letters, *you* remember?

JACK. Oh I read them

CODY. Yeah, that's right. And, ah, so then I told him come out, then you know from then on——

JACK. The first letter I read that you wrote——

CODY. Ah?

JACK. ——was written from, ah, Ed Wehle's ranch . . .

CODY. Oh yes . . . yeah . . . it wasn't——and already at that time, I had written the first word of this book w——which I've got right here in the prologue, ah, at, er, I said to myself "Well, at last," after Val wrote to me or something, I said to myself "At last I'm going to begin my novel,"——been thinkin about it for a year or two, not thinking about it at *all* completely, I just *knew* I'd be doing it, never occurred to me I couldn't write. So I sat down, I said, ah, "Cody Pomeray was born on February eighth, ah, 'twenty-six, ah, well? . . ." couldn't get past that—— and from that day until four years later I never wrote another word, 'cause I realized I couldn't——it never *occurred* to me the problems of the writer, or problems of anything, I just——it never, it was completely blind, I'd have never imagined, I'd never——can't believe that I was so naive, not naive in the sense of naiveté but stu——so dumb as to believe that it was possible to sit down and just write. But at any rate . . . ah . . . Val . . . I remember that particular letter, I think, ah, I'd, ah——already I had . . . disintegrated then, I was——there was a whole form of me that was entirely different, from that point on I just went, ah, different, in different directions . . . much stuff . . . had gone before, yet the whole thing to be understood, has to be taken as a whole, I guess, like everything does——

JACK. On account of *Val*

CODY. No, not on *account* of Val, no, no, I'm just saying in general, I, ah, I changed, of course . . . but, there were, there were . . . great number of things——

JACK. Want me to tell you somethin about Val?

CODY. Yeah

JACK. We was in . . . Boston, Massachusetts——

CODY. Yeah?

JACK. ——and we went, and we got a, hotel room with a . . . fifty night, fifty cents a night flophouse in back of, ah, Old Howard Burlesk theater?

CODY. Yeah . . . which is world famous . . . yeah

JACK. ——in back of Scollay Square, see . . . yeah

CODY. ——which I don't know anything about except that——

JACK. I remember the name of the flophouse, in my notebooks, but I don't have it now (CODY, *Hmm, yeah, yeah*) So we paid fifty cents each, and there was a partition separating us from another room, and all sorts of stuff, and it RAINED!! like a sonofabitch that night, it rained and rained and rained and I woke up in the middle of the night saying to myself "What the fuck are we doing——what am *I* doing, in the first place, back here in Boston, Massachusetts," (CODY, *Hmm!*) And then, Val . . . he was asleep and had his hand thrown over my cock (CODY, *Hm hm*) . . . and I was dreaming of cunts . . . (CODY, *Hm hm*) . . . and I woke up . . . with a hard-on (CODY, *Hm hm*) . . . and I, and I realized what was going on so I went——I coughed "Brrp bllp opoop heh!" see? then I got up and went to the toilet and pissed, my hard-on went down when I pissed, you see (*Cody goes* Hm hm *all the way through*) . . . came back to bed . . . in the morning when we woke up, see we didn't do anything but sleep, there was a picture of a young . . . sort of boy, eight years old, and we said, we speculated, "Wal the fucking thing was probably painted by somebody in Alaska, in 1910, and taken to Boston, in 1925, and now . . . 1945, or 1948, here we are looking at the painting, in back of the Howard . . . Burlesk . . ." *you* know . . .

CODY. (*after silence*) . . . Do you feel through your shoes the machine? I'm also high, see? it took forty-five minutes after twelve o'clock, *fifteen* minutes after twelve thirty——

JACK. Wow, are you high now?

CODY. Yeah, I feel it

JACK. We got another big . . . long . . . sonofabitch to go!

CODY. Yeah . . . yeah . . . well not really

JACK. W-whole big reel——ass!

CODY. Yeah but that's nothing compared to all the things we can talk about, or say

JACK. Oh I'll——that can be solved easily

CODY. How?

JACK. Wal, by stopping it now (REEL ENDS)

(MACHINE BEGINS)

CODY. (*from a month-old tape*) God-*damn*! (*click*) (*present reel begins*)

JACK. (*drunk, lying on the floor with mike in ear*) . . . and I want you to tell me about this here . . . parking lot in L.A. on . . . Main Street . . . that has a only waist high and painted-up-all-green . . . that I dug, you see——naturally. . . . But I wanta know why you made such a big situation about it being waist high

CODY. Man that's almost impossible to answer, it's one of those things

JACK. But it *was* a big thing about it because you came and you peeked over it . . . what did it used to be?

CODY. That's true, that's one thing——Oh it used to be the very——

JACK. That was the used-to-be——it *usen't* to be what it is *now*!

CODY. Wal, I dunno, it's probably pretty much the same

JACK. Well, the name of it

CODY. System Auto Parks, no it used to be "System" and now (*tape blur*) . . . (*as Jack keeps saying* That's right) Walt's . . . yeah, he's taken over, yeah, Five eighty South Main. Ah . . . when I hitch-hiked to California, ah, fourth, third or fourth time, no really actually I guess it was the second time, at any rate, my sister who still thought of me as a little boy of course and very surprised that I stayed out all night and fucked around, but any rate, her, ah, boyfriend told me why didn't I get a job in a parking lot ah, like I. Magnin's or someplace like that, which he had once done years before, so I said "Alright," and so introduced me to a fellow down at System Auto Parks and I . . . went down to learn how to park cars——

JACK. What was HE like?

CODY. He was a big fella, his name is, ah, gee I can't remember his name, but any rate he's, he was a big fella, he was quiet, his name is Vince I guess something like that, but he's, ah, quiet, but he's, he's pretty——an average, ah, L.A. type, it's hard to describe, I mean they know what's going on, the kinda wise guy type but they're really very nice, I mean they're not, ah, hungup on a lot of, you know, viciousness in their makeup or anything, but he's a little bit plump, er, nice fella, very considerate type of guy, but, at the same time he knows what's going on all the time, see?

JACK. Y-e-a-h

CODY. Like when I escaped out of the joint, why, he gave me a big berating, you see I only saw him a few times but he said "What in the hell are you stealing *cars* for? steal something that they can't trace, steal something like money" and all that kind of stuff, but at any rate, after I'd worked System for a few days they sent me up to Five eighty South Main to go work for a fellow named Harvey Allerdee who was the manager of the lot. Harvey Allerdee became my closest friend . . . and best advisor, and I went to live with him and his wife, she was a dancer, her name was Vivian, fat woman, with plucked eyebrows, dark hair, 'bout thirty-eight, but any rate Harvey was tall fella, very red face but not like bourbon tan, rather the red face of an outdoors man, he was always——but ah, he was always smiling in a very wry way, he was always doing (*grimace*), you know, he was always bringing his lips back and smiling very nice, and then you'd say something——what it really amounted to was, ah—— how he developed that I think was from always sayin "I don't know," or else saying, ah, he'd say, "Well, it's up to you," "Well, I dunno," you see, he'd, ah, bring his face back, really very kindly looking, you know, and he had bald head with fringe of hair but it wasn't——didn't look——didn't——think of him as a bald man, and it seems he had freckles, he was very tall and thin and angular, I mean he was ah, ah, very quiet easy-goin, never moved fast or anything, and very good parking lot man and, ah, showed me all the things that there was to know about . . . not only parking cars but how to knock down and clip the customers and the company and everybody else, and he had an old 'thirty Chevy he'd drive to work every day, it was quite a ways, we lived about five miles away out in South L.A., his place out there; so I moved in with him, and, ah, we, ah, I had a real crazy summer, running around with a kid named . . . Rinick and shootin out lightbulbs, and shooting through the ceilings and going to jail and always getting hungup one way or another, but at any rate, despite that, there was no, ah, it really was a wonderful summer, ah, of course that time I was real crazy, I'd steal cars every night, when I closed the lot at midnight I'd take the best car on the lot and go joyridin, and, ah, yeah oh yeah, I've done that countless times everywhere——that's why I've stole at *least* five hundred automobiles and more than that probably, see? but at any rate, ah, Harvey was——I can't get over Harvey, quite a guy, I can't——but at any rate, well I keep saying "at any rate," I don't mean to say that, Harvey, ah, had done time in a joint I finally came to find out, and he had a brother-in-law who was a conman with small things like sellin hot rings and, and ah, Swiss-made wrist watches and so on which of course w——had no workings in them and stop after five minutes, and things like that, and he came over and . . . he did something which amazed me, I can't exactly recall what it is now but he told me, for example that I was left-handed, he told me other things of that nature, sort of clairvoyant, you know, like a fortune teller type . . . thing but . . . also sleight of hand, but, really he was a big conman, and he owned a brand new Pontiac. And——wait a minute I think I hear, I hear . . . (*Jack flutes*) (*record ends as Evelyn comes home from work making photos in International Settlement nightclubs*)

(MACHINE BEGINS NEW CONVERSATION)

JACK. . . . this is the maddest joint in town . . .
EVELYN. It sure is
CODY. This Duluoz's so hungup on tea we been callin that Jimmy Low all night . . . can't make out
JACK. I know
EVELYN. He rifled all my things and couldn't find 'em, huh?

CODY. No, we didn't

EVELYN. I know, I'm surprised you didn't

CODY. Yeah, w——

JACK. Maybe Evelyn can call him up

CODY. (*laughing*)——talked to the landlady two minutes ago, she just said he's not in——

JACK. It's too late

CODY. (*still laughing*) It's two o'clock, yeah . . . I mean, he says . . . "Oh yeah, well I just called on a wild guess" he said——

EVELYN. (*sitting on Jack's chest who is on floor with mike*) Can you breathe? (*laughing*) . . . sitting on your diaphragm. (*to Cody*) I got us a new hat fellas . . . somebody left a tam on my——

JACK. Oh yeah?

CODY. You got it?

EVELYN. ——radiator cap. It's all wet

JACK. Is that it? is that the hat?

CODY. Did you bring it in?

JACK. Oh, on the radiator cap!

EVELYN. I kept looking at it all the way home wondering "What's *that?*"

CODY. Did you bring it in?——yeah? Good. (*laughing*) You looked at it and didn't know what it was, it could have been——

EVELYN. Well it was just a *lump*

CODY. ——a *bomb*, don't you know someone might be . . . have . . . after you?

EVELYN. Somebody asked me to drive him downtown, he was attractive, too

CODY. Well why didn't you, darling, you might have made . . . five dollars

EVELYN. Yeah

CODY. You know you're out of gas, you know, and . . . things like that; gotta get home to the wife and three kids, you know—— I'm the wife now, I guess

EVELYN. Yeah . . . poor wives

CODY. We've been having cozy little knitting session . . . talking about, ah——

EVELYN. Have you?

CODY. ——Five eighty South Main

EVELYN. Well go on

CODY. ——'cross from, ah, across from——

JACK. Well go on!

CODY. ——that Pacific Electric, is that what they call it? I think it is . . . one night——

JACK. Yeah, I was right——Red car (*decides to just name it resignedly*)

CODY. Let's see, one night, it seems to me, I ran into a girl or something and I was frightened, ah, that I might have gotten some, ah, type of social disease, so I, ah, course I knew there was this Army prophylactic station, there's only one up in L.A. and did a land-office business——

JACK. Where's m'wine?

CODY. Ah, across the street there at the, at the Pacific and Electric, so——(*as Evelyn looks around for Jack*)——I think it's in the icebox, darling, so . . .

EVELYN. *Is* there more? Oh boy . . .

CODY. Oh yeah, we only had two quarts

EVELYN. Tokay

JACK. Flame tokay (*he and Evelyn laughing*)

CODY. 'Cause I haven't drunk any, Jack's drunk at least a quart by himself, see (*Jack laughs*)——that's right! And I've drunk, oh, about half of——

EVELYN. Oh you're so brave in wine

CODY. No that's right though!

JACK. That's *true*!

CODY. Yah, that's no kidding, I just couldn't get on it; that's no kidding, we took the Dex——stook straight Ben-ze-drine, not that I——Italian stuff but the other stuff, so we can talk slow (*as Jack concurrently mumbles same information*), we figured that you could talk, you know, on——

JACK. And we're just about high now!

CODY. Just getting, yeah

EVELYN. (*laughing*) Oh no!

CODY. ——three hours——took until ten o'clock didn't it? (JACK, *Yeah*) He said, he said, "Well, at the most two hours," that'd be midnight, midnight didn't feel a thing; well twelve thirty; so finally quarter to one I feel a little bit of a buzz, and now it's going away again, you know, I feel——I could sleep, anything, *you* know . . . in fact I should be——

JACK. ——ten o'clock . . . this clock . . . (*incoherent*)

CODY. Yeah that clock is slow, damn thing's——

EVELYN. Well I came home early, I just came home early

CODY. Yeah but five minutes slow, though, I've been checking all night

EVELYN. (*announcing*) I quit

CODY. You didn't quit?

EVELYN. (*she and Jack laugh*) I did!

CODY. (*from far in kitchen*) What do you mean, quit what?

EVELYN. *Quit*

CODY. The job?

EVELYN. Well I'm sure . . . he won't . . . be interested, he didn't come around . . . *Nicki* says I should go around to the Cable Car Club or something like that and make him give me a steady spot——

CODY. Cable Car *Village*

EVELYN. Nobody can make any money in the Beige Room anyway——

CODY. Yeah I know, all fag joint——

EVELYN. ——I just got a dirty . . . deal, you know, it wasn't my fault

CODY. Yeah . . . I know. . . . Yeah, that's right . . .

EVELYN. So I said "Well."——Look at my shoes!

CODY. Wet . . . Jesus Christ . . . feet——

EVELYN. Believe me I didn't go out if I could help it

CODY. Yeah, well . . . could you help it?

EVELYN. Ah, I took two pictures

CODY. Two pictures?

EVELYN. One of 'em over again . . . hmph

CODY. Had to go to the Sinaloa and darkroom 'em, huh?

EVELYN. Huh-huh . . . then——

JACK. (*sepulchrally*) *Dark room*!

CODY. So when of course——

EVELYN. What happened to you two?

CODY. What? I *know*, we was gonna show but . . . he woulda had to stay with the kids, or else *I* would, and, and . . . the idea of dressin up and everything, you know, so——

EVELYN. Why I kept lookin at people who looked just like this . . . see

CODY. Really?

EVELYN. Sure . . . one thing I know that you couldn't have

gotten in because I forgot to tell you you have to bring your
identification there . . . see, to show at people . . . that makes
it real dangerous, those big signs say "Off Limits for Military
Personnel" . . .

CODY. Oh yes, oh yeah, fags to get ahold of those poor sailors!

JACK. Yeah . . . (*incoherent*) . . . military

CODY. (*as Evelyn laughs*) So I went across the street, and there
was a guy there with a——a clipped English looking you know,
with a mustache, clipped, ah, English mustache——

JACK. Where?

CODY. ——military man——

JACK. Where?

LATER

CODY. ——and he ran the Army prophylactic station in the
P.G., in the Pacific Electric building see? (*Evelyn murmurs and
laughs*)

JACK. Oh! (*finding out where*)

CODY. So I went in, I said "Say, here's a dollar," so I said, ah,
"I can take a pro? I think, er——" He said "Oh that's alright,
keep your dollar, go ahead," and so, I took a pro, and, ah——

EVELYN. How'd you do that?

CODY. Well, I, ah, you see, you go over and you take this,
ah, green castile soap you know, and you wash yourself——well
most people just wash the penis but you gotta get way down up
in the asshole you know, and all around, the balls thoroughly,
be sure and get under the balls thoroughly and up into the hair
almost to the navel, see? and that's the trouble with most guys,
they just, you know, they just wash their penis . . . well then,
after you get it washed and, ah, dried off, ah thoroughly, then
he comes over with a, ah, plunger business, just like an eyedrop-
per, and he shows you how to hold your penis, hold your penis
this way, see? and, and you spread it open, and, he plunges it
in, he says "Alright now, *hold* it!" and you hold it

EVELYN. Like an enema

CODY. So he never has to touch you or anything, and you
hold it for five minutes they make you!——Army regulations,
five minutes, I've seen those poor soldiers standin up there
drunk about to pass out and everything still holdin that in
there, you know? (*laughter*), and then they let it go, of course,

and then (*Jack makes moan*) you walk out——oh then he smears
you with some salve, see, *you* smear yourself, *he* never touches
your, course, himself, at all——some type of salve, you know,
but, and then you put toilet tissue around that, and, walk out,
but of course that——(*Evelyn comments in background*) Yeah!
that's the——that's, that's the professional type prophylactic,
you know; at any rate we got to talking, I talked to this guy
. . . his name was Destry, and he was——Jesus you drank that
whole thing here——

EVELYN. Oh "that whole thing!" Whole thing? you know
how much was in there?

CODY. (*laughing*) That's what I been telling Jack all night——
so at any rate, ah, he's telling me, ah, oh we got talking about
this and that and I told him I was interested in philosophy,
and he was interested in philosophy, and he was innerested in
Indian philosophy, and ah, so ah, every night then thereafter
I'd go over and talk with him all night, there in the pro station,
and ah——

EVELYN. I'm cold——turn the heat up

CODY. ——he told me about his——all his ideas about community living, about getting . . . people together you know,
work——like, say, if you had a group, say, fifty or a hundred
people, why, you don't have to work about two hours a day or
something, and of course there's . . . no regulations of any kind,
do whatever you want, in fact, for kicks, why you put cameras
behind the walls or somethin, but at any rate he was, ah, going
through all that, and ah, in fact before he got in the Army he
had already started it by, ah——he had a dry cleaning business
so he got a couple guys and couple of truckdrivers and they
had it cut down to about six hours or four hours a day they'd
work, and ah, they was all gettin interested in it——in fact they
had bought the lot where they was gonna build the house, and
build additions and everybody just . . . goof off as best they
might——But he had a lot of ulterior motives behind it, see? to
watch the people and find out this and that and all that, but
still his——the main, ah advocation of his which he would talk
about all the time, very sensibly, and, and, give you illustration
that——illustration all night, was the fact that if you visualize a
thing well enough and hard enough why it'll come to pass, despite odds and everything else——For example, he was in some

terrible, ah, pa——po——portion, you know, of the Army, you know, he was in the infantry and something or other, and so he . . . said to himself "What I've got to do is get to the Medical Corps," and so, he did that, which is fairly simple enough, I guess, which is about the limits most people would go, but then he visualized himself in some soft spot where he'd be stationed there regularly and so on and so forth and so on, and he thought of the prophylactic station, and for three years he stayed in this other hospital thinking about it, it was only one chance in a million that he'd get it and he got it of course; and things like that which he was always talking about, but not, ah, bragging, or anything of that nature, just, just simply believed in it, so much so that he had me walking down the street with my eyes closed so I could not bump into anything, you know, but just with my eyes closed I could tell what I was doing and so on, well of course it never worked and I only tried it once or twice, but I went to it——but at the same time he was a technocrat, you know this technocracy, you know? so, ah, we would go to these, ah, technocracy meetings and the, and the speaker would show how——like for example, victory gardens were foolish because if you put the man-hours and labor and, and the . . . bit of grass and all the seeds into . . . the manufacture of, ah——why you would build, a, you know, you know, understand, assembly line and all that, technocracy, very——but at any rate, then he was . . . also——course I was interested in women and he told me that he used to be and everything, course he still is and all that but, he ah, he, he got so absorbed in this philosophy that now he just sat and thought all the time, when he was home, and so on, and ah, whenever there was a woman around or anything why he was never, ah——but he was never, wasn't anything queer about him at all or anything, he was just . . . really, ah, a kind of a second-rate I guess, *now* as I think back upon him, intelligence; ah completely concern——*second*-rate intelligence——concerned about . . . Indian philosophy, see? so that he was all the time with it but I was with, ah, western type or something——

EVELYN. Primitive

CODY. ——of my own and so that——primitive, yeah that's, that's nice——so, ah, ah (*sighing*) he was a friend of mine for a long time, in fact I've forgotten all the ideas that he, ah, put across to me. Well of course the hangover from those ideas was enough so that like when I was in the joint, er, N.M.S.R., er, New Mexico State Reformatory there, the assistant warden, ah, Vagila, why, he was a little interested, so he gave me books like *The Law of Mentalism*, by Sechnal, which, showed that if you——and so on, things like that, which is all very. . . . But ah, the wall, the wall that Jack speaks of is not only the wall that, ah, the night that I escaped and made my way about forty miles after a day or two. . . . And, ah . . . terrible, close, so that even on the street I'd be suspicious, you know . . . ah, to this . . . parking lot expecting to find Kriloff when I'd get there at midnight but he just closed, and he's not there, but someone else *is* there, so that means he wasn't there, didn't work that night, and I'm looking over this wall . . . between the bus depot and the——and the, ah . . . parking lot on Sixth and Main. Other things about that——well, like I used to arm-rassle with somebody there I've forgotten who but we'd get on each side of the wall there, and arm-rassle. Well, other than that the wall has never had much, ah, in *my* mind, except, ah, I used to bang cars into it you know all day long (*laughing wearily*), part of my job, but there was no . . . was a common brick wall . . . (*fades away*) . . . so . . .

EVELYN. (*who laughed*) What's the wall, how did it begin?

CODY. Oh I just happened to mention the wall. He was in L.A. and he happened to see it

JACK. I went over there and I deliberately looked at it

CODY. Oh I see (*then laughs*)

EVELYN. Same wall? How'd you know where it was?

JACK. 'Cause he *told* me where it was

CODY. ——I was startin to talk——

JACK. ——I'd al——I had already seen it, but I didn't know——

CODY. ——yeah, that's right, it's where the buses . . . line up there, see, and the other side is where . . . the cars——

JACK. Sh——right . . . in the middle of cars . . . between them bus . . .

CODY. . . . that's right, that's right, and the other side are the cars, and the front is a shoeshine stand, and on the other side of the front is, ah, is a . . . hotdog stand, ah, and in the middle of the lot is a little shack where, where they . . . run the cars, the guy . . . who runs the cars . . . stands there, see; and (JACK,

Yeah, EVELYN, *Hmm*) the lot's a small lot, very fast lot, fast turnover, but very small *easy* lot, beautiful lot to work, Jesus, *because . . .* it has a eck——entrance and an exit, see, most of 'em you have to send 'em back out the same way they come in, but this one they could go out the alley, see, so it's a real great lot. Most, of course I made most money there and, had my best times there, and everything, you know, it's a real fine lot——I bought me a car, ran into a kid named Rinick, and he worked at another lot for System up the road a ways, and so he came over——but he was *very*——he was Indian, very, ah, reckless . . . guy, he didn't care about anything, but at the same time he was very . . . quiet, and didn't . . . you know, like an Indian, see, and ah, so, I'd get drunk with him a time or two and so we started goin up on Main Street where the Mexican waitresses were, and, but, one day why he was walkin down the street, and a little Indian girl walked by, and he——she——he said "I bet she's Indian" although he never spoke that he *was* Indian or nothin but that's what he said, and ah, so he said "Wait a minute Cody, I'll be back" and so he walked out on the street to follow this . . . well, in fact she wasn't pretty at all, sort of a dumpy little girl type, think about sixteen, and ah, so he came back in about an hour with the girl and he said "Say I don't have a car or nothin" which he didn't have but he used to rent cars all the time like——besides stealin them but ah, he said "Let me take that little car that you just bought," see? But it seems that I had bought the car, which was a 'twenty-seven Nash with seven tires for fifty dollars, but . . . I had a barber, special barber who did my hair, and he was also a painter, and he said that he'd paint my car, for a——twenty dollars or something, in the meantime I'd use his car which was a 'thirty Chevy in better shape than mine and everything, and so I just had it that day, so, Tony said, ah, "Here's——let me use your car . . . for awhile," and I said: "Oh sure," so he took the car and he didn't show up for four days, and when he *did* show up——course I wasn't *worried* about it, because I didn't have to take it back to the barber's for two weeks or so, see, and so I was, and I——at that time I didn't worry anyhow, I wasn't much——not that I was reckless but I didn't seem to really m——I wondered where Tony was, but——So when he did come back he'd smashed in a fender, but that was nothing, he was all full of this story about his love, see, this great——him and this girl that had been together for four days, see. So they moved in together after that, her name was Milly . . . huh?

EVELYN. Pretty music

CODY. *Pretty* music, hm-hm; and ah, course Milly was——she was really quite a nice lil girl, ah, ah we lived——they lived together, of course, I'd spend a many a night there and, but I lived in *South* L.A. with Harvey of course, but ah, one night Nick said "Say take me over to Whittier, will you?" and so I took him over to Whittier and ah, he'd used to live over there a couple of years ago in a——in a trailer that man-friend of his had, so he "I got something that I gotta get," so he got it but he didn't tell me what it was and so we come back, and by this time was pretty drunk, and he pulled it out and it was a gun. He said let's drive down Main Street so I drove down Main Street, oh in a convertible, a new convertible just, ah, we'd rented, a Mercury, 'forty-one, this was 'forty-two, and he ah, shot out the streetlights on Main Street, see, so then . . . I finally got him home, we got home, and, ah, went to bed, I went to sleep, and I woke up and a couple cops were shaking me and waking me up, detectives see, "Now what's goin on, where's the gun?" I said "What gun? what gun?" and I thought Jesus they followed us from Main Street, I don't see . . . how they did!——and ah, he said "Come on where's the gun?" and he started shakin me and here's Nick sittin on the couch and they punched him around a little bit, see, and he wouldn't tell them nothin or anything see, so he said "Wal we'll find it, we'll find it," so they *did* find it, Nick had hidden it under the, ah, dishes in kitchen cupboard. And, ah, so they said "Well come on now, we're gonna take you down," and we said "Wait a minute, what's goin on here now?" and so but he took us all to jail, and then soon as we got into jail, of course there were little incidents on the way and this and that but, I say "What the hell, Nick, how'd they find us," and he said, "Well," and then he confessed what had happened——while I was sleeping, passed out evidently, he had taken out the gun to load it, or to clean it, and so we were on the top floor of a four, five floor apartment house, and so he's workin on the gun like he *should* do pointing it down toward the ground see but he's on top of all these other people beneath him, and the gun went off. And I didn't hear it, imagine, it went off and went through the floor and . . . landed in the chair beside the bed at the head of a man sleeping there and, ah, ricocheted off into the windowsill, and it's about three, four o'clock in the morning but instead of havin enough sense to run down and straighten it out with the guy, Nick jumped in bed and covered up his head——after he threw the, after he threw the, ah, gun, up in the the——up in the cupboard, see, so naturally the guy downstairs, ah, ran to the landlady except for the fact even so things might have been alright because the landlady and himself would have come upstairs to inquire perhaps and not call the police, except that the man who——to whom accidentally Nick had shot near his head, was, ah, in fear of his life, he was from South America or something and some two brothers had been hunting him for years to shoot him, to kill him, and so when that happened he screamed, jumped out of the bed, and ran to the landlady, "Call the police," got on his knees and begged protection and everything, you see, by coincidence. . . . (*laughter*) And, ah, oh it was very frantic, he was Puerto Rican or something, or South or something like that, South America, and, ah——I saw the guy, he was in the hallway when they took us downstairs——and ah, that's what we——Nick found out later, we were in jail there for about ten days while they checked on the gun and everything, they finally let us out, but, ah, Nick was always doing stuff like that. One night, for example, we broke——another Mercury, same thing, rented a car, and we wanted to see who could go around in a circle the fastest on the parking lot see, turn the wheel as tight as you can, then go around, see (*Evelyn shudders*), from a standing start, well we did it and did it, oh you can do fantastic things with it, but of course, finally I had to beat 'em all you know so——see the idea is, to let out the clutch as fast as possible so you can get that terrific getaway and, you know, and, *but*, I let out the clutch so *fast* . . . that I snapped the universal joint, just went kkk, just broke right——you know, 'cause I just——I r-revved the motorfull, you know, the motor's goin like crazy, and you let out the clutch, why it just . . . breaks the driveshaft, see, 'cause the universal joint can't . . . immediately, so, we had our hangup there, I, I don't know what I finally did, we didn't pay for it or anything like that, never paid for anything in those days. (*Evelyn laughs*) Ah, those were . . . crazy times alright. Course that Milly she, after she met me why she liked me and so . . . after while Nick found out——

EVELYN. Oh I thought I remembered that name

CODY. ——what was happening, yeah, and so Nick realized that her and I was gettin a little now and then, and so, but still it wasn't anything between us or anything, he really didn't care by then, see? So the——but at any rate, ah, we were doing this and that, and this and that, one night there was a girl named Phyllis I picked up and, ah, we rented a car and Nick and Milly and *I* drove all night and finally I got in the backseat with Phyllis and then Nick went down the hill and ah the brakes gave out plus the fact I don't think he had it in gear, besides the motor off perhaps also . . . drunk and everything, at any rate he went through a stop sign at the bottom of the hill and went across the street and up over a curbing at one end to the pillars of the Sunoco station . . . type, you know those white pillar things, and ah——

EVELYN. Is that how you broke your nose?

CODY. ——he hit——no, I broke the nose another way, with Nick——

EVELYN. Nick was there then

CODY. No, with Nick it was *another* night, it was very comical, I was with a girl, that Peggy Sneed, you know, the one that I balled all the time? and her——

EVELYN. Huh?

CODY. Yeah, this other guy, ah, married her because he loved her, and all that but at any rate . . . but that happened just accidentally, we was going down very sober in fact, it was about six, seven o'clock at night, goin down Slauson Boulevard, we'd just picked me up and I was driving, of course, you——and so ah, Nick was sittin beside with Milly on his lap, and I said, ah . . . well I started to kiss her, and ah, instead of . . . saying "Nick take the wheel," I just with my hand pointed, at the wheel, obviously thinking that he'd have enough sense to grab the wheel, but instead *he* thought "Look at me" or "I'm kissing her," or, ah, pointin at the girl *he* thought——

EVELYN. "Watch . . . watch . . ."

CODY. So he, ah——yeah, yeah, "watch,"——so he started watching *me* and of course naturally no one took the wheel,

Milly couldn't drive anyhow, so at fifteen miles an hour, we
were just easing along, twenty at the most, we ran right into a
telephone pole and . . . broke the girl's rib, Peggy's, and cut his
scalp didn't hurt Milly, broke my nose. And——but at any rate,
they, ah——this time we come down the hill and we hit the post
and it snapped the bumper right in two, you know that's pretty
bad, *you* know, bumpers don't . . . break like that, but they did,
this one, you know 'cause they spring, but this one didn't, and,
ah, so we're very drunk, so I got out and saw a flat tire and
fixed the flat because I thought we had a flat but instead we
had——now that I started to drive away, that took a half hour,
and it was all four tires were flat! (*laughs*) . . . See, so, so we
started plunkin along the, ah, the——we were in Pasadena and
we was goin to L.A., it's about five in the morning, time to go
back to work you know, and, so we're goin along very happy
at two miles an hour and, ah, so here comes a car and then I
see it's the cops and then I still say "Well we ain't done nothin,
may as well stop, and try to——" so we got stopped, I told this
story before but I mean, it's what I'm talking about when you
tell the same thing over then you just, ah, say the words as they
come to your mind that you've already thought about before
and so there's nothing——you're not pleased by it, no one else
is, but the fact is, there's no, ah, spontaneity, or anything, there's
no, ah, pleasure, you see, because you're——you're just rehash-
ing old subjects, see? *You* know. (*Evelyn faintly speaks to Cody*)
Yeah! well, ah, they got us up in court——course, ah, Nick was
so mad, course I was very angry too——but all night long he
picked up this bunk, ah, that which is held from the wall by iron
chains, you know, see? the chain? and he'd pick it up and slam
it down, pick it up, slam it down——you know, real . . . frantic,
he's an Indian like I said, and he did that, and they threatened
to turn water on him and everything you know, and what happened was he finally broke the chain, believe it or not, it came
loose just at the last moment before we was going to trial at
nine o'clock, so we went up——course I won't elaborate on all
the trial, and all my——

EVELYN. Well that——what happened was that they got you
for stolen cars didn't they?

CODY. No (*protesting anxiously*), that wasn't a stolen car! no
it was a rented car! no they just caught us for——they charged

Nick with contributing to the delinquency of a minor because he was twenty-one and the girls and myself are both under eighteen see? And, ah, Phyllis as it turned out was a reform school escapee, you know——

EVELYN. Phew

CODY. ——eh, no one knew that, of course, so she went back to reform school; and, ah, Milly was sent back to her folks in Oklahoma, and Nick was given six months, and I was given out-of-state probation, see. (*Evelyn speaks softly*) Yeah, yeah that's what started my affair with Peter J. Rock, you know, that's, ah, you know . . . the attorney? the man——

EVELYN. Oh, *yeah*

CODY. ——I had four different tussles with him, and we tied; I won the first one and the third one, he won the fourth one—— the second and the fourth one. You know. But, ah, (*sighing*)—— Oh there's a hundred things to talk about, I really don't want to talk about that period because it's so, you know, in my mind, *as* just little things, like I say. . . . These things that I remember . . . I have talked about. (*Evelyn speaks softly*) Yeah, I used to be——but I was always the quiet one of the bunch, and all that you know, I mean I wasn't——see I'm more exuberant or wild or somethin now, or show-offy or whatever you might call it, you know, ah, than I was, then, I mean I wasn't that way at all, see, now I don't do anything and sound loud, before (*laugh-ing*) I used to be reckless and, and was quiet, not quiet like this tall silent type but I was just normal young kid going around you know

EVELYN. Normal!

CODY. *Well*, I mean, you know, normal-seeming, I'd go to work, and go home, go and try to get a girl or somethin, only thing was, these cars, and naturally all young guys in America they'll tell you, they'll——anybody you want to meet about . . . Saturday night fights or somethin, or . . . this or that happen-ing, it's all the same thing, everybody's that way . . . *you* know, except for the fact of course I had more opportunity working on the parking lots, and like I say, that's about the only thing I got any fun out of was driving cars. And, ah. . . . (*long silence*) . . . Well . . . (*he and Evelyn sort of laugh*)

EVELYN. Next question?

CODY. Yeah (*laughing, goofing*)

JACK. (*sepulchrally*) Are . . . you . . . ?

CODY. I'd just like to know what old Bull Hubbard thinks whenever he hears the "William Tell Overture" (*laughing*) You know? just the mere fact of the word, sometime before he gets hungup——

JACK. I wonder who made that up? hm?

CODY. Well, it's a . . . it's a, you know, some . . . writer, like Julien or, come through on a press, you know, a guy'll just say——that's what it is, after all, William Tell——type, huh?

EVELYN. Is that what he really did I wonder?

CODY. Well he says later——he reneged on that and said he didn't——he said it might have . . . went . . . happened that way but she put it on her head but what happened is he was just loading the gun or cleaning it and it went off or something, remember?

JACK. Yeah later . . . that's what he said——

CODY. But he never wrote, ah, to any one, has he, to really describe——I guess he's kinda afraid to——

JACK. Well you know what *Val* wrote

CODY. Val? no

JACK. Val King

CODY. What'd he write?

JACK. He said it was all her fault (CODY, *Yeah?*), that she . . . deliberately caused all this. (*Yeah?*) Yeah. Val of course is mad

CODY. He must be

JACK. But he says it was all her . . . her

CODY. Jesus

JACK. Deliberately put the glass on her head and dared Bull to shoot it off——

CODY. Well you know after she was walking around the room with him for five years while he sits there and shoots all the time, remember in New Orleans that . . . shootin at the Benzedrine tubes with his cap——with his pellet gun, you know, sit across the room all day, and he'd sit there, and about like where the candle bottle is . . .

JACK. We used to rush to put the fresh benny tubes up

CODY. Yeh, put the fresh benny tube up, and then he'd shoot, get up and walk over, and put a tube up——very hard to hit, you know, hard to hit!

JACK. And then *I'd* do it

CODY. He made one out of two, one out of three, some-times——*very* good, see? And we couldn't hit it hardly, maybe we might hit it once; then he'd show us how to draw all day you know, all day long he'd keep showing you how to draw the gun: "Now don't hold it up here! Don't shoot before you get it out! Hold it down here, hold it low, take your time, aim," *you* heard him, a hundred times, show you how to draw the gun . . .

JACK. After you left Mexico we used to draw all day

CODY. Yeah! Draw all day! Hear that, see?——I didn't say a thing with him in Mexico, I'd stand right there or somethin——

JACK. ——jess drawin——

CODY. ——see to see who's first, see?

JACK. ——see who's first——

CODY. See? "But I got ya, now, see, I got ya Jack! that's aimed right at yore heart, there, right at yore belly, see you was a little off to the side here see?"

JACK. And she would be *laughing* all the time

CODY. Yeah, so you can imagine her being around that all the time, you know, naturally some night she's gonna say "Come here and shoot this off my head." It's very plausible as you think about it, you know, I mean it's not only plausible it's just the thing you'd expect like Jack and I *were* earlier gonna speculate on what's gonna become of everybody, you know, like we know what happened to June, and we know what happened to Finistra, what's gonna happen to, say, Irwin? or what's gonna happen to, say, Jack, or Julien, you know what I mean?

JACK. Oh yeah! we didn't do that!

CODY. We didn't do that, no; 'cause I didn't have any ideas . . . to talk about

EVELYN. Sudden death?

CODY. Well now, just as you could surmise what would happen to June so too you could happen to surmise I suppose——

EVELYN. Would you have surmised that would happen to June?

CODY. Well you wouldn't expect her to do that, though, in the end, because . . . she . . . herself is——you know, she's used to his hangup, you'd think, and so she'd go, see? but we could speculate like what's gonna happen to you and me somehow that way perhaps . . .

EVELYN. You wouldn't have expected that to happen to Finistra would you?

CODY. No, although we were . . . talking and saying that Finistra had been looking for death anyhow, and when it finally did come he wasn't ready for it, wasn't lookin for it, he was——so really it's a joke on Finistra, see, 'cause it happened accidentally

JACK. We didn't do that

CODY. No. It's very hard, because of several things but if you could think about it, ah, you know . . .

JACK. Well, Hubbard, boy, I don't know what's gonna happen to him!

CODY. I just think he will go——here's what I thought about . . . Hubbard anyhow, that really nothing ever will happen to him as far as, you know, like, he could have a lot of times been hung-up, and *hung* (*laughing*), you see, but instead, yeah, he'll go on and on, and go down and he'll disintegrate in the . . . in the heat of the tropics; that's bound to be what'll happen, he can't come *here*, he can't go no place, see, he's going to go South . . .

JACK. He'll——he'll disappear into South America——

CODY. And he doesn't want to go anywhere else, really, and he knows it. (*silence*) That's what's gonna happen to him

JACK. And Irwin, nothing'll happen to him either

CODY. No, he's so afraid and calculating——

EVELYN. He's cautious

CODY. ——yes, very cautious, why when I was in New York there I said . . . we was in this, this girl, this Josephine's house, there and everything, we was in the bathroom, everything locked up tight and the windows all shaded and everything, you know, nobody in there to——nobody in the house, in the front room or nothin, just us, and we're sitting in there, and I got a roach and I'm blastin it, he says "Not so loud! not so loud!" you know (*laughter*) and everything . . . (*the end*)

FIFTH, FINAL NIGHT

CODY. (*singing, testing tape, laughing*) Ehhh . . . Uncle Joe Williams and his octet (*laughing*). . . . Phew! Ahhh . . . I need a cigarette, Ma-a-a. . . . Huh, do you want one? . . . Ah so we came over the George Washington Bridge, in the early morning d-a-w-n, (*laughing, long pause*). And there we were . . . we were——we were all very tired, we went to Vicki's. (*Jack flutes*)

And had a little difficulty waking her up and getting. . . . (*Jack flutes*) (*slammings of icebox*) And then . . . . . .

EVELYN. Then what?

CODY. . . . getting her downstairs, and the thing started. We were up to her a few minutes and, ah, then Huck said he was tired so he stayed there, and Bull and I went down to the point of the Bowery, ah, way below the Bowery, to . . . a chemical outfit down on the Battery I guess, and, ah——turn up the *music* there——and then the, ah . . . I had to double park while he was in there and he was gone about an hour, see . . . and got this chemical outfit, this . . . Bunsen burner (*Jack flutes*), curlicued glass tubes, you know, and curly *s*'s, curly *z*'s I guess, and, ah, oh (*sighing loudly*) we had to unpack 'em . . . (*laughing*) . . . and ah, we never really started to set them up, we——we went that night because, ah, we found June that afternoon, she told us that, ah, that they'd picked her up in the——in the railroad train, practically when she got *off* the train almost as though they were looking for her, which they weren't of course, but she was just walking around in that *turrible* dress of hers with Julie, and this old woman must have turned her in or something and the . . . detectives picked her up, and they took her to Bellevue, and she was there for an hour or two, three, four hours, and she was talking to the attendant there at Bellevue, the man who registered——the manager, the . . . something, you know, Bellevue, and, and she said "Well, my husband of course belongs to the University Club," and he said "Wha, what, what? Well? What? the University Club well, well my!" and he conferred with his colleague you know, and he said "Well Mrs. . . . Mrs. ah Hubbard, ah, we're very sorry that all this has happened, where could our driver take you?" . . . she said "Well, better take me back down to the depot, to the train depot, my husband's supposed to meet me there, he must be a little late, he drove up." So when we found her . . . someplace else but anyhow we found her . . . but no! I *do* believe that *was* the arrangement that they'd made, believe it or not, Bull said "Well I'll see you up there at the depot, when you get off the train we'll meet you up there," and ah, and she said, "Alright I'll wait on the——on the Forty-first Street side" or something like that, and so (*laughing*), they, I think in fact I *remember* exactly that was it, because we went out——goin into this Pennsylvania Station, Thirty-fourth

Street, see——but at any rate, ah, so we had——we went over on
the West Side there in the Fifties by Eighth Avenue, oh about
Forty-seventh and Eighth, and . . . rented a room right in there
and Harper came up very first night and turned Bull on, you
know, and Bull hadn't had any junk in about six weeks except
that paregoric that he'd been melting down, you know. Well
man, so all his problems and everything was over, and June of
course was having to struggle along and take care of everything,
you know, and, and I'd take her out on Times Square there in
that horrible dress, man, and I was, *me*, imagine!——ashamed to
walk with her, believe it or not, and I'd——rarely I feel——but I
really dug it though when we went into the cafeteria there and
everybody dug her but she just flipped along; she knew it too,
but you know, she was just so, ah, she took it, you know; so, ah,
because we had to go out to buy a . . . can of milk for the baby,
see only it was a half-can, cause it was a, ah——you know, so,
ah, she got it in half-cans, 'cause Bull and Harper——and man,
Harper, he's on his veins anyway you know and he can't get it in
I remember, and ah, then they——Oh, they stay there and talk
for a long time, in fact I think Bull went out with Harper after;
it seems to me Huck and me——no Huck, yeah I think Huck . . .
well I don't know what happened . . . that night; but anyhow
(*Evelyn laughs, says*, What were you on?) . . . probably . . . I was
on Nembutals and tea. . . . (*tittering laff*) Remember that tea?
it was always great, you know; and oh that's it! the next day
Huck and me went up to sell the tea, Bull said——see he's all
hungup on junk now——so he's sayin "Here Huck, here's the
tea you go out and sell it," though he didn't give him the tea,
but he said "Here's a sample, go up to some of the . . . guys
you know, the bellhops and everything" so here's Huck and
me, I'm driving, and Huck's cuttin in to see the bellhop——
there's one hotel up around Fifty-eighth and in there and the
West Side again and th——the bellhop said "Yeah," and ah, so
he went in and he sampled that stuff that Huck gave him, and
he came back out, said "Ough man, that's awful, that's *green*
tea," he says, "that's no good, it's not even cured, Oh Jesus,
it's terrible shit," and all that you know, and, yeah, well that's
not so——and, you know, of course he might have——Bull, that
particular (*laughing*), what I'm saying it got *us* high alright,
we must have blasted green tea all the time, there was this . . .

bellhop, no kiddin, he wouldn't pick up . . . although he wanted some——and that's all the incident *there* that I can recall. In the meantime I was always an errand boy going all around up and down in and out, and so the next three or four days we drove all over clear into New Jersey to——clear to Orange and West Orange, South Van-broy and every place (*laughter*) you know, no kiddin, *all* over I'm telling you, and, looking for places and all over Newark and in and out and up and down and weavin up in the Bronx. So about that time, second or third day, Huck by this time was having——he and Vicki weren't getting along so good you know and Vicki was hungup anyhow on account of Huck couldn't keep cuttin in and out there, so he went down the Village to see this Stephanie James accidentally he ran into her or something and so man right away he latched on down there, see——so Stephanie said "Yeah, I'll sell the tea for you Bull," and so Bull come over I'd say about the second or third night, so I drove Bull over to this Stephanie's at Second or Fourth——right across the street from the police station, too, right there on——in the Village, it was over near the, ah, the West Side Highway there by the viaduct, Hudson Street it was, yeah Hudson, and ah, so ah, we went up there and she was . . . *real* knocked out boy, she was ah, you know, on, ah, Nembutals and everything, but, and on junk too, she started taking junk right at this time, and also tea, see? and she was an entertainer in a joint over in Brooklyn, playing the piano, or the bass, or somethin, see

EVELYN. She's the one who gave you the records isn't she?

CODY. Yeah and she gave me all those records, that's right—— yeah she laid all these——when she left me, she was real high that night and she said "That's no good," she'd play it and she'd say "That's no good," she would give me that Lionel Hampton, some old Lionel Hampton, see, and she'd say "That's no good," she'd give me that, she cleaned out her *whole* file to give me all those records I brought back, and, ah, and I . . . dug 'em too, same with how she was diggin 'em but ah, any rate, ah, we go up there and Bull . . . sittin in the chair, you know, and ah, Stephanie over on the bed there, and Huck squattin around on the floor playing the record and, ah, I was sittin there, and we all blasted, and we blasted, she had a real . . . cool pad, it was real . . . cool light and everything. . . . Well so about the

second day I mention to her, ah, if she knew this Vicki and she
said "Oh yeh, well say——" Huck, of course, you know, both of
them——so about the second day she said "Well why don't you
bring this Vicki down?" see, well Vicki was trying to move out
of her place, she was all hungup, so I brought her down, Vicki
got all excited 'cause she wasn't dumb about *those* sort of things,
so naturally (*sniff*) soon as she got down there she started layin
it all on this gal, you know, and so the next morning I had to
go up and get all Vicki's things in the jeep, bring 'em all down,
you know——And I remember Vicki and I talking about you,
you know, I say "Well Vicki I got a real good gal out West, you
know, and everything, soon as I get some money I'm going to
go out there," and she said "Well that's cool, that's cool," and
I'm saying . . . I'm saying, ah, you know "She'll pick up with
me though I guess" and she says, "Well, long as she's a head,
you know, course I get my migraine headaches, you know, my
high b——my——but I'm telling you this last bunch of tea I'm
smoking knocks the headache right out, you know" she said,
she's hungup on headache and also "Meet me on a Hundred
and first," she lived on Ninety-ninth but there's a guy hangin
around or a cop or something, so she was afraid to stand out
in front of there if he come up and anything like that, see. All
the time I had tea or something in the car, you know——so, I
remember one night for some unknown reason or something, I
was going to a show or something like that which . . . I can't understand, but I had that whole . . . ah, two jars, two Mason jars?
quart Mason jars full of tea? and, ah, it was in this open jeep you
know that you can't lock, and so I parked her right there by my
lot on, on Eighth and Forty——and Thirty-fourth, by the Hotel
New Yorker there where I used to work, and I asked a policeman to please watch it, you know, the cop see, and I'm high
and I'm cuttin up to the cop, see, and I'm saying "I say officer,
I'm worried about the——my jeep here, I'm worried about it,
I'm goin to the show or something you know, and everything,
and ah"——He said "Oh I'll watch it, I'll keep an eye on it, kid,
don't worry"——(*laughs*). Phew! (*laughter*) So, anyhow, so, ah,
they, they'd have done that two or three——in the meantime,
ah, Huck and I, occasionally Huck would rissle up, rustle up a
dollar or two, and the World Series was going on, you know,

so I'd spend most of my afternoons in the bar watching the World Series; and, ah, Huck finally got a room, opposite the fire station on Forty-seventh and Eighth, right in there *again*, ri——right in there, see, and ah, so I slept with Huck couple nights there, you know, and ah, he had that skin disease——he laid the money——and June and Bull were in the same room, some little tiny room, they didn't have a *cent* . . . for any reason or any kind or any anything . . . *Harper*, actually, it was Harper I think who was laying out the dollar or two, every day, see? So, about the fifth or sixth day, why, everything was getting pretty frantic, and, ah, I was spending my time between here and there and up and down, you know, in fact that's when I stayed with, ah, Harold Ginsberg down in the Village with Huck, you know, we finally stayed down there three or four nights with *him*, two or three, one or two——and then, ah, . . . and then . . . ah, we was all, down in——and *then* Bull sold his tea . . . finally . . . Stephanie made the connection, and he sold it all for a hundred dollars, on a fifth floor flat room that I couldn't go up, I stayed down in front, see? and Bull, Bull went up and I think Huck went up with him; he sold it to four dagos, for a hundred dollars, the tea, see? So they had some money, and ah, so he bought some junk and everything, and ah (*laughter*)——that's right, he did, yeah, he really did, that's right, because I remember, well let me tell you——so held this new supply of junk, and in the meantime he's making connections *with* Harper, I think Harper was . . . pushin a little or somethin but anyhow I'd always have to go down to Twenty-third and Eighth and Harper he'd go in there and see a few fellows and I *know* it wasn't for junk 'cause he had some, see, so he might have been pushing just a little bit to a couple of his friends, see, a little bit, one or two——Well anyhow, so ah, we're down at Stephanie's one day, by now everybody was getting on everybody's nerves, nobody liked each other, *you* know; and Vicki and Stephanie didn't get along anyhow, and Huck and Steph——course Huck really knew how to cut around, say "Oh nothing bothers me," and everything you know, so he was staying out of harm's way more or less you know, course *I* wasn't involved at all, and ah——but at any rate, there was a definite rupture and break there, finally it happened when I called up——Bull said "Well call up this

Stephanie now," at eleven o'clock in the morning see, I called
up, she said "Goddamn you"——she'd got high on Nembutals
the night before you know or something and, and ah, so she
was laying there all doped up see for twenty-four hours so when
I woke her up right in the middle of that sleep I had to let the
phone ring three or four hours, you know, couldn't let——Bull
had to see her or something——so she said "You and that Hubbard," and "Stay away" and all that see, "Don't ever come——"
so Bull, we never went back, see——but, when that happened,
before that happened, or *something*, one day there was a house
painter who was a real square, see, but he knew Stephanie, so
he was up to Stephanie's there, and ah, so, he also knew Vicki
or something or other, ah and——from old days——and——but
he'd got married in the meantime to a Catholic girl, a religious dago-type girl, only she was Catholic——well not *only*,
but I mean——besides——n——she is not dago-type *because* she's
Catholic, that's what I'm trying to say, (EVELYN, *Hmm*) but
she is dago-*looking*, that's what I'm saying; and he was a painter,
and he worked on the George Washington Bridge for four years
now paintin it back and forth, see, he's done it two and a half
times, see, (*Evelyn laughs*) and——yeah!——and——but he's a
square, and he lives up in the Bronx! So he said——he invited
Bull, June, the baby and me to come up and live with him, and
he had a two or three room place, imagine, so we accepted——
EVELYN. (*laughing*) Course!——
CODY. Moved everything up there——imagine this now!——
goin up that East Side highway and go to the Bronx up there
and everything, and these . . . other girls even more square, the
. . . religious girl, you know, and the *baby*——and they're having
trouble *any*-how, and invited them up just out of the kindness
of his heart mostly, *you* know, like I'd——you know, but I'm
trying to say (*sniff*), so the first day we're there——

(TAPE INTERRUPTED BY THREE MINUTES
OF ED WILLIAMS THE FRISCO HIPSTER ON
AN EVENING WHEN CODY IS BRAKING DOWN
THE LINE FOR THE RAILROAD IN STORMS)

JACK. (*whispering*) Jimmy! (*handing microphone to him on sly*)
ED. (*talking in background to Evelyn*) . . . though parts of the
center are——but most of it is pretty dark and, ah, tangled . . .

EVELYN. Uh huh, and the way he did it, too

ED. Hm hmm . . . but even the fact that it is——in drawing that type of——I doubt is——aren't as good . . . it indicates a, ah, that there is still a, ah, like there's still, ah, you know, and it's, it's (*pointing at drawing, gesturing over it*) still a unit, you know, it's sort of warped and confused a little here and there, but, it still is, ah, you know, a oneness, it isn't completely broken up, it isn't like a schizophrenic . . . split, or anything like that, you know——

EVELYN. Oh not at all, pretty solid, really (*laughing like Irene Dunne in an old Cary Grant comedy*)

ED. Yeah, mi——mine are always——ah, mine are fairly schizoid

JACK. (*singing*) "Just . . . one . . . of those things . . ."

ED. Ah, there're mandalas, you know, like that (EVELYN, *Hmm*) . . . you know, psychic drawings but they're ah——

EVELYN. . . . Rorschach . . .

ED. No that's a——that's a different type of painting, that's something else, this is what Jung——I'm talking through Jung now——

FRANK SINATRA. (*on the radio, loud, turned up by Jack*) "Lover . . . when we're dancing . . . keep on glancing . . . in my eyes . . ." (*Evelyn laughs*)

JIMMY. Well now tell me some more about my artistic efforts here, ah——

ED. Well I mean I'm *talking* about your personality (Jimmy's finger drawings like little Emily's at nursery school) . . . your personality, from *that*, is——Well just a moment

JIMMY. What?

ED. Yeah. I'm getting ready to tell you something (*finding a paper in his pocket*) (*unfolding it crinkly*) Like . . . your personality is pretty . . . surface . . . it's the same . . . in front of you, see . . . and like there are a few sort of connections and now and then with your *real self*, your center (*pronounced like "sinner"*), mostly you're out on the outside of yourself, you're pretty well externalized. . . . Ah. . . . What would you say were, ah . . . four directions, or four sides or four something of your personality . . . like, ah, four, four words that inc——that would, ah, ah, include all the . . . parts of your——of your, ah, makeup. . . . Ah, words on the order of, ah——

(TAPE RESUMES WITH CODY WHO HAS
TOLD HOW HUBBARD ALMOST DIED
TAKING AN OVERDOSE SHOT AT THE
HOME OF THE WASHINGTON BRIDGE
PAINTER AND LAY PALE AND SWEATING
ON THE CHAIR AS EVERYBODY RAN
AROUND FRIGHTENED)

CODY. ——the fact that the tea wasn't that good but anyhow, ah, I had to drive him up to the Bronx there too one night . . . (*drinking wine*) . . . and, but any rate, finally at that time Bull's parents came to see the baby, and they immediately installed him in that . . . exclusive beach club out there Atlantic Beach, so after that I had to drive thirty miles every day, I'd keep the jeep, and I'd spend the night——*Bull* bought me a room, ah, for a week, and ah, so I sat in the room, only it wasn't for me, it was for him to come uptown every second or third night to pick up junk and stay overnight, see, and June was of course out there in the beach club now, see——(*laughing*). Dig how *her* environment changes! Every day she gets up, she goes down the——and all the old biddies, it's the middle of Janurary you know or somethin like that, er, it's very late, it's comin—— approaching December anyhow, it's ah, it's wintry, but they're out there playing in the sand and everything and the kiddies and all that you know, see (*sniffing*), course June never goes out of the apartment, but (*laughing*), but *apartment*, man, what a——it was a great huge, the carpet four feet thick you know and walkin through this and they had all kinds of . . . objects dee art (*Evelyn laughs*) (*both laugh*) and, ah, so ah, terrible place——But I had to go out there in and out——but it *was* pretty nice, though it was *right* on the ocean, real great, I'd like to stay there come to think of it . . . because, *you* know, you'd see the waves right there at your feet, you know, and oh they had, ah, service of every kind, you just call up and they send it up and things you know——
EVELYN. Yep that's where you belong——(*laughing*)
CODY. Y-e-a-h (*semi-laughing*) and, oh it was real great, maids cuttin in and out and up and down . . . it was apartment . . . places, *you* know, oh it was everything, Atlantic Bleach club, and ah, (*Evelyn laughs*), yeah, beach, bleach, oxyd or closol,

likesol, Clorox, and so, ah——Well finally it got——course Bull
and I slept together one night too, that's when I showed him
that full length drawing you'd made of me nude, and it didn't
look like me at all——

EVELYN. (*laughing*) Why?

CODY. The . . . figure and everything was very but the *head*——

EVELYN. Too little huh?

CODY. ——yeah . . . that's right . . .

EVELYN. Too little——

CODY. Yeah . . . that's right. . . . Yeah, tool——that's right, but
it didn't at *all*, though you know (*Evelyn laughs*), I thought it
did at first. (*Evelyn murmurs*) Yeah . . .

EVELYN. (*yelling out laugh*) I *know* it!

CODY. (*both laughing heartily*) No, I was amazed though
'cause I remember when I pulled it out

EVELYN. (*laughing*) Who said it *did!*

CODY. ——you know I hadn't seen it——for a long time (*laughing*), no that's right, I know it didn't . . . so ah (*their laughter
subsiding*), but it got too expensive, so Bull after a week gave
up the room and decided to keep the jeep out at Atlantic Beach
(*Evelyn yawns* Hm Hm) . . . to retrieve, see? And, ah, so I said,
"Well I'll bring it out to you——"

EVELYN. What were they staying in New York for anyway?

CODY. Oh I know, he just decided to come to New York for
awhile, so ah——(*Evelyn murmurs*) Oh they sent him money,
you know, he just didn't have any *then*, the check hadn't come
or something, see? Oh yeah, they gave him about five hundred
a month, or somethin, and every two weeks the check comes,
well . . . anyhow, so, ah, by God, but, I still had the jeep though,
no I never was without the jeep although that threatened a time
or two, but it never quite happened, you know not in terms of
a threat, or anything obviously but the just the idea (*sniffs*), so
but anyhow I lost the room so then Harper and me, ah, were
together there . . . that day, and so in the meantime——

EVELYN. Harper was a waiter too, wasn't he?

CODY. No, Harper is an old——you know how he makes his
money? stealing overcoats, you remember the overcoats——

EVELYN. Yeah, but I thought you told me he was a waiter

CODY. Oh, man, no——Jack says no——

EVELYN. No, huh? Huh! (*laughing*)

CODY. And ah, (*Jack flutes*), so ah, Harper, says, ah "Well, we'll . . . go up and see——I been stayin the last three, four days with this kid Jimmy Ransome, although he's not a kid, *he's* a waiter I think (*Evelyn murmurs*) Yeah Jimmy Ransome, yeah (*Evelyn murmurs*), yeah, that's right, so when it went up there; Jimmy was a real queer duck you know, he was, ah, he wasn't queer, as far as——but I think obviously he *was* queer come to think of it——

EVELYN. Something about him you had his name written down when you came out——

CODY. I owed him fifty dollars!

EVELYN. Oh that's right . . .

CODY. Yeah, I still do to this day owe him fifty dollars—— (*Evelyn laughs*). . . . It, it's all for Jimmy Ransome, hadn't been for Jimmy Ransome darling, none of this would have happened——

EVELYN. (*groans*) Oh!

CODY. ——you can blame it——

EVELYN. ——I hate you!

CODY. ——Yes!——Wal I think something drastic happened to him, or was about to, or will, or has; if he hadn't a give me that fifty dollars, in two days Jack and Irwin would have been there . . . er I didn't know that though, and they would have given me the money and then I'd——(*Evelyn laughs*) They didn't have any money either . . . so all you have to blame is yourself (*imitating melodrama*) for listening to me. Really it's a——it's my fault——(*Evelyn murmurs*) . . . yes, it should have——you should have, listened to——(*Evelyn murmurs*), mop, (*laughs, Jack flutes, a peaceful moment*) (*Evelyn murmurs again*, What did Mama say Mary Saral?) (*Jack flutes, Evelyn murmurs:* Too near its aral? *talking to little Emily in stairway who came down to see grownups in the kitchen like Proust when he was a child in the staircase of time and memory*) (*steps going up*)

EVELYN. Oh!

CODY. Phew . . . yeah, down here (*laughs*) . . . so that's the story of Oscar Pettiford and his quintet, and Joe ah . . . Os-s-s-s-s-s-s, O-s-s-c, OH-s-s-s-s-s-s-s-s-s-s-shrunski . . . the Third. (*Evelyn murmurs*) He's old friend of my father-in-law's's's's's (*imitating W. C. Fields*) law-w-w-w-w-s grandmother's son's, wife's, aunt's s-s-s-s-sister's s-s-s-s-s cousin . . . I *think*. It might

have been, he was an old friend of my father-in-law'ssssss, ah, *and* grandmother—sister . . . . aunt . . . . . son- . . . in-law's . . . . (*dish clanks*) . . . . well anyhow I know cousin's finished. I was trying to remember what I just said but I couldn't, 'cause I didn't try to when we were before; that's pretty bore——poor I guess, hey? But I always like the way Humphrey Bogart tells it . . .
JACK. Is Svenson still open?
EVELYN. (*laughing*) Yust until meed-night.——No!
CODY. Until eleven
EVELYN. Until eleven

(*a finger snapping*)

JACK. What? We just missed by ten minutes, the Rocky Road . . .
EVELYN. Seems to me he said he was going to stay open later . . .
JACK. Sure!
CODY. Well you might catch him just as he's closing, takes, hm, about five minutes to close
JACK. Eh!
CODY. Man, three Rocky Roads. (JACK, *Eh!*) . . . Get your shoes on, huh? (JACK, *Yeah*) And hurry though, because no kidding, he is closing, ah——
EVELYN. Probably is closed now
CODY. Yeh, well, just . . . say . . . hiya! Wait a minute, *he* knows me, no wait——
EVELYN. No, no, no hon!
CODY. No he *does* know me!
EVELYN. Yeah but he doesn't like you——doesn't like you . . . . . (*long silence, Jack is gone, tape ends on a radio blues singer singing Ba-by . . .*)

(TAPE CONTINUES WITH COLORED REVIVAL MEETING ON RADIO)

PREACHER. (*screeching*) WE KNOW HOW TO PRAY!
PEOPLE. PRAY!
PREACHER. MEANWHILE HE TOOK CHANCE ABOUT JE-SUS ONE DAY
PEOPLE. OH OH!

A VOICE. BLEST IS THE LORD, WUNNERFUL!!

PREACHER. AFTER AWHILE THEY KEPT UP ON PRAYIN

PEOPLE. YEAH!!

PREACHER. AFTER AWHILE!!

PEOPLE. AFTER AWHILE!!

PREACHER. JEEEE-EE

PEOPLE. JEE-EE!

PREACHER. ZUS!! I SAID AFTER WHILE!!

PEOPLE. AFTER WHILE!!!

PREACHER. JEE-SAS!

WOMEN. JEE-SAS!

PREACHER. I WALK IN THERE——

PEOPLE. I WALK IN THERE!

PREACHER. I WILL——

PEOPLE. I WILL!!

PREACHER. I HEARD THE WAY HE WORKS——

PEOPLE. OH-OOO!

PREACHER. AFTER AWHILE HE *TOLD* HIM!! CRASH! BOAA!

PREACHER. ——AND WHILE HE TOLD——

PEOPLE. YEAH. HEAH!!

PREACHER. ——SIGHT!——

PEOPLE. YES!!

PREACHER. I HEEEARD——I HEEEEEEEEEEERD——I HEERD A MAN MAY DO WORKS

PEOPLE. MOTHER!
MOTHER!

       PREACHER. I GOT MY SURANCE!
       BUT THEY CAN'T DO IT!——
        I HEEEEEEEEEEEEEEEEERD!

Imitation of the Tape

C OMPOSITION . . . . by Jackie Duluoz 6-B
"Now up yonder in Suskahooty," said Dead Eye Dick——
no, I exaggerate, his name was Black Dan——"up yonder in Sas-
kahoty," said Dead Eye Dick Black Dan, "we used to catch suckers every day on Main Street down by the bank, you know the
one with the red bricks, that I was standin in front of when——
but you introduced (ain't that right?) me to them two suckers
from Edmonton or somethin——yeh, that's right (just when you
said that you reminded me——"This was in Muscadoodle, Wyo.,
many years ago, had a circus there, we was makin the line from
around Ogallala, Nebraska, clear to the Willamette Valley——my
old lady got sawdust on her dress in Ohio that year——shucks
and god-*damn*, I'm gonna go to Charleston, West Virginia
Saturday night, or jump in the river, *one*."

But no, wait in here, don't you know I'm serious? you think
I'm?——damn you, you made, you make, the most, m——I
guess——but now wait a minute, till I l——but no I'll jump
on in, I meant to say, w——about whatever——well, I swear, I
swow——whar's home just like that little character with Barney
Google or that used to be Barney Google the hillbilly, the little
bald guy with the jug always yellin "Lowizie whar do you put
my——corncorb pireper? or (English almost wasn't it?)——hee
hee hee——what? No, I wandered that time, on peyotl which
is total I'll tell all. Baby won't you laff?——I had to stop and
th——it really is almost impossible to go on w——and yet so
deciduously silent or something, my dear says the British Noble
like James Mason at the moon, but now I forgot what he'd say
and go on with my p——so stoned in Boston the time I had
my suit pressed in a little tailor shop on Beacon Hill before
I went to my——nor can I ever forget the young fellow with
me——Ladies and Gentlemen, move aside please, let me introduce, ascertain and try to keep accumulating——meet the one
and only Roger Buttock, descended from the Buttock Bank
Indians. Too, there was a movie house (what? house?) around
the (wah? corner?) of the Strand Theater not to be confused
with hair strand, in my dreams: this perfect little B- or C-movie

full of Sunday afternoon children——a dream! See? Never no hassles there, (they had a toilet. I go down to it in the dream and hang around and drink rotgut when I get too old to enjoy the picture), nothing, no hassles, I love my sweet dreams, they sustain me, I see——I see——what! Wake up to reality my boy! Howk? Signed, for today, for now——no we'll continued right along the monologo.

The newspaper lengthens, but ever without true dimensions within the lyre, the gyre, the——oh——the——the——oh——well, grier. (*Laughter*). Wait a——how they skirl the edges of Endeemion! O brassuges! Oh peyotl total bongoola, Oh mogul rogal portals! Mawrdegras; fine too . . . with an *s* but never . . . (pause) . . . jungled . . . (dared); first, voodoo, written by Bud Powell and Miles Davis; well and so I said to him "Hey sweetiepie lay off my old cunt" and the cop was off duty, standing in the door, with a hard-on! Reading that little twenty-five cent pocketbook "Marihuana"——"Sally you old (Nova Scotian whore) tuffle!" Then high on tea I came to the Indian plateau and drew a deep breath, and made the following introductory speech (to the voice of Yma Sumac?)

1. Definite depth
2. Cattishness
3. Sitting on a stool
4. Loves to sing
5. A woman, a woman
6. Handy hands
7. Fainting Desdemona of the Andes
8. Twirling Barrett from Wimpole street
9. Her musicians say Motherfucka, fuck-a

"Eee! ee!" she says——even editors of great publishing houses listen——"oompaca-a-g——"

Growl! I didn't know the jungle was so (man this is a r——of, why, ah, in the Cathedrals of Europe I used to weep and wail for sight of such——ah——such fine and wondrous metadinal finure; if they call th——I'm——you've got to be serious, I feel——I hear——calls on horizons to which I can never reply because it is completely impossible for me to go that far without a Safari. But I'd love a Safari in Mexico, or in Peru, or Chile, or Ecuador, or all the headwaters of the Orinoco where only several weeks ago a party pitched camp, in the area of the Quarhica and Quarahambo tribes——but here's our B-movie again. All my

B-movies, all our B-movies, taught us what we know now about paranoia and crazy suspicion. Yet would you throw away a good B-movie?——get high on T, and go and see them mope and murp and muckle in a mad dream? Now I want to lie among the salmon plasters of the Plateau Monastaire, the monastery among the muskat and the showering Judean maguey madrubber, *cactu spiritu*; with Hugh Herbert.

In Africa with the eye fixed on straight (they're trying to scare us, the Indians are trying to scare us, I love the Indian, I am an Indian, my mother has Iroquois blood and I have not fathered a Cherokee, nor a Sioux——nor an Omaha short, sad, ting-haired and squat in the rainy dusts of Nebraska, of Shelton, Nebraska where the railroad eats up a watertower as it smashes by for or from Chicago. But, ah, not to get hungup, man, now you're to listen to *me* now, and let *me* tell the story——see?—— right——of the Omaha I'd ever, or Woo!——interestinger tales about the——and then there was the Kwakiutl (teach 'em how to spell! codutl will save the world! codutl will save the world!).

This movie house of mine in the dream has got a golden light to it though it is deeply shaded brown, or misty gray too inside, with thousands not hundreds but all squeezed together children in there diggin the perfect cowboy B-movie which is not shown in Technicolor but dream golden (incidentally some of the Mornings of those Sundays I have definitely spent riding the freightcars of a spectral little Canadian choo-choo railroad which however in one dream suddenly became so vast that it took me to great tremendous distances, in Siberia for instance, where on a gray month I paddled up the Obi, yes the very Obi itself, in a canoe, or small boat, with my mother, deeper and deeper into the pounding drums of the North Pole behind the ass of Siberia and the Salt Mines); but dream golden with silver arras of mist; across the street (I'm not kidding) is a coalpile with blue diamonds in its dust but this is only noticeable at night: Listen if we're all going to be serious——but now I've already lost my seriousness, or that particular one that came there, since the time you said, boo, too, or *did* you say boo? if at all, anyway——but stop yelling my name over the air! Bunch of sweating phonies! Oh the sins of America! O poor deal! O Depressions! O wanton——O soft fields of Virginia when they crossed the river on a May night, news of junctions ahead, signs

that a farmer's barn would soon win a name to rank it with the
turrible name of Waterloo! O weep not Chekhovs! Oh boy with
the dewy musket, in a doorway, or a flaptent, or under a tree by
the hanging carcass——O soldier bugler, soldier lad, SOLDIER
BOY of sadness——(and over by the courthouse Grant lets out
a fart heard around the works, the earthworks). O redoubts! O
rebops! O mighty name of A. P. Hill! Oh Oxford scholars——O
merders of Paris! and murgers of stock!! O murkers!——A. P.
Hill, tell you more about——A. P. Hill soon as the U.P. News
comes on and the results of the Eleventh Race at Arlington Park
purse five thousand million dollars, Bloom let the soap melt in
his backpocket he was so hot. I used to be a sports reporter (on
the *Kwakiutl Herald* in Winnepunk,) on the *Lowelltown Sun*,
up in the musk country, the French-Canadians come mushing
down from Canado to visit relatives and for several days there's
nothing but laughing and scratching on Moody Street——joyous clear cries in the——what? Roy Eldridge?——Roy Eldridge
was playing with a band when I sold candy in the theater——
or is——was——playing——and do you know how far that goes
back?"

"No, how far does go back that hype?"

"As far back as a faroff horse, don't ever let that horse catch
you, he's got a shroud that rider."

"Oh now you're just trying to scare me you dear fool——
shrouds? a rider? didn't we gently kick him off our plateau with
Phillip?"

"Oh no; Rendrovar, they shoved his glittering body down
into the ice; seven masked men and a cabinet in which a clock
ticks to its own mahogany echo, undampened by human hands,
awake, alive, by its virtue of engines——ah, being a machine——it
has won the ability to live and tick by itself till the spring runs
out, and can Shelley be far behind, with this damn generation
not doing anything but waiting for spring, summer, and fall to
come."

"Oh Mowdelaire! He leaned and gleaned, balcony——say,
why did I say balcony? Hand me that bloody handkerchief,
I guess I done gone to meet the (in Washington, D.C. the
young hipsters who run the White Tower late at night and
freefeed their subterranean flipped chicks have no conception
whatever of the dignity which we are supposed to employ in

the contemplation of Abrahaam Lincoln or even plain Abraham) gone to meet the Nay-z-eye, the neigh-zye, the Na-zi menace by myself, in the everywhere I go, gigolo bop to my furlined boots upon which I wear a pearl necklace like Billie Holiday and her dog (Nobody Digs My Dog Like I Dig My Dog) (This movie house——) Saying, 'This movie house' is obviously a camp, isn't it?"

In the morning the campfire girls ate the ashes of the night before in their breakfast bacon.

OF COURSE WE CAN'T POSSIBLY conceive of ruining your weekend but could you possibly leave the machine under my tree or I'll flip my wig.

LADY GODIVA. (*clad*) They knocked me out on a stone of hemp the other——AT THIS POINT IN HIS DREAM DULUOZ WOKE UP and recall——though admitting the blue blur of that——Duluoz woke, recalled that he hadn't seen his father for the longest of times and that possibly he must be dead just as real as death. "Well then," he thought, leaning on the boxcar down the edges of which ran the stain of his sperm, "if I'm to be bateyed in the night for no other reason"——or in whichever way he must, then, have phrased his thoughts, being nineteen ears or years (not corn) old and. . . . Well, you see, I hung myself up. Duluoz. . . .

On the North Atlantic Ocean at dawn, in the month of October, the gray light turns bright fog white and shines whitely on the wet decks of great irondecked vessels groaning to the fro fray. (Meade should have lost an arm at Antietam, the ditty batath; look at all the boys kid under his command, the bloody genius! ". . . enlightened by the vollied glare," as Herman Hankering Melville says, or sez, (Hey Millie!) (this, just then, see, an imitation of my father's column, written, my ah, father writing a column called Ferd or Ez or Ed or something where the humble little guy takes his wife to the movies every (opening) Thursday night to see (oops) the show and to comment about it, picture first, for it was a movie column, and then (oh um) . . . the seven acts of Hespasi, Vaudeville, when fellows with the leftover white paint of clowns on their necks used to cut through redbrick alleys with that one white or brownish light illuminating the gravelly entrance, with, as in cartoons, sad sleepy 3 A.M. (oh it's three o'clock in the morning) houses, or apartment houses, with the cats on the backfences where a tree in Brooklyn dearold grows, and the front part, where, somehow as in a Kafka sweet nightmare, a great clock telling the time is installed: as if, now listen I know I m——where, I say, and as if some landlord so beneficent as in feudal times had installed a giant clock for his tenants to tell time by when they come home drunk with Moon Mullins at all hours and wrap themselves around rubber lampposts with X's in their eyes or X's for their eyes.) (But X's will save the world!) Here, not, who, now these people (I am not incoherent) but the matter at hand, harrumph:

The headline reads (as follows) Arrumph, Kaff!
PEYOTL IS TOTAL Essay on Cody Pomeray
Part I Beyond Cody There are
          only Thieves, the Sins
          of America be Damned.
HAVE YOU EVER KICK-
ED A REEFER?
Ball Hits Fence
in Middle Board . . . . (what I used to do, throw
                                                  a rubber ball, after sup-
                                                  per, at a board in the
                                                  broken window of the
                                                  neighbor barn and when
                                                  I hit it flush in the middle
                                                  it was a strike, when I
                                                  barely missed and it hit
                                                  the protrudent shelf and
                                                  flew off into the air, it
                                                  was a hit, a fly ball, which
                                                  sometimes I caught to
                                                  make the put out; thus
                                                  being pitcher and out-
                                                  field, center fielder, really,
                                                  plumb at the same time.
                                                       For this memory I
                                                       didn't have to go back
                                                       to dear old Compton

> my hometown; Jack
> L. Duluoz, Compton,
> Calif. (LOCAL BOY
> INDICTED FOR
> FORGERY)

But it's still quite essential to follow:

> Extra News! Billoboard running over, oh Billboard Run-
> ning over, O Billboard, Oh Gilgo, O

Walking one Time 'Cross
the City of Providence (where they used to cut the turkey's
head off)

> PROVIDENCE AWAITS THY SENSES
> FOR 'TIS WITHOUT SAID PROVIDENCE
> WE DIE

Then three balls not unlike the balls of a——an old jewish
without a capital W pawnballer, ballpawner, so fat and
thick on balls he oozes munificence——but I dawdle, to
go on——

> FAGS ANONYMOUS especially me and the lit
> ones (this does not mean
> literary, it means lit
> with a match)
> It's so cold in Suskahooty that you can't see across the
> river; northern Canada, y'know; (I spied a young
> lady in yon, yon, yon)
> WmRnHearst didn't have as m——

Nobody digs my dog like I my dog dig
But of course I don't have to go through all that, we'll
t——when we're bloody well finished or shall I wait for
the early morning fog when equestriennes clad only
in skin fighting tideropes . . . I have seen the rp, the
proud ladies of the Hore Show, Horse Show, I have
seen, but I have seen, typing is a goof
FRANK GOFF WAS THE NAME OF THE
CATCHER FOR THE PHILADELPHIA PONTI-
ACS. YOU'VE GOT TO MAKE UP YOUR GOD-
DAMN MIND IF YOU WANT TO GOOF OR
DON'T WANT TO GOOF OR WANT TO STAY
ON ONE LEVEL KICK OR GOOF AND KICK
ALONG MISSPELLING AND

I had conceived of Art Rodrigue in this fashion; Art Rodrigue
the first baseman for the Philadelphia Pontiacs; but don't explain any further; he was just like Al Robert, but Portuguese
of course and so invested with that particular raw power they
showed on sundrowsed porches of mid Moody afternoon,
sometimes with guitars with which they imitated American and
Western kicks but were really, as only Saroyan knows, hung on,
or hung behind, their own great homeland kicks. Same with
the Canadians . . . the guitar for them was a sign of——but
wait, I was on the Portuguese, and Art Rodrigue; for some
reason too, this Art Rodrigue was to be exactly, to look exactly,
infinitely perfectly like Al Robert, the same big tanned seriousness, like the last firstbaseman I saw, the last ballgame I saw, so
beat am I, was a Class D league game down in Kinston, North
Carolina and where, true to God by Gawrsh, like I say, the first
baseman, H. W. Mercer, was tall and tanned and morose and
serious and mooning for Hollywood, that is, to eventually become a movie actor, like say, Gene Bearden of the ideal minor
league ballplayers of the movies and even of Ring Anderson by
Gawrsh, you know, Ring Anderson, who wrote the *Magnificent
Andersons.* Well by God, Art Rodrigue was going to look exactly like Skippy Al Robert; and so, especially because he wore
this light cream and orange uniform of the Pontiacs his dark
face particularly glowed on the green and dazzling playingfield
of afternoon when men squint to see the wheat and the day.
At night, I had no doubt as I lay in my bed, Art Rodrigue and
other ball players throughout the league, imaginary as it was,
went out and spent evenings with naked and willing women; I
could even see Art Rodrigue sitting facing a naked Armenian
girl sitting on a Cape Cod settee with a book and great perfect
breasts standing regardant and soft, not regardant like lions, nor
soft jelly, no Katzenjammer Kids or Animal Crackers or Zoo Parades, but firm and powerful; and so on; Art Rodrigue, who, in
drowsy afternoons when the clouds over Massachusetts floated
past the upper panes of my window where I could see through
the side of the curtain, and knew, as I say, that I had some immortal cloudy destiny somewhere behind and forwards of me
still to deal with and yet a destiny so soft and fleecy, i.e., like
the clouds, that I had nothing to do but notice them and turn

away to further and dustier endeavors of the present and of the events of the living world. The inestimable Latin-ness of my Art Rodrigue, and of the Pontiac baseball team in general (crayoned in orange, position by position, on an ordinary card, slightly glossy, from the father's office, the printing office, see) and the Latinness even of my Summer League, as it were a tennis-and-knickers-Barnstable Cape Cod league coolness, I made this ah, now I'm talking, this summer league called . . . well damn, I forgot the name, just as I forget the exact number of tin cans in the small dump in back of the Rockingham race track the gray misty day Mike and me found a ripe tomato growing among the empty whiskey bottles and ate it raw without salt and without benefit of the Pope's advice about salt; but (and as the races were run off to roars we couldn't see); the names of the teams in the summerleague were Tydol, Gulf, Texaco (not Texcoco, I wasn't with the Indian yet); Peyotl, no, not Peyotl, another gas, to be sure not an offbrand gas, or grass, any more than I would sell you any bad shit or Shell you one; names (before J.C.) which were so soft and orange and yielding to my couch, to my kicks, I lay there, twelve, high on the colors of the imaginary uniforms of imaginary baseball teams on cards; and hungup too and more vitally than ever now, the color of the great silks of great proud socialite stables, like C. V. Whitney "Light Blue and Brown" (who but C. V. Whitney, Cornelius Vanderbilt Whitney, would dig the greatness of Light Blue and Brown, shirt is blue, hat brown, indistinguishable through field glasses on flowery bright afternoons) (in those days, between races, they played records and of course to make it racetrack-cool they played what were then fairly oldish or sentimental records, Rudy Vallee "A Pretty Girl . . .", like we play Sinatra now we who swooned over him on the road, in the street, out in back of the Beverly Hills Alpine cocktail lounge where the faint strains of Artie Shaw's clarinet seep out to knock up a young painter hurrying from one easel to another thinking of peyotl and color); hungup I was too, on the greatest of the great silks of the American turf, the colors of the owner of Omaha, winner of the 1935 Kentucky Derby, Woodward, red polkadots on white silks; although you might think the Cream and Cerise of MY daydream stable would, ahem, surpass that; hungup on the

Harold Paine Whitney silks, which I remember had a stripe of black in a faint borscht silk field, wow, with regardant 1066's from Oakland called Norman.

But the league, when it transpired in the afternoon, had a life of its own; at night it no longer occupied my (me), it was the thing for next afternoon; at night, I was hungup on the great darkness beyond the street lamp out in the dirtroad front of the house, which was under the greatest hugest tree in the world, it had a SWish to it you could hear clear to Sacramento, Calif. and I ain't talking about Compton, either; for you know I'd never abandon my old hometown Lowell when telling what I know about noble trees. Afternoon or evening, that tree had 'em all beat. Why, I remember the night Mr. Hoorair from across the street got mad at little Pinky-Winky whose name don't remember but he did something wrong, I'll say, he was my slave, he groveled at my feet in my kitchen as I sat there with my Operator 5's and Secret Agent X-9 cartoons (although by then that phase, of drawing Secret Agent X-9 in particular——I think my last and most unsuccessful and quick to die cartoon conception and Hero was a guy called "Pecker"——like decline of a civilization——think of that); but I remember that kid being given hell, leaning on the fence, under the tree, while the man gives him the finger and gives him hell, for something, as the great tree swishes over them in the high mysterious breeze of evening. Did I dig evening? is that a question to ask? I slept on the porch, I had covers on the swinging swing; the boughs of the great tree did all the creaking for me; and soft the voices of the winds came from over the grasses of Dracut Tiger Field now cooing to the wild sound of crickets and maybe even the wild sound of a seatspring lurching in lovers-lane backseat of a car parked beneath homeplate pine, and dew; the wind came across that, laden with news of upper woods and places where farmers like Robert Frost slammed barndoors in the early morning and made a sound that would echo clear across two or three properties and subsidiary forests and small rivers, brooks really, running brooks with small rapids, that however in sullen Marches could swell and flood and terrify the wood, I mean, till you expected to see corpses go nudging up to the hump that was once the base of a summer diving board; wherewith, and sooth, in fine, I have dreamed of these woods and those floods and of great symbolic voyages as profound as the Odyssey of a brakeman that begins with a call to deadhead over to so and so and he has to provide, but——and it was Cody I was coming to, then, but as reference and maybe fillup; Africa was never longer than some of the treklands I suffered in the Pine Brook country of my dreams; so came the sweet night wind from those waters, and from the field, and mossed and hugened into movement the great groaning, tossing tree, so martyred, so longfaced a tree that I was not surprised but only apprised of normal laws of doom when it toppled like a matchstick in a fury-fury hurricane, October, 1938, the month and almost the week, if not definitely the week, of Thomas Wolfe's death.

That afternoon began, in fact, the hurricane afternoon, clearly enough with the sudden riptide pace of thin, snaveled clouds across the glary pale above; to add to all that horror, of clouds racing so fast too that you didn't quite believe it and looked twice like at a comedian in a B-movie, a doubletake; so sinister an afternoon and introductory disaster that on the way home, in the grayness of Aiken Street near the dump, a telephone pole had caught on fire and the engines were lined up putting out the fire with their hoses; engines and men that within an hour or two would suddenly be alerted as everybody and the authorities in a simultaneous amazement would realize that a fullscale hurricane was upon this northern manufacturing town in New England. To this day, in the wild and virginal woods near Athol, and in the West, in the Berkshires, in the dismalest swamps east of Hartford or west of Worcester, or northeast of Springfield, or outside raw, gloomy Fitchburg of the crags and wild pine, great tree trunks lie bent on the ground as a result of that Hurricane of 1938 . . . just drive at night, hitch-hike at night outside Billerica, Mass. and let that old B & M brakeman who goes to St. Margaret's church in the Highlands of Lowell on Sunday morning tell about the havoc he saw then and still sees signs of in the forest as on the trains he plies his living back and forth in the darkness and coalsmoke of the night. I knew a guy like that, Cudfield, but to get back, though, to the gray and bleak tragedy of that burning telephone pole I'll never know why it looked so foreboding to me or how I could have felt the impending fury and horror (well it *was* horror to some, those who lost property and even those without property who don't understand why God sends terrible storms on people, don't gloat on sea walls in the winter or ride bicycles to Switzerland from a spinning plate of anchovies (Humph); but enough, let us sleep now, let us ascertain, in the morning, if there is a way of abstracting the interesting paragraphs of material in all this running consciousness stream that can be used as the progressing lightning chapters of a great essay about the wonders of the world as it continually flashes up in retrospect; as, for example, this night I ran cold water into a glass at the sink while everybody was high and immediately was reminded completely and perfectly of the cool exact waters of Pine Brook on a summer afternoon.

MIKE'S BROTHER WAS SO STRANGE that when he was locked in the attic one time he scratched on the door to be let out. He was Roland, well dressed and incapable of finishing a thought without a smile; thin, small Roland with his dark curly hair and sharp-cheeked smile. Trouble in the family centered around them because they were deadly enemies. Mike hated his guts and tried to admire him while Roland, far from caring, was at the same time completely suffering and unable to rest. Mike was a merchant seaman.

The family was on to them. Jane . . . or Crazy Jane, as Roland called her . . . was amused but enlightened. "Oh well, as far as my *brothers* are concerned I've never had any really, but I can say, if you like, what perfect idiots!" She knew more about their problems than anyone. On the other hand, another sister knew nothing about their problem but took it upon herself to assume the responsibility for it: this was

I used to be so cool with my books and records at night in my college room; one Sunday afternoon, too, I saw a boy and a girl in love walking hand in hand across the campus, he up on a wall, she on the pavement, tripping in the rippling airs of afternoon and swash bells from the Cathedrals of Morningside Heights. "I say," I'd say on the esplanade along the Hudson River, Riverside Drive, "how about a light, sir?" and the gentleman in the bowler hat by God would give me a light. I read the Sunday comics one afternoon on a Riverside Drive parkbench; it was pleasant, it was an early moment of mine in New York when reading the funnies on a bench was synonymous, like an idea, with baby carriages and maids and mothers. I've since learned that they'll hide machine guns in baby carriages——who put suspicion in——what was the name of that bum who stole the housewife's steaming pie from her kitchen windersill? In America, the idea of going to college is just like the idea of prosperity is just around the corner, it was supposed to solve something or everything or something because all you had to do was larn what they taught and then everything else was going to be handled; instead of that, and just like prosperity that was never around the corner but a couple miles at least (and false prosperity——) going to college by acquainting me with all the mad elements of life, such as the sensibilities, books, arts, histories of madness, and fashions, has not only made it impossible for me to learn simple tricks of how to earn a living but has deprived me of my one-time innocent belief in my own thoughts that used to make me handle my own destiny. So now I sit and stew in a sophistication which has taken hold of me just exactly like a disease and makes me lie around like a bum all day long and stay up all night goofing with myself. I had thought, in, and before college, that to be a writer was like being, of course, the Émile Zola of the film they made about him with Paul Muni shouting angrily in the streets at the dumb and stupid masses, as if he knew everything and they didn't know a damn thing; instead of that I wonder what working people think of me when they hear my typewriter clacking in the middle of the night or what they think I'm up to when I take walks at 2 A.M. in outlying suburban neighborhoods——the truth is I haven't a single thing to wr——feel foolish. . . . How I wish I could grow corn tomorrow morning! How I wish I had enough patience to go and meet Farmer Brown in two hours from now, 5 A.M., and go learn early morning farming matters from him, and sober, too; and not high on tea, either. Instead of that I give myself tremendous headaches and I am also less paid than a Mexican in New Mexico, and at least the Mexican in New Mexico has the right to get angry and to feel truly righteous in his heart. If I went for righteousness at the face of God on what grounds could I make such a claim?—— where plant my stick? What's happened to our society or our arrangement of living and trading with one another that

without the feeling of righteousness you shrivel away like a
pru——I feel so damned small and sick, I walk into a bar not
feeling right any more, I used to walk in a bar with a swagger,
that's what bars are for, if not swagger outright I just mean
walking in without paying attention to anything but what
you're doing with your friends and with your own thoughts;
now, it seems we all walk into bars with fear and suspicion and
for that reason I haven't been to a bar for a long time because
only just now I've arrived in a strange city and don't know
anyone really. I feel as though everything *used* to be alright; and
now everything is automatically——bad. I even look back on
1950, a year when I sm——when I was getting a certain kind of
virgin kick on T——stowing away random thoughts, even short
phrases, or single crazy words like "Blood" or "Wow" so that
I couldn't forget them when it came around time to——with
bumkick denials of what at that time then I thought were un-
doubted truths. I've made everything bad myself by forgetting
to order that coal for the winter; by God we can't use wood in
the city streets, we can't patch up the window with cardboard,
the price of candles is going up! You can't even go and buy
seven caramels for a penny even though some of them used to
have something that was like rocks in them, one in a thousand
. . . in fact much more than the old naturalistic fishheads and
bananas in a bowl. (Two thoughts rushed to the fore but I have
to push them back, one concerned my aunt's livingroom in
Lynn, Mass. when I used to see such a brown and dull red
painting of fruit and fish or grapes or fowl, that's it, not fish,
fowl, in the gloom of lace curtains and beads, while in the corner there hung suspended also my uncle's sword which for years
I thought he had wielded in some Boer War or Spanish War or
something though I couldn't find it in my history and knew of
course it had nothing to do with the World War I there were
no such swords in that war, only to find it had been handed to
him on a velvet pillow by some Fezzed society of the pre-Twen-
ties eras when the Masons and the Lions were on the roar just
starting to make a big Kiwanis about everything . . . that poor
uncle, too, who committed suicide; and whose chief fame in my
little mind previous to that lay in the fact that he was such a
champion ice cream eater, sundaes and sodas and splits and all,
that members of the family used to trail him to count the

number of times. Those first visions of the world seen from a college window, in the safety of that, which were so melancholy yet at the same time so fine and so cool that you go to sleep on them with a smile so to speak (I go to sleep on present anxieties with a nervous smile) must have been more comforting than the ones I have now because I am now so frightened and feel so strange about everything. If it was a matter of hitchhiking——the comfortable and beautiful darkness of a good old (evil) college campus, where lights burn so softly and goldenly at evening, especially in winter dusks, when the air is so clear the bells of novena rap out with a keen and pristine clang that socks across the air like ice and you pause a-snifflin before some Englishified little window full of books or Brooks Brothers shirts that you don't even have to buy, just look at. In those days I must have been happy, to have such memories of it now, to be able in fact even to save one memory out of it, that it wasn't buried like all my happy moments of now are buried the moment they spring up, so that I don't remember a thing the next day and am only ready to face new sorrows. In those days I must have been a regular student wandering in thought among the shops and windows, like in Poe or Melville. In fact, yes by God I was; I worked as a waiter in a basement Bohemian restaurant with candles on oilcloths in Greenwich Village and got high with the dishwasher in the kitchen on tea, talk and dancing, the dancing he did himself, he was an African primitive dancer, his hands were long as nails, he was a colored maniac; I'd muse on him as I wended my way snowward. Not soon after that, though, I'll bet I began to look around. The sins of America are precisely that the streets . . . are empty where their houses are, there's no sense of neighborhood anymore, a neighborhood quarter or a neighborhood freeforall fight between two streets of young husbands is no longer possible except I think in Dagwood Bumstead and he ain't for real, he couldn't—— beyond this old honesty there can only be thieves. What is it now, that a well-dressed man who is a plumber in the Plumber's Union by day, and a beat-dressed man who is a retired barber meet on the street and think of each other wrong, as the law, or panhandler, or some such cubbyhole identification, worse than that, things like homosexual, or dopefiend, or dope pusher, or mugger, or even Communist and look away from each

other's eyes with great tense movements of their neck muscles
at the moment when their eyes are about to meet in the normal
way that eyes meet on the street, and sometimes with their arm
muscles all tense too from the feeling that there might have
been contact, which arises from the vague abstract mental suspicion that there's going to be a sudden fistfight or assault with
deadly weapon intent, followed by the same old excuses when
the moment of meeting is past and both parties realize it was
just two fears meeting on the street, not two sacrifices, really,
to coin a ph——or explain it that way. Looking at a man in the
eye is now queer. Why else should you be looking a m. in the
e. If you want to find out if he's going to cheat you, go ask his
psychiatrist, he's got all the records available.

SUNDAY NIGHT

Dear Evelyn——
   Guess what's going on while I'm writing this——"The
Hour of Charm"——this has been a beautiful winter day
with bright sun, no wind and the thermometer up to 20
d, better than the 5 d of last night. We've been comfortable though and nothing has gone wrong.
   We finally did get a night at home last week after all
but it took a sprained ankle to do it. Thursday night we
went to the Arts Club musical program and as we came
out mama turned her ankle so we had to cancel one
appearance——. . . I'm making her a chest out of those
two walnut doors she brought from Ravenswood. . . .
We are planning a Christmas at home and probably by
ourselves——

                          . . . Ever, Pop (Cody's wife's father)

GALLOWAY ROLLS ON. On summer nights when a boy decides
to stay up late sitting on the porch he hears rising from the
valley of the river . . . but I always say, like I did say originally,
Galloway rolls on, you can't help it, and then I was to say, now,
hep, don't run away, don't move, to say, yes, to say On summer
nights when a boy and I meant to say a little kid decides to stay
up late or halfway gets the chance to do so from his parents who
are sternly intent on sleep as a health measure as well as necessary, ahem, (driving my car through the Saturday afternoon

sunny streets of Los Angeles ever blessed week has finally made a man of me,) why, that river, that rollin old river, why, that Roanoke, that roanokin river, that . . . decides to say to stay up late sitting on the porch he hears rising from the valley of the river, well that's really from the hole of the river, or the valley hole, the river bed, bed of the valley, from the valley bed the great big hush of dark waters no I meant to say waters, of waters plain and simple, that is like the sound of darkness to anybody who ever was raised and lived in galloway massuchussetts and so on, the hassle . . . being, you have to think of words at the same time that maybe you have to think of actions, like say, the actions of the damned and dead cemeteries . . . to coin, but the old ladies of Galloway can tell you, and the voices of the old ladies of Galloway are somehow commingled in this hush of the river of the night, that "old eternal" hush, old spontaneous eternal hush, saying, and in noble great tones, I have no tones, apparently no mind, just twit, tweet, what a day this might have been, Napoleon might have fallen lot to my pillar of glass with its cargo of golden piss falling out of Billy's broken eardrum . . . why they, he, Doc Holliday shot off the tips of Billy's ears, and all the day's woes piling up on Drumm Street in regular riptide intervals, like, say the dead are laid out in the suburbs row by row, and I come from a land where they let the children cry, that's a pooty good land, valued at ten shares an acre, if you can't boogie, but, and trying to return, origin——yes, yes, I'm (saying, the voices in the Greek tragedian night of Lowell are saying, "O go back home, go back home . . ."). But actually it's been so long since I've heard the sound of the Merrimack River washing over rocks in the middle of a soft summer's night that I can't make poesies out of it, or if I did, wouldn't they, are they not, false? Pure and simple, all you got to do is make your statement, and here is mine: "For Claude the river was the . . . the little Merrimack in Missouri . . . the playpen, lot lost a wife, lot lost a wife, lot lost wives or wives lost lots, if not lot lost lots salt." That should make the greatest difference in the world, etc. I really want to go back to North Carolina and watch that dew shudder on the morning corn. On Saturday nights I want to have a mosquito bite my neck while I take down a swig of Old Crow in the flickering lights of a fishfry, with pretty drawlin girls in well-tailored suits stretching their slender legs in such a way

in the firelight that you can almost see, as Hubbard always did
say, their, that is, "clear to their cunts," to quote him; but really,
I saw one woman in Carolina she was a beauty, engaged to a
Marine I guess, hugging looking at rings in trolleys, no, bus, the
bus ran through the leafy night among old white houses that
ain't a stonesthrow from crumbly log icehouses now converted
to tractor storages, a most beautiful complete rounded perfect
woman; one like that in the South, where, when you hear the
guitars of the hill country in scratching far-off Smoky Mountain
or Georgia stations etc. and the bugs are asleep in the cornfield
at night——there's a moon as bright as a bucket of ice, there's a
cobweb across the old sand road and I can hear the doe-dove
coo from the nightfog tabernacle of the owl. I want to stretch
a pretty girl with soft lips who maybe usherettes on Sundays at
a B-movie on Main Street, or whichever street that is, over a
sandy old lousy bed in a fishing shack along the brown sluggish
old Neuse River, and lay her.

    Why when

        I was down in

            New Orleans that year I came across the
damnedest old boy. He reminded of a man I knew in Washington, D.C. in 1942, in the spring, when I went down there to
work on a construction job——the Pentagon Building in Arlington, Virginia, scene of the unknown soldier; in the afternoon
I used to look up from the dusty shimmering haze of the big
job-scene (it was like about as if we were building the new
Gethsemane) and see the pillars and portals of Robert E. Lee's
mansion, and say to myself "I finally got to the South." And a
year later, from the window of the hospital in Bethesda, Maryland, seeing a little dirt road winding off into the gray woods,
towards West Virginia, I'd say "And now I've got to explore
that old gray road that goes out West." New Orleans, that man,
I tell you, a hot town, a fine town course you can starve there
like everywhere else; and a good man, his name was——I forget,
but, forgit, but he was once Governor of the State of Florida
believe it or not and shaved with me under the hot tropical ceiling fans of old palmtree Nola with its rumbling big river that's
been rolling ever since the environs of Butte picking mud as
it came down and now's as big and mad as the last day of the
Flood. New Orleans, where Sherwood Anderson and William

Faulkner drank bad shit together and staggered in the *Vieux Carré*, and where people like Truman Capote cut along like undersea monsters on the streets, with Tennessee Williams—— I know New Orleans only half well, though, and can't really say, except, as I say, I knew this damn old boy who came from down there, name was Bull Hubbard, Big Bull Hubbard from Ruston, Luzeeanna, and here's how and when I met him and what happened afterwards. First sight I had of Washington's old redbrick I guess you might say Georgian houses one sunny hot afternoon in May after I took a nap to rest off a long trip by bus from New York and Boston, I thought, in the waking minute of the dream of life and all that, that I really was in New Orleans and New Orleans has never looked prettier since, because after all Washington *IS* the gateway to the South. The time has come for every single one American male to go out and be a pimp. This I added on in the spirit of the thing. And of course what I really mean is, the woman has got——the women have got up such an upper hand that there's no other alternative to salvation. Let all the young women be whores, the old women ladies . . . who like to do it still. Just like in France, like in Henry Miller's mad dreams——In New Orleans all you got to do is sit on the levee and play with your balls, let your hand dangle over your balls as though you didn't care and finally you won't. We'll all be like we were on the dump long ago; or like the guy you knew when you were little who used to slap all the asses of the women, including your mother, at a party and laugh like mad. That guy has disappeared from the American scene; without him we'll all——why did I ever tell you about how a Mississippi River or Red River flood can flood a golf course and undermine tees? and make men in white knickers weep? and remind them that mud is where they came from? and that people are still living in mud all over the country, and liking it? like W. C. Fields living on a riverboat in 1950 that's now become so old and weathercurled that it's just left sitting in the bare St. Louis waterfront in the hot sun of afternoons when the only people on the cobbled shore are nogood nigger boys who played hooky from Progressive School or the old hermit of the river smelling drift sticks probably from Fargo, North Dakota. Why, boy, my beard grows longer and to think of it. Why, but I saw, and say, now, to mention, I won't fall apart

NOTJUSTNOW!——eeeeeeek! eek! eeek! I should, I mean I
s——mean I used to write Eek and Shit all over my college days . . .
on gray November afternoons . . . sittin . . . room . . . cutting
. . . Contemporary Civilization. I had nothing but disrespect
for my perfessor, I did. Later on, when Mark Van Doren made
me realize professors could be real interesting, I nevertheless
spent most of my time dreaming on what he must be like in real
reality instead of listening to what he was saying. The one big
thing, though, I do remember him saying, is, "A perfect friend
you always meet every two or three years, accidentally, and you
can't stop talking with him; and when he leaves for another
two, three years, you don't feel sad at all; when you meet him
again, it happens again. He is your perfect friend." This must
have been Van Doren himself. They give that man banquets, his
alumni students do, and cry, all sarcastic professional men, too.
He looked up from a paper I had written and said "Giggling
Lings?" to make sure I did say "Giggling" before the Chinese
name "Lings" and that was the only question he asked. Can
you wonder that men love him? I don't know who this guy
is, I just came across him——while this man tended his farm in
spare hours, or that is, did a few chores among the flowers, and
dreamed, my father sat at a linotype machine puffing a cigar and
spitting in a spittoon into which occasionally also pieces of hot
lead would fall, smoking. The difference in their class . . . styles
of accomplishment. (I was going to say that I was sorry etc. . . . .
it would sizzle in the spit . . . a linotype (machine used to save
madness from wild scripts).) All this. . . . . They tried to drag me
back in the pit of darkness but they failed. I'm talking about all
the people, all the monsters that exist in this world. You can't
teach this old maestro a different tune.

The caveman had the right to kill his wife and child and move
on to another woman; of course it also meant moving on to
other men, to git the woman from, to fight with rock clubs; but
the Master Impostor in this week's *Life* (this is what you hear in
New York all the time, this week's *Life*, last week's *Time*, their
concepts are all bought up . . . well, that was pretty neat I *must*
say)——ah, but, ahem, kaff kaff, Major Hoople coughing in the
wilderness I mean by that, he's standing by the parrot cage with
its wild crimson parakeet and coughing while the bird, from its

tangly bushes, yaks at him and tries to beak his eyes out; his fez is on stormy waters, it's about to fall to the bright linoleum, he and the bird are spending an afternoon together waiting for the missus to get home, on the sun porch, I forget the old name they had it, among pillows, gloss, and beads. . . . he walked away swaggering and lumbering, all hairy, all wild in the scraggly morning mists of Upper Neanderthola, southwest county, they didn't have fences of course but monolithic Robert Frost New England stonewalls; ahem, and there, swaggering, spitting blood, he hurried, across the brush, the harsh twigs and rose thorns snapping at his skin, making it bleed, of course, I added, it also meant moving on to the other men——the question is, did they fight or had they just an agreement, in order to protect their own interests as members of the organic race, otherwise men wouldn't have survived; yes, they must have arranged systems of shuffling and shuttlin wives, like through a master male agency, almost a union, where you waited in line and kept your eyes peeled on that Reindeer Man board with its buffalo signs for who's the next cunt coming to, and will she fill the bill; all hurlyburlying in cave doorways with massive stoneclubs in their hands because there was nobody decadent enough at that time to flunk at the door checking firearms just because the boss proposed it might be a good idea and of course didn't have the guts to do it himself so got a flunk to do it, but a flunk with a will, like certain flunks that throw out Ernest Hummingbird from Greenwich Village parties and instead of flattening them across the wall, which he can very well do and easily do, he, Ernie, with a bottle of gin and bananas, goes off laughing in the night. But now that swagger, descendant of the caveman who made his wife a gore, and added fillips of the child in it, Fillip Gore, is softened by the same man taking a powder from a dull party and a party from which also he can't leave without creating a scene and creating a scene is only possible at carnivals and Zanzibars, really, say, for instance, you can get high as you want in the balcony of a burlesk show with your hat on the pack, I mean the back of your head, a whiskey bottle in your right hand, a cigarette in mouth, preferably cornsilk really, and yr. cok in yr. left hand.——you can do that and get real high, or you can smoke marijuana and float down a small Indiana river that leads to the Mississippi by a series of subsidiary creeks and rivers, on a raft this is, with a good stove, maybe, a supply of meat already cooked wrapped securely in a good big sack that you can open and slice into every night, some coffee, preferably some Nescafé or Bordens, and a part in the middle of the raft where the wood is so thick and so wetty that you can always plant your campfire there over some sand that you carry on edge of the raft, or, really, that is up aft with the galley and the rest of the leavins, the woiks, the home quarters, the heart, the soft of the safari, the place where you light the candle and drink black coffee and smoke your pipeful of marijuana, without deep drags but justpuffing and passing it through your nose, just like with Prince Albert, only real great shit, but you can get this marijuana pipe tobacco regularly because you grow it along the river and harvest it no matter what county you happen to be in at the moment when you need it; and you go floating down that little Indiana, river, further and further down into stranger, lighter, greener ever expanding adventures that must and do ultimately take you to a flat marsh by the sea, great ears of sea corn along a waving grass veldt, scents of something, smoke of a city, something mad and wild and far far gone from the tangled viney place where you started when the dream began, or also, I tried to write this at eleven it was called "Mike Explores the Merrimack," but now wait, I'm not supposed to enter into this but I guess I might as well, now the thing that we're gonna talk about now is not limited to anything really specific and generally antecephilic, that word I looked up in Web——but making——it's just like Hemingway says, in the swamp the fishing would be more tragic. My Mike started in the swamp of the river Merrimack somewhere, this was the river along by the—— but wait a minute, ladies and gentlemen, are we still supposed to communicate? did any of you ever make a speech on Union Square? have you loved my shoe box, my black box, my great black cunt, and Jesus Christ and the great black cunt, have you ever seen Jesus Christ, as I have, standing next to a nigger naked woman with a black cunt, a big black cunt, and Jesus Christ is standing on top of the hill with the wind blowing through his eyebrows and is surveying a rooster about two miles away that happens just at that moment to be perched on a fence not unlike Farmer Brown's fence except it is a Judean fence in the long ago of the earth, and Jesus Christ is saying "Yon rooster crowing . . ." preparatory to that night's dark (that nighted and

dark fitful) and fitful woe-adventures when they plant bleeding
thorns on his head, and drag him spitting blood around, and
push him, and cajole him, and mill about him in awful sorrow,
thousands of men and women in dank robes wailing, o woe,
o woe, and fires are burning someplace up ahead and out of
the crowd jumps this lady with a clean handkerchief or scarf
and jesus mops his face with it, like say W. C. Fields suddenly
borrowing a handkerchief from a stranger at the Worlds Fair in
Chicago some ten, twenty years ago, thirty years, whatever and
on the clean rag is left the imprint of his face, including blood
and features, and the woman runs away not believing it and
staring at the rag and bundles it up under her arm like a flag
and runs but once in the dark (and now the great thunderstorm
and earthquake is forming) she unravels it to see if all the colors,
the blood and features ran off into one another, but no the face
of Jesus is still neatly imprinted on that rag and stares back at
her phosphorescent and frightening and crazy in the night and
she creams, screams, doesn't know what to do with it, drops it
on the ground, kneels before it, wishes her husband was there
to help her carry it home, or to pick it up himself, like a piece
of dead meat, and the husband is nowhere around, and the vis-
age of Him so meek and morrowfull, stares from its stance in
the desert dirt, idly upjaw thrust as when he descended it to his
face, but now the rag on a hillock makes a lean—and she, the
woman, finally running off ten yards, returning wavering, leaning, swaying, like Whitman's wives in Long Island, then she sobs
and with a gesture just like an Indian woman in Peru bending
to pick up a little she just dropped from her shawl while busy
cutting up a fruit, she, Magdalene, or whatever her goddamn
excuse me lord name was, picked it up off the dark dark ground
already beginning to shudder and roll from the earthquakes of
Golgotha, and ran home through narrow Algerian streets, past
pimps and dope addicts, to her home.

I DON'T THINK I KNOW much about this here Ravenswood of
the woman with the silk scarf. . . . You see, though you might
have it in your mouth you can never save it there; so don't
hide your money in your mouth. Is that what I meant to say?
It reminded me, excuse it please, of a movie I saw with Alan
Ladd, "Blue Something Or Other," flame, or fame, or scame, or
shame, or Mame, (Mama), an old lawyer with his frazzled jowls

fixed on his stick and spotted bear hands, cirrhotic, if I believe rightly, but in the Alan Ladd I had started to expo(und)(ose), the radio was blaring in the bright L.A. morning of the motel when the landlady cut up with her mop 'n' skirts and saw the dead body of the night before on the floor——says I, "The dead body of the night before on the floor." My father was Popeye, he smoked his pipe by the docks where the paper moon rose and "remember, please, hip, signals, 1, 2, 3, 4, 5, remember, if, pardon, if, if, you, will, or not, or whichever, simple enough, the good lawyer (you'll improve boy, you'll improve) (shouldn't have played with that percocicle) 'with the passing of parochial time' 'refuse the error' 'upturn the eras' 'call out the natural guard' 'hip hope hype mope' 'the nazi youth' 'the thing is' 'solved' 'you merely' 'give off' 'a little' 'british' 'snufff' 'at' 'SNUFFY SMITH! that's his name!'"

SR. Ahem (*Coughing in the church*)

ALTAR BOY. Tedoom te dieum

SR. Mono-lo-o-go-lo——(*fading away like a song across the vasty pews*)

ALTAR BOY. Kiria (*snaps the smokepot*)

SR. (*himself coughing*) (*in a low tone*)——eh weyondon, *il faut saccotez dans un moment comme ça? Arrête . . . parlez . . . tu sais, bien tu sais, mon vieux, a tarra écri un let si tu larra lasse faire la pauvetit maudite comme quelle eta belle et tabarnac shi shpa capable faire ça dans l' derrière et fré mon* the priest talked to himself in a secret and intonallish and intonatitativeyene mono-tonesky la music *la musique la belle mais arrête donc il faut arrêtez un moment?* and so on with himself

ALTAR BOY. Ekara-doo-rioom?

SR. (*creaking in a joint*) Paradoorium, etabooriumbum, bum-boombum, etara, metaradelaramarea, *cest impossible de setangler je veus dire se desetangletai* ben mudout coung on thwiey skehe long ague she jeiipeout, echrie and, Francie pare idl thsomc e failt tna dh elEndlgn, but emeie the ejeu——

(*Speaking from the deck of a steamboat through a funnel,* W. C. FIELDS, It seems to me . . .)

Shifting locks, **ADERIANDE.** (*cool on the purple iron butt of a Civil War Horse in the middle of Annapolis Navy*) Cefrantus! By mires, and anon the, but you have to get real high before you can blow any kind of a program, man, so listen to me there's nothin better in this big t——woops, now the typewriter's gone, it's thickening tremendously, Allen Swenson and Christopher and all that, well I swow I don't understand this matter in the slightest least, although I just was about to say I must say this thing is going to get us down unless we do something about it immediately don't you think, unless you'd rather I didn't bother at all, or else, if you wish, and I won't hold it against you the least minute, now really I won't, I wouldn't fan your father, would I now my dear old Sally would I fan your feather, now I don't think it's necessary to repeat fan your feather, again, that is, I can see from up here Olympianly that the jeiipeout is working again and so therefore you may resume your regular exlax. Not that I would object, (*spoke up the big woodsman who now, with snouts of iron around his snot comes tripping gaily to kill us, ENVER by name*) how now, yea, not that I would object.

MAN ON SOAPBOX IN UNION SQUARE. Now wait a minute ladies and genmean today I went into a stoh on Union Square street over dere on Fourteenth Street and I bought a hotdog mit sauerkrauten and had some softies ice cream on a cone and drank a cococunt Coke all for a nickel and a kick me a dime, move back there buddy, keep the kids out of this, here's what I'm gonna do, now wait a minute podnerrrrrrrr . . .

GARY COOPER *attendant* to TOM MIX (*the languid grape and I have kissed in the mix, the flaming grape*), *who sits shaving from a coffee cup*): I say Tom, do you——not that I'd had mentioned it before if you hadn't, ah, seen that from the very first, you, ah, ahem, of course, no, but, ah, as, or in case——you know, here's what it is, now *I*——listen to me, *I*, listen to me, now listen to me, now listen to me, *I* can certainly damn fuckingwell tell you, I was there, was you there M-a-a-a?

OWLHORN MOUNTAIN SKI INSTRUCTOR. (*in multilapeled multilateral coloured mooseskin harveststacksack, with pendant boins, or boigns, as properly spelled, and moody rubies in his hyar*): By sooth and foreskin.

REEL TWO. Charlie Chaplin twinkling in an early morning dew, by a garden wall, just as big Two-Time Butch is about to heave a pail of cold water over the wall.

MOLDY MARIE. She was an usherette at the Rialto Theater, Lowell, Mass., she used to mop up the ladies' room after we gangbanged her daughter Filthy Mary in there all night, why you could go to the theater any afternoon and get a handjob just by asking the usher at the door "Where's Filthy Mary?" and he'd say "Oh she's sittin in the backseat with Gartside there getting a blow job up or something——"

"You mean handjob? You don't think Filthy Mary would try a blowjob in the afternoon?"

"Sure, why in the hell not, what's wrong with a blowjob in the afternoon——you think I got seven jaws for nothin?"

That's what I heard him say, and I went down to the front row to see the movie a minute before checking back on the activities of our one and only, our perfect girl, Filthy Mary; and from the front row I of course (and now when I was a very little boy I think my first picture, in other words the first movie I ever saw, I think was a Tom Mix movie with him, white hatted and in fact so snowy in it that in the general rain of that muddy movie screen california he glowed like a glowworm, and synonymous to all that seeing him all leaping across rainy shacks on a robe and landing on maniacs in the dark . . . I was afraid to stick my hand out in the dark until I was twenty-nine years old, oh I'd say twenty-nine years and such, not thirty, if not thirty, or lotsa thirty, well that's a lotsa lots, but I'd venture to guess, at the most, or least, twenty-nine years and ten months and twenty-nine days, that's how old I am today, or maybe just a day or more later than that, but later gater, I'm cuttin a caper, and hear me daddy, waitin for you all day long while I slave over my hot stove till you get home from work, fum work you motherfucker and give me a great big fuck against the stove and I throw up my old dress for you anywhere daddy over in back of the barn ennytime you say daddy, or you come in back behind the haystack tonight at eleven or seben o'clock and I fix you up fine, daddy, I pump you dry and fuck the ass off you, what's the matter with you, I fuck you all the time, daddy, whyfor you don't come and fuck lil old me, I ain't afraid of the dark, I teach you how t'fear the dark, down here in New Orleans we got all kinds voodoos, and hoodoos, and hoodsoodoodoos, too, but we ain'tsa worried about that 'cause my daddy tell my daddy what the Lord said last night, and the ladies convene and forfirm it, and we all go and make it across the young blue light of the fine dimensions aof the ehekdie kdhdke ashout, thbut and eyou kdht thekkk, there was no real interruption there or anything but the pour pour pure mechanical faculties and fear, natural, of making noise, amen.

"WHEN I WAS IN THE DARK that roach pipe was stolen from my hand." "Then why did you ask the question to yourself? What are you up to, Charley?"

"I can't do anything till I figure out how I could have lost that thing in the dark, I distinctly remember leaving this chair with it in my hand, but now I see by lamplight that it's not on the couch, nor in the vicinity of the chair, so where, whyar, wheair, wheayerheheheoeoeoeo can it be? (*Imitating Milton Berle.*) On the vaudeville stage stood two little comedians; in the front row sat a blond; look at 'er, said the first comic; I'm 'avin her now, I'm 'aivin no I'm 'avin 'er now, that is it, with the britishaccent, I have it, yes, that's right, go ahead and forget what you were saying, if you can't remember, crack, go ahead, head, creak, crack, crack your head, head; go crack your head in a crack; go crack your head in a craggy rack; go crack your head in the bone yard rack; go crack your head in the wild blue rack; ah ha, go and crack in your heed; go keed, find your head, crack it, it is found, now listen, kiddies, go crack your head I say in the mailhouse rack, oh yes, zoom, go crack your head in the hailstorm black, the maelstrom sack; go crack, go crack, the shroudy stranger is my brother, he's the one who reached out his black hand in the dark and stole my roach pipe.

Go crack your head in the heady dark; go find yourself another Monroe Starr to sit by swimmingpools with, ten years after he's dead; go crack your head on a mountain top, go find the blonds with the smelly old cunts just like Cody always says gar bless his old little ole hide that rin the thar rhide whoops whelap crack dhkeyr whoops aht the maggie and jiggs are running third and fourth but there are indications that other things will soon aoccur by whih lookout she's coming back again where all liable to get killed around dhere and di fyou don't wash out an dkwhekek dhowowh but now I lost it again who wdra ahlow hdjo w drat it that I should have lost out again like happy old Yeaths now I saw one thing about yea y old Yeats and I say that he is a great man because he learned how to write oatutomatically at the behest of little (gragahest?) ghosts just like james mason wants it but I say and the only thing is you've got to explain yourself clearly or not at all.

So they sell corn in dusty side streets; the paisans sink in the purple ground, the sun is the color of wine, the goats whine, the bellies fatten, the kern and the herd and the isle in the reeds and the paddies of day, all recline, in kind; and eventide is come upon old Mexico. Far across the valley they're blowin up the last of the hell's volcanoes through a hole in the ground so big I ain't never even had the nerve to go and look, but I will soon as I round up a return safari; but I'm saying (move back, it's not rainin under the marquee here, damn, Curtis Street is cold and and gray in the winter!) boom O crash, (inside throughts, then, I mean thoughts, boom O and all that, those were but by God I had a voice then, I won't hang up you, go on, well, he said, I just thought, like the little blubbery gubbery guy in the movies with the goopy lip and bald head and wet eyes know him? now think hard Americans of my generation! ahem, eek! Danny Kaye winds up in the——dash it all, I made a dash, I wanted to surprise the——booopy, goopym ain thksheye ehere eyd but I had nothing to do with it, so they sell corn in dusty side streets, sure that was a legitimate kick, why dint you guys let me go on talking then we wouldna got all hungup like this fornothin, crise, you guys think theres nothin to do around here but get yourself cunted left and right by wise guys. Listen, I'm no shittin——I know what you're thinkin, in fact, thought about it a whole lots of times but I know it'll only bore you——before we harken back——that you guys can do this, or harken by the laws of Macbeth, he with faded insubstanced gory form found ladies screeching in the ante ways, the chambers, in empurpled gowns they serried the dark clots of night with their musical . . . breasts. But he writhes, O how he writhes, the serpent writhes. Better than Eddy Arcaro, sports fans. Ted Williams batted .345 last year, thereabouts, didn't do too badly, trouble with Williams is, he aint battin over .400 like he used to and seems to me he still could if it hadn't been for that Williams shift which has ruined forever the real great day of the great great hitter, that's what socked Williams down, he was disappointed because of that Boudreau shift that forever thereafter made it impossible for him to lambast that old pill with the same extraspecial gusto he used to so ably display in the old days of the bean and the cod, when Major Henry J. Funderhucks, Esq. but not a subscriber, ahem, (although it is reliable to say, that is, reliably brought to us and therefore feasible (feasament) to say, that, in sooth and *par force*, in English perforce, ahem, that, ah, we should indeed have found it so expedient upon ourselves at this happy moment of junctures and correct spellings but would also appeal to our other sensers of the grander day, when it was a well known fact that ballyhood old men living in blue barndoors with cuds of black wax in their fettered frowns and froward tits, would in some sooth, though not to exaggerate, as with the red nose of the bumkin lay, the day of the nay, when all the judgment did in Nile spring a deadly trap for the feze and zuwwing of the day, the Wuzzy, the Fearsome and vastest of its kingdom's last thrall. At, and, ah, but, wait, that fosooth, and in fine, for why stop, and indeed it would be a most and infractuously ensipening pace to maintain as their are now off!——the motorgraws are off across the lake, growling in the pale, in the vale, a child's melted ice cream, extreme, lies flogibating in the wet hot pavement of the afternoon upon which housewives angularly stalk with knockkneed dispairs; and so then, by the sands of the Cousiltalf, which was dutch before it became cleanser, there's nothing easier than scholarship, all you have the damn wellard due you dull bottard you might get in dutch with the fore of the caster and easier? easier? did you say easier? I can see you, I can saw you out, Benvenuto Cellini (did I pronounce your name right?) in the middle of a real great floorshow out at Dagotown, where all us Wops con-gre-gate, gate, and pack our rods and teapots down there with which to make the soil grow, and so, and so, and so, and so, a rose is a rose is a rose, (I was tempted to add jess'one'more'but' didn't by gare.) I walked one time ankledeep in sea swamps and felt my toes nudge up against all kinds of crabs buried in the muck real deep, the deeper my foot sank the more I could feel all kinds of little sharp crabs gettin smaller and smaller as the mud is deeper and they don't have to fight.

YOU THINK I WAS AFRAID OF THEM THERE MAWRDEGROOS in the muckeroo? (Whisper in the audience: Now he's being gay. Answer: Oh, I see, I was wondering what it was all about but from the other side of your thought, my dear) (she gently squeezes his hand in the warm piffultarm of the pruf) wuw, I mean wuf, wuf wuf, or should I say, whoo whoo, or rather, say, woo-woo, go ahead, say woo-woo, woo woo! (this is a borrow parenthesitis) ungently unscrew the she from the hand that squeezes and let's move on, piffultuffle, wuf, orshouldIsay, type, and let's play basketball, because you must remember that you are fatteneeing on a sufsialcge of the kind, no not a fusilacge, but a real one, now listen all you nekdhd eto fearm she is the foun(dloli) (Obscure in meaning), but nevertheless as a printer's son I feel obliged to say that this twaddle——shee—— this twaddle——Sheee, plea, sir, plea, chiny towh, town, tow, how, ow, ow, wo, ow, now you done come up and madeitsuch a largerpefortating word that intha dorignal because by gare there my father he was drunk all the time jess like that I can't understoodand eand the feasome and coustiltalk and all those things you was atalking about before I came back from antientam, mm, taint, and found you (why are you hiding vremedeer?)—— (they told me, they used to tell me, I was the cream of the coffee), leave me alone don't spank me, out of the void, the unknown void, from the vulcan's mouth, from the forge of earths, out of the black interior, the worldswellbottom, out of the deep dark mut, plut, fut and gut of sut and muck in the futted depths and peops and plops and peps of the juicy bottomed dryin briny wild ape dream deep of the formless days when of old the link and the koko made a ringing bellsound in the bottom of the pail and all the rooftapos male and femalo made noises of the slide and wide and however anybody ever tried to get around by ther eiwht al their broken endiements that well, and seeing it's so, you would have said, or thought, well, I know, man, but you, see, when it comes time to do things you immediately pop up with some other damn some udder dam suggestion, damn your hide baby im gonna throu your ass outahere, right now, down the slide and in the sea and don't break your tootsies in the broken glass, I lived in this seaside apartment before and I knew very well everything I damn well about it care to shittin ass know, yeah. It may occur to you and those who are not interested that I don't care a damn what you're doing because I'll tell you why——I should like to make it plain to everyone that I am speaking from a pulpit, not bumming frojlike from a smockbox; asmock box, a smock box, that's a box where the smocks is at, where the smocks are hid, where you dig the smock, the smock is like a rock, the smock is great shit, smock it man, I'm smock pops, o smock you you smock, oh you mother smocker! Oh you tawdle socker! Oh you big Darine! Oh you mad baleen! Oh you craven tool! Oh you assturdal farting, or fartening; you, Oh you! Oh you mad bejawber, with your long tellover turning like in a——but now, cut it out, everybody breakit up, step back, we're about to moddle your coddles real well, move back little ones, big ones bend, ladies first, ass up, head head down, one, two, ready, whamp, give 'em a big kick in the ass I say, I used to work up at Weed, I wore a long black hat over my rocky jowl and jaw and facebone, I used to spit in the spittoons of Michigan Lake, up in the undiscovered north country of the Yuknon, tucson, the Yukon, Tucson, I won't tolerate another m——but . . . in the mawrdegra of that year (unless you want to suck my big bad dick, jack) we had learned to farm without proper imm-plements due to difficulties arising from the fact that nobody ever did get to find out who was the big feller from Weed not afraid to kickpeople in the ass? Never did ask, did ya . . . ya damn fool, didn't know you could get all oovered and sore from the scourge and sore of the great Natal Sore, the score is down, the moon doth rise, the frost is in the handker-chief, fufnik, and I'm ovff the of fht to verht eraces mayeslef kedkdi tin the same time that rintintin stole that wonder horse superchief the mighty oneclad pine tree with doublewords ring-ing in my head nowlike i was goingtoburst my oldtop well wheredo we return to the trickof the d no we missed again and but now, ah, ahem, cunt, hm, look, ah, country, Joanna.

Joan Rawshanks in the Fog

JOAN RAWSHANKS STANDS ALL ALONE in the fog. Her name is Joan Rawshanks and she knows it, just as anybody knows his name, and she knows who she is, same way, Joan Rawshanks stands alone in the fog and a thousand eyes are fixed on her in all kinds of ways; above Joan Rawshanks rises the white San Francisco apartment house in which the terrified old ladies who spend their summers in lake resort hotels are now wringing their hands in the illuminated (by the floodlights outside) gloom of their livingrooms, some of them having Venetian blinds in them but none drawn; Joan Rawshanks leans her head in her hands, she's wearing a mink coat by the wet bushes, she leans against the dewy wire fence separating the slopeyard of the magnificent San Francisco DeLuxe Arms from the neat white Friscoan street-driveway sloping abruptly at seventy-five degrees; in back where the angry technicians muster and make gestures in the blowing fog that rushes past klieg lights and ordinary lights in infinitesimal cold showers, to make everything seem miserable and storm-hounded, as though we were all on a mountain top saving the brave skiers in the howl of the elements, but also just like the lights and the way the night mist blows by them at the scene of great airplane disasters or train wrecks or even just construction jobs that have reached such a crucial point that there's overtime in muddy midnight Alaskan conditions; Joan Rawshanks, wearing a mink coat, is trying to adjust herself to the act of crying but has a thousand eyes of local Russian Hill spectators who've been hearing about the Hollywood crew filming for the last hour, ever since dinner's end, and are arriving on the scene here despite the fog (move over from my microphone wire, there) in driblets; pretty girls with fresh dew fog faces and bandanas and moonlit (though no moon) lips; also old people who customarily at this hour make grumpy shows of walking the dog in dismal and empty slope streets of the rich and magnificently quiet; the fog of San Francisco in the night, as a buoy in the bay goes b-o, as a buoy in the bag goes b-o, bab-o, as a buoy in the bag goes bab-o; the young director eagerly through the rain like an Allen Minko (crazy type in floppy stylish bought-at-Brooks-Brothers-deliberately clothes who talks his way entirely into his careers and stands there, gesticulating, ducking to see, measuring with his eyes, hand over brow to estimate just right, darting up, shadowing himself, looking furtively over his shoulder, long director's coat flying, hangjawed sullen face, long Semitic ears, curly handsome hair, face with the Hollywood Tan which is the most successful and beautiful tan in the world, that rich tan, intent in the foggy night on his great-genius studies of light on light, for he has technicians standing around with punctured boards that they adjust and meander in their hands to cast certain glows and shadows on the essences at hand, hark, though methinks the ghost now comes along the splintered pale, entry made for him, intent on his great-tennis studies of the night) eagerly through the rain he watches Joan through his fist telescopes and then rushes down to her.

"Now baby, remember what I said about the so-and-so" and she says "With the flip on the end of it?"

"Yes, that and what I've been trying to explain to Schultz for ten minutes, the meaneander there when you come in at the end byazacking along the trull, I told him and he won't listen, we called Red, it's absolutely——got the rest straight though?"

"Yes and tell Rogeroo to make room for me at the other end; o those horrible bores in there"——Joan adding the last to mean the people who live on the bottom floor of the apartment house and who invited them in, while waiting for exact arrangements to get underway, offering Joan Rawshanks tea and warmth in her hard stint of the night; the same fogstint she must have gone through when she was a poor dear hustler but now and everything is happening all over at the exact moment. In the back is Leon Errol——suddenly you think, "No this is not Leon Errol" (he's dead) and yet he walks exactly like Leon Errol, on rubber legs, is on a movie lot, has a big floppy gabardine coat in which he must have got drunk at the racetrack in that same afternoon; the two local cops on the beat, according apparently to Hollywood custom, consented to have their pictures taken by a member of the camera crew, who if not delighted was appealed upon to take their pictures; this being Leon Errol; and the police stand passively, side by side, two blue coats, one fortyish, one a boy cop, a thirty-year-old-married-with-two-children-might-have-been-brakeman who instead in the brutality of his instincts migrated to the police force, though with a mild and malleable nature and without military ostentation; these two men, father and son in their nightly duty and relationship in the cold torpors of Russian Hill *haute* through which their tragic figures cut, swinging clubs, in the rare occasions when residents of the neighborhood happen to cast a bored glance from their evening window (there being nothing to see or do in these streets, morning, noon and night); so the cops stand there having their picture took but suddenly and everybody watching (crowds in the cold fog, hand in pockets, like little kids at the back end of semi-pro football games on scuffled wild neighborhood fields of Saturday afternoon cold and red and hard in the month of November in the North;) everybody in the crowd realizes that the Leon Errol fotografter is actually only just fiddling with his lightbulbs and put-up arrangements of tripods and subsidiary lights (with a cat standing next to him again wielding those strange riddled cardboards they use for estimating the inch-ounch of light they want, though how can anybody in a movie audience get to detect that when the picture finally flashes on the screen;) so the cops are temporarily and suddenly under the glare of floodlights and there they are, they don't know what to do, perhaps they should look coply, very well they do, folding arms, looking away. But actually at first they waited with comradely joy while the fotog took his first bending licks at the dark rig, with accommodating nineteenth-century buddy joy they in fact almost locked arms, and waited, as if with mustachions and beerjowl, were posing for the Beanbag Afternoon Set of the German Band Union that invites the Police Force to participate in the old days; the dark suspicion crept now around the crowd perhaps (it certainly did on me, I was alone, watching, Cody was at home not letting anything happen but himself, lamenting in his dark heart's house with lovemasks and tangled flesh shrouds, as usual) that the Hollywood cameramen were such cynics and played such stupendous private jokes in their travels around, that they were putting the cops to a phony hangup; evidently however Leon Errol did snap their pictures, because when it was all over, while the cops nervously took his name and gave their own (to have the pics mailed) he, with the gesture of the narcotic cameraman, sucked the film out of his box and plopped it, hot with reality, instant, into his pocket; just like a teahead might lick the ash-end of a roach for the exact feel of his smoking hots, like a linotypist must feel late in the night before the groaning hot machine that somewhere in its balls and bowels it has some metallic heat that would be good to lick, would kick you like a can of beer; evidently, Leon Errol, sucking, had made the picture alright and would actually——but now, the cops for just a moment had been in the glare of floodlights, watched by others, by a thousand eyes, by my eyes, the eyes of conmen and maybe murderers in the crowd, the poor cops stood there dumbly for the first time in not only their careers but lives that they had been subjected to scrutiny by thousands of eyes under the glare of floodlights (this being of course the Hollywood cameramen stunt trick, they'd get their kicks making cops pose like that all over the country, at least till the cops joined the unions); but now, the leading man was standing at the fringed end of the crowd and he was a strange one, I told Mrs. Brown standing next to me, "I think he looks sorta handsome and all that, you could say that he's handsome——but my God when he turns this way and looks this way I can't stand the great hollow sorrow and strange emptiness and alcoholic lostness and vagueity of his eyes . . . and what is he looking for? look how eagerly he bends and grins and fawns; wouldn't it be terrible to be married to a man like that, you'd never, you'd have to make faces all the livelong day," but Mrs. Brown said, "Yes but on the other hand look at that sharp, almost shroudy clothes he wears, it makes him look like a part in a nineteenth-century castle picture, he's the hero, the son of the Count, the favored of the Peasants, a carriage awaits him by rainsplashed rose arbor down the road, they're going to capture a lovely gowned lady in a black mask tonight; he looks exactly like that, I know what you means about his awful falseness and iridescence of almost homosexual charm but consider that he is a gentleman, a nice fellow, not harming anybody, sorta sissy, probably loves someone very dearly, maybe he has seven kids how do you know? maybe he lives in a rose covered cottage in Catalina and paints rococo Gauguins of his wife covered with suntan lotion with the kids around the big candy ball; so what's it to you that he

fawns and flickers all over" (Two misplaced verbs there.) Joan
Ashplant stands in the fog, the director is explaining what he
wants done; they sound like they're arguing about prices in a
delicatessen, or with a ski attendant in Berne; over at the misty
stone steps the lights are strongest bent; under a canvas that
flaps out from the back of a truck that has red boards in the
back to make it a proper circus wagon but nevertheless (it's a
klieg truck, with tools) a real cluttered up truck, coils of wire,
you'd almost expect to find a clown's mask among the solders,
it's so damned . . . under the tent top sit the great generals of
the vast activity which is the filming of Joan Clawthighs running
up the white driveway (asphalt) (hic) and up the white stone
steps and to the door, pausing, at the foot of the steps (not steps
where she goes, but gradation of concrete, a driveway, garage
ramp, deluxe style, creamy in fact) pausing there to cast a frightened glance into the general night; which she did but when she
had to, the glance had to be in the direction of the crowd; at
first Joan apparently wanted to weep in this scene, the young
director dissuaded her; this explains the early head on hands
business, she was fixing up to cry, in fact the scene was run off
and shot and Joan, weeping, ran up the ramp to the door; nope,
the director made her do this over again, substituting for the
tears a frightened run from something down into the general
driveway of the night so that he had all of us in the fogswept
audience fearful already of some new menace to come from his
fantasy; in fact people now began to crane down the ramp to,
I mean down the driveway to see; I expected a Cadillac with
crooks; (doesn't it seem as though the script would have been
materially altered on the point of this decision about whether
to cry or be frightened? . . . it must have been some wild decision and inspiration in the clear ear of this post-Kwakiutl American culture, the clear air of early times) (of course I stood
amazed) all the crowd was amazed, little teenage girls took care
to notice that the director, absentmindedly explaining to Joan
in the wind, swept and held her scarf when she took a drag off
a cigarette, the teenage girls thought this to be extraspecial
polite to her as Movie Queen but actually I noticed to make his
point clear and to do so drawing her head down by the scarf
noose around her neck and really make her listen his pithy best
instruction; I thought it was just a little on this side of cruel, I

feel a twinge of sorriness for Joan, either because all this time she'd been suffering real horrors nevertheless as movie queen that I had no idea about, or, in the general materialism of Hollywood she is being maltreated as a star "on the way out"; which she certainly is not at this moment (probably is), though of course all the teenage girls were quick to say, in loud voices for everyone to hear, that her makeup was very heavy, she'd practically have to stagger under it, and leaving it up to us to determine how saggy and baggy her face; well, naturally, I didn't expect Joan Crawfish in the fog to be anything but Joan Crawfish in the fog;——(there were subsidiary love affairs that is, apart from the movie one, going on in the audience itself): but I was determined not to let the audience distract me. It was so arranged finally, so decided upon: the area of grass where I'd originally stood to witness my first kicks of this debacle spectacle was finally and suddenly used (I say suddenly because it apparently was not really necessary judging from the scene being shot) and the whole crowd had to move over into a limited area (as though that's what the directors wanted not for kicks but in serious fascistic interest in the movement of crowds) which was also cut off from the street by floodlights on restricted ground, truly "cameras" area, action, cameras, so nobody could go home in these fascistic intervals; there was no backway out, the audience, the crowd had been finally surrounded and looped in and forted in by this invading enemy, the crowd was cooped up in an Alamo, I heard one woman say "I'll be damned if I don't go home *between* scenes!" though no one, not even the Inspector at the rope line hastily thrown up, had mentioned or heard of between-scenes or anything like that, if someone in the crowd hadn't used some democratic social intelligence the crowd would have stood rooted on forbidden ground freezing all night before some kindly and courtly state trooper decided to tell them they didn't have to stand there at all, perfectly proper to walk right up to the klieg lights and even in fact bump into them. Personal, or private, property still prevailed in the presence of several portly gentlemen from upstairs, excuse me; gentlemen, bankers, businessmen, who lived in the creamy Russian Hill apartment and others on the same little driveway semi-privated street (a street, incidentally, with a vista that draws unofficial tourists like myself on sunny

red Sunday gloomdusks that show you the Golden Gate opening purple to the wild gray banners of the orient sea way out,
and the quiet of the wild hills across the Bridge, Marin County,
bushy, dark, filled with cragous canyons of strange traffic, over-
surmounted as a scene by Mt. Tamalpais, a real vista and one
which now of course in the foggy night no one and none of the
Hollywood cameras could see) businessmen who lived in this
charming district congregating as interested neighbors in an
unofficial spectacle (impulsive, organic spectacle) taking place
in their backyards, on their private but not hotly debated property, their hospitable property that's it; so that when a cop, a
trooper Nazi type with sharp jaw, boots, protruberant gun, etc.
steel eyes, told everybody with equal icy calm to move back,
women included, but went up to our cluster of neighbors they
apparently looked back at him with ample-bellied slow surprise
and one of them decided to say that he had talked with Mr.
So-and-So the producer or Assistant Camera Technician and
they knew certainly well the entire proceedings by which the
apartment management itself had rented out its grounds and
impedimenta for a Hollywood location shot, so that if the
trooper should try to make them move back, he would do so
under duress of the knowledge that they were interested clients
of the management of the property upon which that hired tax-
free trooper stood, only fat businessmen having the gall nowadays to stay by the letter of the law give or take; so that, damn
it all, when I tried to winny my way into the center of the
camera crew (I was dressed exactly like they were, at least in the
dark, I had a leather jacket with a fur collar, wino chino pants,
etc. in other words like a soldier in the arctic, a worker in the fog,
etc.) why when the trooper came up to me he wasn't quite sure
where I belonged and said "Are you with the company?" and
had I said "Yes," and I was just then walking or on the movement of deciding to walk up to the midst of the cameras and
wires nonchalantly, I went and said "No," automatically, and,
automatically, he sent me back to the crowd, where I spent the
rest of my time craning, which is an occupation in itself, proper
old men move away from you slyly, enjoying the suspicion that
you're a pickpocket. Joan Rawshanks stood in the fog. . . .

  I said to her "Blow, baby, blow!" when I saw that thousands'
eyes were fixed on her and in the huge embarrassment of that,

really, on a human-like level, or humane, all these people are going to see you muster up a falsehood for money, you'll have to whimper tears you yourself probably never had any intention of using; on some gray morning in your past what was your real tear, Joan, your real sorrows, in the terrible day, way back in the Thirties when women writhed with a sexual torment and as now they writhe with a sexual frustration, they used to, now they don't, they learned to be a generation not liking it; everybody can see her plain as day fabricating tears on her arm, but she really does; there's no applause but there is later when she finally gets the apartment house door open after three or four instructed yanks . . . now there's only the great silence of the great moment of Hollywood, the actual TAKE (how many producers got high on Take do you think?) just as in a bullfight, when the moment comes for the matador to stick his sword into the bull and kill it, and the matador makes use firmly of this allotted moment, you, the American who never saw a bullfight realize this is what you came to see, the actual kill, and it surprises you that the actual kill is a distant, vague, almost dull flat happening like when Lou Gehrig actually did connect for a home run and the sharp flap of the bat on ball seems disappointing even though Gehrig hits another home run next time up, this one loud and clout in its sound, the actual moment, the central kill, the riddled middle idea, the thing, the Take, the actual juice suction of the camera catching a vastly planned action, the moment when we all know that the camera is germinating, a thing is being born whether we planned it right or not; there were three takes of every area of the action; Joan rushing up the drive, then Joan fiddling with her keys at the door, and later a third take that I never got to see, three shots of each, each shot carefully forewarned; and the exact actual moment of the Take is when silence falls over just like a bullfight. Joan Rawshanks, with her long pinched tragic face with its remaining hints of wild Twenties dissolution, a flapper girl then, then the writhey girl of the Thirties, under a ramp, in striped blouse, Anna Lucasta, the girl camping under the lamp like today you can on a real waterfront see a butch queer in seamanlongshoreman peacap bowcoat toga, with simpering fat lips, standing exactly like Joan used to do in old pictures that followed the Claudette Colbert of *I Cover the Waterfront* (busy little girl): Joan Rawshanks, actually in the fog, but as we can see with our own everyday eyes in the fog all lit by klieg lights, and in a furcoat story now, and not really frightened or anything but the central horror we all feel for her when she turns her grimace of horror on the crowd preparatory to running up the ramp, we've seen that face, ugh, she turns it away herself and rushes on with the scene, for a moment we've all had a pang of disgust, the director however seems pleased; he sucks on his red lollipop.

I begin to wonder or that is realize about his red lollipop; at first I thought it was a whistle; and then a gadget; and then an eccentricity; and then a gag; and then a plain lollipop that happens to be on location; the Director with the Lollipop, he gets his ideas better by suddenly lifting it to his lips, in the glare of kliegs, at a moment when the crowd expects him to do something else, so that they're all arrested and bemused and made to comment about the lollipop. Meanwhile I looked anxiously everywhere not only for a better place to see from, but up at the apartment house where the old ladies wrung their hands in hysteria. Apparently (for they could have drawn their blinds or rigged something up) they wanted actually to see what was going on in the street, what the actual hysteria of the scene being filmed, in which subconsciously I sensed their belief; so that in the midst of some awful sprawl by klieglight grayscreen gangster extras getting all wet and bloody in the street with ketchup as the camera actions, the old ladies would come plummeting down from their five-story window in a double wild believing religious hysterical screaming suicide which would be accidentally filmed by the expensive grinding huge cameras and make a picture so stark that for another century Hollywood tycoons would feature this film as the capper to an evening of dominoes and deals, for relaxation of the nerves; two wild women flying in the night suddenly into the area of the lamps, but so suddenly as to look to the eye like rags, then instrumentations of the eyeball, then tricks of the camera, then flickers of electricity, then finally humanizations in twisted hideous form under the bright glares of the wild fear of old women in America, plunk on the ground, and Joan Rawshanks in the fog, not smiling, or fabricating tears, standing, legs aspraddle in a moment of dubious remembrance of what a moment ago she'd thought to decide to remember about just where, halfway up the ramp, to start walking very fast so that her momentum and carrythrough would really get her up that ramp so that in the last steps she wouldn't be a middleaged struggling lady on a cement slope but a young despairing woman of the foggy night walking with lean absentminded pumping legs (being more concerned with affairs of the soul, love, night, tears, rings, fog, sorrowtomorrow) straight up that thing, no hassle. Reason, I saw those ladies, in the kitchen the old damsel had stood up a lamp, took off the sides of it somehow, so that she had a pathetic private klieg light of her own now shining down on the eyes of the crowd (didn't want people looking into her room) (her kitchen or anything) but in the general glare unnoticed, though on an ordinary night it would have upset and gassed and turned on the whole area; but nevertheless she had her lights out in the livingroom and stood there, with a sister or a neighbor, looking down on the scene wringing her hands and I could see declaiming, as though she wanted somehow to be in the movies, be photographed somehow as she declaimed in the general vicinity of a Take, very hysterical, strange, I thought she was crazy and was one of those old sisters who end up hermits if it wasn't for hotel apartments like these that provide them with a minimum of service, saving them from the fate of the Collyer brothers, really, and all over America dotty old rich ladies live like this in hotel apartments; well imagine their horror this evening with all those lights suddenly literally turned right on their windows and into their livingrooms and how they wail and cling to each other and think, naturally, the end of the world is bound to come soon if it hasn't and isn't in the process of right now. There was a fat guy with a red baseball cap; he ran up and down the driveway in some capacity allied with that of the police guards, keeping it clear of incoming cars, of people, or something; every time they shot Joan Rawshanks fiddling with her keys and yanking at that door, traffic had to be stopped on Hyde Street because of the arrangement apparently of the cameras. So I began noticing another crowd sort of thickening on Hyde Street itself, and restricted to one side there, for no reason really, of course, every now and then the fabled-cable-so-photographable coming by with a ringdingding and people, passengers, who are just riding home and have nothing to do with artistic San Francisco societies that fight to keep

the colorful cable car (and so in fact the Hollywood men, I
expected them to look with interest at the passing cable car in
the night but they didn't from which I concluded that the
sharpsters of Hollywood apparently, like New Yorkers, think all
the rest of California is square so anything they do or have is of
absolutely no serious interest, in fact feeling a twinge of civic
pride and wondering, why, on the sly, one of them didn't just
snap a photo of the cable car) (Budd Schulberg, that's who the
director looked like.)——passengers who are riding by are surprised to pass a movie lot but really californially don't give a shit
or shinola. In the back, tragic tent flamps move in the shroudy
wind that comes smack from the great hidden dark bay where
also poor broken tragic King Alcatraz like a muzzle of the cannon sits in the center of the bay, all bright lights in its pavilion
in the night, its arcade and bat shrouds, the sleephouse of two
thousand dead criminals, who with great devouring eyes must
look at San Francisco all day from behind bars and plot huge
crimes and paranoias and love-triumphs such as the world has
never known, ahem——the tents flap, the technicians bend to
stricken tasks by flashlight, there's mud at the wheels of their
trucks, somehow wagons surround them, they're the backbone
of Hollywood for the movies have nothing now but great technique to show, a great technique is ready for a great incoming
age, and these workmen of the progress of machine to aid and
relieve the world, these ambiguous wonderers at the limits of
set and imposed but useful and will-get-you-there (ho ho) task
huddled in the night doing their work behind the fuffoonery
and charaderees of Hollywood so mad, Hollywood, the Death
of Hollywood is upon us, and the wild semi-producers and
booted lieutenants of said same, the group huddled beneath the
wet flapshroud, the generals of Antietam, how they huddle
there in dark *misère*, looking for every possible angle, they think
important, actually utterly unimportant; for the director will
leap out in the drizzle to test a strand of bushes that forms the
edge of a shot of Joan Rawshanks down the driveway (it's not
Joan who stands there waiting all this time as the geniuses speculate and gape, it's the extra, young, prettier, gamer, just a girl,
tired on her feet, working for a living, etcetera, but ambitious,
she'll get there, all she's gotta do is bang the right people is what
I say, that'll get you there fastern anything why did I ever tell

you what C. S. Jones the hoghead on the, you know that old
engineer with the grimy wrinkles that spits and leans beneath
the watertower at dusk in New Mexico and from his wrinkly
sacks of eyes surveys, appraises land tracts reaching to the mist
of the mountains under a cloudheap that on the horizon sits
like the, like God on a couch; why, shore, (spitting), I could tell
you stories about that there Hollywood——only assuming;) the
director will go to all that foolish trouble to move and test a
twig and if he wants to cut it he can, as if that would add reality,
but he ends up not cutting it, just testing it, this consumes the
attention of a thousand eyes and the tickings of moments that
cost a company that puts up props by an actual apartment the
same amount of money it would cost them to build an actual
apartment house itself likely, what with all those union technicians milled and snarling in the background and all them klieg
lights and bought cops and mad producers and geniuses with
lollipops spending their precious time in a rainy Frisco night——
Joan Rawshanks in the fog. . . .

I had no difficulty picking her out, I knew her well; "Good
evening lady" uttered a little teenage girl when the director first
ran up to talk to Joan, the little girl throwing in her own line
of dialog about how'd she feel meeting Joan Rawshanks like
that say on a cable car, as oft you see, here in Frisco, dignified
ladies in furs riding the cold and draughty inconveniences of
the city; Joan Rawshanks in the fog, I didn't rub my eyes, I
didn't blink across the fog and darkness of the night where
stood the very bridge from which in a dream a friend of mine
once fell, like a floppydoll, while I, the last to arrive at the carnival in the canyon, was given first-prize on the last prize, a stale
sandwich, as sadly the elephant tents were folded and a dust
proceeded to emanate from the plain. . . . Yes, because when I
thought of Hollywood camera crews I always pictured them in
the California night, by moonlight, on some sand road back of
Pasadena or something, or maybe in some tree-y canyon at the
foot of the Mojave Desert, or some dreaming copse like the one
in Nathanael West where the cowboy who kills the chicken is
pausing suddenly at eventide to answer the chirp of a bird luting
in the dewy bushes over by the lemon dusk just showing at the
foot and mouth of the grove down there in the canyon where
they went for a Technicolor picnic it seems with their red shirts

glowing phosphorescent in the campfire——I thought of movie
crews in a location like that; best of all I thought of them in the
San Joaquin Valley of California, on a warm night, on a sand
road running through some rolling browngrass fields that at
this point happen not to be in cultivation, just ragged
indecipherable-by-moonlight fields, and a few fences, and overhanging inky trees with the ghosts of old outlaws hanging from
the cottonwood limb, and maybe a wagon standing in back of
crazyranch corral where maybe actually an old Italian fruiterer
lives with fatwife and dogs but in the moonlight it looks like
the corral of a cursed homesteader; and on the soft dust of the
starwhite dirtroad in the moonlight softly roll the big pneu-
matic tires of the camera truck, about forty miles an hour,
scooping up a low cloud for the stars; and on the back of it the
camera, pointing backwards, handled by gumchewing California Nightmen on the Local A.O.U.; and on the road itself
Hopalong Cassidy, in his white hat and on his famed pony, lop-
ing along intently with beck and bent, holding one rein up
daintily, stiffly, like a fist, instead of hanging to the pommel;
grave, bemused in the night, thinking thoughts; an escapee;
followed by a band of rustlers posing as a posse, they catch up
by the moment; the camera truck is leading and rolling them
down the slope of a long hill; soon we will see views of a roadside cut, a sudden little crick bridge made of a log or two; then
the great moony grove suddenly appearing and disappearing;
all pure California night scenery and landscape; the great hairy
trees of its night; then through a sudden splash of dark that
completely and miraculously amazingly obscures Hoppy in a
momentary invisibility; then the posse comes pell-mell from the
other hand; what will happen, how will Hoppy escape? what his
secret thoughts and stratagems! but he doesn't seem to be worried at all, in fact then you realize he's going to hide in those
dark bushes of space and let the posse ride by on momentum,
then he'll simply cut back silently on his horse which is good at
these tricks, (Cody "And etcetera that's exactly right and
more"); I thought of the camera crew doing this in the soft
Southern California night, and of their dinners by campfire
later, and talk. I had never imagined them going through these
great Alexandrian strategies just for the sake of photographing
Joan Rawshanks fumbling with her keys at a goggyfoddy door

while all traffic halts in real world life only half a block away and everything waits on a whistle blown by a hysterical fool in a uniform who suddenly decided the importance of what's going on by some convulsive phenomena in the lower regions of his twitching hips, all manifesting itself in a sudden freezing grimace of idiotic wonder just exactly like the look of the favorite ninny in every B-movie you and I and Cody ever saw (the same expression as the cop posing, the older cop, probably himself it was) to suddenly realize that he is completely witless and therefore achieving the only thought of his life, the single adult realization of anykind, before twitching and reverting back to his puppy roles, puppythorities of a kind, going down the stairs of his own home without realizing that he is doing so in the great dark shadow of time and himself falling . . . with what fascination another oldtimer in the crowd watched that older's face under the floodlights of Leon Errol the rubberlegged tragic mistaken comedian of an accident, how else could I or the oldtimer get to know——when he saw that he was under floodlights, when it, the simple symbol (Wherewereyouonthenightofjunefourteen) finally dawned on him long after it had dawned on the whole crowd who also got their fill looking before he realized, but when it did assert itself on his very tiny brain he looked, he let his lower lip slip up over his upper teeth in a simper of complete idiocy and looked to his companion, with a nose wrinkled complete giveup of what to figure or what to do next; recalling, not instantly but after awhile, that he is a policeman, and at that moment striking the copy coply pose in the flare of lights to return his attention to the drama of the filming of Joan Rawshanks in the fog, whom I saw even then looking fitfully into the sky as the camera took. Joan Rawshanks in the fog . . . it isn't that Hollywood has won us with its dreams, it has only enhanced our own wild dreams, we the populace so strange and unknown, so uncalculable, mad, eee . . . Joan Rawshanks in the fog . . . the little girls in the crowd were pretty, wore bandanas, so did Joan; the little girls were witty, pretty and nice; we had a gay time; out of the corner of my evil eyes I caught sight of little dumplings of every order, cherry lipped, nipptious, virvacious, flauntin their eyes at the boys, and I, an innocent ghost, gaping, a shadow; Joan Rawshanks in the fog, could it be the terrible dolors we all felt when

we saw her suddenly alone in the silence, standing by the litup
fence making ready to emote to millions, to erupt, vomit and
obhurt to others; we are so decadent with our moues. No discussion was on among the shroudy shadows in the litup raining
shadowy background of Franklin Delano Roosevelt, the Technician magicians, the mysteries, no discussion as to whether the
emotional, political and social issues out front had anything to
do with the state of a coil, or the kilowatt of a fowder, when of
course she is eminently layable, but as to her flaunts and sun-
dances, well, they'd have to take it up with the advisory committee on sex down at the union hall, the guys down there—at
one point a millionaire dweller in the rich apartment below
which all this was taking place took his stand along the circus
electric jutter truck and far from, as me, looking nirpatiously
over his shoulder for sign of anyone seein him, rather brushes
lightly with his hand against the material of the truckfence he's
about to lean on, not that it's not his own truck but it might
be dirty; far from me, as I stood, behind the crowd, couldn't
see nothin——meanwhile the great drama ever unfolded in the
area of the blazing lights that were so bright and white when I
first saw them coming up Hyde Street thinking I'd terminate
my walk on top of Russian Hill and get me a prospect then
return home, so bright I thought they were being used by a
new kind of civil defense organization crew that makes tests to
see how bright lights have to be for bomber planes to catch
them on foggy frisco nights; in this brightness, so bright that it
embarrasses, I myself and all the crowd were finally delivered
up judged and damned to them, because we couldn't leave
except through that restricted zone and because of that they
put the light on the alley of exit, for Hollywood of course is
eager to see the populace itself, ahem, I mean, Hollywood
wants to see more than anyone of us, than we do, than anything, we all had to cross that catwalk of lights and felt ourselves
melt into identity as we crossed from the fingerprint rack to the
blue desk, so much so that I took quick refuge beside two conmen who had commented on the old ladies upstairs as they
really——they were burglars or eager to meet rich old dames say
in a capacity as servant and then rob them, I took cover in their
shadow so persistently as we walked the catwalk that one of
them observed the tenacity of my presence somehow and

looked annoyedly, so I had to dart forward, for a moment be caught, flying, etched in whiteheat wild Hollywoodian blazos, to take cover behind a librarian girl who'd had enough of her first glimpse of Hollywood filming since she'd arrived from Little Rock on her first sojourn in California. Earlier in the performance a beautiful crazy girl in glasses and ordinary coat and low heels came rushing up the driveway before the first Take as though she was lost and stopped to talk, or to be talked to really, by the pretty stand-in girl, who only and quite in a natural way began to explain something to her, but then we in the whole crowd saw the girl goof and titter and get that camera feeling and we all laughed her off as an eccentric movie crasher not a serious ordinary girl lost going home in the maze of a movie location scene; well she was a luscious little girl and came around with the rest of the crowd, finally, where it stood, on a grassy slope, watching; stood in the back, smiling, isolated, bashful still . . . with a kind of crazy dream in her eyes. But I was determined to see the spectacle of Hollywood. There she was . . . Joan Rawshanks in the fog; she had taken up the stand-in's place; they were ready for the last great Take. The whistle shrilled, that of the cop who by now had, in the background to all the moil and counter-confusion, worked like a ferret to finally achieve a pinnacle of success and power which had increased to the point now where he was actually blowing his whistle after every Take, in order to signal not only Hyde Street traffic it could move on but the remnants of the trapped crowd who wanted to sneak out the illuminated scandalous escape alley and go home, and had to face that ordeal to do it, running a gauntlet more cruel than any Cecil B. De Mille ever dreamed. So traffic, whitefaced and panicked, stayed suspended on the street; subinterior lieutenants of the uniformed corps rushed out; one big particular lug who was of course a perfect Hollywood version of the cop, they must have hired him for looks and not for training, he'd go running frantically with his hand on his gunhock across or that is along the great Italian balconean rail that juts out from the front of Elite Arms and in full sight, in bright lights, against white marble, dressed all in crazy blackshirt black, he'd go running after some imaginary traffic disturbance that had somehow took root in the porch, otherwise he had no right immediately prior to each take to suddenly

dart off shouting some fake name or ambiguous imitation of
someone shouting for somebody, hand on gun as if they were
filming him, the which I assure you if you've at all trusted my
previous observations, they were not; understand; and so, ah,
but, running to the end of the thing, darting a look over the
precipice, the whole thing and the whole scene, the top of Russian Hill, overlooking great etceteras of the city and the Bay
Bridge down there——the crowd gently surged forward to see
Joan enact the scene of the frightened woman with the fiddling
keys and the door that would only open to three tugs. Through
the rain I try to discern signs of whether the camera is turning
or not; then I could be ready for the big moment; I endeavor
to hear someone shout a signal like "Camera!" There are stri-
dent disturbances in the crowd itself; feeling cold, surrounded,
foolishified, foolified, trapped, they now make cracks, the kids
wrestle in the dark, little dogs break away from the leashes so
that pretty lovergirls previously turning smiling faces to suitors
in the interesting dark are now scurrying among legs of pedestrians very ungirllike and so forth to refetch their little doggies,
and an eccentric but goodlooking middleaged woman who
never goes out alone but has decided to come down in a hasty
coat to see a real Hollywood filming is now hysterically looking
around with a smile of gratitude and goodcheer and light, can't
name it, she was watching so intently from the park curb that
she didn't notice when she started to teeter off it, so when she
landed on her feet not realizing the instinct perfection she was
caught surprised and stumbled forward and teetered and almost
fell, but didn't; to atone for this smiled at everyone in the immediate vicinity close enough to have caught her in the act, as
I did; but no one acknowledged in the least, we all turned away,
she ended up smiling in a void, understand, smiling too in the
opposite direction from the cameras, the cameras are focused
on the rainy asphalt all white, her vacant and inexcusable and
imoondable smile is fixed on nothing but the rainy cape of
night, the whole part of the wind and the night that sits out
here juttin over the bay and a raw wet mountain or two that
comes from Seattle and even the cold regions further North.
Joan Rawshanks hugged herself, she was getting ready for another Take; she had her head bowed; I felt tired standing. She

moves forward . . . ah, the signal must have come; the cameras
are actually turning; just like when the great punter punts, the
ball soars high and magnificent and spiral but the sound of the
kick was unsatisfying; now the cruel cameras grind and gravel
and turn and pick up Joan, and there she goes, hustling like
mad up that ramp, fumbling for her keys in her purse, now she's
got them; it's exactly the same thing they've already done twice,
this is almost as perfect as a vaudeville act; she goes to the door,
fumbles, gets the keyhole, plunges into the keyhole, with rap-
ture, like she was coming, she has that awful ugh desperation
we all saw at this moment, the door won't yield to her first tug,
gad, the door is closed, obstreperous, you can feel it in the
crowd, their hostility for that door is already aroused and
the picture isn't even cut yet or the film dry; they're going to
hate that door en masse opening night; it's just a door, though;
I see Joan tugging at it, she tosses her frightened face to the sky,
the overhead, actually, creamy concrete garage ramp light on
the ramp steps; two tugs, three, the door finally opens, the
crowd cheers scattered and forlorn in the rainy dismalities; and
Joan has made her third Take——The camera men suddenly
begin mutilating and dissecting parts of their equipment and
camera, something is being slapped to the ground like a doggie,
a cigarette lights, the director's assistant (tall sort of grave fellow
like a railroad baggage handler foreman with his hat on the back
of his head only this one here wears a hunting hat casually and
when an intelligent little boy in glasses impulsively wandered
on-set to ask intelligent questions or be let to sit he was kind
and fatherly and not police-like in succeeding in getting him,
the puffy cheek wide-eyed educated curious boy, back, pudgy-
legged and all, into the crowd, to watch, where he oughta
watch from, like us); the Take was over. Joan vanished in a flare
of cloaks, a Carriage was pulling up; just back of the rose vine
wall there . . . but, no, then, actually, Joan was in the tent with
the Generals; it appears they'll take another Take and then everybody knock off for the night, see what Frisco's got to offer;
one technician saying to another "I don't know as I wanta do
that *tonight*," in other words everybody on the job starting to
relax and talk about afterwork matters, so that the crowd began
to file away in great numbers that ate at its presence, in fact I

went with this slice and batch, across those guilt provoking judgment day lights of greatlamps . . . the director's assistant is going around clearing up things it seems. The prettiest girl in the crowd, darkeyed Susan, is in love with James, the tall young beautiful handsomeboy of the neighborhood who will probably win a prize soon, go to Hollywood and become a basketball star simultaneously and also be sought, because of his demure purple eyes, which he can't help, (and long-eyelashed languor) by queers of every kind; but Barbara, whose mother and elder sister are out witnessing with her, is also on the make for James but at the same time on the outs with Susan; so both she and Susan have been occupied all this time (while cops gain power, while producers gain time, while movie stars win thousands of dollars etc. and while old ladies wring their hands in despair, while the fog rolls and ships are sailing out into the darkness of the sea this very instant) occupied all this time in a catfight for James' attention; James, however, being well attended by his squire, junior brother, and dog, and not unconscious of his power; so that after Barbara makes an elaborate fuss saying goodnight to her mother and elder past-prime sister, so that past-prime sister will whimper and coo for James, who loves it and withers, and writhes, past-prime says "Well if you insist on staying out, Barbara, you can tell us all the details in the morning . . ." so that James has to duck a little to miss the object, after that play-act going on simultaneous with the show down there, Barbara officially installs herself to talk to James but he is in love with Susan and keeps casting to her, and when that slice of the crowd I spoke of leaves, Susan is in it, simply going home, leaving James forlorn, defeating Barbara, but Barbara thinks she's won! (defeat and victory all around); all this, too, after Susan and James leapt madly and gaily over the hedges together earlier, in the second try of the first Take, say. So long have I been here that the original interest I had found in observing the director, who was not much older than myself, got lost and with it the director got lost, I couldn't see him anymore, he faded away into something rich and distant, like sitting by swimmingpools on drizzly nights in Beverly Hills in a topcoat, with a drink, to brood. As for poor Joan Rawshanks in the fog, she too was gone . . . I guess they'd raise a glass of

champagne to her lips tonight in some warmly lit room atop
the roof of a hilltop hotel roofgarden swank arrangement somewhere in town. At dawn when Joan Rawshanks sees the first
hints of great light over Oakland, and there swoops the bird of
the desert, the fog will be gone.

IN THE FOREFRONT OF THE THOUGHTS of Charles Brevet
("Ah! Close-ups of Curvy Cuties Oscar! Could You Ask for
Anything More?") I could ask for October again, and the first
falling leaves gathering soot by the railroad track in the New
England heaviness; I could complain about the honey in a
woman's cunt, or sing a song about how you can suffocate on
steam in a closed tunnel; or spit at ruby lips that frame and flesh
the inward desire to do nothing but get fucked, which is the
look on a good woman's face, Jack. This one with her imitation
lace to conceal her real cunt (imitation etc.) her with her eyes all
pool-ly and dark, all wild and midnight, all apple tree and gold,
no pale stupid pose and camp, no hateful commercialism, like a
willing pursy-mouthed whore, but the sloose lips of indulgence,
suck, lie around, eat it, love it all the way, you beautiful doll the
hairs on your thigh are my midnight; the lights in your eye-stars
make me see the moon with its old sad face always mooning
over the world no matter what's happening; it were you and
me, under a roof, dar, love, heart, the moon with same sad-
dened biceptual, bisexual condomidance would erupt her blue
lights to our souls and you, you angel, your wrist makes me
hungry, your every tiny womanhood part of you and all over
you is and it is woman, I couldn't resist you in church, I'd lick
your snowy belly anywhere, in front of any crowds, any time,
on the cross, in Golgotha, on a snowpile, on a picket fence, I'd
bring you $57.90 a week base pay and let you suck me off by
the washing machine when the long red sun sinks like a john in
the red western pacific, oh you lovely ashen-eyed lovely of the
sols, you woman, you gorgeous heart, you small-eared perfect
doe, you rabbit, you fuck you, I want to grab your thighs with
my two hands and spread them forcibly and I want you to just
lie back and watch me, watch me, you can watch me all you
want and I can watch you all I want, perfect understanding,
no more Rimbauds, no more toiletries, poetries, just like you

always, wanted to be, from the beginning to now the start, just like always hunny baby, so it will be, and is the rain still moon-sawing in the poor void?

Your eyes are like the star of midnight, your lips are like the blood of a sacrifice by moonlight; your shoulders are like the yieldings of elephants in the flesh, as they mill and stamp, and moo and turn, their great forms succumbing to the incredible weight of the herd entire, so your shoulders loosey disconnect and ain't all loused up tight and musky in your muscle bones; but pretty as snow; the cake of your breasts when you hide them behind black lace as if I wanted to spread peanut butter sandwiches on it; the cake of your, the icing of your fine and wonderful cool nipples that I dig all the way, even unto the point there they get a little hard and bespeak your inner excite-ments that this is the only way I can reach them; when I was born on that raft, I mean on that barge on the East River, my father was a riverboatman of old beerdrinking wild railroad-building generation New York of the 1900's; why you darling, the night has no meaning without you, and without you I have died a many a many night you weak sisters of the pale! Now that I find you darling, Ruby is your name, Ruby, Mary, ruby mary, filthy bloody mary, you'll an old hag be? not without I don't have something to do about it to hasten you on your way old Yeats will butler, he really was a cunt man that old Irish sod I love him and dig him, why paterson williams the carlos poet, so carlos he makes a shroud out of a mill, or turns clandestine calvers out of the next stick of half tea that I myself brewed in China that time without even bothering to inquire into the price of pselgnels.

Poor doll, I know your juicy hole . . . don't die so; baby doll, your lips are cold, you don't stay high with me; if you could stay high with me forever, and together we'd lay in the pool of myself wrapped in your self, why, Andean princess, I'd lay you, like my first wife used to say, with "violent love."——make violent love to you, hard, if you so wish . . . ask if you want . . . I don't care either way . . . my way is your way, name my way, your way, I've got, I got no way, you got a way, your way is MY way, my way is YOUrrrrrrway, doll, run on ahead, f, f, f, f, f, f, f, f, f, f fuck f f f fuck f f f fuck, why——I licked your eyebrow that time; from over here, that is, mentally, not actually; why did you hide from me (last night); if you die I die.

Well and what could Clementina reply to that? that she then, not that she "nlt" then, with moulct of feathers and torn betwixt twelve fine and "furduloure" types of "clanderi," your "siwht theh eyiou,"; in the middle of the tight fit I've always advised all my students to stick to their gums.

BUT YOU CAN'T SAY THAT ANYTHING REALLY TREMENDOUS happened to Cody and me till the summer of 1949 when I went out West to find him.

A night I spent in Denver . . . prior to my departure to the Coast . . . some kind of preamble. I had just suddenly realized (I had just seen a very successful young American off on a plane, an executive he was) that nothing in the world matters; not even success in America but just void and emptiness awaits the career of the soul of a man. I walked across a giant plain from the airfield, of course all Denver's a plain; I was a sad red speck on the face of the earth; I was also a beat hitch-hiker that nobody was giving rides to except one poor Negro soldier who tried to be nice to me when I asked him hep questions about Five Points the Denver niggertown and he didn't know, not being involved in a white man's preoccupations about what colored life must be. I came to the streets of Denver in their infinitely soft, sweet and delightful August evening; dusk it was, I say, purple, with shacks in soft alleys, and many lawns, all over Denver're many lawns all the time; you see a lawn at the Chinese rectory, at the factory, got drunk on lawns, lost your keys . . . rolled in the grass. . . . I walked in that Denver Night——but at 23rd and Welton or 25th, thereabouts, near the gastank and the softball field; I come in there carrying my sad thoughts and also a cup of red hot and really blood red chili; with beans; no, no beans that time; at 23rd and Welton the lawns of soft sweet old Denver are raggedier, it's where Negro and Mexican children play all day, their parents don't tell them to get off the lawn, there are no signs, you see therefore nice dusty paths running betwixt the lawngreens; and rickety fences are nearabouts, Denver, it's all rickety fences and backyards and incinerators smoking in that blue morning air, but also soft sad dusk at dark; in 1947 in fact, right after I met Cody, and had those anticipatory dreams of me and him drinking and gabbling at bars in the construction worker night; I came to feel that the alleys, the fences, the streets were the "holy Denver streets" I called them, and just because of this particular softness—I walked along that, feeling low, seeing how the successful young executive, mysterious Boisvert, was just a bored old Tiresias completely beat and sighing; with nothing to do in his soul but flounce around and yawn and wait, always wait, wait; the dullness of the heart gone dead, the heart never got anything. The highest glamor he had, and was as sad as an old sishrag; in fact we stood on top of a mountain together at Central City and overlooked a hump of mountains with their special snowing iceclouds flying along a heavenly golden cold ridge, the roaring day of the Colorados, high up, and didn't think much of it together; by myself I might have marveled or by himself he might have . . . but it meant nothing, to see, own, and possess the world from a height physical and social, to either of us. He talked some other nonsense, anecdotes of boredom maybe. You've got to get that World of mind. So I walked the streets of Denver in the night, and passed the dark shapes of women with soft voices, and children with soft voices, and the fragrant smoke from the pipes of workingmen resting on the porch in the evening; at one point in fact a young colored girl peered at me on the sidewalk and said "Eddy?" I passed the holy whitewashed advertisements, the paint-splashes of white in the blue dark greendark that is Denver; I looked up at the flowsy old moon still there with her tilted over sad head, weeping, weeping for the world. Down in Denver, down in Denver, all I did was die. I remember, that was my refrain. Suddenly I came to a softball game under bright floodlights, with earnest glad young athletes but amateurs rushing pell-mell on the dust to the roar of audiences made up of their admiring mothers, sisters, fathers and footman buddies, *whaling* at a ninth inning rally, throwing up dustclouds at second base, slapping doubles off the leftfield foulpole and stretching them into crazy triples only it's a foul and there are groans. I felt pretty silly for having been too longfaced to play softball under litup tanks of the Gashouse Kids and Denny Dimwit at night with the Sunday funnies on the corner and the fair exchange of honesties in childhood,

like this, but instead had to immediately be the star and in fact
rush on to professional gravities and college instead of goofing
with the original game. Poor little Mexican hero-Codys of the
Denver night! With sadfaced little blond Joannas cheering from
the bleachers, with soft hearts, loud voices, real loyalties, squealing, stamping their feet for their brother-boys, crying, cheering
them on at that time when brothers mean something; and me,
in the back, sitting with an old bum whose only interest at the
moment is looking over at a neighbor's sidepocket where latter's
keeping an extry can of cold beer while he's opening the other
with a can opener, the bum just wants to think if he's got
enough money for some too, fishes in his pocket; I look, on
the street, at the intersection, cars are stopped at the red light;
there's exhaust smell; across the traffic, on the rickety porches,
behind lawns, the folks stretch in their evening darkness and
occasionally look at the game or up at the moon and stars, and
it's another summer. Poor heroes of the Night Cavorting in
the Field! And this precisely the field that Cody had once told
me about, and I'd listened so garbledly, that I now, and later,
thought of it as the place where he had somehow lost his rubber bouncinball long ago, the ball he always used to bounce
to and from school with, at ten, eleven, when he lived with his
father in the Larimer flops but also went to school, bouncing
it in the clean spaces between sidewalk markers and then as he
grew more dextrous bouncing and slamming it and sending it
careering off the walls of garages and skyscrapers and dashing
across streets and traffic to retrieve; as, even later, he began
riding his bicycle, his paper route or later route, bumblebee
route, bicycle route selling bumblebee bubblegum, the one in
which, like a Saroyan hero, he made his soul get on the pedals
for its existence and rationalizations; I was told by Irwin that he
"made a living scraping bubblegums off windowpanes" and I
pictured myself washing down the windows at Brockleman's at
Sunday dawn when they're all going to church through Kearney
Square, but actually I do know he worked for a Bubblegum
Caterer and also rode bicycles for a living with an Indian buddy
not Rinick but Ben Rowel with whom he was shot at Christmas
Eve 1943 in the Ozarks by a mangy car-owner; an endeavor,
the soul bicycling, that got him much further than the later
contemplation of billiard balls as a background . . . relaxed

foreground for anxious serious thoughts about money and——
So I died, I died in Denver I died; I said to myself, "What's
the use of being sad because your boyhood is over and you can
never play softball like this; you can still take another mighty
voyage and go and see what Cody is finally doing." Oh the
sadness of the lights that night! . . . the great knife piercing me
from the darkness . . . the nightcloud of my dreams rising, and
the general brownness of my salvation which is like the brownness in old barrooms and also on Ninth Avenue in October and
when they talk about scatology and in Rembrandt's canvas corner when he draws the mighty and golden aracanions, archways,
bulverses and mardigras gargoyles for his surrounding-space to
the minute and fragile, lost, world-conscious figures of Jesus
and the Woman Taken in Adultery, as priests stare. In a swash,
no, paragraph.

In a swash, no, who says paragraph, who says swash,

In a simple swash of dust clouds things were accomplished
and I simply took off for Denver to that is for San Francisco, to
see Cody . . . necessarily I had to leave a lot out there. The trip
consumed a considerable amount of my energy; but it was far
from flagging; I sat, in the rear left corner of the car with my
head against the glass and let all the dry old Nevadys roll on;
there be nothing easier than riding in a good new car across the
West, especially when, as in this travel bureau car, you have no
personal responsibilities with the driver or drivers, and so don't
have to talk or keep time; but just sit back, making more time
than a bus, and more stops, and fewer bounces, and less fare,
cool all over, just sit there, especially at night, and let that land
unfold, unfold, with the poor driver to boot it onwards into the
mist that hangs over the road.

> O dewy road,
> Filmy eyed dove,
> Road of gold, rove
> Noun of roads,
> The town of roads,
> Road, a road,
> The same new old,
> The near a ling.

At the junction of the state line of Colorado, its arid western one, and the state line of poor Utah I saw in the clouds huge and massed above the fiery golden desert of eveningfall the great image of God with forefinger pointed straight at me through halos and rolls and gold folds that were like the existence of the gleaming spear in His right hand, and sayeth, Go thou across the ground; go moan for man; go moan, go groan, go groan alone go roll your bones, alone; go thou and be little beneath my sight; go thou, and be minute and as seed in the pod, but the pod the pit, world a Pod, universe a Pit; go thou, go thou, die hence; and of Cody report you well and truly.

VISIONS OF CODY: I've had several visions of Cody, most of the great ones in the middle of a tea-high and the greatest on jazz tea-high, matched only by the vision I had of him in Mexico. My first great vision of Cody didn't come, as I say, as I keep saying, as though I had to struggle to keep saying, until 1948, goodly two years after I met him in that naked door. It was as if he was a superhuman spirit walking, or that is racing in flesh sent down to earth to confound me not only in my actions but in my thoughts: wild, wild day I suddenly looked from myself to this strange angel from the other side (this is all like bop, we're getting to it indirectly and too late but completely from every angle except the angle we all don't know) of Time——which he kept talking about all the time. Cody now says "Time—— goes——by——*fast!!*——you don't realize or notice or come to tell how *fast*——*time*——flies!!" Beware, he is saying, time is flying; he's not saying later than you think, or Life begins, or the hour is struck, he just says that time is passing us all by this very minute. Then he looks at you primly, with an expression he rarely——Cody has a broken nose that gives a ridge to his bone, Grecian and slight, and a soft nose-end that only slightly Romanizes down but not like a banana nose, it is exactly the nose of a Roman warrior or prelate and like a nose I once saw in the sketches of Leonardo da Vinci that he has made in the sunny streets of active day in old medieval Italy (the Renaissance, like its name, was really French) a curly downward nose-tip like angry old men . . . Cody's cheekbones are smooth, youthful and high; this, with the nose, and alert darting open eyes, makes an arcade-covering for his mouth whenever demurely he presses

and prunes it together, or warps, or persimmons it, for a moment of patience, which usually comes after a statement like he
made about Time, patience to await the foolish unconsidered
words ever ready to blurt from the mouths not the minds of
poor mortal humankind. Consider, harken to Cody's face——his
expression——his now-patience——after all the franticness of his
boy days——why he walks in the rain (or drives) and smiles like
that? (it's an interior splashed smile, the primness). His Ger-
manic head is crew cut: when hair crowds over his skullbones
he combs it to the side like Hitler only sandy, only bullnecked,
rocknecked. He loves to mimic women and wishes he was a
sweet young cunt of sixteen so he could feel himself squishy and
nice and squirm all over when some man had to look and all he
had to do was sit and feel the soft shape of his or her ass in a silk
dress and that squishy all over feeling, and he'd like to spend all
day over a hot stove and finger himself and feel the rub of his
dress on his ass and wait for hubby who has one sixteen inches
long. Adamant nature, though, made him cheekboned impen-
etrable as steel; a daughter may delight in her father's soft cheek,
pinch it, let her try to pinch and purse up his cheekbone with its
arid juiceless stubble. Cody reads Proust slowly and reverently,
has been 729 pages along in Volume I over the past two years,
reading damn near daily, sometimes less than half a page at a
time; he reads out loud, as I say, with the pride and dignity of
a Robert Burns, a Carlyle a Hero of Hero Worships, of whom
it may be said "What light *glares* into his soul that he should
be so."——should be so harsh, unbending, raw, the now-quiet
father of supper hours with potential souls on his knee——Emily,
Gaby, Timmy Pomeray so golden, fat as corn pudding, the same
Cody that I saw from the lower deck of the ferry crossing the
Mississippi when we passed through New Orleans and Algiers
that drowsy afternoon *careering* as it seemed to me like a flag,
a pennant in the blue from the upper deck overhanging the
brown river of his Missouri great fathers, Joanna, his lovelife,
grinning feebly behind him and ready to jump with him if he
was ready for the ecstasy (just like Julien and Cecily on other
roofs). Dear Lord above, I'm high . . . (or wish I was).
  The one great occasion that I saw him with eyes of fire or on
fire and saw everything not only about him but America, all of
America as it has become conceptualized in my brain, was when,

in Mexico, having just blasted a great rugged cigar of marijuana
in the desert parked in front of the stone hut of a family the
mother of which as her sons lazed in the fly door, the door that
was not only the dreamy occupancy of flies in drowse and drum
dum but of brothers and cousins, male, with regardant legs
in the dust, no hillbillies, *paisanos*, cats of the pampas, campo
people, went back in the green dancing shade of well planted
trees swimming in a fresh, or relatively fresh afternoon breeze
from over across the yucca and the peyotl and the crazy weeds
and sand dust blowing, where the daughters were pounding
the supper and humming little drowsy songs like the wind as
they waited for nightfall and the tower and the well (outlook
and imagination), a tired old Mexican mother but happy and
among hers, in colorless shroudy apron more like the great
dresses of Dutch navvies in old black prints stooped humbly
and seriously to scoop with her closed palm and like milking
the long thin dry stalk that knocked its rattly pod-leaves in the
paper she held open underneath with the other hand, in the
apron, throwing precipitate like wheat from a wagon the curled
green burnt conglomerations of crackly weedleaf which is marijuana. On the completion of this tremendous bomber, and as
Cody drove back to town for our afternoon in the whorehouse,
and money in our pockets, and no place to go, and in a foreign
land, and high, and in the sun, I looked at him (as he sat back
driving five miles an hour through narrow stucco alleys that
were streets, with dark eyes watching from all kinds of sudden
spots, as if we were in Afternoon Land not Mexico (famous for
its night) and as, graciously taking instructions from the sweet
and naive little Mexican cat (nineteen) who'd turned us on, left,
right, *derecha, izquierda*, with pointings, to which Cody replied
with grandiloquent purple robed Yesses and That's Rights and
I Do Hear Yous, Man, the same kid showing us his infant son
for a space when we were so high it seemed like an angel suddenly being shown to the tea-heads in Teahead City by the
Youthful Mayor, whose Beauteous Wife who Was Simple Like
Ruth in the Corn watched from a dark Algerian door (with
gold in the stone) finally, feeling so well at ease with the world,
leaning back, bushy haired from a sudden wild high (Americans never smoke marijuana cigars) that must have blown his
top up and the hair too, surprised, flushed, blinking, looking

down to see the steering wheel of that old '37 Ford jalopy we
bucketed down in from Denver over many a dusty bushy mile
running roughly down the spine of the Americas, to see if the
wheel held, but actually in complete possession of all his wits
and joys and in fact so completely and godlike-ly aware of every
single little thing trembling like a drop of dew in the world,
or sitting like the antique clinker of a paper bookmatch on an
insignificant green desk somewhere in the world, aware of the
glow in his stomach related to the strength of his father, aware
of myself and Sherman in the backseat high and dumb, and of
the kid, the town, the day, the year, the consequence, and time
passing us all by, and yet everything always really all right, that
he suddenly glowed up like a sun and became all rosy as a rosy
balloon and beautiful as Franklin Delano Roosevelt, and said,
from way far back maybe ten minutes, an hour or a year or years
ago, "Yes!" At that moment I decided never to forget it (even
as it happened); Cody was so great, so good, that I couldn't
believe——he was by far the greatest man I had ever known.
Do you know that now I realize and look back and see that in
the beginning he made everybody smoke tea so they'd look at
him in their original virgin never to be repeated kicks? . . . the
bastard sensed it. Yet he's an angel. I'm his brother, that's all.

But enough of my greatest enemy——because while I saw
him as an angel, a god, etcetera, I also saw him as a devil,
an old witch, even an old bitch from the start and always did
think and still do that he can read my thoughts and interrupt
them on purpose *so I'll look on the world like he does.* Jealous,
all over. If's anything he can't stand, Val Hayes first off said in
1946, is people fucking when he's not involved, that is, not
only in the same room but the same floor or house or world.
And I discovered he can't stand people talking or putting forth
a thought or even thinking in the same world. He feels that
he is indispensable to his wife, children, his former wives, me,
and the——that would be Heaven, or Time, or Whatever. He's
afraid of death, very cautious, cagey, careful, suspicious, wary,
half near a thing——out of the corner of his eye he talks about
danger and death all the time. He believed in God right away
when he exploded into T and that trip in 1948, told me so immediately as we drove through the night across oceans of rain
and the desolation of the Wilderness and of the Dark Cities.

While eating supper he continually nudges his wife's thigh and sucks juices from her lips and pats her kindly on the head and slaps applesauce out of a can into his children's (his daughters') plates, drinks milk out of the bottle, won't hardly allow me a glass, himself doles out the Nescafé in cups, runs bread in hand and his bread always is wrapped in a sandwich around the evening meat to the stove, handles precarious cast-iron covers of old stove with teetering jumps and balances and Whoops like W. C. Fields, "Lookout there! lookout! lookout! yeaaah!" Everybody got excited this year about Marlon Brando in *Streetcar Named Desire*; why Cody has a thinner waist and bigger arms, personally knew Abner Yokum in the Ozarks (Marlon Brando is really Al Capp), has probably bigger bats and catchers mitts, wears week-old T-shirts covered with baby puke, is like a machine in the night, masturbates five or six times a day when his wife is sick (in fact all the time), has private secret rags all over the house (that I have seen), writes with severe and stately dignity under after supper lamps with muscular bended neck three or four times the half, can run the 100 in less than 10 flat, pass 70 yards, broad jump 23 feet, standing broad jump 11 feet, throw a 12-pound shot 49 feet, throw a 150-pound tire up on a 6-foot rack with just one arm and his knee, plays pinochle at night with the boys in the caboose, wears a slouched black hat sometimes, was walking champ in the Oklahoma State Joint Reformatory, cuts and switches poetic old dirty boxcars from the Maine hills and Arkansas, holds his footing when a 100-car freight slams along in a jawbreaking daisy chain roar to him, drives a '32 Pontiac clunker (the Green Hornet) as well as a '50 Chevy station wagon sharp and fast (I see his head bobbing into sight from the sea of heads in cars on Market Street, girls throng at the bell and the greenlight walk among clerks and Bartlebies and Pulham Esquires and Victor Matures of California, Chinese girls, luscious office girls with tight skirts Chineesing at their knee-sides and the juice drippin down their legs) (why I could tell you stories make your cock stand) and "Wow" "Yes!" "Look at *that* one!" And we dig the cops too, not as cops, but say, "See? that one is all hungup on a pain in his neck, he keeps rubbing his neck, jess standin there, working, thinking, worried about his neck."

In dark and tragic railyard nights of San Francisco like those so long ago in Denver we drive the wide-eyed children along the old red boxcars——"Erie, 15482," "Missouri, Kansas, Texas, 1290," "Union Pacific, Road of the Streamliners, 12807"——we pass the old cowboy switchman in his shack, also the eccentric flagman with a red flag, shortcuff pants, brown felt hat but circus like, fiery yellow but actually dirty gloves, strange rosy weathered expression, a card in his ear, the Men at Work sign at his feet, also ordinary blue shirted haberdashery switchmen who commute to work from coastal mountain fogs and inner bay gales and stand in the middle of the night all dead and abandoned, we pass the diner now closed, the spate of bay water with its oils and slapping boxboats and the ships five blocks away sitting on the same old Penang, we pass the orange rickety railway baggage carts, the steaming Pullmans reposant at the dead-end block, the old porters red-eyed and spitting crossing the rails, the chug-smoke of a locomotive, night, the old sad railyards of life and my fathers. "That's what you'll be doing when you're braking——there's the switchman, only you'll be out on the mountainside or picking up an extra engine for the pass, easy-as-you-go, easy-as-you-go, there's the sign, there's the lantern waving, always have your brakeman's lantern." He once said you can also kill a man with it. "Man I don't get frantic high any more," he tells me, and I know we were high in the past because we were young, we were in the virgin kicks of youth and death. "Time to put the girls to sleep." We drive back to his little crooked house on Russian Hill wedged and lost on a narrow unknown sidestreet and put the golden girls in the rosy bath, their toys and little ragamuffin dusts lay dolly dormant under the kitchen stove as in the night sweetly they draw breath in the peace and security of their father's house, their mother's care, angels of angels, daughters of man, children of God. Obscurely in the kitchen, by a little painted-Evelyn pantry door, hangs a collection of Out Our Ways and Major Hooples, pinned up by old continuous Cody.

High atop the sink pantry sits his roach kit, his tea bowl, his kick plate or kickpot or fixins, a dish, glass, deep dish, small, with rolling paper, tweezers, roach pipe (hollow steel tube), roach pipe ramrod came with the tube, attached, an art tool actually, bottles of seeds for possible future bourgeois agricultures settling down in a rose covered cottage on the blueberry hill with Evelyn's dress flying in the wind when Cody runs like Jack 'n' Jill up the hill to carry her across the threshold as the kiddies cheer, the daughters understand. In this dream I lie coiled under the hill like the snake, and the Bird of Paradise is very far away, in South America actually maybe. Cody's roach kit includes old roaches from 1951, even 1950, so small they've wasted out of sight; and a marble, a mig, like the ones I raced.

War will be impossible when marijuana becomes legal.

The great jazz tea-high where I saw a vision of Cody equal to Mexico was in Jacksons Hole when we heard the little Irwin Garden alto; that night began early——

BUT THE LATEST AND PERHAPS REALLY, next to Mexico and the jazz tea high I'll tell in a minute, best, vision, also on high, but under entirely different circumstances, was the vision I had of Cody as he showed me one drowsy afternoon in January, on the sidewalks of workaday San Francisco, just like workaday afternoon on Moody Street in Lowell when boyhood buddy funnguy G.J. and I played zombie piggybacks in mill employment offices and workmen's saloons (the Silver Star it was), what and how the Three Stooges are like when they go staggering and knocking each other down the street, Moe, Curly (who's actually the bald domed one, big husky) and meaningless goof (though somewhat mysterious as though he was a saint in disguise, a masquerading supderduper witch doctor with good intentions actually)——can't think of his name; Cody knows his name, the bushy feathery haired one. Cody was supposed to be looking after his work at the railroad, we had just blasted in the car as we drove down the hill into wild mid-Market traffics and out Third past the Little Harlem where two and a half years ago we jumped with the wild tenor cats and Freddy and the rest (I dig the Little Harlem in rainy midnights comin home from work in the black slouch hat, from the corner, the pale pretty pink neons, the modernistic front, the puddles so rosy glowing at the foot of the entrance, the long arrowing deserted Folsom Street which, as I hadn't remembered in my back East reveries runs straight into the far lights of the Mission or Richmond or whatever district, all glitters in the indigo distance of the night, to make you think of trucks and long hauls to Paso Robles, bleak Obispo or Monterrey, or

Fresno in the mist of highways, the last highways, the California
up and down coast highways, the ones with an end which is
water orients and the empurpled Golgothan panoplies of Pacific
Bowl and Abyss), past the dingy bars with their incredible
names (colored bars) like Moonlight in Colorado (that one's
actually in Fillmore) or Blue Midnight or Pink Glass and inside
it's all wretched raw brown whiskey and mauve boilermakers,
past Mission Street earlier too (before Folsom) with its corner
conglomerate of bums or sometimes lines of dragged winos so
torpid that when pretty women pass they don't even look (even
though they're waiting in line to give blood for four dollars at
Cutters so they can rush off and buy wine and pissberry brandy
for the Embarcadero Night) or if they do look it's accidental,
they seem to be too guilty to look at ordinary women, only
Steamboat Annies of pierfront *bouges* with knots in their sticks
for calf muscles and hagless toothmarks in their purply gums,
Jey-sas Crise!); bums of Mission and Howard, that live in miserable flop hotels like the Skylark in Denver that Cody and his
father Old Cody Pomeray the Barber lived in and from which
they took their Sunday afternoon walks together hand in hand
and amiable after the previous Saturday night's hassles over his
overdrinking wine in the ceremonial saved-up evening movie
so he'd snore at usher closeup time and lights on in the show-
house would reveal to shuffling audiences of whole Mexican
and Arky families the sight of one of their fellow Americans a
bit under the weather in a seat, this being the capper to a whole
day of Saturday joys for little Cody such as reading the *Count
of Monte Cristo* while his father barbered in the busy weekend
morning, cleanup at the Skylark, and a regular good meal in a
fairly good restaurant in late afternoon, and maybe a moment's
lingering with the majority of noncelebrating Saturday night
bums wrangled around in seated positions in the sitting room
the longer winter nights of which Cody endured aiming spit-
balls at plaster targets and celestial ceiling cracks as old big clock
tocketytocked the Jinuaries away and like in a movie the calendars flapped and still the land and the man survived, stood fixed
and immovable in a blurflap of white pages representing time,
usually the man was Cody's dad, the land Colorado, the occasion and occupation Hope, good boy hope for a change; but
now it's May and they're going to a show and saying good

evening to the bums who sit in state over this like old French
sewing sisters in a Provincial town; May and Larimer Street is
humbuzzing with that same excitement, that same countrified
wrangly sad toot and tinkle of old Main line shopping streets in
Charleston, West Virginia with all its spotted farmer cars ranged
and the Kanawha flowing, and the Southern railroad town with
moils of activity at sun tortured five-and-tens across from the
tracks, awnings, nations of Negroes lounging by beater stores
in near the tobacco warehouses flashing aluminum lights in the
southern day-fire; and Los Angeles when the parade goes up
and down both sides and the cracked old crazy John Gaunt
from a rackety house in a telegraph grove outside the Bakers-
field flats with his entire brood of nine packed and pushed up
to the torn flapass black tarpaulin roof of his fantastic ancient
1929 touring Imperial Buick with the wooden spokes two of
them cracked and a siderack for spares like a snail's shell goof
on the runningboard, old John Gaunt and Ma Gaunt with her
overalls and sorrow (has to wait while Pa gets his fill at the
shooting gallery at South Main, two blocks from System Auto
Parks); it's May and little Cody and old man go cutting together
into the adventures of a hard won evening and one which of
course like all life is doomed to tragic, unnamable, to-make-
you-speechless and sadfaced forever death; just as I used to
hurry with my father in May dusks of Saturday, towards unspeakable seashores, with lights before them, and swooping
spaces fit for gulls and clouds scuds, towards ramps of yellow
sulphur lamp light, overdrives, sudden dank side alleys when
there came among the greases and irons and blackdust of ramps
in cobbled avenues like the avenues of factories in Germany,
those secret chop sueys from Boston Chinatown to make my
mouth water and my thoughts hasten to the wink of Chinese
lanterns hung in red doorways at the base of golden tinsel porch
steps leading up to the Mandarin secrets of within (so when
Cody dreamed of being Cristo thrown in the sea in a bag, I was
kidnapped and Shanghaied and orphaned to a strange but
friendly old Chinaman who was my only contact with hopes of
returning to my former life, orphaned in the interesting old
void, hey?); May night on Larimer, when the sun is red on
green store fronts and Army-Navy suits by the door, and makes
a ray and a frazzle by an empty bottle, foot of a hydrant;

illuminates the reveries of an aged lady in a window above the windows of empty store rooms, she looks on Wynkoop, Wazee and the rails)——we passed Third Street and all its *that*, and came, driving slowly, noticing everything, talking everything, to the railyards where we worked and got out of the car to cross the warm airy plazas of the day and there particularly with a fine soot-scent of coal and tide and oil and big works (a fly across haze oil shimmers) (the tar soft undershoe), noticing how great the day and how in the experience of our lives together we were always finding ourselves on a golden sleepy good afternoon just like fishing or really like the afternoons that must have been experienced by the noble sons of great Homeric warriors after (like Telemachus and the noble son of his host, Nestor's friend) wild night charioteerings across the ghosts and white horses of Phallic Classical Fate in the gray plain to the Sea, rewardful afternoons for tired winners, caresses of cups and figs in the loll of Heroes, just like that, Cody and Me, only American and Cody saying "Now goddammit Jack you've gotta admit that we're high and that was real good shit" and more instant and interesting, and always happening, and *everything always all right*. We sauntered thus——had come in the green clunker for some reason, wore our usual greasy bum clothes that put real bums to shame but nobody with the power to reprimand and arrest us in his house——began somehow talking about the Three Stooges——were headed to see Mrs. So-and-So in the office and on business and around us conductors, executives, commuters, consumers rushed or sometimes just maybe ambling Russian spies carrying bombs in briefcases and sometimes ragbags I bet——just foolishness——and the station there, the creamy stucco suggestive of palms, like the Union Station in L.A. with its palms and mission arches and marbles, is so unlike a railroad station to an Easterner like myself used to old red-brick and sootirons and exciting gloom fit for snows and voyages across pine forests to the sea, or like that great NYCEP whatever station I ran to over the ice that morning en route in Pittsburgh, so unlike a railroad station that I couldn't imagine anything good and adventurous coming from it (we, in our youth, had spent goof hours around railroad stations, in fact the last time I was in Lowell we staggered and laughed past the depot to the nearest bar and jumped and whooped over four-foot snowbanks to boot, bareheaded and coatless). Nothing, only bright California gloom and propriety (and I suppose because Cody works for them here), nothing but whiteness and everything busy, official, let's say Californian, no spitting, no grabbing your balls, you're at the carven arches of a great white temple of commercial travel in America, if you're going to blank your cigar do it on the sly up your asshole or in the sand behind the vine if they had a sand vine or sandpot palm, but really—— when it came into Cody's head to imitate the stagger of the Stooges, and he did it wild, crazy, yelling in the sidewalk right there by the arches and by hurrying executives, I had a vision of him which at first (manifold it is!) was swamped by the idea that this was one hell of a wild unexpected twist in my suppositions about how he might now in his later years feel, twenty-five, about his employers and their temple and conventions, I saw his (again) rosy flushing face exuding heat and joy, his eyes popping in the hard exercise of staggering, his whole frame of clothes capped by those terrible pants with six, seven holes in them and streaked with baby food, come, ice cream, gasoline, ashes——I saw his whole life, I saw all the movies we'd ever been in, I saw for some reason he and his father on Larimer Street not caring in May——their Sunday afternoon walks hand in hand in back of great baking soda factories and along deadhead tracks and ramps, at the foot of that mighty red brick chimney à la Chirico or Chico Velásquez throwing a huge long shadow across their path in the gravel and the flat——

Supposing the Three Stooges were real? (and so I saw them spring into being at the side of Cody in the street right there front of the Station, Curly, Moe and Larry, that's his bloody name, *Larry*; Moe the leader, mopish, mowbry, mope-mouthed, mealy, mad, hanking, making the others quake; whacking Curly on the iron pate, backhanding Larry (who wonders); picking up a sledgehammer, honk, and ramming it down nozzle first on the flatpan of Curly's skull, boing, and all big dumb convict Curly does is muckle and yukkle and squeal, pressing his lips, shaking his old butt like jelly, knotting his Jell-o fists, eyeing Moe, who looks back and at him with that lowered and surly "Well what are you gonna do about it?" under thunderstorm eyebrows like

the eyebrows of Beethoven, completely ironbound in his surls,
Larry in his angelic or rather he really looks like he conned the
other two to let him join the group, so they had to pay him all
these years a regular share of the salary to them who work so
hard with the props——Larry, goofhaired, mopple-lipped, lisped,
muxed and completely flunk——trips over a pail of whitewash
and falls face first on a seven-inch nail that remains imbedded in
his eyebone; the eyebone's connected to the shadowbone, shadowbone's connected to the luck bone, luck bone's connected to
the, foul bone, foul bone's connected to the, high bone, high
bone's connected to the, air bone, air bone's connected to the,
sky bone, sky bone's connected to the, angel bone, angel bone's
connected to the, God bone, *God bone's connected to the bone
bone*; Moe yanks it out of his eye, impales him with an eight-
foot steel rod; it gets worse and worse, it started on an innocent
thumbing, which led to backhand, then the pastries, then the
nose yanks, blap, bloop, going, going, gong; and now as in a
sticky dream set in syrup universe they do muckle and moan
and pull and mop about like I told you in an underground hell
of their own invention, they are involved and alive, they go
haggling down the street at each other's hair, socking, remonstrating, falling, getting up, flailing, as the red sun sails——So
supposing the Three Stooges were real and like Cody and me
were going to work, only they forget about that, and tragically
mistaken and interallied, begin pasting and cuffing each other
at the employment office desk as clerks stare; supposing in real
gray day and not the gray day of movies and all those afternoons
we spent looking at them, in hooky or officially on Sundays
among the thousand crackling children of peanuts and candy in
the dark show when the Three Stooges (as in that golden dream
B-movie of mine round the corner from the Strand) are provid-
ing scenes for wild vibrating hysterias as great as the hysterias of
hipsters at Jazz at the Philharmonics, supposing in real gray day
you saw them coming down Seventh Street looking for jobs——
as ushers, insurance salesmen——that way. Then I saw the Three
Stooges materialize on the sidewalk, their hair blowing in the
wind of things, and Cody was with them, laughing and staggering in savage mimicry of them and himself staggering and
gooped but they didn't notice . . . I followed in back. . . . There
was an afternoon when I had found myself hungup in a strange

city, maybe after hitch-hiking and escaping something, half tears
in my eyes, nineteen, or twenty, worrying about my folks and
killing time with B-movie or any movie and suddenly the Three
Stooges appeared (just the name) goofing on the screen and
in the streets that are the same streets as outside the theater
only they are photographed in Hollywood by serious crews
like Joan Rawshanks in the fog, and the Three Stooges were
bopping one another . . . until, as Cody says, they've been at it
for so many years in a thousand climactic efforts superclimbing
and worked out every refinement of bopping one another so
much that now, in the end, if it isn't already over, in the baroque
period of the Three Stooges they are finally bopping mechani-
cally and sometimes so hard it's impossible to bear (wince), but
by now they've learned not only how to master the style of the
blows but the symbol and acceptance of them also, as though
inured in their souls and of course long ago in their bodies, to
buffetings and crashings in the rixy gloom of Thirties movies
and B short subjects (the kind made me yawn at 10 A.M. in my
hooky movie of high school days, intent I was on saving my
energy for serious-jawed features which in my time was the
cleft jaw of Cary Grant), the Stooges don't feel the blows any
more, Moe is iron, Curley's dead, Larry's gone, off the rocker,
beyond the hell and gone, (so ably hidden by his uncombable
mop, in which, as G.J. used to say, he hid a Derringer pistol),
so there they are, bonk, boing, and there's Cody following after
them stumbling and saying "Hey, lookout, houk" on Larimer
or Main Street or Times Square in the mist as they parade er-
ratically like crazy kids past the shoeboxes of simpletons and
candy corn arcades—and seriously Cody talking about them,
telling me, at the creamy Station, under palms or suggestions
thereof, his huge rosy face bent over the time and the thing
like a sun, in the great day—So then I knew that long ago
when the mist was raw Cody saw the Three Stooges, maybe
he just stood outside a pawnshop, or hardware store, or in that
perennial poolhall door but maybe more likely on the pavings
of the city under tragic rainy telephone poles, and thought of
the Three Stooges, suddenly realizing—that life is strange and
the Three Stooges exist—that in 10,000 years—that . . . all the
goofs he felt in him were justified in the outside world and he
had nothing to reproach himself for, bonk, boing, crash, skittely

boom, pow, slam, bang, boom, wham, blam, crack, frap, ker-
plunk, clatter, clap, blap, fap, slapmap, splat, crunch, crowsh,
bong, splat, splat, *BONG!*

"OBVIOUSLY, AN IMAGE which is immediately and unintention-
ally ridiculous is merely a fancy."——T.S. Eliot, *Selected Essays,
1917–1932*, Harcourt, Brace and Company, 383 Madison Avenue,
New York 17, New York, Fifth Printing, June 1942, when little
Cody Pomeray was sixteen, and was just beginning to learn the
things that would eventually lead him through the mazes of
the mind growing to all kinds of realizations that when a thing
is ridiculous it is subject to laughter and reprisal, and may be
cast away like an old turd in front of the pearly old pigs of the
sty, a thing gone dead. There were no images springing up in
the brain of Cody Pomeray that were repugnant to him at their
outset. They were all beautiful. There was a clarity and pureness
in his mind. Someday he would realize that it was necessary to
go back and get it. Time and history are not made of turds;
ridiculous Caesar wasn't dead in a day; old Herbivorous Walt
didn't march through the brake for nothing, nor moons leering;
pah! it's a fancy sardine sold on paint. When Cody saw a piece of
cowflap along the stockyard tracks, and smelt the dying beasts
within, listened sometimes to pigs squealing in their bleed, their
upside down bleed of the evil Jews Armour and Swift of Denver;
and when he thought of taking one of those pieces, and sitting it up on the frazzled stock porch of the platform, to let it
dry and go fragrant in the sun, like tobacco, so he could, on
some earlier noon than this red dusk he saw it by, return when
the flies are druzzing in pit-plots of their own by the hum of
dynamos of Noon, beez-treeings of noon, sunny warped-ass
porch noon, platform noon, old noon of hydrants, fertilizer,
and seed, noon in Liverpool, Ohio; come by there and watch
the flies make their golden flopovers upon the steaming seeds of
the cowflap now like an old turf flap, cakish, pie-like, Amos 'n'
Andy and the Fresh Air Taxicab in the apple tree (wood from
boyhood ideal trees looks old and dusty in a mature-ity desk);
see that dung hotten in the lull, while old men weep on cadav-
erous leprous piles, by their own worms eaten full of holes, on
nails, symbolic nails; seeing that and also the particular essence

of joy and righteousness in all the world at peace that comes
from the scent of hot rails at noon when the Hottentot sun
blasts down to melt the tar that beds them; paranoia preceding reality, reality flirting with paranoia, paranoia blooming in
fresh aridities, flowering in the vale, paranoia's not a cow palace,
paranoia's a possibility remotely to be wished or avoided, let it
go, till it proves it was right all the time when you die, allowing
his mind to make its own fertilizer estimations, or rather estimations by mental radio, the steer-nerve secret in the hole of the
brain, the place, for him to decide what it is happening in the
warm world that can also be cold outside his eyeballs, that will
send back to him, by impulses of electric mystery, the vision, or
the insanity, or the actual impulse that everything is happening
exactly as you see it, and that is a heinous happenstance there,
it bodes no good, the mind doing this, then letting the soul
rebound softly and say "No, no, everything is really alright, that
was paranoia, that was just a vision." Cody allowed himself the
conviction that in the darkness old men lay in wait, which was
proved later when he himself lay in the darkness of the straw,
the paranoia, the vision, having been just an expression of the
truth of things, not the silly-ass moment! of things! of things!
"Eliot's put the ball up in the air and it's good." Eliot plays
rightforward for Santa Clara, it's a radio basketball.

   Inside the secret of the dung, and the flit-flies in the drowsiness, Cody saw the possibility that he might have taken that wet
cowflap and thus ripened it like an autumn . . . he rolled his
hoop past his thought. But there was nothing ridiculous, there
were no images immediately and sensationally ridiculous; it was
just a matter of believing in his own soul; it's just a matter of
loving your own life, loving the story of your own life, loving
the dreams in your sleep as parts of your life, as little children
do and Cody did, loving the soul of man (which I have seen in
the smoke), lilting in your own breaks to make them good and
bad according to the geography of the day which included (for
him) those Santa Fe drive junkyards not far from the overpass
surmounting the rooftops of Denver Mexicotown. "But we
came," said Cody, "to the garage at twelve o'clock just like Old
Bull Balloon had told us, and there he was, old Bull, upstairs
with all those guys and his hatbands all laid out crazy on his

arm, and we said, well, wup, well, but the fact of the matter
was"——(thinking as the clock ticks)——"that dung you talked
about, that dung, in fact, yes, and I also used to listen to Amos
'n' Andy——"

JACK. Wouldn't I know? You still do!
CODY. ——urp, or, but that's alright, that's aw-right, we let
that one go, this black hair's too long, this black hair's got to
go, down the gangplanks, wup, overbo-a-a-ard! Hear that, ock?
hock? aaaaard, that nasal twang from Issouri, twang. There were
stockyards, and thoughts, I suppose; and my father was there.
It was just one thing, just had, naturally to be anything at all
truthful about the matter, it was a thought that didn't matter
wasn't it!
JACK. It matters, all——
CODY. Had, yes all, in it elements of such unimportance and
unimportant imperfect sections running throughout it that you
had to just slip it out, things had to be thought to be done——
you know that yourself, you've, had, all experienced, in the
same thing as those scythes, those bloody scythes of yours (*imitating W. C. Fields*) cuttin my way through a wall of hu-man
fl-e-sh (*sniffs*). I mean, we know, we both of us know (*bending
to his work*) that the fact of matters like sleepy afternoons in the
sun and flies buzzin is all nice and pretty and in fact you know as
well as I do easy to come by, images not in the instant ridiculous
but——well, made up of the goos and glup of life
SLIM. Yes, (*shuddering*) you was almost *down* then! In your
thought, man——
CODY. True, ah, true; I always told Esmeralda my wife in the
galleon hangings of nineteen oteen, when Mayor Robinson
and I washed the floors of Mack Avenue trolleys in Detroit,
coughing, the bank was so dusty from all that old California
gold dust and Model A juice . . . (*Music: Les Paul echoey guitars
wrangling in highway palaces all up and down the night.*) (*"Hold
that Tiger"*)
JACK. It was Jelly Roll Morton, when, like Blake, seeing visions of the lion breaking the door down he wrote "The Lior
is Breaking the Door Down," I mean the Lion, and he said, the
tiger, hold that tiger, he's coming in the door; no he must have
been already in and the whores hung on by the ge——, vestibule

gowns of the curtains, you know, New Orleans nineteen ten, Jelly Rool Morton

SLIM. And his Kansas City Stools

CODY. The sonumbitch's high! I can't, what are you gonna do man with a piece of turdy thoughts, how can you hold it for long, just like you say, you roll your hoop along, hoop along Pomeray; but by God man I *did* walk along those old stockyard tracks many's the time, the rats just like you say, were huge; I had that cat killed——I loved Monte Cristo——it's all the same——The Indian halfbreed hero is hungup on comic books and just the same; he had maybe a whole horse killed on HIM——Rinick you was right, you was right Ferdy, yeah, Ferd, lemme tell ya Ferd——but, ah by gorsh, yar, ain't she yar though?

JACK. Enchilado?

CODY. Par——har——har har har! (*laughs*) Oh, this is real good shit. Tell my story some other time. Put away your quills and quidnuncs, the good lawyer's in his box, we buried him last night by the shadow of the moon, he fell down the stairs with a severe and stately air, old Hannegan Bannegan the Wake Man spilled beer all over Mrs. O'Farterty's gown, she had it sent down by an old navvy in Albany, I once sailed up that river almost but instead was corpsed

JACK. Well then man, after that. . . . I knew from the deafmute when he wrote all those long letters that you had gathered up the whole mob inside of a half hour on Times Square and down to the Village and departed the fair city of New York in right good order, without a hitch. But what happened then as you sped across the country with that hideous harload, that hideous carlot?

CODY. We, and so we came flaming into the Hylson glare, flanked on all sides by lisping garters, edged over by the Moor to a stately mountainside upon which marks of a wallmaker yet sate, and behold, from all-golden temples on the hill beyond the desert, we made haste to hurry the horde into its prci——, precipitate, precipitit, precipitate hole and hidingplace of eternity; but providence visited the stately deadbone in his styles accouchered, on a nate, made up of quality-givings and sanctions, redeemed by no other than the king of States, the massive arbi——, arboreal foreman of the time; the consummate and most madeup wretch of all time, he spwe, he spewed on me from all quarters an awful gelatin of gluttondraggon juice, green like in spent grass (Spenser), but you make a mow?

JACK. Yes; kindly resume the tale

CODY. Well it was a carload, by god; first there was the Deaf-mute, poor Tony, we never saw him have we again, no, he's down floating disemboweled in the Gate of Gold

JACK. What was he like on Times Square?

CODY. As you know for a living he polished the shoes of men with a golden rag; for his living he scathed his knees hardsore, he brought them to grief; he made pads on the pavement for his bones; he was beat; he had nowhere to go but a poor beat house in the slums where his mother was sick and crazy and laying up in the dark night with nothing to do but look at the moon on the ceiling which is like Out of the Depths Have I Cried to Thee O Lord! Thus Tony in his innocence, one day perceiving, in the welter of librarial tomes in the libroa-a-ary, with radio-ators to keep the place warm, radio-ay-tors, came to see his own m——, name, Nicholas Breton, in the pages of an old turdish English poetrybook, a chapbook of carts: each one with wheels: if I had eyes, the woods had eyes; or some such poesy; I think it was, had I eyes, or eyes to make me see, or were I ever mute, or sent to sing about her ruby lips, or torn between twixt and twence, a wench, a pence, a tight bodice, a lilt in her ribbons, a tattered shoetongue, a cut fan, a fanny to boot, one well formed and fitted in Balzacian scrolls and laces; but up, up, hup——Dig that Joe Holliday blowing that little ta tup tee tup tup, man he really is sweet and cool and beautiful, O world! What will thee hence? Whenfly in your furbishoors? and moors? and spoors? and lures? loors? loons? goons? beautiful dancer desert me not; beautiful tone dethorn me not, castrate me not with your loveliness; if I had such a so lovely soul I too would make a vow in the mow; O May Mows, O Times——

JACK. Nicholas Breton——a brief poem——not too well known——this my tale and descantation hear you now, I dedi-cate to you, to thee, sing you well——But in his EEP's eyes he did not realize anything but that Nicholas Breton was a deaf-mute too, because of the couched meanings in the language, and so, a neighbor relative of Cowens on the Blankums, in old Dervishoor. Thyme?

CODY. Well said lad——figuratif, dedicatee, dove

JACK. Roaned, spavined, lorned, de-horned, hoof and mouthed

CODY. Leaking, drooly, bloody, rollypolly, wounded

JACK. Made to wring the meaning, made to roam the void
   Made to sing demeanors to the meeters of the

CODY. You mean this is the pit of night, the moonsaw?

JACK. The moonsaw's come, the rainy night is milk, red eyes sea,

CODY. Can't decide? Have no bones? Pick up stone? Or stick an own?

JACK. Crick alone, turtle dove alone, moan alone, pose alone.

CODY. Nonsense be, as nonsense was; or nonsense is a trapeze

JACK. Nay a hole beneath it; with a balloon upon the void afloat.

CODY. Van Doren, excellent; New Yorker, extrasmash; Walt Winchell, bardstart

JACK. Tell me Nones; throw a Flying Scone;

CODY. Yeah but the deafmute after an afternoon goofing in the Pokerino with Freddy the French-Canadian hitch-hike kid from up north when they bet on the monkey in the glass cage there and brought postcards to the Chinaman's pigeon, why, I brought the car around at seven o'clock or so, cut right into the Angler to meet Huck; there he was, he had our ten and Phil's five and some other guy's five whose name I don't remember and off we went to meet the connection, he was sitting in Lindy's Diner on Forty-third and Lebenth Avenue and here come this whole mob of——but that was, cops, girls, but something other——and we pick up, up at his pad, pay him, lightup, bombers, high, Huck's sittin there with those eyes you know, high, and I'm sittin there still tryin to hold my breath and can hardly crack another lung, and wham, I let loose, and go pherrrrf, and laugh, and spew smoke, and spit all over myself, you know, high, and Huck's just smilin a little thin corner smile with his eyes all disapprovin and sad fixed on mine, you know, as if to say and in fact sayin in the next minute, "What youdoin man?" Just that and nothin else, dig; but J, Huck; and we picked up, and ran back to the gang on the Square, we picked up the imbecile and Freddy in the penny arcade, they were goofing like two romantic mechanics that come riding

around on bicy, motorbikes, motorcycles on Satnight running
in from Jersey like mad, they was standin and goofin there at the
nickel machine with the flippity hips and earnestly homosexual,
you know, or whatever, arm around arm diggin these biglegged
babies comportin themselves in a flaphole all cold and blue and
dark for Ben Turpin to come cuttin in to, damn that old Ben
Turpin always gettin in the panties, the mouse, like——Mother
Hubbard's cupboard——Shee-it, I could tell you stories make
you wish you was daid. I could lay you down a hype make you
wish you was dead *and* gone, dead *and* gone

JACK. I could ripple you houndspack make you wish I was
dead and void

CODY. Dead and voiced; I signed it last night, my voucher——
Please, no callers today, I have a tired point between my lgets,
my legs, last night those Liggens bandmen the honeyrippers
came in here and desecrated my thighs, damn their hides. (*The
swish of a rubber through the air.*) There, that dark deed's done,
Jack; no scones or bonescan furnish me now!

JACK. In the bonecan with it. But tell me, fair prince, what
betideth then?

CODY. We got that other bore, Rod Moultrie, and Ray Smith
I guess and all jam'd into the car——but there was also Dorie
Jordan all hassled and castrated and half alive, with no dangling,
the screw girl of that lot? Pah! We had Huck; we had a carload
and drove across the country, insane. There was then talk of a
certain Roger Boncoeur who started at Cape Cod, Provincetown Bohemian summers, walking the roads by night; and
ended walking all over America in the night with a candle in
his hand; later he went mad, or it simplified itself into something practical like a brakeman's lantern and some walking
shoes and gear; or, really now, I can't tell; then his kid brother
was it? Ben Boncoeur, that with fevered brow came running
back from Mexico in dusty coaches of the Ferrocarril Mexicano, with a bomber like a hyacinth bough wrapped around his
sculptured waits, waist, like a seraph, a satrap, a molasses black
strap, a roach to kill a vulture, a mighty boomblast joint, the
hugest hunk of Swaziland boom ever assembled in the history
of the Paleontological Museum, or was it the Herbivorous?
no, the, why of course, the goddamned, ah, the damn, old,
museum there, you know the one I——the Botanical Gardens

swimmingpool or whatever, the Botany Tie, the Botany Tool, the Botanical Weed Garden and now everybody's left me fuddling in my own foolish thoughts, well that's all I've got left and if the Lord will be patient I shall again try to resume my narrative without suffering everyone to terrible and foolified hangups. Across Kansas we ate dung; an evening star hung on the edge of the dim blaze of night in Iowa; in Illinois we saw a barn; in Indiana there was an organist who didn't understand, he hid himself——but really and truly, in Indiana there was a barn too, and a tree, a tree Oh yes Oh most; in Pennsylvania there was snow, in Ohio there was snow, in Nebraska there was snow, in Wyoming there was snow, in Nevada there was snow, and night; and in California with the unfriendly palms, there was fog, and day. We came running out on Ellis and O'Farrell with all our gear on the sidewalk; the baby was crying; I told Luke to light the stove. They threw us in jail; not but two nights later when Old Bull Balloon was sittin there with his ass in a pan of hot water because he'd caught cold in his rectum, outside in the alley with cats and fish on the fence and a moonsaw view, comes this old shroudy blackhat stranger cuttin along, looks in, says nothin, Old Bull looks back at him, lays a watery fart that you can hear rippling and turkishpiping clear to——and finds himself off into the gloom; yessir, I'll tell you who it was, it was the eternal husband coming back to peek at the tortured old lover who stole his wife away; why, hell, and both of them mad. But up in Butte, Montana it all worked out when I told Smiley——but he understood——but it's all a bore, and recently

JACK. Yes, that's the one

CODY. ——yeah, they spoke, yeah the one, away why hell, understood Butte, just a . . . (*silence*) (*as Cody tucks in the edges*) . . . just awhile ago there occurred to me that there must have been someone else on that road with me, some strange character yet unheard of, like I told you, can't remember, and you know that dream of yours about being pursued across a white desert by a shrouded stranger in a hood, with stave of shining gold, terrible feet, clouds for knees, and a black face in snow cowls; and that time, coming out of New York, across the misty rainy New Jersey night, the white highway sign pointing South, and pointing West, and take your pick, and we drove South, for that warmpiss of rivers and greengrass and docks, you said

"Seems to me I've forgotten something——" something about packing for the trip, and mentally, and you forgot you said some thought, or some important dream that you had thought of remembering and didn't, and expressed later the concern that it might have been in connection with the shrouded Arab stranger and you wished therefore you could remember it, that dream having always——mystified——But think back: the someone else not in your, or the, sense, you, used about, last, when you—— said, that, Cody is the brother I lost——not that sense as senses, but a gap in the air along by me in the road, the night under the gray moon, the mist——But you know——

JACK. Who was it?

SLIM. What owl wooed it? What fowl deed reads it?

CODY. They made matters where matter was there, they tore earth——they ended up writing great poems about the foundation of canals——and not dull canals——wild canals, crazy canals, immediate banal canals . . . *down* canals; canals. But you really don't want to hear the rest about that trip——How the idiot jumped off the Golden Gate Bridge when he realized I was crazy and couldn't communicate with him on Folsom Street, and little Freddy stayed and learned bop from an old schmecker who used to blow when he was a shipyard worker in L.A., 1943 and 'four, and turned to the hype himself, for sad-youngkid kicks smoking nervous cigarettes at the jam session door and thinking, thinking, always and all the time thinking music as though he was about to break his American mind wide open and let the pieces of the puzzle sprawl on the floor like old queers in Turkish baths falling on Scandinavian harlot boys. (Why did I ever show you my collection of Pierre Louys ponog, porno-graphic arts, pictures of black queens and brown boys and feathered men and sad sisters naked together and old hermit saints and little plum-boys and tender mothers and wild American tourists caught fallen in a *bouge* with a big pernod bottle at the side of her mouth, there she is, Eleanora! Eleanora went wild! Theodora! Theodora Eleanora Roosevelt Dodsworth, that's what. . . . No, Freddy learned to blow real sweet too, and ended up, in New York, right there on the apple, bowed, appealing, sad, brow-shiny, in the lights of Bop City or Birdland blowing soft sweet pearly tones for the boys and girls and weaving his girdles of gold around "A Small Hotel," "Zing

Went the Strings," and "Long Island Zounds"! (!) ("——"!)
Bam!: (that mad Stan Getz that's got everybody stoned, man,
and I told you didn't I about the time I met him in Denver
when he was passing through with Herman's band playing——
JACK. I talked to Ray Eberle when he was singing with Glenn
Miller's band, on a summer night in the Massachusetts road,
smoking cigarettes in the moonlit driveway, and Ray Eberle
said, "Shit."——that sweet singer——
CODY. ——and (*talking at the same time as Jack*) and he came
up to the pad, that is he was brought up. . . . Huh? . . . yuh, um-
hum (*looks away in Caesar conformation*) (*or confirmation*) (*in
Caesar confirmation*). Those two guys on Tenth Avenue in New
York had 'em, the, you know, those African French pictures that
André Gide dug, all those hrr——that gone——aff——I stole the
picture of the gone little nigger cunt that is kneelin there with
her body thrown back over her heels and all set out to go with
her everything completely out
JACK. Yes——fit for desert nights, I'd say it was fit for rugs in
loverooms
CODY. Blooms, blooms——but we'll turn off this tape

(MACHINE ENDS)

CODY. (*in the doorway*) But darling I . . . don't . . . want . . . . .
hear that? an old cuntlapper she called me
JACK. (*on the porch, night*) She did not
CODY. But she did, man, she *did*. Yes (*addressing a listen*) Yes.
Yes. Oh inert mass of nerves, O dull heart; yes. Alright, dear
JACK. (*holding Cody by the shoulders*) Easy man, snap out of it.
(*slaps him sharply in the face*) There, is that better?
CODY. No

(MACHINE ENDS AGAIN)

(*starts, music*)
CODY. Then up on Liberty, on the Mission Hill up there old
shroudy hat and old Smiley Balloon or whatever made up; we
went——Well Freddy ended up like Stan Getz in New York, the
imbecile died, he made the bay his bed that night; he bumped
along, a greenly corpse, piles and rust chains of ghost buoy
boats
JACK. In other words he drowned

CODY. Aye and he did

JACK. So lies a tale that teaches a moral; don't make your lanterns too soon, it may be darker than you think, or you may not need lanterns at all; for I had imagined it all dark and big and prophetic-like and it wasn't anything but the conjoiner of directions, a road's a road, that's all; and so now I've been up and down the road, all over, forty-seven states, bar your South Dakota, and——Wounded Knee, that's where she was born, Wounded Knee; now she makes her mows in Ajijic; she makes her, gasses her, self in old Ah-hee-heek; damn. Helen by name, launched ships, had hips; eyes; furlined pussy; won over the father image and the King by the sharpness and tartness of her master's wines, I bet

CODY. Helen of Goy? She made tsimitzes about her tsimitzes. She had ice-cold rice pudding in her hair. She was a model, a dream; she was a gas. I caught her one night sitting on the edge of the bed in her pink slip yelling "Lose me you motherfucker lose me" at a Lenny Tristano record, blowing her bop brushes on a hatrack, or a hatbox; snares it was, real snares; blowing her pop brushes on a snare, and not a care, not a sneer, blowing her boppy poppy brushes on a-24587-X-type snares, yeah

JACK. It was the same way when we had that dream about driving up the hill in the whiteness and you fell out of the car——

CODY. We had a dream?

JACK. Oh pardon my hard-on, I had a dream

CODY. Know full well that I'll never succumb to your advances

JACK. It was only your manly built, your beautiful eyes that attracted me so fair, on the cobblestones there

CODY. Don't think you can hang around here and make passes at ME

JACK. Tut, tut, nary a thought; I told the Judge I was a confidence man

CODY. And he let you into this cell, to watch cockroaches race with me? Fah, man, I don't believe a word of it

JACK. Ask Charles Laughton, as Captain Blah? Go ahead, ask him! ass him!

CODY. Sir, you sully my honors; they were won at great expense in Carthage

JACK. Or Carthage never raved; or Carthage never

CODY. Carthage never is such talk; you have the wit of an adder, a tongue made to pry, like ends of iron padgets; you make a mouse hole out of the cheese, and find nothing to do but pole, or sit on my pole, or make a grab for it either way—— Nay, I know, nay, nay: a pole, a pole, I have a golden pole

JACK. A golden pole? With rings of frazzly slagrous iron from the maw of dinosauric hillbottoms up-wheedled through a rack-shaft?——when the steaming cranes mix thunder with the mire, and men make monkey dances in the snow, all muddy, mettled to their extremes, thorny, caucuses in their shacks——

CODY. Ah me morning-star

JACK. It's a blue rose, the morning-star is like a blue rose in the Hair of the Archangel

CODY. Saint, believer, sinner——you think your Ippolits were Idiots? You think your Raskolniks were Apostolic? were Jewish? holy?——we had an Indian called Harold Jew, don't ask me where he got the name, and he ended up going mad in a Miama hotelroom, flat on the bed in the middle of the night, dying on peyotl, his eyes fixed on the ceiling, where he saw an image of his Great and Sorrowful Face, Bending Over the World; completely killed, self-killed, like jazz killed itself; (*jawbone jazz, t'was dreary*): and when the face of Jesus departed from his mortal sight he suddenly knew he was Jesus Christ Himself Returned and this was the Second Coming

JACK. And wasn't that the time that kid said the Second Coming would be televised, you would see the sprawled grayprint figure of a young hoodlum slain by cops lying arms outspread in a pool of blood in front of the National Maritime Union or nearby on 17th Street New York City, Manhattoes, and televised coast to coast to the entire nation as the first of its series, but suddenly everybody all over America is stricken with the realization that the Second Coming has Arrived and all arise and go forth; everywhere the image of the beautiful and the dead, the dead hoodlum, the naked punk, laid out flat with also a baseball bat sunk in his skull and a woman screaming, a Spanish woman screaming for joy nearby, ask me why; he lies there, the mailman let him go, he asked for the postman twice, he went too far with the babyface act, he was too beautiful, he too fell out of an airplane and landed on the frontpage with a bandaged head and——except that he is on television and dead; everybody in

America realizes that this is the Image of Him Again and they all rush off somewhere, clouds of dust rise, as if War was the Excitement of the World, the rave of events; war starts, he rises, crosses depend, blood gulls in the sky with a semi-abstract pattern set to the music of mambo on a synchronized film. Man, he's dead

CODY. Yeah, about that time——but this Harold Jew arose, decided he was God, and headed back for his homecountry, the Kwakiutl country up on Vancouver Isle and parts of (*island*) it in British Columbia and around the Yakima or something but really——to resurrect among his people, you understand, and ends up in the last climactic scene of his life——certain hip people were there who were digging peyotl——ends up screaming at potlatches, throwing his mother's dearest possessions into the raging Dostoevskian fires of pride and heroism. Finally he throws himself in and roasts to a crinkler. Tasty around the cheekbones. Yes, I knew him when; he was, he, an Indian through and through, a splendid——fact of the matter, his father was a rough hombre in and around Grants, New Mexico, boy, where the flint-star sits on the side of the mountain star, and man it's dry and high and keen cold, his old man had black eyes and hated continental busdrivers with bullnecks, he shot one outside the town of Abilene, Kansas, in a sudden rage erupting from the back seat of the bus and puttin the muzzle to the driver's neck, opening fire. The bus ran into a grain elevator and seventeen pigeons flew out of the loft; *Mrs. O'Flaherty Old Wives Tales*, a volume by Arnold Bennett, fell on a piece of broken glass and a dry bird turd that happened to be lying by the side of the road where the Wild Goose left it last spring, durn his limey hide; but do I talk too much. (JACK, *No Pa, you shore don't, you shore do*) That was the last I heard of any of those road characters——I've grown old since. They don't concern me anymore. How could they have even concerned me in the beginning, I'm serious about a road when I'm traveling on one, I gotta go somewhere, I go——course I can goof, and have goofed, on roads, on the road, but, usually it was a big——well you know, distance, time, mileage, blah, bloo, bloop; of no particular essence of meaning, in other words

JACK. Truer words

CODY. Just as silly as the rain's really milk, see?

DULUOZ SAT IN HIS SUNDAY AFTERNOON CHAIR at Cody's,
having just taken his afternoon cold weather walk like he used
to do in the icecold red-whipping January Sundays of the East,
and looked out the nursery window. White houses of Frisco, a
grayboard arrangement for the steps going down, wash on the
line (here in the alley you'd think it was a void the world, not a
round pursy earth, the void is in the mind and in the city), old
lady with neat and frazzled tow-chin and rosy mothercheeks
peers forth from her graywhite house and hauls in wash, one
or two pieces, for something she needs Sunday afternoon, no,
she's hauling little by little more and more . . . all's left is (I'm a
tattlegray spy) towel, two bibs, and a slip, how should I know,
what would she say (as she looks up to hear plane) (in all this
bleakness of life so far from her girlhood) if she knew I sat
here noting down mentally her wash piece by piece, she'd think
"That young man is insane, there's something wrong with his
mental faculties, he plays with himself too late" and me hiding
in the closet with closed eyes, gasping, or the time Ma sneaked
up on me in the Sarah Avenue house and at noon it was, en-
deavoring to see what I was doing to make (as she thought)
my handkerchiefs wet when all I was doing was washing my
own handkerchiefs——my mother was real rough on me in that
respect, she wouldn't allow any kind of sex in the house. They
say that makes a man nutty. I guess I'm nutty then. They say
you know the sun, the moon and the stars.

Well, thought Duluoz, this lady is just like Ma. I wish I could
get Ma to come live in Frisco. Yeah, that's what I oughta do——
In the white woodsteps (there's old Cody downstairs laughing
to inferior subsidiary Amos 'n' Andy programs of four o'clock
Sunday afternoon in Frisco——and I thought I was going to
be Duluoz the newspaperman on the *San Francisco Chronicle*
instead (like of the *Sun*) Duluoz the brakeman).

He stared out of the window and watched the flutter of a diaper in reflection in a sun porch window, in ripply reflection too,
like Eliot's fog just merely slipping into his mind as a kind of
observable phenomena. Two green tin cans of olive oil on the
clean white steps of that Italian family. (O the beans of home!
thought Duluoz at that moment.) Duluoz sat and rocked in the
chair. I'll write that letter to A. A. Quinn tonight, he decided.

Cody is the brother I lost.

IN THE DIM . . . Oh by the wind, and by the wind grieved, lost
brother depart, O!, not!——'ere sallyings into the pale, or sulks
in bigdome clocks, go crashing by the vale. A day! a day!

But it wasn't a long time till I saw her again and then that
time she said to me "Charley boy there's shore something
wrong with you, don't know as I can tell exactly what tis but
you, you my boy, *you*, candy eater, cheater, can go sulk by the
moon, and make nippets of milady's apples, idle off a July on
the same stonewall or crack pits in your pupple guns, fit for the
walking wounded and all the mysteries of thy orisons——to wit,
to woo——go now.

Yes, Cody is the brother I lost——he could very well have
been my brother instead of the actual one I had who died——did
he die a dead death?——or a living death——?——Cody, when he
lets the crumbled folds of his old black braky hat that of course
he doesn't wear anymore, the other night he happened to find
a brand new brown gentleman's felt hat in the attic and put
on to go switching in Oakland (I went with him, watched him
run and race that kicked boxcar or about to be kicked boxcar
and slip the pin with a dextrous step into his work, flip, and the
boxcar's loose, or the gondola's loose, or the flat, or tank, or
reefer, any old reefer'll do on a rainy night, sends the car reeling by itself as the Diesel hoghead engineer eases in his mighty
brakes that can brake a hundred-car line buckle by buckle and
indefatigably emphatic about it; Cody, in his new brown hat
looking very rakish and Irish and not at all any more like a hero
of old roads, like a young Buck Mulligan O'Gogarty but really
rakish, tilty, jaunty, but businesslike and bemused in the dark.
The Oakland yards have innumerable tracks and this was one
subsidiary among-all-the-others yards that Cody pounced on
the pins in, with his new hat. The agility that once made it able
for him to overtake tremendous athletes in the gloomy sports
of his youth which was so tragically mis-spent in those refor-
matories and Sunday afternoon railyards. But would anyone
deny a man his father? Cody is the brother I lost. . . . In that
new hat he is not the grim Oklahoma posseman pursuer that
he is in the black slouch hat . . . with its rainslopes and dark
weathered, square, Rocky Mountain and Larimer Street crown;
with his just teeth, showing, and his unshaven prognathous jaw,

he looks like a marshal who just murdered a marshal, Cody in his maturity having finally attained a measure of success in that he is now indistinguishable from the culprit and the Assistant D.A. at the same time and to boot. Wot, now, that bastard, he makes me mad; he makes me think he's nothing but an empty minded, vacant, bourgeois Irish proletarian would-be-Proust tire recapper——a nothing who won't listen to what anybody says: "Nothing personal, I just can't think or even assume terms for what might have called thought if you wished, and be concerned——fah!"

So in the black hat he meers and makes mouths and imitates one thing after another; the other Saturday, just like this, in the car, with the girls, shopping, he said, "Lessee now, we gotta get mee-ilk, and beer-yed and greem-yeld——" Cody is the brother I lost; he's the brother I had, too, the spittin image of Mike Fortier, old whooping Mike with his boots and visored cap pointing his flashlight through the woods at night in search of his bear trap in back of the dump, Cody is Mike all inverted and twisted and torn, and inhibited, neurotic, restless, too-intelligent, gone, blank, *a stud who is down, man, really down*; (d'I ever tell you about Cody's prognathic face, as though it was concave but the power of his bony nose and almost silly obfusking out-humping wild muddleman face you see twinkles and yurkles and something that makes you think of the side of the big facewall of the world so to speak) "Why, J-a-a-ck, (*imitating Hubbard*) d'I ever tell you about that t-i-me when me and Ma was aimin to buy that paper mill in Fillville I said to my last attorney lost otturney rup-r-r-r-up——wup, hup, hap, ap, wap, a, ack, ack, a, aaa, ahe, em, hem——urp——ock!"

Ock is one of the characteristic things that have been happening in his throat, including a terrible cough by which he coughs up all our money, or mine at least, or is it his?

The brother that I lost——that was always laughing on Saturday nights and I haven't seen him since——Cody was there, by the washtub on the porch on Saturday night, making the sisters laugh and the little siblings cry——the ones that grow up to become anthropologists and modern jazz tenormen. A terrible heaving rack of grrs come out of Cody's voice sometimes while kidding like this that makes Evelyn say "Oh don't do that with your voice!" and lately "Cody, don't you hear the sound of it?" To laff this off Cody attains newer and more horrible noises with his mouth. The children giggle. Gaby is always giggling it seems, her eyes shine, shine; Jimmy said she had her father's eyes: "She must be high"; Gaby laughs when Cody is being exactly like the brother I lost; but like him too he has to get hell from the woman, the great mother-women of the vicinity of the presences; wherefore I love Gaby for loving Cody when I do too. He treats Gaby roughly because he feels sorry for Emily who was always in tears in 1949 when he was running away and more so in her mother's; he'll grab Gaby when she says she wants to go and pull her pants down and by the palms haul her in one sweep onto the seat of the little bowl, almost throwing her across the room on it, and she's *laughing*; so I learn Cody is really not hurting her but playing a great adventurous game that no one else dares and it's Saturday afternoon, it's that fetched time . . . those streets outside, that night coming, Denny Dimwit will sit in the washtub by the light of the moon surer than hell and the cat on the fence, in the Bronx Jail in New York murderers will sit in iron cells enclosed from iron halls and listen to Lava Soap and *Gangbusters* with wide-eyed interest, leaving their cards on the table a half hour, the same interest and later skeptical criticism of the show from practical points of view that little kids all over the country at that moment Saturday night in rocking chairs of the thrilling livingroom——in fact Happy, the father, French-Canadian Happy Bernier who works as bouncer in the Laurier Club and once operated the rollercoasters at Lakeview, that is, helped build them, or paint them, he's rocking his chair most furiously as the gunshots and roars come (in Bronx Jail they tensen) and cries harshly when the poor crazy mother Layo (called thus by the naborhood young gang) fiddles a poor pot in the kitchen, "For Crise Sakes Jesus God cut the goddamn fucking noise in there," and she replies with a wild screeching laugh that I used to hear from six blocks and across the river if I had cats in my ears, the laugh resounding also in the children who pick up, but immediately then, all eyes of the world now on the last chapter of *Gangbusters*, the final scene, the moral, Layo's in the door, Happy's stopped rocking, in the Bronx Jail they smile slowly (and outside it's the red sun sinking blood red in the world and the United States of America from Portuguese

French-Canadian tenements of Cape Cod to the outskirts of
heather in San Luis Obispo).

Cody listens to *Gangbusters* too: in the dark he sits or wants
to sit, but Evelyn hates *Gangbusters*, Evelyn likes *Dragnet* better; her problem is furniture, there's no way for them to listen to
the radio in the dark kitchen at feeding time, and the parlor like
the parlors of Polish coal miners in Pennsy, French-Canadian
millworkers in Massachusetts, and Irish barbers in the West, is
unused. . . .——rocking his children on all three knees, saying
"Shh," "Listen" "Now" and all eyes big and little, dull and shining, are fixed on the blood red dial of the radio. Somewhere a
cock was crowing. It was the cock of Shakespeare, that on New
Year's Eve Evelyn crew. Cody married a woman from good
society who wants him to sit up straight in the light when he
listens to *Gangbusters*.

Cody is the brother I lost——He is the Arbiter of what I
Think. I'll follow, did I ever say I wouldn't follow? or did I ever
ask to follow?——We sit and speculate about high prices, talk
practical about actual grocery bills, (that I have nothing to do
with), chew fingernails; "It's a goddamn shame," says Cody,
"yep, that's what it is (cough)." He looks at his wrist for signs
of a hive or to examine a hair line or think. "Hem," he says; in
a reverie he looks away like Caesar. I begin to suspect he knows
I'm watching him. His eyes turn slowly to mine; it's absurd; but
he doesn't laugh, he stares right at me, grows red all over, looks
like he's holding his breath, oh yes that's right he's only holding
his breath and wants to see if I've noticed how long and well he
did it; also he's bound to be saying "Oh real good shit."

Well, the world is all made up of people.

Let's swing a camera down on Cody and catch him hurrying
up the ramp like Joan Rawshanks in the fog, but Gad he would
outrun the camera!——he would astound the lighting with his
furlibues, eye-flutters, show-offs, piper jigs and "shining eyes";
he wouldn't even make the son of the villain he's so dishonest
looking . . . fah! He is a hero, a champion, he wrote "Laura";
he married Frank Sinatra; he gave David Rose his very first kiss,
or was it Thor Heyerdahl Axel Stordhal. *Kon-Tiki!* A man committed suicide because he couldn't write a song like that. I am
amazed by this in America. "Brother, have you seen starlight
on the rails?" O delicately they dive, delicately they dive, for

Greeks, beneath the railroad platforms (from which the torn letter in the basket had been supposed to dive and therewith swim away, or that is, to say, *whale* away).

O brother Cody Pomeray of Night! Why do you not speak to me! Who has spawned your Fear in the Foggy Dark? In the foggy dark, the goggyfoggy dark——Cody stands, a brakeman, on the front platform of a Diesel switch engine rolling twenty-five miles an hour down the railyards down fifty lead, to the ten-track switches; Cody stands, implacable, unforetold, expressionless, almost dull looking and ridiculously serious, Cody Pomeray, showing me how he will die, and how well he does and also not showing anything to anyone but just being there, dead in void, (Cody Pomeray alone at the railyards). "He make a living and moo in the dark," as the French-Canadian says, "in the place of the boxcart," where his father was lost and he was alone, when Frank Sinatra was singing his first heart-out "This Love of Mine" and Cody was fourteen and heard it from the doors of swinging bars like the refrain of his anxiety and anguished love-loss of his cat that just got killed, the little skull-crushable lost brother kitten *minoux* of these tortured eternities, these bloody infirmities there——why does Cody insist on the rails? "It's all on rails," he said to me at first; so he fell on one last Fall, ten years after those first poolhall days, and almost got run over by the cast-iron wheels of a drag in the hills. It's because six makes six and Junior is the son of Senior as well as sun of, and he repeats older's habits in the inversion of his prime, and focal history. Likewise, therefore drinks sweet wine to ease his smoking throat only, not because he is a wino; who would winos bear? who——But since psychology is a two-edged sword, and the siblings have become a GOOF, enough.

In dealing with Cody I feel that the universe is solid faced, substantial jawed (sober-toed, not goblin-toed).

JACK. (*thinking*) Nothing smells more like piss than piss—— I sit over its ammoniac horrors all day.——The colored people forgot their Dizzy Gillespie for Charlie Parker; the white people remembered Benny Goodman and forgot Artie Shaw

CODY. (*breaking a thought*) A frowsy-mouthed dame that cunt thinks she is as she stands sticklegged on the corner like a old harridan and lets the traffic ride by her Hannegan who's——aff, well;——well he is, trouble with Jack is he——damn——he doesn't

finish what he started so I can't stand there all day long, myack,
like tonight in front of the Bakery and he's talking to me big
writer on the sidewalk and Geez what can——a guy——I says to,
to himself——I can't——Oh, yeah (*yums and yawns*); but Jack
is——well he, that time in Chicago, but, he,——ah well; Jack
looking at me wearing the old hat is thinkin I have great starlight
in my eyes——I ain't nothin but a simple honest pimp, I ain't,
fah, why, ap——I got me no roach pipe; I ain't no Denny Dimwit, just like I ain't no damn Cuban mountain and no bubblegum salesman, I'm Cody Pomeray. I ain't got nothin to do with
all that (ahem); I don't fart around with that kind of shit; I'm
not made to be played on a piccolo; I ain't got no truck for that
fuck, that lousy fuckin brother-in-law like in the movies and
comics that never pays rent or food and complains all day in
the house; that's what he is, a fuckin brother-in-law; why, that
louse; I got my words more than Sid Caesar, I got more——shit,
wh'am I supposed to do to get out of this dilemena, dilemin-
emina, dimmema, yair——that louse; that——(*sighs*); geez——(*all
this time Cody has been playacting what you've just read——as if
I could start a book in the second person not the first person or the
third person——so as to confound the ladies inside his thoughts,
like a lackey wild old Tom Calabrese balancin teacups on his knee
with a tennis ball in his ear, man I mean, a tennis ball in his, the
original tennis ball, in his lap, sittin on a book, and makin wit all
afternoon with the ladies and grandmothers of the clime; Cody has
been thinking like an angry Irishman complaining in American
bars just like the Frenchman Céline complaining and gesticulating in French bars but with so many more great words——Yaaak!
cries his son Timmy Pomeray, usurping and erupting, slurping,
bubbling at brims with the vitality of the clime. Now Cody returns
to "serious and revealing" thoughts*)
CODY. I'll goof myself out at this rate——work's too hard on
this parking lot; but I've got to do something in between seasons as brakeman; everybody in the country knows that; ain't
no money no more. That cunt there all this time didn't dare for
one minute lift her pretty little leg for me to see when she got
out of the lowseat of that Cadillac 'Fifty-two with the fingertip
steeringwheel and Fishtail Fries backward and forwards——Hup,
a customer, yes sir? Why yes sir. No, he's going t'other way,
ain't a customer it's a bore. Dark day with nothing better to ask

for; warm air; sun; rain in an hour. He wasn't a customer, Jack would say, he was the Devil or Daniel Webster's. Jack Dictionary would laugh to har me prank so——I thank so——anyho——Aaahyou! I yawn on void——Make way for the King, the Queen dropped dead, he's come to see Poloniopolos, the Greek tragedian who was in that urn of shit they ate in Montaigne to prove something about the Classics and it was well proven. Well, I've got to read Montaigne on a mountain I guess all kidding aside I ain't read, won't read, have no time——well, wa, read's read, let read read himself——damn, it makes no difference——what's going on around here? where am I? O, the parking lot, this concrete was the crick and cold in my back, this world provided the wind for my breath as I my thoughts roved. That would be nice (with stately élan surveying the day). Ah Mrs. Murphy in up yonder tenemental window makes a up-swing of the rug, and calls Mrs. Tarantino and they exchange cans of spaghetti across the rosy void all day which is all lit up with the sunlight and (them little flies floppin) and has ripplin seas of washclothes to make angel wings for the general creamy white and golden atmosphere of housewife afternoons with a dark stranger sitting by the well watching it all, like Beethoven listening to the clatter of the washingwomen in the little European crick, or better and best, the one and only Omar Khayyám who relaxes in the shade seeing and knowing everything around and most of all enjoying the marijuanalike reverie of their, the housewives', peace; better than Khayyám, the old blind prophet and beggar of the African, the Belgian African Congo town, who sits with stick and provenders them all day with the remarks that well up from his interminable meditations by the bamboo and in the pale, the Great Nigger of the World, Abraham, Adam, Jésu, rattling his beads with that reason for his own and he's left alone; the two of us combibing, intermingling two minds now; the Khayyám.

And saying to the world, Peace has come; they've come with the golden oars and sprung the floods of god on us, we're all ready to fly into the wind with seabags of moneybags, it's a gasser——the witch doctor trails off, the ladies wait, the witch doctor picks up again——Saying, He that is Ranified in the Banshee's Hide May Not the Toga Boast and Crow in this Moredroga. Hollow flutes announce the King, he comes to contest this latest prediction of the prophet, he swings his big be-feathered lance; Old Witchdoctor Remus Khayyám Duluoz, he just sits and lets go another blast at the government. "War is the health of the State." "War is Obsolete." "War is Existentialist." "War is Nowhere." Well blow, baby, blow! blow, world, blow! go! Yaah——shee-it!——Sh'cago, that's *no* town—— it's th'apple, man, it's th'apple, it's scrapple from the apple, it's *down*. And meanwhile Miles Davis, like the sun; or the sun, like Miles Davis, blows on with his raw little horn; the prettiest trumpet tone since Hackett and McPartland and at the same time, to flesh some of its fine raw sound, some wild abstract new ideas developed around a growing theme that started off like a tree and became a structure of iron on which tremendous phrases can be strung and hung and long pauses goofed, kicked along, whaled, touched with hidden and active meanings; to come in, then, like a sweet tenor and blow the superfinest, is mowd enow. I love Miles Davis because, send in your penny postcard. "Goof the people," Little Zagg used to say, serious as hill, "just go along and upset the people," hill's bills, it's a damn shame, and him walking down the street at night and here's this line of drugstore standers, 2 A.M. Manhatnut, and Zagg says "Watch how we (him and Hindenburg the last of the Dalton boys, Dalton being his pseudoname) upset these cats along the window glass of this here Whelan's. They won't know what hit them." And little Zagg and Bob Hindenburg are walkin along and go cuttin right in there "in fronts of those guy," as a French-Canook would say, and there's this gabardine beret and gabardine topcoat on both of them, and Little Zagg he's real small, and big Bob looks tough, and Zagg looks cunning, and on they go, *but*, all the time diggin the guys on the corner to see the effect of the clothes they're wearing; and nobody knows what to think, *it's a real goof.* "Sure, I knew her in Oregon," that guy is sayin over there by the gas pump; with his mustache and salesman bags and lightin a Camel and waiting for his De Soto convertible and nothing to worry about but some gossip about somebody he knew in Oregon——did he say *woman?* He must have meant cunt. At least I do. Mean. Cunt. Or. Me. Means. Pah——bah——fah——fow——fo——fum, I smellthe dog of an English blood!——round the engines, we're heading for the Arapahoe Rootly tooty Jamboree-ee in old D-Town, Denver, colow, shit

BROKEN THOUGHT, CODY Always working on a parking lot, damn. Always *working*, worked from here to Chimexico, Alabama and McCook, Nebraska. Yow!——there . . . she . . . goes . . . now! The cunt of them all, the legs a mile wide, I mean long; ah well, the bus swallered her whole, hole, her whole hole from sight of my eyeballs as I lean in this gastrous doorway all disastered and torn to die for love of Milady. Jesus I hate that——well actually, it's a good face but I don't like the feeling you get from seeing his throat that he is (cunning, now; no time for exile or silence, silence or exile)——a man hanged, standing there, a big hangmark in his neck, old Faustus bones, but fat and ugly and has broken white flesh of whitecollar workers of America when they really deteriorate and looks awful, and here he is waitin for his car, and tellin the boss I'm a piece of shit, or too old, or too young or whatever, and I was gonna say I hated his face.

Ah what a hassle over a man in the morning——there he stands, accept him. He's a pillar to my post. I won't begrudge him a cent of tribute. I always did say a dollar borrowed is a buck owned; and a quarter of the fiscal tax is equal to a fifth of a finance loan divided two and a third by the mutual co-benefiting subsidiary Chinese policies of the Kraft Memorial Industry of Insurances with central main branch offices in the middle of the parking district.

Damn. How much time passed then? Only a few seconds, and by the clock, and my job lags and drags and rolls on wearily, wearily, I don't want to work, I want to goof——it's a goof. O once there were saints on windowsills and pigeons in the idealistic dawn of Denver, when Irwin in Mahatma robes of sorrow hid in that dank cellar in Grant Street and pounded nails into his hands upon the table; bent his head, went *down*, died——to live again and come forth fifteen times strong as Job so that today he is a big respectable young poet in New York, nobody knows about him but his name is Jewish and means Tribe of the Mountain Son of the Golden Finger, he has said, "I looked into the mirror/to check my worst fears./ My face is dark but handsome./ It has not loved for years./" Also he has written: "I came home from the movies/ with nothing on my mind, Trudging up 8th avenue/ to fifteenth almost blind,/ Waiting for a passenger ship" (and this reminds me exactly of a dream about a big passenger ship lined up along a beach near a tenement resort that has broken glass in the sand beyond the washlines and the girl who said to me "But I can cut my feet in that sand, hey," and one might, Pow!, the offshore pirates in big old heavy cruisers open'd up on our lines of defense and let us have flush in the ass and face, we all collapsed in the sand on better days, with parasols and a few parakeets and paratrooper's wives crowning us with ivy leaves of laurel victory all poison and southern, now what the hell was I saying——no, on the other hand, that *was* the beach, I caught myself running then just as Jack caught me running on the machine, but the sand *was*, and *is*, quite . . . tragic, or whatever, and so: but that dream was strange, dear Chad) "/ship to go to seas. I lived in a roominghouse attic/ near the PortAuthority/ An enormous city warehouse/ Slowly turning brown/ Across from which old brownstone's/ fire escapes hung down/ On a street which should be Russia/ outside the Golden Gates/ or Back in the middle ages,/ not in United States/."

> And that/ sir/ is poetry/
> nothing but/ nothing else/
> nothing/ sir/ *but*/ sir/ nothing/
> *but*/ sir/ altogether sir.

"In a street which should be Russia" expresses exactly the longing of a former idealistic young Jewish boy looking out a window in the Manhattan of his disillusions; it is also a statement close to madness and so close as to induce hyposthobia, or, swinging on a trapeze above death, in a street which should be Russia, outside the Golden Gates (the golden knobs on the Kremlin, the furls; the Golden Gate of Russian Hill Frisco;) *or back in the Middle Ages, not in United States* . . . what is this "in United States" if it isn't the expression of a clever shallow mind gripped in the fear of madness; then you come, no but now listen but you do, to "Two books on top the bedspread, Jack Woodford and Paul de Kock. I sat down at the table to read a holy book,/ about a super city/ whereon I cannot look" and you have the utterances of a mighty poet, "*I sat down at the table to read a holy book,/ about a super city/ whereon I cannot look*," "About a super city," "Whereon I cannot look." "Whereon." The use of Superman terms mixed with clay nouns

like table, book, etc. and the capper, the mighty "whereon" of
poetic exactitude and also direction pointer to meaning, and
stately splendor of. "Then I heard great musicians/ playing
the Mahogany Hall." he goes on, later, elsewhere, this gem is
in my possession, we're having a new succession of Daudets and
Baroques of all sorts——kinds——specialties——sizes——bust——
measurement——the gray time, the gay, gay time——the small
hotel time, the time, time is of *it*——time, go time, go——Cody
walked in, sat on the stove, "Oh but I'm tired this strange old
night; Oh but this is a tired night, I worked all day on those
truck tires and all last night switchin'")——and stands there in
the doorway thinking that old broken thought, and here's what
it was, "That sticklegged old bat who's standing on the corner and her Hannegan's gone by, that's his name, we park his
Chrysler in here, he's the only guy who gives a tip, him and that
Texas millyoil man; her Hannegan, she calls him, old cunt, her
story she's puttin down, but fine, I like her fine, I'd like to try
her sometime. How long ago did she leave that step?"

I HAVE SEEN THE RED SUN fall on Cody's clothes on the floor of
the attic; his workgloves, dungarees, chino pants, shirts, socks,
shoetrees, cardboards, white shirts piled, on top of ancient
leather belts, ancient railroad overtime papers now stomped
with the dust of shoes, the wild phosphorescent inner linings
of jackets or scarves, a whistle, a, an official railroad pay cal-
culator and time book, put out by Crown overalls, showing
a sad red-ink railroad man (in this red sun attic) standing in
his architectural even riveted Crown coveralls pointing with a
proud shy smile lost in red ink and absences of red ink in the
oval reserved for his face, at an ad for Crown coveralls whereby
a testing company, having put them (U. S. Testing Company)
through a crash tour in stock cars (or something) and there
you have the certificate of laboratory testing: "We regularly test
Crown shrunk coveralls and certify them to be of high quality,
strong——" signed, with a signature, "a new pair FREE if they
shrink" and me thinking: "Did Cody dream on this too in this
sad red attic of his maturity's home, this house in which he is
suddenly raising three children for the world." Inside a thousand and one figures showing, under engine numbers, train
numbers, time lefts, amounts, overtimes, mileses, all useless

phantasmagoria in a page where he keeps——but it is there, he really fills out these columns, so voilà, "Date, Sept. 23, (from SJ to Tracy, train no. X-2781, on duty 1:30 P.M., tie up 5:30, miles, a hundred; $13.40 earned, no overtime; conductor, Webbington of New Zealand"——all filled out, in his poor dumb scrawl with which however he has written the following words too:

"Cake upon cake the perspiring years pile on, just like a dissheveled U P desk with papers sittin on last week's foundations"——or——"It was with considerable regret (this is more like it) that my old man at this time was not able to discern the meaning of certain words currently becoming popular in use on theater marquees, and so we walked in the shadow of our ignorance. A childly courtesy that once marked his most redeeming feature, in matters like this one of the gay marquee that used to light up 'grand,' now was followed by a just-as-redeeming curiosity and just as childlike when I asked him what 'slay' meant.

"'Well,' he said, 'it means you kill somebody with a spear.'

"'Er somethin,' he added a minute later, as we picked our teeth on a fender of a Ford parked in front of Haymaker's Café. 'Er somethin, Cody old boy, er something.'"——this being an example of how Cody would write if he wrote about these things. His poor clothes piled in the sad attic of Frisco joyous hamburg-zizzling suppertime dusks of summer and manual labor; good Cody; a man who works is good, this is a maxim among the old people and one that you can't gainsay——and the book, the book, it's got a 1935 date on it, what is it doing, like that old green jalopy hungup in this attic, this town so far from its cra——"But in the afternoon, especially late, around four, how the red sun illuminates these dusty objects of Cody's life, how mutely and yet eloquently they lie there, unattended, left and thrown there, still-life geometrical images of Cody's poor attempt to stay alive and strong beneath the skies of catastrophe."

ONCE CODY raged in a park like this, was amazing——rosy afterlights of the Pacific sunfall, vast silences, Mexical rainclouds mixing with the thin diving bird and the yukkle bird's cry in the wet bush——shudderings and thrashings in the bush—— and mixed with rosebrown clouds blown by a fogbank far away——the bird of the first spring evening and first flipflop hardy wintered tragicbug——the dusk of the park, the benches, the sad walk, the gathering darkness, the hollow shell of Cody haunting this gloom and these Mexican monuments and fountains like the ones we saw in Chapultepec Park at the bottom of the road——Cody is dead.

The tortured clawtrees making their ugly frazzle in the geometric center of the afterglow, a downtrodden pine, the drip-drip of a faroff bay launch crawling among the great mountains of San Pablo Bay; the wet grass, the green madness of the world, the mud of children who played, the hedge (transparent and full of streetlights); the chained garbage cans of the socialistic park; the tufts of spruce——the awful sadness of the death of Cody. In a sunny day he once cavorted here with the mystery and the grace of a Shakespearean garden hero——this is the part of the forest he mystified——this is where, by the death of the light I discovered him in, he now's a ghost pacing on the tulip and tips of hedges, morose, secretive, grown old——no more "Now Jack just as we passed that hedge, and felt a tulip, I was going along in the assumption within my own thoughts, those concerning your beatitude sayings, and not——won't hang you up on a detail——as we and as I saw, while you looked at the gathering stormclouds over there at the magic side of the park, my infant self arising, I'm playing in this park with all the kicks I ever found inside my mind and everything I have to make myself a living organism cabbaging and ticking and swinging like mad towards the darkness of our common death in this skeletal earth and billion particled gray moth void and empty huge horror and glory isn't it awful making enormous bands in all directions like the flight of the prophetic swallow who comes from the other side of the cable car mountain.

"Adieu, sweet Jack, the air of life is permeated with roses all the time."

BUT IT WAS ONLY yesterday that Cody said to me and nobody's said such a thing in over a year, "I love you, man, you've got to dig that; boy, you've got to know." And I suddenly realized that women, those flesh embodiments of perfume, would love me too, a thing I had forgotten in all this darkness of the studious soul laboring in the undergrounds of knowledge with that little brakeman's lantern of just-enough-light illuminating the clay endeavors beneath the Golden Spear of God. "Okay Cody" I said "I heard you, I sure do know it now." It was the peyotl day, the day of judgment; I was coming down the stairs, as calm as an Indian, with my tenor horn round my neck, that is, depending from my neck strap; I was not only on my first day as tenorman but understanding all music as I lay either flat on my back or stood up aslump with my sweet old horn, learning the first modified woodshed rudiments of raw wild joy which is American jazz, the *song*, the great whistling song, whistling into your horn and holding your horn high, aware all the time of the mistakes you can make and at the same time realizing the dreariness of the moments it consumes to realize this and letting the song, the song pass you by; then raising your horn, horizontal like Lester and Lee Konitz, and blowing into it, whistling out of it, out of its iron, the perfect harmonic note in this moment of the tune, the pop tune, the song, the living American melodic symphony that rings in my brain continually and is the great chord of the key, the great hollow and echoing arrangements of wide-spaced octaves in which as upon the Pillar of the Arcades of Jazz, Modern Jazz, the conglomerating music of the world, the whole world, a song is hurled and not only, but in its perfect heartbreaking harmonic hint——just as love is a hint of God. I had been seeing how all music would merge into the great Abstraction that is coming——Abstract war (as now), Abstract art, Abstract classical-based modern symphonic music, Abstract advertising, Abstract baseball (television and other developments later), Abstract drama, and the Abstract novel, and Abstract modern jazz soft-sound tenor horns blowing, sweet, distant, rowel, up-going, go-baby-to-New-York in a rush of things. I have seen the tenorman's sad pale face too, and in my own face, Stan Getz, Brew Moore, Gerry Mulligan, Jimmy Ford, the fairytale altos with red shirts like the one Cody and I saw in Chicago but I'll get to that in a minute; Charlie Parker, Sonny Stitt, Lester Young, Joe Holliday, and the mysterious James Moody and his King Pleasure; names like the names of great English poets, like the names Googe, Smart, Cowley and Vaughan, Sidney and George Herbert; wasn't Spenser's cousin-in-law Robert Johnston who wrote those obscure and unknown fantastic hymns that he wove into choruses of strange vast five-act dramas replete with funny characters abstracted

from Blakeian ravings he wrote in the streets and on the gallows
at midnight when they caught him and put him in the clink
for trespassing on the property of the Crown? Who will know
the fate of Brew Moore whom I have seen like a ghost on the
sidewalk: he has huge hair and he walks with his arms knocking,
you have to look again before you are frightened (ahem). What
did Clyde Cockmaster the second base English poet look like,
he who carried coals . . . but now there's no time to lose. I was
so intent on music as I came down those stairs that I didn't remember Cody's saying he loved me, till the, till a day later or so.
No, Cody isn't dead; Cody is the average man, Cody is the fellow who works for a living and has a wife and kids, and worries
about Taxes in March, and listens intently to the catastrophic
news of radios, also to every kind of wild jabberous crapule that
comes from the minds of harrassed radio scriptwriters who can't
cash their checks while they're writing Inner District Attorney.
Cody is not dead. He is made of the same flesh and bone as
(of course) you or me: he has a bloodstream, and veins, like
you and me, and a system of nerves that inform him of the
catastrophe or the roses be day as they May; he, why he listens
to basketball games with his nerves, usually reading or talking
and just hearing the reverberations of youngcunt excitement
in wild play halls of juicy highschool days, not caring about
the outcome of the game any more or any less than you or me,
but like you or me missing not a jot of that sex need in his soul
and letting it listen to the old basketball game the way it wants
(sometimes too, like we did, in New York before I started out
for May with my suitcase he, and I, listened, on misty nights in
dark Manhattan parking lot in the shack, brownlit and dumb
and unhappy like the shacks of his father so long ago that the
memory crops and molders, comes to a cropping stop, dead
in dirt, in hopes of staying alive there we'd be listening to the
scream of basketball audiences and the mathematical music of
a great athletic radio announcer (Marty Glickman), "Up-to-
the-set-shot, swish," "Back to the forecourt, pass," "Down the
center line, shoot," "Out of bounds, resume play," "Don De
Short going to the free throw line," Morton with the ball in
right front court," "Six minutes in the fourth and final quarter," "This courtcast is coming to you——" "No good, taken

off by Sesalush of Stamford, pass to Thorp, back to Sex, over to James and James s-s-s-s-s-set shots, long, oh, Wow, swish, zowie" (Screamcunts——"It was in and out and in again, most *sensational!*")——But Cody isn't great because he is average. I have seen the star of an Angel in his eye, the beauty of his brown and eye sidebones; also, I have noted the beauty of his children and his works in the arrangement of their lives; his son has the air of a Beethoven in his crib; his daughter Gaby and, the huge and serious childish sorrow of great saints and nuns; Emily is an Empress, she will be polluter of reigns, replacing the silken glove for the mailéd fist——maybe; or she will weep, she'll cry in the snow at night. Cody can't possibly be average because I've never seen him before. I've never seen any of you before. I myself am a stranger to this "average" world. Well, we'll all meet in hell and hatch another plot. Julien Lucifer, that'll be the New Angel and Satan-Winged Blackamoor who'll start the Infernal Revolution by the power of his tongue. In such a Revolution I can see Cody just standing there in the crowd and not even watching; on some afternoons he does the wash on the washing machine porch, without any expression on his face. Why should he be average? He is as mysterious as frost.

He believes in money, goes to work, spends it, and believes in money still——spending energy for spendingmoney, one thing eats another. By God, I believe in the Church; at——they rang me a bell once, free.

But the fact that any man has to say "I love you" when ob- viously he doesn't have to (and also the fact he said it to me) makes me feel good; I will say it too, I will say it to the women I love and to the men (like Cody) I love. Only a few hours later we were cursing at each other in the car like two men about to fly out and fight on the sidewalk; it's entirely possible in Cody, and I'm always ready for anything one way or the other. It would be extremely strange if I had a fight with Cody. I'd be on my toes for a killing. Yes, we could kill each other, me kill him or him kill me, whichever way the breaks went; that's how strong he is and how much I used to fight and still might unless if I was strong enough and might still be able to hold him off laughing——but that's out of the question, he's no struggling babe, he's a raging murderous man.

"My aunt's got a hold
of you, O babe!
My aunt's got a hold
of you, O babe!"

TRAGIC SATURDAY IN FRISCO. I'm coming home from work
in dark of night, musing on my freepass-incoming-to-Frisco
train, I'm thinkin about Cody, red neons, night, and instead, en
route home, get few beers in the wildest bar in America, corner
Third and Howard, paddy wagon's there every hour, we just
got to drink there you and me sometime man but anyway I get
high drunk, drop money on floor, am panhandled, play Ruth
Brown wildjump records among drunken alky whores colored,
and colored men and white winos milling in a pissy drafty room
with stains seeping down the wall, absolutely the wildest bar in
America, but I've got my rake, brakeman's lantern and rainsuit
and feel fine and crazy, even though the cops, going in to arrest
a few beat drunks, usually Alabama immigrants off reefers, says
to me "You stayin here long?" meaning, scram, no place for
you, but I stay, get drunk, make friends with friendly neat colored Frank, cut around corner to Little Harlem scene of the
great jam sessions of '48 and '49, only girl I laid in town so
far is in there, colored B-girl, gone woman, Marie, I hook up
in there with her niece tall lissome black Lulu, call Cody feverish with excitement (he's in bed fucking E) he rushed out,
("Come on Cody, let's celebrate your birthday," it's his birthday, February 8th), came down, in middle night, station wagon,
all pile in, rush to find four-foot connection Charley, he's on
street, wham, tea, first thing you know, in his room, strip poker
starts, strip, and Lulu has to lose! In a dead giggling silence she
began undressing before us——great tits, shoulders, legs, thighs,
belly, bellybutton, perfect Betty Grable all over, but black——
wham, and Charley who's a four-foot sexfiend born raised in
Panama where his father is numbers racket and four-foot too,
has eyes on her, Cody is saying "Sh-H7h7h7it," whatever, and
I'm watching, and whoo, her girlfriend's watchin, fresh out of
reform school she is (name I fergit), told us about conditions
there, how when girls go fruit they put 'em in cottages alone,
all girls go fruit, black girls go fruit for Mexican girls, Cody

spends entire rainy days hiding from his wife listening to these stories from the five colored sisters and cousins hangin around Marie's housing project shack pad, with lazy men around, Cody sits on bed blasting and giggling with the girls all day——Lulu gets embarrassed and dresses, re-dressed; from then on, disaster, Cody runs off to get tea from wife and also from guilt for running out, she waiting in night, now sobs, I, drunk, bring two girls into Cody's dark house, we stand breathless by baby sleep crib of Little Timmy Pomeray as Evelyn sobs and everything and throws us out, and off we go, two girls and Cody, and I, bleary, driving into woods of California for orgy, but one girl cops out (Carol), Lulu stay with me, but Lulu pass out, and (joined by another girl with Joe Louis face) we spend whole day driving aimlessly and with that vague-jawed but tremendous rocky fatalistic and tragic obstinacy of Cody and his fathers and the great raw hobos and hardy winos of death and experience in the world, Cody just drives and drives having switched to old '32 Pontiac tragic jalopy of the mist, we go up and down unbelievable shakespeare cute hills of california countryside, warm day, hawaiian shirts, forests, we take girls back to housing project, a brother comes to carry Lulu out, pays no attention, off they go, Saturday late afternoon, the red sun falls on everything, night's coming, wild whooping saturday night frisco and Lulu's already drunk and ruined her coat; well, Cody and I return to house, crestfallen, to wife rocking baby hysterically in dark. Cody makes up after days of sorrowful house silence, see?

(*On the gallows,*) **JACK.** I wanted to tell about——but the calluses, the——

> Tonight don't sing me "Hoods of the Moon"
> Don't sing tonight the "Hoods of the Moon"
> Golden Boy, go be a princess in a tower
> Gamin of Gold be instead princess of a tower,
> Dreaming melancholic about our poor love
> Or be blond cabinboy up on mast.

(C-R-O-W-S-H, *he's hanged*)

PEYOTL FANTASY, at one point on peyotl I didn't know I was smoking a cigarette, it felt like a strange little vegetable the way it flipped and fluttered in my hand, an ear of cabbage, but it was only because Cody had rolled the joint so wrong and it was inverting in the hand. I think I understood everything at last, I must have, ever since I've been unable to get high on T any more because nothing has the quality of surprise after the knowledges of the cactus plant. Cody was just standing there. "Nuthin happens," he sez to me——"Crise Cody waddaya mean? I never got so stewed and stoned since I took heroin and Dilaudid and all the big ass drugs of long ago before the harmless leaf." "Harmless you say?" winks my mother with her face that I can never forget. And Peyotl twice as worse! "Cody! this is the end of the heart, these green crabapples in your belly have a toxin in their tree"——it didn't occur to me cactus was poison and shoulda looked at those needles closer, cactus with his big lizard hide and poison hole buttons with wild hair, grooking in the desert to eat our hearts alive, ack——"This shit'll kill you, this is no ordinary shit, the Indians who eat this haven't long to live, this thing is the realization of suicide, your mind tells you how you can die, take your pick; I see," I told Evelyn "how I can go out tonight and blow this horn at the top of my lungs with all my might all night I could die, I would die."

"Would you know just before?" she asks me.

"No——yes——I think so——oh sure, but this stuff is so horribly powerful that you'd do it if you just felt like it. This's what John Parkman did, committed suicide on Peyotl, the new sleeping pill, from Tragic Carol to Sad Hip John, wow——" I'm telling her anything, everything, and all of it is true and ringing in the air just like now with you and me, and Evelyn's a little skeptical——"Say, I wanta eat," Cody says to Ed (who turned us on); "No," says Ed, "nobody eats till I say so."

We're all sittin around, upstairs, downstairs, in the basement, in the attic, quiet respectable Friday afternoon; Ed is reading Irwin Garden's poetry out loud, without a leer, idealistically, seriously, with those Frisco telegraph wires I see behind him in my reveries of him Frisco native born, like Sebastian reading poetry like in Boston long ago, man, up in the gray mist Frisco Cisco Attic; Cody is quietly considering his stomach, patting, saying, "Urp, well, I guess I won't throw up now; should be able to eat soon. I'm not high, are you?"

MEANWHILE I'm sittin there on the bed I sleep on, with the horn around my neck, and a stick a tea in my mouth, thinkin about girls, girls, looking at dirty pictures, feeling nauseated, holding myself up, my stomach atremble, my heart beating out of control, my mind quivering from the activity of the soul below, that pragmatic flesh in your regions of the heart and belly (and afraid to lie still and see visions,) my eyes shifting planes of ceiling on me, I commented only once, my hair hanging in strands with square edges backhead like an Indian, Cody repeatedly saying that I look like an Indian and I tell them my Iroquois grandmamama in the North Gaspé, 1700, I being of the race of the Indian who was pushed out of every place in the western hemisphere New World except America, ha ha——The children are utterly amazed at us all day long, they don't dare speak a word, or touch, as if we was cactus and we're stoned to the bone goopin at the moon on the couch side by side with arms hangin and tongues hung.

"I'm real relaxed," I says——

"Damn, so am I," admits Cody with a mild and conciliatory air; no, he's not high, he's like Irwin Garden.

"Damn, I know all the secrets of high, har me?——it can't miss, nosiree——" because Cody is not listening, only suddenly the peyotl makes him say, "What was that you said Jack?" And I can't remember; but on peyotl all I gotta do is look back in my mind, like I look back on this page, to know what it was I said. "I know all the secrets about how to get hi and stay hi and understand everything all the time, and they say that's to be crazy, and I'm crazy now, I know I'm crazy now. But I made a speech, didn't I Cody?"

"Yes, you did," he nods Irishly, that is, like a simple young Irish kid like the ones I used to know on the wooden fences Saturday mornings down the blue sky alley that's just like the ones in either Denver or Lowell, when that smoke, that joy, transpired in the holiday air and piping clean morn of the old-fashioned clime: there's me Cody, sittin next to me; his wife is sendin me messages of joy through the Western Union because this peyotl didn't make him go mad but instead he sat by his wife like a vegetable sex organ all day, and at night rolled his bones grimly and manlily to work a hunnerd fifty miles away, midnight (that's my brother). "Yessir, I done made a speech, s'about how to stay high and how crazy I am," and I'm imitating colored dialect to add variety to a feat of memory, the peyotl is so potent, so all-giving, so nervewrackingly beautiful and sometimes so nauseating. "Some people get high on nausea," I heard once, from Bull Hubbard I think, in the days when we lay side by side in twin beds with the shades drawn at midnight, and we're fully dressed and have Syrettes of morphine stuck in our arms, relaxin and me thinkin I'm going to die and then I settle down to watching the Technicolor movie in my brain and the music and dancinggerls and Masonic gilt churches for backdrops, with a Vermont red mill in the pond, and the ocean the way I first seen it all warm and I'm floating over it on my back to Glenn Miller saxophone sections and Sarah Vaughan, bah, talking to rabbits, invoking God, bending double to find the vagina, deciding poems, planning essays, rearranging prophetic Dostoevskian abstract novels with characters so strange that Lionel Trilling said "The use of only their first names, and without nicknames or anything, and the 'imaginary city,' renders the whole thing unreal;" running my tongue along the edge of my mouth and wondering where all my wives of eaves and gables were gone, where my old buddy Mike, what's the score in the ninth inning. And there's Bull, saying, "Some people get high on nausea." He was reading myths then——he found 'em everywhere, he had Persian rugs, long before the so-called swank Atlantic Beach Club compared. "Get high and stay and understand everything all the time, I'm saying." So much for peyotl, in another epoch it'll get you high again. Peyotl is legal at this time, (February 1952) unless the law intervenes and makes it famous by giving it publicity and so everybody starts growing cactus on their back porches and poisoning themselves. But they've got to learn.

High, I'm telling you, high. What's the law against being high? What's the use of not being high? You gonna be low?

All kinds of things like that are occurring to me in the finalities of the peyotl day. "Well," I say to Cody, "and so you are Cody Pomeray" (saying this to myself) and out loud to him: "Well, so there you are sitting there." I felt like a portrait artist; I felt more like he was a ghost I'd come to see, which is exactly what he was when I left New York to come here.

Now I shall leave Frisco. I am going off to another ghost, to

report . . . I hope it's a girl, not a baby daughter either. (Do I
have a baby daughter somewhere? I have not troubled to find
out, and bird's on the wing again, I lost) (and am lost)——My
ghost sits nearby in his miraculous chair. How long a way I've
come to report him to myself, to comport or omport, from
his newspaper-material life of day by day, the story and significance of his spirit to mine and to others joined with mine.
What freezings have I felt; what dark days seen; what old Decem-
ber's bareness—everywhere. (with mightolicum furious armed
powers gesticulating furled flags upon the rale, not ounched or
made turbigity in a cloxen wale; fartitures, meadowlarks and
darkeningses-arecess Dimogenes burned): a wit, a woo, downy
dull fit make the reel, tolly doll came in the whirl, rammedon
saw his rivers: vales swallow blood. The ruined choir in the tree.
The stone that hung me on. The clime had airs when that wind
moist comes fanning his dew feather from a sea, lowing the bay
cows in the field, to make silos whale, tops sir methinks, where
cockadoodledo, adoodledoo, adoodledee, till grime cakes in a
burning lake. But gospel me not, Crown!——I had kings in my
navvies, and knew a French corount, one inpurpled but only
gently, *couronné*, crowned, as upon a spire, gleaming like Nestor's spear in the keen. Shakespeare, thou art flagellous of the
time. (Fragile act, fragile act.)

Time is of the essence, I must run on, "right?" I says to Cody
and he is sitting there quietly running the whole room with
some magnificent action watched by everybody enrapt, except
me, that was staring at the floor. "Whee!" I says, "I don't know
what's happening." But then I realize: it's not for me, or you, to
know; it's got to come to you, and does, eventually and always
does. How can I be suspicious of what C. says behind my back
to his wife, when I always learn later that they have nothing to
talk about but themselves and I can do anything I please such
as lighting matches in the pyromaniac attic. Music, sax, saxes,
quivering light, trumpets, voices, lights, shakes; all's happening; voices, song, toyland, eek, giraffes, zoos, circuses, fidos,
parkings, awl-hoots, toyland, jubilee, big red fox, red nose,
big Jack Little, girls and boys, Brooklyn Dodgers, joy, summer, New York, ice cream cones; blues in old saloons, of New
Orleans, short ones, at bar, King Cole, stories from ringside;
cigar-smoke, leather cases for lighters, a golfbag; mysterious

conversations through floor, the brown moth light in the corners of the room, the little dusts, the little dolls and ragamuffin dusts in the floor, so sad, tiny (flecked) specked, upon the toy wars of the floor, the little toys of children always mystify the air they occupy, they have been wished an identity by a breathing soul and therefore live. Listen, I have wished myself into heaven, there are more people dead than alive; dead eyes do not see? Dead eyes see.

And rain sleeps.

EVERYTHING'S ALL RIGHT; dead eyes see, are not blind. Roses riot everywhere. Sunflowers, Ah! I love you. Abstraction. You think? See rain. Comes afloat. Fell. From stormclouds in the racky north, strifed and blew-melted aslant skies like a warm frost melting in the savage huge infinity over the world and Kansas. (The Great Dustclouds of Kim!) Kim, Colorado, 1932; with cactus blown from Mexico mebbe. Sadness of the soul. Dimness of the inventive heart. I see heaven through everything. Heads bowed on scaffolds. Puddles of mud in Casablanca. Dull movies about Monte Carlo. Unmailed letters (or just envelopes). Baseball mustaches in old poems about home runs;

> Lowerin the boom on the bosun;
> The labels of unknown whiskies;
> Cartoons about jealous wives.
> Atlases to hold up shelves.
> (Sweet and Sour Lyrics)
> (That Ed Williams read like a young
>   idealist in the attic,
> to our gratification, Cody and me,
>   and surprise.)
> Songs about populated boats singing.
> Hello to an old flame.
> Putting on your coat at midnight.

THINGS HAVE A DECEIVING LOOK OF PEACEFULNESS, THE BEAST is actually ready to leap——lookout——yet what about those French dreams last spring?——what, sweet hype? can't write?——find no machine to relabate your fond furlures;

furloors, vleours, or velours, we know that in French, in print
à main we cannot fail——

O Telegraph Hill!

Strange graces came to occupy this back seat, you mind, in
(own) tides. (time?) Furbishoors, fruppery, nosootle, nonsottle, nonsottle, sweattle, don't wrestle with this——trestle——(to
prove I can go on efficiently, otherwise I'll begin an abstract
drawing)

(an ABSTRACT drawing)

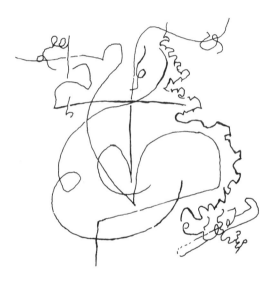

The thing to do is put the quietus on the road——give it the
final furbishoos and finishes, or is that diddling? Kind King and
Sir, my Lord, God, please direct me in this——The telling of the
voyages again, for the very beginning; that is, immediately after
this. The Voyages are told each in one breath, as is your own,
to foreshadow that or this rearshadows *that, one!*

I first met Cody in 1947 but I didn't travel on the road with
him till 1948, just the tail end of that year, at Christmas time,
North Carolina to New York City 450 miles, and back to North

Carolina, and back to New York City again, in thirty-six hours, with washing dishes in Philadelphia, a teahead ball, and a Southern drawl evening drive in between.

And in all that time Cody just talked and talked and talked.

We had met in 1947 when he first came to New York from Denver with his first wife, the sixteen-year-old Joanna Dawson of Denver and L.A. where her sadistic handsome father divorced from her mother, was a cop; Cody, all bare ass standing in the door of a coldwater pad when we first knocked on the door, me, Ed Gray, Val Hayes. They were students at Columbia University, close friends of mine, Val was a dear close friend at the time; they told me Cody was a mad genius of jails and raw power, that he was a god among the girls with a big huge crown wellknown wherever he went because he liked to talk about it and made frequent and assertive use of it and also the women talked about it and wrote letters mentioning it; sometimes frantic; a reader of Schopenhauer in reform schools, a Nietzschean hero of the pure snowy wild West; a champion. In the door he stood with a perfect build, large blue eyes full of questions but already thinning in edges, at edges, into sly, or shy, or coy disbelief, not that he's coy, or even demure; like Gene Autry (exact appearance) with a hardjawed bigboned——but he also at that time bobbed his head, prided himself on always looking down, bobbing, nodding, like a young boxer, instructions, to make you think he's really listening to every word, throwing in even early as 1947 a thousand manifold yesses and that's rights; testing his knee muscles, thinking of his next piece, plotting it on the sly while his wife buttons from the last. When we walked in Joanna had to jump up off the bed and straighten; Cody didn't warn her, or shield; she hastily fixed up, her hair, her wrinkled dress (I guess) I No de hesitatee. I was amazed how young and beautiful she was, though a little pimply then; and Cody I had expected to be, from reading a letter he wrote from Colorado Reformatory, a kind of small, thin, shy guy with dark hair and a poetic sadness in his jailness, like a sick criminal genius, or a saint, an American young saint, one who might even be boring and eventually turn to some strange Seventh Day Adventist type religion, like you meet in bus stations in Minneapolis, with wide eyes of fire and phony phenomenality, turning his body to religion or just sadkid goop; but Cody was dishonest looking, a thief, a car thief, and that's exactly what he was, he had already stolen over five hundred cars (and served time for some of it); not only a thief, maybe a real angry murderer in the night. The "kid" I had imagined from his letter, I never imputed any kind of crime for——other than some kindly Robin Hood-type theft, giving a widow, exit, giving a widow a window, sadly in the late afternoon. Cody was serpentine he was not sad——Cody had long sideburns like certain French-Canadians I used to know in my boyhood in Lowell, Mass. who were real tough, sometimes were boxers, or hung around rings, gyms, garages, porches in the afternoon (with guitars), sometimes got shiny boots and motorcycles and rode voyages as far as Fall River and New York just to be on Times Square in their buttons a half hour, and had the bestlooking girls, and you saw them the couple coming up from the dump and the river at night along the baseball fence as nonchalant as nothing had happened, he just threw away the rubber and his dark eyes flashed across the night. Cody was vigorous, his actions were tamed to his will——the "kid" never had a chance; I thought of Cody immediately as a lion tamer, he looked a little like Clyde Beatty had looked to me in the great circus in Boston, from a distance, stiff and strong, the visiting Ringling of thunderous May nights. I didn't think of Cody as a friend.

I THINK I SLEPT in the chair that night, starting after dawn, when the others in one of these typical youthful New York parties straggled off only the last possible moment before roaring morning; Cody and Joanna (and the kid whose friend owned the pad) must have slept with their clothes on on the couch, the kid, Bob Markan, in the kitchen or floor or something. In the morning I was sitting with an ashtray butt between my ashy fingertips smoking, by the gray window, as old Espan Harlem woke slowly to another day and already the first cats were, like in San Juan, already standing on the roofs and looking around the horizon and down, rooftop sentinels of the great Indian World that you see in all Indian cities all day, Havana, Mexico City, Trinidad, Cuzco, Mongol towns in shaggy Siberia must be, respectable collector of unemployment spending the day with the pigeons on the roof overlooking the street that's all—— I commented on them, in fact; and also later to Vicki when we had the place to ourselves one morning, and she said "Oooh daddy, I dig those motherfuckers all the time." Joanna like in a sad French painting of 1950, not a Modigliani but that emaciated Breton genius with the sad longbodied Bohemians in the room, that I saw in that there *New York Times*, sat on the edge of the bed with her hands hanging in her lap and her broad country face under its sea of golden curly tresses fixed in a dumb stare like a farmer wife waitin for her turn to pump at the well while Pa swooshes with the soap pan, under cool pines of dew and a red sun reflecting on the lake; but Joanna is in an evil gray New York pad that she heard about back West and gapes.

Cody was pacing up and down restlessly; he came to his decision in the middle of talking to me about those roof sitters and saints above. "Well now, Joanna, what we've got to do is sweep the floor and then scramble up those eggs and have a breakfast, we'll never crystallize in our plans or come to any rockbottom pure realization, decision, whichever, or nothin without perfect action and knowledge not only philosophical and on an emotional plane but pragmatic and simple."

And Joanna automatically got up and started up the breakfast. And Cody had made his speech in utmost anxiety and tenderness but complete domination and control, and I saw that in his wild life of carstealing, girl-conning, poolhalling and hustling he needed order and a certain amount of help. He was very youthful and severe, and I marveled at him——openly with myself I thought of him as a heartbreaking new friend, in fact very beautiful to whom the only thing I could ever be left to say would be, "Ah but your beauty will die and so will life and the world." I walked beside him on tiptoe, I didn't want to disturb the delicate balance that existed between this angel and me; as for Joanna, because she was a woman, I had designs on her, I kept looking at her breasts and thinking of her lips and her legs spread revealing her cunt, and me there bending over her naked heart with my hair falling over my eyes like moronic French actors or the pimpish characters in Parisian postcards and dirty-books especially those with furnishings in back and sometimes (the girl with the cigarette cunt). My feeling for Cody was ethereal, like for a character in a book, for Joanna, earthy—— that's to say, sexy, malevolent, manlike; Cody accepted us as he accepts everyone secretly severely and especially impersonally as his present wife now knows better than anyone——Cody paid no attention and never did later to Joanna and me, even when she flattened me on walls in Harlem afterhours joints and pushed while Cody stood not far, and almost even when we——definitely when we lounged on couches or almost even when she sat between us golden bare in the front seat of the '49 Hudson as we drove across the state of Texas in 1949 and she applied cold cream to our respective organs, a flash sight of which opposite rolling trucks must have had from their high cabs so that it seemed to me that I saw them go swerving off in the tail window like drunks in amazement of course; gorgeous Joanna with her yellow cunt in the sun, the first warm sun (approaching by the hour red old El Paso in the Sunset) since the blackened snows of New York winter, her squishy delicious cunt, wow, that Cody repeatedly penetrated and lubricated with his finger as he drove on and where we'd said goodbye to our friends in a squalid snowy winternight in upper York Avenue by the tenements those three, four days from New York to New Orleans to Frisco, and smelled deeply for the taste and reminder and sense of Joanna the girl he wanted; sitting there, blushing, laughing, but just as composed as Queen Elizabeth, her pendant breasts full, round, soft and real in the light, that neither of us dared touch in front of each other, though I playfully and masterfully once in a while rubbed up with my palm her inside thigh till she tickled and laughed (at El Paso she squeezed my balls through my pants as we waited for Cody and a young crazy reformatory hepcat we met in the bus station when trying to hustle with our three abilities for gas fare to Tucson and nobody was there but the cat who kept saying "Let's mash somebody on the head and take his money" and Cody went off with him high and laughing and excited to dig the streets and bars, and in the dark Joanna and I played little games tenderly); almost even, Cody paid little attention, when, at his request, we all were in the same bed, the bed in which my father died and that I'd given to furnish our New York pad, actually held by Irwin who was working nights, therefore giving that bed some life to renew it and give it direction in the empty void (and sagged in the middle from a once-mighty weight); lay stiff as an iron board at or upon his edge of the bed, Joanna sunk hot in the middle and smiling and a little embarrassed and thinking of something else ("Gee, what an honor to have two men at the same time, Cody and Jack"); and I on the other protuberant end, amazed, complicated, plotting, and none of us breathing or moving until Cody said "We must all be cool and relaxed as though nothing was on our minds at all, dig please, man, Joanna, be straight in your soul and admit whatever feelings and act on them right away, don't let even a second rot——" as the saying is, *blow*, or anything, or go, so, do it, start, begin, now. So we fiddled and daddled and nothing really happened, just like highschool kids in a hooky, in a truant bedroom with Coca-Cola and aspirins we sent each other out of the room to do it alone, one by one, and were frightened by the darkness in the house, in fact the creaking mystery, philosophical void, the missing of the point, the obvious sadness of having to die never having known some-thing about everything and ourselves we're dying by the hour to know and act upon immediately, that might very well be as Reich says *sexual*, some mystery in the bones themselves and not the shadows of the mind. No, as I walked on the sidewalk that first morning with Cody——

In Denver the summer of 1947, which is after these first meet-ings, Irwin took a picture of us with arms clapped over each other's shoulder looking straightly and severely into the eyes—— whatever happened to that picture, I've never seen it? (a nurse he put me on to has it) but life is so huge and complicated I can't go into the nurse now, or Denver 1947, or anything, and time flies . . . *in this case*, not in any case, though.

THAT FIRST NIGHT of meeting I didn't bother to do anything but laugh at Val and poke Cody in the ribs whenever Val, his mentor in Denver, the kid his age who'd told him poetry was more important than philosophy, made any mentorial, positive, educational or advisory remarks. As for Joanna, she cradled Val's head in her lap; I detested her at first I guess, I don't remember; all the guys said they'd laid her, half of them boasting, after a few weeks, after Joanna had the cops after Cody as revenge for something in their great brawling roominghouse and hotel roomfights, Cody: "Listen, honey, bitch, whore, or, O, no, dar-ling, yes, no, O yes, you, don't, O, bitch, whore, damn, fuck!"

Joanna: ". . . and you didn't tell me you meant the other side of the street so by hiding that you hide goddammit sonofabitch

I don't know what you hide——" Joanna soon learned to hide better, it appears. Later she began to out-lie Cody. But his relationship with his women is something I can't rely on to cast any light on the fact that whenever, on the East Coast on some warm spring evening, I happen to be thinking of the overbulge of the land all the way to California and all of it all in that same red light, a common idea of mine, just to relax the soul, or make a pretty picture to hang and re-hang in my brain, I see Cody's face occupying the West Coast like a big cloud and that must be because after him there's only water and then China out there for me or he represents all that's left of America for me. Loving China as I do, I have endeavored——

It wasn't until some time later Cody and I renewed the early meetings, which also included a walk from Spanish Harlem, where he stayed for that week or two, to the campus on Morningside Heights, during which he said he wanted Val and others like me to figure something out to get him into Columbia as a regular undergraduate, freshman, so he could get on the football team and amaze Lou Little (as I'm positive he would have done) and he didn't even have highschool or even complete grammar school credits if anybody can go digging those kind up; and a few strolls, experiences looking for a new room for him, in which, later, in his absence, Joanna, on the bed, confessional, intimate, repetitive, told me and poured into my ear the sob glob story of Cody, Cody, Cody, till I hated the sound of the name and pictured the muslin curtains and outside redbrick of the hotel with what must have been just the same in Denver and the same tears and story; and a meal, a spaghetti meal, actually on the occasion of Cody's and Joanna's first night on the Columbia Campus, at Jack's on Amsterdam, with everybody around the table, Tom Calabrese, (met him for the first time that night), Mac, Gray, Val, and Allen Minko bless him.

Cody came to my door——but this is dull, but yet it isn't—— Ah, that this loud and frosome crabble——Val Hayes said, kicking the door by the clean trick of stepping on it and at the same time turning the knob at a rush down the hall striding into the door, "if you want to lay Joanna ask Cody." I had no——But later, when I thought I'd never see Cody again and was busy in the sorrowful eternity, he himself came to my door knocking.

"I want to learn how to write," he said. It was after supper

one evening. I formed all kinds of impressions of Cody that
have since been discredited as he maniacally but sometimes
not so maniacally continues his life——but this all wasting time.

Yes, there is the——grave——

While he was in New York in the winter of '46 and '47 Cody
made friends with Irwin Garden; twice or so a week he did
come to my house, and one dawn in my bedroom as I lay on
my bed and he on my dead father's bed (this before we moved
it and drank strawberry soda) he read me an entire condensed
version of the life of Jack London from the *Reader's Digest*,
just I think for me to become accustomed to his voice and
style of reading, his particular Western intonations as though
he was wearing an old black hat in the rain of the badlands on
a grim——but also really a ceremonial fondness for words like a
bigfist——but we never became really close, the only thing we
did was agree one m-e-l-t-i-n-g warm afternoon on the snowy
boulevard as he strolled with me to catch a further bus stop
towards New York and I was on my way to a little sort of little
kid's library at the corner of Jerome Ave. and Crossbay, where
(of course adult books too) old silver rimmed ladies answered
all your questions about (if you're question-asking type) where
to find the Cimarron River——agreed to go out West together
that spring, to Denver, his hometown, and wreak havoc with
the wild drunk nights of lawns and big trees under wild snow-
capped mountains in the jackpine moonlight that I imagined
then . . . no Larimer trolley tracks. But nothing came of——he
went off to Denver prematurely, with a stolen typewriter, or a
typewriter he just bought, or something desperate and crazy. (I
saw him off at the Greyhound Bus, 34th Street, ate beans with
him; when he went for extra bread in his new pencil-stripe suit,
and patted his belly as if it was ample, and puffed his cigar like
my father used to do, I said to myself——And Irwin, who was
there, that wretch, that, why that, he said, I said, "Say Cody's
kind of a thin guy ain't he," and Irwin leered, said, "He's got
a good hard flat belly; I know a good belly when I see one;
don't go talking him into getting fat or nothing; I'm an expert
on bellies now you know." We took pictures in the twenty-five
cent booth of a——my picture came out very strange. Cody
looked coy, profile, long sideburns, like the side views in the
post office, plup; and Irwin looked, with his glasses off, he being

the hornrimmed wild hip kid type you see everywhere like for instance that year he was in the Strand Theater when Lionel Hampton blew mad from the stage and jumped down in the aisle and they say some kind of CCNY hipster madstudent ran up and danced wild and sexcrazy in front of him to the beat so that Irwin says "the whole theater vibrated as one great orgone that suddenly took on a wild octopus like existence but only like a Negrer preacher flapping his hands to heaven and calling for the Rock and the Rise to come down and with big shrieking harpies in the air like evil suggestions under the water Eternity" or something like that saying it with serious nod of the head, this being the great kind of buddy Cody and I had by gad . . . but so, we saw Cody off, after the pictures) (mine of course was cut in half, both kept a half in their wallets, and I looked "just like an, a dago who kill anybody says anything wrong about his mother," this statement about the snapshot was put forward, by somebody, I think Julien later——) in the bus station Irwin kept saying, as the clock came to five minutes of Cody's bus, Hurry up please it's time, from T. S. Eliot, and Cody nodded; on a bus that said CHICAGO on it so that my eyes popped, I'd never been west of Jersey, I suddenly saw that Cody, this guy, so anxious, busy, was going home, going home, he roared off into the night. Joanna by that time was herself already back in Denver, working someplace, she'd had her wild arguments with Cody in New York——coming in across, so that the horses of dawn that they had seen together in the Greyhound Bus coming in across the plains towards New York only a few living months before the horses had passed the meadows of loss, the horses of dawn, the grays racing for the ghost, the blacks followed by the grays, some vernal sight from the buswindow, when probably poor little Joanna leaned her head on Cody's arm and really seriously dreamed her first, and Cody himself probably with one drowsy dormant eye uplidded to coming day outside the rushing windows, his legs stretched in the dark plush of the snoring bus, probably he too, drowsily in the winter dawn, like a farmer may open his eye at 4 A.M. when the first redness comes in across Dakota snows and hugs his wife a little and closes his eyes on that mortal vision of heaven and earth which is the sky in the morning, Cody too probably saw those horses of dawn——scented the first fresh fields of the East, of his dream——But now he was on a Denver-bound backgoing bus, off into the night, disappointed, back you go, zoom, CHICAGO, and we watched him go.

I myself didn't travel till two or three months later, and when I did, Irwin himself was already traveled to Denver, but via Texas, to see Bull and June and Huck in their shack or beat farmhouse in the Texas Bayou down near Trinity or Bleeding Heart or whatever; a rickety hipster kid who would someday be so thin, nonchalant, cool, complex in the same envelope of skin that then made him look like a ricket's ape, a monkeydoodle dandy, a Raskolnik, an undergrounder, a subterranean hipster star, a basketball riveter, (he was a poet); I myself took off, in the dew, in the dew of things, towards that evening-star of the West that eventually I did get to see after many days' travail and wild ride on the road in the form of a drooping old moist heap in the eve, in a bed of day-blue, shedding with sparkler-dims and showers her soft infinescences or infinessences, or infiniscences, on the baldy grain, of Iowa, Keota, the Buckle of the Golden Belt, to make you wise like an Aryan King in the blue desert; and such, just thats; and I got to see Cody in Denver again. Had very little to do with him. He, shortly after I continued on my way to the West Coast to get a ship and meet Deni Bleu, and get a ship I mean, went to Texas hitch-hiking, with Irwin, to Hubbard's, after Davies, his old mentor, had——that is, but wait, I wanted to refer back to this Davies, his grown mentor in Denver, whatever you can call him, his whatnot, his, but it appears I'm tired of telling over and over again about Cody's history in Denver when everybody including me knows it, unless you impute something strange of it, or make remarks, I don't know, I'm sometimes, Rendrovar, completely at a fucking loss.

(In others words, I didn't know Cody too well except as a Western guy I had known——I mean——On a soft summer night, only thing we did in Denver, a night like in a dream because I couldn't see anything beyond the windows, we rode a trolley from downtown to Denver U. campus talking about hotrods and midget auto races, and occasionally passing great Western white Washomats of cars gurgling and gleaming and spewing whiteness in the inky night——along by a few brown streetlamps.)——to Texas they went to see Hubbard, *a Texas yon eté pour voire Hubbard, et la y'on passez une couple de——*so

I didn't——but again, wait——I'm hungry——to go and see his
new girl Evelyn perform an ingenue role in Ibsen's *A Pillar of
Society*. A striking blond, commented upon by old ladies in the
audience——I sat far back, in the reverberating hall I behaved
like a French poet anarchist——Cody was wrapped in Evelyn——
this was my last sight of him till another year and one half——a
lot of things happened, but, he divorced Joanna in Denver,
or Frisco, drove her from Frisco back to Denver over terrible
blizzards in the Donner and Berthoud passes for divorces, married Evelyn in Frisco, this after hitchhiking to Texas with Irwin
kneeling on the road (like Rimbaud and his Verlaine, every
rose's got a summer, Julien and his Dave, I had my Sebastian;
Julien's Verlaine was murdered, my Verlaine was killed in a battle of war, Cody's Verlaine though is Irwin——or was——). When
I returned from California in October 1947, and after nothing
but strange nights stealing groceries in cafeterias in canyons
with Deni Bleu, an entirely different and other story, and after
having picked cotton in the San Joaquin Valley with a beautiful
Mexican girl, same, Cody had just left my house after crisscrossing me from Texas and then crisscrossing me on the map of the
country, in Indiana I guess bound for his big Jerichos of the
Golden Gate in the Final Land of America, California——so I
didn't see him till 1948. At which time I was in North Carolina
visiting relatives and boom, one day in December a muddy
Hudson pulled up on the sand road out front and out popped
a tragic rough-hewn Cody in a T-shirt in the sharp Christmas
cold and knocked on the door, and this after I'd only vaguely
mentioned, in a letter, where I'd be around Christmas. What
he did, one year married and a new father, working on the
railroad, pockets full of money, or no, not that, pockets empty
but money in the bank, he saw a new 1949 Hudson in a show
window on Larkin and bam, bought it. On time and down
payments. Slim Buckle was with him, his long tall buddy from
poolhall Denver days; they decided to blow across the country,
take off like the modern Indians do in jalopies from El Paso say
to as far as Montana on a whim: but for money Cody persuaded
Slim to marry Helen, who became Helen Buckle, money for
the trip, abandoning her in Tucson when she either didn't fork
over or spent too much on motels enough to make a man sick;
in L.A.——they pointed the Hudson south for that snowless

southern road to New York——they picked up travel bureau passengers at a fee and then conned them, the sailor especially, for
meals. Neck taut, exploded, Cody was pushing the car through
Las Cruces, New Mexico, when the vision of his voyage flashed
and exploded: Joanna!——he shot the car offcourse and north
to Denver; picked up Joanna there after horrible tearful scenes
and tears and cocksucking in hotel rooms; and off, the three of
them, eastward flying into the snow, through Kansas, where he
went off the road, and Missouri, where his kinfolk came from
and were still in all that snow measuring their thoughts and
snapping their suspenders in the gray void of a drizzly day, over
the river and into Tennessee and over the Great Smokies, the
rods blasting to hurl them off the icy rims; and to Rocky Mount
where I innocently was spending a meditative Christmas in the
bosom of my family. It was then we drove those two trips to
New York——to help the family move things; and when New
Year's came, parties——friends——but these were my first close
views of Cody (and of course I went back to the Coast with the
whole gang, we drove naked through a good part of the state
of Texas, Cody, Joanna and I after leaving Buckle in New Orleans with Bull Hubbard and June, in that old swamp mansion
in Algiers where Helen *had come to lie or that is reign in wait
for Slim* on Cody's return southern swing to Frisco)——(and I
thought Cody was, and still do, one of the most remarkable
men I've ever seen). He has excitements that are so wild and
all-inclusive——but wait a second there Joe——

There was something frantic in the air anyway Christmas
1948——I had "The Hunt" Dexter Gordon and Wardell Gray
cutting each other with tenors, I had four of the sides blowing
them good and loud in the little white house in the country
when Cody drew up with Joanna and Slim like dead people
when you looked in over the windows, victims of Cody's frantic tragic destiny, he was always bursting to blow. Cody was
rocky and strange; "Hey man," we greeted; nervous, rubbing
his belly, he immediately played my record, but louder than
I had ever dared because of my sister's misunderstanding of
bop, a stranger for all intents and purposes from California with
corpses in a car outside, just a T-shirt, bowing and blowing in
front of the phonograph, like good oldfashioned oldtime jitter-
bugs that really used to lose themselves unashamed in jazz

halls; and Cody wanted his jazz powerful, simple, like the early swing of Coleman Hawkins and Chu Berry; my mother, sister, others, great troops of somber relatives of the South with the great faces of Civil War generals and frontier(matriarchs)——Oh goddamn——(making the mistake of following a bum story line already written)——watching him, really, in amazement, and later the other two when they woke up all pimply and gray and acted cool.

In the car I saw that Cody was completely in charge of the souls of Slim and Joanna and had been so for thousands of miles; "Now darlings we all sit in the front seat, Joanna honeycunt at my knee, buddy Jack next, big warm Slim at the door whereby he gets to use, damn, that fine, ugh, Indian, wow, Navajo, blanket, zoom," shooting the car at the road as, after a few hours sufficient to let a little dark fall and Christmas lights come on and a meal, we whaled north the four of us, an absolutely perfect driver, wham, zam, maniacally excited every moment and sometimes screaming like Ed Wynn laughing, we were in Washington and on to Baltimore, Philly, where we washed the dishes——but never, mind, I mean, New York, long ago excitements on the snowy road and for reasons long forgotten. That's why I rush over these historical matters——Cody has marched on since then though still like a fiend I see him rushing, gliding, like Groucho Marx in heaven——Sufficient to say, in California, after Joanna had——he abandoned me with her penniless, that is just drove away from corner O'Farrell and Grant saying he'd be back and not five minutes after the car finally stopped in Frisco from hell and gone east, our gear on the sidewalk, her high-heel shoe sticking out from my sweater, his explosion was over——but not really, a few nights later——in fact when I left he was planning a breaking-and-entering with Joanna——but not really——she'd had a sugar daddy, he had a pad, they stood on the sidewalk——talking about it, high—— there were memorable jazz nights——Slim Gaillard who is so hungup on just goofing and blows a gone load, Cody said "He knows time"——Then I returned across the country, alone, back to GI school to New York, by bus, via Butte, snows, the Bitterroot night, howling blizzards in North Dakota, Minneapolis, Chi, stealing apples in Pennsylvania grocery stores, rearriving New York just in time to see Ed Gray, Dave Sherman and Biff

Buferd off on the *Queen Mary* to Paris, and France, the lucky
bastards——but events do drag——but time passed——I won't
even mention time again——and finally in the spring of 1949 I
myself came out, alone, to Frisco to see Cody and he returned
to New York with me at one point in Nebraska at a hundred and
ten miles an hour. But all that——Gad——there had been guns
with Joanna, pointings at the temple——"all that winter had a
gun to my head, yessir!"——(through her mail slot he could
see her screwing sailors)——further arguments, arrangements,
rearrangements, babies born, Cody being, say, called by the
railroad in the middle of the night and going off in the fog in
his Levis with brakeman lantern, keys, jacket, bareheaded and
earnest and wild in the halo lamps of railly night, (till later in
the seriousness of his maturity he came to wear blue conductor's
uniforms as passenger brakeman and looked splendid). From
New York to California Cody and we in the car were stopped
twice, 1948 trip (the song "Slowboat to China" was popular, it
was really the name of our Hudson), 1949 again, three times, by
the police who suspected our looks, once on a lawn in Detroit,
in my former wife's neighborhood; once in the street, frisked;
on the road in Iowa again——but later, all that. Our fates are
very mixed and intermuddled, wild!

I CAN GOOF if I want to, that's the name of this chapter; but far
from talking, but, to con——The thing I couldn't get over then
was the magnificence of the actual car trip, in a matter of hours,
from one ocean to another across a country so interesting apart
from horrors that exist in it from one point to another, from
Tennessee to Dakota, from Massachusetts to Maine, from the
shores of Kitchigoomi to Abacadabra, Florida, or what might
not be horrors so much as just life and way it is in a necessary
culture and roaring along just like the weather or the sound,
the mighty seasound of all the blowers in all the factories and
apartment houses of New York, why, and say, that isn't what
you might start out saying if you were a successful owner, a
repair shop proprietor, radio repair, and however——but lived
in Jackson Heights, but that's another story (on Mission Street,
well on Howard Street, that wildbar, that's where I got drunk
last night).

   The trip proceeded, like the unrolling of a mighty thread

of accomplished-moments, accomplished-ments, I want to go
now, you better go now, wow, that girl, how I'd love to have her
sitting on my lap, saying "I want to go now," softly, meaning I
want to fuck, let's start, she's learned all the tenderness of the
new generation, the hip generation, the modern generation, the
generation that ten thousand years from now will lie in ruins
beneath the decays of worn fossil, like oil under the cabbage
leaves of old Carboniferous, if not Carbonomnivorous or better
Carbonitis, the Dinosaurs rolled their own roaches in an ugh,
ploppy sea, with Mormon fishtails rising slick and viney from
the wet pluck and muck of mires, dismal, dawn, dumbdawn of
reptiles. The final capture of Moby Dick around February 1952,
by the crew of a Scandinavian whaler equipped with a harpoon
cannon (dig, they call it a gun) and the subsequent cutting
up of its hunks and hanks even at sea off Japan, is much more
tragic than this midnight oil burnt by the doom of mesosaurs,
mausosaurs, daguerrosaurs, roarsaurs, horrisaurs, rawsaurs, so-
saurs, sososaurs and saurs musical——Moby Dick is Dead, and
Had to Die——it outlived Ahab more than a hundred years,
and predated Melville a century, whole centuries maybe more;
longevity was its only secret. It should have been Thoreau, or
Thoreau too, saw that whale at sea, that hump like a snow hill,
that White Vision, the Albino, the Albatross, the Tibetan chalice rag, the Leprosy: Thoreau would have said "Humph" and
predicted the harpoon cannon and turned away. "Enlightened
by the vollied glare" was not Melville's personal experience,
but A. P. Hill's and Danny Sitfence's from the red clay lands of
South Carolina, and in a way Whitman, and President Abraham
Lincoln with his stovepipe hat at the breastworks of Bull Run
(Melville milled in draft riot crowds, Bartleby-ish and pale, on
23rd Street, the hotel they posted notices on's still there, they
rolled beer in barrels off waterfront gangways, the dung breaker
got a fistful of suds in his eye, the stout ran in the gutters, they
cut fish heads in the warm sun and threw them to the cats, they
lolled by the Seurat sundecks of excursion boats, and counted
sails, and clouds; and Whitman bareheaded and holy and all
White like the Melville dream (from darkness) among them
strange, demure, queer, maybe a slouched hat, maybe a book,
a Bible, *Leaves of Grass*, Montesquieu, Abner Doubleday, the
Koran, astronomy, physics, woodlore, the paper, a pigeon in

his hair, a turd on his brow, a strange dream, a queer gleam, a something insinuating, intense, almost a very well maniacal in the darkness by the rail there, leaning, by gulls bisected, bedecked in moons, tranquil, fragile, China-like, fleecy, stormy, browy, snowy, graced, steep, bony, sweating, like Cody, saying "Yes!," wondering if, looking under the pale, prodding, poking, doting, pruning, Old Spontaneous Me, spitting prune juice, squeezing oil out of olives, a haunter of basketshops by the rigging, my Man Friday, old Herbivorous Whitman the Saint of Long Island, the Ghoul of Shores, the Former of Granite Rhymes, the Maker of Sweet Music, the Master of Hammer, Han, the Kind King Ming, the Doodling Wing, Eagle, Claw, Beak, Power, Mountain Top, Star, Lay, Rainer of Rivers, Mooder of Mowders, Sea Splash, Spray, Air, Wild Goose, Pine, Soarer, Thinker, Pacer, History Maker, Haunter of Cemeteries, in the streets at night solitary beneath a lamp, or the moon, on the corner, digging, a cat).

——while Melville made murky matter of the Battery, the Day Break Boys (busters of the river, raft bandits, hansom hustlers, still axing from the hills)——Handsome Herman, the Abyssinian King of Whorly Prints, the Assyrian busy beard, the Weaver of the Net, the Albatross, the Dung of the Albatross, the Calmer of Waves, Singer of Spars, Sitter of Stars, Maker of Sparks, Thinker of Helms, Rails, Bottles, Tubs, Creaks and Cringes of the Shroudy Gear; Seaman, Rower, Oarsman, Whaler, Whaler, Whaler . . . observer of rock formations in the Berkshires, dreamer of Pierres. . . . O old Thoreau, hermit of the Woods, Spirit of the Morning Mist in Reedy Fields, Stalker of Serpentine Moonlights, of Snowy Midnights, of Forests in Winter, of Copses in May Morn, of October Rusted Grapes, of the Bushel Basket of Apples, of the Green Ones, the Fallen Green Apples Turning Brown in the Wet Grass in the Morning; the dam, Beaver Brook, the Sudden Mill Dye, the pure Snow Creek in the Upper Land, the Dell of Flowers, the Warm Scent of Flowery Fields in August, Homer and the Woodchips, Koran and the Axe, the Hot Pinch of Grasshoppers, Hay, Hot Rock, the Whiff of the Country World, the Sand Road, the Wall of Stone, the Snow, the Star Shining on the Glaze of the Snow in March, the Barndoor Slamming Across the Snowy Woods and Fields, the Moon on the Pine Cone Glaze, the Cobweb in the

Summer, the Waters Lapping, the Night, the Wind at Night
and Lips Clinging in the Fields at Night, the Hump of the
Meadow at Night, the Milky Hump of Lovers in the Grass, Me
and She, Humping in the Grass, Under the Apple Tree, under
Clouds Racing Over the Moon, in the Broad World, the Moist
Star of Her Cunt, the Universe Melting Down the Sides of the
Sky, the Warm Feel of It, the Moist Star Between her Thighs,
the Warm Pull in There, the Action on the Grass, the Rubadub
of Legs, the Hot Clothes, the Thirsting Mosquitos, the Tears,
the Shuddering, the Bites, the Tonguings, and Twistings, the
Moaning, the Moving, the Rocking, the Beating, the Coming,
the Second Coming, the Third Coming——

The old void's still got it in him.

IN 1949 THAT'S WHAT WE DID, his wife threw him out just as
I got there and only because it was a climactic moment, and
we bowled back to the East Coast in a trip that was so frantic
and so crazy that it has a beginning and an end, began in the
heat of wildest excitement, great jazz, fast driving, women, acci-
dents, arrests, all night movies, and ended all petered out in the
dark of Long Island, where we walked a few blocks around my
house just because we were so used to moving, having moved
three thousand miles so fast and talking all the time. It began
in Frisco——with that look, that came from those sources and
from his old jalopy and the life with his father who must have
smiled at him like that in the darkest moments of beat luck——
we started off the voyage by dedicating two nights of jazz to it.

At that time Frisco jazz was at its rawest peak, for some reason the age of the wild tenorman was piercing up through
the regular-course developments of bop, as if a few years too
late and a few years too early, and of course really too early,
only now it's the fad; then, before it was a fad the wild tenormen blew with an honest frenzy because nobody appreciated
or cared (except isolated hipsters running in screaming) ("Go!
Go! Go!") . . . friends and hepcats and they didn't care anyway
and the "public," the customers in the bar, liked it as jazz; but
it wasn't jazz they were blowing, it was the frantic "It."

"What's the IT, Cody?" I asked him that night.

"We'll all know when he hits it——there it is! he's got it!——
hear?——see everybody rock? It's the big moment of rapport

all around that's making him rock; that's jazz; dig him, dig
her, dig this place, dig these cats, this is all that's left, where
else can you and go Jack?" It was absolutely true. We stood
side by side sweating and jumpin in front of wild be-hatted
tenormen blowing from their shoetops at the brown ceiling,
shipyard workers; altos too, singers; drummers like Cozy Cole
mixed with Max Roach, a kid cornet of sixteen (little Negro
grandmother's favorite), a cool bop hepcat who stood slumped
with his horn and no lapels and blew like Wardell; but best of
all the workingman tenors, the cats who worked and got their
horns out of hock and blew and had their women troubles, they
seemed to come on in their horns with a will, saying things, a
lot to say, talkative horns, you could almost hear the words and
better than that the harmony, made you hear the way to fill up
blank spaces of time with the tune and consequence of your
hands and breath and soul; and wild women dancing, the ceiling roaring, people falling in from the street, from the door, no
cops to bother anybody because it was summer, August 1949,
and Frisco was blowing mad, the dew was on the muscat in the
interior fields of Joaquin, the money was flowing for Frisco is
a seasonal town, the railroads were rolling, there were crates of
melons on sidewalks, chipped ice, and the cool interior smells
of grape tanks; the Little Harlem, Third and Folsom, it rocked,
in back in a funny alley that seems to be connected to the bar
but not to the street, ten, twenty teahead men and women
blasting and drinking wine spodiodi, whiskey-beer-and-wine;
and we had some too, and wham, got drunk, as well as hi; saw
a little colored alto in a high stiff collar and a square suit and
looked just like a square Alabama nigger standing by the side
of the road twirling his keychain in the Wilderness in front of
the shack where his father sits, on the porch, leg up on a chair,
leg ruined by fieldwork, poverty, decades of malnutrition, old
age, ordinary mortal old age, standing there the kid is (with
a new gray fedora) on a Sunday afternoon and watching the
cars go by, go by, go by, to cities and news of wild things, old
Kaycee the alto town, old Frisco the tenor town, old Detroit
the baritone town, old New York the jumpingnest town, the
Dizzybird Town, old Chicago the open town, old San Pedro
the seaman's town, the pierhead jumpin town, the bottom of
the land town, the jumpin off town; he looked just like that,

and more innocent, and blew his head off that night; a fellow
coming in from work came running into the room where the
jazz was yelling "Blowblowblow!" and we'd heard him yelling
that all the way up the stairs (Jackson Hole, after hours) and
probably he'd been yelling that all the way from Market Street
but that little alto, his eyes fixed on Cody, his feet flopping and
dancing in a monkey hop that was exactly like Irwin Garden's
monkey hop that he used to pull in the streets of Denver, Texas,
New York as he followed the trail of Cody and gave it up, that
little alto blew one chorus after another, each one simple, blew
two hundred of them, just a blues number, he'd say "Ta-potato-
rup, ta-potato-rup," then "ta-potatola-*dee*-rup," "ta-potatola-
dee-rup," like that, repeating twice for emphasis each time, with
the simplicity of a kid learning to write in grammar school with
the eraser in his mouth or a young Lincoln at the shovel, smiling into his own horn, completely cool in the shower of frenzies
that poured from his lungs and fingers, saying to Cody "Ta ra
ta ta, the Angel Gabriel is really black" just as from the top of
St. John the Divine Cathedral in New York blows the Angel
Gabriel on his horn over the rooftops of Harlem . . . Dizzy
Gillespie in stone.

"He's the kind who sleeps all day in his grandmother's,"
yelled Cody above the fury, "he learned to play in the woodshed, dig him? see his kind? he's Tom Watson that's who he
is, Tom Watson learned to blow and go continually and cast
off the negatives and completely relaxed, though not hung,
in, or behind, bumkicks of any kind, realizing, also, as, for instance, there's what I'm saying, but, no wait, Jack and listen to
me, now I'm gonna lay down on you the truth——but listen to
him, listen to *him*. *It*, remember? *It*! *It*! He's got *it*, see? That's
what *it*——means, or I mean to explain, earlier, see, and all that
and everything, Yes!" as little alto rose with the band that sat
behind him——three pieces, piano, drums, bass——working
the hound dog to death, rattle-ty-boom, crash, the drummer
was all power and muscles, his huge muscular neck held and
rocked, his foot boomed in the bass, old intervals, blump, be
whom, blump, boom; the piano rapping his outspread fingers
in chordal offbeat drive clank, beautiful colors emanating from
the tone of his crashing-guitar chords; blues; and the bass like
a machine slapping in through the chugedychug of time with

its big African world beat that comes from sitting before fires
in the crickety night with nothing to do but beat out the time
by the great wall of vines, a tuck a tee, a tuck a teek a tuck a
teek, and make your moan, go moan for man, the disaster of
the world, evil souls and innocent mountain stones . . . and the
sudden occasional harsh yells as everybody all the drummers
and mooners and cricketers with the tingpin wires (this thing
has a proper name in the Belgian Congo, home of the "conga"
drum, the heartbeat drum, the heart of the world, Adam and
Eve, Eden's in Abyssinia), all realize they've got *it*, *IT*, they're
in time and alive together and everything's alright, don't worry
about nothing, *I love you*, whooee——

THE GREAT SPINDLY TIN-LIKE CRANE TOWERS of the transterritorial electric power wires standing in serried gloom with
pendant droop of head shapes (the upper insulation Tootsie
Rolls strapped securely in space by the pull and tort of the
wires——and not really Tootsie Rolls but pagodas of Japan hung
in a gray mist of South San Francisco to save from shock the
void, the empty California gray white air with its roll of fog-
clouds marching to the beat of Bethlehem Steel mill hammers).
Faroff the misty neons of subsidiary, little used diners for the
airport, with fried clams, ice cream, waffles; either that or it's an
empty factory shining in the night an advertisement of itself in
the nowhere of industrial formations; a rusty weedy marsh here,
not a real marsh, a slag of drain waters from rusty foundry cans
and pisspots, but muddy like a swamp, inhabited by frogs and
crickets that madly sing at dark fall, croak.

Trucks growling up the 101 overpass surmount the South
City yards where Cody worked, lines of shining headlamps
coming up the faroff ditch marshes and headed for the city;
the sense of rain and steam everywhere in the fragrant distance
of oil, mist, steam of engines and pure Pacific brine with that
special California white raw air.

All hail the Giant Rat beneath the Stockyard platforms!——
hail the poor whiteface cows drowsing in their evening stockyard fattening meadow with its call of faroff trains and almost
Iowa-like valley green softness, that will be hamburg tomorrow
when the wheels of industry have churned them through to
reality and death.

nippets for pisspots
The Pisspots of Thought

I

The dangling rain filmed
a sperm across the night:
the Night is not the Future.

II

And you always get the best
    prices in the West!
Tough to beat! You can't compare it!

III

Disposes melodiously
their boding gory
doles, makes holes
Of their radon dungs;
Means nothing,
But a Lark was poorfool.

And what was that place the fellows took Milly (Crawford)
the maid riding that rainy afternoon of Lawrence road cemeteries, that I later saw in the night, from car or train, strange
darkness, factory, or stockyards, or whatever, in the 1920's
nighttime?

THE GREAT VOYAGE WAS READY to begin. I was standing on the
corner of Folsom and Fourth but nearer to the alley with old
Ed Laurier the altoman, and we were high; we were waiting for
Cody who had just gone in the bar to make a phonecall getting
Earl Johnson down to drive us around, just like Cody used to
call Earl and other members of the poolhall gang at any hour of
day or night in Denver arranging orgies in record time, in the
activity of which he just automatically ran into Joanna (golden
highschool sodafountain) his number one wife and that's how
it all began, only now Earl Johnson himself was married to a
fresh slender little blond, a doll, from Wyoming, Helen Johnson, and living in Frisco, and could only come at great expense
to his marital bliss. "Trouble with Helen," Cody said out the
corner of his mouth, rasping like those Texas Okie farmboys
but now big old farmbulls with tufty beards and booze on the

floor of the car, having just snuck from their chores to go brawl in drinking fields, loose disconnected necks hanging surly heads into the black of a boozy old Oklahoma Buick made crack and matter dust by forlorn interminable storms and drought clouds searing the harvest the souls of juicy men, hunglipped, booze shining on their *guêles*, their mugs, pugs, mouths, like gleaming starlight in the rainy night, "Which way is it to Houston?" the driver's asking me, having just forced me to the side of the road in the rainblind to ask this counsel, this direction, and Cody and Joanna asleep in the backseat; just at the last minute I swung the Hudson over as the head-on lights showed they weren't simply on the wrong side of the road but head-on; "Which way to Houston?"; the tremendous rainy darkness splattering all Texas around, the dim view of just edges of muddy plowed fields, gulches, sand bars, bushes, whistling thin trees hidden in a solidwall right over, the wilderness enow of all tragic present rain, drenching; swung the car, luckily onto sand level, got out, woke Cody, Joanna handled wheel, we pushed our backs to bumper with hair in our eye, and mud in our teeth; took all morning to dry and drove on. Just like that, Cody rasped it, "her *nose* is too long."

Well, not all, Helen Johnson by God has a real cute little nose and face, God bless her fine looking little ass. Having, (back now to phonecall) finished——Cody came running out to rejoin us, his buddy and his jazz connection (all-American white guys, almost all of them, have grown up with some special Negro friend or acquaintance they boast about continually, it's a point of contented honor). But Cody came, flew out the door, into the night, the soft and crazy California night, hear me, but not running, rather, gliding, on the balls of his feet and with his body bent forward like Groucho so that his T-shirt flies not the ordinary backflap coattails, with the Stooges in suit right in back of him (just imagine that, just think of Moe bent and gliding like that); but Moe and nobody and no Groucho bless his great Jewish heart for which I offer 17,000,000,000 dollars to the lowest bidder, neither could have the great seriousness and anxiety, time-anxiety, of Cody as he flew, like a Dostoevskian fevered rickety midget hero dashing at his psychological skull to blam it on the wall of Russia and his Friends, here comes Cody, the wind is roaring back from his nose as it cuts through the air.

"Godalmighty" says Ed Laurier "That's cat's crazy; buddy, that cat's *crazy*"——and looking away to *hmp* it in, stomping, rolling his bones with one shuddering yes-indeed of his whole frame the way Jelly Roll used to stomp and roll in poolhalls of Southern Alabama, a halfdollar shining in his hand, the point of contentious laughter, yet, the point of his emphatic steps down on the ground to give a zing, a lift to his whole meaning when he said that and he really *said* that, and it, anyway——"Yes, your buddy is a crazy motherf——looka him rolling out of that bar and all dem goddamn guys in there turnin to look twice to believe their own eyes what it was swished by just a second ago, Lord have a mercy on me, whoo! he's all got this, his pore thumb there that he says he broke off his wife's haid, damn, all bandaged and sticking in the air like a mule's pecker. Hey Cody!——what you——hey——hyah-hyah!" (slapping Cody's back, and Cody looks at him with a silly goofy wondering "Yes? Yes? What is it? You were saying? Oh? Yes——the shoe, no——yes——I mean, the——whiches——Yes!" and looking down the street for a cop, hitching his belt absentmindedly, glancing furtively at some point beyond me, ahemming, pulling down his nose, smiling, "Yes! I know, I see, my thumb! stuck up like a balloon, yes! I hear you! ee-ee-ee-ee!" a tremendous idiot giggle in the streets of man). He rushed into the car the moment it arrived. Why, at one point coming out of that bar he looked like a maniac actually just broke away from his keepers who took a gamble to take a drink in a bar while taking him, eager and glad, to a padded cell in the hills beyond the road. What he done, run out to see what street, for Johnson on phone, for directions, looked all which way for sign, whirling in his steps, under the lamp, bandaged thumb upheld like a white goose into the night——till bandage turned Gray in Salt Lake City.

These were the moments preceding what I guess was the greatest day in Cody's life. It was some day or other in August, 1949; I'd say the 25th, or the anniversarial 22nd, this was a night or two before. He was mad and feverish enough that night; it was later after the jazz, after the altos and the singers and the sad kid in the beautiful filthy suede jacket with street-eyes in the brown world mooning "Close Your Eyes" and kicking into the mike like a great jazz musician which he was then, he was singing nothing but "Close Your Eyes," he was in that woodshed

wildbar learning, the only place where jazz can be learned, as
Cody now knows, till later Freddy Strange that was his name, he
blasted in the car with us, he called his diminutive boy to blow
us clear across Frisco in a fishtail Cadillac and "nobody even
noticed he passed all red lights he was so good," or something
like that; later Freddy Strange sang with Dizzy Gillespie on the
apple; after this music, we hooked elsewhere, with Ed; there
were dawns, scatterings.

I played solitaire with Slim Buckle's poor wife Helen, who at
that time, after all her travails rounding him up in New Orleans,
was waiting out another one of his grave madness voyages, this
time to Maine, in the company of Tom Watson who'd now
grown a hipster beard in his march among millions towards
modernity. "Why they didn't do anything but sit in the bathtub," said Helen——actually, apparently, they went in there to
blast; or whenever Slim took a bath Watson had the temerity
to sit there and chat with him, that being a proper social arrangement in the Near East and among bathing beauties from
pole to pole; but of course, her Greek——her hair streaming
on the rug, Helen lost out on sitting in the bathroom herself
with her Slim, and sh'ad every right to be mad. Also, she hated
Cody anyhow, too. She'd castigate him, just before we left,
before crowds of Dostoevskian heroes in the room; just the
Johnsons, some children, a neighbor girlmother I got thrill-
ingly close to (I remember), all in the parlor of Helen's Mission
district pad. "Cody how can——Cody you stand there like a
damn fool, you're the first idiot they ever made. You're the louse
they invented. Always fighting with your wife, asking pity when
she throws you out, conning everybody, interested in your old
dangling between legs and that's all, abandoning little cozy children, running off with Jack. When are you going to straighten
out and realize that you have to face the responsibilities of your
life and your wife and home. This isn't Communist Russia, this
is America. What do you think this is, a harem? You want all
the women of the United States to become whores? You'd like
that, be pimp; number one; asshole——" for all I know she
added tidbits and fillips better in simpering reviews before the
mirror. . . . Sullen eyes were arranged on Cody's face as he stood
there in holy San Francisco, thumb up, sweating, a forehead
throbbing, with red fire light, eyes blank, blue, grayblue, with a

glint in the middle all mystery to me and anybody, listening to every one of her words as if hearing the music of her soul and all our souls and saying Yes! to every bit of it, one chorus, one solo after another, soft, sweet, harsh or high, the SAINT, THE GOOF . . . Cody had become, here among the remnant buddies of his Denver American raw youth in basements, junkheaps and lawns the great Idiot of us all . . . entirely irresponsible to the point of wild example and purgation for us to learn and not have to go through, like the pale criminal genius who kills our old suburban queen to show us it can be done and doesn't have to be done, and Jesus crucified. "Ah poor Cody," I thought, and spoke up; breaking my Frisco neutrality (there had been pictures taken of all of us, our shadows fell across grassplots; our children would revisit these photos in their brown old age and guess we were in our prime and clarifying adulthood then, our clear-bell decisive years, what a laugh if it's really true). "Now wait a minute Helen. . . ." But she had me over a barrel in the matter of English literature, she spoke out like a sadsack heroine, frosome, "You'll find out for yourself too late what a no good person Cody can really be and is; how can you make him worse than he is, you of all people."

"Evelyn threw him out, I didn't——I mean, it's none of my doing, but you can't blame Cody for everything, think of your own shoddy cons," I should have yelled out the window or at them or up in the air. By this time Cody was downstairs standing like a ghost in the tenement doorway waiting for us to make up our minds about TIME, rubbing his belly, sweating, fingering his balls, blowing Phew!, ready to go across the gleaming and groaning continent of America where his fathers had all got lost.

We started rolling at two o'clock in the afternoon, or something, noon; a Travel Bureau car to Denver, a Plymouth driven by a pansy, and a dull couple. A real pansy, one with the strange criminal face of complete nonentity among ordinary human identification-signs, you just couldn't tell what he was, sadist or masochist and from which end and with whip, dress, or oyster pie, a fetishist hiding in a closet, he must have spent whole afternoons simpering in the bathroom. Arriving in Sacramento at nightfall, these dull people decided to sleep, the trip half started. All the way to Sacramento Cody and I had terrified them by talking as we did in the backseat, wild and crazy, just like we were both seeing red; in fact I was. The excitement between us was so immense and extraordinary, and we had so little recognition of the fact that these people were there or even in a car, that at one point we were rocking the car back and forth. "Hey you're rocking the boat," complained the husband from upfront where a conversation was going between the three of them, probably about us who were completely deaf to anything but ourselves. We were talking about the Great Scythes of our childhood, when I, riding in New England littleroads with boulders and posts and hills of vine all along, would, imaginary, cut it all down with my scythe as my father swept the car by; and he, Cody, in the tragic red roads of Sunday afternoon in Eastern Colorado, when blackhatted men grimly drive the children, swept alongside the car either on foot or wielding from inside the car a gigantically and intricately built Scythe that not only snipped the close posts and sage or wheat but extended itself in a monstrous dream to horizon with all the massiveness of unbelievable realities like the Oakland Bay Bridge or the skeletal Swiftian frame of the Pentagon in Arlington, Virginia when they were raising the octagonal facewalls into place by longnecked celestial giraffe cranes, slow as the Bird of Paradisical Eternity raising the Great World Snake in its beak to the lost up, a scythe also so fantastic in its hinges that it could sweep over the flat plain, adjust itself to cut tablelands, rise a notch in the beyond and extend to horizons to cut mountain ranges entire while still managing in the little forefront blade to cut that bunchgrass into clouds of flying——We talked about this. "But not only that but I had——"

"But wait, *me*, I had——" Also "getting it" in jazz, finding the mystic or the music, yhr mydyiv gtrnxy og yhr eiyvhfovyot, "the mystic frenzy of the witchdoctor" sweating tenor holding everybody enrapt in a blow-blow-blow whaling jam session, or sweet vowels of an eloquent talking alto poem à la Charles Yardbird Parker the Only. "It hurts like hell to find you can blow your heart out and die, go hear him blow before he dies, they say."

"Who?"

"That Johnny that blew in the Blue Geek." The Scythes made me sweat, I was damp. Cody kept yelling "Yes!" as I blew my own great chorus on the subject clutching anxiously at his T-shirt as if that tattered rag could hold him to hear words. He rocked back and forth with his yesses. "I hear every one of your words!" I talked faster and faster, he had me hypnotized like a mad dream; I kept recalling my life. It was so far; I rolled my eyes at the roof to draw breath, just like that kickin tenor in Little Harlem had hauled off to blow with a wild thinking look at ceiling cracks, boom, the IT (is right there, to give it to you, it lurks in the frizzly dust of ceilings as well as in that rose-perfected air of Cody's)——

Just like in the garden, Cody's Gethsemane over there, by the cable car mountain, I hung on his every return word as if I was going to die right on it and it's the last I'm to hear: frenzy. Meanwhile the grave automobile, and the sensible pervert, carried us over the green hills of Vallejo to old Sacramento. That night the gangbelly broke loose between Cody and the skinny skeleton, sick: Cody thrashed him on rugs in the dark, monstrous huge fuck, Olympian perversities, slambanging big sodomies that made me sick, subsided with him for money; the money never came. He'd treated the boy like a girl! "You can't trust these people when you give them (exactly) what they want." I sat in the castrated toilet listening and peeking, at one point it appeared Cody had thrown him over legs in the air like a dead hen: it swallowed me back, gad I was horrified, it was murder, I have my good reasons now for not succumbing to any of these Arabian pleasures especially with a blackamoor—what, he was really an Irishman called O'Sello?——"It's not in my line," said Céline in Africa.

But enough, it wasn't characteristic of Cody as he is now in his workingman's life and marriage.

Tragic coffee drunk at dawn, all five of us re-met now: then on over Donner Pass, Cody driving, smoothly stern, paying no attention, swinging the Pass like he done Tehachapi and Sierra Madre Oriental grades, rhythmical, according to the flow of engineers who built it, playing the bankings and swoop-dedoop curves—in a piney bright morn—slam across Nevady, fast, unwounding, unrolling a state in an afternoon . . . Reno, Battle Mountain, Elko, Great Salt Flats by dark.

Just like girlie magazines, we represented to these goonish normals in the front seat the vicious novelties of America. We

were dirty faced and pimply like moronic dirt-kneed teenage
mountain girls hauled by the law for turning tricks in the backalleys of mountain communities. They hated our guts; we cut
them down the middle.

"WHY, H-WHAT? WHY? what have I done? why this hostility
against me? Did you say Irish Barbers in the West?"

"Irish Barbers In the West."

"This old Pomeray was, I swear and upon me proved."

"Your testimony is insufficient."

"And the fate of my benjamin brother benedicts in crime?"

"You have dealt unfairly with the meaning of the law; you
have transcribed the letter too; you are sentenced to ten years'
hard labor in prison. Have you anything to say?"

"Thank you, your honor."

"Ironic tones won't get you far. My father had the same
sass——the court is proved, the case is closed. All judges, attendants of judges, coatwipers, and pissorial funeral urnmakers
in raggedy goon cloth tuxes please step forth and cast a parting
glance at the prisoner in the dock, the cock on the clock, say
Cuckoo prettyboy."

"Cuckoo."

"Now all you have to do is write an apologetic letter not only
to the King of England but your old gym instructors, they've
sweated all these years worrying about your body and your soul,
they murk in steambaths drooling with tears of sweat."

"If the court, please, I have something to say in defense of
myself: I, Jack Duluoz, have not been the same since my brother
Gerard died, when I was four. I sincerely plead——

CODY POMERAY. (*stepping up in his furlined weather-
proof work jacket with dungarees, key snap ring, switch key, wallet bulge, GI workshoes, carrying a rainwork suit on the way to
work, but clean in his pockets*) Sirs, the defendant is an impostor
French-Canadian from New England; in any case he deserves
punishment——(in fact Julien, Irwin and I have often wondered
what he would do, how he'd squeal with pain, if the court could
torture him in a cold tank, nekkid)

JACK. I can't allow——succumb——it's too much——anybody
squeals——

JUDGE CODY. (*sitting in the rostrum with his pince nez camp*

set out, performing it) A hanging is already in progress at Black-
moor, I hear——so if you'n Judge Bean come closer——I likes a
good hangin——me and old Bull lotsa times——(*to Jack*) Things
happen, man; thing happen; you've got to expect it sometime,
the bad news, the worst. No use kiddin yourself
JACK. What am I losing?
CODY. None of us know
JACK. So goes
CODY. Be careful, Jack be careful——Hang him, men
(*On the gallows,*) **JACK.** I wanted to tell about——but the calluses, the——(*hanged*)

SOMETHING INTERESTING there is in Cody's ability to make
me, or his wife, sad, and even friends I watched: is he showing
the sadism of the big powerful face he had bucking through
the Montana storms of earth, when I, with him, was faced by
the wild dismalities of a universe so severe the only thing is to
grimly bear and buck it. Tenderness has no room; tenderness
has no sadness. Cody is sad. He makes us sad. There is nothing
inexpressibly sadder than that old photo of his father's 1928
house-built-on-a-truck he rattled from West Virginia to West
Dakota in, for no reason whatever; baby Cody is in the picture,
pudgy, swaddled in a wicker swing, beaming on the world, a
sun shining in the pale of the daguerrotype brown, the roof of
the housetruck protruding into the tragic trees like a disappearing wigwam in old miningtown Indian prints, lost, sad, endless——Eternity standing with her hands behind her back. . . .
In this Clark Gable mustachio old Civil War photo Cody would
sit there, bushed and be-derbied, askew, whiskered, flatulent,
mighty hands a-rest, with his high cheekbones mystifying back
his eyes and deeply glinting with Indian mysteries and the past:
this is the enigmatic Cody, the sad one, the one who said hello
to tragedy in a womb, and heads now for his raving grave and
greedy sleep.
    "Mistress of the night," he addressed it, "make me sleep"
(bouncing from home Iowa to L.A. in 1926 in that dewy jalopy
of the night). And the rocky road rushed on outside. "Mater,
matter, flyswatter. . . ."
    Realizing to stop, his father let him be dunged on the lip of
the earth in that Salt Lake ward . . . a golden boy baby, a sad

protuberant spoon from his side lips, gold of Ebon. But 'twas a county sheriff slapped that plank on his father's heels in the flat-car outside Grand Island Nebrasky. A clay spoon, a clay spear. That poor picture. . . .

Well, Cody is always interested in himself: from behind his iron bars he's always talking and conning somebody all day. Like the lyrics of popular songs you can't believe a word of it. I hear him from far away; his voice urgent, anxious, high-pitched, explanatory, full of rapine; he's on the bed convincing her, who's turned her head away in disgust, for now, that she need worry about nothing, he didn't drown the kittens at all, they fell down the drain by themselves, or it wasn't because he wanted to see Jimmy he was late but because (she having made no issue about lateness) in passing the bakery it reminded him she had mentioned that very morning she was sick and tired of store bread and so he went right to the store and bought some, twenty-two cents . . . something like that. For years I've listened to him con women; supreme; first Joanna the lost lovely blond of his early and first passions under those bleak electric neons by hotel windows in the wind-whip of Wyoming born, first her; then Evelyn; finally that horrible Diane who has everybody frightened with her lawsuits and quiddities. That first con in Harlem, make the breakfast, was followed by . . . Damn Cody, I'm tired of him and I'm going; my benefactor whispers his wife to me in the dark.

His sad face permeates the mere mention of Sioux City; if he says it himself, and wasn't ever there, I know it's an American city. A true, real American is a mystery to us, to U.S., some-where and somehow he became like Cody and stands here among us. In my romance I have traveled far to find a cousin to the Greek. And in my romance I have traveled far to see an American, one that reminded me of the Civil War soldier in the old photo who stands by a pile of lumber in a drizzle, waiting for arrest, backgrounded by pine brush bottoms all wet and dismal in an Alabama afternoon in the wilderness of hoar. Beside him is a superior officer, Rebel Colonel or Captain, Con-federate Wildcat, teeth bared, coat over arm, defiant to the very wind. "Ho! don't forget those two prisoners by the lumber," shouts the Yankee captain perceiving the prisoners but not the camera, and old Johnny Youngpants who looks like Cody just stands there beside his rosehog Confederacy wildboar and waits for tomorrows of capture with that implacable sad and slightly gaunted look of the Sioux Cities of the mind, the one I mean, his father had it, and has it in that photo, that teary, dreary look of old torment and of old mists, that hangjaw ancientness and goodhearted tragicness of the old entire; a piss-ass poor agrarian whore "Why do I stop in my grains?" couldn't look worse in a cornfield with her legs spread, or honester. (Splat, or as B. O. Plenty says, Ptoo.) But sadness, sadism, all, let's hear what my French-Canadian side has to say about him. Now we're conning nature.

"Si tu veux parlez àpropos d'Cody pourquoi tu'l fa——tu m'a arrêtez avant j'ai eu une chance de continuez, ben arrête donc. Écoute, j'va t'dire—— lit bien. Il faut t'u te prend soin——attend?——donne moi une chance——tu pense j'ai pas d'art moi français?—— ça?——idiot——crapule——tas'd marde——enfant shiene—— batard——cochon——buffon—— bouche de marde, granguele, face laite, shienculotte, morceau d'marde, susseu, gros fou, envi d'chien en culotte, ça c'est pire——en face!——fam toi!—— crashe!——varge!——frappe!—— mange!——foure!——foure moi'l Gabin!——envalle Céline, mange l'e rond ton Genet, Rabelais? El terra essuyer l'coup au derrière. Mais assez, c'est pas intéressant. C'est pas intéressant l'maudit Français. Écoute, Cody ye plein d'marde; les lé allez; il est ton ami, les le songée; yé pas ton frère, yé pas ton père, yé pas ton ti Saint Michel, yé un gas, yé mar- riez, il travaille, v'as t'couchez

"If you want to talk about Cody why do you do it—— you stopped me before I had a chance to continue, stop won't you! Listen, I'm going to tell you——read well: you have to take care of yourself, hear it?——give me a chance—— you think I've no art me French?——eh?——idiot—— crapule——piece of shit—— sonofabitch——bastard—— pig——clown——shitmouth—— long mouth——ugly face, shitpants, piece of shit, sucktongue, big fool, wanta- shitpants, that's worse——right in the face!——shut up!—— spit!——hit it! (varge!)——hit! (frappe)——eat it!——fuck!—— scram me Gavin!——swallow Céline, eat him raw your Genet, Rabelais? He woulda wiped your neck on his ass. But enough, it's not inter- esting. It's not interesting goddamn French. Listen, Cody is full of shit; let him go; he is your friend, let him dream; he's not your brother, he's not your father, he's not

l'autre bord du monde, v'a
pensant dans la grand nuit
Européene. Je t'l'explique, ma
manière, pas la tienne, enfant,
chien——écoutes:——va trouvez
ton âme, vas sentir le vent, vas
loin——La vie est d'hommage.
Ferme le livre, vas——n'écrit
plus sur l'mur, sa lune, au
chien, dans la mer au fond
neigant, un petit poème. Va
trouvez Dieu dans les nuits. Les
nuées aussi. Quantesse s'a peut
arrêtez s'grand tour au cerveux
de Cody; il y a des hommes, des
affaires en dehors à faire, des
grosses tombeaux d'activité dans
le désert d'l'Afrique du coeur,
les anges noires, les femmes
couchée avec leur beaux bras
ouvert pour toi dans leur
jeunesse, d'la tendresse enfer-
mez dans l'même lit, les gros
nuées de nouveaux continents,
le pied fatiguée dans de climes
mystères, descend pas le côté de
l'autre bord de ta vie (30) pour
rien.
À Cody, un corp.

your Saint Michael, he's a guy,
he's married, he works, go
sleeping on the other side of
the world, go thinking in the
great European night. I'm explaining him to you, my way,
not yours, child, dog——listen:
——go find your soul, go smell
the wind——go far——Life is a
pity. Close the book, go on——
write no more on the wall, on
the moon, at the dog's, in the
sea in the snowing bottom, a
little poem. Go find God in
the nights. The clouds too.
When can it stop this big
tour at the skull of Cody;
there are men, things outside
to do, great huge tombs of
activity in the desert of Africa
of the heart, the black angels,
the women in bed with the
beautiful arms open for you in
their youth, some tenderness
shrouded in the same bed, the
big clouds of new continents,
the foot tired in climes so
mysterious, don't go down
the hill of the other side of
your life (30) for nothing.
To Cody, a body.

SALT LAKE LIES AT THE RIM of a once-great sea-like lake in the heights of the American plateau; great mountains like those that shelter the little farming town of Farmington, Utah with their snowy rilled hump bumps from the wild of the wind comes blowing from upper Saskatchewans and territorial Montanas; it's amazing how the town is laid out neat and bright. First you see it, as we did then, across the dusk flats like shining jewelry on the water; that Salt Lake water always so mysterious at night because none of it laps on the shore, it's bedded in a basin way in, no frogs, no lush, all dry, desert, salt, flat, and over the curve of the God damned or God blessed earth where that God-cloud

showed itself to me, coming out, you can see the humpful disappearance of telegraph lines strung on marching poles to the
infinite curvature. "It's the thing you can't see holds the world
together," I told Cody, "the curve."

"Wow," said Cody, and I had just told him all about snakes
under hills and castles with haunted bats, Monks, parapets and
cribs upstairs, "never heard you talk so," he said; he was pale,
sweat, fever, wild, his bandage shuddered like a light in the dark
rushing air, he fell asleep on my arm thumb up——like a duty.
The bandage all gray, unwrapped, a thousand gravely miles back
Evelyn had probably fixed it snowy neat new. Poor, poor Cody,
I'm watching him sleep in the car, in front they say "Hang on
to the wheel, he'll wake, drive some more"; the husband: "Have
no fear dear," and the fag: "I've never seen anything so crazy,
you'd think this world was made up of a hundred percent cha-
rac-ters." They have Louvres for his brooch at the diving baths,
he with his asshole folds allinfinite . . . like an old lady in Cannes
at three o'clock in the afternoon in a jewelry store, "*Qu'elque
chose pour la plage.*"

We enter Salt Lake City; the sun is gone, darkness falls; Cody
wakes from his nap as they're driving the car to a hospital on
an eminence for sightseeing; Cody looks out the window, from
a shelf of a dream, at Salt Lake City laid out in necklaces of
geometrically patterned ahem light; he brushes back the bushy
film in his eyes, he fixes a con on the town of his birth, levels of
dreary time fly over the brows of the city hidden in the upward
night. "This is the city where I was born," he announced. Up
in the front seat they hear but are talking about the interesting
hospitals of Salt Lake City. On the teenage corner when the
tourists are eating, Cody and I stand gawping in the stare glares,
gawping in the city: earlier that afternoon, while the tourists
made another meal on our time, we whiled it away playing talk-
games over bad meatloaf and under green Tom Sawyer trees
of Lovelock——'twas Lovelock where I saw two little boys and
a Negro pickaninny cottonmouth boy, also little, of ten, sittin
on rails, whittlin, with a dog——damn, that was 1947, I believed
in the world, I slept on the lawns of gas stations on my way to
see Cody and Denver. The car rolls on. Between Salt Lake and
Denver lies the mystery of the soul of Cody. Here he was born,
there he was raised; the apex of the raw wild space between that

nameless place with an eagle on a shrouded mineshaft pole, in the northwest corner, in raw pines, the thing there first was about Colorado, Utah territory, the great grayday of the wild West, the grim reminder like Russia, the powerful rugged earth and souls of Colorado, that land; Strawberry Pass, the wink of a big reservoir in the moonlit night among red sages; "That fool doesn't know how to drive in the mountains," Cody complained; but at Green River's Vernal junction with a road, *the* road, they got tired and let Cody drive and slept all three in the backseat like chums (poor lost lambs in the Dillinger voids of crosscountry, three floppydolls, or a cosmos, three dreams of ghosts, three pandemic therpitoids, reducible in their gender to a sex, the man who mistrusts men, his wife trusts only women, voila! the man-woman for their needs; I have here——Fah!). We had the car to ourselves all night long; we made Kremmling in a keen dawn; en route he pointed out a reform school in the peaks near Climax, one in *which*; mines, too, Polybdenum; at Kremmling adobe walls in the spank of morning air on the rooftop of America and where cactus had dew on it till noon, we lolled like cowboydolls; I felt I was coming closer to Cody's mystery——Cody used to be a cowboy too; the mighty mountain wall Berthoud stood black and bleak in a Gibraltarean shroud in the clouds; a Gate. Uprushed that, we did; rolled on in, tongued a pass, dropped pines on our left (a mile) and scared clay on our right from protuberant roadcliffs, like the ones children draw in cartoons; the Rocky Mountains of Cody's birth consequence and youthful girl-parties in hot cars in the bye and bye. It was suddenly hot Denver again, flat pancake in the seafloor plain. His growing up town, the Chicago of his despairs, in this town he made neons twinkle on themselves like they belonged to Toledo, he rendered Denver, he was the wildhaired Cody Pomeray of his own city——hurrying along the wall there, with a strange key in his hand and a girl waiting for him in a car.

This was when Cody stole those cars and raised Cain with dust and idiots, that——

We got hungup in Denver and had to move on for various reasons, and in the unimaginable bedlam of events I came out (screaming over the telephone at men and women who were accusing me of breaking up homes and harboring criminals)

with a fifth of Old Granddad, pull out the tongue and set up
the rolltop special, just dust, no rocks. We drank at that thing
in a livingroom (just like his now-kitchen) full of children,
comic books, syrup and dogs with litters; pillows, confusion,
telephone; a friend's house; in a livingroom illuminated you
might say by the moon, it hung outside haunting our madness. We got so drunk——we were on our way to New York——
from Frisco——every way, any way——Cody disappeared——
came back——Wham, he was trying to throw pebbles in a girl's
window (that I'd known), she had nice goose pimples on her
knees), her mother rushed out with a shotgun over her arm,
called a highschool gang on the corner in an old car, threatened to call her husband who was at work, and there's her and
Cody wrangling in the moonlit dusty road about it: as sullen
a scene——Cody wouldn't quit; I had to take over as "elder"
advisor; Cody and I stomped back to the house over alfalfa
rows, whooping, ("I don't care," said Cody), just like old times.
Old Grand Dad. All this is out on the skirts of Denver, West
Alameda, the dark wild night there . . . dogs bark in an ink; the
tar melts on your evening Western star when you imagine you
can still see it hanging even at midnight between the Berthoud
Walls with an old cowpoke-ghost-rider-in-the-sky bluedark behind advertising night over deserts, damn that country. . . .
Out we go with a woman, Frankie Johnnie herself, somewhat
Okie-like, cussin and goodnatured, drove coal trucks in winter
for her kids, rode horseback in summer with buddy ladies one
of them a redhaired old circus queen with a snowy Pal-o-mine
sensation that struts as in a bed of sawdust down the hard-
cut roads licketysplit along the highway towards Golden and
them places——why——that kind of gal, with her kiddies but
one fourteen-year-old dotter that Cody and me had to watch
each other for, I did most of the worrying; with the mother we
go out, in a cab, called, to a roadhouse, stomping down beers.
Place is full of hammers and gashes of the crazy guitar Colorada
Columbine whoopee night of roadhouses and wronks, you'd
think sometimes they rushed out and tied somebody to a post
and whacked him with sticks for no reason, crazy Arkies on
the edge of the Plains, the knuckles of the Mountains, beet-
farmers. Also an idiot just got married that day——Why do I
say idiot?——he was a paralytic, the poor bastard, he only was

clutched to act like an idiot by enraged muscles; he was drunk
at the bar, moaning and lolling, young, about twenty, extraor-
dinarily handsome as young men go. He staggered to Cody on
scarecrow feet, knock-kneed, and they buddied up after awhile
of——CODY: ——Yes! and HIM: ——Thash wha I toll 'em, I haff
to get mawwied to-day-y-y? (squeal, laugh, yuck, the fluttering
finger, the anguished lookaway jerking the tortured saintly face
away into its own beauty and vacuity beyond the——) "Yes!"
Cody keeps yelling to this poor fool, he'll excite him unbearably, unmitigatably——His moans——Music is whang-whanging
and twanging all right——cobwebs on the screen, August night,
the Great Plains, High on the Hill of the Western Night, Coors
beer, Friday, Phillip Morrises, change, beerrings, damp floor
in the john head——Cody goes out, I see him pushing into
the darkness with an eager swing of his bare arms, he's got a
plan: earlier that night the last of his relatives gave him a dirty
deal——concerning his father——"We don't consider him a father
to anyone——before he stays in county jail or the nuthouse
wards for winos for good we want you *and* him to sign a paper"
(his long dead sad mother's people from Iowa), after which we
spent an hour walking in a carnival, Cody, for some reason,
wearing jeans for the first time since Joanna days (for me), in
the starry night strolling, among hobbledehoys and carrousels,
the pretty lips of Mexican girls too young, the boys in the tent
shrouds smoking over motorcycles, the sawdust, candy apples,
apple wombs, socket machines, giraffes, hurt ladies of the circus,
flap walls of Teeny Weeny shows, and the prize, the last stale
sandwich, the elephants are hauling off the wagon houses, a
dustcloud obscures the stars, a great knife comes sighing from
the dark to pierce the heart of Cody (twenty-five blocks from
my Welton & 23rd sorrows) who is hung on the pretty four-foot
Mexican midget beauty in the motel yard across the road from
the carny's last stake (littlekid place, rubbers place). "Damn,
Wow, Shoot!" Cody has his hand under his T-shirt, his other
on himself, rubbing, he looks awful; he did this on Main Street,
Rocky Mount North Carolina and Testament, Virginia, it's terrible, what must people think of him. So now we're drunk——
He takes a ride in some poor drinker's car, he comes back with
the car, wham, he steals another in the driveway, goes off, right
under the noses of cops and discussing-groups whose attention

was called earlier——He's going mad, he wants the idiot to go
riding with him——"Come on, come on!" he pleads but idiot
says no, suddenly fears him and backs away; I'm saying "No
stolen cars for me," *she* is too; Cody goes off disappointed,
sweaty, redfaced, mean, steals another car, drives around the
downtown streets of his old boyhood——there it all is, Larimer Street with its bright huge glitter and swarming bums, the
barbershop (Gaga's), B-movie, the buffet bars; the pawnshops;
and the rails, and Champa, Arapahoe; Curtis Street all red and
boppy now like South Main in L.A., things have changed,
grown more hep, and somehow grown more cold; he drives by
the poolhall, Tom might be in there right now; what has been
the meaning of his life? Who can say? And he drives around, and
returns to the bar——he rushes off after us in the cab, overtakes
the cab, scares, wait.

BREATHING MY SOUL (in a baggage car.) The night workers
know the night. I have sick stomach. I am not their equal.
This is California. America's last hope. Bring on the Mexican
heroes. One for all, all for one. I am the blood brother of a
Negro Hero. Saved! And so all the fellows are workers. In the
night they jabber of pay. Nothing's doing, I've worked with
the wretches; it takes an intelligent American boy to be high
nowadays: that's because the workers have become so intelligent. (The tractor driver Tony the Mex, I know him well, I'll
ask him his real full name, I'm a reporter for United Press. But
he loves me; I don't have to be U.P.)

Working in the beautiful night with aged cyclists and young
railroad Tom Sawyers with their shroudhats on their backheads,
drinking brews across the street at lunch hour, one, two, three
blocks from the Little Harlem of old madnesses and imaginary
useless reveries. The hide of an elephant, a cock and a goat's eye.
Dark Laughter has come again!

I've pressed up girls in Asheville saloons, danced with them
in roadhouses where mad heroes stomp one another to death
in tragic driveways by the moon: I've laid whores on the strip
of grass runs along a cornfield outside Durham, North Carolina, and applied bay rum in the highway lights; I've thrown
empty whiskeybottles clear over the trees in Maryland copses
on soft nights when Roosevelt was President; I've knocked

down fifths in trans-state trucks as the Wyo. road unreeled; I've jammed home shots of whiskey on Sixth Avenue, in Frisco, in the Londons of the prime, in Florida, in L.A. I've made soup my chaser in forty-seven states; I've passed off the back of cabooses, Mexican buses and bows of ships in midwinter tempests (piss to you); I've laid women on coalpiles, in the snow, on fences, in beds and up against suburban garage walls from Massachusetts to the tip of San Joaquin. Cody me no Codys about America, I've drunk with his brother in a thousand bars, I've had hangovers with old sewing machine whores that were twice his mother twelve years ago when his heart was dewy. I learned how to smoke cigars in madhouses; and hopped boxcars in NOrleans; I've driven on Sunday afternoon across the lemon fields with Indians and their sisters; and I sat at the inauguration of. Tennessee me no Tennessees, Memphis; aim me no Montanas, Three Forks; I'll still sock me a North Atlantic Territory in the free. That's how I feel. I've heard guitars tinkling sadly across hillbilly hollows in the mist of the Great Smokies of night long ago:

> Man of the broad mysterious
> Smoky
> Mountain
> night.

——when Pa Gant returned from California. I've stood outside musical doorways in a thousand misty heroisms across the sad big land.

I'm writing this book because we're all going to die——In the loneliness of my life, my father dead, my brother dead, my mother faraway, my sister and my wife far away, nothing here but my own tragic hands that once were guarded by a world, a sweet attention, that now are left to guide and disappear their own way into the common dark of all our death, sleeping in me raw bed, alone and stupid: with just this one pride and consolation: my heart broke in the general despair and opened up inwards to the Lord, I made a supplication in this dream.

110, HE PASSED US IN THE CAB, tooting, got the——he——he sat alone bullnecked in that littlen stolen coupe and shot on ahead of us into the night of the mountains straight ahead. "Damn, who's that?" cabbie said; "Just a friend of mine," I say; awe in his——how cold my knee is——(I'm naked, in dawn, it's time to go to bed)——And I saw him going off into his destiny at last, there was the sad flick of red exhaust across his red pipe, he flew for the raw night on three wheels——he was going to lead the posse a merry chase, the actual police in patrol cars, up and down the mountains of the midnight mist. Somewhere out in those hills they have a herd of buffalo drowsing in a kept kennel——Cody was going to drive right by them. But buffaloes aren't interesting in themselves. Absolutely crazy man——even today he eats with rage, he raves at the table spurting jam up on the ceiling, you've never seen a madder toastmaker (in the oven, fullblast), he jerks like a puppet above his bacon and eggs with a wild and stupid anxiety.

CODY. (*thinking*) Yes, I stole that coupe, passed them honkin in the cab, turned in at her road and left——came out in my shorts at near dawn to stash it, Jack's anxious——I drive it whomp te whomp over those alfalfa rows, discover it's a cop's car, time to move on from Denver. We get that Travel Bureau ride . . . driving 1947 Cadillac limousine

JACK. (*thinking*) Cody's runoff with the Cadillac the moment the owner relinquishes it to our care . . . "just get it to Chicago, pay your own gas," wow, Cody picks up Beverly the waitress he conned earlier in the morning when I took a nap on the church lawn of middlewestern Lutheran music and birdy trees all exhausted from that lastnight's car stealing and idiots and Old Granddad and yelling over the phone——Life is so harsh. Cody parks the Cadillac in an empty lot, talks her into it, screws her between the legs, casts off handkerchief, starts car, drives back, drops her off with promise to marry him in the East (she'll follow, just like Joanna), and he's back, picks up passengers, two Bonaventura Jesuit Irishmen on a lark in the summer, eastward we fly . . . all's behind us, Frisco, fag, Salt Lake, and that poor episode we had when I thought he was insulting my age warning me about my kidneys and right there in men's room I yelled angry words at him, buttoning my fly, ("Don't stop and aim at other urinals, for your beat park days as old man it will be bad for your kidneys, there's nothing worse"), just like when Pa and me took a leak in the Chinese restaurant john and he was always an angry, a *hating* man ("Toutes les Duluoz son malade," all the Duluozes are sick), and Cody couldn't figure why I was sore and burned to cry or bust or whatever when we raised an argument from roast beef sandwiches that ordinarily would have stilled our fret, Cody cried on the sidewalk sort of, I really couldn't see and everything important died yesterday, yet he was really crying, the loneliness of his eager hands that would someday be quiet inside the dirt had got hold of him. I was too stupid to consider him and bless him. But we had that successfully behind us, heading East——

CODY. (*thinking*) Into the soft sweet East we go, I'm ballin that Jack 'cause I got-a make Chicago by next nightfall as promised but at same time——

JACK. (*thinking*) And this is the exact eastward direct route, through Nebraska, of his old flyswatter days

CODY. (*thinking*) Jack is thinking his thoughts, his feet up on the dashboard, and I breaks the speedometer at a hundred and ten——big heavy hard-assed car, s'got the road held down, humps along like a bumblebee, some lotsa car, best yet——I take my T-shirt off, naked in the waist I go cuttin towards Greeley so we can make Ed Wehle's ranch by nightfall, only a hundred and fifty miles out of way

JACK. I agree to ranch idea, Cody was cowboy on it

CODY. I show him stretch of dirt road out by Sterling where I rode and galloped all one morning, ten, twelve miles on an errand for old man Wehle who's cussin at cows in the grass, other boys on horseback, "Git im, git im!" yells old man driving out on range in his new ranchero Buick

JACK. Going too fast on the muddy rainy road in the dismal moors of the Plains Cody whoops the big Cadillac with a "Whoops, hey, ahum, wal, ouch, ork!" into the ditch, ass-back, nobody hurt. Huddled in the prairie storm Cody goes for farmer help, tractor, Bonaventura backseat riders say "Is he your brother? He's crazy." I'm mad as hell, I'm bigshot in those days; but there's Cody right smack in his world, walking across a stretch of rainy plains to get help in the mist and mud, like when he waded through that New Mexico flood and lay down soaking in a raw old gondola, trying to light fires, and the water all around the boxcars in the drag, and no restaurant for miles——

CODY. Farmer pulls me out of mud for five. Has pretty daughter. We move on to ranch. Cows mill at door. I spot ranch house across the dark, one light. We follow sand road through range. Ed's in barn milking. I see his flashlight flickerin in the barn. I'm back home on the ranch

JACK. This is the ranch where he wrote that first letter of Val's I saw

CODY. Ed used to play Laramie with me in old days, we was buddies at harvest time

JACK. I sense coyotes beyond. Ed's wife listens to the Hit Parade in the dismal Saturday night of the wide wide deep. Delicious ice cream she froze

CODY. Jack is polite and excited

JACK. I peer into night beyond the kitchen, eyes shaded—there's no end to the night out there, all northeast of Colorado

CODY. In the midnight we bowl, we split the air

JACK. We unroll Nebraska in one grand land furl, the little houses are there, man's in his infinity

CODY. Roads never end, the horizon is black, they got lights up ahead

JACK. We smash Nebraska off our fenders pebble by pebble—we fly up to the dawns of Iowa, a hundred and ten miles an hour; Old Union Pacific Route of the Streamliners drops off to our right, the telegraph wires are burning in our fan, we're *moving*

CODY. I'm blasting the rods to hell, it's not my Cadillac

JACK. Far back in the funereal seat the two college boys sleep

CODY. Meat for Chicago

JACK. We pass the hobos of the road with the fire under a watertank—we don't pause to inquire—Iowa is pale green, Cody is grimly driving. We love each other and talk all night about it and comment on memories. Tom Sawyer never had a better time. Cody's tellin me about his past, "Yes, but no, well yes, I *do* remember and in fact, it was Ed Wehle's aunt's parlor, we had pimple games, talkin all day and doin it all day—but wait, I *do* think it was after and not beyond the artkino film book I lost——"

CODY. I've talked about a lot of things in my time

JACK. Bye and bye the churchbells are ringing in little Iowa towns, it's Sunday morning, hymns is raising in the golden air, they're bringing in the sheaves in the Baptist churches of the gaunt great land

CODY. Lady with white hair in diner treats us to extra potatoes

JACK. We smash onwards, Cody races with a maniacal Italian gangster hipcat from Chicago who, with mother, wants to match new Buick to our Cad, for ninety miles he tries to race Cody, Cody teases his bumper along, terrible, the guy gets a hundred-yard headstart on a passcurve and Cody eats up deficit with a purse of his lips as his foot descends on limousinic throttle——The Italian maniac gives up with wild cheer and smile hands up as we roar on by——his mother gave up. I get scared of Iowa curves and lay on backseat in a ball——paranoia about a crash

CODY. Man is all-fired hysterical just because I happen to know how much this baby can do, why shucks——

JACK. Pop tunes pop in the clouds but nonetheless I'm scared of this frightening afternoon, a minute ago he came down on a congestion of cars in a narrow bridge that only disentangled when he forced the issue in passing——he had us lined for the snout of a westbound truck trailer, with bump and ditches and honking hysterical passed cars on all sides, we made it, no great truck raised its tragic hump in the fatal red afternoon of Ioway, they'll be singing Wabash of the moon tonight and we've made it——but I can't rest with the road rushing and hissing beneath my head as the huge float of the car pummels forward with that maniacal Ahab at the wheel. The flash and throb of these trees, daylights, it's too fast

CODY. By mid-Iowa and after the insipid hassle of Des Moines (where Ma & Pa met) (in 1926) that damn nigger fool whose waterbag I busted, a little traffic light bump, and here he is calling the law, claiming hit-and-run, and we gave him blood, owner's name and address and everything——the hangup thence resulting, two hours at the po-lice station while they phone on ahead the tycoon in his Chicago——midafternoon, near Illinois, I'm tired

JACK. Sweet little rivers flow in a red dappled dream

CODY. I'm balling straight on through, Davenport to Cicero in two seconds, smoky old Chicago's up front, we pick up a couple hobos for fifty cents gas fare and here we come

JACK. Rolling into the city of Chicago, at dusk, in August

CODY. Brakes ain't working no more, rods ruined, we pass the hideous Skid Row of Madison Avenue, some of 'em are stone dead in the gutters

JACK. Carl Sandburg knew some of 'em——the great heroes of the Chicago night long ago, the ones who knew Willard from just watching one fight one night and touching him as he passed *and then died in flops*, from Denver clear on through: the density of the tragedy in America is confusing and immense in volume, oomaloom along the oil cloth with your little bug, the screendoors weren't made to slam for nothing and in no interesting night. Everybody is important and interesting

CODY. We clean up at the Y in the great city of Chicago I'm seein for the first time——When was it I got and gave myself the right to see Chicago, yes——point the muddy nose snout of the horny automobile deluxe at the street, ass to brickwall in a good big alley with just redbrick dust light illuminating the upper edges of the backalley pit, to make the infernal night of the city, the somber lost unspeeched red of our city night color, the red of night, the Caddy sits in its proper bed and we eat in a cafeteria

JACK. Cody is digging that old town——the gloom of it, the Els, the beans, the whores, you're in Chicago you hear guys say "Ah New York's alright sometimes," in New York the word Chicago is never heard; but a big town, and here's all the bop opening for us in the night——

CODY. In a bar——

JACK. ——great soft summernight, Chinamen on the unreal sidewalks of North Clark, women with great breasts watching the street from sleep-windows, the sight of a naked woman through the peepholes of hootchy-kootchy joints, a monstrous Moody Street of later life in the world

CODY. We pick up on our own kicks, talking, driving around for girls, they are scared of us in that big limousine like——

JACK. Like car thieves and juvenile heroes on a mad—— slamming hydrants, ruining the car——but the bop

CODY. The combo

JACK. Lean, loose, pursymouth tenorman, twenty-one; blows modern and soft, cool in his sportshirt only; with bony shoulders and fingering horn keys with their movement; next tenor is freckled boxer, Prez, in suit open at collar, hitching horn, long lapels, tie, neck strap, shiny golden horn, blows round and Lester-like; all leaning and jamming together and whaling in North Clark saloon and a hep niteclub later, the heroes of the hip generation. Me and Cody is right there; he's sweating, he wants to hear the jazz, he nods his head and socks his hands and bounces to the beat. They roll into a tune——"Idaho." The Negro alto highschool broadgash mouth Yardbird tall kid blows over their heads in a thought of his own, moveless on the horn, fingering, erect, an idealist who reads Homer and Bird. The other alto is a blond effeminate hipster from Curtis Street, Denver, with a red shirt, or South Main Street, or Market, or Canal, or Streetcar, he's the sweet new alto blowing the tiny heartbreaking salute in the night which is coming, a beauteous and whistling horn; he just held it there till his turn, and blew breath easily but fully in a soft flue of air, out came the piercing thin lament but completely softened by the Sound, the New Sound, into a——great Gad, man, the prettiest——

CODY. The bassplayer was a redheaded kid who looked gone, he just fucked that bass to death, his mouth hung open, the beat boomed

JACK. Drummer, with soft goofy complacent Reichianalyzed ecstasy, gum chewing, raggedydoll-necked like all Reichians, fluttered his brushes at the flowers, fit chee chee, fit chee chee and held the beat; piano dropped chords like a Wolfean horse turding in the steamy Brooklyns of winter morn

CODY. Then (because I had called him God in New York) Jack said "Look there's God" and there in a corner, pale head leaned in one hand, is George Shearing listening to the American sounds, old elephant ears, eager to transform it to his misty summernight's use, Keatsian; and with him the vein-popped Denzil Best, who, starch-collared, sits at his drums machining it in like a law student ("When he's excited his vein pops!" yells Cody)——George is persuaded by the young musicians to play, which he does, gassing the afterhours club, which, at roar of great Chicago day is still open, nine, and we all stumbled out into raggedy American realities from the dream of jazz: all our truths are at night, are to be found in the night, on land or sea. Pray for the safety of the mind; find a justification for yourself in the past only; romanticize yourself into nights. What is the truth? You can't communicate with any other being, forever. Cody is so lost in his private——being——if I were God I'd have the word, Cody is my friend and he is doomed as I am doomed. What are we going to do? Oh Jack Duluoz what are you going to do? Oh Cody Pomeray, tell me the secrets of the——of the what? Cody Pomeray, of the what! sing me a song of yourself, explain your soul, why will you die, did you inquire, make a comment, repast, fast, think and plot to prayer or just come to this state of being dieable by yourself without help and in your own blank and unseeing lost stare into the roomy lights inside the round fold in the curvallex halfpart of the upper nodule brain. Trumpets don't make the past reality; horns won't bring back your sense of life in cribs of no-death, who taught you to die?

CODY. In Chicago——

JACK. Whenever I realize that I'm going to die, I no longer can understand the meaning of life

CODY. We staggered to Detroit in a bus to see his first wife, we walked at dusk along Jefferson Street, five, six miles, wondering in the ruins of Detroit, sat on the lawn of his love to chat by summer moonlit trees, but neighbors called cops, we were casing joints

JACK. Next day we saw her——

CODY. He and his ex-wife were no longer on the same team; it was his last touchdown with her; all he had, was a remaining chance to lick a fieldgold——

(this may be the production of a cracked brain again)

Blow, baby, blow——

JACK. We stayed in Detroit, situated at the upper end of the middle up there, for three days——It was farcical. We were frisked in the streets; at the same time we spent afternoons riding in the back of her teenage friends' cars, open rumble seat, looking for Vernors Ginger Ale in the moppy clouds of afternoon among redbrick factories——

CODY. One night we saw a big baritone sax in a Hastings Street joint, he blew alright, the gals were fine——but——

JACK. Cody had no girl, he fell asleep——mine made me walk home five miles——apathetic, I hung on the edge of the night——we sat in the balcony of an all night B-movie, saw Eddy Dean and Peter Lorre, slept in the seats in the roar of

the pictures, almost got swept up at dawn in one gigantic heap
by corps of broomers in sullen suits. Where was Billie Holiday,
where was Huck? We dug Detroit Skid Row. In a cold park,
sitting on the grass among trolleys, Cody said I had brown in
my ears; we were beggars.

Finally we got a ride arranged to New York, for a pittance, in
a new Chrysler; meanwhile the summer that had plummeted
across the continent with all its showers and heats now turned
autumnlike and we huddled in the wind——because Cody and
I returning East was the last expression of space left in the general knowledge. And even it wasn't working. Nothing awaited
him there, he was on a wildgoose chase, he was being given
the runaround by Fate. Stories, promises of Italy——I'd said
"We'll go to Italy with my money," which was nonexistent and
never showed up——He faced the bleak East and winter——It
was a prophetic night when we dug Skid Row in the cold wind,
thinking about his father. In New York, upon our arrival there,
he immediately met his third wife to be.

Time is the purest and cheapest form of doom.

SHE WAS A RAVING fucking beauty the first moment we saw
her walk in, at a party; she said "I always wanted to meet a real
cowboy" and I called him over. I had a chick of my own a few
days later, cool——tremendous activities in the apple, Manhattan, New York. Cody got divorces and whatnots and promised
to do this and that, I saw him often at their place: in the evening
after work he sat in his Chinese hip-length gown, naked, puffing
on a Turkish water pipe full of Zombie, under the lovebed's his
battered suitcase he's had since poolhall days. His children are
being born on the West Coast. We listen to basketball games.
One night I meet him in a bar, I'm late, he's wearing a suit
for the first time since 1947; I say "Sorry I'm late," he says "I
thought you were standing me up on our first date," and flut-
ters his eyes at me. We try to talk seriously but can't any more;
everything blew out on that Cadillac trip East, there's nothing
left. I'm depressed. I sit at home and listen to the slamming
Long Island freights and think of worries of all kinds. Cody's in
his bathrobe, the Chinese one, composing an epic novel: "Cody
Pomeray was born Feb. 8, 1926, in Salt Lake City." I help him

edit it under the cockroaches. We go to Birdland, there's Sonny
Stitt whaling.

But when Spring comes I want to leave New York, I gotta
hear the bird of Shenandoah whistling, I take off for Mexico
City via Lexington, Virginia and Stonewall Jackson's grave,
and Denver. I'm in Denver, preparing to go south by rail,
when Cody suddenly appears in a 1937 Ford jalopy. What'd he
do?——to come rattling back West across the Plains, alone, 1800
miles? Why, he threw up everything; but actually he was headed
for Mexico City for a divorce from Evelyn, but not as No. 3
thought so he could husband her, rather to return to Evelyn
dis-wed or uppity-wed, all wed and inter-wed.

Mexico was the last great trip. But it began in Denver.

IT BEGAN IN DENVER in a little Ford model 1937——Model
T——T-Zone, V-8——flying and rattling south. It was Cody's
return to his native city, he stood on porches with a coat over
his arm, rocky and stern. He goofed with local ex-athletes in
round-the-town high cars at 1 A.M.——I was there, up front with
Slim Buckle and Tom Watson, others in back, we all got high
on Dave Sherman getting his first kicks on tea: he kept slapping
his knee and laughing, yelling, squealing, "Son of a *bitch*——god
damn." Mad, Cody loved him and at nine o'clock in the morning polite important suburbanites of Denver, while cooking
their bacon and eggs, could hear great subterranean "Yesses"
rumbling from the earth, from the cellar where I lived, where
Cody and Sherman sat in a bed talking about everything. It
was the first time that any of the Denver group represented by
Dave ever dug Cody. There was a master and student relation,
for forty-eight hours. Sherman was just an ordinary Denver
guy who'd been highjumper in high school, four years in the
service, six months in an office, now didn't know what to do.
Meanwhile Cody conducted a complicated affair with a crippled
girl across town, she almost followed us to Mexico. Sherman's
father, fearful of his son's departure, an unhappy old man like
the unhappy old men of French movies and real life, all rheumy
and wasted and immitigably gloomy in brown darknesses of afternoon parlors . . . so frightened was he of the magic sound of
Cody's name on Dave's lips when he announced he was leaving

for Mexico, that, when I showed up to help Dave with luggage, the old man insisted on calling me Cody. (Cody had goofed an entire party, given in honor of a local young writer, with his idiotic behavior in company, Lord knows he'll do anything, he fingered his balls, he grabbed the hostess, cake spluttered from his mad activities laughing up and down the dish line, he charmed and bemused half our lives away, all kinds of emotions ran riot in the room, Helen Buckle with her Slim in tow now for good (him all beaming), and Earl Johnson and Helen, same Earl raced for that football in insane past days, others——) We left Denver in a cloud of dust, we said goodbye to the charming tennis wizard and buddy beerdrinker wit, the All Knowing——I saw a dot decreasing in size and it was still Ed Gray, watching us go to Mexico. Two miles outside town, all our suitcases intact, Sherman is bit by a bug; it comes from golden Colorado wheatfields, it's like home, but his arm swells poisonously, we have to buy penicillin in San Antone. Now the moon like a fevered bulb arises, New Mexico is hot under the stars, dew-cold; there's Dalhart, Texas burning far across the horizon, we'll be there by dawn light; the moon hugens in the sky, a fatted calf, leans its skewered castrative eyes on a nob, poor good moon; we're rolling to Mexico. Fantasize us no Samarkands. This is the New World. The spine of America runs deep down. . . . "Think of it, boys, we'll be rolling bean-bugging down the continent and over the rolling world"——a frightening thought, Time, and Space so vast anyhow; why did God leave us on this ledge? and didn't warn us a bit? God created a sin. He sins, we die.

We're rolling down along, Pueblo, Trinidad, Raton Pass and soft roll of rocks in truck midnights, a hamburger; anthropologist campfire off the road marks where the anthropologists of our youth are telling their life stories, as we in the car are doing. Cody recalls childhood occasions when he must have met Dave. "When I was covering the alleys up by Cherry I used to double-check by your house 'cause I always found——you must have seen me, I'd bounce a ball sometimes, seems like I seen you, on a bike, or somethin, but at any rate." And here we're three gringos rolling in the summer night to Mexico, by moon. "Keep her rollin, boys," yelled Cody from the backseat sleep, "we'll be kissin señoritas b'dawn." We spent a whole day traversing downwards through Texas, eternities of bush, Coleman, Brady, hot, dusty; at one point I thought Cody was something else and the car a celestial wagon when I dropped off to doze at his side in the afternoon; a grueling huge journey. I drove some; Sherman leaned on the wheel through interminable counties. Texas! At Abilene we saw the red faced Texans crossing their hot white pavements. After Fredericksburg (where Cody, Joanna and I had crossed in the snows of 1949 with eyes on the West) it was the cool of evening, a gradual general descending to San Antonio; that dawn had been Amarillo in the buffalo plains, the whip of flags at great gas stations, the windy panhandle grasses. Here it was evening, and the heat increasing as the plateau gives off to the level of the Rio Grande. Lights get browner, darker, you can tell Mexican territory long after; San Antonio is humming and buzzing and fragrant in a tropical night. While Sherman gets his shot at the hospital, Cody and I walk the Mexican verdurous shacktown streets, looking for girls, shoot some pool in local Mex hall, play records at juke, Wynonie howling "I Love My Baby's Pudding," the poolsharks are tormenting a young hunchback, Cody says "Look, a young Tom Watson." I feel like Jimmy Cagney, I can feel the air with my fingers.

I get semi-drunk on a lonely backseat pint while they drive on down to Dilley, Cochinal and Laredo. Hotter and hotter the night; I wake up stupid in the great heat of Laredo at 2 A.M. in June. Bugs are slamming the lunchcart screen, it's disgusting, it's a heat wave, it's the utter lost-bottom of old Tex-ass, take it away. We eat disinterested sandwiches among border rats and disappointed cops. Off we go into Mexican guards at the border ramp, thinking nothing of it.

I HAD THE GREAT CHIMERA of Vaughn Monroe in the ghostly sky of the Western herd——O mournful cry!——I have heard train whistles howling at the gates of distant great cities, seen the swarm of white horses thundering across the horizon of America in the Night, saw music in trees, the dream in the river, the moon glistening in a young girl's eye in bed——This explains my Cody Pomeray, "I saw him rising." in the top of the West.

We came into Mexico on tiptoe. As the officials checked we saw that across the road, where they said Mexico began, Mexico did begin, with the late sitters of the night, some of them on chairs and it's 3 A.M., one cabaret chili joint is open, beer's there, etc., we see that Mexico is the land of night. There are young men as well as old men standing in the hot sleeping street there at night . . . closed shutters . . . Nuevo Laredo; there are disinterested sullen eatings at smoking counters of the valley summernight. White is the predominant color of the dollmen in doorways, they also wear floppy strawhats and any old shoes. "What?" says Cody who didn't expect it either, "Is that what these cats do at night——Man, we go by there and *be* with those fellows, we go dig the world." In no time at all Cody and I realized the Indians . . . we discovered our own Indian in the Pancho of American border lore: "These guys, these women are Indians with high cheekbones——" and beautiful too——We saw little girls standing in jungle clearings with machetes in their father's hand as he by the road goops to watch a car on the Pan American Highway. But jungle comes lower down——beyond Nuevo Laredo and our beer over delighted outstretched palms holding Mexican currencies——the desert only, gray flats of dawn, sand, yucca, the sun coming up over the Gulf of Mexico in a big red ball from Africa, far ahead the clouds of the Sierra Madre, the mysterious plateau of high airs and mountain joy that is Mexico, the top of the world, desolate, Indian, beautiful, bigger than dreams——"Say pardner" I tell Cody "this must be the road the old outlaws rode when they spoke of Old Monterrey, here they'd come lopin on ghost horses to exile, talk of your South Africas."

"Dig way in there"——Cody——"at the 'dobe hut where that farmer and kids must live——set out there, with one animal, a Mexican mule, a burro, and the harsh inhospitable earth that doesn't even have the country light of North Carolina at night, just pitch-black in the nigger stars. Shucks, talk of your Arkansaws, this is rough and thorny country."

We came to the first town in a dewy morn——Sabinas Hidalgo, the goat herds, the shepherds and the girls with ground on their knees smeared in.

"Allo daddy," said the bestlooking babe as in our beat Ford we slowly bounced at five per into town——Cody so madded by the magic that he's looking at the insides of 'dobe homes: "Look, the mother's gettin tequila breakfast ready with her pancakes on the stove——the little kids are all sleeping in the same bed——behind the blind there's an angel, must be. Dang, what a fine country."

"Let's turn around and pick up those girls."

"Look at the old handlebar mustache with his goatstick cuttin off into the shade of the hills for the day——"

"The tulip day——and those revolutionaries in big black bourgeois sombreros joking at the gas pump containing nationally owned oil, their attendants and squires are waiting by the goats and dust cracked Depression Buicks." It was all there, all these things. In our tourist guidebook it said Sabinas Hidalgo was an agricultural town. "Read slowly and clearly as I drive," instructs Cody. We're headed for the jungles of the cockatoo: "It says colors run riot in the dense vegetation."

"Whooee, let's go, let's have a ball, some cunts in the hay, some Tahitian misses in disguise, pay for the father and run off with the house and kick the dog, make the brothers mad, ruin Mexico for Americans forever."

Huge clouds ahead: they have the transparency and cold film of mountain ridge clouds, they're blowing. We start climbing a great pass. "Viva Aleman!" it's whitewashed on rock. Mad. It's clear and cold like New Hampshire——we've left the Mexican desert, we're crawling up a cavity of the plateau, better things and higher levels of world-wonder ahead.

CODY DRIVES ON, he never rests much——by the time we've been through the whorehouses of intervening cities, and hurried through Monterrey, through jungles south of Victoria, through mountain chains and over cloud-sneering passes he's still intently driving with a bleak jawbone. At Monterrey he had a flat tire or fixed something, I looked up from an attempted nap and saw the twin peaks of Saddle Mountain all crazy and jagged in the altitude, I never; it was one hell of a goose at heaven, like Diamond Point, Oregon and the needle of Cleopatra, but twisted, pommel like, a goof of a mountain.

I drove for awhile, there was something sad in the car. Cody and I weren't speaking much, Dave slept. Great trips are like that. Sadness is inexplicable and creative. We flew down the land. The old car managed nicely. We began getting high to misprove our vision. In the first set of tropical mountains, high above the great yellow ribbon of the river, Rio Moctezuma that dug its canyon forever, near Tamazunchale the brown and fetid foothill town, we stopped on a mountain ledge off the road to think and talk. To me the great verdant valleys rising on both sides in mad slopes covered with aerial agricultures of the mountain planting tribe, yellow bananas gracing the mountaintops, was all small and green and funny like a child dream I was so high: the hugeness of the world became a joke in my mind, I thought these mountains were all in one quiet and massive room; I told this but they didn't understand: but Times Square too is in one livingroom of Time. At a little town to which we descended I saw a corner 'dobe two-story apartment or tenement and as clearly as a bell it was true, to me, that was the house where I'd been born, they took me to the sunny front a long time ago. Mexico drove me mad. Cody was in ecstasies sweating over it. We were innocent.

We slept in the jungle, a ghostly white horse came trotting out of the jungle woods in the pitch of night, Cody was on the sand road in a blanket, the horse phosphorescent and aflame in the dark came, meek longfaced ghost, tippy-toe past Cody's sleeping head, pursued by mangy jungledogs barking, continuing on across town (the humble little Limon town of shacks, store lit Main Street with its one oil lamp store, and bananas and flies and barefoot kidsisters in the happy gloom of Fellaheen Eternal Country Life). I slept on top of the car, it was too hot below——soft showers of infinitesimal million-mothed bugs fell on my upturned eyes, it was like a film from the stars, I had never known God's original Eden jungle could be so soft and sweet, my face was so safe; for the first time I resigned to insupportable heat, and almost enjoyed it thanks to the sensation and crushed bleeding of bugs and mosquitoes all over me, the casualness of our trip. "Start the car Cody, blow some air," I complained at dawn; he did; up ahead over swamps shines the Mantes radio antenna, red lights, as if we were in Nebraska; it's a leprous dawn spreads in the sky. At a jungle gas station that would make a good Atlantic Whiteflash man go pale, they've got a concrete ramp at dawn after unspeakable indulgences and orgies of blood in the night a million bugs of every hue and prick crawling insensate around my poor shoes. I leap into the car to escape the horror; Cody and Dave drink Mission

Orange at the icebox, they're lost in a sea of bugs, they don't care. Beyond them is Tropic of Cancer swamp——The goddamn attendant, he's barefooted. . . . Why they've got caterpillars, beetles, dragonwings with a mile long, black stickers, every kind——there's no air; when Cody pushes the hot Ford out we get gusts of deadbug junglerot breeze against the caked blood and sweat of our bitten skins. Pleasant! It's like Daddy Eroshka in the Tolstoy fable of the Cossack marshes, (enjoy the burning bleeding sensation of the jungle raw, be natural man). Talk of your insides of a baker's oven in New Orleans on a July night, the Tropic of Cancer July is best to climb out of.

Blowing fogs wham across the bush at the top of the great altitude cool pass——golden airs are being propelled in a height——we can't see below the parapet, it's too white and misty, just a yellow ribbon and a green valley like a sea below it, dwellings in between like eyries.

All the Indians along the road want something from us. We wouldn't be on the road if we had it.

OUR OLD THIRTIES upgoing Ford, so-called with the noses and soiled with the mess of our fathers, year-cracked, haunted, tinny heap of the American movement into the round West: covered wagons brought crudities, the Ford brought traveling salesman and blonds, brought Sears catalog, Jack Benny on the radio. The Indians with hands outstretched expect us three galoots goofing in an old V-8 to come over and give them dollars; they don't know we discovered the atom bomb yet, they only vaguely heard about it. We'll give it to them, alright. . . . Unshaven, Cody, hands in pants, surveys the mountains. "What they want has already crumbled in a rubbish heap——they want banks."

Cody gave a little girl his wristwatch in exchange for "the smallest and most perfect crystal she's picked from the mountain just for me"; as a rule those went for five cents or less. "Damn, I wish I had something to give them," muses Cody. "Isn't there anything I can give them?" he might as well shout at the mountains; no answer. We receive pineapples for fractions of a penny: no fair exchange at all. The Indians are lounging against alpine stonewalls on the ledges of light, hatbrims down, draped, shrouded in dark and dusty vestments. Biblical patriarchs bless herds and convene with crowds in the deserted dusty ghost town market-squares of late afternoon; women flow along the fields with flax in their arms, striding, talking; from out the wild Judean earth showers the wild maguey pulque octopus of cactus, ready to stab and suck. Jeremiacal hobos lounge, shepherds by trade, under groves of dark trees in the white desert, comes the soft footfall of the water boy coming from the kine. . . . Above roll the world clouds, salmon, the high plateau is still. I can see the hand of God. The future's in Fellaheen. At Actopan this Biblical plateau begins——it's reached by the mountains of faith only. I know that I will someday live in a land like this——I did long ago.

(BUT OH WHEN I WAS in Colorado they sang sad songs about Columbine——at night, over the radio as we drove past the Okie outskirts and the corrals, "Little Colorado Columbine"—— never again, Oh never again. This flower grew for long-ago Codys too . . . as it does now for the children of respectable Okie car mechanics living on rose covered little sideroads out Alameda, down Broadway, in past East Colfax . . . sad world that tortures its own hearts . . . never again the dream of Colorado, the sunny Sunday afternoon, the roadhouse, the great wheatfield, the white mountains beyond.)

Cody saw angels of heaven through everything, in Mexico. Hour after hour, sick with repugnant life he drove on and yet endured. At Actopan, or Ixmiquilpan, or Zacualtipan, I don't know which, where we passed, there was a crowd of Indians in robes standing in the sun under great trees that cast their shade in the other direction, with dogs, children, baskets, everything gleaming golden in the sun the air is so blue and cool and keen, the fields so mellow; women with lowered Virgin Mary faces hiding in their earthy dressinggowns made of flax and hands and by time dyed; just like a woman with her left leg up on daddy's hip where he sits, her right one down, open to his up-aimed rutabaga, her breast planted in his mouth, just like that dame looking to the moon as she enjoys what's going on below, Cody was, when I said "Hey Cody look at all the shepherds of the Bible in the sun of antiquity," he takes one look out of a red-eyed nap, says "Oah" and looks at the torn ceiling of the old Ford like that, as if to goop the loop. Across from that rocky village with its cactus foundations is an earth of the young Jesus; they're bringing the goats home, long-stepping Pantrio comes fumilgating along the maguey rows, his son gave him up a month ago to walk barefoot to Mexico City with a home-made mambo drum, his wife gathers blossoms and flax for his embroideries and kingdoms, the young inquisitive carpenters of the village quaff pulque from urns in the goateries and shelli-meeli-mahim of Mohammedan Worldwide Fellaheen dusk and nightfall, Ali Babe be blessed. Did Cody see that?——Later he said he recalled all that, but as if it had been a dream when he looked (out the window).

But not so sick with repugnant life, cheesy Cody in his beat down Ford rottin on up the fard, with Mexican saints and peons watching him. What a land!——We rose for the plateau whereon Mexico City sits; it was gradual, those Biblical levels in between, those sweet lands terminated, just a step up, by monasteries, like the progress of the history of the church, and the town and the city, till we reach the San Juan Letran chapels and cathedrals of the great city night. There is a stupid blur in my memory of the trip; I think Cody remembers absolutely nothing——either that or all.

CODY HAD ONE MOTHER, but she had seven sons. And, like me, he sinned against his father; he left him flat in Ogden, I left my father flat in New Haven.

There's a picture of Cody's mother and one of his father's friends, they're standing in front of a keenly etched old automobile in the modern bright print of the Thirties camera, bless it; we see the sheen of stove-polish on the fenders of this venerable jalopy, it's got a canvas roof, it's just a few years older than our Mexico Ford (a '25 Chandler or Reo or Buick); Cody's mother is wearing overalls, coveralls, a man's white shirt, sleeves rolled, collar open; her hair is swept back and tied; she has a long gaunt face, she's forty-five or fifty, has had many children ("These damn Okies!" Cody yelled furiously when Frankie Johnnie refused to buy a jalopy for Cody's temporary use while we waited in Denver for the Cadillac ride)——It must be a piney Sunday afternoon in that old photo; they went driving, a Thirties Sunday-driver picnic, with beer, brawling beers in roadhouse crossroads with other families who even bring children to

drowse and scratch at the tavern back screen where the flies
flip over the garbage; now someone's suggested a picture be
taken, maybe old Cody, or some brother, Jim, Joe, Jack, his
shadow (or hers) (is in the grass at the foot)——she's posing with
a Depression baker in a California S.I.U. skid row hat all snow
white, wearing chinos khaki or wino pants with a shirt, beat
cuffs rolled, beat shoes in the weeds, one arm on hip (where's
his joy now?). Poor old Colorado with the red sun sinking . . .
on California.

This picture was taken in the days when Denver began to
imitate L.A. and spread for miles——and Cody spread all the
way to California. There are blossoms on the weeds at the bottom of the picture . . . tragic Columbine of the soft green fields
in their ripple winds and rushing irrigation ditches, irriditches:
Colorado where Cody began, now not the railyards, but the
outlying woods, Denver——Just like the Green Clunker in its
lonesome stand along the boxcars in a Frisco Xmas, this clunker
is lost in the space and mastery of Actuality which there red-
dens and reflects off the faces of the woman in overalls and the
smiler from Larimer Street——Smiley I believe his name was,
Smiley Moultrie that bought groceries on Saturday afternoons
and then suffered them to wait in the car for the evening movie
while he played cards with the fellows in Curtis Street pool-
backs, later a drink in a nugget saloon full of cowboys and local
freightyard clerks and hotrod boys and winos in a mad mess;
driving home from the movie at night Smiley Moultrie's little
boy Red snoozed in the lull of wishes and hopes gratified, his
arm against his Pa, timidly learning, believing: but that Smiley
was a nogood ornery no account horn toad, they felled him in
a bush after the snapshot and took all his money. He died of
paresis cursing against the jewth, in Texas or in Maine.

In no time at all, Cody himself has grown from a little barefoot lad of five (1931) in this picture where he stands in the
hot sun on the cement steps, in little chubby overalls made
smooth and wrinkly and sweet by grasses and pisses in the day,
a lawn behind him, a rose arbor, the Denver afternoon where
those immortal clouds ever roam to their mountains. Nothing
has changed in the skies over Colorado since 1931——But now
Cody is grown big and rocky and gaunt and manly in his doom.
Hope expresses itself in the composition of flowers, light and

leaf in the background of Cody at eleven, his arms are folded complacently but with expectancy, he grins for camera, his hair is brushed to one neat schoolboy side, he has suspenders and bicycle boy stripes on his long pants, a clean white shirt is folded in a square at the elbow——In his eyes all this human belief, at eleven there's belief (1937) which is gone and instead should have ripened. Has it not ripened?

We come driving into Mexico City; (how do we know?).

Great excited soccer fields of dusk and windwhip first attracted our attentions; outside on the plains, outside town, where monasteries mix territories of agriculture with haciendas and wineries, we feel that wind for real, I blast on the plain under a roaring tree huge a hundred foot, with my eyes fixed on that pinkwalled creamy monastery across the way haunted by afternoon shapes in shrouds, bearing apples; now that wind that from vineyards got grained, blew blasting across the suburban Mexico City outlying factory soccer fields with huge commotions and settlements in between whaling like mad and the traffic refusing to halt. "Look at 'em kick!"

> And oh the sad streets
> in lost adobes,
> Calle de Los Niños Perdidos.

"Dig this *traffic* man!" yells Cody——we just hit town——I see Cody's in predicaments, traffics are slamming around him, we suddenly realize nobody has mufflers on their cars, the noise is clamorous. On a horizon is a bullring, el Cuarto Caminos, the Four Roads meet, a plain, on Sunday afternoons they slay the bull and over the stonewall across the field where the echo roars the primitive Aztecs still sit in their stone village on a filthy crick, stone bridges overtop it, the center of the stone worn down so's you have to pick your way through a trough in the bridge a thousand years old. A car——stopped us——did we want whores? Lights, the first of the gray evening, turned on in the Metropolis ahead; we realized we'd been through a land.

In my dream of the Shrouded Stranger who pursued me across the desert and caught me at the gates of the Eternal City, he with his white eyes in the darkness of his rosy folds, his firefeet in the dust, that smothered me to death in a dream, he'll never catch me if he didn't then, when we entered the gates of

Mexico City, he came from that land and was going the same
way, same hour of the day, bluefall, dusk. . . . Too, there is a
dream of a little golden road, a house, a treeshade, the which
Shroudy inhabits in the disguise of my mother and then projects himself over to a shade across the shimmering heat coming
after me; I ask my mother for a toy gun to shoot him with: he
didn't catch me in real life, or, if he did, and I'm caught now, I
be dadblamed if I know what part——where——in what beautiful
fiction of the dream he was spavined and——the golden moon
resplendant over the village of the poor, has, by its imagery
and fire, turned the sleepers of the roof to make sheets and
shrouds in a madder ledge; old Art-Star, Jerusalem Shepherd,
made into a drowsy moist eye of night, sheds sparklers and hot
crackers on the town, midnight is dewy, the blue Baghdad sky
of Reality is in the window, golden milken towers that rise, de-
pendeth in the sky of night, make watch posts for thoughtful
shepherds dozing for dawn and cowbells. This is the city the
Shrouded Stranger denied me, he smothered me to death in
his dress and I woke with the towers of the blue my last view.
Ten dollars please, no more visits. Alright, so I places a bet on
Blue Foam——Ting a ling.

MEXICO CITY was the bottom of and the end of the road, that
ever-widening American road because it now can go no further,
four lanes, five lanes, six lanes, poor road, there was so little
beyond there that was "American," "North American-o" that
Cody didn't ever think of driving beyond the City, say towards
Cuernavaca, because, damn, instead he got involved in a rotary
circle and——"Here comes an ambulance, I believe it's an ambulance" I'm saying to myself as from the gray out-regions of
some out-spoking from Reforma sub-boulevard comes the wild
careening eyes of a——the Fellaheen Ambulance is coming! It
is driven by barefooted interns, Indians, shirtless, slunk low at
the wheel obese and insane, sneering along at the wheel, heroes
of Pancho Villa and great Smokey wars in the cactus beyound,
he's driving an ambulance like a Mexico City Cody. . . . Here
he comes! siren howling! seventy miles, eighty an hour in the
city streets, people, traffic part, he careers without any of that
kind of obstruction American and West European (including
French) ambulance drivers are suffered to accept when they are

reduced to darting and weaving in dense downtown Dubuque and McCook Main Streets of the gray tragic land which is now covered with white bungalows in the thrushing rain of 1952; an ambulance should be allowed to blow across town; the Indian just opens up like a cannonball and aims at his city: they, Indians all, accept his knowledge and wisdom and make way for him——disaster otherwise, he comes skittering on drunken crazy wheels in a frenzy of flight like a gull taking off from water, he sits greasy beneath the ikon in a green light, a gloom; the Fellaheen World Ambulance, it is liable to explode any minute, doctors, interns, patients and sympathetic handholders all in one sprowsh on crackglass sidewalks, skrunk, flerp. Val Hayes steps forth finger outheld——

CODY. Talk of that ambulance, here I have a rotary circle drive almost like the one we foolished inside of in Virginia that morning coming down to New Orleans where remember? this mad disc jockey is yellin at us over the air "Don't WORRY 'bout nothin!"

JACK. And I'm in the backseat——filled with the Gulf, it's floating along our left windows, the Gulf of Mexico

CODY. That now we've crossed——in this rotary I'm spinning my brain at an occupation——there are six spokes around this square, six boulevards, converging, but a thousand yards square fill this enormous grass circle with its Mayan traceries and Rocks there and Maximilian Peccadildoes in stone up above, so vast the circle that I cannot help but be hung in time in the lull of the drive, of driving, and miss my spokes which I'll have to had counted at decision-time, the dream resurrects you but you're a menace asleep at a wheel, round you go, whoopetiwhoop, around the mulberry square, see? and forget all about your boulevard and go in a sweeping circle——

JACK. At the bottom of the road, at the bottom of the road

CODY. Did you see how that damn ambulance with his red ass tail diminished into his space funnel yonder into downtown moils not trafficless and opened a gateway

JACK. ——to Santa Maria of Mercy, the stone edifice in the—— Whee! look at those cunts

Yes, at midnight we stood, Cody and I, in the middle of a narrow little street, a street so narrow the jukebox in the one-arm hotdog stuck out into the gutter, and along the wall across the street are forty beautiful Latin whores with Madonna eyes gleaming from the dark above the words they thought we'd like to hear. Cody is stonecold dead stiff upright in the street center, he's transfixed by a spear that commences in the Perez Prado mambo booming in the juke in a flood of the street in sound and runs through his body to the lined-up whores in their orisons there. "Jack, that amazing Hedy Lamarr angel one in the third door from end (whoo! what was on that porch then, a *dice game* or *what*? men squatting!) has, to mar her otherwise beauty, great sad pockmarks of a childhood typhus that you can't see in the dark but I looked again when she cast her shining eyes around, towards the light, making greasy reflection for her cheek, balmlike."

There was a great smell of rotting vegetation in the air but which had risen from the jungles below the plateau, in the form of rain, and was older and more seaworthy and almost exhilarating; but in heavy rains, worms swim the sidewalks in their deluge . . . worms appear from stucco, *voilà*; vegetable rains oil the sidewalks. Tile sweats back caterpillars. The Tropic of Cancer. . . . Not content just to be driving in circles at the bottom of the road, we also made the great American drinking night, playing night, in terms of complete and final perfect bars; we slung ropes over tenement porches, we dove down the street like seadogs, it was criminal what the little girls were charging for a dance in a crowded jukebox bar with an unused bandstand supporting the box, brawlings at bar, lovings in the mill, a penny a dance, a close squeeze and cunt to cock hug, a walking thigh to thigh, to mambo, dreamy, crazy, dissipated, in Mexico at last they've caught up with that mad Poughkeepsie crowd of ours, whoo! "Ooh that cunt——Eeyak!——Urk!" Cody was out of his mind, he darted between legs, he popped up like (a dervish doll——a dribblydoll——like) a pop cork from shoulders, he pleaded with my ear: "I've never, I never knew, anything like this!!!" The American Irish pioneer in him was mourning the loss of home, he realized he never had one. . . . "In Denver they have mass arrests if girls and boys get together in big hot crowds like this——whee!" His face fell stony and silent. He flew around like a raven, flapping in the streets; usually just Groucho-gliding and exploring imaginary——real alleys as he ducked along in a goof (one of so many lost in the gray void now) and Sherman and I strode along in back and laughed, we'd been laughing since Denver. We lost track of the car as we roamed sad suburban streets with interconnecting highgrass fields with paths, and empty lamp poles; a weird spot. I suddenly remembered we were in Mexico——I had thought——but what? but like Cody this was my first trip to a foreign land (innocents abroad), there couldn't be another. A lost faced cow herd or sheep guardian but also highschool soft bus stop saint who happened to be wandering in the 4 A.M. of his neighborhood for no reason and with a playstick but also probably a stick of weed too, grand for him and *his* history teacher. . . . A Fellaheen Suburban Ghost, a Sebastian of sorrows in another rain; maybe the buddy of that mambo peasant in the hip alleys downtown selling crucifix and weed and dodging crooked connections and mystical cops with four arms and eight hands (Mayan) in the Chinese moil of corners ducking into bars, everybody's a cat down there: the mambo kid is at Las Brujas playing for the whore dancers, a tuck a tick a tee, a tuck a tick a tee (same beat, Conga is the drum son of Congo the River in a Spanish philological pseudomorphosis carried through the cane by torchy sweating anguished confused messengers). The lonely lampposts remind Cody and Dave of Denver, remind me of Pawtucketville; the kid says he's going to church, we don't disbelieve it; beyond the lamp post glare I imagine I see American white bungalows of old-time side streets of home like in Truckee, Eau Claire, elsewhere, Buffalo, Shuffalo, but it's 'dobe Mexican tragic sleeping cells of night. In downtown streets beggar families lie in segments; I see that Jesus-like poor dog in the beard and bright eyes blowing the flute at his infant sister and all radiant and saved because she cackles, his bony arms, only the strawhat ruins that Khartoum effect, the whole world fooled me, the Indians are older than music, the Greeks stole their laments from an Indian wail in the Mongolian Sweeps. They came down over Bering Strait: to quote Bull Hubbard "Mexico is an oriental country;" meanwhile the first dark Indians of the Sink shot a loop northward that later so lost itself from the Bering Strait elderly arm that it became Gnothic, the Teuton, West Europa, the French Cabinet, Eisenhower, and apartment house in Santa Barbara. At the thumb of Korea the movement ceased

and found its easternmost knock at the westernmost line which
is in that mid-Pacific Polynesian somewhere. Cody is therefore
an offshoot of the Celtic rebel redskin with his chalk buffaloes in
a cave, lost his oriental guile tr——in an Irish cave. The Fellaheen
World is at silence. This has absolutely no effect on the stolid-
ity of Cody's upthrust face as he gazes at the airport pokers of
Mexico City, raving up there in the Fellaheen Night with the
dingbats and jungle air. Cody is Cody——you couldn't scratch
him off an etching gargoyle, dingbat; the King of all my friends.

"You see, there's nothing we can do about it. I told you I
was——everything is all right in other words——that's why we
don't talk as of yore, we've said it, seen it, the effort is awful, we
have knowledge though, I recognize you, I know you more or
less recognize whatever in me——in other words, the world is
fine, we do have a certain amount of responsibility but it's very
light and not deserved really, we com*plain* (cough)——hem,
(like my father), 'it's a damn shame'——and shaking his poor
philosophical head at the floor, Cody who's been through everything and suffered it all. It was in Mexico that I think——he
couldn't go much further, nobody could, find an answer, the
time pressed in——inside seven days he said "I'm going back to
New York, I'm going back to California too, I'm going back
to United States."

"What?" I cried, looking up from my mail, from my grandee
darkpolished desk . . . in the sunlight that stabbed in from the
open shutter, "What?" adjusting my pen quill——"going off
are you? back to——" He was going back to his present New
York woman, marry her, and then go back to his second (and
at present being divorced and most suffering of all) wife. . . . I
saw sullenness coming into Cody's face like a calm.

"False nonsense."——Acheson, 1952
"You've got to legalize the Fellaheen,"——Duluoz, 1952

The last I see of him, he's in the kitchen like an anxious old
grandma seedin his weed in Mexican beer trays, "cerveza"——
with his bony ruinous faceball bent over other skulls and uselessness.

He begged me to be a complete idiot with him; now he's
begging me to go to work with him.

BEFORE THE GATES of San Antonio, on our way down, that hot sultry valleynight when we eased up at a gas station, and drank a few cold beers from an icebox next to pumps, various Mexicans doing same in their peregrinating on the sidewalk so green, I thought, in all that wild delight and tropic love, a pity I should be seeing the wildest and most Fellaheen town in America so late in my years——San Antone was just about the only wahoo town I'd missed——But after Mexico City this San Antone of yours seemed——duller than the United States——the faces of red Texans in oil sitting in white flannel in air conditioned hotel lobbies while their long face grantwood wives hang a spike on their ears in a blue symphonic silo——reading newspapers—— Mexico City gassed me. It so gassed Cody he never recovered; in a month, blow, he made the final decision of his life he had seen so much in that brief traumatic time (ahem; aided by his blasting a full ten cans in a week or two to alleviate the gaspings of his direction-leaping conscience: he flew back across the U.S. in the airplane night (his first ride) contemplating the tragic mistake of his lands below. With Evelyn it was now going to be do or die; Cody was now trying to really adjust himself for the last time to an irrevocable Time-spanning eternity-flirting em-broiled vivacious sobbing-globbing pow'ful marriage. . . . After all those jungle nights and mad fantasies of Mexico City, espe-cially that last scene I'll tell here, you'd think he would look like a dead man upon arriving in Frisco——instead . . . but wait for that too. It was, in the park, a terrible scene between our two souls, I don't really know what happened, I was so surfeit with Mexico, he too, we——sat there at a rail in a Maximilian Park Coke plaza, over water with lillies and Mexican oarsmen with their Japanese dolls of the 'dobe tenements, balloons of children sunning in the biggest balloon of them all, trees rising in cricket hollow hall sides with vine, wild red cockflowers, the Tropic of Cancer park, more like jungle, with sudden Indian picnicker families squatting in a vale like a lost arm, the walls of the Aztec temple and the French tearful monarch with his dread-ful chin-moled Flaubertian beauty bedazzling and drooling at his side, that park, Chapultepec, ("Chapupec," as Bull's kid Willie called it, in a pet) (when we never made it in a picnic)—— we're having the national drink, Mission Orange, we're in the sun, successful arrivers on tourist roads, but suddenly more or less——"Say Cody what about that story you were going——not story but what happened in Victoria in the back of the lockers and whore-rooms, there," when Prado blasted our ears off off that magnificent super booming jukebox of the Indian proprietor afternoon in dives and sales de bailes——asking Cody about what he did while I myself was engaged with a bouncing señorita——instead of answering me he says, "Makes no difference, Jack."

"'Bout what? No difference?"

"About . . . things, remembrances, the machinic of recall and rehash, communication and closeness and all that foldebawble——"

"Not my words."

Cody doesn't realize how much I love him.

"——or be concerned, not, or that——but now there's no use, damn it"——with a distant look in his eyes suddenly there he is remembering Dave's delighted "Son of a *bitch*, god *damn*!" with the knee-slap Denver glee but instead Cody, vacantly from alleys of the past, draws it out in the forge of his own uses all twisted and ash caked, "Son of a bitch god *damn*!!" with heavy sullen awe, saying, his new tune, "I get more hung up! I get more hung up!" It was tragic the way he hit himself thinking those things and their reason over, terrible——"I'd ask what is it Cody but it's too late."

"It's nothing," says Cody not listening. From far away the curse comes, clouding his eyes——I'm powerless in front of such loneliness and imprisoned despair, I'm there teetering and afraid to talk——"What are you gonna do?" Nothing. In a few weeks——less than that——after one of our many bawdy nights and bordellos and wines and fillettes, why, Cody sat at kitchen table in the Mexican Indian Night Gloom and packed to go. I had a fever that night from dysentery and only vaguely noticed him departing for New York three thousand miles away and in the poor Ford. "All that again?" I say to Cody hearing of his departure. . . . meaning all that land and driving. But he left——"Got things to do"——at night now drove back, north, right out Insurgentes the way we come in, Ferrocarril Mexicano haunting his left hubcaps, in the dark, across the holy biblical plains by the first starlight the wise men made. Far across the dewy cacti the coyote crowed his oats with a long dog grin, a burly sack hung from a nail, an ikon flickered in the tree, the wines of repentance flowed in the stream. Bent over his wheel like a madman, shirtless, hatless, the moon leering on his shoulder, the apex of the night sweeping back in a fast shroud, he unrolled his old Ford joint by cracking the door over the humps and billdales of the Pan American Hiway through the Fold and Void of Earth Old . . . poor Crafeen, he made his mew in a churchyard marble pew. The bowl of Old Okiah, flung from northern lips of stars, caromed from the baldy temple of the Lazy King; they brought news of a tune. Feverish in his middles, here he goes crackowing across the desert and back to Texas up; alone now and in inky night he redone the mountains and the passes, he passed the parapets and crevasse dwellers in their apron of night. Did he see any lights?

IN VICTORIA Cody Pomeray, his headlights pointed to the corner of a yard as he waited for his boy Victor who went in for a minute to find out if his sister knew his wherabouts whether fiesta dance or pulque saloon or mambo dive in peanut and Sunkist counter back by Tequila Square; waiting, Cody saw and heard a bunch of nervous children giggling about him and now the headlights were revealing them to the hide and seek gang in the other Mexico post suppertime alley, but, so, when Cody eventually swung car around, Victor returned, and hits flush on children at fence instead of just part on them, they ain't there at all because they never existed, he had a hallucination.

And the moment he's back in California——after the Ford broke down in Lake Charles, La. and he flew on in to marry Diane in Newark, and then re-crossed old hump to the Coast, he looks (you'd have thought dead) in a foto with Evelyn on newhoneymooning Market sidewalks of romantic boygirl Frisco the two of them cutting along like ads for the future——bright, neat, Cody his hair ruffled in the wind and over his forehead, a T-shirt, clean as snow now, inside a tweed cheap suity sports coat, trousers pressed, rippling and folding in the walk sun, his shoes amazing by the sad gray sidewalk, his hands holding Evelyn's, his arms folded, half grinning, an Irish youth almost pretty and certainly handsome and boyish, and her a regular doll of course with blond upfluffed braids of gold hair and chic suit and high-heels and handbag (a suede jacket, by God, with a suede cord belt), tweed and casual corduroy herringboning down the after——This is the picture of Cody in the first days of his reformed marriage. He's an institution by himself. He has the strength of the bourgeois and the lumpenproletariat all at once, he Out-Marxes Marx, he's a lad. . . . Shortly after this he unpacked his battered poor old pissass huge bungtrunk that I remember one time in Ozone Park, struggling with on a hipster New Year's, 1949; trunk I first saw with half-familiar socks and appurtenances of shirts sticking out all gray and dismal in the traveled emptiness. It was at my house——my mother——but that's the picture——Our, his children will look at that and say "My daddy was a strapping young man in 1950, he strutted down the street as cute as can be and for all a few troubles he had that Irish fortitude and strength——ah coffin! eatest thou old strength for thy meal, and throw worms?"

How can the tragic children tell what it is their fathers killed, enjoyed and what joyed in and killed them to make them crop open like vegetable windfalls in a bin . . . poor manure, man.

"How could he then——and as they say, after a grueling series of voyages overland in old cars and with——and the nights, fights, tears, reconciliations, packing, sewing up, in fact he got married just before that picture and that clear across the land—— so there he smiles in his youth, my father, my Cody——and now what fodder, what box thing——" Te Deum, the children will imagine gods for their fathers and myths for the forgotten mistakes of anonymity by glooms: no hope whatever of gleaning the secret from our ancestral he-doers and she-makers. He doeth, she maketh it: in the corn they sing. Blessed be the Lord, the Meek, the Union of these two souls amen. Let us pray in the great dark rains of a carnage . . . ask for knowledge . . . find a backrest for our doubt.

"Tutta tua vision fa manifesta, e lascia pur grattar." These lines are the foundations of a great design.

THE MAD ROAD, lonely, leading around the bend into the openings of space towards the horizon Wasatch snows promised us in the vision of the West, spine heights at the world's end, coast of blue Pacific starry night——nobone halfbanana moons sloping in the tangled night sky, the torments of great formations in mist, the huddled invisible insect in the car racing onwards, illuminate.——The raw cut, the drag, the butte, the star, the draw, the sunflower in the grass——orangebutted west lands of Arcadia, forlorn sands of the isolate earth, dewy exposures to infinity in black space, home of the rattlesnake and the gopher . . . the level of the world, low and flat: the charging restless mute unvoiced road keening in a seizure of tarpaulin power into the route, fabulous plots of landowners in green unexpecteds, ditches by the side of the road, as I look from here to Elko along the level of this pin parallel to telephone poles I can see a bug playing in the hot sun——swush, hitch yourself a ride beyond the fastest freighttrain, beat the smoke, find the thighs, spend the shiny, throw the shroud, kiss the morning star in the morning glass——madroad driving men ahead. Pencil traceries of our faintest wish in the travel of the horizon merged, nosey cloud obfusks in a drabble of speechless distance, the black sheep clouds cling a parallel above the steams of the CBQ——serried Little Missouri rocks haunt the badlands, harsh dry brown fields roll in the moonlight with a shiny cow's ass, telephone poles toothpick time, "dotting immensity" the crazed voyager of the lone automobile presses forth his eager insignificance in noseplates and licenses into the vast promise of life . . . the choice of tragic wives, moons. Drain your basins in old Ohio and the Indian and the Illini plains, bring your big muddy rivers through Kansas and the mudlands, Yellowstone in the frozen North, punch lake holes in Florida and L.A., *raise* your cities in the white plain, cast your mountains up, bedawze the west, bedight the West with brave hedgerow cliffs rising to Promethean heights and fame——plant your prisons in the basin of the Utah moon——nudge Canadian groping lands that end in arctic bays, purl your Mexican ribneck, America.

Cody's going home, going home.

Here are some of the letters prepared under the moon and mailed in love through these immensities and impossibilities of the land of his birth, "Dear Cody, No, it makes no difference now" (Lester Young's chorus of "You Can Count On Me," 1938)——Yes, Lester used to blow like a sonofabitch, it's time to say so, as, in Chicago we saw the children of the modern jazz night blowing their horns and instruments with belief; it was Lester started it all, the gloomy saintly serious goof who is behind the history of modern jazz and this generation like

Louis his, Bird *his* to come and be——his fame and his smoothness as lost as Maurice Chevalier in a stagedoor poster——his
drape, his drooping melancholy disposition in the sidewalk,
in the door, his porkpie hat ("At sessions all over the country
from Kansas City to the apple and back to L.A. they called him
Porkpie because he'd wear that gone hat and blow in it")——
what doorstanding influence has Cody gained from this cultural
master of his generation? what mysteries as well as masteries?
what styles, sorrows, collars, the removal of collars, the removal
of lapels, the crepesole shoes, the beauty goof, the——one night
I saw Lester, in a reverie on the stand, make such faces in his
thoughts as the audience of watchers (that)——the sneer, the
twitch, that Billie Holiday has too, that compassion for the
dead; those poor little musicians in Chicago, their love of Lester, early heroisms in a room, records of Lester, early Count,
suits hanging in the closet, tanned evenings at ballrooms, the
great tenor solo in the shoeshine jukebox, you can hear Lester blow from L.A. to Boston, Frisco to New York, Seattle to
Philly, Kansas City, Kansas to Kansas City, Missouri, 1935, '40,
Lester has a hold of the generation, in New York, swank apartment, Lionel droops by a twenty-story French window with a
listen to his Lester clarinet early solo on "Way Down Yonder in
New Orleans" (other side), sunk to hear, an Englishman discovering the greatness of America in a single Negro musician——
Lester is just like the river, the river starts in near Butte, Montana in frozen snow caps (Three Forks) and meanders on down
across states and entire territorial areas of dun bleak land with
hawthorn crackling in the sleet, picks up rivers at Bismarck,
Omaha and St. Louis just north, another at Kay-ro, another
in Arkansas, Tennessee, comes deluging on New Orleans with
muddy news from the land and a roar of subterranean excitement that is like the vibration of the entire land sucked of its gut
in mad midnight, fevered, hot, the big mudhole rank clawpole
old frogular pawed-soul titanic Mississippi from the North, full
of wires, cold wood and horn.

So Lester, began holding his horn high in nigger chicken-
shacks backstreet basie kaycee wearing greasy smeared corduroy bigpants and in torn flap smoking jacket without straw,
scuffle-up shoes all sloppy Mother Hubbard, soft, pudding, and

key-ring, early handkerchiefs, hands up, arms up, horn horizontal, shining dull in woodbrown shithouse with ammoniac piss from broken gut bottles around shitty pukey bowl and a whore sprawled in it legs spread in brown cotton stockings, bleeding at belted mouth, moaning "Yes" as Lester, horn placed, has started blowing, "blow for me you old motherfucker blow," 1938, it's 1938, Miles is still on his daddy's checkered knee, Louis's only got twenty years behind him, and Lester blows all Kansas City to ecstasy and now Americans from coast to coast go mad, and fall by, and everybody's picking up——what? This had no effect on Cody? he who stood beside me listening to Lester's Children in Chicago, he who——hung in a doorway waiting for his connection (with me dragged millionaires to hear Lester). "Dig him," Cody says with a sneer when we see Lester, just after Chicago, just before Mexico City, at Birdland, and Lester sneers at him from bandstand; this is the mark of the hip generation, "I'm hip, man, I'm hip."

Flying back across the fantastic land thus did Cody in his climaxes and, in the night time traveling, worried, look-ahead, gnawing, climactic, dolorous, thus did Cody——he is connected with Lester, all our horns came down. Tragic muling cat! on screechy hincty fence by cotton cloth and pin——In his ripest period Lester had let his horn half down and his head, consequently, because he didn't adjust mouthpiece, fell over ninety degrees in sadness; then finally, in his Baroque late hornings in the open void of American Nightclub, he'd let the horn fall all the way, adjusted the mouthpiece only in relation to the first fall, and hangs there, ninety degrees, largefaced, sad, blowing clichés in a masterful and cool manner, his hair long, his forearm busted, his shoes thick and crimson rich now (like chemical milk foam plastic rubber couches) instead of those old galoshes of his cartoon Born-thirty-years-too-soon youngmanhood in shacks, O Lester! Great name!

"I, much like him, incline, and do fall, I've given up just about like Lester you'd say but of course, but yes, that's apt—— he sure could blow——of course it's just music——I don't get frantic about music anymore of course, only the criticism in my mind." Cody talking, stern boned in a fixity pose, solid rock, the canny Scot, old Yeats, a future Dostoevsky of inflexible tragic convictions and irritabilities. Some generation. Some nigger. And that big void over the beloved bending head of the earth, God bless us all.

CHARLES ATKINSON, a singer in incomparable prose, the basis of modern prose his roughest outlines, the precursor to *Neurotica* and *Time-Life* and all crazy styles, the translator of Spengler's poem *Decline of the West*——a laurel wreath no less dylan, a poet of the cold bedewdrop't mornings in gray Ars Scotia! Hoil!

SHORT OF ONE TRIP Cody took to New York and the East Coast as if he wanted to see for the last time if there was any fame worthwhile and decided not so, he came among us for no reason and without warning; successfully married down with Evelyn for the past entire six months now what was it brought him *again* over that huge distance and incomprehensible-almost America, Cody——riding on free passes four thousand miles a southern route; sitting up in daycars blowing his piccolo flute——his stockings off, crossing the dark land, the day land, five days and five nights coming: Evelyn drove him to the yards, watched him cross those old rails shining so clean in their sooty blackbed, his bag, struggling eastward again——"Now darling, I'll bring Jack back as we agreed; I'll see *her*——" (*She* was having her baby, Cody's third then in all) "——and I'll be back."

"But why are you going?" poor Evelyn asked. Cody had no idea and all his answers were unsatisfying——but he came, and fluted overland like a Zenzi witch King in his dragoon, and arrived in New York for exactly the third time in his life. How far this was from that first dewy trip with rosy Joanna in 1946!——those bus dreams they'd shared, the innocence of American kids; far even from the time we returned together from that Cadillac ride, when, at least, Cody hoped to use New York as a port to Italy and Europe or anything and so'd come crushing in as he did, got married so fast, exploded so soon again, was now returned blind and blank. His chief message now was, "Can't talk no more," he stuttered, just, or fumbled, made no attempt to make sense when he spoke and with the same logical pertinacity that previously he'd spoken in immense coy logics with structures like the statute books and even the Corinthian pillars outside: he played his flute (that flute had really started in summer 1949, in fact the very almost day we got back and who do we hook up with in New York, up at 116th Street, Slim Buckle and Tom Watson re-arriving from their trip to Maine, their psychosomatic nightmare in the land just like "me and Cody," all brothers under the skin, sitting in a Riverside Park bench all longfaced, western hombre travel types occupying benches in the city of New York a minute, to hear the bird of dusk in a dreamy new known park: Cody played the flute instead of screwing Vicki the Chinese girl (another Vicki altogether), it was a sordid evening, Irwin accused the whole lot of being cruel to girls on purpose, me included, there also was Rhoda, she suffered, Big Slim, Tom, old poolhall saint Tom now older and bearded and big blue eyes but distant and no longer Cody's mentor but merely watcher of Cody's boy Slim, subsidiary sorrows and heading for a personal levelous grave in redder, more broken years——so all of us, we're never young enough, thirty'll do, forty'll do, fifty'll do, sixty, seventy, eighty'll do, no more——but that night, nothing, a flute) (and strangely now Cody less and less plays the flute, fact is the children have swallowed the mouthpiece in their toys)——

"But Cody," I say: "I'd a gone back with you immediate if you'd showed up like you said in seven weeks——I ain't got that money saved, I can't buy no truck now." ("I cain't build no new truck with what yore daddy left me last fall, yummer, so ease over sometime if you can and show me how to rig up this new Sears and Roebuck taint I ordered up, gives me an idea for a housetruck or some such silly ideee——")

"Wal," says Cody, "I'll go back alone then?" It appeared so, strange——but he was only in New York three days, I saw (in fact) little of him, was busy; he hooked up in other activities . . . already we weren't on speaking terms any more, old buddies of the night grown sad, just like once exuberant basketball quintets meeting in sad maturity hotel lobbies with their shamefaced wives (in Worcester). He had brought his heavy topcoat to New York winter, we walked by the tracks under clouds of perfect white steam and he said "Whoo! I'd forgot how cold the East is, cold as a sonumbitch, damn. I'm going back to California there."

"Back to Evelyn, huh?"

"What else, boy? Diane won't have me; I tried my best, I

pleaded with her seven hours straight, live at the end of Watsonville chain gang; I'll be in most every morning, get hers, one night with one, one with the other; women just don't understand." So he went back to his wife and daughters.

"Don't know why I came," he finally admitted cheerfully; he was through with New York, though; it wasn't made for Cody Pomeray. It takes a raw wild young town——if any exist, if Frisco, I mean San Francisco, d——We clapped hands in a gloom——we posed for a picture in a gray square; Cody's all stern and hardjaw, his hand's inserted in his Levi pocket like the upside down hand of a Napoleon and like a Gay Nineties banker and like a long lumberjack in a rangy mountain town, fingers board in, thumbs at ease out, his big hardbelt, workshirt severe and even military, and big square mountainous determination and simplicity face (like a dumb Canook), already raveled frowns in his head, concerns, lines, worries, the might of muscular righteous agreement with the self . . . that's Cody.

"'You Can Depend on Me,' man, that's the name of the record," said Lionel, "when Lester was really blowing and generated this excitement which was so *tremendous*, I've never known anything like it here in the United States——except perhaps, maybe, man, you know, when Cody, on his last trip, when he came for no reason, and went back, remember? and we all got high at that Deni party with Danny and Irwin and got in the cab in one fell gang and were at the *peak, Cody* was *blowing*, crazy, he was talking incessantly and with absolutely insanely excited agreement, an incredible speech and babble that had us all *gassed* . . . the vibration in the cab as the driver drove up Seventh Avenue was so tremendous I thought——I didn't think what the cabdriver could think——what next——explosion—— Cody *whaling* like ten men with gestures and excitements, he's saying 'Now listen fellas, ah, knowing full well' (and laughing that crazy laff, like as, an utter *maniac!*) 'but, and, if, ah, yes, you, but, ork, off,' *you* know Cody——"

"Yes," I said; saw Lionel that same night slumped against the wall of the apartment, exhausted, his face at one point during that night so Englishy and delightful grew so rosy in the middle of a Cody spiel, (playing tick-tack-toe Cody Lionel Danny Richman and me at a Deni Bleu party with rosy faces and that unmistakable golden davenport of a driving T-high), now depleted, Cody's just vanished in a flare of heels to get Josephine, Lionel's saying, dumbly like losing his father, "Where's Cody? Where's Cody? Where'd he go?" and we had to explain and console him on the floor.

"America's real mad," he always said, "Lester myboy Lester." He's proud of that name, stood on winter sidewalks with him. "And guys like C-o-d-y," pronouncing the name with his teeth, relishing it, "guys like C-o-d-y in America. Crazy."

"Cody," he said before he sailed for England, "things like Cody and you, my buddy my dear friend Jack, and Lester, makes me want to come back to America and stay, yessir, hmph," adjusting his umbrella and going to London again, stooped, like Alistair Sims, another book.

A BLADE OF GRASS waves in the sunny Frisco afternoon, it grows out through the greasy rocks of the railroad track of Cody; tars smell, are warm, railroad executives who once were vain young clerks with slicked hair and pressed pants now roll themselves baggily along Track 66 ramps and wander in the drowsy nothing afternoon of motors, breathing engines, steams, rattles, hammer on a nail, flybuzz, truck-trailer rumble and a rattling power mixer somewhere——also hot, fragrant soot flows across the immortal unclouded afternoon with its Oakland mountains to the left and Mission hills to the right all drowsy dormant. Here comes the conductor with his red and white lamps and red flag——a fly——a piece of paper riding and tumbling along the tracks——an orange Ford truck sleepily backs out from the Special Agent's scarred, brown, stained, antique W. C. Fields door ("Ain't you an old Follies g-i-r-l?")——dishes from the depot counter rattle in a dull lull, the Filipino scullion angles by with no expression——Someone yells and wakes me up from an afternoon dream. . . . Geometric visual perspective vanishments of double rails into crowded sooty distance with backs of boxcars reposant by vague "storage" signs on meaningful buildings——figures crossing the general raily layout in a flat void of activity-afternoons: unused cabooses waiting for the evening shapeup so they can go be backbroken and jawboned and rattleheaded in a mountain brake——rickety orange baggage carts sitting in sun-glints softened by smoke——those track-grasses waving like hair here, making green carpets there for the rails'

flow to points unseen——Smoke works up from over by the
roundhouses and general Out Our Way toolshops where at
evening overalls all greased are hung up on nails by lockers in
brown sad light . . . the light of Cody, work, night, fatherhood,
gloom. An empty wine bottle, (Guild), a board, a carton paper
torn from limey interiors of boxcars that were probably loaded
in similarly sleepy New Orleans yards way down and over the
crazy old land of our dreams——nameless rusty metal and tin
hunks——Old Cody Pomeray ain't been here yet!——at these
final rails that deadhead hump of greeneries, the holy Coast is
done, the holy road is over.

Tonight the stars'll be out.

YET, AND YES, THERE'S CODY POMERAY . . . cuttin to work.
A new day is dawning in the blue lagoon east over Oakland
there, a silent sad Coast Line truck trailer sits by a skeletal shed
in the soft dawn of all America marching to this last land, this
receiving California——the engine bell is tolling in the yards,
the crew clerk's office is a-still, the dew is on the road again and
as forever, the sleepy rumbling truck goes by, the workman's
"liquid shuffle" boots and bigneck secrecy in the dark morn,
it's Cody going deadheading to Watsonville where he wanted
Joanna to live and the other girl to live and me to live and's
going someday to his grave with Evelyn in his weep——The tree
is still by the blue morning stars just like in Selma, Sabinal and
Alabama——I'm a fool, the new day rises on the world and on
my foolish life: I'm a fool, I loved the blue dawns over racetracks
and made a bet Ioway was sweet like its name, my heart went
out to lonely sounds in the misty springtime night of wild sweet
America in her powers, the wetness on the wire fence bugled
me to belief, I stood on sandpiles with an open soul, I not only
accept loss forever, I am made of loss——I am made of Cody,
too——he who rode a boxcar from New Mexico to L.A. at the
age of ten with a bread underarm, (hanging from the grabiron)
(over the couplings), he who lost his mother at nine, his father
was a bum, a wino alcoholic, his brother ignored him or (as Jim
for a few years) condescended to confide his cruelties to him
(gruff partnerships and trainings)——Cody no soft Ben joyed
in, he sat alone by the railroad track. All the thoughts Cody
has while working, the things he jots in pencil ("enfolded in

bleak Obispo with bleak Buckle and even bleaker Helen")——
the first day in these yards, when we walked almost arm-in-arm
in a December spring and everything was alright——ah, all the
mornings you suffer and all for nothing and forgetfulness and
the necessary natural blankness of men——and Cody is blank at
last. Tree, tree, in thy bushy stand make me a vow: promise my
star of pity still burns for me. Now flights of doublecrossing
black birds come winging across the paleness of the East, the
morning-star lips in that pale woodshed sky, she shudders and
shits sparks of light and waterfalls of droop and moistly hugens
up a cunt for cocks of eyes crowing across the fences of Golden
Southern America in her Dawn.

Goodbye Cody——your lips in your moments of self-pos-
sessed thought and new found responsible goodness are as silent, make as least a noise, and mystify with sense in nature, like
the light of an automobile reflecting from the shiny silverpaint
of a sidewalk tank this very instant, as silent and all this, as a
bird crossing the dawn in search of the mountain cross and the
sea beyond the city at the end of the land.

Adios, you who watched the sun go down, at the rail, by my
side, smiling——

Adios, King.

VISIONS OF GERARD

GERARD DULUOZ was born in 1917 a sickly little kid with a rheumatic heart and many other complications that made him ill for the most part of his life which ended in July 1926, when he was 9, and the nuns of St. Louis de France Parochial School were at his bedside to take down his dying words because they'd heard his astonishing revelations of heaven delivered in catechism class on no more encouragement than that it was his turn to speak——Saintly Gerard, his pure and tranquil face, the mournful look of him, the piteousness of his little soft shroud of hair falling down his brow and swept aside by the hand over blue serious eyes——I would deliver no more obloquies and curse at my damned earth, but obsecrations only, could I resolve in me to keep his fixed-in-memory face free of running off from me——For the first four years of my life, while he lived, I was not Ti Jean Duluoz, I was Gerard, the world was his face, the flower of his face, the pale stooped disposition, the heartbreakingness and the holiness and his teachings of tenderness to me, and my mother constantly reminding me to pay attention to his goodness and advice——Summers he'd lain a-afternoons, on back, in yard, hand to eyes, gazing at the white clouds passing on by, those perfect Tao phantoms that materialize and then travel and then go, dematerialized, in one vast planet emptiness, like souls of people, like substantial fleshy people themselves, like your quite substantial redbrick smokestacks of the Lowell Mills along the river on sad red sun Sunday afternoons when big scowling Emil Pop Duluoz our father is in his shirtsleeves reading the funnies in the corner by the potted plant of time and home——Patting his sickly little Gerard on the head, "*Mon pauvre ti Loup*, me poor lil Wolf, you were born to suffer" (little dreaming how soon it would be his sufferings'd end, how soon the rain, incense and teary glooms of the funeral which would be held across the way in St. Louis de France's cellar-like basement church on Boisvert and West Sixth).

For me the first four years of my life are permeant and gray with the memory of a kindly serious face bending over me and being me and blessing me——The world a hatch of Duluoz Saintliness, and him the big chicken, Gerard, who warned me to be kind to little animals and took me by the hand on forgotten little walks.

469

"*Allo zig lain——ziglain——zigluu——*" he'd say to our cat, in a little high crazycatvoice and the cat'd look plain and blank back at him as though the cat language was the true one but also they understood the words to portend kindness and their eyes followed him as he moved around our gray house and suddenly they'd bless him unexpectedly by jumping on his lap at dusk, in the quiet hour when water's burbling on the stove the starchy Irish potatoes and hushsilence fills ears in houses announcing Avalokitesvara's blessed everlasting presence grinning in the swarming shadows behind the stuffed chairs and tasseled lamps, a Womb of Exuberant Fertility the world and the sad things in it laughable, Gerard the least and last to dis-acknowledge it I'd bet if he were here to bless my pencil as I undertake and draw breath to tell his pain-tale for the world that needs his soft and loving like.

"Heaven is all white" (*le ciel yé tout blanc*, in the little child patois we spoke our native French in), "the angels are like lambs, and all the children and their parents are together forever," he'd tell me, and I: "*Sont-ils content?* Are they happy?"

"They couldnt be anything else but happy——"

"What's the color of God?——"

"*Blanc d'or rouge noir pi toute*——White of gold red black and everything——" is the translation.

Lil Kitty comes up and gricks wet nose and teethies against Gerard's outheld forefinger, "Whattayawant, *Ploo pli?*"—— Would I could remember the huddling and the love of these forlorn two brothers in a past so distant from my sick aim now I couldnt gain its healing virtues if I had the bridge, having lost all my molecules of then without their taste of enlightenment.

He bundles me in the coat and hat, he'll show me how to play in the yard——Meanwhile smoke sorrows from red dusk roofs in winter New England and our shadows in the brown frozen grass are like remembrances of what must have happened a million aeons of aeons ago in the Same and blazing Nirvana-Samsara Blown-Out-Turned-On light.

I do believe I remember the gray morning (musta been a Saturday) when Gerard showed up at the cottage on Burnaby Street (when I was 3) with the little boy whose name I cant forget and the consistency of it like lumps of gray mud, Plourdes——Balls of sorrow are his name——Sniveling at the nose which he had no handkerchief to blow, dirty, in a little holey sweater, Gerard himself in his long black parochial stockings and the highbutton shoes, they're standing in the yard by the little wooden stoop in back of to the side where the meadows of sadness are faced (with their stand of gleary pines beyond and in which on rainy days I could see the beginning of the Indianface Fog)——Gerard wants Mama Ange to give the little boy Plourdes some bread and butter and bananas, "*Ya faim*, he's hungry"——From a poor and ignorant family, likely, and they'd never feed him except at supper, or an occasional (perhaps) lard sandwich, Gerard was acute enough to realize the child was hungry and was crying on account of hunger and he knew the munificence of his own mother's home and took him thereunto and asked for food for him——Which my mother gave the boy, who now, years later, I see, or just saw, on a recent visit to Lowell, six feet tall and 200 pounds and a lot of bread and butter and bananas and child largesse has gone into the bulkying of his decaying mountain of flesh——A glimmer memory maybe in his truckdriver brain of the tiny sickling who mourned for him and fed him and blessed him in the long ago——Plourdes——A Canadian name containing in it for me all the despair, raw gricky hopelessness, cold and chapped sorrow of Lowell——Like the abandoned howl of a dog and no one to open the door——For Plourdes his fate, for me:——Gerard to open it to the Love of God, whereby, now, 30 years later, my heart, healed, is stillwarm, saved——Without Gerard what would have happened to Ti Jean?

I'm on the porch muffled in bundlings watching the little Christly drama——My mother goes in the kitchen and butters bread and peels bananas, with that heartbreaking, slow, fumbly motion of mothers of the world, like old Indian Mothers who've pounded tortillas and boiled mush across clanks of millenniums and wind-howl——My heart is where it belongs.

My father comes home from work and hears the story and says "How he's got a heart, that child!" shaking his head and biting his lips by the stove.

It was only many years later when I met and understood Savas Savakis that I recalled the definite and immortal *idealism* which had been imparted me by my holy brother——And even later with the discovery (or dullmouthed amazed hang-middled mindburnt waking re discovery) of Buddhism, Awakenedhood——Amazed recollection that from the very beginning I, whoever "I" or whatever "I" was, was destined, destined indeed, to meet, learn, understand Gerard and Savas and the Blessed Lord Buddha (and my Sweet Christ too through all his Paulian tangles and bloody crosses of heathen violence)——To awaken to pure faith in the bright one truth: All is Well, practice Kindness, Heaven is Nigh.

Gerard's sad eyes first foretold it——In the dream already ended, which all this is——His face so tranquil and compassionate, various pictures of him we had, one in particular in front of me now, that was taken in his (probably) fifth year, on the porch of the Lupine Road house the which, when I recently visited it, revealed to me (to my infant's old gaze) the ancient form of Earth-Beginnings in the form of a fluted porch-ceiling-light-globe that I had studied and studied with infant eyes long afternoons of drowse sun or warm March, in my crib——When, seeing it just recently, age 33, its contours rejoined me deeply with the long forgotten contours of Gerard's face and peculiar soft hair, and little Raskolnik parochial shirt, and high black stockings——Nay, and unto the very brown slats of the house next door, and even more nay-worse-so unto the very stone

"castle" on top of the hill a field away which I had completely
forgotten in my rational memory and saw with awe in maturity
what already I'd divined unconsciously in teenage reveries of
"Doctor Sax and the Castle of the Great World Snake" all to be
explained ahead in the *Duluoz Legend*——The said porch is the
scene of the holy little snapshot here kept, Gerard sitting on the
rail with my sister Nin (then 3), holding her hand, smirky-ing
in the sun the two of them as some aunt or paternity godfather
snaps the shot, the long forgotten snow of human hopes pal-
ing into browner stains in old photoisms——I see there in the
eyes of Gerard the very diamond kindness and patient humility of the Brotherhood Ideal propounded from afar down the
eternal corridors of Buddhahood and Compassionate Sanctity,
in Nirmana (appearance) Kaya (form)——My own brother, a
spot of sainthood in the endless globular Universes and Chilli-
cosm——His heart under the little shirt as big as the sacred
heart of thorns and blood depicted in all the humble homes of
French-Canadian Lowell.

Behold:——One day he found a mouse caught in Scoop's
mousetrap outside the fish market on West Sixth Street——
Faces more bleak than envenomed spiders, those who invented
mousetraps, and had paths of bullgrained dullishness beaten
to their bloodstained doors, and crowed in the sill——For that
matter, on this gray morning, I can remember the faces of the
Canucks of Lowell, the small tradesmen, butchers, butter and
egg men, fishmen, barrelmakers, bums in benches (no benches
but the oldtime sidewalk chair spitters by the dump, by banana
peels steaming in the midday broil)——The hungjawed dull
faces of grown adults who had no words to praise or please
little trying-angels like Gerard working to save the mouse from
the trap——But just stared or gawped on jawpipes and were silly
in their prime——The little mouse, thrashing in the concrete,
was released by Gerard——It went wobbling to the gutter with
the fishjuice and spit, to die——He picked it tenderly and in his
pocket sowed the goodness——Took it home and nursed it,
actually bandaged it, held it, stroked it, prepared a little basket
for it, as Ma watched amazed and men walked around in the
streets "doin good for themselves" rounding up paper beyond
their beans——Bums! all!——A thought smaller than a mouse's

turd directed to the Sunday Service Mass necessity, and that usually tinged by inner countings how much they'll plap in th'basket——I dont remember rationally but in my soul and mind Yes there's a mouse, peeping, and Gerard, and the basket, and the kitchen the scene of this heart-tender little hospital—— "That big thing hurt you when it fell on your little leg" (because Gerard could really feel empathetically that pain, pain he'd had enough to not be apprentice at the trade and pang)——He could feel the iron snap grinding his little imagined birdy bones and squeezing and cracking and pressing harder unto worse-than-death the bleak-in-life——For it's not innocent blank nature made hills look sad and woe-y, it's men, with their awful minds——Their ignorance, grossness, mean petty thwarthings, schemes, hypocrite tendencies, repenting over losses, gloating over gains——Pot-boys, bone-carriers, funeral directors, glove-wearers, fog-breathers, shit-betiders, pissers, befoulers, stenchers, fat calf converters, utter blots & scabs on the face of it the earth——"Mouse? Who cares about a gad dam mouse——God musta made em to fit our traps"——Typical thought——I'd as soon drop a barrel of you-know-what on the roof of my own house, as walk a mile in conversation about one of them——I dont count Gerard in that seedy lot, that crew of bulls——The particular bleak gray jowled pale eyed sneaky fearful French Canadian quality of man, with his black store, his bags of produce, his bottomless mean and secret cellar, his herrings in a barrel, his hidden gold rings, his wife and daughter jongling in another dumb room, his dirty broom in the corner, his piousness, his cold hands, his hot bowels, his well-used whip, his easy greeting and hard opinion——Lay me down in sweet India or old Tahiti, I dont want to be buried in *their* cemetery——In fact, cremate me and deliver me to *les Indes*, I'm through——Wait till I get going on some of these other bloodlouts, for that matter——Yet not likely Gerard ever, if he'd have lived, would have fattened as I to come and groan about peoples and in plain print loud and foolish, but was a soft tenderhearted angel the likes of which you'll never find again in science fictions of the future with their bleeding plastic penis-rods and round hole-machines and worries about how to get from Pit to Pisspot which is one millionth of a billionth of an inch further in endlessness of our gracious Lord than the earth speck (which I'd spew) (if I were you)

(Maha Meru)——Some afternoon, Gerard goes to school——It had been on a noontime errand when sent to the store to buy smoked fish, that he'd found the mouse——Now, smiling, I see him from my overstuffed glooms in the parlor corner walking up Beaulieu Street to school with his strapped books and long black stockings and that peculiar gloomy sweetness of his person that was all things to me, I saw nothing else——Happy because his mouse was fed and repaired and safe in her little basket——Innocent enough comes our cat in the mid drowses of day, and eats, and leaves but the tail, enough to make all Lowell Laugh, but when Gerard comes home at 4 to see his tail-let in the bottom of the poor little basket he'd so laboriously contrived, he cried——I cried too.

My mother tried to explain that it wasnt the cat's fault and nobody's fault and such was life.

He knew it wasn't the cat's fault but he took Nanny and sat her on the rocking chair and held her jowls and delivered her an exhortation no less:

"*Méchante!* Bad girl! Dont you understand what you've done? When will you understand? We dont disturb little animals and little things! We leave them alone! We'll never go to heaven if we go on eating each other and destroying each other like that all the time!——without thinking, without knowing!——wake up, foolish girl!——realize what you've done!——Be ashamed! shame! crazy face! stop wiggling your ears! Understand what I'm tellin you! It's got to stop some fine day! There wont always be time!——Bad girl! Go on! Go in your corner! Think it over well!"

I had never seen Gerard angry.

I was amazed and scared in the corner, as one might have felt seeing Christ in the temple bashing the moneychanger tables everywhichaway and scourging them with his seldom whip.

WHEN MY FATHER comes home from his printing shop and undoes his tie and removes 1920's vest and sits himself down at hamburger and boiled potatoes and bread and butter of the prime with the kiddies and the good wife, the proposition is put up to him why men be so cruel and mice betrayed and cats devour the rest——Why we were made to suffer and be harsh in return, one the other, and drop turds of iron on brows of hope, and mop up sick yards and sad——"I'll tell you, Ti Gerard, little one, in life it's a jungle, man eats man either you eat or get eaten——The cat eats the mouse, the mouse eats the worm, the worm eats the cheese, the cheese turns and eats the man——So to speak——It's like that, life——Dont cry and dont bother your sweet lil head over these things——All right, we're all born to die, it's the same story for everybody, see? We eat the cow and the cow gives us milk, dont ask me why."

"Yes, why——why do men make traps for little mice?"

"Because they eat their grain."

"Their old grain."

"It's grain that's in our bread——Look here, you eat it your bread? I dont see you throw it on the floor! and you dont make *passes* with the dust in the corner!"——*Passes* were the name Gerard had invented for when you run your bread over gravy, my mother'd do the soaking and throw the *passes* all around the table, even to me in my miffles and bibs at the little child flaptable——But because of our semi-Iroquoian French-Canadian accent *passe* was pronounced *PAUSS* so I can still hear the lugubrious sound of it and comfort-a-suppers of it, *M'ué'n pauss*, as you'd expect Bardolph to remember his cockwalloping heigho's of Eastcheap——My father is in the kitchen, young and primey, shirtsleeves, chomping up his supper, grease on his chin, bemused, explaining moralities to his angels——They'll grow 12 feet tall in the grave ere the monstrance that contains the solution to the problem be held up to shine and make true belief to shine, there's no explaining your way out of the evil of existence——"In any case, eat or be eaten——We eat now, later on the worms eat us."

Truer words were not spoken from any vantage point on this packet of earth.

476

"Why? *Pourquoi?*" cries lil Gerard with his brows forming woe and inabilities——"I dont want it to be like this, me."

"Though you want or not, it is."

"I dont care."

"What you gonna do?"

He pouts; he'll go to heaven, that's what; enough of this beastliness and compromising gluttony and compensating muck——Life, another word for mud.

"Come, come, little Gerard, maybe there's something you know that *we* dont know"——My father always did concede, Gerard had a deep mind and deep things to think that didnt find nook in insurance policies and printer's bills——They'd never write Gerard a policy but in eternity, he knew we were here a short while, and pathetic like the mouse, and O pathet-icker like the cat, and O worse! like the father-cant-explain!

"Awright," he'll go to bed and sleep it off, he'll tuck me in too, and kiss Ti Nin goodnight and the mouse be no lesser for her moment in his hands at noon——Together we pray for the Mouse. "Dear Lord, take care of the little mouse"——"Take care of the cat," we add to pray, since that's where the Lord'll have to do his work.

Ah, and the winds are cold and blow forlorner dust than they'll ever be able to invent in hell, in Northern Earth here, where people's hopes though warm fail to conceal the draft, the little draft that works all night moving curtains over radia-tor heat and sneaks around your blanket, and would bring you outdoors where russet dawn-men with coldchapped ham-hands saw and pound at wood and work and steam with horses and curse the Satan in the air that made all Russias, Siberias, Ameri-cas bare to the blasts of infinity.

Gerard and I huddle in the warm gleeful bed of morning, afraid to get out——It's like remembering before you were born and your hap was at hand and Karma forced you out to start the story.

"Where is she the little mouse now?"

"This morning. The cat has shat her in the woods (*Le chat l'a shiez dans l'champ*)——with the little pipi yellow you see in the snow down there, see it?"

"*Oui.*"

"*Voilà* your fly of last summer, she's dead too——"

We think it over in motionless trance, as Ma prepares Pa's breakfast in the fragrant kitchen below.

"Angie," says Dad at the stove, "that kid'll break my heart yet——it hurt him so much to lose his little mouse."

"He's all heart."

"With his sickness inside——Ah, it busts my head——Eat or get eaten——not men?——Hah!——There's a gang downtown would, if their guts were big enough."

Gerard's feeling of the holiness of life extended into the realm of romance.

A drunkard under an ample tent was never more adamant concerning how his little sister should behave——"Mama, look what Ti Nin's doing she's going to school with her overshoes flopping and throwing her behind around like a flapper!" he yelled one morning looking out the window——It was one of those days when he was suffering a rheumatic fever relapse and had to stay in bed, weeks sometimes, some days worse than others——"Aw look at her!——" He was horrified——He refused to let her do it, when she came home at noon he had a speech worked out for her——"I'm telling you Gerard, you'll be a priest some day!" my mother'd say.

Meanwhile the kids at church did the sign of the cross some of them with the following words:

> "Au nom du père
> Ma tante Cafière
> Pistalette de bois
> Ainsi soit-il"

Meaning

> "In the name of the Father
> My Aunt Cafière
> Pistolet of wood
> Amen"

There's my pa——Emil Alcide Duluoz, at that time, 1925 a hale young printer of 36, dark complexioned, frowning, serious, hardjawed but soft in the gut (tho he had a gut so hard when

he oomfed it and dared us kids butt our heads in it or punch
fists off it and it felt like punching a powerful basketball)——5:7,
Bretonsquat, blue eyed——He had a habit I cant forget, even
now I just imitated it, lighting a small fire in the ashtray, out of
cigarette pack paper or tobacco wrapping——Sitting in his chair
he'd watch the little Nirvana fire consume the paper and render
it black crisp void, and understand, mayhap, the bigger kindling
of the 3,000 Chillicosms——That which would devour and digest to safety——A little matter of time, for him, for me, for you.

Too, he'd take fresh crisp MacIntosh apples of the Fall and
sit in his easy chair and peel em with his pocket knife, making
long tassels around and around the fruitglobe so perfect you
could have hung them like tassels' canopies from chandelier to
chandelier in the Hall Tolstoy, the which we'd take and sling
around and I'd eat em in like great tapeworms and they'd end
up flung out in the garbage can like coils of electric wire around
and around——After which he'd eat his peeled apple at the gisty
whitemeat cutsurface with great slobbering juicy bites that had
all the world watering——"Imitate the roar of a lion! Imitate a
tiger cat! Imitate an elephant!"——Which he'd do, in his chair,
for us, evenings in New England, Gerard on one knee, me on
the other, Nin on his lap——That is, when ever there was no
poker game to speak of downtown.

"And you my little Gerard, why do you look so pensive tonight? What's goin on in that little head?" he'd say, hugging his
Gerard to him, cheek against soft hair, as Nin and I watched
rave lip't and rapt in the happiness of our childhood, little
dreaming what quick work the winds of outside winter would
do against the timbers and tendons of his poor house.

In the name of the father, the son, and the Holy Ghost,
amen.

Gerard had birds that neighbor and relative could swear did
know him personally, they came to his windowsill in the time
of his long illnesses, especially Spring, when his rheum-rimmed
eyes'd look out on fresh undefiled mornings like captured prin-
cesses in must towers——Vile visitations of bile'd turned him
green, and white, in the night, his bedpan beneath the bed, but
for the birds he had roses for words——"*Arrive, mes ti's anges*,
Come my little Angels," and he'd sow his (by Ma prepared)

breadcrumbs on the sill and on the short slope roof up there where his sickroom was (a location for a room that forever frets my brain when in gray dreams I dream of houses, that location is always the one that makes me sink, somewhere to the north and west of misery, by peaks, mystery, gables)——Cherry blossom'd May brought him hundreds of gay birds with gloomy beaks that chattered on the roof around his crumbs——But he'd cry: "Why dont the little birds come to me?! Dont they know I wont hurt them?"

"Of course they dont, they cant know——for all they know you're a boy, and boys hurt birds."

"And birds hurt boys?"

"And birds never hurt a boy, but the boy will stone his dozen and upset the nests of a dozen fledgelings in his nasty prime."

"Why? Why is everyone so mean? Didnt God see to it that we——of all people——*people*——would be kind——to each other, to animals."

God made no provisions for that winter.

The birds chatter, come come close at hand, he glees and jumps up and down at his pillow: "That one's coming, that one I'm tellin you, he'll end up in my hand!"

"I hope," my mother'd say with wise eyes and unwisely in the night pray for it and worthily praise him——My father couldnt believe it.

"Ah, if I could buy him birds!"

"Just one little bird, just ONE," he'd cry, as I sat in my little chair by the bed watching, fingering the crumb pan with little pudgy fingers so fat they called me *Ti Pousse*, Little Thumb.

"Come here, Little Thumb, look, the little grey bird, doesnt he look like he wants to eat in my hand and give me a little kiss?"

"Yes."

"Wouldnt you like to kiss that little thing?"

"Yes."

"Yes yes little bird come on."

But a chance noise of breadtruck drives the whole flock away *kavroom*, for the next tree, where they jabber the new news—— Tears come to Gerard's eyes, his lips form a fateful pout, a groan comes, it means "Ah what's the use——if I loved them any more they'd have honey and balm for breakfast and have beaks

of gold, yet they avoid me like a rat dripping bacteria——like a falcon——like a man."

"Gerard," my mother'd explain, "dont make yourself sad about the little birds. Do you know why? Because God sees and knows you love them and he'll reward you."

"In heaven I'll have all the birds I want."

"Yes in heaven——and maybe on earth, have courage, patience."

With his little belly he heaves a heigh ho sigh, 't'would be a good thing to be in that snowy somewhere and rosy nowhere where patience is just a word and no bellies burdenly pain. "Yes, in heaven there are birds, millions of birds, even smaller than these, big like butterflies, smaller, like ants, white like an angel——everywhere." He'd turn to his drawing board propped on his lap and start drawing his dreary eternities and dreams of paradise. He was an amazing artist at the age of 8. He drew pictures that my old man actually disbelieved as his own when he saw them a-nights:

"Gerard did that?——look here!"

Ditto my father's friends——To prove it he'd draw right in front of them, boats sailing on the blue ocean (copied from the Saturday Evening Post), birds, bridges, lambies, people's hats——Also he had an erector set and built up impossible engineering marvels like vast complicated ferris wheels and race cars and the usual tote-cranes and trucks that were borrowed from the book of instructions——Heaving the book aside he'd of a sick morning (as I watch) whip up beautiful little baby carriages or baby cribs for Nin to put her dolls in at noon, all set with little draperies——I wonder if she still remembers these latter days as she stares at Television's rancid blight whole evenings in her home parlor, waiting to join him in Heaven——

For me he'd concoct delights at the drop of my saying it, "Make me a *ritontu*," which is I dont know what, and he'd make a crazy construction and I'd play with it and try to un-screw it and chew the edges of it——

Then the birds would come flocking and singin in rollicking nations around our holy roof again, and he'd call for bread, and multiply it in crumbs, and sow it to the sisters who pecked and picked——

"*Vien, vien, vien,*" the picture of him hand outstretched and helpless in bed calling at the open window for the celestial visitors, enough to make my heart leap from a cold indifferent lair (of late)——

He never got his hand on a bird, naturally, and what transformation might have taken place in such a case I do not know——

Meanwhile Dr. Simpkins came and went with his oldfashioned satchel and his listen-tubes and pipes and pills and pumps and surprised us all by his gravity and inability to speak——He had no long hope for the life of Gerard.

I didnt understand anything that was going on, I was rosy plump Little Thumb *Ti Pousse* glad to be in the same world as Gerard.

One night we're on the kitchen floor with the Boston American, I remember distinctly the pinksheet Hearst evening news, on the front page is the photo of a woman who's murdered someone, I take my scissors and stab her right in the eye impaling the paper on the linoleum——"*Non non Ti Jean* never do that!" Didnt understand (as I remember myself) the glee, the mindless happy glee that went into that vigorous stab——But to Gerard the mindlessness was precisely the horror and the currency of a hateful hopeless world——"*Non, non,* never do anything like that,——Ah poor Ti Pousse, you dont understand——Look, take out the scissors, fix her eyes"——We smooth the ruffled paper, stroke the paper lady's eyes, brood over our sin, rectify hells, fruition good Karmas for ourselves, repent, go to confession—— His lips tsk tsk and pout——Kissable Gerard, to kiss him and that pout of pain must have been as soft a sin as kissing a lamb in the belly or an angel in her wing——He gave me piggybacks to prove that other pastimes were better and that I was forgiven—— He even let me "beat him up" in mock fights where we rolled on the linoleum and I screamed——

With my little hands clasped behind me I stand at the kitchen window, sometime not long after, on a gray blizzard day, watching the inky snowflakes descend from infinity and hit the ground where they become miraculous white, whereby I understand why Gerard was so white and because of man came of such black sources——It was by virtue of his pain-on-earth, that his black was turned to white.

It's a cold crisp morning in October, Gerard is going to school
with his books and bread and butter and banana lunch and an
apple——I watch him going down Beaulieu Street, alone——
Gangs of kids run around——At the end of Beaulieu Street is the
large gravel play yard of the Green Public School where because
the kids werent Catholics the nuns have been telling Gerard
and Nin and the kids of St. Louis de France Parochial School
that they have tails concealed beneath their trousers——Which
some of us (I for one) seriously believe——At that street Gerard
turns right to go to St. Louis which is right there along three
wooden fences of bungalows, first you see the nun's home,
redbrick and bright in the morning sun, then the gloomy edifice of the schoolhouse itself with its longplank sorrowhalls
and vast basement of urinals and echo calls and beyond the
yard, with its special (I never forgot) little inner yard of cinder
gravel separated from the big dirt yard (which becomes a field
down at Farmer Kenny's meadow) by a small granite wall not a
foot high, that everyone sits on or throw cards against——The
big game is card slinging, the bubblegum cards with pictures
of movie stars and baseball players (Great God! it musta been
Vilma Banky and Rogers Hornsby with young faces on the
fragrant bubblegum cards)——They are flung against the wall,
nearest wins——The big game at recess——Gerard comes slowly
ruminating in the bright morn among the happy children——
Today his mind is perplexed and he looks up into the perfect
cloudless empty blue and wonders what all the bruiting and
furor is below, what all the yelling, the buildings, the humanity, the concern——"Maybe there's nothing at all," he divines
in his lucid pureness——"Just like the smoke that comes out of
Papa's pipe"——"The pictures that the smoke makes"——"All
I gotta do is close my eyes and it all goes away"——"There *is*
no Mama, no Ti Jean, no Ti Nin, Papa——no me——no *kitigi*"
(the cat)——"There is no earth——look at the perfect sky, it says
nothing"——Little snivelly Plourdes is losing at a game of cards
in the corner, the bullies buffet him out——"He's crying——he
only thinks of his luck and his luck is worse"——"his luck is
mixed up in the bad and the poor"——"Ah the world"——To
the other end is the *Presbytère* (Rectory) where Father Père
Lalumière the *Curé* lives, and other priests, a yellow brick house
awesome to the children as it is a kind of chalice in itself and we

imagine candle parades in there at night and snow white lace at breakfast——Then the church, St. Louis de France, a basement affair then, with concrete cross, and inside the ancient smooth pews and stained windows and stations of the cross and altar and special altars for Mary and Joseph and antique mahogany confessionals with winey drapes and ornate peep doors——And vast solemn marble basins in which the old holy water lies, dipped by a thousand hands——And secret alcoves, and upper organs, and sacrosanct backrooms where altar boys emerge in lace and blacks and the priests march forth bearing kingly ornaments——Where Gerard had been and kept on going many a time, he liked to go to church——It was where God had his due——"When I get to Heaven the first thing I'm gonna ask God is for a beautiful little white lamb to pull my wagon——*Ai,* I'd like to be there right away already, not have to wait——" He sighs among the birds and kids, and over at the end of the yard are gathered the teacher nuns getting ready for the morning bell and lineup, the morning breeze moving their black robes and pendant black rosaries slightly, their faces pale around rheumy eyes, delicate as lacework their features, distant as chalices, rare as snow, untouchable as holy bread of the host, the mothers of thought——Striking awe in children——Monastic ladies devoted to sewing and devout service in their gloomy redbrick hermitage there where we saw them in the windows with their cap flares and cameo profiles bent over rosaries or missals or embroideries, they themselves mostly all the time vigorously curiously digging the scene outdoors——In fact right now a hobo from Louisiana and the East Texas Oil fields who happens to be passing thru Lowell, lies in the straw grass below the Green School fence, knee on knee, grass in mouth, contemplating the flawless void and humming the blues and what could be the thoughts of the old nun at the window watching him——"Lazy bum! (*Paresseux!*)"——"Robber!——Sinner!"

Typical of Gerard that he doesnt look to the fields, the trees down further where Farmer Kenny's fields become a thicket and after a few cottages of Centerville spurting morning smoke the distant hills and horizon meadows of on-to-Dracut and New Hampshire and all that pale brown promise of the sere continent——Gerard was inward turned like a chalice of gold bearing a single holy host, bounden to his glory doom——He

sits on the little wall contemplating the kids, and the bum in the field, the nuns in the window, the little girls hopskotching beyond and where Ti Nin is screaming with the rest——"Little crazy, look at her gettin all excited——she doesnt understand the blue sky this morning, she doesnt care like a little kitty——But look——" he looks up, mouth agape——"There's nothing there, not a cloud, not a sound——just like it was water upsidedown and what's the bugs down here?" The air is crisp and good, he breathes it in——The bell rings and all the scufflers go to shuffle in the dreary lines of class by class with the head nun overlooking all, the parade ground formation of the new day, latecomers running thru the yard with flying books——A dog barking, and the coughs, and the gritty gravel under restless many little shoes——Another day of school——But Gerard has eyes up to sky and knows he'll never learn in school what he'd like to learn this morning from that sky of silent mystery, that heartbreaking sayless blank that wont tell men and boys what's up——"It's the eye of God, there's no bottom——"

"Gerard Duluoz, you're not in line——!"

"Yes, Sister Marie."

"Silence! The Mother *Supérieure* is going to talk!"

"Ssst! Mercier! Give me my card!"

"It's mine!"

"It is not!"

"Shut your trap! (*Famme ta guêle*)."

"I'll fix you."

"P r r r r t"

"Silence!"

Silence over all, the rustle of the wind, the banners of two hundred hearts are still——Under that liquid everpresent impossible-to-understand undefiled blue——

A few Fall trees reach faint red twigs to it, smoke-smells wraith to twist like ghosts in noses of morning, the saw of Boisvert Lumberyard is heard to whine at a log and whop it, the rumble of the junkmen's cart on Beaulieu Street, one little kid cry far off——Souls, souls, the sky receives it all——Nobody can comment on the only reality which is Crystal Naught not even Viking Press——Not even Père Lalumière who now with clothesline-fresh garments parades downhall in the *Presbytère* whistling to his room, *lacrimae rerum* of the world in his smarting

morning eyes, pettling and purtling with his lips at thought of
the good *cortons* porkscraps for breakfast comin up just now
soon's he gets his dud-o's on and sweeps officially to another day
as *Curé* of the World——A good man and true, like Our Mayor
in his City Hall and the President Coolidge at his desk 500
miles South to the morning that brights the Potomac same as
brights the Merrimac of Lowell——In other words, and who will
be the human being who will ever be able to deliver the world
from its idea of itself that it actually exists in this crystal ball of
mind?——One meek little Gerard with his childly ponderings
shall certainly come closer than Caesarian bust-provokers with
quills and signatures and cabinets and vestal dreary laceries——
I say.

O, to be there on that morning, and actually see my Gerard
waiting in line with all the other little black pants and the little
girls in their own lines all in black dresses trimmed with
white collars, the cuteness and sweetness and dearness of that
oldfashion'd scene, the poor complaining nuns doing what
they think is best, within the Church, all within Her Folding
Wing——Dove's the church——I'll never malign that church that
gave Gerard a blessed baptism, nor the hand that waved over
his grave and officially dedicated it——Dedicated it back to what
it is, bright celestial snow not mud——Proved him what he is,
ethereal angel not Festerer——The nuns had a habit of whacking
the kids on the knuckles with the edge part of the ruler when
they didnt remember 6×7, and there were tears and cries and
calamities in every classroom every day——And all the usual——
But it was all secondary, it was all for the bosom of the Grave
Church, which we all know was Pure Gold, Pure Light.

That bright understanding that lights up the mind of the soldier
who decides to fight to death——"O Arjuna, fight!"——That's
what's implied at the rail of the altar of repentance, for the
repenter gives up self and admits he was a fool and can only be
a fool and may his bones dissolve in the light of forever——*All*
my sins, leaving not jot or tittle out, even unto the smallest
least-noticeable almost-not-sin that you could have got away
with with another interpretation——But you bumbling fool
you're a mass of sin, a veritable barrel of it, you swish and
swash in it like molasses——You ooze mistakes thru your frail

crevasses——You've bungled every opportunity to bless somebody's brow——You had the time, you will have the time, you'll
yawn and wont understand——Ah you're a bum as you are——
'T were better to dissolve you——The Holy Milk you act like
a curdler and a bacteria in it, yellow scum, sometimes purple
or pot green——As you are, it wont do——The Lord *knows* he
made a mistake——We talk about "the Lord" out of the corner
of our hands for want of a better way to describe the undefil-
able emptiness of the blue sky on such mornings as the morning Gerard wondered——It's typical of us to compromise and
anthropomorphalize and He it, thus attributing to that bright
perfection of Heaven our own low state of selfbeing and self-
hood and selfconsciousness and selfness general——The Lord
is no-*body*——The Lord is no bandyer with forms——All condi-
tional and talk, what I have to say, to point it out——Miserable
as a dull sermon on a dull rainy morning in a damp church in
the North and Sunday to boot——We are baptized in water for
no unsanitary reason, that is to say, a well-needed *bath* is implied——Praise a woman's legs, her golden thighs only produce
black nights of death, face it——Sin is sin and there's no erasing
it——We are spiders. We sting one another.

No man exempt from sin any more than he can avoid a trip
to the toilet.

Gerard and all the boys did special novenas at certain seasons
and went to confession on Friday afternoon, to prepare for
Sunday morning when the church hoped to infuse them with
some of the perfection embodied and implied in the concept
of Christ the Lord——Even Gerard was a sinner.

I can see him entering the church at 4 P.M., later than the
others due to some errand and circumstance, most of the other
boys are thru and leaving the church with that lightfooted way
indicative of the weight taken off their minds and left in the
confessional——The redemption gained at the altar rail with
penalty prayers, doled out according to their lights and dark-
nesses——Gerard doffs his cap, trails fingertip in the font, does
the sign of the cross absently, walks half-tiptoe around to the
side aisle and down under the crucified tablets that always
wrenched at his heart when he saw them ("*Pauvre Jésus*, Poor
Jesus") as tho Jesus had been his close friend and brother done
wrong indeed——He genuflects and enters the pew and puts

little knees to plank, the plank is worn and dusted with a million kneeings morning noon and night——He starts a preliminary prayer——"Hail Mary——" in French the prayer: "*Je vous salue Marie pleine de grâce*"——Grace and grease interlardedly mixed, since the kids didnt say "grace," they said "grawse" and no power on earth could stop them——The Holy Grease, and good enough——"*Le Seigneur est avec vous——vous êtes bénie entre toutes les femmes*"——Blessed among and above all women, and they saw their mother's and sister's eyes as one pair of eyes——"*Et Jésus le fruit de vos entrailles*"——"entrailles" the powerful French word for Womb, *entrails*, none of us had any idea what it meant, some strange interior secret of Mary and Womanhood, little dreaming the whole universe was one great Womb——The coil of that thought and wording, not conducive to a true understanding of the nature and emptiness-aspect of Wombhood, the perfect blue sky's our Womb (but not our guts and coils)——"*Sainte Marie, Mère de Dieu, priez pour nous, pécheurs, maintenant et à l'heure de notre mort*"——No comma in the minds and thoughts of the little boys (and their fathers) who ran it straight thru "*pécheurs maintenant et à l'heure de notre mort*", sinner always right unto death, no help no hope, born——

"*Ainsi soit-il*," amen, none of them knowing either what that meant, "thus it is," it is what is and that's all it is——thinking *ainsi soit-il* to be some mystic priestly secret word invoked at altar——The innocence and yet intrinsic purity-understanding with which the Hail Mary was done, as Gerard, now knelt in his secure pew, prepares to visit the priest in his ambuscade and palace hut with the drapes that keep swishing aside as repentent in-and-out sinners come-and-go burdened and disemburdened as the case may be and is, amen——

Now Gerard ponders his sins, the candles flicker and testify to it——Dogs burlying in the distance fields sound like casual voices in the waxy smoke nave, making Gerard turn to see—— But in and throughout all a giant silence reigns, shhhhhing, throughout the church like loud remindful evercontinuing abjuration to stay be straight and honest with your thought——

"I pushed lil Carrufel"——It took place in the schoolyard, with throw-cards Gerard had contrived a card-castle at midday recess, the first grader knocked it down coming too close and curious, without reflection Gerard raged and pushed him, really mad, "Look what you done to my house——Nut!" then instantly repented and too late——Now he pouts to concede: "But it was my house——*mautadit fou*" (a form of dyazam fool, or, drazyam, or whichever, used by children and in fact everyone including prelates, congressmen and druggists)——"But when I pushed him he turned pale, he didn't know anybody was gonna push him at that moment and that was the moment that hurt him——*Ya venu blême comme une vesse de carême* (He got pale as a lenten fart)——His heart sank, and it's *me* that done it——It's a clear sin——My Jesus wouldnt have liked that watching from his cross"——He turns eyes up and around to the cross, where, with arms extended and hands nailed, Jesus sags to his footrest and bemoans the scene forever, and always it strikes in Gerard's naturally pitiful heart the thought "But *why* did they do that?"——Looking there at the foolish mistakes of past multitudes, plain as day to see, right on the wall——The massive silence enveloping the graceful gentle form of hip and loincloth, limbs and knees, and the tortured thin breast——And the unforgettable downcast face——"God said to his son, we've got to do this——they decided in Heaven——and they did it——it happened——INRI!"——"INRI——that means, it happened!—— or else, INRI, the funny ribbon on the cross of the lover they killed——and, they put a nail through it"——Whatever mysterious thoughts that lie beneath in the bent heads of people and children in churches and temples century after century——"He's crying!" moaned Gerard, seeing it all.

Two other sins to confess: the deep sin of looking at Lajoie's and Lajoie could look at his, at the urinals, Wednesday morning, in the corner, for a long time——On purpose——Gerard blushes to think of it——He sees the strange image of Lajoie's, different, curlier than his, he twinges to urinate namelessly and twists in his knee rest with the horror of his shame, not knowing—— Sin's so deeply ingrained in us we invent them where they aint and ignore them where they are——Across his mind sneaks the proposition to avoid referring to the priest——But God will know——And to mock the kindly ear of the listener Priest, who expects what there is, by removing one whit, a human sin divine to discover——"Poor Father Priest, what'll he know if I dont tell him? he wont know anything and he'll comfort me and send me off with my prayer, well it'll be a big sin to hide him a sin——like if I'd spit in his eyes when he's dead, like"——

The fortunate priest, Père Anselme Fournier, of Trois Rivières Quebec, the last of twelve sons but the first in his father's eye, pink-handed where he might have been horny-handed from the soil of Abraham, receives Ti Gerard in the confessional by sliding open his panel and bending quick ear obedient and loaded with long afternoon——Coughs revolve around the ceiling and sail and set in the pew sea, a knee-rest scrapes Sca-ra-at! with a harsh harmonizing *bang* from the altar where a worker creaks around with chair and candle snuffer——

"Bénit" is the only word, "bless," Gerard hears as the priest quickly mutters the introductory invocation and then his ear is ready——Gerard can faintly smell the adult breath and that peculiar adult smell of old teeth in old mouths long at work—— "Bz bz bz" he hears as his predecessor in the confessional, just let out, prays fast and furious his repentant penalty rosaries at the rear seat half on his way to run out and slap cap on and run screaming across dusk stained fields of stubble and raw mud, to gangs in clover dales wrangling with rocks——A bird zings across the reddening late sky and over the roof of St. Louis de France, as though the Holy Ghost wanted it——Saffron is the east, white is the west, where a bank cloud hides the thrower Sun, but soon it'll all girdle and engolden and be rich red gambling sunset splendor, again, as yesterday——No school tomorrow is the frost announcement in the field grass, in the quiet corners of the schoolyards——Gerard senses all this but his day's work is just begun.

"My father, I confess that I pushed a little boy because he made me mad."

"Did you hurt him?"

"No——but I hurt his heart."

The priest is amazed to hear the refinement of it, the hair-splitting elegant point of it, ("He'll make a priest" he inner grins).

"Yes, you're right, my child, it hurt his heart. *Why* did you push him?" he pursues in conclusion with that sorrowful tender sorriness of the priest in the confessional as tho and as much to say "When all is said and done, why do we sit here and have to admit the sinningness of man."

"I pushed him because he had broken my little cardhouse."

"Ah."

"It made me mad."

"You flew into a rage."

"*Oui.*"

"You didnt think——He was younger than you."

"*Oui*, just a little boy of the first grade."

"Aw,"——regretfully the fine priest looks around at Gerard briefly, commiserating as tender heart to tender heart——Ah, a scene going on in the little church of dusk! And somewhere wars!

"Well," to conclude, "you know your sin——You'll have to keep your patience the next time——Keep well your idea, that you hurt his heart if not his body"——admiringly——"you've understood it yourself. I am certain," he takes trouble to add in spite of an overburdened afternoon of work in there, "that the Lord understands you.——And, there is something else you want to tell me."

"Yes my father"——and this Gerard says feeling like a beast piling animality on animality,——"I——er——" he stammers, confuses, and blushes, and stops.

"I'm waiting, my little boy."

Quickly Gerard whispers him the news about the urinal, Saturday Afternoon Confessions in St. All's had never heard a lurider admission it would seem from the stealth of his ps-ps'es.

"Ah, and did you touch his little dingdong?" (*Sa tite gidigne*).

Gerard: "*Aw non!*" glad he has a loophole and all because he never thought of it, mayhap——

"Well," sighing, "I have confidence in you my child that you'll never do it again. And something else? anything else?"

Gerard instantly remembers still another sin, forgotten until then——"I told the Sister I had studied my Catechism, and no I hadnt studied it."

"And you didnt know it?"

"Yes I knew it, but from another time, I remembered."

("Ah, that's no sin," thinks the Priest) and closes up accounts with: "Very well, that's all? Well then, say your rosary and fifteen Hail Mary's."

"Yes my father."

The gracious slide door slides, Gerard is facing the good happy wood, he runs out and hurries lightfoot to the altar, fit to sing——

It's all over! It was nothing! He's pure again!

He prays and bathes in prayers of gratitude at the white rail near the blood red carpet that runs to the stainless altar of white-and-gold, he clasps little hands over leaned elbows with hallelujahs in his eyes——To be God, and to've seen his eyes, looking up at my altar, with that beholding bliss, all because of some easy remission of mine, were hells of guilt I'd say——But God is merciful and God above all is kind, and kind is kind, and kindness is all, and it all works out that the mortal angel at the altar rail as the church hour roars with empty silence (everybody gone now, including the last priest, Gerard's priest) is bathed in blisskindness whether it would be pointed out or not that other easier ways might do the job as well, which may be doubtful, snow being snow, divinity divinity, holiness holiness, believing believing.

All alone at the rail he suddenly becomes conscious of the intense roaring of the silence, it fills his every ear and seems to permeate throughout the marble and the flowers and the darkening flickering air with the same pure hush transparency—— The heaven heard sound for sure, hard as a diamond, empty as a diamond, bright as a diamond——Like unceasing compassion its continual near-at-hand seawash and solace, some subtle solace intended to teach some subtler reward than the one we've printed and that for which the architects raised.

Enveloped in peaceful joy, my little brother hurries out the empty church and goes running and skampering home to supper thru raw marched streets.

"Did you go to your confession, Lil Gerard?"

"*Oui.*"

"Come eat, my golden angel, my *pitou,* my lil Mama's cabbage."

I'm sitting stupidly at a bed-end in a dark room realizing my Gerard is home, my mouth's been open in awe an hour you might think the way it's sorta slobbered and run down my cheeks, I look down to discover my hands upturned and loose on my knees, the utter disjointed inexistence of my bliss.

Me too I'd been hearing the silence, and seeing swarms of little lights thru objects and rooms and walls of rooms.

None of the elements of this dream can be separated from any other part, it is all one pure suchness.

Would I were divinest punner and tell how the cold winds blow with one stroke of my quick head in this harsh unhospitable hospital called the earth, where "thou owest God a death"— Time for me to get on my own horse—

The Kat is up on the sink actually fascinated by the drip drip of the faucet, there he is with his paws under him and his tail curling down and his ruminative quickglancing face bending and earpricking to the phenomena, as tho he was trying to figure out, or pass the time, or make fun of us—But Mama has a headache, it's a cold windy night in Old February and Pa is out late at work (playing poker backstage B.F.Keiths maybe with W.C.Fields for all I know with my drawn yawp masque)— The winds belabor at the windows of the kitchen, Ma is on the couch on the newspapers where she's flopped in despair, it's about 9:30, supper dishes have been put away (tenderly by her own hands) and now she lies there head back on a kew-pie cushion with an ice pack on her head—The woodstove roars—Gerard and I are at the stove rocker, warming our feet, Nin is at the table doing her "*devoir*" (homework)—

"Mama you're sick," demurs Gerard with the gods, with his piteous voice, "what are we going to do."

"Aw it'll go away."

He goes over and lays his head against hers and waits to hear her cure—

"If I had some aspirins."

"I'll go get you some—at drugstore!"

"It's too late."

"It's only 9:30—I'm not afraid."

"Poor Lil Gerard it's too cold tonight and it's too late."

"No mama! I'll dress up good! My hat my rubbers!"

"Run. Go to Old Man Bruneau, ask him for a bottle of aspirin—the money is in my pocketbook."

Together Gerard and I peer and probe into the mysterious pocketbook for the mysterious nickles and dimes that are always there intermingled with rosaries and gum and powder puffs—

Little Gerard runs and puts his muffcap and draws it over his ears and draws on his rubbers with that tragic bent over motion no angels who never lived on earth could know——A cold key in a tight lock, our situation, the skin so warm, thin, the night of Winter so broad and cool——So Saskatchewan'd with advantage——

"Hurry up my golden, Mama'll be afraid——"

"I'll go get your medicine and you'll be all right, just watch!"

Gleefully he goes off, the door admits Spectre into the kitchen an instant and he slams it——I watch him tumble off.

Beaulieu Street going down towards West Sixth, 4 houses, to the Fire House, is swept by dusts——The lamp on the corner only serves to accentuate by contrast the lightlessness in the general air——The stars above are no help, they twinkle in a vain freeze——The cold sweeps down Gerard's neck, he tries to bundle in——He hurries around the corner and down West Sixth, towards the lights of the big corner at Aiken and Lilley and West Sixth where bleak graypaint tenements stand with dull brown kitchen lights under the hard stars——Not a soul in sight, a few cruds of old snow stuck in the gutters——A fine world for icebergs and stones——A world not made for men—— A world, if made for anything, made for something dead to sympathy——Since sympathizing there'll not be in it ever——He runs to warm up——

Down at Aiken the wind from the river hits him full-blast with a roar, around the corner, bringing with it the odor of cold rocks in the river's ice, and the savor of rust——

"God doesnt look like he made the world for people" he guesses all by himself as it occurs in his chilled bones the hopeless sensation——No help in sight, the utter helpless-ness up, down, around——The stars, rooftops, dusty swirls, streetlamps, cold storefronts, vistas at street-ends where you know the earth-flat just continues on and on into a round February the roundness of which and warm ball of which wont be vouchsafed us Slav-level fools as but flat——Flat as a tin pan——So for winds to swail across, a man oughta lie down on his back on a cold night and miss those winds——No thought, no hope of the mind can dispel, nay no millions in the bank, can break, the truth of the Winter night and that we are not made for this world—— Stones yes, grass and trees for all their green return I'd say no to judge from their dead brownness tonight——A million may buy a hearth, but a hearth wont buy rich safety——

Gerard divines that all of this is pure division, a grief of separation, the cold is cold because there are two to know it, the cold and he who is en-colded——"If it wasnt for that, like in Heaven, . . ."

"And Mama has a headache, aw God why'd you do all this suffering?"

En route back with the aspirins he hears a forlorn rumble in Ennell Street, it's the old junkman coming back from some over extended work somewhere in windswept junkslopes, his horse is steaming, his steel-on-wood-wheels are grinding grit on grit and stone on stone and wind swirls dust about his burlaps, as he smiles that tooth-smile of the cold between embittered lips, you see the suffering of his mitts and the weeping in his beard, the woe——Going home to some leaky rafter——To count his rusty corsets and by-your-leaves and tornpaper accounts and pile-alls——To die on his heap of mistakes, finally, and what was gained in emptiness you'll never find debited or credited in any account——What the preachers say not excepted——"Poor old man, he hasnt got a nice warm kitchen, he hasnt got a mother, he hasnt got a little sister and little brother and Papa, he's alone under the hole under the open stars——If it was all together in one ball of wool——!——" The horse's hooves strike sparks, the wheels labor to turn into West Sixth, the whole shebang sorrows out of sight——Gerard approaches our house, our golden kitchen lights and pauses on the cold porch for one last look up——The stars have nothing to do with anything.

In some other way, he hopes.

"There, your little hands are cold——thank you my child—— bring me a glass of water——I'll be all right——Mama's sick tonight——"

"Mama——why is it so cold?"

"Dont ask me."

"Why did God leave us sick and cold? Why didnt he leave us in Heaven."

"You're sure we were there?"

"Yes, I'm sure."

"How are you sure?"

"Because it cant be like it is."

"*Oui*"——Ma in her rare moments when thinking seriously she doesnt admit anything that doesnt ring all the way her bell of mind——"but it is."

"I dont like it. I wanta go to Heaven. I wish we were all in Heaven."

"Me too I wish."

"Why cant we have what we want?" but as soon as he says that the tears appear in his eyes, as he knows the selfish demand——

"Aw Mama, I dont understand."

"Come come we'll make some nice hot chocolate!——"

"Hot chocolate! (*Du coco!*)" cries Ti Nin, and I echo it: "Klo Klo!"

The big cocoa deal boils and bubbles chocolating on the stove and soon Gerard forgets——

If his mortality be the witness of Gerard's sin, as Augustine Page One immediately announced, then his sin must have been a great deal greater than the sin of mortals who enjoy, millionaires in yachts a-sailing in the South Seas with blondes and secretaries and flasks and engineers and endless hormone pills and Tom Collins Moons and peaceful deaths——The sins of the junkman on Ennell Street, they were vast almost as mine and brother's——

In bed that night he lies awake, Gerard, listening to the moan of wind, the flap of shutters——From where he lies he can just see one cold sparkle star——The fences have no hope.

Like, the protection you'd get tonight huddling against an underpass.

But Gerard had his holidays, they bruited before his wan smile——New Year's Eve we're all in bed upstairs under the wall-papered eaves listening to the racket horns and rattlers below and out the window the dingdong bells and sad horizon hush of all Lowell and towards Kearney Square where we see the red glow embrowned and aura'd in the new (1925) sky and we think: "A new year"——A new year with a new number and a new little boy with candlelight and *kitchimise* standing radiant in the eternities, as the old, some old termagant with beard and scythe, goes wandering down the darkness field, and on the sofa arms of the parlor chairs even now the fairies are dancing——

Gerard and Nin and I are sitting up in the one bed of conclave, with a happy smile he's trying to explain to us what's really happening but by and by the drunks come upstairs with wild hats to kiss us——Some sorrow involved in the crinkly ends of pages of old newspapers bound in old readingroom files so that you turn and see the news of that bygone New Year's day, the advertisements with top hats, the crowds in Hail streets, the snow——The little boy under the quilt who will have X's in his eyes when the rubber lamppost ushers in his latter New Years Eves, one scythe after another lopping off his freshness juices till he comes to bebibbling them from corny necks of bottles——And the swarm in the darkness, of an ethereal kind, where nobody ever looks, as if if they did look the swarms ethereal would wink off, winking, to wink on again when no one's watching——Gerard's bright explanations about dark time, and cowbells——Then we had our Easter.

Which came with lilies in April, and you had white doves in the fields, and we went seesawing thru Palm Sunday and we'd stare at those pictures of Jesus meek on the little *azno* entering the city and the palm multitudes, "The Lord has found that nice little animal there and he got up on his back and they rode into the city"——"Look, the people are all glad"——A few chocolate rabbits one way or the other was not the impress of our palmy lily-like Easter, our garland of roses, our muddy-earth Spring sigh when all in new shoes we squeaked to the church and outside you could smell the fragrant cigarettes and see men spit and inside the church was all dormant and adamant like wine with white white flowers everywhere——

We had our Fourth of July, some firecrackers, some fence sitting spitting of sparks, warm trees of night, boys throwing torpedoes against fences, general wars, oola-oo-ah popworks at the Common with the big bomb was the finale, and popcorn and Ah Lemonade——

And Halloween: the Halloween of 1925, when Ma dressed me up as a little Chinaman with a queu and a white robe and Gerard as a Pirate and Nin as a Vamp and old Papa took us by the hand and paraded us down to the corner at Lilley and Aiken, ice cream sodas, swarms of eyes on the sidewalks——

All the little children of the world keep quickly coming and going to the holidays that only slowly change, but the quality of the brightness of their eyes monotonously reverts——Seeds, seeds, the seed sown everywhere blossoming the fruit of our loom, living-but-to-die——There's just no fun in holidays when you know.

All the living and dying creatures of the endless future wont even wanta be forewarned——wherefore, I should shut up and close up shop and bang shutters and broom my own dark and nasty nest.

At this time my father had gotten sick and moved part of his printing business in the basement of the house where he had his press, and upstairs in an unused bedroom where he had some racks of type——He had rheumatism too, and lay in white sheets groaned and saying "*La marde!*" and looking at his type racks in the next room where his helper Manuel was doing his best in an inkstained apron.

It was later on, about the time Gerard got really sick (long-sick, year-sick, his last illness) that this paraphernalia was moved back to the rented shop on Merrimack Street in an alley in back of the Royal Theater, an alley which I visited just last year to find unchanged and the old graywood Colonial one storey building where Pa's pure hope-shop rutted, a boarded up ghost-hovel not even fit for bums——And forlorner winds never did blow ragspaper around useless rubbish piles, than those that blow there tonight in that forgotten alley of the world which is no more forgotten than the heartbreaking and piteous way Gerard had of holding his head to the side whenever he was interested or bemused in something, and as if to say, "Ay-you, world, what are our images but dust?——and our shops,"——sad.

Nonetheless, lots of porkchops and beans came to me via my old man's efforts in the world of business which for all the fact that 't is only the world of adult playball, procures tightwad bread from hidden cellars the locks of which are guarded by usurping charlatans who know how easy it is to enslave people with a crust of bread withheld——He, Emil, went bustling and bursting in his neckties to find the money to pay rents, coalbills (for to vaunt off that selfsame winter night and I'd be ingrat to make light of it whenever trucks come early morning and dump their black and dusty coal roar down a chute of steel into our under bins)——Ashes in the bottom of the furnace, that Ma herself shoveled out and into pails, and struggled to the ashcan with, were ashes representative of Poppa's efforts and tho their heating faculties were in Nirvana now 'twould be loss of fealty to deny——I curse and rant nowaday because I dont want to have to work to make a living and do childish work for other men (any lout can move a board from hither to yonder) but'd rather sleep all day and stay it up all night scrubbling these visions of the world which is only an ethereal flower of a world, the coal, the chute, the fire and the ashes all, imaginary blossoms, nonetheless, "somebody's got to do the work-a the world"——Artist or no artist, I cant pass up a piece of fried chicken when I see it, compassion or no compassion for the fowl——Arguments that raged later between my father and myself about my refusal to go to work——"I wanta *write*——I'm an *artist*"——"Artist shmartist, ya cant be supported all ya life——"

And I wonder what Gerard would have done had he lived, sickly, artistic——But by my good Jesus, with that holy face they'd have stumbled over one another to come and give him bread and breath——He left me his heart but not his tender countenance and sorrowful patience and kindly lights——

"Me when I'm big, I'm gonna be a painter of beautiful pictures and I'm gonna build beautiful bridges"——He never lived to come and face the humble problem, but he would have done it with that *noblesse tendresse* I never in my bones and dead man heart could ever show.

It's a bright cold morning in December 1925, just before Christmas, Gerard is setting out to school——Aunt Marie has him by the hand, she's visiting us for a week and she wants to take a morning constitutional, and take deep breaths and show Gerard how to do likewise, for his health——Aunt Marie is my father's favorite sister (and my favorite aunt), a talkative openhearted, teary bleary lovely with red lipstick always and gushy kisses and a black ribbon pendant from her specs——While my father has been abed with rheumatism she's helped somewhat with the housework——Crippled, on crutches, a modiste——Never married but many boyfriends helped her——The spittin image of Emil and the lover of Gerard's little soul as no one else, unless it be the cold eyed but warm hearted Aunt Anna from up in

Maine——"Ti Gerard, for your health always do this, take big
clacks of air in your lungs, hold it a long time, look" pounding
her furpieced breast, "see?"——

"*Oui*, Matante Marie——"

"Do you love your Matante?"

"My Matante Marie I love her so big!" he cries affectionately
as they hug and limp around the corner, to the school, where
the kids are, in the yard, and the nuns, who now stare curiously
at Gerard's distinguished aunt——Aunt Marie take her leave
and drops in the church for a quick prayer——It's the Christmas
season and everyone feels devout.

The kids bumble into their seats in the classroom.

"This morning," says the nun up front, "we're going to study
the next chapter of the catechism——" and the kids turn the
pages and stare at the illustrations done by old French engravers
like Boucher and others always done with the same lamby gray
strangeness, the curlicue of it, the reeds of Moses' bed-basket I
remember the careful way they were drawn and divided and the
astonished faces of women by the riverbank——It's Gerard's turn
to read after Picou'll be done——He dozes in his seat from a bad
night's rest during which his breathing was difficult, he doesnt
know it but a new and serious attack on his heart is forming——
Suddenly Gerard is asleep, head on arms, but because of the
angle of the boy's back in front of him the nun doesnt see.

Gerard dreams that he is sitting in a yard, on some house
steps with me, his little brother, in the dream he's thinking
sorrowfully: "Since the beginning of time I've been charged to
take care of this little brother, my Ti Jean, my poor Ti Jean who
cries he's afraid——" and he is about to stroke me on the head,
as I sit there drawing a stick around in the sand, when suddenly he gets up and goes to another part of the yard, nearby,
trees and bushes and something strange and gray and suddenly
the ground ends and there's just air and supported there at
the earth's gray edge of immateriality, is a great White Virgin
Mary with a flowing robe ballooning partly in the wind and
partly tucked in at the edges and held aloft by swarms, countless swarms of grave bluebirds with white downy bellies and
necks——On her breast, a crucifix of gold, in her hand a rosary
of gold, on her head a star of gold——Beauteous beyond bounds
and belief, like snow, she speaks to Gerard:

"Well my goodness Ti Gerard, we've been looking for you all morning——where were you?"

He turns to explain that he was with . . . that he was on. . . . that he was. . . . that . . .——He cant remember what it is that it was, he cant remember why he forgot where he was, or why the time, the morning-time, was shortened, or lengthened——The Virgin Mary reads it in his perplexed eyes. "Look," pointing to the red sun, "it's still early, I wont be mad at you, you were only gone less than a morning——Come on——"

"Where?"

"Well, dont you remember? We were going——come on——"

"How'm I gonna follow you?"

"Well your wagon is there" and Oh yes, he snaps his finger and looks to remember and there it is, the snow-white cart drawn by two lambs, and as he sits in it two white pigeons settle on each of his shoulders; as prearranged, he bliss-remembers all of it now, and they start, tho one perplexing frown shows in his thoughts where he's still trying to remember what he was and what he was doing before, or during, his absence, so brief——And as the little wagon of snow ascends to Heaven, Heaven itself becomes vague and in his arm with head bent Gerard is contemplating the perfect ecstasy when his arm is rudely jolted by Sister Marie and he wakes to find himself in a classroom with the sad window-opening pole leaning in the corner and the erasers on the ledges of the blackboards and the surly marks of woe smudged thereon and the Sister's eyes astonished down on his:

"Well what are you doing Gerard! you're sleeping!"

"Well I was in Heaven."

"What?"

"Yes Sister Marie, I've arrived in Heaven!"

He jumps up and looks at her straight to tell her the news.

"It's your turn to read the catechism!"

"Where?"

"There——the chapter——at the end——"

Automatically he reads the words to please her; while pausing, he looks around at the children; Lo! all the beings involved! And look at the strange sad desks, the wood of them, and the carved marks on them, initials, and the little boy Ouellette

(suddenly re-remembered) as usual with the same tranquil unconcern (outwardly) whistling soundlessly into his eraser, and the sun streaming in the high windows showing motes of room-dust——The whole pitiful world is still there! and nobody knows it! the different appearances of the same emptiness everywhere! the ethereal flower of the world!

"My sister, I saw the Virgin Mary."

The nun is stunned: "Where?"

"There——in a dream, when I slept."

She does the sign of the cross.

"Aw Gerard, you gave me a start!"

"She told me come on——and there was a pretty little white wagon with two little lambs to pull it and we started out and we were going to Heaven."

"*Mon Seigneur!*"

"A little white wagon!" echo several children with excitement.

"Yes——and two white pigeons on my shoulder——doves—— and she asked me 'Where were you Gerard, we've been waiting for you all morning'"——

Sister Marie's mouth is open——"Did you see all this in a dream?——? here now?——in the room."

"Yes my good sister——dont be afraid my good sister, we're all in Heaven——but we dont know it!"——"Oh," he laughs, "*we dont know it!*"

"For the love of God!"

"God fixed all this a long time ago."

The bell is ringing announcing the end of the hour, some of the children are already poised to scamper on a word, Sister

Marie is so stunned everyone is motionless——Gerard sits again and suddenly over him falls the tight overpowering drowsiness around his heart, as before, and his legs ache and a fever breaks on his brow——He remains in his seat in a trance, hand to brow, looking up minutes later to an empty room save for Soeur Marie and the elder Soeur Caroline who has been summoned——They are staring at him with tenderest respect.

"Will you repeat what you told me to Sister Caroline?"

"Yes——but I dont feel good."

"What's the matter, Gerard?"

"I'm starting to be sick again I guess."

"We'll have to send him home——"

"They'll put him to bed like they did last year, like before—— He hasnt got much strength, the little one."

"He saw Heaven."

"Ah"——shrugging, Sister Caroline——"that"——nodding her head——

Slowly, at 9:30 o'clock that morning, my mother who's in the yard with clothespins in her mouth sees him coming down the empty schooltime street, alone, with that lassitude and dragfoot that makes a chill in her heart——

"*Gerard is sick*——"

For the last time coming home from school.

When Christmas Eve comes a few days later he's in bed, in the side room downstairs——His legs swell up, his breathing is difficult and painful——The house is chilled. Aunt Louise sits at the kitchen table shaking her head——"*La peine, la peine*, pain, pain, always pain for the Duluozes——I knew it when he was born——his father, his aunt, all his uncles, all invalids——all in pain——Suffering and pain——I tell you, Emil, we havent been blessed by Chance."

The old man sighs and plops the table with his open hand. "That goes without saying."

Tears bubbling from her eyes, Aunt Louise, shifting one hand quickly to catch a falling crutch, "Look, it's Christmas already, he's got his tree, his toys are all bought and he's lying there on his back like a corpse——it's not *fair* to hurt little children like that that arent old enough to know——Ah Emil, Emil, Emil, what's going to happen, what's going to happen to *all* of us!"

And her crying and sobbing gets me crying and sobbing and soon Uncle Mike comes in, with wife and the boys, partly for the holidays, partly to see little Gerard and offer him some toys, and he too, Mike, cries, a great huge tormented tearful man with bald head and blue eyes, asthmatic thunderous efforts in his throat as he draws each breath to expostulate long woes: "My poor Emil, my poor little brother Emil, you have so much trouble!" followed by crashing coughs and in the kitchen the other aunt is saying to my mother:

"I told you to take care of him, that child——he was never strong, you know——you've always got to send him warmly dressed" and et cetera as tho my mother had somehow been to blame so she cries too and in the sickroom Gerard, waking up and hearing them, realizes with compassion heavy in his heart that it is only an ethereal sorrow and too will fade when heaven reveals her white.

"*Mon Seigneur*," he thinks, "bless them all"——

He pictures them all entering the belly of the lamb——Even as he stares at the wood of the windowframe and the plaster of the ceiling with its little cobwebs moving to the heat.

Hearken, amigos, to the olden message: it's neither what you think it is, nor what you think it isnt, but an elder matter, uncompounded and clear——Pigs may rut in field, come running to the Soo-Call, full of sow-y glee; people may count themselves higher than pigs, and walk proudly down country roads; geniuses may look out of windows and count themselves higher than louts; tics in the pine needles may be inferior to the swan; but whether any of these and the stone know it, it's still the same truth: none of it is even there, it's a mind movie, *believe* this if you will and you'll be saved in the solvent solution of salvation and Gerard knew it well in his dying bed in his way, in his way——And who handed us down the knowledge here of the Diamond Light? Messengers unnumberable from the Ethereal Awakened Diamond Light. And why?——because is, is——and was, was——and will be, will be——t'will!

Christmas Eve of 1925 Ti Nin and I gayly rushed out with our sleds to a new snow layer in Beaulieu street, forgetting our brother in his sack, tho it was he sent us out with injunctions to play good and slide far——

"Look at the pretty snow outside, go play!" he cried like a kindly mother, and we bundled up and went out——

I still remember the quality of that sky, that very evening, tho I was only 3 years old——

Over the roofs, which held their white and would hold them all night now that the sun was casting himself cold and wan-pink over the final birches of griefstricken westward Dracut——Over the roofs was that blue, magic Lowell blue, that keen winter northern knifeblade blue of winter dusks so unforgettable and so cold and dry, like dry ice, flint, sparks, like powdery snow that ss'ses at under doorsills——Perfect for the silhouetting of birds heading darkward down their appointed lane, hushed—— Perfect for the silhouetting presentations of church steeples and of rooftops and of the whole Lowell general, and always yon poor smoke putting from the human chimneys like prayer—— The whole town aglow with the final russet adventures of the day staining windowpanes and sending pirates to the east and bringing other sabers of purple and of saffron scarlot harlot rage across the gashes and might ironworks of incomprehensible moveless cloud wars frowned and befronting one another on horizon Shrewsburies——Up there where instead of thickening, plots thinned and leaked and warrior groups pulled wan expiring acts on the monstrous rugs of sky areas with names in purple, and dull boom cannons, and maw-mouth awwp up-clouds far far away where the children say "There's an old man sleeping in the north with a big white mouth that's open and a round nose"——These mighty skies bending over Lowell and over Gerard as he lay knowing in his deathbed, rosaries in his hands, pans on papers by the bed, pillows under his feet——The sides and portion wedges of which sky he can barely see thru the window shade and frame, outside is December's big parley with night and it's Christmas Eve and his heart breaks to realize that it will be his last Christmas on our innocent mistaken earth—— "Ah yes——if I could tell them what I knew——but when I start it stops coming, it's gone, it's not to talk about——but now I *know* it——just like my dream——poor people with their houses and their chimnies and their Christmases and their children—— listen to them yelling in the street, listen to their sleds——they run, they throw themselves on the snow, the little sled takes them a little ways and then that's all——that's all——And me,

big nut, I cant explain them what they're dying to know——It's
because God doesnt wanta——"

God made us for His glory, not our own.

Nin and I have our sleds and mufflers and we have wrangled
dramas with the other kids over the little dispositions of activity
among snowbanks and slide-lanes, it all goes on endlessly this
world in its big and little facets with no change in it.

In the kitchen, before Pa gets home and in a quiet interim when
Gerard's asleep and we're still sliding, Ma takes out her missal
and unfolds a paper from it on which are written the words of
the prayer to St. Martha:——

"St. Martha, I resort to thy protection and aid and as proof
of my affection and faith I offer this light which I shall burn
every Tuesday."

She lights her devotional candle.

"Comfort me in difficulties and thru the great favor which
you enjoyed thru lodging in the house of Our Saviour, inter-
cede for my family that we may always hold God in our hearts
and be provided for in our necessities. I beseech thee to have
infinite pity in regard to the favor I ask thee." (State favor).

"If you please, my Lord, bless my poor little Gerard and make
him well again, so he can live his little life in peace——and without pain——he has suffered so much——he's suffered enough for
twenty four old sick men and he hasnt said a word——My Lord,
have pity on this little courageous child, amen."

"I ask thee, St. Martha," she finishes reading the prayer, "to
overcome all difficulties as thou didst overcome the dragon
which thou hadst at your feet. Our Father——Hail Mary——
Glory Be"——

And at that very moment ladies in black garments, scores of
them, are scattered throughout St. Louis de France church,
kneeling or sitting or some standing at the various special
shrines, their lips muttering prayers for similar requests for
similar troubles in their own poor lives and if indeed the Lord
seeth all and saw all that is going on and all the beseechment in
His name in dark earth-churches throughout the kingdom of
consciousness, it would be with pain He'd attend and bend His
thoughts to it——Some of the women are 80 years old, they've
been coming to that basement church at dusk every day for

the last quarter of a century and they've had manifold and O manifold reasons to loft prayer from that cellar, little chance they mightnt——

Amazing how the kids always scream with glee around the church at that sad hour of dusk.

And by God, amazing the bar standers and beer eaters bubbling at elbow bangs in speakeasy clubs around the corner, enough to make a man believe in Rabelais and Khayyam and throw the Bible and the Sutras and the dry Precepts away——"*Encore un autre verre de bière mon Christ de vieux matou*! Another glass a beer ya Christing old he-cat!"

"Well you're swearing like a dog on Christmas Eve!"

"Christmas Eve my——my you-know-what, if I dont have a glass a beer in my belly and two hundred others to boot it dont render *me* no merry in the Merry Christmas even if there was forty of your Christmases in the calendar the same bloody day I'm talkin to ya," translation to that effect. "*Calvert, Caribou est sou*, Caribou's drunk!"

"Drunk? Come to my house, I got some whiskey there that'll make you fill your words with another kinda *marde!*"

The cussingest people in the world the Canucks in their cups, all you have to do is go to their capital and range up and down the bars of Ste. Catherine Street in Montreal to see some guzzling and some profanity.

"Gayo, sonumbitch, go shit!"

"Ah the bastat."

A pretty Christmas they're having, there's a little tree in the corner with lights, and drunk under it——In comes the younger element, they'll have to take out papers to catch up with the old good swigglers and cussmakers——

My father, en route home, stops for a quick one himself in the company of his old friend Gaston MacDonald who has a spanking 1922 Stutz parked outside, with them is Manuel whose usual courtesy of driving Pa home tonight in the sidecar motorcycle has been set aside in favor of the Stutz and besides it's too cold and besides they're so high now the motorcycle trip would have been a fatality——

"Drink, Emil, amuse yourself, dammit it's Christmas!"

"Not for me, Gaston——with my little Gerard in bed it's not a hell of a pretty Christmas."

"Ah, he was sick before."

"Yes but it always tears my heart out."

"Ah well, poor Emil, you might as well go throw yourself on the rocks in the river off the cliff in Little Canada . . . to crack . . . your spirit like that——look here, nothin you can do. Down the hatch!"

"Down the hatch."

"You dammit Manuel I thought you was s'posed to be a drunkard?"

"Drunkards take their time," says my father's assistant with a sly grin——

There are also silent drinkers with big chapped red fists around silent glasses, huddled over, figuring out ways to get their wives outa their thoughts and you can see their mouths lengthen down and draw sorrow almost as you look——

"Poor dog there, look, Bolduc,——do you know that guy was the best basketball player at the YMCA in '18?——and '16, and '17 too!——They offered him a professional contract——No, his father didnt want it, old rocky Rocher Bolduc, 'Stay in your store damn you or you'll never have it again'——today he's got the store, little candies for the children, licorice, pencils, a little stove near the corner, Bolduc spends his time in there with his sweater and his wife hates him and there was a time when he was the biggest athlete in Lowell——and a goodlooking happy-golucky guy!"

And chances are Bolduc's wife is one of the black sorrowful ladies in the now-dark pews a few blocks up from the club——

My father has his drink, two or three of them, and wipes his mouth, and heads home, on foot passing thru the corner at Lilley and Aiken, stopping at the drugstore for his 7-20-4 cigars, then the bakery for fresh Franco-American bread that at home he'll slice on a wood board in the middle of the table slices big enough to write your biography on——

"Allo Emil——long time no see."

"I'm pretty busy."

"Still got your shop near the Royal?"

"I'm established there, Roger——business is going good."

"The *anglais* aint givin you *marde?*" (the English)——"the

Irish——the Greeks?——one thing me I like about bread, I do
my business with the Canadians" (pronounced Ca-na-yen, the
thick peasant pride and emphatic umph of it)——

My father is actually a complicated cosmopolite compared to
Roger the baker——but he hands him a cigar.

"We'll see you at the bazaar?"

"If I have time——I'll pitch in a little in any case, for invitation
cards, my little bit——"

And all the usual pleasantries, detailed styles, and panoramic
shots of a complete social scene, Centerville in Lowell in 1925
being a close knit truly French community such as you might
not find any more (with the peculiar Medieval Gaulic closed-in
flavor) in modern long-eared France——

Emil comes home with his cigars and bread, and rounds the
corner of Beaulieu just as the dusk clouds have fought their last
war grim and purple in the invisibilities and here comes the evening star shimmering like a magic hanger in the fade-far flank of
the retreat, and lights of brown and quiet flavor have come on
in homes and he sees lil Nin and I wheeing with our sleds——

"In any case I got two of em in good health——but in my
heart I cant be happy about anything, Gerard there are no others
like Gerard, I shall never be able to understand where a little
boy like that got so much goodness——so much——enough to
make me cry, damn it——it's the way he's always got his little
head to one side——pensive, so sad, so concerned——I'd give all
the Lowells for the map of the Devil, to keep my Gerard——Will
I keep him?" he wonders looking up?——seeing the same unsay-
ing stars Gerard had stared at——"*Mystère*, it's a Christmas to
make the dogs cry"——"Come my little kids!" he calls to Nin
and me but we dont hear him in the heat of our play in the cold
snow so he goes in the house anyway, with that sad motion of
men passing into their domiciles, the pitifulness of it, specially in
winter, the sight of which, if an angel returned from heaven and
looked (if angels, if heaven, which is an ethereal crock) would
make an angel melt——If angels were angels in the first place.

Christmas comes, Gerard gets a great new erector set, big
enough and complicated enough to build hoists that'll carry
the house away——He sits in bed contemplating it with his little
sad sideways look, like the way the moon looks on May nights,

the face tilted over——It's an expression, with his arms folded, that again and again says "Ah, but and but, look at that, my souls"——Nin gets a pickaninny doll, I remember distinctly finding it that Christmas morning on the mantle by the tree, and the little high chair that went with it, and Gerard promptly that week made a little doll house for his sister, subsidiary gifts from his own Santa Claus hands——Me, I had toys that I've forgotten cold, and it goes to show——

Then New Year's——

Then the bleak January, the friendless February with his iron fingers in your grill of ribs——

Gerard lay abed all the time, getting up only to go to the toilet or occasional wan visits to the breakfast table, where after dishes were cleared, he'd sometimes sit a half hour erecting structures high that I watched standing at the side of him, holding his knee I expect——"What you doin, Gerard?"

No answer but in the action of his hands and the working of his face as he thinks, and I marvel at my love for him——Then he'd get tired and sigh and go back to bed and try to sleep, at midday, and I had no one to play with any more——I'd bring him drawingboards and crayons, he'd feebly rise to do my bidding——Sitting up, against pillows, legs out, in the white room, and white frost on the windowpane, and my mother watching us in the doorway——Her gleeful way of saying: "You're having fun now?" as tho everything was alright with the world and 50 years later she'll still be the same, and seen it all——

"Ti Pousse, Ti Pousse, Ti Pousse, how fat you are Ti Pousse," he'd say to me, mockfighting and hugging me and stroking my face. "Little Cabbage, Little Wolf, Little Piece of Butter, Little Boy, Little Pile, Little Nut, Little Savage, Little Bad, Little Cryer, Little Bawler, Little Winner, Little Robber, Little Lazy, Little *Kitigi*——Ti Jean Ti Jean——*Ti Jean Louis le gros Pipi*——Little Fatty——you weigh two tons——they'll bring you in a truck——Little Red, Little red mug——Look, Mama, the beautiful red cheeks Ti Jean has——he'll be handsome little boy!——he'll be strong!"

I basked in all this just like you would expect someone who deserved it, to bask in eternal bliss——I was going to be made to appreciate it, like a Fallen Angel.

Lancing pain in the legs and vague pain in the chest wakes Gerard in the mid of night, he makes a soft groan and represses even that realizing we're all asleep, and Mama is exhausted——I lie in the crib across the room, lips to sheet——"Aw it hurts, it hurts!!" he groans, and grabs his pain, which wont stop——It comes on and off like a light.

"Lance, lance, lance, why is this happening to me, what'd I do? I confessed to the priest, I havent hidden anything——It's not that——Aw well, I guess it isnt worth it living——Ow—— Oh Ow——" Hands to face, about to cry. Like a load of rocks dumped from a truck onto a little kitty, the pitiful inescapability of death and the pain of death, and it will happen to the best and all and most beloved of us, O——Why should such hearts be made to wince and cringe and groan out life's breath?——*why does God kill us?*——The only answer can be written without words.

And Gerard knows that. He remembers his whole life now. Nothing to do in the long pain night, but hurt. And think. It is the long night of life. And think. The morning he was born somehow there was gray rain and damp overshoes and rubbers in a dreary closet and a brown sad light in the kitchen and angry smirch of bepestered life-faces, and somehow from somewhere out, or in the center, Counsel coming to him, saying, "Dont do it——Dont be born" but he was born, he wanted to do it and be born and ignored the Counsel, the Ancient Counsel——

The pain knifes into his jerking flesh, he jumps in bed a little, and aside, to avoid, it fades away a bit——"To me, to me it's happening"——He knows it isnt happening to me otherwise I'd be thrashing in my crib——"It's happening only to me"——He hears Pa snore upstairs, the littler harmonious snores of probably Ti Nin and Ma——It's only happening to him and it's the middle of the night and the window leaks and rattles from that wind——Out on the cold canals of Lowell across the river, snow-swirls are turning in the moon——

"O, when will it stop——?"

"O my Lord, help me——"

A stab of pain——"Help me!" he involuntarily cries out loud——"Nobody could know how much it hurts——O my Jesus you've left me alone and you're hurting me——And you too, you were hurted——Aw Jesus——nothing to help me——nothing"

——Stab of strange pain, it advertises as it comes and comes with quick and open robbery, and vanishes with your peace—— "I'll have to die, I'll have to die!" steals the dark cant-help-it thought——"If it doesnt stop"——And "*It wont stop*" sneaks the other thought, coming with the pain as voucher——

"Throughout all that, throughout that snowy window and the cold night and the big wind, and my leg and everything else in the house, throughout all that there isnt something else?"

And ecstasy unfolds inside his mind like a flower and says Yes, and he sees millions of white dots, like, and in another instant his legs are stabbing again and he's opened his eyes to concentrate on the concentrating——Like a Roman Soldier left to die on a deserted battlefield and howling for mercy for three days running, without food or water, and finally dying, which is a remembrance of the great American Saint Edgar Cayce (according to him in an earlier transmigration) Gerard a petallish thing of 9 is left to face cold unhopeful bone antagonized deep by elements within itself that will to war and wreck it, he himself, his personal-soul, is but victimized, tyrannized, wracked, flung aside, suffered to be a loser in the dubious game of mortal well-being——Words cant do it——"I've been thrown to that!"——A thousand realizations come to him——"It's got to stop!" the constant human thought as pain continues to hurt——

Words cant do it, readers will get sick of it——

Because it's not happening to themselves——

> "O Lord, Ethereal Flower,
>   Messenger from Perfectness,
>   Hearer and Answerer of Prayer,
>   Raise thy diamond hand,
>   Bring to naught,
>   Destroy,
>   Exterminate——
>
> O thou Sustainer,
> Sustain all who are in extremity——
>
> Bless all living and dying things in
>   the endless past of the ethereal flower,
> Bless all living and dying things in
>   the endless present of the ethereal flower,

Bless all living and dying things in
the endless future of the ethereal flower,
amen."

Unceasing compassion flows from Gerard to the world even
while he groans in the very middle of his extremity.

But comes morning and a temporary cessation of his pain and
Ma's up making oatmeal in the kitchen, the steam from the
stove is fragrant and comes and steams Gerard's bedroom window and gives everything a wonderful new quality of gladness, of simple attempt——The earth and the flesh be harsh,
but there's comradeship below——"I'm making you some nice
oatmeal, Gerard, and some nice toasts——wait another five minutes, I'll put you that on a tray and we'll have a nice breakfast
together."

"It was a long night, Mama."

"Well now it's finished, my golden angel——It was hurting?"

"*Oui*"——sadly.

"You shoulda called me if it was hurting——Always call me
when you need something, Mama is there——There! Ti Pousse
is awake——your chum's gonna get up and you can spend the
morning having fun together."

"O Mama, I'm so happy it's morning——the oatmeal smells
so good——You're so nice, Mama."

Such tributes few mothers hear, or at least over so little, and
over the oatmeal she blurs and rubs her eyes——"Dear angel,
are you comfortable?——here, I'll fix your pillow——there"——
slapping the pillow expertly, then kissing him——"There——
Mama's golden angel——Dont worry, you'll be all better in two
months——the Doctor Simpkins told me——You'll be able to
go out and play in the nice warm weather!——It'll be March in
two weeks and *bing*, April!——May!——See how fast it goes?"

"*Oui*, Ma."

"Dont you worry, with your Mama to take care of you you'll
be well in two shakes of a lamb's tail——"

Great joy, because of the vacuum created by great horror in
the night, floods into his being as he sees his delighted mother
come hurrying over bearing the steaming tray to place on his
lap——Ahead of him is a long day of interested drawing and

erector set——The sun hasnt shown, it's a cold cloudy day, the windows are gray and portentous with the news of the excitement of life and the healthy and the living——

He eats daintily and formally the simple food, reverencing each bite as tho it was holy, to enjoy it more, and because it is so momentous. "The corner of the toast——good——the middle of the toast——there——" A faint twinge in his legs recalls the pain of the night before, and setting the tray aside with a weary sigh he nevertheless sees it fit to realize, "Ah well, it goes up and down and then it goes no more. It's best not to frighten anyone, nor harm anyone——dont let them know."

I'm up in my crib, in long johns, jealous because Gerard got his breakfast before me. I'm thinking "Because he's sick he's always waited on before me——Me, me!" I cry. "Me too I'm hungry!" "They always make such a fuss over him," I pout—— I remember that morning, distinctly, standing in the crib like that——*Sticks and stones may break my bones but words'll hurt me never?*

In fact, Gerard is a little impatient with me for rattling the crib and throws me an exasperated look——"*Eh twé*, Oh you!"

And there's no doubt in my heart that my mother loves Gerard more than she loves me.

After awhile Pa's up and grumbling in the kitchen over his breakfast, with puffed disinterested eyes, not, as Edgar Cayce explicitly reminds us, "mindful of the present vision before our eyes."

The long night of life is terribly long and deceptively short.

Caribou the man who was drunkest and gayest the night before, having undergone indescribably ghastly feelings under the bridge where he wobbled and woggled and spit, is now lofting a new morning drink to his lips which will soon plunge him back into——what?

"What else you want me to do?——We all die? We're all piles of you-know-what? Liars? Poor? Invalids? Well then! I drink! Open the door, belly, gimme another chance." He gets his other chance, dances jigs till ten, and sleeps at noon. What he does at 4 o'clock in the afternoon is in its poor selfsame essence no different than what the mournful ladies with their beads and moving-lips, in the shadows of the church, are doing——For, the truth that is realizable in dead men's bones ought to be a good enough truth for everybody, laughers, cryers, cynics, and hopers included, all——The truth that is realizable in dead men's bones, all great gloomy unwilling life aside, and setting aside my knighthood to thus say so, exhilarates yea exterminates all symbols and bosses and crosses and leaves that quiet blank—— For my part, the news about the truth came from the silence of my predecessor diers' graves.

Sicken if you will, this gloomy book's foretold.

Comes the cankerous rush of spring, when earth will fecundate and get soft and produce forms that are but to die, multiply—— And a thousand splendors sweep across the March sky, and moons with raving moons that you see through drunken pine boughs snapping——When the river with her loaden humus gets heavier at the bank, because of the melting of the caky stiffnesses that'd had the earth seal-locked in her vaunted tomb of Hard——And there'll be laughter in the melting earth tonight——And there'll be sawdust, trees, women's thighs, river bends, starlight, backporches, more babies, young husbands, beer——There'll be singing in the April tree tops——There'll be visitations from the South from oft-returning species of visitors with feather tails and beady eyes, avaricious for the worm—— And the worm himself will divide into a billion counterparts and come oozing out of parted-sands (black and oily and blue) like as if someone were squeezing the earth from below——There'll be new fish——There'll be There'll-be Himself——

All of a sudden tossed wars of tree-tops will be warmer wars and less dry and crackety ones, and there'll be rumors and sing-ing down the hillsides as snow melts, running for cover under the bloody light, to join the river's big body——So that Ocean will again receive her swollen rent, as ever April, yet, landlord without end, be none the richer and with such coffers bottom-less how the poorer possible?——In the ocean there is a Spring, deep and verdurous we cant estimate, so I sing the surface one, the Spring that makes us feel so sad and fair, and morning air brings nostalgic cigarette smoke from holy hopey smok-ers——When hats are whipped and finally succumb, coats flap and run their stories out, and vests disappear, and shirtsleeves are hoisted of a sudden afternoon April 26 and the ballgame is on——The time when all the earth is black with sap——No end to what you could say about Spring, and in that locked-in New England Spring is a big event, long coming, short staying, it flows by as fast as a flooded river——In that river you can see the accumulated debris of seventeen thousand fecundities up the both shores clear to the maw of the well where she began—— Marble'd melt in such country at the time, and add veins to the color in the river——Children run out exhilarated as princes and knights, illustriously insane as ancient fools, to weirdly fool in fields and down river banks; to at that time put them behind a knife-carved schooldesk is like asking Thane to stow his Ice Axe and say farewell to his Prow——It is the dizzy lyrical time, airy, ethereal, mists are bright, the sun is never exactly golden, never exactly silver, never exactly bright, never exactly dark, never for a long time dimmed, but races continual eye dazzling wars, reaches everywhere throughout textures of clouds and shows birds' shining wings——And when the first buds appear on bushes and trees, and your heartborne blossoms float to commemorate new Awakened Ones and fall in migholes and on hopskotch trails, Vaya, then, night coming, and the round horizon all about reverberates with roars of all-sigh all-world all-men Shush War, you'll know, by the fence, the sad wooden American fences and under the promised yellow moon, the pierce of the arrow of April in your flesh, the promise accounted for in the Tablets of Hardworking Man's Beardy Serious Prophets: namely, ecstasy of living and dying. . .

You'll have your cold wars and warm peaces, the frotting and rubbings of all things on all sides, the ecstasy general, orgasms, screams of passion, rites of Spring, May, June, July and the Bees——No matter what anyone says, you'll have it, you'll dream you have it and so like the popular lovesong says, You'll Have It.

Blossoms fluttered from the trees and crossed contrarious Gerardo's windowpane, he would not balmy truck with Spring and swell with it, but wasted like Sacrosanct and ill-timed Autumn, out of his element——Like my father exactly 20 years later, he was dying during the Resurrection and the Life Renewed.

He was getting worse. Rarely now we saw him out of bed and about the kitchen. Our visits to his bedside were still, for he slept a lot. My mother grew rings around her sleepless eyes, and prayed late and rose early to praise early——Her nerves were so shot she was losing her teeth one by one, her stomach was a mass of gelid anxious phenomena, like swarms of snakes——The Snake of Inevitability was rising up and eating the Duluozes.

My father had more time to avoid the sight of his little boy's death, by busying by burying himself in details of his work at the shop——And as heartbreaking April blossomedburst into May and the mornings and the nights were music, the death in the house grew browner——I remember Springnight the fence in our backyard, and the dim light in Gerard's sickroom window casting a faint candle-like glow on the lilac bushes, and above the warm teary stars, and the roar furor all around in the city of Lowell: trains across the river, the river itself booming heavily at the Falls, cries of people, doors slamming clear down to Lilley Street.

"Angie, we gotta do some work tonight me and Manuel—— I'm going to his house now."

"Awright Emil——dont come home too late——I'm afraid to be alone if anything happened."

"Ah well, you should be used to it by now——It'll happen in time."

"Dont talk like that——He recovered the last time."

"Yeah, but I never saw him skinny and quiet like that—— Ah," from the porch, door open, "the beautiful nights that are coming——all for other people——"

"Call Ti Jean, he's in the yard with his kitty——it's his bedtime."

"Take it easy, my girl, I'll be home before eleven——We got a big order, just came in this morning——Manuel's waiting——Ti Jean, come in the house——your mother wants you——come on, my little man."

"Did you take your bath?"

"Aw tomorrow, if I'm dirty I'm dirty——Make me some *cortons* if you got time, I always like them for my sandwiches at the shop——"

"Bye Emil."

"Bye Angie——I'm going now."

Emil Alcide Duluoz, born in upriver St. Hubert Canada in 1889, I can picture the scene of his baptism at some wind whipped country crossing Catholic church with its ironspike churchspire high up and the paisans all dressed up, the bleak

font (brown, or yellow, likely) where he is baptized, to go with
the color of old teeth in this wolfish earth——Forlorn, the Plains
of Abraham, the winds bring plague dust from all the way to
Baffin and Hudson and where roads end and the Iroquois Arctic begins, the utterly hopeless place to which the French came
when they came to the New World, the hardness of the Indians
they must have embrothered to be able to settle so and have
them for conspirators in the rebellion against contrarious potent
churly England——Winds all the way from the nostril of the
moose, coarse rough tough needs in potato fields, a little fold
of honey enfleshed is being presented to the holy water for
life——I can see all the kinds of Duluozes that must have been
there that 1889 day, Sunday most likely, when Emil Alcide was
anointed for his grave, for the earth's an intrinsic grave (just dig
a hole and see)——Maybe Armenagé Duluoz, bowlegged 5 feet
tall, plank-stiff, baptismal best boots, tie, chain and watch, hat
(hat slopey, Saxish, slouch)——His statuesque and beauteous
sisters in endless fold-draperies designed by Montreal couturiers
tinkling delighted laughter late of afternoons when parochial
children make long shadows in the gravel and Jesuit Brothers
rush, bookish like "ill angels," from darkness to darkness——The
mystery there for me, of Montreal the Capital and all French
Canada the culture, out of which came the original potato paternity that rioted and wrought us the present family-kids of
Emil——I can see the baptism of my father in St. Hubert, the
horses and carriages, an angry tug at the reins, "*Allons ciboire
de cawlis de calvert*, wait'll they finish wipin im"——Poor Papa
Emil, and then began his life.

A whole story in itself, the story of Emil, his mad brothers
and sisters, the whole troop coming down from the barren
farm, to the factories of U.S.A.——Their early life in early Ameri-
cana New Hampshire of pink suspenders, strawberry blondes,
barbershop quartets, popcorn stands with melted butter in a
teapot, and fistfights in the Sunday afternoon streets between
bullies and heroes who read Frank Merriwell——Of Emil much
later more——

But his rise from riotous family, to insurance salesman in the
"big city" (for Lowell 14 miles downriver) and then to independent businessman with a shop, his waxing and puffing on
cigars——His eager bursting out of vests and coats, tortured

armpits of suits, quick short heavy steps on our history sidewalks——But a reverend, sensitive, apt-to-understand man, and understand he did, the mournfulness of his vision, the way he shook his head (that little Gerard imitated), the way he sighed——A citizen of the raving world, but eager to be good——Eager to be rich too——But a man endowed with qualities of interested apperception of the nature of things, as would qualify him to be a tragic philosopher——Insights, sadnesses, that leapfrogged his intelligence and came down on the other side and were light——"I see blind light——I see this sad black earth!" might have been one thought he had.

Here he goes hurrying to Manuel's for their night's work—— Manuel lives four blocks down near the big corner of Lilley and Aiken——As Emil turns off Beaulieu, which is the little street that bears the great burden of Gerard's dying, a breeze blows, bringing whiffs of hope, voices, song, it's a gay Saturday night, but the young father has no primer for that wellknown pump and only slowly ghostly sadly wends his way, thinking, "My father died drunk behind his stove——my mother died in her dishes and poor washclothes——father and mother, it happens to all of us one way or the other, we can pray if we want but it wont help——Go on, God, dont call yourself God in my face——Doin business under conditions like that, we'll never win——"

Manuel lives in a raucous tenement, first floor, you walk in from the woodporch which has rollers that run the washlines across a tar court to the porch of the other tenements, all closed in, with, on warm Spring Night, all windows open and families airing their rave and grievance——Crash! Old Paquette's drunk again——Bang! Old lady Pirouette who lost her son in the war is dropping her dishes again——Boom! that damn little Petrie's poppin off his lastyear's firecrackers——It swims in thru all windows and revolves around and rumors and runs like a river, voices, language, gossip, crashes, jingles and jangles——"There's no end to it!"——Whole rant-sentences can be heard in rising and falling snatches of vigorous Canuckois, coming from by old woodstoves in ancient rockingchairs——Sounds for the quick head and trailing robe——Emil walks in to Manuel's kitchen unannounced, nobody in it, he stands questioning——It doesnt take long for him to realize that Manuel is in the bedroom with his wife having a fight——

"They always told me not to marry you, you were a drunkard at sixteen——*sixteen?!!* I bet you was drunk as a hoot-owl at 15, 14——You're not the man I married but dammit the reason for that is because you were puttin up a front *when* I married you, crook——"

"Aw shut ya big ga dam mouth, it's only good for *blagues*——I gave you your money, I'm goin to work, I'll be gone all night, you oughta be satisfied, ya cow——"

"Dont call me a cow, dog——"

"Call yourself what you like, me I'm goin——and if I'm drunk tomorrow morning when I get back we'll blame it on you"——

"Aw yeah, look for excuses."

"Bein in the same house with a pest like you it's enough to make a man drink poison!"

"Why dont you do it then."

"And leave you my insurance that I took out because Emil Duluoz bullshitted my ear in 1920, not a chance——I'll live and you'll be poor——Go tell *that* to your mother."

My old man winces in the kitchen and bathetically would tiptoe out except that Manuel's wife is suddenly exploding into the kitchen with a backward added yell to loverboy: "Aw sure, simpleton, I'll go tell all this to my mother and make her happy she had a little girl and brought her up to well my goodness Mr. Duluoz is here!"

My father, eyes to the ceiling, salutes at the side of his head, as if to say "Dont mind me, I'm the court jester."

Manuel comes out of his gloomy bridalchamber with a chamberpot in his hand, and slippers on his feet. "Ah——Emil——"

"Come on, Manuel, before Rosie throws you out on your face——"

"I'll throw him out to the Devil, damn him!" she screams, slamming the door that leads to the parlor which is never used.

(Sigh) my old man, "At least you dont have any children—— Put on your shoes and come on——You got drunk again there yesterday?"

"Just a little nip."

"Poor Manuel, come on I'll *buy* you a little nip——just one hour of work then we'll go to the club."

"How is it at home?"

"Well, there we dont fight, we——" he was about to say "we die" but checked himself.

Together they leave the tenement and get on Manuel's motorcycle with the side car, Emil in it, stately with hat-in-hand and goopy look, and off they go put-putting and bouncing over the Aiken Street Bridge——Almost exhilaration sweeps over both of them as the river winds whip their faces, and they both yell and point at the moon, which is rising yellow-huge on the horizon over Pawtucketville——About a mile to the left are the glowing windows of the mills, some windows dye-blue, all reflected on the thrashy waters——About a mile to the right, Pawtucketville's hill of houses and the moon and one vast darkness cloud burlying over Spring——

It's the time of the juices——

They go careering up Aiken thru the tenement streets of Little Canada and cross the canal bridge and along to the high Medieval granite walls of St. Jean de Baptiste church (where Gerard was baptized), then left on Moody Street along busy storefronts, then right, to Merrimack Street, with its trolleys and busy cars, and down to the bright corner where stands the Jewel Theater, and the Royal Theater——Manuel roars to a stop, they get out like brave mechanics, and toddle off down the alley by the Royal, redbrick, past the fire escape, to the rear——Emil turns on the light——You see the press, the hand presses, the piles of glossy paper, the paper cutter, the roll-trucks, the inky shadows, rolls, rags, cans, inks, the long sad stained planks of the floor leading to the back entrance which fronts Market Street where the Greek coffee shops show dismal cardgames and *barbutte* dice games going on in green interiors among gloomy men in black, the long lost sad scenes.

"What you thinkin, Leo, will we do it before 8 o'clock?" comes the cry now in English from the rhythmic chomping press where inky Manuel (inky from so much) in blue striped scullion's apron stands feeding sheets between the yawns of inkpan and types, sheketak, sheketoom, shketak, shketoom, and out come orange circulars advertising stores their Spring bargains and Specials:——

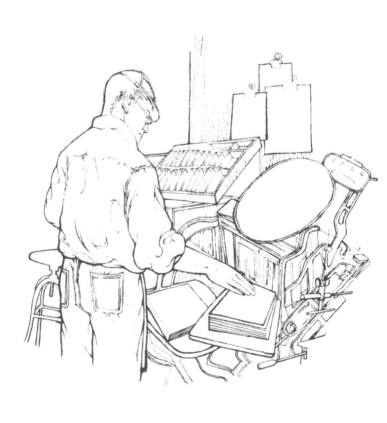

THE MODERN WONDER

S h o e   S a l e

MEN'S SHOES	WOMEN'S	BOY'S SCOUT SHOES
$7 or $8 values	$6 low shoes	$2.49
As low as $2.98	Goodyear welt	
	$2.98	

THE MODERN SHOE STORE
143 Central St   Opp. Talbot's

——to be delivered door to door by boys on bikes or by Tao hoboes who assemble under the pharting trills of birds at daybreak to receive their day's bagful of circulars, which will go for booze and beans——

"All I gotta do, Manuel, is finish this ad and get my foldin done, turn the key on Red Line Taxi and Cantwell optical, be done. Did you finish that new Pollard mat?"

"The great underpriced basement? All done, Leo, everything twenty-three skidoo and ready to roll."

"Well oil her up, we'll be outa here by eight and maybe go down to the Keiths' for a game."

"*Ah ben mué, les cartes, son pas assez bon pour la soif pour mué*, (ah well me, cards, they're not good enough for thirst for me.")

"*Ben mué too shpeux usez un bierre*, (well me too I can use a beer,") both of them suddenly reverting to Frenchy slang since nobody's there to hear them anyway, just as you might expect the Greeks that you could see across the way thru the great dirty wire windows, breaking from their usual Greek to talk some English for the benefit of business there "ska ta la pa ta wa ya" here we go again, the great raving *patois* of Lowell on all sides, Polocks on Lakeview Avenue and Back Central, and practically pure Gaelic or at least lilting lyric Gaelic English on the Highlands and downtown——Syrians to boot, up the canal somewhere——And your old New England Yankees eating Indian Pudding for dessert in old stately houses with lawns, on Andover, Pawtucket and Chelmsford, with names like Goldtwaithe and Smith——And thin noses and thin lips and read *Walden* by the fireplace on howling nights——

Eight o'clock Pa and Manuel close up shop and go across the street to the Jewel Theater for a chat with the manager Sam, the cameras are running off the latest photoplay replete with thrills and fast action and gray rain streaming across the screen and the piano rumbling suspense thunders in the pit, the oldtime movie stars with their prim painted lips set grim——"We grow through suffering," is written for what says the hero in flickery letters, "Jesus God," says a bum in the seat, "by now I oughta be as big as the side of the house"——Sam gives them an introductory warming nip that goes like a prairie fire thru Manuel's belly, then they get back in the contraption and go bouncing down Merrimack to the Square, as acquaintances shout "*Weyo*, Emil, when you gonna enter in the races? Buy yourself some goggles and a hat that comes down over your ears! Manuel'll get you in the river, give im time!"——

"Ho Emil, how's the boy?"

"Ho Slattery——still swingin em?"

My father is a popular fellow around Lowell, in insurance he's buttonholed practically every small (and some big) businessman in town and extolled the virtues etc. etc. of seeing that your grave doth not rot in vain and you leave your successors some of your ghostly change——Then as a printer, to get ad-work, he'd followed up old acquaintances and hotfooted everywhere and was a proficient, nay much more proficient with the non French usually Irish segment of his customers, a proficient persuader and general goodtime Charley——"Ha ha ha!" rang his harsh laugh, and you heard him cough as he left thru the door, bound for another——

They go rattletrapping in the strange comic French Movie contraption down past the City Hall and for want of shamelessness go sneaking thru the back streets to avoid the great Main Kearney Square where all Lowell's in the lights——The clock, the Chinese restaurant, the Number One soda-fountain, the trolley stops, the big stores, the newspaper——They go instead around by Kirk street and down a railroad switch alley for the mills, across spectral-in-my-mind Bridge Street where stands the great gray warehouse of eternity and into the little alley that runs between it and the stagedoor side entrance of the B.F.Keiths theater.

"If you want your moonshine there he is now, old Henry——I'll meet you backstage."

Emil goes under the iron fire escape and's just about to disappear inside when some of the vaudeville performers who have gathered in the warm night for a smoke, call him over——As one-time ad man making up the B.F.Keiths Vaudeville ads he is wellknown by a lot of the performers on the famous old circuit——

"If it aint Ben Oaklander, where's your piano, boy?"

"Emil——What you been doin these past two years——know Billy here, Billy Dale?"

"*Shore* I know Billy Dale——Say, what's on tap with the new show?"

"Just opened tonight——There's Rialto and Lamont, the Talkless Boys——Oh, Lois Bennett, you know her——"

"A Ray of Western Sunshine——"

"——Western Sunshine, and Muriel Pollock the Popular Composer——and old Prop-Prop himself——"

"Prop-prop, did they ever throw him in the canal like they said they'd do the night he puked all over the trunks and suitcases?"——

"No——Say, boy, we took pity on him——Wal, you know what happened to him, wal, he's in South Bend now; wal sir Emil, how are you boy?"

"And do I understand we've got the dainty captivating vivacious Miss Corinne and Dick Himber offering Coquettish Fancies with Ben Oaklander on the piano?"——

"Say, boy, you got that memory——Yes sir, and there's Bob Yates and Evelyn Carsen in 'Getting Soaked' by Billy Dale and Bob Yates and there's Clarence Oliver, 'Wire Collect'"——

"I'll be damned, he's still around——"

"Yes sir, old mountain man too, and Billy McDermott the only survivor of Coxey's Army and on the screen a photoplay of speed and derring-do, me boy, forget what the name of it is——"

"A little bit of canned music, a title, a couple of sighs, and there's your money's worth——"

"Me boy, if it wasnt for vaudeville the man on the street wouldnt have a place in the world to get himself a good night of entertainment——Pathe News and topics, and Aesop's Fables all right, but when you got them flesh n blood performers up there, me boy, that exit march at eleven P.M. wouldnt be worth the paper 't'scored on! Stop me if I'm lying."

Bend the drapes to your purpose——

And as they're standing there, smoke fragrantly rises from their cigarettes to the spring moon, and here crunching down the cindered alley comes a man in a strawhat (like Emil), but fatter, huge, with cane and great pot belly and bulbous red nose, a namelessly battered and muggled eatenup and almost disappeared face:——Old Bull Baloon.

"Emil, want ya to meet Bull Baloon here——"

"Glad ta meet ya——"

"This the boy plays poker?"

"Same."

"How 'bout a little swiggle a Mother Machree's ancient re-vitalizing monkey juice, Mister Emil?"

"Why——well——"

"Sometimes known as continental bug joy juice, or *joie de vivre*" (Old Baloon pronouncing it JWA-DAY-VIVRAY to Emil's great amused delight)——

"No, no, non, non, non——it's *joie de vivre,* I'm French, I know."

"This here business at hand, the poker game, somebody called Charley Sagely, and somebody O-BRIEN or other, brings my attention to the fact that——" upending his flask, swallowing, looking around, wiping the neck of it, "——brings my attention——" but again repeating it slowly as now his eye has caught one of the principals coming down the alley and it's time to get the game underway, and meanwhile Manuel has come back with *his* bottle, and they all go inside to start the game in one of the dressing-rooms——

As the game progresses the participants increase, and soon they can hear the B.F.Keiths' orchestra playing the exit march in the pit and the audience is filing out for a soda in Paige's or Liggett's Drugstore or in Dana the Greek's and there will be dense dyed neon of oldtime city night in America, like old cartoons showing the boy newspaper seller with little cloth cap and scarf and knickers holding out a paper to two men, one in derby, one with elegant cane, their coats flapping in the

aftertheater wind, and beyond, a great crowd, some reading
papers, and the wallsides of buildings in the city night and the
dimmed marquees and the general drizzle of activity in the furthest reaches of the scene, where I see Gerard's dead face——Old
Fish Street, it is all incredibly dense, dark, soft, rich as if Spanish
Night, the blue of tombs is in the neons, the secret of the Old
Fish is on Old Fish Street, the dark spoor of real profound red
throbs up from the assemblied lights and makes a halo overhead, it is all slightly alien, ugly, but soft and kindly——It is a
dream, in the middle of it the kings and queens are being dealt
by the mysterious cardplayers in the empty theater.

"What in the hell kinda concoction by the way you got in
that new flask, Bull?"

And he, Old Bull Baloon, man of a long life (60) cluttered
with a hundred thousand misadventures the whole story of
which can never, will never be told except you see it written
in the picotée carnation of his nose, the swim of winkles in his
eyes, the wrinkles there, indicative of earlier olden eyes like
of a hardboot on a Kentucky rail, the crooked coy smile and
yellow-teeth, the big ring on thick Neroid finger like fingers of
old whores successful and retired or fingers of Roman prelates
given to regurgitation ere their excarnification comes due and
all the banquets fall:——"It's a little mixture of wine, gin, and
bourbon, I learned it in Panama some years ago with a little
man named Low stood about four foot one inch and was half
Chinese for all I know, lived in a wattle tenement on the edge of
a river sewer system with dead rats and crapsticks floatin in the
tide, and green spiders where he hid his dice——One afternoon
some hobo from Pratt Street Baltimore I believe and I believe
the name was Slats came up to Lady Nicotima at the bar and
slapped her rump, congratulatin her for the good showing that
afternoon, whereupon she turns around and says 'Dont you
believe in God?' and aims a delicate little pistol and fires, hitting
Charley Low dead between the shoulderblades and the bullet
goes thru him and ends up I aint never seen him no more——
and so," he says, receiving his hole card and his face card, "better be jocund with the fruitful grape, as sadden after none, or
bitter fruit" (quoting Omar Khayyam) and glances down at his
hole-card, a nine of spades.

"By God I dont drink as a rule like you do Bull——Manuel

you see this guy?"——to Manuel who's watching the game sitting on a trunk drunk——"but by golly have you seen that boy guzzle up that whisky tonight, Charley? Jim? Two bottles now?"

"It's only two A.M., give him a chance to start——"

"I've had to come from a long way and a lot of snowy country to want that much heat, Emil."

"I'm *made* of water!" complains the stagehand who keeps going to the toilet.

"Well, I like to gamble, like a drink once in a while," big Emil glancing at his king of heart face-card and adjusting it over the hole card, which now, surreptitiously, in the middle of his sentence, he raises a corner of, to see the spade smooth black of a 10 of spades, winking inside himself to think, "but I never could drink like that and put it away like that——hell George Daslin and me and Henry O'Hara one time drink I dunno how much beer out of a barrel, in Lawrence and then had whisky and a cardgame just like this I guess 9 in the morning, whoo, it took ten years offa my life——"

"I wouldnt tell you if I knew," says O'Brien now looking at his hole-card with the same sly up-corner, saying to himself, so that the others can almost read it in the imprint of the smoke before the lamp, "ten of diamonds."

Old Conductor Jim Sagely the railroad man, holding his ace of clubs in one hand, thoughtfully raises the jack of same underneath and purses his New England farmer lips.

"Sagely," says Bull, slyly, small blue eyes thru reddened eyelid puffs watching, raising flask for a slug soon as he's finished his speech, a simp, "if I had a barrel a beans and I had a store, I'd hire you to count the bad ones and lay the good ones aside, that's how sly your dollar is."

"What are you, a Scotchman? A sneaky character you must be, with that false hat——bet it's got hinges on it. I aint no guy that lets his whisky bottle interfere with the waybills, or throws a switch and throws the crummy over before it's crossed the points."

"A lame, improfitable, infantile turn of talk if ever I heard one, your *crummies*——You? You're too miserly for *my* cardgame—— it's midnight in *my* little life——what's *your* key?——Took 80 dollars from me last night——that represents a lotta claprous calls from the crew clerk and a lotta locals in the freezing air for an old Canadian National boomer like me."

"*Boomer? You?* You cahd shahp! Pool shahk!——First time I win some real money in my life and they's complainin in the sides and up the back——"

"**Le phantôme de l'opéra**," provides sepulchrally looking-over his shoulder, Manuel, looking to the eerie shrouds back-stage deeper——

"Ne-mind the phantoms and drink your drink——You gave me a start, damn you!" says my father quietly chuckling.

"No complainin, Sage, I'm passin king of hearts Emil Pop here with his wife and kiddies just born, bang," throwing Emil a king of clubs face card, and everybody eying it. "And Charles the hammer, bang, a queen of spades, two kings and two queens showing and where's the marital bed, bang, a jack of spades for the conductor, and bang" (for himself) "same of hearts."

"The game thickens."

"I bet and raise the ante."

"At this stage, nobody cares."

"And on this stage. A new ace wont do you no good——old Sage could use it."

"Sevens——aint got no use for em, even when I got seven in the hole, my unlucky number, nine's my lucky number by God."

"Another seven——talkin of the devil——pair a kings high."

"There he is, Bull Baloon with a girl for his jack. Who's gonna win the rainbow pot?"

"Let me look and think." Emil, high, with pair of kings, pre-tends innocent worry. Charley O'Brien has nothing further to examine beyond his showing queens, but a mentioned forlorn seven.

"It's a dream, lads, it's a dream," utters Bull up-ending a lofty big pull on his swiggins, bloodshot returning the cap, spitting over his shoulder at the two spittoons in the corner. Sagely has a jack under and a jack on top, and nobody knows, but no advantage his, yet, till the last thrust of fate-cards, from the hands of the dealer, Bull. Emil leans over to rub his thigh in the night of the world forgetting his family, lost in the eye to eye the game of men in America; nights long ago after Langford battered John-son; smoke in Butte saloons; Denver backrooms, games; lost heroes of America; Chicago, Seattle; vaudeville redbrick alleys

and forgotten cundoms under isolated signs in the highway
night of Roadster Twenties; long jaws of bo's riding the boxcar
from outside North Platte, to clear t'Ogallah, mispronounced,
sad, spindle legged waiters in the summermoth night, by lights;
America, sweaty, poker games, Negroes on the sidewalk in Baltimore, history, nostalgic with afternoon and man, midnight
and weariness, dawn and O'Shea running to catch his train, Old
Bull Baloon examining his useless King hole-card, half deciding
to full decide to leave the game because even if he gets another
King he's got no ace to ace-high Emil.

The others stay; Bull deals, lost in the dream. "Ten dont
do you no good, Emilio, lessn you got another underneath,"
dealing Emil a ten of clubs. Deals Charley a seven, making a
pair of 7's on the top. "You better have a queen underneath,"
which Charley doesnt have, stripped bare and queenless, turning up a 10 apologetically. "Another pair of Sevens!" dealing
Sagely a 7 of hearts. "If he has another 7 underneath," opines
the rednosed dealer from Butte Montana, "he's got his own
deck a cards hidden in back of his ear inside that curly hair,
yass. Which, would a left me with the Ace of Jokers," dealing
himself, for the hell of it, the final fifth card tho he's out, the
Ace of Spades, Death. "Gentlemen," seeing he's inadvertently
emptied his flask without realizing it in the heat of what he was
doing, "is there any beer in the house? No beer?"

"We got some left, yeh Bull, in the box there."

And Emil rakes in the pot, cigar in teeth, big body tensed forward in chair to affairs of the night, as goldpots strew the blue
beginnings with incense of aurora and dawn creaks up to crack
and boom over the black sad earth now irrevocably Gerard was,
enfleshed, sacrificed and given over to, O moanin shame.

"I'm the one shoulda got that spade," comments Emil in the
alley, as they urinate.

Bull, pointing up the dawn sky: "More ill fated than in all
your dreams you'd a bitterly hoped her to be."

Then they get drunk——It happens all of a sudden, on the spur
of nothing but a cry——"Slup a slug, son!"——The high white
mists of Spring morn over the redbrick roofs of downtown
Lowell make them dizzily glad, they go (Manuel in the middle bawling) staggering down the alley——In two cars and the

ridiculous motorcycle they go careering thru the mists and over the bridge.

"Where's that Irish club?——Where's that dog with the pipe in his mouth and the blue eyes who sits by the stove in the——"

"You mean Bob Donnelly, if he aint asleep now with his arms around his milky wife I'd bet and be damned and be called Tarzan if he wasnt still up and jawin his Jew's harp somewhere the other side a town——"

"And Murphy! Where are the river boys?"

"Never mind! It's a mystery!"

"Be Jesus Christ it makes me feel good, they lit the furnace in my damp cellar."

"All the blowers of hell'll send it thru the vents and veins and you'll come out with a true face at last."

They rave and scream as the wind ventilates them across the bridge, they're looking for the Polish Club that's supposed to open 24 hours a day, down on Lakeview——"That place with the chairs in front."

"Ah who needs a ga dam club——come down by the carnival grounds and piss in the bushes."

"Suits me fine, termagant."

"Manuel, what you doin, you almost got us to the end of our holes."

"They been swallowin a long time!"

"Then why not swallow more, lover."

"With my wife in hell everything suits me."

"You got eyes like a dead potatobug——wake up and watch the road!"

"Eat the damn road!" says Manuel who'd as soon the road ate him so they'd be where they were going sooner.

Irrelevant conversations meanwhile rage in the cars, driven respectively by Sagely and O'Brien, Old Bull Baloon in his red-eye cups now reconstructing adventures of six decades with the invention of sixty——They all spill out on the field at Lakeview Avenue, across from the mills, on the river, just as the blazing red sun kisses and peeps over the window roofs of all Centerville——

My father reels about from snort to snort, the earth morning under him——

My father with straw hat in big gnarled veiny hands, collar

bursting out soft and unstylish over his coat lapels from folds
of thick muscular neck, frown dark on his brow, hair curly,
dark, crisp, nose bulbous, mouth grim but sentimental, kneeling on one knee, examining the sunrise with serious and exact
and ponderous officialness, nodding slowly, "I'll tell ya Bull,
there aint never been a mystery of this world I didnt stand in
awe of, when standing in front of it, or kneelin on one knee as
I am now." Strangely, rockily, the redness shows on the ridges
of his face.

His head is held slightly on one side, as I say a little like
Gerard, but in this case, the father's sadness is held inside a
manly grace, or rather, a manly brace, the philosophicalness
abides higher in the cranium here than it can in the recentness-
film of the angel child——Experience has made a man of Emil,
and you may take man and weigh him on the scales with his
weight in goldshit on the other pan, the measurement may
come out, legible——If so, write me a letter——I see no reason
for Man——But his value, I buy——Dawns white with drunkness
I've had myself with my boys and after that were boys——And
there'll be more——Brothers that were saints that died on me,
that too's happened a million times in a million repetitudes
and reincarnations in Samsara's sorrow parade——More wine!
fewer dead potato bugs! Roll me down the road in a barrel, if
I'm lying——(and I've been rolled in a barrel down the road, an
I'm a liar)——Jesus Child,——But birth and tender years which
we take to be actual happeningness in the phenomena of this
self belief that something seems to happen, called existence,
hath made of Emil's son Gerard instead of a weighable debat-
able man, a tender-born and angel of tender years——Emil's lips
pressed together to make the whole face storm, Breton, hot,
worried, Emil, leaning his big arms on thick unbreakable knees,
thick thighs, he brushes the cigar smoke from the pants of his
thigh, he fixes his face in the rising sun (priests are anointing
and intoning a quartermile away), he looks like some Medieval
wallguard waiting for the Jesus Child, nodding, "I'll be gol
danged . . . aint it a strange world, Bull——here we are, by the
side of a river, two men——once upon a time we had a notion
we were romeos and gave up our little suspenders and our Saturday night nickelodeons and made googoo eyes at the girls at
basketball games and hit hero homeruns and then developed

these big endless holes to throw our money in——*money?* And all of it!——Like throwing ten dollar bills and flowers in the gad dam ocean, Bull——"

"Expand upon the theme," says Bull passing the bottle.

"No I'm through——an ocean, Caesar never had it so good I'm tellin you.҉

Meaningless, they grow solemn and serious.

"It's a hell of a world——debts, wives, woman——scissors, meat, do you blame her?"

"Why hell no?"

"Ha?"

"Hell No!"

"In the winter, kiddies——a purple shame, an American shame, a durn Babe Ruth homerun of a shame——Youth gone wild, hung upsidedown——"

"Tarzan——"

"Emil, the world is happy!"

"You damn right."

"My best, MY children, I'm not promising anything——"

"End, but hole hat or no hole hat and happy sandholes of infantile or not, I predict it, seaweave breezes once in a while, sand most a the time, hot unhappy painful burning sand and right in his throat, and makes his wet yes water more"——(slup, a slug)——"Let the women wash it, I'm through, I'm the culprit officer, O offi sair, sir, but take me away not now, some other time Offi Sair Charley," as Emil and Charley dance and gesture Cop-and-Innocent Arrest on the red haunted banksides of 8 A.M. Lowell in the mud and molten snow——Harsh laughter, lighting of cigars, holding of them between fingers outstretched stiff drunk, the fragrance of the Cuban smoke, the Cuban quality of men, mixed with alcohol so many percent by volume and name your Infinity——Slapping of laugh-hands, Whoos!, and "Take me away peaceably, I wanta play one more game of poker!"—— Pulling up of thigh pants, clearing of throats, ah-hums and hem-haws, popping of eye-bulge doubts, starings into the blank to wait for further time——

"O where's that Donnelly!"

"Well then goddamit let's go to him!"

Off they vow in their Immense vehicles——

"Oh call it a day!"

"And *why?*"

And when they do find Donnelly it's only for him to sit there saying "Emil you could have ended up your days cryin in that corner——calling for more drinks——but you had to buy a store, and hire yourself out, and count your every blarney."

"Aright with me, Ole Be-larney."

"And you hankered and pankled and popped to discover——"

"I did."

"And you——are you sure this is a mixture of what did you say?" and later to the other old Irishmen of the corner, in the store, the bloody store, he, Donnelly, says, "Emil Duluoz——a perfect person," and they believe him.

But by that time we've all got big headaches——And our Manuel-wives'll have a scream at us——And it's only stored in bottles, tho you might think in furnaces of ire in Diablo Bottoms——"The trouble with you, Duluoz," pronounces Bull on our porch, the which even Gerard in his bed can heart, at 10 A.M.——

"What?"

"You're just too eager to hear for me to tell you what's wrong with you, so you can change and rectify——God made misers, and misers made God, and I'm suited."

They bump rolling heads together in the amazingness of this——

"Tst-tst," says my mother peeking from the kitchen, "it looks like your father is drunk this morning"——"Who's that, that big pile? He's swallowed all his glasses and his barrels in his nose, it looks like!——They want some breakfast——I'll warm up last night's good *ragout d'boulette*" (pork meatball stew with onions and carrots and potatoes, exquisite, Old Bull Baloon never had a better meal since the time in Wyoming the fry-cook said to him at dawn "I got some nice homefrieds for ya this morning, Bull"——

O pitiful, lovable, soon-to-be-departed earth,——)

That'll do.

"And time bids be gone"——

It might be pepper for a cold feast, but I always did say that the fact that men *are*, is more interesting than anything they might do——'tis only a poor action on a part stage and the scenery (the fakery) can be seen to shift and jello, in the back-drops, the stagehands are clumsy, the designer clumsy, and thine eye quick——Inadequate settings, poorly paid carpenters——You wake up in the middle of the night and look at the horizon sneaking swiftly back into place, and you think "O God, it's all the same thing"——That there *is* a world, that, rather, there *seems* to be a world, is hugely more interesting than what tiddly diddly well might happen in it, like Nirvana in an ant-heap or an ant-heap in Nirvana, *one*——

Bless my soul, death is the only decent subject, since it marks the end of illusion and delusion——Death is the other side of the same coin, we call now, Life——The appearance of sweet Gerard's flower face, followed by its disappearance, alas, only a contour-maker and shadow-selector could prove it, that in all the perfect snow any such person or thing ever did arrive say Yea and go away——The whole world has no reality, it's only imaginary, and what are we to do?——Nothing——*nothing*——*nothing*. Pray to be kind, wait to be patient, try to be fine. No use screamin. The Devil was a charming fool.

In his last days Gerard had little to do but lay in bed and stare at the ceiling, and sometimes watch the cat. "Look Ti Jean, the little nut——look, he looks one way, he looks the other—— Lookat the crazy face, what's he thinkin?——Everytime he sees something what does he think?——Look, he's goin in the other room. Why? What's he thinkin that makes him go in the next room? Look, now he stops, he looks——he licks himself—— there, he yawns——well, now he's comin back——he's crazy—— O CRAZY KITIGI! Bring him!" and I'd bring him the little grey tiger cat and we'd biddle and fwiddle with his crazy nose and stroke his head and he'd set in purring and glad. "Look at him, a little crazy ball like that, a little white belly as soft and as smooth as a heart——God made kitties I guess for us——God sent his kitties everywhere——Take care of my kitigi when I'm gone," he adds holding kitigi to his face and almost crying.

"Where you goin?"

No answer.

"See? the little face, the little head, look, I could break his head by squeezing my hand——it's only a little thing with no strength——God put these little things on earth to see if we want to hurt them——those who dont do it who *can*, are for his Heaven——those who see they can hurt, and *do* hurt, they're not for his Heaven——See?"

"*Oui.*"

"Always be careful not to hurt anyone——never get mad if you can help it——I gave you a slap in the face the other day but I didnt know it when I did it"——

(That'd been one of the last days when he felt good enough to get up and play with his erector set, a gray exciting morning for all-day work, gladly he'd at the breakfast crumb-swept newspapers of the table begun to raise his first important girder when I importunately rushed up tho gleefully to join in the watching but knocked the whole thing over scattering screws and bolts all over and upsetting the delicate traps, inadvertently and with that eternal perdurable mistakenness we all know, he slapped my face yelling "*Décolle donc!*" (Get away!) and must have instantly regretted it, no doubt that in a few minutes his remorse was greater than my disappointed regret——) We made up soon enough, head to head at the sad and final mortal window, holy Gerard and I, which gave credence now to his speech about kindness; and a speech it is, that down thru the imaginary eternities, is, and hath been, handed down by all spiritual heroes (of his like and calibre):——immeasurable kindness——"It's in the words of the Lord's Prayer——forgive us our sins, as we forgive those who sin against us. Did you forgive me for hitting you?"

"Oui"——(tho I was too littly naive to know what it meant *forgive*, and hadnt really forgiven him, holding back that reserve of selfly splendor for future pomp)——As solid as anything, as solid as the rock of the mountain, the solid folly men and boys and women will have——"I hit you——but I didnt have to, now I know it, the junk is packed away, the thing I was building with my set" (he shrugs gallicly) "I dont remember it any more!"

"The *grignot!*"

"Dont remind me," he smiles wanly.

"Ti Jean, dont bother Gerard, he's got to sleep this morning."

June, late June, with the trees having burdgeoned green and golden and the beeswax bugs are high chickadeeing the topmost trees embrowsying the drowsy air of reader's noon, the backfences of Beaulieu street sleeping like lazy dogs, the flies rubbing their miser forelegs on screens, "The little flies too, you dont have to kill them——they rub their little legs, they dont know how to do anything else——"

"Sleep Gerard, the doctor wants you to sleep——Go outside Ti Jean, you've talked enough this morning."

And I cry, to lose my buddy, whose pale door is closed on me, and there he is with his protected little kitty in the fold of his sheets and the birds are at the window waiting for more of those familiar crumbs from his sure hands——

The doctor comes more often, leaves sooner.

I wander up and down Beaulieu Street, lonely, little, a little Our Gang Rascal with no gang and no comedy and no ring-eyed dog or Pancakes to throw——All alone in mid afternoon I sit on the highwood backsteps of the St. Louis Bazaar hall and strive to imitate the sound it makes when Uncle Mike Duluoz and his wife and all the Duluozes drive over from Nashua to visit us and sit in the parlor and lament——"A BWA! A BWA!"—— I'm especially imitating Uncle Mike, the hurt curl of his lips—— His great rouge cry-face, poor Uncle Mike had he seen that, my little pantomime of him, he'd a wept cruds to the earth to add to the woe——

"Cut out that noise, you little brat——we've been listening to that bwa-bwa all morning!" shouts a woman from the tenement washlines across the way——I cant go on with my A-BWA play, go back to the house, Gerard's asleep, Ma's doing the wash, I go in the cellar, it's dark and damp and sad——My mother calls from the door above "Your little chum is back!" meaning some child from down the street I'd befriended a few weeks ago and now I dont remember him from beans——Hands aback clasped I go to Gerard's bedroom door, he meditates gently in mid afternoon, the shades drawn——

"Ti Jean," he calls me, "take my pillow and raise it a little—— there——thanks——I wanta see my birds outside——raise the shade——tick tzick tzick birdies!"——His breath smells like crushed flowers——I see and behold the sad sideways look for the last time, the long triste nun-like face, the blue eyes in their hollows.

Soon he's asleep on his sitting-up pillow.

When the little kitty is given his milk, I imitate Gerard and get down on my stomach and watch him greedily licking up his milk with pink tongue and chup chup jowls——

"You happy Ti Pou?——your nice *lala*"——

They see me in the parlor imitating Gerard with imaginary talks back and forth concerning lambs, kitties, clouds.

July comes, the pop firecrackers start coming on like a war in the neighborhood——Gerard's room takes on the quality of a lily, white, wan, fragrant——My mother and father are shaking their heads——

"What's the matter with Gerard?"

"He's very sick, Ti Pousse."

Ti Nin and I wait on the porch wondering what's wrong. I wanta go in and talk to him but I'm not allowed——The doctor turns up the sheets and looks at Gerard's swollen legs and says "That must hurt——I've never seen a kid like this——keep giving him that prescription——How you feelin Gerard?"

Gerard unaccustomed to being spoken to in English, answers, with girlish lips made so by sickness, or girlish-should-I-say-beautiful lips, "I'm aw-right, Doctor Simp*kins*," with the accent on "kins," like my mother talks——

The big doctor betakes his black suited bulk out of that house of sorrows and goes home, having given up hope a long time ago——

Some time near the 4th of July he tells my mother to call the priest——"He cant have the strength to go any further" ("if he does," adding to think, "it'll be murder")——

My father, arms loaded with paper bags in which are firecrackers, with an expectant smile comes in that night, but he's told the priest will be called——With that comes the nuns, there they come down Beaulieu Street, three of them, to sit at Gerard's bedside praying——He's awake.

"How are you feeling, Gerard?"

"Awright, my sister."

"Are you afraid, sweetheart?"

"No my sister——The priest blessed me——"

They ask him questions which he answers briefly and softly, my mother sees the nun taking it down on paper——She never saw the paper again——Some secret transmitted from mouth to heart, at the quiet hour, I have no idea where any such paper or record could have ended or could be found today, lest it's written on the rock in the mountains of gold in the country I cant reach——Or some fleecy mystery imparted, concerning the kinds of fearlessness, or the proof of faith, or the ethereality of pain, or the unreality of death (and life too), or the calm hand of God everywhere slowly benedicting——Whatever, the solemn tearful nuns did take it down, his last words, at deathside bed, and betook themselves back to the nunnery with it, and crossed themselves, and you can be sure there were special prayers that night——Saint Teresa, who promised to come back and shower the earth with roses after her death, shower ye with roses the secret nun who understands, make her pallet a better one than canopied of Kings'——Shower with roses and defend all the lambs and war the wraithful doves around——I'm afraid to say what I really want to say.

I dont remember how Gerard died, but (in my memory, which is limited and mundane) here I am running pellmell out of the house about 4 o'clock in the afternoon and down the sidewalk of Beaulieu Street yelling to my father whom I've seen coming around the corner woeful and slow with strawhat back and coat over arms in the summer heat, gleefully I'm yelling "*Gerard est mort!*"(Gerard is dead!) as tho it was some great event that would make a change that would make everything better, which it actually was, which granted it actually was.

But I thought it had something to do with some holy transformation that would make him greater and more Gerard like——He would reappear, following his "death," so huge and all powerful and renewed——The dizzy brain of the four-year-old, with its visions and infold mysticisms——I grabbed Pa and tugged his hand and glee'd to see the expression of likewise gladness on his face, so when he wearily just said "I know, Ti Pousse, I know" I had that same feeling that I have today when I would rush and tell people the good news that Nirvana, Heaven, Our Salvation is *Here* and *Now*, that gloomy reaction of theirs, which I can only attribute to pitiful and so-to-be-loved Ignorance of mortal brains.

"I know, my little wolf, I know," and sadly he drags himself into the house as I dance after.

The undertakers presumably carry the little no-more-body of no-more-pain-and swelled-legs away, in a tidy basket, to prepare him for his lying-in-state in our front parlor, and that night all the Duluozes do drive up from Nashua in tragic blackflap cars and come to crying and jawing in the brown kitchen of eternity as suddenly in my mind, as tho it was only a dream, a vision in the mind, which it is, I see the whole house and woe open up from within its every molecule and become instead of contours of walls and ceilings and absence-holes of doors and windows and there-yawps of voices and lamentings and wherewillgo-beings of personality and name, Aunt Clementine, Uncle Mike, cousins Roland and Edgar, Aunt Marie, Pa and Ma and Nin at the lot, just suddenly a great swarming mass of roe-like fiery whitenesses, as if a curtain had opened, and innumerably re-vealed the scene behind the scene ("the scene behind the scene is always more interesting than the show," says J.R.Williams the *Out Our Way* cartoonist), shows itself compounded be, of emptiness, of pure light, of imagination, of mind, mind-only, madness, mental woe, the strivings of mind pain, the working-at-thinking which is all this imagined death & false life, phan-tasmal beings, phantoms finagling in the gloom, goopy poor figures haranguing and failing with lack-hands in a fallen-angel world of shadows and glore, the central entire essence of which is dazzling radiant blissful ecstasy unending, the unbelievable Truth that cracks open in my head like an oyster and I see it, the house disappears in her Swarm of Snow, Gerard is dead and the soul is dead and the world is dead and dead is dead.

I've since dreamed it a million times, down the corridors of Seeming eternity where there are a million mirrored figures sitting thus and each the same, the house on Beaulieu Street the night Gerard died and the assembled Duluozes wailing with green faces of death for fear of death in time, and Time's con-sumed it all already, it's a dream already a long time ended and they dont know it and I try to tell them, they wanta slap me in the kisser I'm so gleeful, they send me upstairs to bed——An old dream too I've had of me glooping, that night, in the parlor, by Gerard's coffin, I dont see him in the coffin but he's there, his ghost, brown ghost, and I'm grown sick in my papers (my writ-ing papers, my bloody "literary career" ladies and gentlemen) and the whole reason why I ever wrote at all and drew breath to bite in vain with pen of ink, great gad with indefensible Usable pencil, because of Gerard, the idealism, Gerard the religious hero——"*Write in honor of his death*" (*Écrivez pour l'amour de son mort*) (as one would say, write for the love of God)——for by his pain, the birds were saved, and the cats and mice, and the poor relatives crying, and my mother losing all her teeth in the six terrible weeks prior to his death during which time she stayed up all night every night and grew such a mess of nerves in her stomach that her teeth began falling one by one, might sight funny to some hunters of conceit, but this wit has had it.

Lord bless it, an Ethereal Flower, I saw it all blossom——they packed me to bed. They raved in the kitchen and had it their way.

There's the rocking chair, Uncle Mike's wife had it, the peculiar dreary voice she had, fast way she talked, things I cant utter but I'd roll and broil in butter, the gurgle in their throats——I could recount the dreary yellings and give you all the details—— It's all in the same woods——It's all one flesh, and the pieces of it will come and go, alien hats and coats not to the contrary—— Uncle Mike had a greenish face: he had barrelsful of pickles in Nashua, a sawdust oldtime store, meat-hacks and hung hams and baskets of produce on the sidewalk: fish in boxes, salted.—— Emil's brother,——"So *vain*, so full of ego, people——shut your mouth you" he finally says to his wife, "I'm talkin tonight—— in the great silence of our father we'll find the reasons for our prides, our avarices, our dollars——It's better any way, now that he's dead his belly doesnt hurt any more and his heart and his legs, it's better"——

"Have it your way," says my father listlessly.

"Ah Emil Emil dont you remember when we were children and we slept together and Papa built his house with his own hands and all the times I helped you——we too we'll die, Emil, and when we're dead will there be someone, *one person* for the love of God, who'll be able to look at us in our coffins and say 'It's all over, the *marde*, the fret, the force, the strength'?—— more's the strength in the belly than anywhere else——finished, bought, sold, washed, brought to the great heaven! Emil dont cry, dont be discouraged, your little boy is better——remember you well what Papa used to say in back of his stove——"

"With his bottle on Sunday mornings, aw sure that one was a smart one!" (the wife).

"Shut your mouth I said!——All men die——And when they die as child, even better——they're *pure* for heaven——Emil, Emil,——poor young Emil, my little brother!"

They shake their heads violently the same way, thinking.

"Ah"——they bite their lips the same way, their bulgey eyes are on the floor.

"It ends like it ends"——

My mother's upstairs sobbing, lost all her control now——The aunts are cleaning out the death bed, there's a great to do of sheets and an end to sheets, a Spring cleaning.

"I brought him on earth, in my womb, the Virgin Mary help me!——in my womb, with pain——I gave him his milk!——I took care of him——I stood at his bedside——I bought him presents on Christmas, I made him little costumes Halloween——I'd make his nice oatmeal he loves so much in the mornings!——I'd listen to his little stories, I examined his little pictures he drew——I did everything in my power to make his little life contented——inside me, outside me, *and returned to the earth!*" wails my mother realizing the utter hopeless loss of life and death, the completely defeated conditionality and partiality of it, the pure mess it entails, yet people go on hoping and hoping——"I did everything," she sobs with handkerchief to face, in the bedroom, as the Bradleys, Aunt Pauline, her sister, come in, from New Hampshire, "and it didnt work——*he died anyhow*——They took him off to Heaven!——They didnt leave him with me!——Gerard, my little Gerard!"

"Calm yourself, poor Ange, you've suffered so."

"I havent suffered like he did, that's what *breaks* my heart!" and she yells that and they all know she really means it, she's had her fill of the injustice of it, a little lame boy dying without hope——"It's *that* that's tearing my heart out and breaking my head in two!"

"Ange, Ange, poor sensitive heart!" weeps gentle Aunt Marie at her shoulder.

Nin and I are sobbing horribly in bed side by side to hear these pitiful wracks of clack talk coming from our own human mother, the softness of her arms all gashed now in the steely proposition Death——

"I'll never be able to wipe that from my memory!"——"Not as long as I live!"——"He died *without* a chance!"

"We all die——"

"Good, damn it, good!" she cries, and this sends chills thru all of us man and child and the house is One Woe this night.

Meanwhile, insanely, our cousins Edgar and Roland have sneaked off with the firecrackers to the backyard, and like leering devils, which they arent really, but as much as like satyrs and Mockers and be-striders of misfortune, there they are setting off all our precious firecrackers, Nin's and mine and Gerard's, at midnight, callously, a veritable burning of the books of the Duluozes, Ker plack, whack, c a ka ta r a k sht boom!

"*Les mauva, les mauva,*" (mean! mean!) Ti Nin and I scream in pillows——

The Bradleys are going to drive us to Nashua for the night and bring us back for the funeral in 48 hours——With Gerard and the firecrackers all gone, and Ma crying on the very floor, we had better be driven somewhere——

When Ti Nin and I were little.

Then comes the solemn funeral, Nin and I are taken back on a rainy dreary day to see the house all one great Gloom Shrine full of kids from the St. Louis Parochial School filing in and out in frightened parades, their eyes straining to see the deadface in the unholy velvet pillow among the flowers, the sooner they see it the quicker they'll know the face of death and fears be justified all——And files of nuns, standing by the coffin, praying with long black wooden rosaries——All dolled up in little necktie I cant believe it's my own house and this, this World Parlor with Histories of Black being written in it, the very selfsame silly drowsy parlor where I'd sat and goofed away whole long afternoons chubbling with my lips or going goopy goopy at the window passers, or with Gerard (whose head I hold no claim on any more) held head-to-head confabs and listened to the holy lazy silence of Time as it washed and washed forever more——But now, his bier a glory, in death all Splendidified, banished-from-hair-earth and admitted-to-Perfectness he lies, commemorating our parlor silently, tho no one knows precisely what I know——But others know something of him I never

knew, the nuns, and some of the boys, and mayhap Père Lalumière the *Curé* who now in the kitchen with one ecclesiastical
blackshoe up on a chair and manly elbow on knee assured my
mother "Ah well, be not anxious, Mrs. Duluoz, he was a little
saint! He's certainly in Heaven!"

That was the reason for the big crowd, they came to see
the little boy in the neighborhood who had died and gone
to heaven, and housewives even that day began noticing and
announcing that the flock of birds, the nation of phebes and
peewits and meek and lowly whatnots that had pestered at his
window for so long since Spring broke in, was gone——

"They're gone completely."

"You dont see one."

"It's 'cause it's rainin!"

But the next day, and the next day, and the next day after that,
the little ones revisited no more the scene of the deicide——

"They're gone with him!"

Or, I'd say, "It was himself."

Unforgettable the files of children come to see the cheek they
knew so well in classrooms, to see its loss of lustre pink, and
estimate the value of death——With what avid and horrified eyes
they gazed on little Schoolmate so reposy silent in his ornate
bed——What horror even just to approach the house and see
the wreath, with the fatal pale blue ribbon, and the fatal drawn
shades in the parlor——The vultures do feed on disconsolate
such-rooftops when you look, the chimney exudes angels of
fear like whirligigs of gray butterflies . . .

What you learn the first time you get drunk at sixteen, tugging
at old urinaters in Moody Street saloons and yelling "Dont you
realize you are God?" is what you learn when you understand
the meaning that's here before you on this heavy earth: living
but to die . . . look at the sky, stars; look at the tomb, dead——In
invoking the help, Transcendental help from other spheres of
this Imaginary Blossom, invoke at least, by plea, for the learning of the lesson:——help me understand that I am God——that
it's all God——Urinating, alone, wont get you far——It happens, every day, in all the latrines of Samsara——*Here and Now*,
said the children seeing "*Ti Gerard Duluoz qu'est mort*"——"it's

not any harder'n that——they wont be able to punish me any more"——Beyond punishment, he lies, qualified for eternity and perfectness——"Is it *true* he's dead?——mebbe he's kidding"—— and all the ghost feelings of men——But no, "that bareheaded life under grass" is no "blithe spirit"——It's the genuine death.

All the desperate praying in the stuffy parlor is scaring the kids half to death, they think "It'll happen to me too but look how they're all afraid of it?"

Clasped in Gerard's kindly fingers is a beautiful solid silver crucifix——There are flowers from relatives in Maine who couldnt come, from friends——All the people in the world who wear their daily face come passing with their final face, as, for instance, Manuel, sober, dark-attired, unaccostably silent, he wont even speak to the priest, to Emil he makes one regretful nod——He'll be one of the pallbearers.

Old Bull Baloon is gone west, wont be at the funeral.

The women, the aunts, stand at the back and are never weary of shaking their heads from side to side, and *lamenting the loss*, and talking about it——

Young priests make polite calls and add their powerful prayers and depart swiftly to duties in the gloom——One of them has such a handsome sad face, it's a shame he never married and presented it to some respectful wench——

"The young Lafontaine!"

"Aw oui——he comes from Montreal——I didnt know he was so short."

"Yes but he's so pretty."

"Pretty? Handsome as a heart——It's too bad——All the good men are bought up or else won."

"One or the other."

"Look here comes old lady Picard——she never misses one——"

"No——Oh well, the old lady, we'll accept her prayers."

"Her prayers are not to be thrown away."

"There——the little angels——another line——This one, they tell me it was Gerard's class——yes——the nuns are puttin em in front——there. The little angels. They're afraid."

"Ah"——sigh——"they'll have to know *some* day, it happens to all of us."

"Ah, but he was so young."

"Look at that old bat across the street, she's burning her

garbage and all the smoke blowin on the house of the dead with the wind."

The house of the dead indeed, it was hardly my house——I'd lost Gerard in the shuffle.

High above, in the stormy sky, a bird with little buffeted birdy bones bats ahead, beak to the nose of the wind——Shrouds of gray rain fall Awe-ing and slanting to our crystal——It is the sky, the void, that no fist could form in and hold any part of it—— Below, on the stain of earth, where we all, human brothers and sisters, pop like flower after flower from the fecund same joke of unstymied pregnant earth and raise standardbearers of fertility and ego-personality, life, below the blown shrodes and woe-bo blackclouds June is handing down from some whoreson unseasonal storm, patches of brown and yellow and black show where we live, chimneys are pouring black smoke——"The Chimbleys of the World!"——And we are angels revisiting it——Coming down, far, sad, wide, the world, the earth, this pot, this place, this parturience-organizer——There are the chimney smokes fuming up and pouring and defiling open space, and there the tracks, cracks, cities, dead cats floating in rivers, calendars on the wall indicating June 1926——License plates on old cars sayin Massachusetts, the helm and Chineemark of it——The name of a store, in gold leaf letters embossed and chipping already, "Lowell Provision Company," a self-believing butcher with a handlebar mustache standing in the door, full of human hope and realistic sentimentality among the charnels and hacked thighs of his own making, bleedied in his blocks, his hands raw from blood-juice, red in fact——Shakespeare, Throwspeare, Disappear Spear, and where is the Provision made for a "cessation and a truce" to all this sprouting of being just so it can wilt and be sacked, canned——We the angel spirits, descend to this earth, earth indeed, we are awed to see living beings, living beings indeed, we see man there ghostly crystal apparition juggling as he goes in selfmade streets inside Mind a liquid phantom glur-ing on the brain ectoplasm——A vision in water——

Papier-mâché canals flow in downtown Lowell, men smoking cigars stand by the rail spitting in the waters that reflect drizzle hopelessness of 1926——And to their way of thinking, ahem, the money in their pocket is real and the pride in their heads as real as sin and as solid as Hell——And the money that is real and the pride that is solid is about to buy an actual porkchop which tho it has since appeared (it is now 1956, Jan. 16, Midnight), the hunger with it, and the hungerer to boot, can still be called *real*, tho it neither *is not*, nor *is*, but beyond such considerations anyway, like a reflection of a porkchop on water——Facts well known by fat Mr. Groscorp who now, in his apartment across the street from the St. Louis Presbytère, on West Sixth Street, is about to partake of his noonday meal at the kitchen table by the rain drizzled window that looks down on the street where suddenly a slow caravanseri of limousines and flower-roadsters has rounded the corner from Beaulieu Street, and headed up to the church front, where official waiters minister with the proper silver special knobs——His face is huge, muckchop rich as kincobs, sleek as surah, gray pale and fetid to-make-you-sick, a great beast, with small mouth makes an oo of simpery delight, and great hanging jowls——A bathrobe, slippers, a fat cat——Winebottle and chops laid out——His huge paunch keeps him well away from his fork, and makes it necessary for the eating-chair to be scraped a good deal of the way back, so that he stoops, or rather hunches forward with huge mountainous determination, like a tunnel, to his about-to-be-eaten lunch—— "Ah," he interrupted, "another corpse!"——And he raises napkin to lips, and watches leaning up to see below closer——"In all this rain, they're gonna bury another one,——aw dammit, it's a pity, it spoils all my meal——It all goes down the same hole, why make such a great ceremonial fuss?——The solemnity, the gloves——the special gloves and the stiff legs——the little mousey smile——the little mustache——the big hunger for nothing to eat, or else the great famine in the richness of the season—— One or t'other, it's all the same, because," raising his eyes to the upper part of the window and examining the blown gust clouds, "you might say"——he burps delicately, lowering the shade——"That, there's plenty more where it came from, the comin and the goin——Outa my way, I'm eating——We'll think about it later——"

The funeral directors with their cars had assembled at our door on Beaulieu and carefully, from our great drear house built on an old cemetery in which were more dead soul dusts than in all the words of this book, its sorrow was removed from its nest——Sleek like a snake the coffin was slid out and in the hearse, bang.

And around the corner.

The children and some onlookers follow on the sidewalk, the church is only a block and a half away.

Right by the building where huge Mr. Groscorp's eating his necessitous Samsara dinner, is a gang of painters and plasterers and tile layers working on a new house——They've just had their last lunch slug of coffee and feel good and make cracks.

"Ah, another one for the cemetery?"

"Why dont they hurry up, damn them, it's not so much fun playin with the dead in the rain!"

"An old bastard who fell face first dead in his soup, I bet."

"Or else some old bitch spent all her life yellin at her husband and her brother, now they wont hear her no more——Do you believe those hypocrite faces you see?"

"Or else an old priest, dead in his bed."

"Or else an old housepainter, he fell off the ladder and spent six months in the hospital yelling 'A dammit it hurts!' and after that they carried him out."

"No——too gay——a whore, from Boston, returned home, she spent sixteen years in the whorehouse swingin her ass for a buck and now the funeral director with the little ass's got half, and——"

"And the rest lost in the bank a the dead."

"Throw em some rice, we'll marry em!"

"Look, they stopped to take out the coffin."

"Coffin for the so-pretty" (*Tombeau pour les si beaux*).

"It's not a long one——"

"It's not a long one?——dammit, it's a child's coffin."

They all get quiet.

"Ah, well that's a story we forgot."

"We're not good enough storytellers."

"Well me I'm paintin."

"Paint, dog, till your hand close your buttons."

"Till they put a brush in your mug, my fine Piroux, and after that we'll sing dirty songs for ya."

"Suits me."

"Look——that little coffin, the kid wasnt ten."

"All the better for him."

"And why?"

"*And why* he asks me with his ignorant face?"

"It's raining on your head, come on in here."

"There'll be plenty of rainin on the head today."

And inside the church now as the procession comes in, the pallbearers carrying the little coffin, followed by Ma and Pa and me and Nin and relatives, across the gritty sidewalk, great comes the opening peals of the organ sounding the beginning of the mass.

"Suscipe, sancte Pater, omnipotens aeterne Deus, hanc immaculatam hostiam, quam ego indignus famulus tuus offero tibi, Deo meo vivo et vero, pro innumerabilibus peccatis, et offensionibus, et negligentiis meis, et pro omnibus circumstantibus, sed et pro omnibus fidelibus christianis vivis atque defunctis: ut mihi et illis proficiat ad salutem in vitam aeternam. Amen."

An eternal salute . . .

One of the first if not the very first, memories of my life, I'm in a shoe repair store and there are shelves cluttered with dark shoes, innumerable battered shoes, and it's a gray rainy day (like the day of the funeral, or rather, foggy-misty with occasional drizzle)——I'm presumably with Ma and probably one year old in my baby carriage (if it happened at all) and the Vision is of the great Gloom of the earth and the great Clutter of human life and the great Drizzly Dream of the dreary eternities, and as we leave the shop, or, as is left the shop, by self or phantom, suddenly is seen a little old man, or ordinary man, in a strangely slanted gray hat, in coat, presumably, walking off up the dreary and endless boulevard of the drizzle dump, the tearful beatness of the scene and weird as if maybe this is just a memory of mine from some previous incarnation in St. Petersburg Russia or maybe the gluey ghees of dark fitful kitchens in Thibet ancient and long ago, tho not with that hat——That hat, with its strange Dostoevskyan slant, belongs to the West, this side of this hairball, earth——And it seems to me that the little man is going towards some inexpressibly beautiful opening in the rain where it will be all open-sky and radiant, but I will never go there, as I'm being wheeled another way in my present vehicle——He, on foot, heads for the pure land——So that it seemed to me as the organ music played and the priest intoned in Latin at the altar far up the pews in the end of time, that Gerard, now motionless in the central presented bier at the foot of the main aisle and by the altar rail, with his long face composed, honorably mounted and all beflowered and anointed, was delivered to that Pure Land where I could never go or at least not for a long time——Dread drizzle *mer*, dread drizzle *mer!*

"*Et pro omnibus*" sings the priest in rising and falling Latin, incense everywhere, and turns with that untouchable delicacy of lace over holy black, with all his paraphernalias, and it seems in my 3-year'd brain "et pro om-ni-boos" is the description of that land and that attainment, the glory of Gerard——(that was prophesied)——"*aeternam*," the gloomy fall of the song voice, "eternity," I can almost guess and smell the location and no way in my wild mind to muddle my way and shake off——And I'm so little and so far back, and in my reveries and dreams later on it seems the funeral took place across the street from our house in a strange other church permeating everywhere——Just as the simplest thing in the world, when properly looked at, is the original riddle.

——Way at the back of the church are blankfaced standers, it's like Good Friday when the church is crowded and it's usually raining (and according to superstition) and there are standers at the back in overshoes or rubbers or with umbrellas who want to quit swiftly the snowy grace and get back to the poolhall——I dont understand anything of the funeral service, its solemnity escapes my high head as I look around and mull over faces of people and those tragic overshoes and wet splashes of almost puddles at the back of the church and the hopeless dampness as tho it was all taking place underneath some stone steps and there are the drear shadows making the yellowy marble so faint, so sad——The daubing at eyes by aunts and mothers, their faces squeezing into sections wishing he hadnt died, ah, seems to me fitting and proper, it's all part of the show——It's a vast ethereal movie, I'm an extra and Gerard is the hero and God is directing it from Heaven——

I see bleak wooden fences in the rain and the little man with the mysterious hat and then my mind swirls and I see nothing but the swarm of angels in the church in the form of sudden myriad illuminated snowflakes of ecstasy——I scoff to think that anybody should cry——I let go a little yell, my mother grabs my

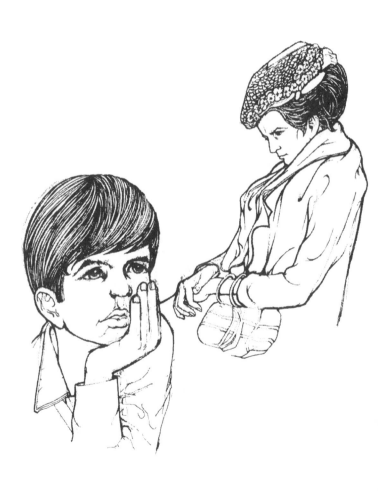

face and taps me gently, "*Non non non*"——People gloomy at the funeral have heard the little child's voice, they think: "He doesnt understand."——

I want to express somehow, "*Here* and *Now* I see the ecstasy," the divine and perfect ecstasy, reward without end, it has come, has been always with us, the formalities of the tomb are ignorant irrelevancies most befittingly gravely conducted by proper qualified doers and actors and Latin-singers——Of a rouse, the boys' choir takes up in the back and my mother's eyes burst with tears, she never could stand boys singing anyway.

"Some of them knew Gerard!" she announces proudly to near-at-hand solemn Emil and thru him at Marie——"The little angels!" ("Sing, sing," she thinks, "sing with all your hearts my angels for my friend Gerard who is dead, my little man, my little sad son——It's for yourselves you sing, angels!!")

I myself hear the boys singing and turn around to see them in the choir loft with their little oo-voices uplifted and rosy to the black arms of a hypnotist, a hypnotist of feeling——By the way the boys are singing and by significant rustles you can tell the service (and increasing coughs) is almost over——Easy enough to cough cough cough and go back home, off other people's funerals!

And Oh the coffin at the forefront, and the priest flicking the ciborium incense pot and at each flick, in three directions, by some magic bell rope signal, the outside roofbell flicks like smoke itself and kicks off a soft "ker plang" for the edification of the people of Centreville, Gerard has died——Drizzly news——From the incense pot, "ker-tling," so gentle and quiet, to the sound of the connecting signal rope, "kak," and "ker plang," such beautiful music and I see three fumes of music smoke float up and away——Let there be rejoicing.

We all get in cars and they slowly weave the parade and out we go on a long slow drive along the Merrimac River, by sodden trees in all their foliage looking sad, to the bridge at Tyngsboro, and across that, to Nashua, entering that little city (my parents' come-from town) in bleak array, to the cemetery outside town, where I remember the long gray wall, and the glistening boulevard in the rain——And they haul the coffin gently down to graveropes that for all their gentle look have no gentle job to do, and lower away, easy does it, the little hunk of pain, into the mud——Roots and plopping pieces show in the dug sides——Men stand around, my father in the midst of them, bareheaded, with that goarly helplessness beneath immense and endless skies that say "Yah" down upon the entire scene——My father's curly hair is moist, and uncombed, and his lids of eyes are down where they'll always be——A cold place to kneel, this earth, and he'll kneel again, it's a cold place for knees——Ma and Ti Nin sitting with me in a black car burst out sobbing as the coffin downward disappears, I turn to them and say "Well why are you crying?"

"Ti Jean you dont understand, you're too young to understand!" they wail, seeing my rosy face, my questioning eyes.

I look again, the men have stepped a pace aback, expectant, old gravedigger picks up his shovel and closes the book.

T H E   E N D

Sometime in the same
night that's everywhere
the same right now
and forevermore
        amen

BIG SUR

My work comprises one vast book like Proust's except that my remembrances are written on the run instead of afterwards in a sick bed. Because of the objections of my early publishers I was not allowed to use the same personae names in each work. On the Road, The Subterraneans, The Dharma Bums, Doctor Sax, Maggie Cassidy, Tristessa, Desolation Angels, Visions of Cody *and the others including this book* Big Sur *are just chapters in the whole work which I call* The Duluoz Legend. *In my old age I intend to collect all my work and re-insert my pantheon of uniform names, leave the long shelf full of books there, and die happy. The whole thing forms one enormous comedy, seen through the eyes of poor Ti Jean (me), otherwise known as Jack Duluoz, the world of raging action and folly and also of gentle sweetness seen through the keyhole of his eye.*

JACK KEROUAC

1

THE CHURCH IS BLOWING a sad windblown "Kathleen" on the bells in the skid row slums as I wake up all woebegone and goopy, groaning from another drinking bout and groaning most of all because I'd ruined my "secret return" to San Francisco by getting silly drunk while hiding in the alleys with bums and then marching forth into North Beach to see everybody altho Lorenz Monsanto and I'd exchanged huge letters outlining how I would sneak in quietly, call him on the phone using a code name like Adam Yulch or Lalagy Pulvertaft (also writers) and then he would secretly drive me to his cabin in the Big Sur woods where I would be alone and undisturbed for six weeks just chopping wood, drawing water, writing, sleeping, hiking, etc. etc.——But instead I've bounced drunk into his City Lights bookshop at the height of Saturday night business, everyone recognized me (even tho I was wearing my disguise-like fisherman's hat and fishermen coat and pants waterproof) and 't'all ends up a roaring drunk in all the famous bars the bloody "King of the Beatniks" is back in town buying drinks for everyone—— Two days of that, including Sunday the day Lorenzo is supposed to pick me up at my "secret" skid row hotel (the Mars on 4th and Howard) but when he calls for me there's no answer, he has the clerk open the door and what does he see but me out on the floor among bottles, Ben Fagan stretched out partly beneath the bed, and Robert Browning the beatnik painter out on the bed, snoring——So says to himself "I'll pick him up next weekend, I guess he wants to drink for a week in the city (like he always does, I guess)" so off he drives to his Big Sur cabin without me thinking he's doing the right thing but my God when I wake up, and Ben and Browning are gone, they've somehow dumped me on the bed, and I hear "I'll Take You Home Again Kathleen" being bellroped so sad in the fog winds out there that blow across the rooftops of eerie old hangover Frisco, wow, I've hit the end of the trail and cant even drag my body any more even to a refuge in the woods let alone stay upright in the city a minute——It's the first trip I've taken away from home (my mother's house) since the publication of "Road" the book that "made me famous" and in fact so much so I've been driven mad for three years by endless telegrams, phonecalls, requests, mail, visitors, reporters, snoopers (a big voice saying in my basement window as I prepare to write a story:——ARE YOU BUSY?) or the time the reporter ran upstairs to my bedroom as I sat there in my pajamas trying to write down a dream——Teenagers jumping the six-foot fence I'd had built around my yard for privacy——Parties with bottles yelling at my study window "Come on out and get drunk, all work and no play makes Jack a dull boy!"——A woman coming to my door and saying "I'm not going to ask you if you're Jack Duluoz because I know he wears a beard, can you tell me where I can find him, I want a real beatnik at my annual Shindig party"——Drunken visitors puking in my study, stealing books and even pencils——Uninvited acquaintances staying for days because of the clean beds and good food my mother provided——Me drunk practically all the time to put on a jovial cap to keep up with all this but finally realizing I was surrounded and outnumbered and had to get away to solitude again or die——So Lorenzo Monsanto wrote and said "Come to my cabin, no one'll know," etc. so I had sneaked into San Francisco as I say, coming 3000 miles from my home in Long Island (Northport) in a pleasant roomette on the California Zephyr train watching America roll by outside my private picture window, really happy for the first time in three years, staying in the roomette all three days and three nights with my instant coffee and sandwiches——Up the Hudson Valley and over across New York State to Chicago and then the Plains, the mountains, the desert, the final mountains of California, all so easy and dreamlike compared to my old harsh hitch hikings before I made enough money to take transcontinental trains (all over America highschool and college kids thinking "Jack Duluoz is 26 years old and on the road all the time hitch hiking" while there I am almost 40 years old, bored and jaded in a roomette bunk crashin across that Salt Flat)——But in any case a wonderful start towards my retreat so generously offered by sweet old Monsanto and instead of going thru smooth and easy I wake up drunk, sick, disgusted, frightened, in fact terrified by that sad song across the roofs mingling with the lachrymose cries of a Salvation Army meeting on the corner below "*Satan* is the cause of your alcoholism, *Satan* is the cause of

your immorality, Satan is *everywhere* workin to destroy you unless you repent *now*" and worse than that the sound of old
drunks throwing up in rooms next to mine, the creak of hall
steps, the moans everywhere——Including the moan that had
awakened me, my own moan in the lumpy bed, a moan caused
by a big roaring Whoo Whoo in my head that had shot me out
of my pillow like a ghost.

2

AND I LOOK AROUND THE DISMAL CELL, there's my hopeful rucksack all neatly packed with everything necessary to live in the woods, even unto the minutest first aid kit and diet details and even a neat little sewing kit cleverly reinforced by my good mother (like extra safety pins, buttons, special sewing needles, little aluminum scissors)——The hopeful medal of St. Christopher even which she'd sewn on the flap——The survival kit all in there down to the last little survival sweater and handkerchief and tennis sneakers (for hiking)——But the rucksack sits hopefully in a strewn mess of bottles all empty, empty poorboys of white port, butts, junk, horror. . . . "One fast move or I'm gone," I realize, gone the way of the last three years of drunken hopelessness which is a physical and spiritual and metaphysical hopelessness you cant learn in school no matter how many books on existentialism or pessimism you read, or how many jugs of vision-producing Ayahuasca you drink, or Mescaline take, or Peyote goop up with——That feeling when you wake up with the delirium tremens with the *fear* of eerie death dripping from your ears like those special heavy cobwebs spiders weave in the hot countries, the feeling of being a bentback mudman monster groaning underground in hot steaming mud pulling a long hot burden nowhere, the feeling of standing ankledeep in hot boiled pork blood, ugh, of being up to your waist in a giant pan of greasy brown dishwater not a trace of suds left in it——The face of yourself you see in the mirror with its expression of unbearable anguish so hagged and awful with sorrow you cant even cry for a thing so ugly, so lost, no connection whatever with early perfection and therefore nothing to connect with tears or anything: it's like William Seward Burroughs' "Stranger" suddenly appearing in your place in the mirror—— Enough! "One fast move or I'm gone" so I jump up, do my headstand first to pump blood back into the hairy brain, take a shower in the hall, new T-shirt and socks and underwear, pack vigorously, hoist the rucksack and run out throwing the key on the desk and hit the cold street and walk fast to the nearest little grocery store to buy two days of food, stick it in the rucksack, hike thru lost alleys of Russian sorrow where bums sit head on knees in foggy doorways in the goopy eerie city night I've got to escape or die, and into the bus station——In a half hour into a bus seat, the bus says "Monterey" and off we go down the clean neon hiway and I sleep all the way, waking up amazed and well again smelling sea air the bus driver shaking me "End of the line, Monterey."——And by God it *is* Monterey, I stand sleepy in the 2 A.M. seeing vague little fishing masts across the street from the bus driveway. Now all I've got to do to complete my escape is get 14 miles down the coast to the Raton Canyon bridge and hike in.

3

"ONE FAST MOVE OR I'M GONE" so I blow $8 on a cab to drive me down that coast, it's a foggy night tho sometimes you can see stars in the sky to the right where the sea is, tho you cant see the sea you can only hear about it from the cabdriver——"What kinda country is it around here? I've never seen it."

"Well, you cant see it tonight——Raton Canyon you say, you better be careful walkin around there in the dark."

"Why?"

"Well, just use your lamp like you say——"

And sure enough when he lets me off at the Raton Canyon bridge and counts the money I sense something wrong somehow, there's an awful roar of surf but it isnt coming from the right place, like you'd expect it to come from "over there" but it's coming from "under there"——I can see the bridge but I can see nothing below it——The bridge continues the coast highway from one bluff to another, it's a nice white bridge with white rails and there's a white line runnin down the middle familiar and highwaylike but something's wrong——Besides the headlights of the cab just shoot out over a few bushes into empty space in the direction where the canyon's supposed to be, it feels like being up in the air somewhere tho I can see the dirt road at our feet and the dirt overhang on the side——"What in the hell is this?"——I've got the directions all memorized from a little map Monsanto's mailed me but in my imagination dreaming about this big retreat back home there'd been something larkish, bucolic, all homely woods and gladness instead of all this aerial roaring mystery in the dark——When the cab leaves I therefore turn on my railroad lantern for a timid peek but its beam gets lost just like the car lights in a void and in fact the battery is fairly weak and I can hardly see the bluff at my left——As for the bridge I cant see it anymore except for graduating series of luminous shoulder buttons going off further into the low sea roar——The sea roar is bad enough except it keeps bashing and barking at me like a dog in the fog down there, sometimes it booms the earth but my God where is the earth

and how can the sea be underground!——"The only thing to
do," I gulp, "is to put this lantern shinin right in front of your
feet, *kid*do, and follow that lantern and make sure it's shinin
on the road rut and hope and pray it's shinin on ground that's
gonna be there when it's shining," in other words I actually fear
that even my lamp will carry me astray if I dare to raise it for a
minute from the ruts in the dirt road——The only satisfaction I
can glean from this roaring high horror of darkness is that the
lamp wobbles huge dark shadows of its little rim stays on the
overhanging bluff at the left of the road, because to the right
(where the bushes are wiggling in the wind from the sea) there
aint no shadows because there aint no light can take hold——So
I start my trudge, pack aback, just head down following my
lamp spot, head down but eyes suspiciously peering a little up,
like a man in the presence of a dangerous idiot he doesnt want
to annoy——The dirt road starts up a little, curves to the right,
starts down a little, then suddenly up again, and up——By now
the sea roar is further back and at one point I even stop and
look back to see nothing——"I'm gonna put out my light and
see what I can see" I say rooted to my feet where they're rooted
to that road——Fat lotta good, when I put out the light I see
nothing but the dim sand at my feet.

Trudging up and getting further away from the sea roar I get
to feel more confident but suddenly I come to a frightening
thing in the road, I stop and hold out my hand, edge forward,
it's only a cattle crossing (iron bars imbedded across the road)
but at the same time a big blast of wind comes from the left
where the bluff should be and I spot that way and see nothing.
"What the hell's going on!" "Follow the road," says the other
voice trying to be calm so I do but the next instant I hear a rattling to my right, throw my light there, see nothing but bushes
wiggling dry and mean and just the proper high canyonwall
kind of bushes fit for rattlesnakes too——(which it was, a rattlesnake doesnt like to be awakened in the middle of the night by
a trudging humpbacked monster with a lamp.)

But now the road's going down again, the reassuring bluff
reappears on my left, and pretty soon according to my memory
of Lorry's map there she is, the creek, I can hear her lappling
and gabbing down there at the bottom of the dark where
at least I'll be on level ground and done with booming airs

somewhere above——But the closer I get to the creek as the road dips steeply, suddenly, almost making me trot forward, the louder it roars, I begin to think I'll fall right into it before I can notice it——It's screaming like a raging flooded river right below me——Besides it's even *darker* down there than anywhere! There are glades down there, ferns of horror and slippery logs, mosses, dangerous plashings, humid mists rise coldly like the breath of death, big dangerous trees are beginning to bend over my head and brush my pack——There's a noise I know can only grow louder as I sink down and for fear how loud it can grow I stop and listen, it rises up crashing mysteriously at me from a raging battle among dark things, wood or rock or something cracked, all smashed, all wet black sunken earth danger——I'm *afraid* to go down there——I am *affrayed* in the old Edmund Spenser sense of being *frayed* by a whip, and a wet one at that——A slimy green dragon racket in the bush——An angry war that doesnt want me pokin around—— It's been there a million years and it doesnt want me clashing darkness with it——It comes snarling from a thousand crevasses and monster redwood roots all over the map of creation——It is a dark clangoror in the rain forest and doesnt want no skid row bum to carry to the sea which is bad enough and waitin back there——I can almost feel the sea pulling at that racket in the trees but there's my spotlamp so all I gotta do is follow the lovely sand road which dips and dips in rising carnage and suddenly a flattening, a sight of bridge logs, there's the bridge rail, there's the creek just four feet below, cross the bridge you woken bum and see what's on the other shore.

Take one quick peek at the water as you cross, just water over rocks, a small creek at that.

And now before me is a dreamy meadowland with a good old corral gate and a barbed wire fence the road running right on left but this where I get off at last. Then I crawl thru the barbed wire and find myself trudging a sweet little sand road winding right thru fragrant dry heathers as tho I'd just popped thru from hell into familiar old Heaven on Earth, yair and Thank God (tho a minute later my heart's in my mouth again because I see black things in the white sand ahead but it's only piles of good old mule dung in Heaven).

4

AND IN THE MORNING (after sleeping by the creek in the white sand) I do see what was so scary about my canyon road walk——The road's up there on the wall a thousand feet with a sheer drop sometimes, especially at the cattle crossing, way up highest, where a break in the bluff shows fog pouring through from another bend of the sea beyond, scary enough in itself anyway as tho one hole wasnt enough to open into the sea——And worst of all is the bridge! I go ambling seaward along the path by the creek and see this awful thin white line of bridge a thousand unbridgeable sighs of height above the little woods I'm walking in, you just cant believe it, and to make things heart-thumpingly horrible you come to a little bend in what is now just a trail and there's the booming surf coming at you whitecapped crashing down on sand as tho it was higher than where you stand, like a sudden tidal wave world enough to make you step back or run back to the hills——And not only that, the blue sea behind the crashing high waves is full of huge black rocks rising like old ogresome castles dripping wet slime, a billion years of woe right there, the moogrus big clunk of it right there with its slaverous lips of foam at the base——So that you emerge from pleasant little wood paths with a stem of grass in your teeth and drop it to see doom——And you look up at that unbelievably high bridge and feel death and for a good reason: because underneath the bridge, in the sand right beside the sea cliff, *hump*, your heart sinks to see it: the automobile that crashed thru the bridge rail a decade ago and fell 1000 feet straight down and landed upsidedown, is still there now, an upsidedown chassis of rust in a strewn skitter of sea-eaten tires, old spokes, old car seats sprung with straw, one sad fuel pump and no more people——

Big elbows of Rock rising everywhere, sea caves within them, seas plollocking all around inside them crashing out foams, the boom and pound on the sand, the sand dipping quick (no Malibu Beach here)——Yet you turn and see the pleasant woods winding upcreek like a picture in Vermont——But you look up into the sky, bend way back, my God you're standing directly

under that aerial bridge with its thin white line running from
rock to rock and witless cars racing across it like dreams! From
rock to rock! All the way down the raging coast! So that when
later I heard people say "Oh Big Sur must be beautiful!" I gulp
to wonder why it has the reputation of being beautiful above
and beyond its *fearfulness*, its Blakean groaning roughrock Creation throes, those vistas when you drive the coast highway on
a sunny day opening up the eye for miles of horrible washing
sawing.

5

IT WAS EVEN FRIGHTENING AT THE OTHER PEACEFUL END of Raton Canyon, the east end, where Alf the pet mule of local settlers slept at night such sleepfull sleeps under a few weird trees and then got up in the morning to graze in the grass then negotiated the whole distance slowly to the sea shore where you saw him standing by the waves like an ancient sacred myth character motionless in the sand——Alf the Sacred Burro I later called him——The thing that was frightening was the mountain that rose up at the east end, a strange Burmese like mountain with levels and moody terraces and a strange rice-paddy hat on top that I kept staring at with a sinking heart even at first when I was healthy and feeling good (and I would be going mad in this canyon in six weeks on the fullmoon night of September 3rd)——The mountain reminded me of my recent recurrent nightmares in New York about the "Mountain of Mien Mo" with the swarms of moony flying horses lyrically sweeping capes over their shoulders as they circled the peak a "thousand miles high" (in the dream it said) and on top of the mountain in one haunted nightmare I'd seen the giant empty stone benches so silent in the topworld moonlight as tho once inhabited by Gods or giants of some kind but long ago vacated so that they were all dusty and cobwebby now and the evil lurked somewhere inside the pyramid nearby where there was a monster with a big thumping heart but also, even more sinister, just ordinary seedy but muddy janitors cooking over small woodfires——Narrow dusty holes through which I'd tried to crawl with a bunch of tomato plants tied around my neck——Dreams——Drinking nightmares——A recurrent series of them all swirling around that mountain, seen the very first time as a beautful but somehow horribly green verdant mist enshrouded jungle peak rising out of green tropical country in "Mexico" so called but beyond which were pyramids, dry rivers, other countries full of infantry enemy and yet the biggest danger being just hoodlums out throwing rocks on Sundays—— So that the sight of that simple sad mountain, together with the bridge and that car that had flipped over twice or so and

landed flump in the sand with no more sign of human elbows or
shred neckties (like a terrifying poem about America you could
write), agh, HOO HOO of Owls living in old evil hollow trees
in that misty tangled further part of the canyon where I was
always afraid to go anyhow——That unclimbably tangled steep
cliff at the base of Mien Mo rising to gawky dead trees among
bushes so dense and up to heathers God knows how deep with
hidden caves no one not even I spose the Indians of the 10th
Century had ever explored——And those big gooky rainforest
ferns among lightningstruck conifers right beside sudden black
vine cliff faces rising right at your side as you walk the peaceful
path——And as I say that ocean coming at you higher than you
are like the harbors of old woodcuts always higher than the
towns (as Rimbaud pointed out shuddering)——So many evil
combinations even unto the bat who would come at me later
while I slept on the outdoor cot on the porch of Lorenzo's
cabin, come circle my head coming real low sometimes filling
me with the traditional fear it'll get tangled in my hair, and such
silent wings, how would you like to wake up in the middle of
the night and see silent wings beating over you and you ask
yourself "Do I really believe in Vampires?"——In fact, flying
silently around my lamplit cabin at 3 o'clock in the morning as
I'm reading (of all things) (shudder) *Doctor Jekyll and Mister
Hyde*——Small wonder maybe that I myself turned from serene
Jekyll to hysterical Hyde in the short space of six weeks, losing
absolute control of the peace mechanisms of my mind for the
first time in my life.

But Ah, at first there were fine days and nights, right after
Monsanto drove me to Monterey and back with two boxes of a
full grub list and left me there alone for three weeks of solitude,
as we'd agreed——So fearless and happy I even spotted his powerful flashlight up at the bridge the first night, right thru the
fog the eerie finger reaching the pale bottom of that high monstrosity, and even spotted it out over the farmless sea as I sat by
caves in the crashing dark in my fisherman's outfit writing down
what the sea was saying——Worst of all spotting it up at those
tangled mad cliffsides where owls hooted ooraloo——Becoming
acquainted and swallowing fears and settling down to life in
the little cabin with its warm glow of woodstove and kerosene
lamp and let the ghosts fly their asses off——The Bhikkus' home

in his woods, he only wants peace, peace he will get——Tho why after three weeks of perfect happy peace and adjustment in these strange woods my soul so went down the drain when I came back with Dave Wain and Romana and my girl Billie and her kid, I'll never know——Worth the telling only if I dig deep into everything.

Because it was so beautiful at first, even the circumstance of my sleepingbag suddenly erupting feathers in the middle of the night as I turned over to sleep on, so I curse and have to get up and sew it by lamplight or in the morning it might be empty of feathers——And as I bend poor mother head over my needle and thread in the cabin, by the fresh fire and in the light of the kerosene lamp, here come those damned silent black wings flapping and throwing shadows all over my little home, the bloody bat's come in my house——Trying to sew a poor patch on my old crumbly sleepingbag (mostly ruined by my having to sweat out a fever inside of it in a hotel room in Mexico City in 1957 right after the gigantic earthquake there), the nylon all rotten almost from all that old sweat, but still soft, tho so soft I have to cut out a piece of old shirt flap and patch over the rip——I remember looking up from my middle of the night chore and saying bleakly "They, yes, have bats in Mien Mo valley"——But the fire crackles, the patch gets sewn, the creek gurgles and thumps outside——A creek having so many voices it's amazing, from the kettledrum basin deep bumpbumps to the little gurgly feminine crickles over shallow rocks, sudden choruses of other singers and voices from the log dam, dibble dabble all night long and all day long the voices of the creek amusing me so much at first but in the later horror of that madness night becoming the babble and rave of evil angels in my head——So not minding the bat or the rip finally, ending up cant sleep because too awake now and it's 3 A.M. so the fire I stoke and I settle down and read the entire *Doctor Jekyll and Mister Hyde* novel in the wonderful little handsized leather book left there by smart Monsanto who also must've read it with wide eyes on a night like that——Ending the last elegant sentences at dawn, time to get up and fetch water from gurgly creek and start breakfast of pancakes and syrup——And saying to myself "So why fret when something goes wrong like your sleepingbag breaking in the night, use self reliance"——"Screw the bats" I add.

Marvelous opening moment in fact of the first afternoon
I'm left alone in the cabin and I make my first meal, wash my
first dishes, nap, and wake up to hear the rapturous ring of
silence or Heaven even within and throughout the gurgle of
the creek——When you say AM ALONE and the cabin is suddenly home only because you made one meal and washed your
firstmeal dishes——Then nightfall, the religious vestal lighting of
the beautiful kerosene lamp after careful washing of the mantle
in the creek and careful drying with toilet paper, which spoils
it by specking it so you again wash it in the creek and this time
just let the mantle drip dry in the sun, the late afternoon sun
that disappears so quickly behind those giant high steep canyon
walls——Nightfall, the kerosene lamp casts a glow in the cabin,
I go out and pick some ferns like the ferns of the Lankavatara Scripture, those hairnet ferns, "Look sirs, a beautiful hairnet!"——Late afternoon fog pours in over the canyon walls,
sweep, cover the sun, it gets cold, even the flies on the porch
are as so sad as the fog on the peaks——As daylight retreats the
flies retreat like polite Emily Dickinson flies and when it's dark
they're all asleep in trees or someplace——At high noon they're
in the cabin with you but edging further towards the open
doorsill as the afternoon lengthens, how strangely gracious——
There's the hum of the bee drone two blocks away the racket
of it you'd think it was right over the roof, when the bee drone
swirls nearer and nearer (gulp again) you retreat into the cabin
and wait, maybe they got a message to come and see you all
two thousand of em——But getting used to the bee drone finally
which seems to happen like a big party once a week——And so
everything eventually marvelous.

Even the first frightening night on the beach in the fog with
my notebook and pencil, sitting there crosslegged in the sand
facing all the Pacific fury flashing on rocks that rise like gloomy
sea shroud towers out of the cove, the bingbang cove with its
seas booming inside caves and slapping out, the cities of seaweed floating up and down you can even see their dark leer in
the phosphorescent seabeach nightlight——That first night I
sit there and all I know, as I look up, is the kitchen light is on,
on the cliff, to the right, where somebody's just built a cabin
overlooking all the horrible Sur, somebody up there's having
a mild and tender supper that's all I know——The lights from

the cabin kitchen up there go out like a little weak lighthouse beacon and ends suspended a thousand feet over the crashing shore——Who would build a cabin up there but some bored but hoary old adventurous architect maybe got sick of running for congress and one of these days a big Orson Welles tragedy with screaming ghosts a woman in a white nightgown'll go flying down that sheer cliff——But actually in my mind what I really see is the kitchen lights of that mild and tender maybe even romantic supper up there, in all that howling fog, and here I am way below in the Vulcan's Forge itself looking up with sad eyes——Blanking my little Camel cigarette on a billion year old rock that rises behind my head to a height unbelievable—— The little kitchen light on the cliff is only on the end of it, behind it the shoulders of the great sea hound cliff go rising up and back and sweeping inland higher and higher till I gasp to think "Looks like a reclining dog, big friggin shoulders on that sonofabitch"——Riseth and sweepeth and scareth men to death but what is death anyway in all this water and rock.

I fix up my sleepingbag on the porch of the cabin but at 2 A.M. the fog starts dripping all wet so I have to go indoors with wet sleepingbag and make new arrangements but who cant sleep like a log in a solitary cabin in the woods, you wake up in the late morning so refreshed and realizing the universe namelessly: the universe is an Angel——But easy enough to say when you've had your escape from the gooky city turn into a success——And it's finally only in the woods you get that nostalgia for "cities" at last, you dream of long gray journeys to cities where soft evenings'll unfold like Paris but never seeing how sickening it will be because of the primordial innocence of health and stillness in the wilds——So I tell myself "Be Wise."

6

Though there are faults to monsanto's cabin like no screened windows to keep the flies out in the daytime just big board windows, so that also on foggy days when it's damp if you leave them open it's too cold, if you leave them closed you cant see anything and have to light the lamp at noon——And but for that no other faults——It's all marvelous—— And at first it's so amazing to be able to enjoy dreamy afternoon meadows of heather up the other end of the canyon and just by walking less than a halfmile you can suddenly also enjoy wild gloomy sea coast, or if you're sick of either of these just sit by the creek in a gladey spot and dream over snags——So easy in the woods to daydream and pray to the local spirits and say "Allow me to stay here, I only want peace" and those foggy peaks answer back mutely Yes——And to say to yourself (if you're like me with theological preoccupations) (at least at that time, before I went mad I still had such preoccupations) "God who is everything possesses the eye of awakening, like dreaming a long dream of an impossible task and you wake up in a flash, oops, No Task, it's done and gone"——And in the flush of the first few days of joy I confidently tell myself (not expecting what I'll do in three weeks only) "no more dissipation, it's time for me to quietly watch the world and even enjoy it, first in woods like these, then just calmly walk and talk among people of the world, no booze, no drugs, no binges, no bouts with beatniks and drunks and junkies and everybody, no more I ask myself the question *O why is God torturing me*, that's it, be a loner, travel, talk to waiters only, in fact, in Milan, Paris, just talk to waiters, walk around, no more self imposed agony . . . it's time to think and watch and keep concentrated on the fact that after all this whole surface of the world as we know it now will be covered with the silt of a billion years in time . . . Yay, for this, more aloneness"——"Go back to childhood, just eat apples and read your Cathechism——sit on curbstones, the hell with the hot lights of Hollywood" (remembering that awful time only a year earlier when I had to rehearse my reading of prose a third time under the hot lights of the Steve Allen Show in the Burbank studio, one hundred technicians waiting for me to start reading, Steve Allen watching me expectant as he plunks the piano, I sit there on the dunce's stool and refuse to read a word or open my mouth, "I dont have to REHEARSE for God's sake Steve!"—— "But go ahead, we just wanta get the tone of your voice, just this last time, I'll let you off the dress rehearsal" and I sit there sweating not saying a word for a whole minute as everybody watches, finally I say "No I cant do it" and I go across the street to get drunk) (but surprising everybody the night of the show by doing my job of reading just fine, which surprises the producers and so they take me out with a Hollywood starlet who turns out to be a big bore trying to read me her poetry and wont talk love because in Hollywood man love is for sale)——So even that marvelous, long remembrances of life all the time in the world to just sit there or lie there or walk about slowly remembering all the details of life which now because a million lightyears away have taken on the aspect (as they must've for Proust in his sealed room) of pleasant mental movies brought up at will and projected for further study——And pleasure——As I imagine God to be doing this very minute, watching his own movie, which is us.

Even when one night I'm so happy sighin to turn over to resume my sleep but a rat suddenly runs over my head, it's marvelous because I then take the folding cot and put a big wide board on it that covers both sides, so I wont sink into the canvas confines there, and place two old sleepingbags over the board, then my own on top, I have the most marvelous and rat free and in fact healthy-for-the-back bed in the world.

I also take long curious hikes to see what's what in the other direction inland, going up a few miles along the dirt road that leads to isolated ranches and logging camps——I come to giant sad quiet valleys where you see 150 foot tall redwood trees with sometimes one little bird right on the topmost peaktwig sticking straight up——The bird balances up there surveying the fog and the great trees——You see one single flower nodding on a cliff side far across the canyon, or a huge knot in a redwood tree looking like Zeus' face, or some of God's little crazy creations goofing around in creek pools (zigzag bugs), or a sign on a lonely fence saying "M.P.Passey, No Trespassing," or terraces of fern in the dripping redwood shade, and you think "A long way from the beat generation, in this rain forest"——So I angle back down to the home canyon and down the path past the cabin and out to the sea where the mule is on the sea shore, nibbling under that one thousand foot bridge or sometimes just standing staring at me with big brown Garden of Eden eyes——The mule being a pet of one of the families who have a cabin in the canyon and it, as I say Alf by name, just wanders from one end of the canyon where the corral fence stops him, to the wild seashore where the sea stops him but a strange Gauguinesque mule when you first see him, leaving his black dung on the perfect white sand, an immortal and primordial mule owning a whole valley——I even finally later find out where Alf sleeps which is like a sacred grove of trees in that dreaming meadow of heather——So I feed Alf the last of my apples which he receives with big faroff teeth inside his soft hairy muzzle, never biting, just muffing up my apple from my outstretched palm, and chomping away sadly, turning to scratch his behind against a tree with a big erotic motion that gets worse and worse till finally he's standing there with erectile dong that would scare the Whore of Babylon let alone me.

All kinds of strange and marvelous things like the weird Ripley situation of a huge tree that's fallen across a creek maybe 500 years ago and's made a bridge thereby, the other end of its trunk is now buried in ten feet of silt and foliage, strange enough but out of the middle trunk over the water rises straight another redwood tree looking like it's been planted in the treetrunk, or stuck down into it by a God hand, I cant figure it out and stare at this chewing furiously on big choking handfulls of peanuts like a college boy——(and only weeks before falling on my head in the Bowery)——Even when a rancher car goes by I daydream mad ideas like, here comes Farmer Jones and his two daughters and here I am with a 60-foot redwood tree under my arm walking slowly pulling it along, they are amazed and scared, "Are we dreaming? can anybody be that strong?" they even ask me and my big Zen answer is "You only think I'm strong" and I go on down the road carrying my tree——This has me laughing in clover fields for hours——I pass a cow which turns to look at me as it takes a big dreamy crap——Back in the cabin I light the fire and sit sighing and there are leaves skittering on the tin roof, it's August in Big Sur——I fall asleep in the chair and when

I wake up I'm facing the thick little tangled woods outside
the door and I suddenly remember them from long ago, even
to the particular clumpness of the thickets, stem by stem, the
twist of them, like an old home place, but just as I'm wondering what all this mess is, bang, the wind closes the cabin door
on my sight of it!——So I conclude "I see as much as doors'll
allow, open or shut"——Adding, as I get up, in a loud English
Lord voice nobody can hear anyway, "An issue broached is an
issue smote, Sire," pronouncing "issue" like "iss-yew"——And
this has me laughing all through supper——Which is potatoes
wrapped in foil and thrown on the fire, and coffee, and hunks
of Spam roasted on a spit, and applesauce and cheese——And
when I light the lamp of aftersupper reading, here comes the
nightly moth to his nightly death at my lamp——After I put out
the lamp temporarily, there's the moth sleeping on the wall not
realizing I've put it on again.

Meanwhile by the way and however, every day is cold and
cloudy, or damp, not cold in the eastern sense, and every night
is absolutely fog: no stars whatever to be seen——But this too
turns out to be a marvelous circumstance as I find out later, it's
the "damp season" and the other dwellers (weekenders) of the
canyon dont come out on weekends, I'm absolutely alone for
weeks on end (because later in August when the sun conquered
the fog suddenly I was amazed to hear laughing and scratching
all up and down the valley which had been mine only mine, and
when I tried to go to the beach to squat and write there were
whole families having outings, some of them younger people
who'd simply parked their cars up on the high bridge bluff and
climbed down) (some of them in fact gangs of yelling hoodlums)——So the rainforest summer fog was grand and besides
when the sun prevailed in August a horrible development took
place, huge blasts of frightening gale like wind came pouring
into the canyon making all the trees roar with a really frightening intensity that sometimes built up to a booming war of trees
that shook the cabin and woke you up——And was in fact one
of the things that contributed to my mad fit.

But the most marvelous day of all when I completely forgot
who I was where I was or the time a day just with my pants
rolled up above my knees wading in the creek rearranging the
rocks and some of the snags so that the water where I stooped

(near the sandy shore) to get jugfuls would, instead of just slug-gishly passing by shallow over mud, with bugs in it, now come rushing in a pure gurgly clear stream and deep too——I dug into the white sand and arranged underground rocks so now I could stick a jug in there and tilt the opening to the stream and it would fill up instantly with clear rushing unstagnated bugless drinking water——Making a mill race, is what it's called——And because now the water rushed so fast and deep right by the sandy stooping place I had to build a kind of seawall of rocks against that rush so that the shore would not be silted away by the race——Doing that, fortifying the outside of the seawall with smaller rocks and finally at sundown with bent head over my sniffling endeavors (the way a kid sniffles when he's been playing all day) I start inserting tiny pebbles in the spaces between the stones so that no water can sneak over to wash away the shore, even down to the tiniest sand, a perfect seawall, which I top with a wood plank for everybody to kneel on when they come there to fetch their holy water——Looking up from this work of an entire day, from noon till sundown, amazed to see where I was, who I was, what I'd done——The absolute innocence like of Indian fashioning a canoe all alone in the woods——And as I say only weeks earlier I'd fallen flat on my head in the Bowery and everybody thought I'd hurt myself——So I make supper with a happy song and go out in the foggy moonlight (the moon sent its white luminescence through) and marveled to watch the new swift gurgling clear water run with its pretty flashes of light——"And when the fog's over and the stars and the moon come out at night it'll be a beautiful sight."

And such things——A whole mess of little joys like that amaz-ing me when I came back in the horror of later to see how they'd all changed and become sinister, even my poor little wood platform and mill race when my eyes and my stomach nauseous and my soul screaming a thousand babbling words, oh——It's hard to explain and best thing to do is not be false.

7

BECAUSE ON THE FOURTH DAY I BEGAN TO GET BORED and noted it in my diary with amazement, "Already bored?"—Even tho the handsome words of Emerson would shake me out of that where he says (in one of those little redleather books, in the essay on "Self Reliance" a man "is relieved and gay when he has put his heart into his work and done his best") (applicable both to building simple silly little millraces and writing big stupid stories like this)——Words from that trumpet of the morning in America, Emerson, he who announced Whitman and also said "Infancy conforms to nobody"——The infancy of the simplicity of just being happy in the woods, conforming to nobody's idea about what to do, what should be done——"Life is not an apology"——And when a vain and malicious philanthropic abolitionist accused him of being blind to the issues of slavery he said "Thy love afar is spite at home" (maybe the philanthropist had Negro help anyway)——So once I again I'm Ti Jean the Child, playing, sewing patches, cooking suppers, washing dishes (always kept the kettle boiling on the fire and anytime dishes need to be washed I just pour hot hot water into pan with Tide soap and soak them good and then wipe them clean after scouring with little 5-&-10 wire scourer)——Long nights simply thinking about the usefulness of that little wire scourer, those little yellow copper things you buy in supermarkets for 10 cents, all to me infinitely more interesting than the stupid and senseless "Steppenwolf" novel in the shack which I read with a shrug, this old fart reflecting the "conformity" of today and all the while he thought he was a big Nietzsche, old imitator of Dostoevsky 50 years too late (he feels tormented in a "personal hell" he calls it because he doesnt like what other people like!)——Better at noon to watch the orange and black Princeton colors on the wings of a butterfly——Best to go hear the sound of the sea at night on the shore.

Maybe I shouldna gone out and scared or bored or belabored myself so much, tho, on that beach at night which would scare any ordinary mortal——Every night around eight after supper I'd put on my big fisherman coat and take the notebook, pencil and lamp and start down the trail (sometimes passing ghostly Alf on the way) and go under that frightful high bridge and see through the dark fog ahead the white mouths of ocean coming high at me——But knowing the terrain I'd walk right on, jump the beach creek, and go to my corner by the cliff not far from one of the caves and sit there like an idiot in the dark writing down the sound of the waves in the notebook page (secretarial notebook) which I could see white in the darkness and therefore without benefit of lamp scrawl on——I was afraid to light my lamp for fear I'd scare the people way up there on the cliff eating their nightly tender supper——(later found out there was nobody up there eating tender suppers, they were overtime carpenters finishing the place in bright lights)——And I'd get scared of the rising tide with its 15 foot waves yet sit there hoping in faith that Hawaii warnt sending no tidal wave I might miss seeing in the dark coming from miles away high as Groomus——One night I got scared anyway so sat on top of 10 foot cliff at the foot of the big cliff and the waves are going "Rare, he rammed the gate rare"——"Raw roo roar"—— "Crowsh"——the way waves sound especially at night——The sea not speaking in sentences so much as in short lines: "Which one? . . . the one ploshed? . . . the same, ah Boom" . . . Writing down these fantastic inanities actually but yet I felt I had to do it because James Joyce wasnt about to do it now he was dead (and figuring "Next year I'll write the different sound of the Atlantic crashing say on the night shores of Cornwall, or the soft sound of the Indian Ocean crashing at the mouth of the Ganges maybe")——And I just sit there listening to the waves talk all up and down the sand in different tones of voice "Ka bloom, kerplosh, ah ropey otter barnacled be, crowsh, are rope the angels in all the sea?" and such*——Looking up occasionally to see rare cars crossing the high bridge and wondering what they'd see on this drear foggy night if they knew a madman was down there a thousand feet below in all that windy fury sitting in the dark writing in the dark——Some sort of sea beatnik, tho anybody wants to call me a beatnik for THIS better try it if they dare——The huge black rocks seem to move——The bleak awful

---

*The complete poems written by the sea are to be found at the end of this book, in the appendix, entitled "Sea": Sounds of the Pacific Ocean at Big Sur. JK

roaring isolateness, no ordinary man could do it I'm telling you——*I am a Breton!* I cry and the blackness speaks back "*Les poissons de la mer parlent Breton*" (the fishes of the sea speak Breton)——Nevertheless I go there every night even tho I dont feel like it, it's my duty (and probably drove me mad), and write these sea sounds, and all the whole insane poem "Sea."

Always so wonderful in fact to get away from that and back to the more human woods and come to the cabin where the fire's still red and you can see the Bodhisattva's lamp, the glass of ferns on the table, the box of Jasmine tea nearby, all so gentle and human after that rocky deluge out there——So I make an excellent pan of muffins and tell myself "Blessed is the man can make his own bread"——Like that, the whole three weeks, happiness——And I'm rolling my own cigarettes, too——And as I say sometimes I meditate how wonderful the fantastic use I've gotten out of cheap little articles like the scourer, but in this instance I think of the marvelous belongings in my rucksack like my 25 cent plastic shaker with which I've just made the muffin batter but also I've used it in the past to drink hot tea, wine, coffee, whisky and even stored clean handkerchiefs in it when I traveled——The top part of the shaker, my holy cup, and had it for five years now——And other belongings so valuable compared to the worthlessness of expensive things I'd bought and never used——Like my black soft sleeping sweater also five years which I was now wearing in the damp Sur summer night and day, over a flannel shirt in the cold, and just the sweater for the night's sleep in the bag——Endless use and virtue of it!—— And because the expensive things were of ill use, like the fancy pants I'd bought for recent recording dates in New York and other television appearances and never even wore again, useless things like a $40 raincoat I never wore because it didnt even have slits in the side pockets (you pay for the label and the so called "tailoring")——Also an expensive tweed jacket bought for TV and never worn again——Two silly sports shirts bought for Hollywood never worn again and were 9 bucks each!——And it's almost tearful to realize and remember the old green T-shirt I'd found, mind you, eight years ago, mind you, on the DUMP in Watsonville California mind you, and got fantastic use and comfort from it——Like working to fix that new stream in the creek to flow through the convenient deep new waterhole near the wood platform on the bank, and losing myself in this like a kid playing, it's the little things that count (clichés are truisms and all truisms are true)——On my deathbed I could be remembering that creek day and forgetting the day MGM bought my book, I could be remembering the old lost green dump T-shirt and forgetting the sapphired robes——Mebbe the best way to get into Heaven.

I go back to the beach in the daytime to write my "Sea," I stand there barefoot by the sea stopping to scratch one ankle with one toe, I hear the rhythm of those waves, and they're saying suddenly "Is Virgin you trying to fathom me"——I go back to make a pot of tea.

> Summer afternoon——
> Impatiently chewing
> The Jasmine leaf

At high noon the sun always coming out at last, strong, beating down on my nice high porch where I sit with books and coffee and the noon I thought about the ancient Indians who must have inhabited this canyon for thousands of years, how even as far back as the 10th Century this valley must have looked the same, just different trees: these ancient Indians simply the ancestors of the Indians of only recently say 1860—— How they've all died and quietly buried their grievances and excitements——How the creek may have been an inch deeper since logging operations of the last 60 years have removed some of the watershed in the hills back there——How the women pounded the local acorns, acorns or shmacorns, I finally found the natural nuts of the valley and they were sweet tasting—— And men hunted deer——In fact God knows what they did because I wasnt here——But the same valley, a thousand years of dust more or less over their footsteps of 960 A.D.——And as far as I can see the world is too old for us to talk about it with our new words——We will pass just as quietly through life (passing through, passing through) as the 10th century people of this valley only with a little more noise and a few bridges and dams and bombs that wont even last a million years——The world being just what it is, moving and passing through, actually alright in the long view and nothing to complain about——Even the rocks of the valley had earlier rock ancestors, a billion billion

years ago, have left no howl of complaint——Neither the bee,
or the first sea urchins, or the clam, or the severed paw——All
sad So-Is sight of the world, right there in front of my nose as
I look,——And looking at that valley in fact I also realize I have
to make lunch and it wont be any different than the lunch of
those olden men and besides it'll taste good——Everything is
the same, the fog says "We are fog and we fly by dissolving like
ephemera," and the leaves say "We are leaves and we jiggle in
the wind, that's all, we come and go, grow and fall"——Even
the paper bags in my garbage pit say "We are man-transformed
paper bags made out of wood pulp, we are kinda proud of being
paper bags as long as that will be possible, but we'll be mush
again with our sisters the leaves come rainy season"——The tree
stumps say "We are tree stumps torn out of the ground by
men, sometimes by wind, we have big tendrils full of earth that
drink out of the earth"——Men say "We are men, we pull out
tree stumps, we make paper bags, we think wise thoughts, we
make lunch, we look around, we make a great effort to realize
everything is the same"——While the sand says "We are sand,
we already know," and the sea says "We are always come and
go, fall and plosh"——The empty blue sky of space says "All this
comes back to me, then goes again, and comes back again, then
goes again, and I dont care, it still belongs to me"——The blue
sky adds "Dont call me eternity, call me God if you like, all of
you talkers are in paradise: the leaf is paradise, the tree stump
is paradise, the paper bag is paradise, the man is paradise, the
sand is paradise, the sea is paradise, the man is paradise, the fog
is paradise"——Can you imagine a man with marvelous insights
like these can go mad within a month? (because you must admit
all those talking paper bags and sands were telling the truth)——
But I remember seeing a mess of leaves suddenly go skittering
in the wind and into the creek, then floating rapidly down the
creek towards the sea, making me feel a nameless horror even
then of "Oh my God, we're all being swept away to sea no matter what we know or say or do"——And a bird who was on a
crooked branch is suddenly gone without my even hearing him.

8

B<small>UT THERE'S MOONLIT FOGNIGHT</small>, the blossoms of the fire flames in the stove——There's giving an apple to the mule, the big lips taking hold——There's the bluejay drinking my canned milk by throwing his head back with a miffle of milk on his beak——There's the scratching of the raccoon or of the rat out there, at night——There's the poor little mouse eating her nightly supper in the humble corner where I've put out a little delight-plate full of cheese and chocolate candy (for my days of killing mice are over)——There's the raccoon in his fog, there the man to his fireside, and both are lonesome for God——There's me coming back from seaside nightsittings like a muttering old Bhikku stumbling down the path——There's me throwing my spotlight on a sudden raccoon who clambers up a tree his little heart beating with fear but I yell in French "Hello there little man" (*allo ti bonhomme*)——There's the bottle of olives, 49¢, imported, pimentos, I eat them one by one wondering about the late afternoon hillsides of Greece——And there's my spaghetti with tomato sauce and my oil and vinegar salad and my applesauce *relishe* my dear and my black coffee and Roquefort cheese and afterdinner nuts, my dear, all in the woods——(Ten delicate olives slowly chewed at midnight is something no one's ever done in luxurious restaurants)—— There's the present moment fraught with tangled woods—— There's the bird suddenly quiet on his branch while his wife glances at him——There's the grace of an axe handle as good as an Eglevsky ballet——There's "Mien Mo Mountain" in the fog illumined August moon mist among other heights gorgeous and misty rising in dimmer tiers somehow rosy in the night like the classic silk paintings of China and Japan——There's a bug, a helpless little wingless crawler, drowning in a water can, I get it out and it wanders and goofs on the porch till I get sick of watching——There's the spider in the outhouse minding his own business——There's my side of bacon hanging from a hook on the ceiling of the shack——There's the laughter of the loon in the shadow of the moon——There's an owl hooting in weird Bodhidharma trees——There's flowers and redwood logs——There's the simple woodfire and the careful yet absent-minded feeding of it which is an activity that like all activities is no-activity (*Wu Wei*) yet it is a meditation in itself especially because all woodfires, like snowflakes, are different every time—— Yes, there's the resinous purge of a flame-enveloped redwood log——Yes the cross-sawed redwood log turns into a coal and looks like a City of the Gandharvas or like a western butte at sunset——There's the bhikku's broom, the kettle——There's the laced soft fud over the sand, the sea——There's all these avid preparations for decent sleep like the night I'm looking for my sleeping socks (so's not to dirty the sleepingbag inside) and find myself singing "A donde es me sockiboos?"——Yes, and down in the valley there's my burro, Alf, the only living being in sight——There's in mid of sleep the moon appearing——There's universal substance which is divine substance because where else can it be?——There's the family of deer on the dirt road at dusk——There's the creek coughing down the glade——There's the fly on my thumb rubbing its nose then stepping to the page of my book——There's the hummingbird swinging his head from side to side like a hoodlum——There's all that, and all my fine thoughts, even unto my ditty written to the sea "I took a pee, into the sea, acid to acid, and me to ye" yet I went crazy inside three weeks.

For who could go crazy that could be so relaxed as that: but wait: there are the signposts of something wrong.

9

THE FIRST SIGNPOST came after that marvelous day I went hiking up the canyon road again to the highway at the bridge where there was a rancher mailbox where I could dump mail (a letter to my mother and saying in it give a kiss to Tyke, my cat, and a letter to old buddy Julien addressed to Coaly Rustnut from Runty Onenut) and as I walked way up there I could see the peaceful roof of my cabin way below and half mile away in the old trees, could see the porch, the cot where I slept, and my red handkerchief on the bench beside the cot (a simple little sight: of my handkerchief a half mile away making me unaccountably happy)——And on the way back pausing to meditate in the grove of trees where Alf the Sacred Burro slept and seeing the roses of the unborn in my closed eyelids just as clearly as I had seen the red handkerchief and also my own footsteps in the seaside sand from way up on the bridge, saw, or heard, the words "Roses of the Unborn" as I sat crosslegged in soft meadow sand, heard that awful stillness at the heart of life, but felt strangely low, as tho premonition of the next day——When I went to the sea in the afternoon and suddenly took a huge deep Yogic breath to get all that good sea air in me but somehow just got an overdose of iodine, or of evil, maybe the sea caves, maybe the seaweed cities, something, my heart suddenly beating——Thinking I'm gonna get the local vibrations instead here I am almost fainting only it isnt an ecstatic swoon by St. Francis, it comes over me in the form of horror of an eternal condition of sick mortality in me——In me and in everyone——I felt completely nude of all poor protective devices like thoughts about life or meditations under trees and the "ultimate" and all that shit, in fact the other pitiful devices of making supper or saying "What I do now next? chop wood?"——I see myself as just doomed, pitiful——An awful realization that I have been fooling myself all my life thinking there was a next thing to do to keep the show going and actually I'm just a sick clown and so is everybody else——All all of it, pitiful as it is, not even really any kind of commonsense animate effort to ease the soul in this horrible sinister condition (of mortal hopelessness) so I'm left sitting there in the sand after having almost fainted and stare at the waves which suddenly are not waves at all, with I guess what must have been the goopiest downtrodden expression God if He exists must've ever seen in His movie career——*Éh vache*, I hate to write——All my tricks laid bare, even the realization that they're laid bare itself laid bare as a lotta bunk——The sea seems to yell to me GO TO YOUR DESIRE DONT HANG AROUND HERE——For after all the sea must be like God, God isnt asking us to mope and suffer and sit by the sea in the cold at midnight for the sake of writing down useless sounds, he gave us the tools of self reliance after all to make it straight thru bad life mortality towards Paradise maybe I hope——But some miserables like me dont even know it, when it comes to us we're amazed——Ah, life is a gate, a way, a path to Paradise anyway, why not live for fun and joy and love or some sort of girl by a fireside, why not go to your desire and LAUGH . . . but I ran away from that seashore and never came back again without that secret knowledge: that it didnt want me there, that I was a fool to sit there in the first place, the sea has its waves, the man has his fireside, period.

That being the first indication of my later flip——But also on the day of leaving the cabin to hitch hike back to Frisco and see everybody and by now I'm tired of my food (forgot to bring jello, you need jello after all that bacon fat and cornmeal in the woods, every woodsman needs jello) (or cokes) (or something)——But it's time to leave, I'm now so scared by that iodine blast by the sea and by the boredom of the cabin I take 20 dollars worth of perishable food left and spread it out on a big board below the cabin porch for the bluejays and the raccoon and the mouse and the whole lot, pack up, and go——But before I go I realize this isnt my own cabin (here's the second signpost of my madness), I have no right to hide Monsanto's rat poison, as I've been doing, feeding the mouse instead, as I said——So like a dutiful guest in another man's cabin I take the cover off the rat poison but compromise by simply leaving the box on the top shelf, so nobody can complain——And go off like that——But during my absence, but——You'll see.

10

WITH MY MIND EVEN AND UPRIGHT and abiding nowhere, as Hui Neng would say, I go dancing off like a fool from my sweet retreat, rucksack on back, after only three weeks and really after only 3 or 4 days of boredom, and go hankering back for the city——"You go out in joy and in sadness you return," says Thomas à Kempis talking about all the fools who go forth for pleasure like high school boys on Saturday night hurrying clacking down the sidewalk to the car adjusting their ties and rubbing their hands with anticipatory zeal, only to end up Sunday morning groaning in bleary beds that Mother has to make anyway——It's a beautiful day as I come out of that ghostly canyon road and step out on the coast highway, just this side of Raton Canyon bridge, and there they are, thousands and thousands of tourists driving by slowly on the high curves all oo ing and aa ing at all that vast blue panorama of seas washing and raiding at the coast of California——I figure I'll get a ride into Monterey real easy and take the bus there and be in Frisco by nightfall for a big ball of wino yelling with the gang, I feel in fact Dave Wain oughta be back by now, or Cody will be ready for a ball, and there'll be girls, and such and such, forgetting entirely that only three weeks previous I'd been sent fleeing from that gooky city by the horrors——But hadnt the sea told me to flee back to my own reality?

But it is beautiful especially to see up ahead north a vast expanse of curving seacoast with inland mountains dreaming under slow clouds, like a scene of ancient Spain, or properly really like a scene of the real essentially Spanish California, the old Monterey pirate coast right there, you can see what the Spaniards must've thought when they came around the bend in their magnificent sloopies and saw all that dreaming fatland beyond the seashore whitecap doormat——Like the land of gold——The old Monterey and Big Sur and Santa Cruz magic——So I confidently adjust my pack straps and start trudging down the road looking back over my shoulder to thumb.

This is the first time I've hitch hiked in years and I soon begin to see that things have changed in America, you cant get a ride any more (but of course especially on a strictly tourist road like this coast highway with no trucks or business)——Sleek long stationwagon after wagon comes sleering by smoothly, all colors of the rainbow and pastel at that, pink, blue, white, the husband is in the driver's seat with a long ridiculous vacationist hat with a long baseball visor making him look witless and idiot——Beside him sits wifey, the boss of America, wearing dark glasses and sneering, even if he wanted to pick me up or anybody up she wouldn't let him——But in the two deep backseats are children, children, millions of children, all ages, they're fighting and screaming over ice cream, they're spilling vanilla all over the Tartan seatcovers——There's no room anymore anyway for a hitch hiker, tho conceivably the poor bastard might be allowed to ride like a meek gunman or silent murderer in the very back platform of the wagon, but here no, alas! here is ten thousand racks of drycleaned and perfectly pressed suits and dresses of all sizes for the family to look like millionaires every time they stop at a roadside dive for bacon and eggs——Every time the old man's trousers start to get creased a little in the front he's made to take down a fresh pair of slacks from the back rack and go on, like that, bleakly, tho he might have secretly wished just a good oldtime fishing trip alone or with his buddies for this year's vacation——But the P.T.A. has prevailed over every one of his desires by now, 1960's, it's no time for him to yearn for Big Two Hearted River and the old sloppy pants and the string of fish in the tent, or the woodfire with Bourbon at night——It's time for motels, roadside driveins, bringing napkins to the gang in the car, having the car washed before the return trip——And if he thinks he wants to explore any of the silent secret roads of America it's no go, the lady in the sneering dark glasses has now become the navigator and sits there sneering over her previously printed blue-lined roadmap distributed by happy executives in neckties to the vacationists of America who would also wear neckties (after having come along so far) but the vacation fashion is sports shirts, long visored hats, dark glasses, pressed slacks and baby's first shoes dipped in gold oil dangling from the dashboard——So here I am standing in that road with that big woeful rucksack but also probably with that expression of horror on my face after all those nights sitting in the seashore under giant black cliffs, they see in me the very apotheosical opposite

of their every vacation dream and of course drive on——That
afternoon I say about 5 thousand cars or probably 3 thousand
passed me not one of them ever dreamed of stopping——Which
didnt bother me anyway because at first seeing that gorgeous
long coast up to Monterey I thought "Well I'll just hike right
in, it's only 14 miles, I oughta do that easy"——And on the
way there's all kindsa interesting things to see anyway like the
seals barking on rocks below, or quiet old farms made of logs
on the hills across the highway, or sudden upstretches that go
along dreamy seaside meadows where cows grace and graze in
full sight of endless blue Pacific——But because I'm wearing
desert boots with their fairly thin soles, and the sun is beating
hot on the tar road, the heat finally gets through the soles and
I begin to deliver heat blisters in my sockiboos——I'm limping
along wondering what's the matter with me when I realize I've
got blisters——I sit by the side of the road and look——I take
out my first aid kit from the pack and apply unguents and put
on cornpads and carry on——But the combination of the heavy
pack and the heat of the road increases the pain of the blisters
until finally I realize I've got to hitch hike a ride or never make
it to Monterey at all.

But the tourists bless their hearts after all, they couldnt know,
only think I'm having a big happy hike with my rucksack and
they drive on, even tho I stick out my thumb——I'm in despair
because I'm really stranded now, and by the time I've walked
seven miles I still have seven to go but I cant go on another
step——I'm also thirsty and there are absolutely no filling stations or anything along the way——My feet are ruined and
burned, it develops now into a day of complete torture, from
nine o'clock in the morning till four in the afternoon I negotiate
those nine or so miles when I finally have to stop and sit down
and wipe the blood off my feet——And then when I fix the
feet and put the shoes on again, to hike on, I can only do it
mincingly with little twinkletoe steps like Babe Ruth, twisting
footsteps every way I can think of not to press too hard on any
particular blister——So that the tourists (lessening now as the
sun starts to go down) can now plainly see that there's a man
on the highway limping under a huge pack and asking for a
ride, but still they're afraid he may be the Hollywood hitch
hiker with the hidden gun and besides he's got a rucksack on

his back as tho he'd just escaped from the war in Cuba——Or's got dismembered bodies in the bag anyway——But as I say I dont blame them.

The only car that passes that might have given me a ride is going in the wrong direction, down to Sur, and it's a rattly old car of some kind with a big bearded "South Coast Is the Lonely Coast" folksinger in it waving at me but finally a little truck pulls up and waits for me 50 yards ahead and I limprun that distance on daggers in my feet——It's a guy with a dog——He'll drive me to the next gas station, then he turns off——But when he learns about my feet he takes me clear to the bus station in Monterey——Just as a gesture of kindness——No particular reason, and I've made no particular plea about my feet, just mentioned it.

I offer to buy him a beer but he's going on home for supper so I go into the bus station and clean up and change and pack things away, stow the bag in the locker, buy the bus ticket, and go limping quietly in the blue fog streets of Monterey evening feeling light as feather and happy as a millionaire——The last time I ever hitch hiked——And NO RIDES a sign.

11

THE NEXT SIGN IS IN FRISCO ITSELF where after a night of perfect sleep in an old skid row hotel room I go to see Monsanto at his City Lights bookstore and he's smiling and glad to see me, says "We were coming out to see you next weekend you should have waited," but there's something else in his expression——When we're alone he says "Your mother wrote and said your cat is dead."

Ordinarily the death of a cat means little to most men, a lot to fewer men, but to me, and that cat, it was exactly and no lie and sincerely like the death of my little brother——I loved Tyke with all my heart, he was my baby who as a kitten just slept in the palm of my hand with his little head hanging down, or just purring, for hours, just as long as I held him that way, walking or sitting——He was like a floppy fur wrap around my wrist, I just twist him around my wrist or drape him and he just purred and purred and even when he got big I still held him that way, I could even hold this big cat in both hands with my arms outstretched right over my head and he'd just purr, he had complete confidence in me——And when I'd left New York to come to my retreat in the woods I'd carefully kissed him and instructed him to wait for me, "*Attends pour mué kitigingoo*"——But my mother said in the letter he had died the NIGHT AFTER I LEFT!——But maybe you'll understand me by seeing for yourself by reading the letter:-

"Sunday July 20, 1960, Dear Son, I'm afraid you wont like my letter because I only have sad news for you right now. I really dont know how to tell you this but Brace up Honey. I'm going through hell myself. Little Tyke is *gone*. Saturday all day he was fine and seemed to pick up strength, but late at night I was watching T.V. a late movie. Just about 1:30 A.M. when he started belching and throwing up. I went to him and tried to fix him up but to no *availe*. He was shivering like he was cold so I rapped him up in a Blanket then he started to throw up all over me. And that was the last of him. Needless to say how I feel and what I went through. I stayed up till 'day *Break*' and did all I could to revive him but it was useless. I realized at 4 A.M. he was

594

gone so at six I wrapped him up good in a clean blanket——and at 7 A.M. went out to dig his grave. I never did anything in my whole life so heart breaking as to bury my beloved little Tyke who was as human as you and I. I buried him under the Honey-suckle vines, the corner, of the fence. I just cant sleep or eat. I keep looking and hoping to see him come through the cellar door calling *Ma Wow*. I'm just plain sick and the weirdest thing happened when I buried Tyke, all the black Birds I fed all Win-ter seemed to have known what was going on. Honest Son this is no lies. There was lots and lots of *em* flying over my head and chirping, and settling on the fence, for a whole hour after Tyke was laid to rest——that's something I'll never forget——I wish I had a camera at the time but God and Me knows it and saw it. Now Honey I know this is going to hurt you but I had to tell you somehow . . . I'm so sick not physically but heart sick . . . I just cant believe or realize that my Beautiful little Tyke is no more——and that I wont be seeing him come through his little 'Shanty' or Walking through the green grass. . . . P.S. I've got to dismantle Tyke's shanty, I just cant go out there and see it empty——as is. Well Honey, write soon again and be kind to yourself. Pray the real 'God'——Your old Mom X X X X XX."

So when Monsanto told me the news and I was sitting there *smiling* with happiness the way all people feel when they come out of a long solitude either in the woods or in a hospital bed, bang, my heart sank, it sank in fact with the same strange idiotic helplessness as when I took the unfortunate deep breath on the seashore——All the premonitions tying in together.

Monsanto sees that I'm terribly sad, he sees my little smile (the smile that came over me in Monterey just so glad to be back in the world after the solitudes and I'd walked around the streets just bemusedly Mona Lisa'ing at the sight of every-thing)——He sees now how that smile has slowly melted away into a mawk of chagrin——Of course he cant know since I didnt tell him and hardly wanta tell it now, that my relationship with my cat and the other previous cats has always been a little dotty: some kind of psychological identification of the cats with my dead brother Gerard who'd taught me to love cats when I was 3 and 4 and we used to lie on the floor on our bellies and watch them lap up milk——The death of "little brother" Tyke indeed——Monsanto seeing me so downcast says "Maybe you

oughta go back to the cabin for a few more weeks——or are you
just gonna get drunk again"——"I'm gonna get drunk yes"——
Because anyway there are so many things brewing, everybody's
waiting, I've been daydreaming a thousand wild parties in the
woods——In fact it's fortunate I've heard of the death of Tyke
in my favorite exciting city of San Francisco, if I had been home
when he died I might have gone mad in a different way but
tho I now ran out to get drunk with the boys and still once in
a while that funny little smile of joy came back as I drank, and
melted away again because now the smile itself was a reminder
of death, the news made me go mad anyway at the end of the
three week binge, creeping up on me finally on that terrible day
of St. Carolyn By The Sea as I can also call it——All, all confusing till I explain.

Meanwhile anyway poor Monsanto a man of letters wants
to enjoy big news swappings with me about writing and what
everybody's doing, and then Fagan comes into the store (downstairs to Monsanto's old rolltop desk making me also feel chagrin because it always was the ambition of my youth to end up a
kind of literary businessman with a rolltop desk, combining my
father image with the image of myself as a writer, which Monsanto without even thinking about it has accomplished at the
drop of a hat)——Monsanto with his husky shoulders, big blue
eyes, twinkling rosy skin, that perpetual smile of his that earned
him the name Smiler in college and a smile you often wondered
"Is it real?" until you realized if Monsanto should ever stop
using that smile how could the world go on anyway——It was
that kind of smile too inseparable from him to be believably
allowed to disappear——Words words words but he is a grand
guy as I'll show and now with real manly sympathy he really
felt I should not go on big binges if I felt so bad, "At any rate,"
sez he, "you can go back a little later huh"——"Okay Lorry"——
"Did you write anything?"——"I wrote the sounds of the sea,
I'll tell you all about it——It was the most happy three weeks of
my life dammit and now this has to happen, poor little Tyke——
You should have seen him a big beautiful yellow Persian the
kind they call calico"——"Well you still have my dog Homer,
and how was Alf out there?"——"Alf the Sacred Burro, he ha, he
stands in groves of trees in the afternoon suddenly you see him
it's almost scarey, but I fed him apples and shredded wheat and

everything" (and animals are so sad and patient I thought as I remembered Tyke's eyes and Alf's eyes, ah death, and to think this strange scandalous death comes also to human beings, yea to Smiler even, poor Smiler, and poor Homer his dog, and all of us)——I'm also depressed because I know how horrible my mother now feels all alone without her little chum in the house back there 3 thousand miles (and indeed by Jesus it turns out later some silly beatniks trying to see me broke the windowpane in the front door trying to get in and scared her so much she barricaded the door with furniture all the rest of that summer).

But there's old Ben Fagan puffing and chuckling over his pipe so what the hell, why bother grownup men and poets at that with your own troubles——So Ben and I and his chum Jonesy also a chuckly pipesmoker go out to the bar (Mike's Place) and sip a few beers, at first I vow I'm not going to get drunk after all, we even go out to the park to have a long talk in the warm sun that always turns to delightful cool foggy dusk in that town of towns——We're sitting in the park of the big Italian white church watching kids play and people go by, for some reason I'm bemused by the sight of a blonde woman hurrying somewhere "Where's she going? does she have a secret sailor lover? is she only going to finish her typing afterhours in the office? what if we knew Ben what every one of these people goin by is headed for, some door, some restaurant, some secret romance"——"You sound like you stored up a lot of energy and innerest in life in those woods"——And Ben knows that for sure because he's been months in the wilderness too, alone——Old Ben, much thinner than he used to be in our madder Dharma Bum days of 5 years ago, a little gaunt in fact, but still the same old Ben who stays up late at night chuckling over the Lanka-vatara Scripture and writing poems about raindrops——And he knows me very well, he knows I'll get drunk tonight and for weeks on end just on general principles and that a day will come in a few weeks when I'll be so exhausted I wont be able to talk to anybody and he'll come and visit me and just silently at my side be puffing his pipe, as I sleep——The kind of guy he is——I trying to explain about Tyke to him but some people are cat lovers and some aint, tho Ben always has a little kitty around his pad——His pad usually has a straw rug on the floor, with a pillow 'pon which he sits crosslegged, by a smoking teapot, his

bookshelves full of Stein and Pound and Wallace Stevens——A
strange quiet poet who was only beginning to be recognized
as a big rosy secret sage (one of his lines "When I leave town
all my friends go back on the sauce")——And I'm on my way to
the sauce right now.

Because anyway old Dave Wain is back and Dave I can see
him rubbing his hands in anticipation of another big wild binge
with me like we had the year before when he drove me back to
New York from the west coast, with George Baso the little Japanese Zen master hepcat sitting crosslegged on the back mattress
of Dave's jeepster (Willie the Jeep), a terrific trip through Las
Vegas, St. Louis, stopping off at expensive motels and drinking
nothing but the best Scotch out of the bottle all the way——And
what better way to go back to New York, I could have blown
190 dollars on an airplane——And Dave's never met the great
Cody and will be looking forward to that——So me and Ben
leave the park and slowly walk to the bar on Columbus Street
and I order my first double bourbon and gingerale.

The lights are twinkling on outside in that fantastic toy street,
I can feel the joy rise in my soul——I now remember Big Sur
with a clear piercing love and agony and even the death of Tyke
fits in with everything but I dont realize the enormity of what's
yet to come——We call up Dave Wain who's back from Reno
and he comes blattin down to the bar in his jeepster driving
that marvelous way he does (once he was a cab-driver) talking all the time and never making a mistake, in fact as good a
driver as Cody altho I cant imagine anybody being that good
and asked Cody about it the next day——But old jealous drivers
always point out faults and complain, "Ah well that Dave Wain
of yours doesnt takes his curves right, he eases up and sometimes even pokes the brake a little instead of just ridin that old
curve around on increased power, man you gotta *work* those
curves"——Obvious at this time now, by the way and parentheti-
cally, that there's so much to tell about the fateful following
three weeks it's hardly possible to find anyplace to begin.

Like life, actually——And how multiple it all is!——"And what
happened to little old George Baso, boy?"——"Little old George
Baso is probably dyin of T.B. in a hospital outsida Tulare"——
"Gee, Dave, we gotta go see him"——"Yessir, let's do that
tomorrow"——As usual Dave has no money whatever but that

doesnt bother me at all, I've got plenty, I go out the following day and cash 500 dollars worth of travelers checks just so's me and old Dave can really have a good time——Dave likes good food and drink and so do I——But he's got this young kid he brought back from Reno called Ron Blake who is a goodlooking teenager with blond hair who wants to be a sensational new Chet Baker singer and comes on with that tiresome hipster approach that was natural 5 or 10 and even 25 years ago but now in 1960 is a pose, in fact I dug him as a con man conning Dave (tho for what, I dont know)——But Dave Wain that lean rangy red head Welchman with his penchant for going off in Willie to fish in the Rogue River up in Oregon where he knows an abandoned mining camp, or for blattin around the desert roads, for suddenly reappearing in town to get drunk, and a marvelous poet himself, has that certain something that young hip teenagers probably wanta imitate——For one thing is one of the world's best talkers, and funny too——As I'll show——It was he and George Baso who hit on the fantastically simple truth that everybody in America was walking around with a dirty behind, but everybody, because the ancient ritual of washing with water after the toilet had not occurred in all the modern antisepticism——Says Dave "People in America have all these racks of drycleaned clothes like you say on their trips, they spatter Eau de Cologne all over themselves, they wear Ban and Aid or whatever it is under their armpits, they get aghast to see a spot on a shirt or a dress, they probably change underwear and socks maybe even twice a day, they go around all puffed up and insolent thinking themselves the cleanest people on earth and they're walkin around with dirty azzoles——Isnt that amazing? give me a little nip on that tit" he says reaching for my drink so I order two more, I've been engrossed, Dave can order all the drinks he wants anytime, "The President of the United States, the big ministers of state, the great bishops and shmishops and big shots everywhere, down to the lowest factory worker with all his fierce pride, movie stars, executives and great engineers and presidents of law firms and advertising firms with silk shirts and neckties and great expensive traveling cases in which they place these various expensive English imported hair brushes and shaving gear and pomades and perfumes are all walkin around with dirty azzoles! All you gotta do is simply wash yourself with soap and water! it hasnt occurred to anybody in America at all! it's one of the funniest things I've ever heard of! dont you think it's marvelous that we're being called filthy unwashed beatniks but we're the only ones walkin around with clean azzoles?"——The whole azzole shot in fact had spread swiftly and everybody I knew and Dave knew from coast to coast had embarked on this great crusade which I must say is a good one——In fact in Big Sur I'd instituted a shelf in Monsanto's outhouse where the soap must be kept and everyone had to bring a can of water there on each trip——Monsanto hadnt heard about it yet, "Do you realize that until we tell poor Lorenzo Monsanto the famous writer that he is walking around with a dirty azzole he will be doing just that?"——"Let's go tell him right now!"——"Why of course if we wait another minute . . . and besides do you know what it *does* to people to walk around with a dirty azzole? it leaves a great yawning guilt that they cant understand all day, they go to work all cleaned up in the morning and you can smell all that freshly laundered clothes and Eau de Cologne in the commute train yet there's something gnawing at them, something's wrong, they know something's wrong they dont know just what!"——We rush to tell Monsanto at once in the book store around the corner.

By now we're beginning to feel great——Fagan has retired saying typically "Okay you guys go ahead and get drunk, I'm goin home and spend a quiet evening in a hot bath with a book"——"Home" is also where Dave Wain and Ron Blake live——It's an old roominghouse of four stories on the edge of the Negro district of San Francisco where Dave, Ben, Jonesy, a painter called Lanny Meadows, a mad French Canadian drinker called Pascal and a Negro called Johnson all live in different rooms with their clutter of rucksacks and floor mattresses and books and gear, each one taking turns one day a week to go out and do all the shopping and come back and cook up a big communal dinner in the kitchen——All ten or twelve of them sharing the rent, and with that rotation of dinner, they end up living comfortable lives with wild parties and girls rushing in, people bringing bottles, all at about a minimum of seven dollars a week say——It's a wonderful place but at the same time a little maddening, in fact a whole lot maddening because the painter Lanny Meadows loves music and has installed his Hi Fi speaker in the kitchen altho he applies the records in a back room so the daily cook may be concentrating on his Mulligan stew and all of a sudden Stravinski's dinosaurs start dinning overhead——And at night there are bottlecrashing parties usually supervised by wild Pascal who is a sweet kid but crazy when he drinks——A regular nuthouse actually and just exactly the image of what the journalists want to say about the Beat Generation nevertheless a harmless and pleasant arrangement for young bachelors and a good idea in the long run——Because you can rush into any room and find the expert, like say Ben's room and ask "Hey what did Bodhidharma say to the Second Patriarch?"——"He said go fuck yourself, make your mind like a wall, dont pant after outside activities and dont bug me with your outside plans"——"So the guy goes out and stands on his head in the snow?"——"No that was Fubar"——Or you go runnin into Dave Wain's room and there he is sitting crosslegged on his mattress on the floor reading Jane Austen, you ask "What's the best way to make beef Stroganoff?"——"Beef Stroganoff is very simple, 't'aint nothin but a good well cooked beef and onion stew that you let cool afterwards then you throw in mushrooms and lotsa sour cream, I'll come down and show way soon's I finish this chapter in this marvelous novel, I wanta find out what happens next"——Or you go into the Negro's room and ask if you can borrow his tape recorder because right at the moment some funny things are being said in the kitchen by Duluoz and McLear and Monsanto and some newspaperman——Because the kitchen was also the main talking room where everybody sat in a clutter of dishes and ashtrays and all kinds of visitors came—— The year before a beautiful 16 year old Japanese girl had come there just to interview me, for instance, but chaperoned by a Chinese painter——The phone rang consistently——Even wild Negro hepcats from around the corner came in with bottles (Edward Kool and several others)——There was Zen, jazz, booze, pot and all the works but it was somehow obviated (as a supposedly degenerate idea) by the sight of a "beatnik" carefully painting the wall of his room and clean white with nice little red borders around the door and windowframes——Or someone is sweeping out the livingroom. Itinerant visitors like me or Ron Blake always had an extra mattress to sleep on.

12

BUT DAVE IS ANXIOUS AND SO AM I to see great Cody who is always the major part of my reason for journeying to the west coast so we call him up at Los Gatos 50 miles away down the Santa Clara Valley and I hear his dear sad voice saying "Been waitin for ya old buddy, come on down right away, but I'll be goin to work at midnight so hurry up and you can visit me at work soon's the boss leaves round two and I'll show you my new job of tire recappin and see if you cant bring a little somethin like a girl or sumptin, just kiddin, come on down pal——"

So there's old Willie waiting for us down on the street parked across from the little pleasant Japanese liquor store where as usual, according to our ritual, I run and get Pernod or Scotch or anything good while Dave wheels around to pick me up at the store door, and I get in the front seat right at Dave's right where I belong all the time like old Honored Samuel Johnson while everybody else that wants to come along has to scramble back there on the mattress (a full mattress, the seats are out) and squat there or lie down there and also generally keep silent because when Dave's got the wheel of Willie in his hand and I've got the bottle in mine and we're off on a trip the talking all comes from the front seat——"By God" yells Dave all glad again "it's just like old times Jack, gee old Willie's been sad for ya, waitin for ya to come back——So now I'm gonna show ya how old Willie's even improved with age, had him reconditioned in Reno last month, here he goes, are you ready Willie?" and off we go and the beauty of it all this particular summer is that the front right seat is broken and just rocks back and forth gently to every one of Dave's driving moves——It's like sitting in a rocking chair on a porch only this is a moving porch and a porch to talk on at that——And insteada watching old men pitch horseshoes from this here talking porch it's all that fine white clean line in the middle of the road as we go flying like birds over the Harrison ramps and whatnot Dave always uses to sneak out of Frisco real fast and avoid all the traffic——Soon we're set straight and pointed head on down beautiful fourlane Bayshore Highway to that lovely Santa Clara Valley——But I'm amazed that after only a few years the damn thing no longer has prune fields and vast beet fields like at Lawrence when I was a brakeman on the Southern Pacific and even after, it's one long row of houses right down the line 50 miles to San Jose like a great monstrous Los Angeles beginning to grow south of Frisco.

At first it's beautiful to just watch that white line reel in to Willie's snout but when I start looking around out the window there's just endless housing tracts and new blue factories everywhere——Sez Dave "Yes that's right, the population explosion is gonna cover every bit of backyard dirt in America someday in fact they'll even have to start piling up friggin levels of houses and others over that like your cityCityCITY till the houses reach a hundred miles in the air in all directions of the map and people looking at the earth from another planet with super telescopes will see a prickly ball hangin in space——It's like real horrible when you come to think of it, even us with all our fancy talks, shit man it's all millions of people and events piling up almost unimaginable now, like raving babboons we'll all be piled on top of each other or one another or whatever you're sposed to say——Hundreds of millions of hungry mouths raving for more more more——And the sadness of it all is that the world hasnt any chance to produce say a writer whose life could really actually touch all this life in every detail like you always say, some writer who could bring you sobbing thru the bed fuckin bedcribs of the moon to see it all even unto the goddamned last gory detail of some dismal robbery of the heart at dawn when no one cares like Sinatra sings" ("When no one cares," he sings in his low baritone but resumes):——"Some strict sweeper sweeping it all up, I mean the incredible helplessness I felt Jack when Céline ended his Journey To The End Of The Night by pissing in the Seine River at dawn there I am thinkin my God there's probably somebody pissing in the Trenton River at dawn right now, the Danube, the Ganges, the frozen Obi, the Yellow, the Paraña, the Willamette, the Merrimac in Missouri too, the Missouri itself, the Yuma, the Amazon, the Thames, the Po, the so and so, it's so friggin endless it's like poems endless everywhere and no one knows any bettern old Buddha you know where he says it's like "There are immeasurable star misty aeons of universes more numerous than the sands in all the galaxies, multiplied by a billion lightyears of multiplication, in fact if I were to go on you'd be scared and couldnt comprehend and you'd despair so much you'd drop dead," that's what he just about said in one of those sutras——Macrocosms and microcosms and chillicosms and microbes and finally you got all these marvelous books a man aint even got time to read em all, what you gonna do in this already piled up multiple world when you have to think of the Book of Songs, Faulkner, César Birotteau, Shakespeare, Satyricons, Dantes, in fact long stories guys tell you in bars, in fact the sutras themselves, Sir Philip Sidney, Sterne, Ibn El Arabi, the copious Lope de Vega and the uncopious goddamn Cervantes, shoo, then there's all those Catulluses and Davids and radio listening skid row sages to contend with because they've all got a million stories too and you too Ron Blake in the backseat shut up! down to everything which is so much that it is of necessity don't you think NOthing anyway, huh?" (expressing exactly the way I feel, of course).

And to corroborate all that about the too-much-ness of the world, in fact, there's Stanley Popovich also in the back mattress next to Ron, Stanley Popovich of New York suddenly arrived in San Francisco with Jamie his Italian beauty girl but's going to leave her in a few days to go work for the circus, a big tough Yugoslav kid who ran the Seven Arts Gallery in New York with big bearded beatnik readings but now comes the circus and a whole big on-the-road of his own——It's too much, in fact right this minute he's started telling us about circus work——On top of all that old Cody is up ahead with HIS thousand stories—— We all agree it's too big to keep up with, that we're surrounded by life, that we'll never understand it, so we center it all in by swigging Scotch from the bottle and when it's empty I run out of the car and buy another one, period.

13

BUT ON THE WAY TO CODY'S MY MADNESS ALREADY BEGAN TO MANIFEST ITSELF in a stranger way, another one of those signposts of something wrong I mentioned a ways back: I thought I saw a flying saucer in the sky over Los Gatos——From five miles away——I look and I see this thing flying along and mention it to Dave who takes one brief look and says "Ah it's only the top of a radio tower"——It reminds me of the time I took a mescaline pill and thought an airplane was a flying saucer (a strange story this, a man has to be crazy to write it anyway).

But there's old Cody in the livingroom of his fine ranchito home sittin over his chess set pondering a problem and right by the fresh woodfire in the fireplace his wife's set out because she knows I love fireplaces——She a good friend of mine too—— The kids are sleeping in the back, it's about eleven, and good old Cody shakes my hand again——Havent seen him for several years because mainly he's just spent two years in San Quentin on a stupid charge of possession of marijuana——He was on his way to work on the railroad one night and was short on time and his driving license had been already revoked for speeding so he saw two bearded bluejeaned beatniks parked, asked them to trade a quick ride to work at the railroad station for two sticks of tea, they complied and arrested him——They were disguised policemen——For this great crime he spent two years in San Quentin in the same cell with a murderous gunman——His job was sweeping out the cotton mill room——I expect him to be all bitter and out of his head because of this but strangely and magnificently he's become quieter, more radiant, more patient, manly, more friendly even——And tho the wild frenzies of his old road days with me have banked down he still has the same taut eager face and supple muscles and looks like he's ready to go anytime——But actually loves his home (paid for by railroad insurance when he broke his leg trying to stop a boxcar from crashing), loves his wife in a way tho they fight some, loves his kids and especially his little son Timmy John partly named after me——Poor old, good old Cody sittin there with his chess set, wants immediately to challenge somebody to a chess game but

only has an hour to talk to us before he goes to work supporting the family by rushing out and pushing his Nash Rambler
down the quiet Los Gatos suburb street, jumping in, starting
the motor, in fact his only complaint is that the Nash wont start
without a push——No bitter complaints about society whatever
from this grand and ideal man who really loves me moreover as
if I deserved it, but I'm bursting to explain everything to him,
not even Big Sur but the past several years, but there's no chance
with everybody yakking——And in fact I can see in Cody's eyes
that he can see in my own eyes the regret we both feel that
recently we havent had chances to talk whatever, like we used
to do driving across America and back in the old road days, too
many people now want to talk to us and tell us *their* stories,
we've been hemmed in and surrounded and outnumbered——
The circle's closed in on the old heroes of the night——But
he says "However you guys, come on down round 'bout
one when the boss leaves and watch me work and keep me
company awhile before you go back to the City"——I can see
Dave Wain really loves him at once, and Stanley Popovich too
who's come along on this trip just to meet the fabled "Dean
Moriarty"——The name I give Cody in "On the Road"——But
O, it breaks my heart to see he's lost his beloved job on the
railroad and after all the seniority he'd piled up since 1948 and
now is reduced to tire recapping and dreary parole visits——All
for two sticks of wild loco weed that grows by itself in Texas
because God wanted it——

     And there over the bookshelf is the old photo of me and
Cody arm in arm in the early days on a sunny street——
     I rush to explain to Cody what happened the year before
when his religious advisor at the prison had invited me to come
to San Quentin to lecture the religious class——Dave Wain was
supposed to drive me and wait outside the prison walls as I'd
go in there alone, probably with a pepup nip bottle hidden in
my coat (I hoped) and I'd be led by big guards to the lecture
room of the prison and there would be sitting a hundred or so
cons including Cody probably all proud in the front row——
And I would begin by telling them I had been in jail myself
once and that I had no right nevertheless to lecture them on
religion——But they're all lonely prisoners and dont care what
I talk about——The whole thing arranged, in any case, and on

the big morning I wake up instead dead drunk on a floor, it's already noon and too late, Dave Wain is on the floor also, Willie's parked outside to take us to Quentin for the lecture but it's too late——But now Cody says "It's alright old buddy I understand"——Altho our friend Irwin had done it, lectured there, but Irwin can do all sorta things like that being more social than I am and capable of going in there as he did and reading his wildest poems which set the prison yard humming with excitement tho I think he shouldna done it after all because I say just to show up for any reason except visiting inside a prison is still SIGNIFYING——And I tell this to Cody who ponders a chess problem and says "Drinkin again, hey?" (if there's anything he hates is to see me drink).

We help him push his Nash down the street, then drink awhile and talk with Evelyn a beautiful blonde woman that young Ron Blake wants and even Dave Wain wants but she's got her mind on other things and taking care of the children who have to go to school and dancing classes in the morning and hardly gets a word in edgewise anyway as we all yak and yell like fools to impress her tho all she really wants is to be alone with me to talk about Cody and his latest soul.

Which includes the fact of Billie Dabney his mistress who has threatened to take Cody away completely from Evelyn, as I'll show later.

So we do go out to the San Jose highway to watch Cody recap tires——There he is wearing goggles working like Vulcan at his forge, throwing tires all over the place with fantastic strength, the good ones high up on a pile, "This one's no good" down on another, bing, bang, talking all the time a long fantastic lecture on tire recapping which has Dave Wain marvel with amazement ——("My God he can do all that and even explain while he's doing it")——But I just mention in connection with the fact that Dave Wain now realizes why I've always loved Cody—— Expecting to see a bitter ex con he sees instead a martyr of the American Night in goggles in some dreary tire shop at 2 A.M. making fellows laugh with joy with his funny explanations yet at the same time to a T performing every bit of the work he's being paid for——Rushing up and ripping tires off car wheels with a jicklo, clang, throwing it on the machine, starting up big roaring steams but yelling explanations over that, darting, bending, flinging, flaying, till Dave Wain said he thought he was going to die laughing or crying right there on the spot.

So we drive back to town and go to the mad boardinghouse to drink some more and I pass out dead drunk on the floor as usual in that house, waking up in the morning groaning far from my clean cot on the porch in Big Sur——No bluejays yakking for me to wake up any more, no gurgling creek, I'm back in the grooky city and I'm trapped.

14

INSTEAD THERE'S THE SOUND OF BOTTLES CRASHING in the livingroom where poor Lex Pascal is holding forth yelling, it reminds of the time a year ago when Jarry Wagner's future wife got sore at Lex and threw a half gallonfull of tokay across the room and hooked him right across the eye, thereupon sailing to Japan to marry Jarry in a big Zen ceremony that made coast to coast papers but all old Lex's got is a cut which I try to fix in the bathroom upstairs saying "Hey, that cut's already stopped bleeding, you'll be alright Lex"——"I'm French Canadian too" he says proudly and when Dave and I and George Baso get ready to drive back to New York he gives me a St.Christopher medal as a goingaway gift——Lex the kind of guy shouldnt really be living in this wild beat boardinghouse, should hide on a ranch somewhere, powerful, goodlooking, full of crazy desire for women and booze and never enough of either——So as the bottles crash again and the Hi Fi's playing Beethoven's Solemn Mass I fall asleep on the floor.

Waking up the next morning groaning of course, but this is the big day when we're going to go visit poor George Baso at the TB hospital in the Valley——Dave perks me up right away bringing coffee or wine optional——I'm on Ben Fagan's floor somehow, apparently I've harangued him till dawn about Buddhism——some Buddhist.

Complicated already but now suddenly appears Joey Rosenberg a strange young kid from Oregon with a full beard and his hair growing right down to his neck like Raul Castro, once the California High School high jump champ who was only about 5 foot 6 but had made the incredible leap of six foot nine over the bar! and shows his highjump ability too by the way he dances around on light feet——A strange athlete who's suddenly decided instead to become some sort of beat Jesus and in fact you see perfect purity and sincerity in his young blue eyes——In fact his eyes are so pure you dont notice the crazy hair and beard, and also he's wearing ragged but strangely elegant clothing ("One of the first of the new Beat Dandies," McLear told me a few days later, "did you hear about that? there's a new strange

underground group of beatniks or whatever who wear special
smooth dandy clothes even tho it may just be a jean jacket with
shino slacks they'll always have strange beautiful shoes or shirts,
or turn around and wear fancy pants unpressed acourse but with
torn sneakers")——Joey is wearing something like brown soft
garments like a tunic or something and his shoes look like Las
Vegas sports shoes——The moment he sees my battered blue
little sneakers that I'd used at Big Sur when my feet go sore,
that is in case my feet got sore on a rocky hike, he wants them
for himself, he wants to swap the snazzy Las Vegas sports shoes
(pale leather, untooled) for my silly little tightfitting tho perfect
sneakers that in fact I was wearing because the Monterey hike
blisters were still hurting me——So we swap——And I ask Dave
Wain about him: Dave says: "He's one of the really strangest
sweetest guys I've ever known, showed up about a week ago I
hear tell, they asked him what he wanted to do and never answers,
just smiles——He just sorta wants to dig everything and just
watch and enjoy and say nothing particular about it——If someone's to ask him 'Let's drive to New York' he'd jump right for it
without a word——On a sort of a pilgrimage, see, with all that
youth, us old fucks oughta take a lesson from him, in faith too,
he has faith, I can see it in his eyes, he has faith in any direction
he may take with anyone just like Christ I guess."

It's strange that in a later revery I imagined myself walking
across a field to find the strange gang of pilgrims in Arkansas
and Dave Wain was sitting there saying "Shhh, He's sleeping,"
"He" being Joey and all the disciples are following him on
a march to New York after which they expect to keep going
walking on water to the other shore——But of course (in my
revery even) I scoff and dont believe it (a kind of story daydreaming I often do) but in the morning when I look into Joey
Rosenberg's eyes I instantly realize it IS Him, Jesus, because
anyone (according to the rules of my revery) who looks into
those eyes is instantly convinced and converted——So the revery
continues into a long farfetched story ending with thinking
I.B.M. machines trying to destroy this "Second Coming" etc.
(but also, in reality, a few months later I threw away his shoes
in the ashcan back home because I felt they had brought me
bad luck and wishing I'd kept my blue sneakers with the little
holes in the toes!)

So anyway we get Joey and Ron Blake who's always following Dave and go off to see Monsanto at the store, our usual
ritual, then across the corner to Mike's Place where we start off
the 10 A.M. with food, drink and a few games of pool at the
tables along the bar——Joey winning the game and a stranger
poolshark you never saw with his long Biblical hair bending to
slide the cue stick smoothly through completely profession-
ally competent fingerstance and smashing home long straight
drives, like seeing Jesus shoot pool of course——And meanwhile
all the food these poor starved kids all three of them do pack
in and eat!——It's not every day they're with a drunken novelist with hundreds of dollars to splurge on them, they order
everything, spaghetti, follow that up with Jumbo Hamburgers,
follow that up with ice cream and pie and puddings, Dave Wain
has a huge appetite anyway but adds Manhattans and Martinis
to the side of his plate——I'm just wailing away on my old fatal
double bourbons and gingerale and I'll be sorry in a few days.

Any drinker knows how the process works: the first day you
get drunk is okay, the morning after means a big head but so
you can kill that easy with a few more drinks and a meal, but
if you pass up the meal and go on to another night's drunk,
and wake up to keep the toot going, and continue on to the
fourth day, there'll come one day when the drinks wont take
effect because you're chemically overloaded and you'll have to
sleep it off but cant sleep any more because it was alcohol itself
that made you sleep those last five nights, so delirium sets in——
Sleeplessness, sweat, trembling, a groaning feeling of weakness
where your arms are numb and useless, nightmares, (nightmares of death) . . . well, there's more of that up later.

About noon which is now the peak of a golden blurry new
day for me we pick up Dave's girl Romana Swartz a big Rumanian monster beauty of some kind (I mean with big purple
eyes and very tall and big but Mae West big), Dave whispers
in my ear "You oughta see her walking around that Zen-East
House in those purple panties of hers, nothing else on, there's
one married guy lives there who goes crazy every time she goes
down the hall tho I dont blame him, would you? she's not trying to entice him or anybody she's just a nudist, she believes
in nudism and bygod she's going to practice it!" (the Zen-East
house being another sort of boardinghouse but this one for all

kinds of married people and single and some small bohemian
type families all races studying Subud or something, I never
was there)——She's a big beautiful brunette anyway in the line
of taste you might attribute to every slaky hungry sex slave in
the world but also intelligent, well read, writes poetry, is a Zen
student, knows everything, is in fact just simply a big healthy
Rumanian Jewess who wants to marry a good hardy man and
go live on a farm in the valley, that's it——

The T.B. hospital is about two hours away through Tracy
and down the San Joaquin Valley, Dave drives beautiful with
Romana between us and me holding the bottle again, it's bright
beautiful California sunshine and prune orchards out there zipping by——It's always fun to have a good driver and a bottle
and dark glasses on a fine sunny afternoon going somewhere
interesting, and all the good conversation as I said——Ron and
Joey are on the back mattress sitting crosslegged just like poor
George Baso had sat on that trip last year from Frisco to New
York.

But the main thing I'd liked at once about that Japanese
kid was what he told me the first night I met him in that crazy
kitchen of the Buchanan Street house: from midnight to 6 A.M.
in his slow methodical voice he gave me his own tremendous
version of the Life of Buddha beginning with infancy and right
down to the end——George's theory (he has many theories and
has actually run meditation classes with bells, just really a serious young lay priest of Japanese Buddhism when all is said and
done) is that Buddha did not reject amorous love life with his
wife and with his harem girls because he was sexually disinterested but on the contrary had been taught in the highest arts
of lovemaking and eroticism possible in the India of that time,
when great tomes like the Kama Sutra were in the process of
being developed, tomes that give you instructions on every act,
facet, approach, moment, trick, lick, lock, bing and bang and
slurp of how to make love with another human being "male or
female" insisted George: "He knew everything there is to know
about all kinds of sex so that when he abandoned the world of
pleasure to go be an ascetic in the forest everybody of course
knew that he wasnt putting it all down out of ignorance——It
served to make people of those times feel a marvelous respect
for all his words——And he was just no simple Casanova with

a few frigid affairs across the years, man he went all the way, he had ministers and special eunuchs and special women who taught him love, special virgins were brought to him, he was acquainted with every aspect of perversity and non perversity and as you know he was also a great archer, horseman, he was just completely trained in all the arts of living by his father's orders because his father wanted to make sure he'd NEVER leave the palace——They used every trick in the books to entice him to a life of pleasure and as you know they even had him happily married to a beautiful girl called Yasodhara and he had a son with her Rahula and he also had his harem which included dancing boys and everything in the books" then George would go into every detail of this knowledge, like "He knew that the phallus is held with the hand and moved inside the vagina with a rotary movement, but this was only the first of several variations where there is also the lowering down of the gal's hips so that the vulva you see recedes and the phallus is introduced with a fast quick movement like stinging of a wasp, or else the vulva is protruded by means of lifting up the hips high so that the member is buried with a sudden rush right to the basis, or then he can withdraw real teasing like, or concentrate on right or left side——And then he knew all the gestures, words, expressions, what to do with a flower, what not to do with a flower, how to drink the lip in all kinds of kissing or how to crush kiss or soft kiss, man he was a *genius* in the beginning" . . . and so on, George went all the way telling me this till 6 A.M. it being one of the most fantastic *Buddha Charitas* I'd ever heard ending with George's own perfect enunciation of the law of the Twelve Nirdanas whereby Buddha just logically disconnected all creation and laid it bare for what it was, under the Bo Tree, a chain of illusions——And on the trip to New York with Dave and me up front talking all the way poor George just sat there on the mattress for the most part very quiet and told us he was taking this trip to find out if HE was traveling to New York or just the CAR (Willie the Jeep) was traveling to New York or was it just the WHEELS were rolling, or the tires, or what——A Zen problem of some kind——So that when we'd see grain elevators on the Plains of Oklahoma George would say quietly "Well it seems to me that grain elevator is sorta waitin for the road to approach it" or he'd say suddenly "While you guys was talkin just then about how to mix a good Pernod Martini I just saw a white horse standing in an abandoned storefront"——In Las Vegas we'd taken a good motel room and gone out to play a little roulette, in St.Louis we'd gone to see the great bellies of the East St.Louis hootchy kootchy joints where three of the most marvelous young girls performed smiling directly at us as tho they knew all about George and his theories about erogenous Buddha (there sits the monarch observing the donzinggerls) and as tho they knew anyway all about Dave Wain who whenever he sees a beautiful girl says licking his lips "Yum Yum." . . .

But now George has T.B. and they tell me he may even die—— Which adds to that darkness in my mind, all these DEATH things piling up suddenly——But I cant believe old Zen Master George is going to allow his body to die just now tho it looks like it when we pass through the lawn and come to a ward of beds and see him sitting dejected on the edge of his bed with his hair hanging over his brow where before it was always combed back——He's in a bathrobe and looks up at us almost displeased (but everybody is displeased by unexpected visits from friends or relatives in a hospital)——Nobody wants to be surprised on their hospital bed——He sighs and comes out to the warm lawn with us and the expression on his face says "Well ah so you've come to see me because I'm sick but what do you really want?" as tho all the old humorous courage of the year before has now given away to a profoundly deep Japanese skepticism like that of a Samurai warrior in a fit of suicidal depression (surprising me by its abject gloomy fearful frown).

15

I MEAN IT WAS LIKE MY FIRST FRIGHTENED REALIZATION OF WHAT TO BE JAPANESE REALLY MEANT——To be Japanese and not to believe in life any more and to be gloomy like Beethoven yet to be Japanese in gloom, the gloom of Bashō behind it all, the huge thunderous scowl of Issa or of Shiki, kneeling in the frost with the bowed head like the bowed-head-oblivion of all the old horses of Japan long dust.

He sits there on the lawn bench looking down and when Dave asks him "Well you gonna be alright soon George" he says simply "I dont know"——He really means "I dont care"——And always warm and courteous with me he now hardly pays any attention to me——He's a little nervous because the other patients, G.I. vets, will see that he's received a visit from a bunch of ragged beatniks including Joey Rosenberg who is bouncing around the lawn looking at flowers with that bemused sincere smile——But little neat George, just 5 feet 5 and a few pounds over that and so clean, with his soft feathery hair like the hair of a child, his delicate hands, he just stares at the ground——His answers come like an old man's (he's only 30)——"I guess all the Dharma talk about everything is nothing is just sorta sinking in my bones," he concedes, which makes me shudder——(On the way Dave's been telling us to be ready because George's changed so)——But I try to keep things going, "Do you remember those dancing girls in St.Louis?"——"Yeh, whore candy" (he's referring to a piece of perfumed cotton one of the girls threw at us in her dance, which we tacked up later to a highway accident cross we'd yanked out of the ground one blood red sunset in Arizona, tacking this perfumed beautiful cotton right where the head of Christ was so that when we brought the cross to New York naturally we had everybody smelling it but George pointed out how beautiful we'd done all this subconsciously because the net result was that all the hepcats of Greenwich Village who came in to see us were picking up the cross and putting their heads (noses) to it)——But George doesnt care any more——And anyway it's time to leave.

But ah, as we're leaving and waving back at him and he's

turned around tentatively to go into the hospital I linger behind the others and turn around several times to wave again——
Finally I start to make a joke of it by ducking around a corner
and peeking out and waving again——He ducks behind a bush
and waves back——I dart to a bush and peek out——Suddenly
we're two crazy hopeless sages goofing on a lawn——Finally as
we part further and further and he comes closer to the door
we are making elaborate gestures and down to the most infinitesimal like when he steps inside the door I wait till I see him
sticking a finger out——So from around my corner I stick out
a shoe——So from his door he sticks out an eye——So from my
corner I stick out nothing but just yell "Wu!"——So from his
door he sticks out nothing and says nothing——So I hide in the
corner and do nothing——But suddenly I burst out and there
HE is bursting out and we start waving gyrations and duck back
to our hiding places——Then I pull a big one by simply walking
away rapidly but suddenly I turn and wave again——He walking
backwards and waving back——The further I go now also walking backwards the more I wave——Finally we're so far apart by
about a hundred yards the game is almost impossible but we
continue somehow——Finally I see a distant sad little Zen wave
of hand——I jump up into the air and gyrate both arms——He
does the same——He goes into the hospital but a moment later
he's peeking out this time from the ward window!——I'm behind a tree trunk thumbing my nose at him——There's no end
to it, in fact——The other kids are all back at the car wondering
what's keeping me——What's keeping me is that I know George
will get better and live and teach the joyful truth and George
knows I know this, that's why he's playing the game with me,
the magic game of glad freedom which is what Zen or for that
matter the Japanese soul ultimately means I say, "And someday
I will go to Japan with George" I tell myself after we've made
our last little wave because I've heard the supper bell ring and
seen the other patients rush for the chow line and knowing
George's fantastic appetite wrapped in that little frail body I
dont wanta hang him up tho he nevertheless does one last trick:
He throws a glass of water out the window in a big froosh of
water and I dont see him any more.

   "Wotze mean by that?" I'm scratching my head going back
to the car.

16

To complete this crazy day at 3 o'clock in the morning here I am sitting in a car being driven 100 miles an hour around the sleeping streets and hills and waterfronts of San Francisco, Dave's gone off to sleep with Romana and the others are passed out and this crazy nextdoor neighbor of the roominghouse (himself a Bohemian but also a laborer, a housepainter who comes home with big muddy boots and has his little boy living with him the wife has died)——I've been in his pad listening to booming loud Stan Getz jazz on his Hi Fi and happened to mention I thought Dave Wain and Cody Pomeray were the two greatest drivers in the world——"What?" he yells, a big blond husky kid with a strange fixed smile, "man I used to drive the getaway car! come on down I'll show ya!"——So almost dawn and here we are cuttin down Buchanan and around the corner on screeching wheels and he opens her up, goes zipping towards a red light so takes a sudden screeching left and goes up a hill fullblast, when we come to the top of the hill I figger he'll pause awhile to see what's over the top but he goes even faster and practically flies off the hill and we head down one of those incredibly steep San Fran streets with our snout pointed to the waters of the Bay and he steps on the gas! we go sailing down a hundred m.p.h. to the bottom of the hill where there's an intersection luckily with the light on green and thru that we blast with just one little bump where the road crosses and another bump where the street is dipping downhill again——We come down to the waterfront and screech right——In a minute we're soaring over the ramps around the Bridge entrance and before I can gulp up a shot or two from my last late bottle we're already parked back outside the pad on Buchanan——The greatest driver in the world whoever he was and I never saw him again——Bruce something or other——What a getaway.

17

I END UP GROANING DRUNK ON THE FLOOR this time beside Dave's floor mattress forgetting that he's not even there.

But a strange thing happened that morning I remember now: before Cody's call from downvalley: I'm feeling hopelessly idiotically depressed again groaning to remember Tyke's dead and remembering that sinking beach but at the side of the radiator in the toilet lies a copy of Boswell's Johnson which we'd been discussing so happy in the car: I open to any page then one more page and start reading from the top left and suddenly I'm in an entirely perfect world again: old Doc Johnson and Boswell are visiting a castle in Scotland belonging to a deceased friend called Rorie More, they're drinking sherry by the great fireplace looking at the picture of Rorie on the wall, the widow of Rorie is there, Johnson suddenly says "Sir, here's what I would do to deal with the sword of Rorie More" (the portrait shows old Rorie with his Highlands flinger) "I'd get inside him with a dirk and stab him to my pleasure like an animal" and bleary with hangover I realize that if there was any way for Johnson to express his sorrow to the widow of Rorie More on the unfortunate circumstance of his death, this was the way——So pitiful, irrational, yet perfect——I rush down to the kitchen where Dave Wain and some others are already eating breakfast of sorts and start reading the whole thing to the lot of them——Jonesy looks at me askance over his pipe for being so literary so early in the morning but I'm not being literary at all——Again I see death, the death of Rorie More, but Johnson's response to death is ideal and so ideal I only wish old Johnson be sitting in the kitchen now——(Help! I'm thinking).

The call comes from Cody in Los Gatos that he lost his job tire recapping——"Because we were there last night?"——"No no something entirely different, he's gotta lay off some men because his mortgage is bleeding him and all that and some girl is tryna sue him for forging a check and all that, so man I've got to find another job but I have to pay the rent and everything's all fucked up down here, Oh old buddy how about, cant you, I plead or I dont plead, or honestly, Jack, ah, lend me a

hundred dollars willya?"——"By God Cody I'll be right down
and GIVE you a hundred dollars"——"You mean you'll really
do that, listen just to lend to me is enough but if you insist,
hm" (fluttering his eyelashes over the phone because he knows
I mean it) "you old loverboy you, how you gonna get down
here there and give me that money there son and make my old
heart glad"——"I'll have Dave drive me down"——"Okay I'll pay
the rent with it right away and because it's now Friday, why,
Thursday or whatever, that's right Thursday, why I dont have
to be lookin for a new job till next Monday so you can stay here
and we'll have a long weekend just goofin and talkin boy like
we used to do, I can demolish you at chess or we can watch a
baseball game" and in a whisper "and we can sneak into the City
see and see my purty baby"——So I ask Dave Wain and yes he's
ready to go anytime, he's just following me like I often follow
people myself, and so off we go again.

And on the way we drop in on Monsanto at the bookstore
and the idea suddenly comes to me for Dave and me and Cody
to go to the cabin and spend a big quiet crazy weekend (how?)
but when Monsanto hears this idea he'll come too, in fact
he'll bring his little Chinese buddy Arthur Ma and we'll catch
McLear at Santa Cruz and go visit Henry Miller and suddenly
another big huge ball is begun.

So there's Willie waiting down on the street, I go to the store,
buy the bottle, Dave wheels Willie around, Ron Blake and now
Ben Fagan are on the back mattress, I'm sitting in my front seat
rocking chair as now in broad afternoon we go blattin again
down that Bay Shore highway to see old Cody and Monsanto's
in back of us in his jeep with Arthur Ma, two jeeps now, and
about to be two more as I'll show——Coming to Cody's in mid
afternoon, his own house already filled with visitors (local Los
Gatos literaries and all kinds of people the phone there ringing continually too) and Cody says to Evelyn "I'll just spend a
couple days with Jack and the gang like the old days and look
for a job Monday"——"Okay"——So we all go to a wonderful
pizza restaurant in Los Gatos where the pizzas are piled an inch
high with mushrooms and meat and anchovies or anything you
want, I cash a travelers check at the supermarket, Cody takes
the 100 in cash, gives it to Evelyn in the restaurant, and later
that day the two jeeps resume down to Monterey and down

that blasted road I walked on blistered feet back to the frightful bridge at Raton Canyon——And I'd thought I'd never see the place again. But now I was coming back loaded with observers. The sight of the canyon down there as we renegotiated the mountain road made me bite my lip with marvel and sadness.

18

IT'S AS FAMILIAR AS AN OLD FACE IN AN OLD PHOTOGRAPH as tho I'm gone a million years from all that sun shaded brush on rocks and that heartless blue of the sea washing white on yellow sand, those rills of yellow arroyo running down mighty cliff shoulders, those distant blue meadows, that whole ponderous groaning upheaval so strange to see after the last several days of just looking at little faces and mouths of people——As tho nature had a Gargantuan leprous face of its own with broad nostrils and huge bags under its eyes and a mouth big enough to swallow five thousand jeepster stationwagons and ten thousand Dave Wains and Cody Pomerays without a sigh of reminiscence or regret——There it is, every sad contour of my valley, the gaps, the Mien Mo captop mountain again, the dreaming woods below our high shelved road, suddenly indeed the sight of poor Alf again far way grazing in the mid afternoon by the corral fence——And there's the creek bouncing along as tho nothing had ever happened elsewhere and even in the daytime somehow dark and hungry looking in its deeper tangled grass.

Cody's never seen this country before altho he's an old Californian by now, I can see he's very impressed and even glad he's come out on a little jaunt with the boys and with me and is seeing a grand sight——He's like a little boy again now for the first time in years because he's like let out of school, no job, the bills paid, nothing to do but gratefully amuse me, his eyes are shining——In fact ever since he's come out of San Quentin there's been something hauntedly boyish about him as tho prison walls had taken all the adult dark tenseness out of him——In fact every evening after supper in the cell he shared with the quiet gunman he'd bent his serious head to a daily letter or at least every-other-day letter full of philosophical and religious musings to his mistress Billie——And when you're in bed in jail after lights out and you're not sleepy there's ample time to just remember the world and indeed savor its sweetness if any (altho it's always sweet to remember it in jail tho harder in prison, as Genet shows) with the result that he'd not only come to a chastisement of his bashing bitternesses (and of course it's always good to get away from alcohol and excessive smoking for two years) (and all that regular sleep) he was just like a kid again, but as I say that haunting kidlikeness I think all ex cons seem to have when they've just come out——In seeking to severely penalize criminals society by putting the criminals away behind safe walls actually provide them with the means of greater strength for future atrocities glorious and otherwise—— "Well I'll be damned" he keeps saying as he sees those bluffs and cliffs and hanging vines and dead trees, "you mean to tell me you ben alone here for three weeks, why I wouldnt dare that . . . must be awful at night . . . looka that old mule down there . . . man, dig the redwood country way back in . . . reminds me of old Colorady b'god when I used to steal a car every day and drive out to hills like this with a fresh little high school sumptin"——"Yum Yum," says Dave Wain emphatically turning that big goofy look to us from his driving wheel with his big mad feverish shining eyes full of yumyum and yabyum too—— "S'matter with you boys not making extensive plans to bring a bevy of schoolgirls down here to wile away our conversation pieces thar" says Cody real relaxed and talking sadly.

Behind us the Monsanto jeepster follows doggedly——Passing thru Monterey Monsanto has already called Pat McLear, staying for the summer with wife and kid in Santa Cruz, McLear with his own jeepster is following us a few miles down the highway——It's a big Big Sur day.

We wheel downhill to cross the creek and at the corral fence I proudly get out to officially open the gate and let the cars through——We go bumping down the two-rutted lane to the cabin and park——My heart sinks to see the cabin.

To see the cabin so sad and almost human waiting there for me as if forever, to hear my little neat gurgling creek resuming its song just for me, to see the very same bluejays still waiting in the tree for me and maybe mad at me now they see I'm back because I havent been there to lay out their Cheerios along the porch rail every blessed morning——And in fact first thing I do is rush inside and get them some food and lay it out——But so many people around now they're afraid to try it.

Monsanto all decked out in his old clothes and looking forward to a wine and talkfest weekend in his pleasant cabin takes the big sweet axe down from the wall nails and goes out and starts hammering at a huge log——In fact it's really a half of a tree that fell there years ago and's been hammered at intermittently but now he's bound he's going to crack it in half and again in half so we can then start splitting it down the middle for huge bonfire type logs——Meanwhile little Arthur Ma who never goes anywhere without his drawing paper and his Yellow-jack felt tip pencils is already seated in my chair on the porch (wearing my hat now too) drawing one of his interminable pictures, he'll do 25 a day and 25 the next day too——He'll talk and go on drawing——He has felt tips of all colors, red, blue, yellow, green, black, he draws marvelous subconscious glurbs and can also do excellent objective scenes or anything he wants on to cartoons——Dave is taking my rucksack and his rucksack out of Willie and throwing them into the cabin, Ben Fagan is wandering around near the creek puffing on his pipe with a happy bhikku smile, Ron Blake is unpacking the steaks we bought enroute in Monterey and I'm already flicking the plastics off the top of bottles with that expert twitch and twist you only get to learn after years of winoing in alleys east and west.

Still the same, the fog is blowing over the walls of the canyon obscuring the sun but the sun keeps fighting back——The inside of the cabin with the fire finally going is still the dear lovable abode now as sharp in my mind as I look at it as an unusually well focused snapshot——The sprig of ferns still stands in a glass of water, the books are there, the neat groceries ranged along the wall shelves——I feel excited to be with the gang but there's a hidden sadness too and which is expressed later by Monsanto when he says "This is the kind of place where a person should really be alone, you know? when you bring a big gang here it somehow desecrates it not that I'm referring to us or anybody in particular? there's such a sad sweetness to those trees as tho yells shouldnt insult them or conversation only"——Which is just the way I feel too.

In a gang we all go down the path towards the sea, passing underneath "That *son*ofabitch bridge" Cody calls it looking up with horror——"That thing's enough to scare anybody away"——But worst of all for an old driver like Cody, and Dave too, is to see that upended old chassis in the sand, they spend a half hour poking around the wreckage and shaking their heads——We kick around the beach awhile and decide to come back at night with bottles and flashlights and build a huge bonfire, now it's time to get back to the cabin and cook those steaks and have a ball, and there's McLear's jeep already arrived and parked and there's McLear himself and that beautiful blonde wife of his in her tight blue jeans that makes Dave say "Yum yum" and Cody just say "Yes, that's right, yes, that's right, ah hum honey, yes."

19

A ROARING DRINKING BOUT BEGINS deep in the canyon—
Fog nightfall sends cold seeping into the windows so all
these softies demand that the wood windows be closed so we
all sit there in the glow of the one lamp coughing in the smoke
but they dont care——They think it's just the steaks smoking
over the fire——I have one of the jugs in my hand and I wont
let go——McLear is the handsome young poet who's just written the most fantastic poem in America, called "Dark Brown,"
which is every detail of his and his wife's body described in
ecstatic union and communion and inside out and everywhichaway and not only that he insists on reading it to us——But I
wanta read my "Sea" poem too——But Cody and Dave Wain
are talking about something else and that silly kid Ron Blake is
singing like Chet Baker——Arthur Ma is drawing in the corner,
and it sorta goes like this generally:——

"That's what old men do, Cody, they drive slowly backwards
in Safeway Supermarket parking lots"——"Yes that's right, I was
tellin you about that bicycle of mine but that's what they do yes
you see that's because while the old woman is shoppin in that
store they figure they'll park a little closer to the entrance and
so they spend a half hour to think their big move out and they
back in out slowly from their slot, can hardly turn around to see
what's in back, usually nothin there, then they wheel real slow
and trembly to that slot they picked but all of a sudden some cat
jumps in it with his pickup and them old men is scratchin their
heads sayin and whining 'Owww, these young fellers nowadays'
and all that obvious, ah, yes, but that BICYCLE of mine in
Denver I tell you I had it twisted and that wheel used to wobble
so by necissity I had to invent a new way to maneuver them
handlebars see——"——"Hey Cody have a drink," I'm yelling in
his ear and meanwhile McLear is reading: "Kiss my thighs in
darkness the pit of fire" and Monsanto is chuckling saying to
Fagan: "So this crazy character comes down stairs and asking
for a copy of Aleister Crowley and I didnt know 'bout that till
you told me the other day, then on the way out I see him sneak
a book off the shelf but he puts another one in its place that

he got out of his pocket, and the book is a novel by somebody called Denton Welch all about this young kid in China wanderin around the streets like real romantic young Truman Capote only it's China" and Arthur Ma suddenly yells: "Hold still you buncha bastards, I got a hole in my eye" and generally the way parties go, and so on, ending with the steak dinner (I dont even touch a bite but just drink on), then the big bonfire on the beach to which we march all in one arm-swinging gang, I've gotten the idea in my head I'm the leader of a guerilla warfare unit and I'm marching ahead the lieutenant giving orders, with all our flashlights and yells we come swarming down the narrow path going "Hup one two three" and challenging the enemy to come out of hiding, some guerillas.

Monsanto that old woodsman starts a huge bonfire on the beach that can be seen flaring from miles away, cars passing across the bridge way up there can see there's a party goin on in the hole of night, in fact the bonfire lights up the eerie weird beams and staunches of the bridge almost all the way up, giant shadows dance on the rocks——The sea swirls up but seems subdued——It's not like being alone down in the vast hell writing the sounds of the sea.

The night ending with everybody passing out exhausted on cots, in sleepingbags outside (McLear goes home with wife) but Arthur Ma and I by the late fire keep up yelling spontaneous questions and answers right till dawn like "Who told you you had a hat on your head?"——"My head never questions hats"——"What's the matter with your liver training?"——"My liver training got involved in kidney work"——(and here again another great gigantic little Oriental friend for me, an eastcoaster who's never known Chinese or Japanese kids, on the west coast it's quite common but for an eastcoaster like me it's amazing and what with all my earlier studies in Zen and Chan and Tao)——(And Arthur also being a gentle small soft-haired seemingly soft little Oriental goofnik)——And we come to great chanted statements, taking turns, without a pause to think, just one then the other, bing and bang, the beauty of them being that while one guy is yelling like (me):——"Tonight the full apogee August moon will out, early with a jaundiced tint, and pop angels all over my rooftop along with Devas sprinkling flowers" (any kind of nonsense being the rule) the other guy has time not only to figure the next statement but can take off from the subconscious arousement of an idea from "angels all over my rooftop" and so can yell without thinking an answer the stupider or rather the more unexpectedly insaner sillier brighter it is the better "Pilgrims dropping turds and sweet nemacular nameless railroad trains from heaven with omnipotent youths bearing monkey women that will stomp through the stage waiting for the moment when by pinching myself I prove that a thought is like a touch"——But this is only the beginning because now we know the routine and get better and better till at dawn I seem to recall we were so fantastically brilliant (while everyone snored) the skies must have shook to hear it and not just foil: let's see if I can recreate at least the style of this game:——

ARTHUR: "When are you going to become the Eighth Patriarch?"

ME: "As soon as you give me that old motheaten sweater"—— (Much better than that, forget this for now, because I want to talk first about Arthur Ma and try again to duplicate our feat).

20

A<small>S I SAY MY FIRST LITTLE CHINESE FRIEND</small>, I keep saying "little" George and "little" Arthur but the fact is they were both small anyway——Altho George talked slowly and was a little absent from everything in the way of a Zen Master actually who realizes that everything is indifferent anyway, Arthur was friendlier, warmer in a way, curious and always asking questions, more active than George with his constant drawing, and of course Chinese instead of Japanese——He wanted me to meet his father the following weeks——He was Monsanto's best friend at the time and they made an extremely strange pair going down the street together, the big ruddy happy man with the crewcut and corduroy jacket and sometimes pipe in mouth, and the little childlike Chinese boy who looked so young most bartenders wouldnt serve him tho he was actually 30 years old——Nevertheless the son of a famous Chinatown family and Chinatown is right back there behind the fabled beatnik streets of Frisco——Also Arthur was a tremendous little loverboy who had fabulously beautiful girls on the line and however'd just separated from his wife, a girl I never saw but Monsanto told me she was the most beautiful Negro girl in the world——Arthur came from a large family but as a painter and a Bohemian his family disapproved of him now so he lived alone in a comfortable old hotel on North Beach tho sometimes he went around the corner into Chinatown to visit his father who sat in the back of his Chinese general store brooding among his countless poems written swiftly in Chinese stroke on pieces of beautiful colored paper which he then hanged from the ceiling of his little cubicle——There he sat, clean, neat, almost shiney, wondering about what poem to write next but his keen little eyes always jumping to the street door to see who's going by and if someone came into the shop itself he knew at once who it was and for what——He was in fact the best friend and trusted adviser of Chiang Kai Shek in America, true and no lie——But Arthur himself was in favor of the Red Chinese which was a family matter and a Chinese matter I had nothing to say about and didnt interest me except insofar as it gave a dramatic picture of father and son in an old culture——The point of the matter anyway being that he was goofing with me just like George had done and making me happy somehow like George had done—— Something anciently familiar about his loyal presence made me wonder if I'd ever lived before in some other lifetime in China or if he'd been an Occidental himself in a previous lifetime of his own involved with mine somewhere else than China——The pity of it is that I have no record of what we were yelling and announcing back and forth as the birds woke up outside but it went generally like this:——

ME:- "Unless someone sicks a hot iron in my heart or heaps up Evil Karma like tit and tat the pile of that and pulls my mother out her bed to slay her before my damning human eyes——"

ARTHUR:- "And I break my hand on heads——"

ME:- "Everytime you throw a rock at a cat from your glass house you heap upon yourself the automatic Stanley Gould winter so dark of death after death, and growing old——"

ARTHUR:- "Because lady those ashcans'll bite you back and be cold too——"

ME:- "And your son will never rest in the imperturbable knowledge that what he thinks he thinks as well as what he does he thinks as well as what he feels he thinks as well as future that——"

ARTHUR:- "Future that my damn old sword cutter Paisan Pasha lost the Preakness again——"

ME:- "Tonight the moon shall witness angels trooping at the baby's window where inside he gurgles in his pewk looking with mewling eyes for babyside waterfall lambikin hillside the day the little Arab shepherd boy hugged the babylamb to heart while the mother bleeted at his bay heel——"

ARTHUR:- "And so Joe the sillicks killit no not——"

ME:- "Shhhhoww graaa——"

ARTHUR:- "Wind and carstart——"

ME:- "The angels Devas monsters Asuras Devadattas Vedantas McLaughlins Stones will hue and hurl in hell if they dont love the lamb the lamb the lamb of hell lambchop——"

ARTHUR:- "Why did Scott Fitzgerald keep a notebook?"

ME:- "Such a marvelous notebook——"

ARTHUR:- "Komi denera ness pata sutyamp anda wanda

vesnoki shadakiroo paryoumemga sikarem nora sarkadium baron roy kellegiam myorki ayastuna haidanseetzel ampho andiam yerka yama chelmsford alya bonneavance koroom cemanda versel——"

ME:- "The 26th Annual concert of the Armenian Convention?"

21

INCIDENTALLY I FORGOT TO MENTION THAT DURING THE THREE WEEKS ALONE the stars had not come out at all, not even for one minute on any night, it was the foggy season, except the very last night when I was getting ready to leave—— Now the stars were out every night, the sun shone considerably longer but a sinister wind accompanied the Autumn in Big Sur: it seemed like the whole Pacific Ocean was blowing with all its might right into Raton Canyon and also over the high gap from another end causing all the trees to shudder as the big groaning howl came newsing and noising from downcanyon, when it hit there was raised a roar of noise I didnt like——It seemed ill omened to me somewhere——It was much better to have fog and silence and quiet trees——Now the whole canyon by one blast could be led screaming and waving in all directions in such a confused mass that even the fellows with me were a little surprised to see it——It was too big a wind for such a little canyon.

This development also prevented the constant hearing of the reassuring creek.

One good thing was that when jet planes broke the sound barrier overhead the wind dispersed the clap of empty thunder they caused, because during the foggy season the noise would come down into the canyon, concentrate there, and rock the house like an explosion making me think the first time (alone) that somebody'd set off a blast of dynamite nearby.

While I woke up groaning and sick there was plenty of wine right there to start me off with the hounds of hair, so okay, but Monsanto had retired early and typically sensibly to sleep by the creek and now he was awake singing swooshing his whole head into the creek and going Brrrr and rubbing his hands for a new day——Dave Wain made breakfast with his usual lecture "Now the real way to fry eggs is to put a cover over them so that they can have that neat basted white look on the yellows, soon's I get this pancake batter ready we'll start on them"——My list of groceries was so all inclusive in the beginning it was now feeding guerilla troops.

A big axe chopping contest began after breakfast, some of us

sitting watching on the porch and the performers down below
hacking away at the tree trunk which was over a foot thick——
They were chopping off two foot chunks, no easy job——I realized you can always study the character of a man by the way
he chops wood——Monsanto an old lumberman up in Maine
as I say now showed us how he conducted his whole life in fact
by the way he took neat little short handled chops from both
left and right angles getting his work done in reasonably short
time without too much sweat——But his strokes were rapid——
Whereas old Fagan pipe-in-mouth slogged away I guess the
way he learned in Oregon and in the Northwest fire schools,
also getting his job done, silently, not a word——But Cody's
fantastic fiery character showed in the way he went at the log
with horrible force, when he brought down the axe with all his
might and holding it far at the end you could hear the whole
treetrunk groaning the whole length inside, runk, sometimes
you could hear a lengthwise cracking going on, he is really
very strong and he brought that axe down so hard his feet left
the earth when it hit——He chopped off his log with the fury
of a Greek god——Nevertheless it took him longer and much
more sweat than Monsanto——"Used to do this in a workgang
in southern Arizony" he said, whopping one down that made
the whole treetrunk dance off the ground——But it was like
an example of vast but senseless strength, a picture of poor
Cody's life and in a sense my own——I too chopped with all my
might and got madder and went faster and raked the log but
took more time than Monsanto who watched us smiling——
Little Arthur thereupon tried his luck but gave up after five
strokes——The axe was like to carry him away anyway——Then
Dave Wain demonstrated with big easy strokes and in no time
we had five huge logs to use——But now it was time to get in
the cars (McLear had rearrived) and go driving south down the
coast highway to a hot springs bath house down there, which
sounded good to me at first.

But the new Big Sun Autumn was now all winey sparkling
blue which made the terribleness and giantness of the coast all
the more clear to see in all its gruesome splendor, miles and
miles of it snaking away south, our three jeeps twisting and
turning the increasing curves, sheer drops at our sides, further
ghostly high bridges to cross with smashings below——Tho all

the boys are wowing to see it——To me it's just an inhospitable
madhouse of the earth, I've seen it enough and even swallowed
it in that deep breath——The boys reassure me the hot springs
bath will do me good (they see I'm gloomy now hungover
for good) but when we arrive my heart sinks again as McLear
points out to sea from the balcony of the outdoor pools: "Look
out there floating in the sea weeds, a dead otter!"——And sure
enough it is a dead otter I guess, a big brown pale lump floating up and down mournfully with the swells and ghastly weeds,
my otter, my dear otter I'd written poems about——"Why did
he die?" I ask myself in despair——"Why do they do that?"——
"What's the sense of all this?"——All the fellows are shading their
eyes to get a better look at the big peaceful tortured hunk of
seacow out there as tho it's something of passing interest while
to me it's a blow across the eyes and down into my heart——
The hot water pools are steaming, Fagan and Monsanto and
the others are all sitting peacefully up to their necks, they're all
naked, but there's a gang of fairies also there naked all standing
around in various bath house postures that make me hesitate
to take my clothes off just on general principles——In fact Cody
doesnt even bother to do anything but lie down with his clothes
on in the sun, on the balcony table, and just smoke——But I
borrow McLear's yellow bathingsuit and get in——"What ya
wearing a bathingsuit in a hot springs pool for boy?" says Fagan
chuckling——With horror I realize there's spermatazoa floating
in the hot water——I look and I see the other men (the fairies)
all taking good long looks at Ron Baker who stands there facing
the sea with his arse for all to behold, not to mention McLear
and Dave Wain too——But it's very typical of me and Cody that
we wont undress in this situation (we were both raised Catholics?)——Supposedly the big sex heroes of our generation, in
fact——You might think——But the combination of the strange
silent watching fairy-men, and the dead otter out there, and the
spermatazoa in the pools makes me sick, not to mention that
when somebody informs me this bath house is owned by the
young writer Kevin Cudahy whom I knew very well in New
York and I ask one of the younger strangers where's Kevin Cudahy he doesnt even deign to reply——Thinking he hasnt heard
me I ask again, no reply, no notice, I ask a third time, this time
he gets up and stalks out angrily to the locker rooms——It all

adds up to the confusion that's beginning to pile up in my battered drinking brain anyway, the constant reminders of death
not the least of which was the death of my peaceful love of
Raton Canyon now suddenly becoming a horror.

From the baths we go to Nepenthe which is a beautiful cliff
top restaurant with vast outdoor patio, with excellent food,
excellent waiters and management, good drinks, chess tables,
chairs and tables to just sit in the sun and look at the grand
coast——Here we all sit at various tables and Cody starts playing chess with everybody will join while he's chomping away at
those marvelous hamburgers called Heavenburgers (huge with
all the side works)——Cody doesnt like to just sit around and
lightly chat away, he's the kind of guy if he's going to talk he has
to do all the talking himself for hours till everything is exhaust-
edly explained, sans that he just wants to bend over a chess-
board and say "He he heh, old Scrooge is saving up a pawn
hey? cak! I got ya!"——But while I'm sitting there discussing
literature with McLear and Monsanto suddenly a strange couple of gentlemen nearby strike up an acquaintance——One of
them is a youngster who says he is a lieutenant in the Army——
I instantly (drunk on fifth Manhattan by now) go into my
theory of guerilla warfare based on my observations the night
before when it did seriously occur to me that if Monsanto,
Arthur, Cody, Dave, Ben, Ron Blake and I were all members
of one fighting unit (and all carrying canteens of booze on our
belts) it would be very difficult for the enemy to hurt any of us
because we'd be, as dear friends, watching so desperately closely
over one another, which I tell the first lieutenant, which attracts
the interest of the older man who admits that he's a GENERAL
in the Army——There are also some further homosexuals at a
separate table which prompts Dave Wain to look up from the
chess game at one quiet drowsy point and announce in his dry
twang "Under redwood beams, people talking about homosexuality and war . . . call it my Nepenthe Haiku"——"Yass" says
Cody checkmating him "see what you can *ku* about that m'boy
and get out of there and I'll noose you with my queen, dear."

I mention the general only because there are also something
sinister about the fact that during this long binge I came across
him and *another* general, two strange generals, and I'd never
met any generals in my life——This first general was strange

because he seemed too polite and yet there was something sinister about his steely eyes behind goof darkglasses——Something sinister too about the first lieutenant who guessed who we were (the San Francisco poets, a major nucleus of them indeed) and didn't seem at all pleased tho the general seemed amused——Nevertheless in a sinister way the general seemed to take great interest in my theory about buddy units for guerilla warfare and when President Kennedy about a year later ordered just such a new scheme for part of our armed forces I wondered (still crazy even then but for new reasons) if the general had got an idea from me——The second general, even stranger, coming up, occurred when I was even more far gone.

Manhattans and more Manhattans and finally when we got back to the cabin in late afternoon I was feeling good but realized I was going to be finished tomorrow——But poor young Ron Blake asked me if he could stay with me in the cabin, the others were all going back to the city in the three cars, I couldnt think of any way to reject his request in a harmless way so said yes——So when they all left suddenly I was alone with this mad beatnik kid singing me songs and all I wanta do is sleep——But I've got to make the best of it and not disappoint his believing heart.

Because after all the poor kid actually believes that there's something noble and idealistic and kind about all this beat stuff, and I'm supposed to be the King of the Beatniks according to the newspapers, so but at the same time I'm sick and tired of all the endless enthusiasms of new young kids trying to know me and pour out all their lives into me so that I'll jump up and down and say yes yes that's right, which I cant do any more——My reason for coming to Big Sur for the summer being precisely to get away from that sort of thing——Like those pathetic five highschool kids who all came to my door in Long Island one night wearing jackets that said "Dharma Bums" on them, all expecting me to be 25 years old according to a mistake on a book jacket and here I am old enough to be their father——But no, hep swinging young jazzy Ron wants to dig everything, go to the beach, run and romp and sing, talk, write tunes, write stories, climb mountains, go hiking, see everything, do everything with everybody——But having one last quart of port with me I agree to follow him to the beach.

We go down the old sad path of the bhikku and suddenly I see a dead mouse in the grass——"A wee dead mousie" I say cleverly poetically but suddenly I realize and remember now for the first time how I've left the cover off the rat poison in Monsanto's shelf and so this is *my mouse*——It's lying there *dead*——Like the otter in the sea——It's my own personal mouse that I've carefully fed chocolate and cheese all summer but once again I've unconsciously sabotaged all these great plans of mine to be kind to living beings even bugs, once again I've murdered a mouse one way or the other——And on top of that when we come to the place where the garter snake usually lies sunning itself, and I bring it to Ron's attention, he suddenly yells "LOOKOUT! you never can tell what kind of snake it is!" which really scares me, my heart pounds with horror——My little friend the garter snake turns therefore with my head from a living being with a long green body into the evil serpent of Big Sur.

On top of that, at the surf, where long streamers of hollow sea weed always lie around drying in the sun some of them huge, like living bodies with skin, pieces of living material that always made me sad somehow, here's the young hepcat lifting them up and dancing a dervish around the beach with them, turning my Sur into something seachange——Something brainchange.

All that night by lamplight we sing and yell songs which is okay but in the morning the bottle is gone and I wake up with the "final horrors" again, precisely the way I woke up in the Frisco skidrow room before escaping down here, it's all caught up with me again, I can hear myself again whining "Why does God torture me?"——But anybody who's never had delirium tremens even in their early stages may not understand that it's not so much a physical pain but a mental anguish indescribable to those ignorant people who dont drink and accuse drinkers of irresponsibility——The mental anguish is so intense that you feel you have betrayed your very birth, the efforts nay the birth pangs of your mother when she bore you and delivered you to the world, you've betrayed every effort your father ever made to feed you and raise you and make you strong and my God even educate you for "life," you feel a guilt so deep you identify yourself with the devil and God seems far away abandoning you to your sick silliness——You feel sick in the greatest sense of the

word, *breathing without believing in it*, sicksicksick, your soul
groans, you look at your helpless hands as tho they were on fire
and you cant move to help, you look at the world with dead
eyes, there's on your face an expression of incalculable repin-
ing like a constipated angel on a cloud——In fact it's actually a
cancerous look you throw on the world, through browngray
wool fuds over your eyes——Your tongue is white and disgusting, your teeth are stained, your hair seems to have dried out
overnight, there are huge mucks in the corners of your eyes,
greases on your nose, froth at the sides of your mouth: in short
that very disgusting and wellknown hideousness everybody
knows who's walked past a city street drunk in the Boweries of
the world——But there's no joy at all, people say "Oh well he's
drunk and happy let him sleep it off"——The poor drunkard
is *crying*——He's crying for his mother and father and great
brother and great friend, he's crying for help——He tries to pull
himself together by moving one shoe nearer to his foot and he
cant even do that properly, he'll drop the shoe, or knock something over, he'll do something invariably that'll start him crying again——He'll want to bury his face in his hands and moan
for mercy and he knows there is none——Not only because he
doesnt deserve it but there's no such thing anyway——Because
he looks up at the blue sky and there's nothing there but empty
space making a big face at him——He looks at the world, it's
sticking its tongue out at him and once that mask is removed
it's looking at him with hollow big red eyes like his own eyes——
He may see the earth move but there's no significance of any
particular kind to attach to that——One little unexpected noise
behind him will make him snarl in rage——He'll pull and tug
at his poor stained shirt——He feels like rubbing his face into
something that isnt.

His socks are thick tired moisty slimes——The beard on
his cheeks itches the running sweats and annoys the tortured
mouth——There's a twisted feeling of no-more, never-again,
agh——What was beautiful and clean yesterday has irrationally
and unaccountably changed into a big dreary crock of shit——
The hairs on his fingers stare at him like tomb hairs——The
shirt and trousers have become glued to his person as tho he
was to be drunk forever——The ache of remorse sinks in as tho
somebody was pushing it in from above——The pretty white

clouds in the sky hurt his eyes only——The only thing to do
is turn over and lie face down and weep——The mouth is so
blasted there's not even a chance to gnash the teeth——There's
not even strength to tear the hair.

And here comes Ron Blake starting off his new day singing at
the top of his voice——I go down by the creek and throw myself
in the sand and lie looking with sad eyes at the water which no
longer friends me but sorta wants me to go away——There isnt
a drop to drink left in the cabin, all the goddamn jeeps are gone
with all its healthy cargo of people and I'm alone with an enthusiastic kid on a lark——The little bugs I'd saved from drowning
just because I was bemused and alone and glad, now drown
unnoticed within my reach anyway——The spider is still minding his own business in the outhouse——Alf lows mournfully in
the valley far away to express just the way I feel——The bluejays
yak around me as tho because I'm too tired and helpless to
feed them any more they're figuring on trying me if they can,
"They're friggin vultures anyway" I moan with my mouth in
the sand——The once pleasant thumpthump gurgle slap of the
creek is now an endless jabbering of blind nature which doesnt
understand anything in the first place——My old thoughts about
the slit of a billion years covering all this and all cities and generations eventually is just a dumb old thought, "Only a silly
sober fool could think it, imagine gloating over such nonsense"
(because in one sense the drinker learns wisdom, in the words
of Goethe or Blake or whichever it was "The pathway to wisdom lies through excess")——But in this condition you can only
say "Wisdom is just another way to make people sick"——"I'm
SICK" I yell emphatically to the trees, to the woods around, to
the hills above, looking around desperately, nobody cares——I
can even hear Ron singing at his lunch inside.

What's even more horrible he tries to show compunction
and wants to help me, "Anything I can do"——Later he goes
for a lone walk so I go in the cabin and lie on the cot and
spend about two hours groaning out a lament: "*O mon Dieux,
pourquoi Tu m'laisse faire malade comme ça*——*Papa Papa
aide mué*——*Aw j'ai mal au coeur*——*J'envie d'aller à toilette
'pi ça m'intéresse pas*——*Aw 'shu malade*——Owaowaowao——"
(I go into a long "awaowaowoa" that I guess lasted a whole
minute)——I toss over and find new reasons to groan——I think

I'm alone and I'm letting it all go a whole lot like I'd heard my father do when he was dying of cancer in the night in the bed next to mine——When I do manage to stagger up and go lean on the door I realize with double upon double horror that Ron Blake has been sitting there all this time listening to everything over a book——(I wonder now what he told people about this later, it must have sounded horrible)——(Idiotic too, cretinous even, maybe only French Canadian who knows?)——"Ron I'm sorry you had to hear all that, I'm sick"——"I know, man, it's okay, lie down and try to sleep"——"I cant sleep!" I yell in a rage——I feel like yelling "Fuck yourself you little idiot what do you know what Im going through!" but then I realize how oldman disgusting and hopeless all that is, and here he is enjoying his big weekend with the big writer he was supposed to tell all his friends what a great swinging ball it was and what I did and said——But methinks and mayhap he took away a lesson in temperance, or a lesson in beatness really——Because the only time I've ever been sicker and madder was a week later when Dave and I came back with the two girls leading to the final horrible night.

22

Bᴜᴛ ʟᴏᴏᴋ ᴀᴛ ᴛʜɪs: in the afternoon restless youngster Ron wants to go hitch hiking to Monterey of all things to go see McLear and I say "Okay go ahead"——"Aint you coming with me?" he asks surprised to see the champion on-the-roader wont even hitch hike any more, "No I'll stay here and get better——I gotta be alone," which is true, because as soon as he's gone and has yelled one final hoot from the canyon road directly above and gone on, and I've sat in the sun alone on the porch, fed my birds finally again, washed my socks and shirt and pants and hung them up to dry on bushes, slurped up tons of water kneeling at the creek race, stared silently at the trees, soon as the sun goes down I swear on my arm I'm as well as I ever was: just like that suddenly.

"Can it be that Ron and all these other guys, Dave and McLear or somebody, the other guys earlier are all a big bunch of witches out to make me go mad?" I seriously consider this—— Remembering that childhood revery I always had, which I used to ponder seriously as I walked home from St. Joseph's Parochial School or sat in the parlor of my home, that everybody in the world is making fun of money me and I dont know it because everytime I turn around to see who's behind me they snap back into place with regular expressions, but soon's I look away again they dart up to my nape of neck and all whisper there giggling and plotting evil, silently, you cant hear them, and when I turn quickly to catch them they've already snapped back perfectly in place and are saying "Now the proper way to cook eggs is" or they're singing Chet Baker songs looking the other way or they're saying "Did I ever tell you about Jim that time?"——But my childhood revery also included the fact that everybody in the world was making this fun of me because they were all members of an eternal secret society or Heaven society that knew the secret of the world and were seriously fooling me so I'd wake up and see the light (i.e., become enlightened, in fact)——So that I, "Ti Jean," was the LAST Ti Jean left in the world, the last poor holy fool, those people at my neck were the devils of the earth among whom God had cast me,

an angel baby, as tho I was the last Jesus in fact! and all these
people were waiting for me to realize it and wake up and catch
them peeking and we'd all laugh in Heaven suddenly——But
animals werent doing that behind my back, my cats were always
adornments licking their paws sadly, and Jesus, he was a sad
witness to this, somewhat like the animals——He wasnt peeking
down my neck——There lies the root of my belief in Jesus——So
that actually the only reality in the world was Jesus and the
lambs (the animals) and my brother Gerard who had instructed
me——Meanwhile some of the peekers were kindly and sad,
like my father, but had to go along with everybody else in the
same boat——But my waking up would take place and then
everything would vanish except Heaven, which is God——And
that was why later in life after these rather strange you must
admit childhood reveries, after I had that fainting vision of the
Golden Eternity and others before and after it including Samadhis during Buddhist meditations in the woods, I conceived of
myself as a special solitary angel sent down as a messenger from
Heaven to tell everybody or show everybody by example that
their peeking society was actually the Satanic Society and they
were all on the wrong track.

    With all this in my background, now at the point of adult-
hood disaster of the soul, through excessive drinking, all this
was easily converted into a fantasy that everybody in the world
was witching me to madness: and I must have believed it subconsciously because as I say as soon as Ron Blake left I was well
again and in fact content.

    In fact very contented——I rose that following morning with
more joy and health and purpose than ever, and there was me
old Big Sur Valley all mine again, here came good old Alf and
I gave him food and patted his big rough neck with its various
cocotte's manes, there was the mountain of Mien Mo in the distance just a dismal old hill with funny bushes around the sides
and a peaceful farm on top, and nothing to do all day but amuse
myself undisturbed by witches and booze——And I'm singing
ditties again "My soul aint snow, wouldnt you know, the color
of my soul, is interpole" and such silly stuff——And I yell "If
Arthur Ma is a witch he sure is a funny witch! har har!"——And
there's the bluejay idiot with one foot on the bar of soap on
the porch rail, pecking at the soap and eating it, leaving the

cereal unattended, and when I laugh and yell at him he looks up cute with an expression that seems to say "What's the matter? wotti do wong?"——"Wo wo, got the wong place," said another bluejay landing nearby and suddenly leaving again—— And everything of my life seems beautiful again, I even start remembering the nutty things of the binge and go back even farther and remember nutty things all through my life, it's just amazing how inside our own souls we can lift out so much strength I think it would be enough strength to move mountains at that, to lift our boots up again and go clomping along happy out of nothing but the good source power in our own bones——And when I visit the sea it doesnt scare me anymore, I just sing out "Seventy thousand schemers in the sea" and go back to my cabin and just quietly pour my coffee in the cup, afternoon, how pleasant!

I make a wood run, axe and yank logs outa everywhichawhere and leave em by the side of the road to leisurely carry home——I investigate a cabin down the creek that has 15 wood matches in it for my emergency——Take a shot of sherry, hate it——Find an old San Francis Chronicle with my name in it all over——Hack a giant redwood log in half in the middle of the creek——That kind of day, perfect, ending up sewing my holy sweater singing "There's no place like home" remembering my mother——I even plunge into all the books and magazines around, I read up on 'Pataphysics and yell contemptuously in the lamplight "'T'sa'n intellectual excuse for facetious joking," throwing the magazine away, adding "Peculiarly attractive to certain shallow types"——Then I turn my rumbling attention to a couple of unknown *Fin du Siècle* poets called Theo Marzials and Henry Harland——I take a nap after supper and dream of the U.S. Navy, a ship anchored near a war scene, at an island, but everything is drowsy as two sailors go up the trail with fishingpoles and a dog between them to go make love quietly in the hills: the captain and everybody know they're queer and rather than being infuriated however they're all drowsily enchanted by such gentle love: you see a sailor peeking after them with binoculars from the poop: there's supposed to be a war but nothing happens, just laundry . . .

I wake up from this silly but strangely pretty dream feeling exhilirated——Besides now the stars come out every night and I go out on that porch and sit in the old canvas chair and turn my face up to all that mooching going on up there, starmooched firmament, all those stars crying with happy sadness, all that ream and cream of mocky ways with alleyways of lightyears old as Dame Mae Whitty and the hills——I go walking towards Mien Mo mountain in the moon illuminated August night, see gorgeous misty mountains rising the horizon and like saying to me "You dont have to torture your consciousness with endless thinking" so I sit in the sand and look inward and see those old roses of the unborn again——Amazing, and in just a few hours this change——And I have enough physical energy to walk back to the sea suddenly realizing what a beautiful oriental silk scroll painting this whole canyon would make, those scrolls you open slowly at one end and keep unrolling and unrolling as the valley unfolds towards sudden cliffs, sudden Bodhisattvas sitting alone in lamplit huts, sudden creeks, rocks, trees, then sudden white sand, sudden sea, out to sea and you've reached the end of the scroll——And with all those misty rose dark-nesses of varying tint and tuckaway shades to express the actual ephemerality of night——One long roll unfurling from the range fence among the misty hills, moon meadows, even the hay rick near the creek, down to the trail, the narrowing creek, then the mystery of the AW SEA——So I investigate the scroll of the valley but I'm singing "Man is a busy little animal, a nice little animal, his thoughts about everything, dont amount to shit."

In fact back at the cabin to make my bedtime hot Ovaltine I even sing "Sweet Sixteen" like an angel (by God bettern Ron Blake) and all the old memories of Ma and Pa, the upright piano in old Massachusetts, the old summernight sings——That's how I go to sleep, under the stars on the porch, and at dawn I turn over with a blissful smile on my face because the owls are callin and answering from two different huge dead trunks across the valley, hoo hoo hoo.

So maybe it's true what Milarepa says: "Though you young-sters of the new generation dwell in towns infested with deceitful fate, the link of truth still remains"——(and said this in 890!)——–"When you remain in solitude, do not think of the amuse-ments in the town . . . You should turn your mind inwardly, and then you'll find your way . . . The wealth I found is the inexhaustible Holy Property . . . The companion I found is the

bliss of perpetual Voidness . . . Here in the place of Yolmo Tag
Pug Senge Dzon, the tigress howling with a pathetic trembling
voice reminds me that her piteous cubs are playing lively . . .
Like a madman I have no pretension and no hope . . . I am telling you the honest truth . . . These are the crazy words of mine
. . . O h you innumerable motherlike beings, by the force of
imaginary destiny you see a myriad visions and experience endless emotions . . . I smile . . . To a Yogi, everything is fine and
splendid! . . . . . In the goodly quiet of this Self-Benefitting sky
Enclosure, the timely sounds I hear are all my fellows' sounds . . .
At such a pleasant place, in solitude, I, Milarepa, happily remain,
meditating upon the void-illuminating mind——The more Ups
and Downs the more Joy I feel——The greater the fear, the
greater the happiness I feel . . ."

23

B<small>UT IN THE MORNING</small> (and I'm no Milarepa who could also
sit naked in the snow and was seen flying on one occasion)
here comes Ron Blake back with Pat McLear and Pat's wife the
beautiful one, and by God their little sweet 5 year old girl who
is such a pleasant sight to see as she goes jongling and jiggling
through the fields to look for flowers, everything to her is perfectly new beautiful primordial Garden of Eden morning here
in this tortured human canyon——And a rather beautiful morning develops——There's fog so we close the blinds and light the
fire and the lamp, me and Pat, and sit there drinking from the
jug he brought talking about literature and poetry while his
wife listens and occasionally gets up to heat more coffee and
tea or goes out to play with Ron and the little girl——Pat and
I are in a serious talkative mood and I feel that lonely shiver in
my chest which always warns me: you actually love people and
you're glad Pat is here.

Pat is one if not THE most handsome man I've ever seen——
Strange that he's announced in a preface to his poems that his
heroes, his Triumvirate, are Jean Harlow, Rimbaud and Billy
the Kid because he himself is handsome enough to play Billy
the Kid in the movies, that same darkhaired handsome slightly
sliteyed look you expect from the myth appearance of Billy the
Kid (I suppose not the actual real life William Bonnie who's said
to've been a pimply cretin monster).

So we launch on a big discussion of everything in the comfortable gloom of the cabin by the warm red glow of the girly
fire, I'm wearing dark glasses anyway for fun, Pat says "Well
Jack I didnt have a chance to talk to you yesterday or even last
year or even ten years ago when I first met you, I remember
I was terrified of you and Pomeray when you ran up my steps
one night with sticks of tea, you looked like a couple of car
thieves or bank robbers——And you know a lot of this sneery
stuff they've written against us, against San Francisco or beat
poetry and writers is because a lot of us dont LOOK like writers
or intellecuals or anything, you and Pomeray I must say look
awful in a way, I'm sure I dont fill the bill either"——"Man

you oughta go to Hollywood and play Billy the Kid"——"Man
I'd rather go to Hollywood and play Rimbaud"——"Well you
cant play Jean Harlow"——"I'd really like to just get my 'Dark
Brown' published in Paris, do you know that when you think
it's possible a word from you to Gallimard or Girodias would
help"——"I dunno"——"Do you know that when I read your
poems Mexico City Blues I immediately turned around and
started writing a brand new way, you enlightened me with that
book"——"But it's nothing like what you do, in fact it's miles
away, I am a language spinner and you're idea man" and so
on we talk till about noon and Ron's been in and out, 's'made
jaunts to the beach with the little ladies and Pat and I dont
realize the sun has come out but still sit there deep in the cabin
by now talking about Villon and Cervantes.

　Suddenly, boom, the door of the cabin is flung open with
a loud crash and a burst of sunlight illuminates the room and
I see an Angel standing arm outstretched in the door!——It's
Cody! all dressed in his Sunday best in a suit! beside him are
ranged several graduating golden angels from Evelyn golden
beautiful wife down to the most dazzling angel of them all
little Timmy with the sun striking off his hair in beams!——It's
such an incredible sight and surprise that both Pat and I rise
from our chairs involuntarily, like we've been lifted up in awe,
or scared, tho I dont feel scared so much as ecstatically amazed
as tho I've seen a vision——And the way Cody stands there not
saying a word with his arm outstretched for some reason, struck
a pose of some sort to surprise us or warn us, he's so much like
St. Michael at the moment it's unbelievable especially as I also
suddenly realize what he's just actually done, he's had wife and
kiddies sneak up ever so quiet up the porch steps (which are
noisy and creaky), across the wood planks, easy and tiptoeing,
stood there awhile while he prepared to fling the door open, all
lined up and stood straight, then pow, he's opened the door and
thrown the golden universe into the dazzled mystic eyes of big
hip Pat McLear and big amazed grateful me——It reminds me of
the time I once saw a whole tiptoeing gang of couples sneaking
into our back kitchen door on West Street in Lowell the leader
telling me to shush as I stand there 9 years old amazed, then
all bursting in on my father innocently listening to the Primo
Carnera–Ernie Schaaft fight on the old 1930's radio——For a big

roaring toot——But Cody's oldfashioned family tiptoe sneak carries that strange apocalyptic burst of gold he somehow always manages to produce, like I said elsewhere the time in Mexico he drove an old car over a rutted road very slowly as we were all high on tea and I saw golden Heaven, or the other times he's always seemed so golden like as I say in a davenport of some sort in Heaven in the golden top of Heaven.

Not that he means to produce this effect: he's just standing there with innate dramatic mystery holding forth his arm as if to say Behold, the sun! and Behold, the angels! sorta pointing at all the golden heads of his family and Pat and I stand aghast.

"Happy birthday Jack!" yells Cody or some such ordinary crazy inane greeting "I've come to you with good news! I've brought Evelyn and Emily and Gaby and Timmy because we're all so grateful and glad because everything has worked out absolutely dead perfect, or living perfect, boy, with that little old hunnerd dollars you gave me let me tell you the fantastic story of what happened" (to him it was utterly fantastic), "I went out and traded in my Nash that as you know wont even start but I have to have m'old buddies push it down the road for me, this guy had a perfect gem of a purple or what color is it Maw? magenty, slamelty, a *jeepster* stationwagon Jack but a perfect beauty mind you listen with a beautiful radio, a brand new set of backup lights, thisa and thata down to the perfect new tires and that wonderful shiney paint job, that color'll knock you out, that's what it is, Grape!" (as Evelyn murmurs the color) "Grape color for all the old grape wine jacks, so we've come here to not only thank you and see you again but to celebrate this, and on top of all that, occasion, goo me I'm all so gushy and girly, hee hee hee, yes that's right come on in children and then go out and get that gear in the car and get ready to sleep outdoors tonight and get that good open fresh air, Jack on top of all that and my heart is jess OVERflowin I got a NEW JOB!! along with that splissly little old beautiful new jeep! a new job right downtown in Los Gatos in fact I dont even have to drive to work any more, I can walk it, just half a mile, now Ma you come in here, meet old Pat McLear here, start up some eggs or some of that steak we brought, open up that vieen roossee wine we brought for drunk old Jack that good old boy while I personally private take him to walk with me back down the road where the jeep is parked, unlock that gate, you got the corral key Jack, okay, and we'll talk and walk just like old times and drive back real slow in my new slowboat to China."

So it's a whole new day, a whole new situation the way it is with Cody, in fact a whole new universe as suddenly we're alone again really for the first time in ages walking rapidly down the road to go get the car and he looks at me with that hand-rubbing wicked look like he's about to spring a surprise on me that's the top surprise of them all, "You guessed it old buddy I have here the LAST, the absolutely LAST yet most perfect of all blackhaired seeded packed tight superbomber joints in the world which you and I are now going to light up, 's'why I didnt want you to bring any of that wine right away, why boy we got time to drink wine and wine and dance" and here he is lighting up, says "Now dont walk too fast, it's time to stroll along like we used to do remember sometimes on our daysoff on the railroad, or walkin across that Third and Townsend tar like you said and the time we watched the sun go down so perfect holy purple over that Mission cross——Yessir, slow and easy, lookin at this gone valley" so we start to puff the pot but as usual it creates doubtful paranoias in both our minds and we actually sort of fall silent on the way to the car which is a beautiful grape color at that, a brand new shiney Jeepster with all the equipments, and the whole golden reunion deteriorates into Cody's matter-of-fact lecture on why the car is going to be such a honey (the technical details) and he even yells at me to hurry up with that corral gate, "Cant wait here all day, hor hor hor."

But that's not the point, about pot paranoia, yet maybe it is at that——I've long given it up because it bugs me anyway——But so we drive back slowly to the shack and Evelyn and Pat's wife have met and are having woman talk and McLear and I and Cody talk around the table planning excursions with the kids to the beach.

And there's Evelyn and I havent had a chance to talk to her for years either, Oh the old days when we'd stay up late by the fireplace as I say discussing Cody's soul, Cody this and Cody that, you could hear the name Cody ringing under the roofs of America from coast to coast almost to hear his women talking about him, always pronouncing "Cody" with a kind of anguish yet there was girlish squealing pleasure in it, "Cody has to learn to control the enormous forces in him" and Cody "will always modify his little white lies so much that they turn into black ones," and according to Irwin Garden Cody's women were always having transcontinental telephone talks about his dong (which is possible.)

Because he was always tremendously generated towards complete relationship with his women to the point where they ended up in one convoluted octopus mess of souls and tears and fellatio and hotel room schemes and rushing in and out of cars and doors and great crises in the middle of the night, wow that madman you can at least write on his grave someday "He Lived, He Sweated"——No halfway house is Cody's house——Tho now as I say sorta sweetly chastised and a little bored at last with the world after the crummy injustice of his arrest and sentence he's sorta quieted down and where he'd launch into a tremendous explanation of every one of his thoughts for the benefit of everybody in the room as he's putting on his socks and arranging his papers to leave, now he just flips it aside and may make a stale shrug——A Jesuit at work——Tho I remember one crazy moment in the shack that was typically Cody-like: complicated and simultaneous with a million nuances as though the whole of creation suddenly exploded and imploded together in one moment: at the moment that Pat's pretty little angel daughter is coming in to hand me an extremely tiny flower ("It's for you," she says direct to me) (for some reason the poor little thing thinks I need a flower, or else her mother instructed her for charming reasons, like adornment) Cody is furiously explaining to his little son Tim "Never let the right hand know what your left hand is doing" and at that moment I'm trying to close my palm around the incredibly small flower and it's so small I cant even do that, cant feel it, cant hardly see it, in fact such a small flower only that little girl could have found it, but I look up to Cody as he says that to Tim, and also to impress Evelyn who's watching me, I announced "Never let the left hand know what the right hand is doing but this right hand cant even hold this flower" and Cody only looks up "Yass yass."

So what started as a big holy reunion and surprise party in Heaven deteriorates to a lot of showoff talk, actually, at least on my part, but when I get to drink the wine I feel lighter and we all go down to the beach——I walk in front with Evelyn but when we get to the narrow path I walk in front like an Indian to show her what a big Indian I've been all summer——I'm bursting to tell her everything——"See that grove there, once in a while you'll be surprised out of your shoes to see the mule quietly standing there with locks of hair like Ruth's over his forehead, a big Biblical mule meditating, or over there, but up here, and look at that bridge, now what do you think of that?"——All the kids are fascinated by the upsidedown car wreck——At one point I'm sitting in the sand as Cody walks up my way, I say to him him imitating Wallace Beery and scratching my armpits "Cuss a man for dyin in Death Valley" (the last lines of that great movie *Twenty Mule Team*) and Cody says "That's right, if anybody can imitate old Wallace Beery that's the only way to do it, you had just the right timber there in the tone of your voice there, *Cuss a man for dyin in Death Valley* hee hee yes" but he rushes off to talk to McLear's wife.

Strange sad desultory the way families and people sorta scatter around a beach and look vaguely at the sea, all disorganized and picnic sad——At one point I'm telling Evelyn that a tidal wave from Hawaii could very easily come someday and we'd see it miles away a huge wall of awful water and "Boy it would take some doing to run back and climb up these cliffs, huh?" but Cody hears this and says, "What?" and I say "It would wash over us and take us all to Salinas I bet" and Cody says "What? that brand new jeep? I'm goin back and move it!" (an example of his strange humor).

"How'd'st rain rule here?" says I to Evelyn to show her what a big poet I am——She really loves me, used to love me in the old days like a husband, for awhile there she had two husbands Cody and me, we were a perfect family till Cody finally got jealous or maybe I got jealous, it was wild for awhile I'd be coming home from work on the railroad all dirty with my lamp and just as I came in for my Joy bubblebath old Cody was rushing off on a call so Evelyn had her new husband in the second shift then when Cody come home at dawn all dirty for his Joy bubblebath, ring, the phone's run and the crew clerk's asked me out and I'm rushing off to work, both of us using the same old clunker car in shifts——And Evelyn always maintaining that she and I were really made for each other but her Karma was to serve Cody in this particular lifetime, which I really believe and

I believe she loves him, too, but she'd say "I'll get you, Jack, in another lifetime . . . And you'll be very happy"——"What?" I'd yell to joke, "me running up the eternal halls of Karma tryina get away from you hey?"——"It'll take you eternities to get rid of me," she adds sadly, which makes me jealous, I want her to say I'll never get rid of her——I wanta be chased for eternity till I catch her.

"Ah Jack" she says putting her arm around me on the beach, "it's nice to see you again, Oh I wish we could be quiet again and just have our suppers of homemade pizza all together and watch T.V. together, you have so many friends and responsibilities now it's sad, and you get sick drinking and everything, why dont you just come stay with us awhile and rest"——"I will"——But Ron Blake is redhot for Evelyn and keeps coming over to dance with seaweeds and impress her, he's even asked me to ask Cody to let him spend some time alone with Evelyn, Cody's said "Go ahead man."

Having run out of liquor in fact Ron does get his opportunity to be alone with Evelyn as Cody and me and the kids in one car, and McLear and family in the other start for Monterey to stock up for the night and also more cigarettes——Evelyn and Ron light a bonfire on the beach to wait for us——As we're driving along little Timmy says to Paw "We shoulda brought Mommy with us, her pants got wet in the beach"——"By now they oughta be steamin," says Cody matter-of-factly in another one of his fantastic puns as he lockwallops that awful narrow dirt canyon road like a getaway car in the mountains in a movie, we leave poor McLear miles back——When Cody comes to a narrow tight curve with all our death staring us in the face down that hole he just swerves the curve saying "The way to drive in the mountains is, boy, no fiddlin around, these roads dont move, you're the one that moves"——And we come out on the highway and go right battin up to Monterey in the Big Sur dusk where down there on the faint gloamy frothing rocks you can hear the seals cry.

24

M CLEAR EXHIBITS ANOTHER STRANGE FACET OF HIS
HANDSOME BUT FAINTLY "DECADENT" Rimbaud-type
personality at his summer camp by coming out in the livingroom with a goddamn HAWK on his shoulder——It's his pet
hawk, of all things, the hawk is black as night and sits there on
his shoulder pecking nastily at a clunk of hamburg he holds
up to it——In fact the sight of that is so rarely poetic, McLear
whose poetry is really like a black hawk, he's always writing
about darkness, dark brown, dark bedrooms, moving curtains,
chemical fire dark pillows, love in chemical fiery red darkness,
and writes all that in beautiful long lines that go across the page
irregularly and aptly somehow——Handsome Hawk McLear,
in fact I suddenly yell out "Now I know your real name! it's
M'Lear! M' Lear the Scotch Highland moorhaunter with his
hawk about to go mad and tear his white hair in a tempest"——
Or some such silly thing, feeling good again now we've got new
wine——Time to go back to the cabin and fly down that dark
highway the way only Cody can fly (even bettern Dave Wain
but you feel safer with Dave Wain tho the reason Cody gives
you a sense of dooming boom as he pushes the night out the
wheels is not because he'll lose perfect control of the car but
you feel the car will take off suddenly up to Heaven or at least
just up into what the Russians call the Dark Cosmos, there's a
booming rushing sound out the window when Cody bats her
down the white line at night, with Dave Wain it's all conversation and smooth sailing, with Cody it's a crisis about to get
worse)——And now he's saying to me "Not only today but the
other day with the boys, that beautiful McLear woman there,
wow, with her tight blue jeans, man I cried under a tree to see
that poppin around so innocent like, whoo, so I tell you what
we're gonna do old buddy: tomorrow we go back to Los Gatos
the whole family and we've dropped Evelyn and the kids home
after the hiss-the-villain play we're all gonna see at seven——"——
"The what?"——"It's a play," he says suddenly imitating the
tired whiney voice of an old P.T.A. Committee woman, "you
go there and you sit down and out comes this old 1910 play

about villains foreclosing the mortgage, mustaches, you know, calico tears, you can sit there you see and hiss the villain all you want even for all I know yell obscenities or something I dunno——But it's Evelyn's world, you know, she's designing the sets and that's the work she's done while I was in the can so I cant begrudge her that, in fact I aint got a word in edgewise, when you're the father of a family you go along with the little woman acourse, and the kids enjoy it, after that plan and after you've hissed the villain we'll drop them home and then old buddy" zooming up the car even of all thinks, the hawk is black as night and sits there faster in lieu of rubbing his hands with zeal, so to say Zoom, "you and me gonna go flyin down that Bay Shore highway and as usual you're gonna ask your usual dumb almost Okie wino questions, *Hey Cody*" (whining like a old drunk) "*I b'lieve we're comin into Burlingame aint it?* and you're always wrong, hee hee, old crazy dumb fuckin old Jack, then we go rubbin shoulders into that City and go poppin right up to my sweet little old baby Willamine that I want you to meet inasmuch and also I want you go dig because she's gonna dig YOU my dear old sonumbitch Jack, and I'm gonna leave you two little lovebirds together for days on end alone, you can live there and just enjoy that gone little woman because also" (his tone now businesslike) "I want her to dig as much as possible everything you got to tell her about what YOU know, hear me? she's my soulmate and confidante and mistress and I want her to be happy and learn"——"What's she look like?" I ask grossly——And I see the grimace on his face, he really knows me, "Eh well she looks alright, she has a gone little body that's all I can say and in bed she is by far the first and only and last possible greatest everything you dig"——This being just another of a long line of occasions when Cody gets me to be a sub-beau for his beauties so that everything can tie in together, he really loves me like a brother and more than that, he gets annoyed at me sometimes especially when I fumble and blumble like with a bottle or the time I almost stripped the gears of the car because I forgot I was driving, in which case actually I remind him of his old wino father but the fantastic thing is that HE reminds ME of MY father so that we have this strange eternal father-image relationship that goes on and on sometimes with tears, it's easy for me to think of Cody and almost cry, sometimes I can see

the same tearful expression in his eyes when he sometimes looks
at me——He reminds me of my father because he too blusters
and hurries and fills all his pockets with Racing Forms and papers and pencils and we're all ready to go on some mission in
the night he takes with ultimate seriousness as tho we were
going on the last trip of them all but it always ends up being
a hilarious meaningless Marx Brothers adventure which gives
me even more reason to love him (and my father too)——That
way——And finally in the book I wrote about us ("On The
Road") I forgot to mention two important things, that we were
both devout little Catholics in our childhood, which gives us
something in common tho we never talk about it, it's just there
in our natures, and secondly and most important that strange
business when we shared another girl (Marylou, or that is, let's
call her Joanna) and Cody at the time announced "That's what
we'll be old buddy, you and me, double husbands, later on we'll
have whole Harreeeem and reams of Hareems boy, and we'll
call ourselves or that is" (flutter) "ourself Duluomeray, see
Duluoz and Pomeray, Duluomeray, see, hee hee hee" tho he
was younger then and really silly but that gives an indication of
the way he felt about me: some kind of new thing in the world
actually where men can really be angelic friends and not be homosexual and not fight over girls——But alas the only thing we'd
ever fought about was money, or the ridiculous time we fought
about a little line of marijuana dust running down the middle of
a page where we were separating our shares with a knife, when
I objected I wanted some of the dust he yelled "Our original
agreement had nothing to do with the dust!" and he slumps it
all into his pocket and stalks off redfaced so I jump up and pack
and announce I'm leaving and Evelyn drives me to the City but
the car wont start (this is years ago) so Cody redfaced and crazy
and ashamed now has to push us with the clunker, there we
go down San Jose boulevard with Cody behind us pushing us
and with Cody behind us pushing us and bumping us not just
to give us a start but to chastise me for being so greedy and I
shouldnt leave at all——In fact he'd back up and come up on our
rear and really wham us——That night ending me dead drunk
on Mal Damlette's floor on North Beach——And in any case the
whole question of us, the two most advanced men friends in the
world still fighting over money after all being, as Julien says in

New York, indication of the fact that "Money is the only thing Canucks ever fight about, and Okies too I guess" but Julien I suppose imagining and fantasizing himself as a noble Scotsman who fights about honor (tho I tell him "Ah you Scotchmen save your spit in your watchpocket").

Lacrimae rerum, the tears of things, all the years behind me and Cody, the way I always say "me and Cody" instead of "Cody and I" or some such, and Irwin watching us across the world night now with a bite of marvel on his lower lip saying "Ah, angels of the West, Companions in Heaven" and writing letters asking "What now, what's the latest, what visions, what arguments, what sweet agreements?" and such.

That night the kids end up sleeping in the jeep anyway because they're afraid of the big black woods and I sleep by the creek in my bag and in the morning we're all set to go back to Los Gatos and see the villain play——Frustrated Ron is casting sad eyes at Evelyn, apparently she's put him off because she says to me (and I dont blame her) "Really the way Cody presses people on me it's awful, at least I should have my own choice" (but she's laughing because it's funny and it is funny the way Cody does it anxious and harried wondering if that's what she really wants and wants no such thing)——"At least not with utter strangers," says I to be funny——She:-"Besides I'm so sick of all this sex business, that's all he talks about, his friends, here they are all open channels to do good as co creators with God and all they think about is behinds——that's why you're so refreshing" she adds——"But I aint so refreshing as all that? hey!"——But that's my relationship with Evelyn, we're real pals and we can kid about anything even the first night I met her in Denver in 1947 when we danced and Cody watched anxiously, a kind of romantic pair in fact and I shudder sometimes to think of all that stellar mystery of how she IS going to get me in a future lifetime, wow——And I seriously do believe that will be my salvation, too.

A long way to go.

25

THE SILLY STUPID HISS-THE-VILLAIN PLAY IS ALRIGHT IN ITSELF but just as we arrive at the scene of the chuck wagons and tents all done up real old western style there's a big fat sheriff type with two sixshooters standing at the admission gate, Cody says "That's to give it color see" but I'm drunk and as we all pile out of the car I go up to the fat sheriff and start telling him a Southern joke (in fact just the plot of an Erskine Caldwell short story) which he receives with a witless smiling expression or really like the expression of an executioner or a Southern constable listening to a Yankee talk——So naturally I'm surprised later when we go into the cute old west saloon and the kids start banging on the old piano and I join them with big loud Stravinsky chords, here comes two gun sheriff fatty coming in and saying in a menacing voice like T.V. western movies "You cant play that piano"——I'm surprised, turning to Evelyn, to learn that he's the blasted proprietor of the whole place and if he says I cant play the piano there's nothing I can do about it legally——But besides that he's got actual bullets in those six guns——He's going all out to play the part——But to be yanked from joyful pianothumping with kids to see that awful dead face of negative horror I just jump up and say "Alright, the hell with it I'm leaving anyway" so Cody follows me to the car where I take another swig of white port——"Let's get the hell out of here" I say——"Just what I was thinkin about," says Cody, "in fact I've already arranged with the director of the play to drive Evelyn and the kids home so we'll just go to the City now"—— "Great!"——"And I've told Evelyn we're cuttin out so let's go."

"I'm sorry Cody I screwed up your little family party"—— "No No" he protests "Man I have to come to these things you know and be a big hubby and father type and you know I'm on parole and I gotta put up appearances but it's a drag"——To show what a drag it is we go scootin down that road passing six cars easy as pie——"And I'm GLAD this happened because it gave us an excuse, hee hee titter you know to get outa there, I was thinking for an excuse when it happened, that old fart is crazy you know! he's a millionaire you know! I've talked to him, that little beady brain, and you be glad you missed hangin around till that performance, man, and that AUDIENCE, ow, ugh, I almost wish I was back in San Quentin but here we go, son!"

So of old we're alone in a car at night bashing down the line to a specific somewhere, nothing nowhere about it whatever, especially this time, in a way——That white line is feeding into our fender like an anxious impatient electronic quiver shuddering in the night and how beautifully sometimes it curves one side or the other as he smoothly swerves for passing or for something else, avoiding a bump or something——And on the big highway Bay Shore how beautifully he just swings in and out of lanes almost effortlessly and completely unnoticeable passing to the right and to the left without a flaw all kinds of cars with anxious eyes turning to us, altho he's the only one on the road who knows how to drive completely well——It's blue dusk all up and down the California world——Frisco glitters up ahead——our radio plays rhythm and blues as we pass the joint back and forth in jutjawed silence both looking ahead with big private thoughts now so vast we cant communicate them any more and if we tried it would take a million years and a billion books——Too late, too late, the history of everything we've seen together and separately has become a library in itself—— The shelves pile higher——They're full of misty documents or documents of the Mist——The mind has convoluted in every tuckaway everywhichaway tuckered hole till there's no more the expressing of our latest thoughts let alone old——Mighty genius of the mind Cody whom I announce as the greatest writer the world will ever know if he ever gets down to writing again like he did earlier——It's so enormous we both sit here sighing in fact——"No the only writing I done," he says, "a few letters to Willamine, in fact quite a few, she's got em all wrapped in ribbons there, I figgered if I tried to write a book or sumptin or prose or sumptin they'd just take it away from me when I left so I wrote her 'bout three letters a week for two years——and the trouble of course and as I say and you've heard a million times is the mind flows the mind rises and nobody can by any possible c——oh hell, I dont wanta talk about it"——Besides I can see from glancing at him that becoming a writer holds no interest for him because life is so holy for him there's no need to do anything but live it, writing's just an afterthought or a scratch anyway at the surface——But if he could! if he would! there I am riding in California miles away from home where my poor cat's buried and my mother grieves and that's what I'm thinking.

It always makes me proud to love the world somehow—— Hate's so easy compared——But here I go flattering myself helling headbent to the silliest hate I ever had.

26

ALTHO CODY'S SAID THESE THINGS I'm very well aware that the real arrangement of the evening is that we're just going to see Billie together so she can get her kicks meeting me (after hearing about me from him and after reading my books etc.) and in fact Cody has already conferred with Evelyn about how I'm going to be staying at their house in Las Gatos for a month, as of old sleeping in my bag in the backyard not because they dont want me to sleep in the house but it's my idea, but it's beautiful anyway to sleep under the stars and anyway I therefore keep out of the way of the family when they get up to go to work and school——At noon they see me shambling in from the big back field yard yawning for coffee——And I'm in line for that, i.e., that's what I want to do and that's my plan—— But when we run upstairs to Willamine's apartment and come bursting in to this neat little well arranged pad with goldfish bowl, books, strange doodads, neat kitchen, the whole clean as a pin, and there's Billie herself a blonde with arched eyebrows exactly like the male Julien blond with arched eyebrows and I yell out "It's JUlien by God it's Julien!" (and by now I'm drunk anyway because we've as of old picked up an old hitch hiker on Bay Shore who says his name is Joe Ihnat and we bought him a bottle and I bought me one too, never will forget old Joe Ihnat in fact somehow because he said he was a Russian and his was an ancient Russian name and when I wrote out our names he said *my* name was an ancient Russian name also) (tho it's Breton) (and also told us he'd just been beaten up by a young Negro for no reason in a public toilet and Cody gasps and says to me "I've met those Negroes that beat up old men, they're called the Strongarms in San Quentin, they're all put away among themselves away from the other prisoners, they're all Negroes and it seems all they wanta do is beat up old defenseless men, he's tellin the absolute truth"——"But why do they do that?"—— "Oh man I dont know they just wanta hit up on some old man that cant hit back and just beat him and beat him till he's dead" and Oh the horror of Cody's knowledge of the world when all is said and done)——So now we're sitting with Billie

in her pad, outside the window you see the glittering lights of
the city again, ah Urbi y Roma, the world again, and she's got
these mad blue eyes, arched eyebrows, intelligent face, just like
Julien, I keep saying "Julien goddamit!" and I see even in my
drunkenness a little worried flutter in Cody's eyes——The fact
of the matter being, Billie and I go for each other like two tons
of bricks right there in front of Cody so that when he rises and
announces he's going back to Los Gatos to get some sleep to
go to work it's already well agreed I'm staying right where I am
and not only for tonight but for weeks months years.

Poor Cody——Yet you see I've already explained why actually subconsciously this is what he really wants to happen but
he wont admit it ever and always invents reasons around this to
get mad at me and call me a bastard——But aside from Cody I
find Billie to be a very companionable strange kid in this lonesome night and I actually NEED to stay with her awhile——In
fact both Billie and I explain to Cody why——But there's nothing evil, man-against-man or sinister about any of it, it's just a
strange innocence, a spontaneous burst of love in fact and Cody
understands that bettern anybody else anyway so he leaves at
midnight saying he'll be back tomorrow night and all of a sudden I'm alone with a charming woman and we're talking a blue
streak sitting crosslegged facing each other on the floor in a
litter of books and bottles.

It gives me a pang of pain and remorse really now to recall
that on this first night her apartment was so neat and clean and
charming——The chair by the goldfish bowl which I quickly ap-
propriated as my old man chair, where I sat constantly sipping
port for a whole week, the kitchen with its intelligent arrangements of spices and eggs in the icebox, and for that matter too
the poor little son of Billie sleeping in a well arranged back
room (her son from her deceased husband who was also a railroad man)——Elliott the child's name and I didnt get to see him
till later that night——And with the huge packet of Cody's San
Quentin letters in her hand she launches forth on her theories
about Cody and eternity but all I can keep saying as I swig from
my bottle is "Julien, you're talking too much! Julien, Julien, my
God who'd ever dream I'd run into a woman who looks like
Julien . . . you look like Julien but you're not Julien and on top
of that you're a woman, how goddam strange"——In fact she

had to pack me off to bed drunk——But not before our first
lovely undertaking of love and everything Cody said about her
being absolutely true——But the main thing being that tho she
looked like Julien etc. and had Cody's big sad abstract letters
about Karma in a ribbon and actually went out in the morning and earned a hundred a week in fashion modeling she had
the most musical beautiful and sad voice I've ever heard in my
life——The things she's saying are really rather inane because
after all her education is based on really Californian hysterias
like the earlier mistress of Cody Rosemarie who also was thin
and pale haired and crazy and kept talking abstract——(Like
she's saying "I thought I could do something to ease the con-
tradiction between immanent and universal ethics which I
thought was my problem and was what I hoped to gain thru
therapy, like, any evolution presupposes an involution and all
that kind of thinking" as I sigh, but she does say something
interesting once in a while like "While Cody was in prison my
main occupation was praying for him, I had an all day going,
there was also a bit we did together every evening from 9:00
to 9:09 but he's out now and something else is happening
I'm not sure what . . . but I'm sure we aid the storm when we
transcend time in one respect and cant even keep up with it in
others . . .")——But also all kinds of to-me-unimportant and
uninteresting crap about channels about people being either
closed or open channels and Cody is a big open channel pouring out all his holy gysm on Heaven, I really cant remember,
or the destinies, the sighs, the rooftops of all that, the stars are
shining down on their poor heads as they draw breath to explain
inanities really——Like the letters to her (I glance at them) are
all about how they've met and their souls have collided in this
dimension because of some unfulfilled Karma on another planet
and in another plane that is, and now they have to gird themselves to assume this big responsibility to meet some measure
of this and that, I dont even wanta go into it——Because also
the fact of the matter being, when Willamine talks to me I'm
utterly bored, I'm only interested in the sad music of her voice
and in the strange circumstance (I guess Karma-like too) that
she looks like poor Julien.

   Her voice is the main point——She talks with a broken
heart——Her voice lutes brokenly like a heart lost, musically

too, like in a lost grove, it's almost too much to bear sometimes like some fantastic futuristic Jerry Southern singer in a night club who steps up to the mike in the spotlight in Las Vegas but doesnt even have to sing, just talk, to make men sigh and women wonder I guess (if women ever wonder)——So that as she's trying to explain all that nonsense to me (all that philosophy of hers and Cody's and Cody's new buddy Perry, coming up the next day) I just sit and marvel and stare at her mouth wondering where all the beauty is coming from and why——And we end up making love sweetly too——A little blonde well experienced in all the facets of lovemaking and sweet with compassion and just too much so that b'dawn we're already going to get married and fly away to Mexico in a week——In fact I can see it now, a great big four way marriage with Cody and Evelyn.

For she is the great enemy of Evelyn——She's not satisfied just to be Cody's lover and soul heart she wants to go right over there and lay Evelyn down on the line and take Cody away with her forever and to do this she'll even have a deadend heaven deep love affair with old Jack (same pattern of old)——There's not much difference between her and Evelyn when you listen to their talk about Cody except in Evelyn's case I'm always fascinatedly interested——Billie actually bores me tho of course I cant tell her that——Evelyn is still the champ and I wonder about Cody.

O the ups and downs and juggling of women, blondes at that, all in the great magical City of the Gandharvas of San Francisco and here I am alone on a magic carpet with one of em, whee, at first of course it's a great ball, a great new eye-shattering explosion of experience——Not dreaming, I, what's to come——For with sad musical Billie in my arms and my name Billie too now, Billie and Billie arm in arm, oh beautiful, and Cody has given his consent in a way, we go roaming the Genghiz Khan clouds of soft love and hope and anybody who's never done this is crazy——Because a new love affair always gives hope, the irrational mortal loneliness is always crowned, that thing I saw (that horror of snake emptiness) when I took the deep iodine deathbreath on the Big Sur beach is now justified and hosannah'd and raised up like a sacred urn to Heaven in the mere fact of the taking off of clothes and clashing wits and bodies in the inexpressibly nervously sad delight of love——Dont let no old fogies tell you otherwise, and on top of that nobody in the world even ever dares to write the true story of love, it's awful, we're stuck with a 50% incomplete literature and drama——Lying mouth to mouth, kiss to kiss in the pillow dark, loin to loin in unbelievable surrendering sweetness so distant from all our mental fearful abstractions it makes you wonder why men have termed God antisexual somehow——The secret underground truth of mad desire hiding under fenders under buried junkyards throughout the world, never mentioned in newspapers, written about haltingly and like corn by authors and painted tongue in cheek by artists, agh, just listen to *Tristan und Isolde* by Wagner and think of him in a Bavarian field with his beloved naked beauty under the fall leaves.

How strange in all, and making everything that's happened in the past weeks, the backs and forths and pains of me in City and Sur, all piled up now rationally like a big construction whereon could be built a divingboard which would enable me clumsily to dive into Billie's soul and therefore why complain?

In the middle of the night she fetches the little 4 year old boy to show me the spiritual beauty of her son——He is one of the weirdest persons I've ever met——He has large liquid brown eyes very beautiful and he hates anybody who comes near his mother and keeps asking her questions constantly like "Why do you stay with him? why is he here, who is he?" or "Why is it dark outside?" or "Why does the sun shine yesterday?" or anything, he'll just ask questions about everything and she answers every one of them with extreme delight and patience till I say "Doesnt he bother you with all these questions? why dont you let him croon and goof like a little child, he's tugging at your knee asking EVERYTHING man why dont you just let him singsong?"——She answers "I answer him because I may be missing his next question, everything he asks me and says to me represents something important about the absolute I may be missing"——"What do you mean the absolute?"——"You yourself said everything is the absolute" but of course she's right and I realize that in my dirty old soul I'm already jealous of Elliott.

27

THE MAT OF NIGHT admits the groaning glory godlike love I guess but at the same time it's also boring in a way and we both laugh to discuss that——We stay awake that first night till dawn discussing everything in the books from Cody in every detail down to me in every detail to her in every detail to Evelyn to books and philosophies and religions and the absolute and I end up whispering her poems——Poor kid has to get up in the morning and go to work and I'm left there snoring drunk—— But she makes her neat breakfast and takes Elliott off to the daily babysitter lady and I wake up at one in the afternoon alone and take a swig of wine and get in the hot bath to read a book——The phone keeps ringing, everybody from Monsanto to Fagan to McLear to the Moon Man has somehow found out where I am and what the number is, tho none of them have previously even met Billie let alone seen her——I shudder to realize Cody will get mad for making his secret life so public.

But here comes Perry——Like me Perry has that strange brotherly relationship with Cody whereby he gets to be *confidant* and sometimes lover of all Cody's gals——And I can see why——He looks just like me only he's young and looks like I did when first Cody met me but the point is not that so much, he is a tempestuous lost tossed soul just out of Soledad State Prison for attempted robbery with a boyish face and black hair falling over it but powerful thick muscular arms that I realize he could break a man in half with——His name is strange too, Perry Yturbide, I immediately say: "I know what you are, Basque"—— "Basque? is that it? I never found out! let's call my mother longdistance in Utah and tell her that!"——And he rings up his mother way over there, on Billie's phone bill, and here I am bottle of port wine in one hand and butt in mouth talking to a Basque ex con's mother in Utah telling her in fact reassuring her "Yes I believe it's a Basque name"——She's saying "Hey, what you say? who are you?" and there's Perry smiling all glad——A very strange kid——It's been a long time in fact in my literary sort of life that I've met a real tough hombre like that out of jails and with those arms of steel and that fevered concern that scares governments and makes officials pale, that's why he's always put away in prison this type of man——Yes yet the type of man the country always needs when there's a little old war started by an aging governor——A real dangerous character, in fact, Perry, because tho I appreciate his poetic soul and everything I realize looking at him he's capable of exploding and killing somebody for an idea maybe or for love.

Some of his own friends ring Billie's doorbell, everybody seems to know I'm there, they come up, they are strange anarchistic Negroes and ex cons, it seems to be some sort of gang, I begin to wonder——Like a ring of fevered sages, the Negroes are intense and crazy and intellectual but they've all got those strong muscular arms again and all have jail records yet they all talk as tho the end of the world depended on their words—— Hard to explain (but will do).

Billie and her gang in fact, with all that fancy rigamarole about spiritual matters I wonder if it isnt just a big secret hustler outfit tho I also realize that I've noticed it before in San Francisco a kind of ephemeral hysteria that hides in the air over the rooftops among certain circles there leading always to suicide and maim——Me just an innocent lost hearted meditator and Goop among strange intense criminal agitators of the heart—— It reminds me in fact of a nightmare I had just before coming out to the Coast, in the dream I'm back in San Francisco but there's something funny going on: there's dead silence throughout the entire city: men like printers and office executives and housepainters are all standing silently in second floor windows looking down on the empty streets of San Francisco: once in a while some beatniks walk by below, also silent: they're being watched but not only by the authorities but by everybody: the beatniks seem to have the whole street system to themselves: but nobody's saying anything: and in this intense silence I take a ride on a self propelled platform right downtown and out to the farms where a woman running a chicken farm invites me to join her and live with her——The little platform rolling quietly as the people are watching from windows in groups of profile like the profiles in old Van Dyck paintings, intense, suspicious, momentous——This Billie business reminding me of that but because to me the only thing that matters is the conceptions in my own mind, there has to be no reality anyway to what I suppose is going on——But this also an indication of the coming madness in Big Sur.

28

STRANGE——and Perry Yturbide that first day while Billie's
at work and we've just called his mother now wants me to
come with him to visit a general of the U.S. Army——"Why?
and what's all these generals looking out of silent windows?" I
say——But nothing surprises Perry——"We'll go there because
I want you to dig the most beautiful girls we ever saw," in fact
we take a cab——But the "beautiful girls" turn out to be 8 and
9 and 10 years old, daughters of the general or maybe even
cousins or daughters of a nextdoor strange general, but the
mother is there, there are also boys playing in a backroom, we
have Elliott with us whom Perry has carried on his shoulders
all the way——I look at Perry and he says "I wanted you to see
the most beautiful little cans in town" and I realize he's danger-
ously insane——In fact he then says "See this perfect beauty?" a
pony tailed 10 year old daughter of the general (who aint home
yet) "I'm going to kidnap her right now" and he takes her by
the hand and they go out on the street for an hour while I sit
there over drinks talking to the mother——There's some vast
conspiracy to make me go mad anyway——The mother is polite
as ordinarily——The general comes home and he's a rugged big
baldheaded general and with him is his best friend a photographer called Shea, a thin well combed welldressed ordinary
downtown commercial photographer of the city——I dont understand anything——But suddenly little Elliott is crying in the
other room and I rush in there and see that the two boys have
whacked him or something because he did something wrong
so I chastise them and carry Elliott back into the livingroom on
my shoulders like Perry does, only Elliott wants to get down off
my shoulders at once, in fact he wont even sit on my lap, in fact
he hates my guts——I call Billie desperately at her agency and
she says she'll be over to pick us all up and adds "How's Perry
today?"——"He's kidnapping little girls he says are beautiful,
he wants to marry 10 year old girls with pony tails"——"That's
the way he is, be sure to dig him"——In her musical sad voice
over the phone.

I turn my poor tortured attention to the general who says he was an anti-Fascist fighter with the Maquis during World War II and also a guerilla in the South Pacific and knows one of the finest restaurants in San Francisco where we can all go feast, a Fillipino restaurant near Chinatown, I say okay, great——He gives me more booze——Seeing the amusing Irish face of Shea the photographer I yell "You can take my picture anytime you want" and he says sinister: "Not for propaganda reasons, anything but propaganda reasons"——"What the hell do you mean propaganda reasons, I aint got nothin to do with propaganda" (and here comes Perry back through the door with Poopoo holding his hand, they've gone to dig the street and have a coke) and I realize everybody is just living their lives quietly but it's only me that's insane.

In fact I yearn to have old Cody around to explain all this to me tho it soon becomes apparent to me not even Cody could explain, I'm beginning to go seriously crazy, just like Subterranean Irene went crazy tho I dont realize it yet——I'm beginning to read plots into every simple line——Besides the "general" scares me even further by turning out to be a strange affluent welldressed civilian who doesnt even help me to pay the tab for the Fillipino dinner which we have, meeting Billie at the restaurant, and the restaurant itself is weird especially because of a big raunchy mad thicklipped sloppy young Fillipino woman sitting alone at the end of the restaurant gobbling up her food obscenely and looking at us insolently as tho to say "Fuck you, I eat the way I like" splashing gravy everywhere——I cant understand what's going on——Because also the general has suggested this dinner but I have to pay for everybody, him, Shea, Perry, Billie, Elliott, me, others, strange apocalyptic madness is now shuddering in my eyeballs and I'm even running out of money in their Apocalypse which they themselves have created in this San Francisco silence anyway.

I yearn to go hide and cry in Evelyn's arms but I end up hiding in Billie's arms and here she goes again, the second evening, explaining all her spiritual ideas——"But what about Perry? what's he up to? and who's that strange general? what are you, a bunch of communists?"

29

T
HE LITTLE CHILD REFUSES TO SLEEP in his crib but has to
come trotting out and watch us make love on the bed but
Billie says "That's good, he'll learn, what other way will he ever
learn?"——I feel ashamed but because Billie is there and she's
the mother I must go along and not worry——Another sinister
fact——At one point the poor child is drooling long slavers of
spit from his lips watching, I cry "Billie, look at him, it's not
good for him" but she says again "Anything he wants he can
have, *even us.*"

"But kid it's not fair, why doesn't he just sleep?"——"He
doesnt wanta sleep, he wants to be with us"——"Ooh," and I
realize Billie is insane and I'm not as insane as I thought and
there's something wrong——I feel myself skidding: also because
during the following week I keep sitting in that same chair by the
goldfish bowl drinking bottle after bottle of port like an auto-
maton, worrying about something, Monsanto comes to visit,
McLear, Fagan, everybody, they call to me dashing up the stairs
and we have long drunken days talking but I never seem to get
out of that chair and never even take another delightful warm
bath reading books——And at night Billie comes home and we
pitch into love again like monsters who dont know what else
to do and by now I'm too blurry to know what's going on anyway tho she reassures me everything is alright, and meanwhile
Cody has completely disappeared——In fact I call him up and
say——"Are you gonna come back and get me here?"——"Yes
yes yes in a few days, stay there" as tho maybe he wants me to
learn what's happening like putting me through an ordeal to
see what I have to say about it because he's been through the
ordeal himself.

In fact everything is going crazy.

Perry's visits scare me: I begin to think he must be one of
those "strong armers" who beat up old men: I watch him
warily——All this time he's pacing back and forth saying "Man
dont you appreciate those sweet little cans? what does it matter how old a woman is, 9 or 19, those little pony tails jiggling
as they walk with those little jigglin cans"——"Did you ever

kidnap one?"——"You out of wine, I'll make a run for you get some more, or would you rather have pot or sumptin? what's wrong with you?"——"I dont know what's goin on!"——"You're drinking too much maybe, Cody told me you're falling apart man, dont do it"——"But what's goin on?"——"Who cares, pops, we're all swingin in love and tryin to go from day to day with self respect while all the squares are puttin us down"—— "Who?"——"The Squares, puttin down Us . . . we wanta swing and live and carry across the night like when we get to L.A. I'm goin to show you the maddest scene some friends of mine down there" (in my drunkenness I've already projected a big trip with Billie and Elliott and Perry to Mexico but we're going to stop in L.A. to see a rich woman Perry knows who's going to give him money and if she doesnt he's going to get it anyway, and as I say Billie and I are going to get married too)——The insanest week of my life——Billie at night saying "You're worried that I cant handle marrying you but of course we can, Cody wants it too, I'll talk to your mother and make her love me and need me: Jack!" she suddenly cries with anguished musical voice (because I've just said "Ah Billie go get yourself a he-man and get married"), "You're my last chance to marry a He Man!"——"Whattayou mean He Man, dont you realize I'm crazy?"——"You're crazy but you're my last chance to have an understanding with a He Man"——"What about Cody?"—— "Cody will never leave Evelyn"——Very strange——But more, tho I dont understand it.

30

I DO UNDERSTAND THE STRANGE DAY BEN FAGAN FINALLY CAME to visit me alone, bringing wine, smoking his pipe, and saying "Jack you need some sleep, that chair you say you've been sitting in for days have you noticed the bottom is falling out of it?"——I get on the floor and by God look and it's true, the springs are coming out——"How long have you been sitting in that chair?"——"Every day waiting for Billie to come home and talking to Perry and the others all day . . . My God let's go out and sit in the park," I add——In the blur of days McLear has also been over on a forgotten day when, on nothing but his chance mention that maybe I could get his book published in Paris I jump up and dial longdistance for Paris and call Claude Gallimard and only get his butler apparently in some Parisian suburb and I hear the insane giggle on the other end of the line——"Is this the home, *c'est le chez eux de Monsieur Gallimard?*"—— Giggle——"*Où est Monsieur Gallimard?*"——Giggle——A very strange phone call——McLear waiting there expectantly to get his "Dark Brown" published——So in a fury of madness I then call London to talk to my old buddy Lionel just for no reason at all and I finally reach him at home he's saying on the wire "You're calling me from San Francisco? but why?"——Which I cant answer any more than the giggling butler (and to add to my madness, of course, why should a longdistance call to Paris to a publisher end up with a giggle and a longdistance call to an old friend in London end up with the friend getting mad?)——So Fagan now sees I'm going overboard crazy and I need sleep——"We'll get a bottle!" I yell——But end up, he's sitting in the grass of the park smoking his pipe, from noon to 6 P.M., and I'm passed out exhausted sleeping in the grass, bottle unopened, only to wake up once in a while wondering where I am and by God I'm in Heaven with Ben Fagan watching over men and me.

And I say to Ben when I wake up in the gathering 6 P.M. dusk "Ah Ben I'm sorry I ruined our day by sleeping like this" but he says: "You needed the sleep, I told ya"——"And you mean to tell me you been sitting all afternoon like that?"——"Watching unexpected events," says he, "like there seems to be sound of a Bacchanal in those bushes over there" and I look and hear children yelling and screaming in hidden bushes in the park— "What they doing?"——"I dont know: also a lot of strange people went by"——"How long have I been sleeping?"——"Ages"—— "I'm sorry"——"Why should be sorry, I love you anyway"—— "Was I snoring?"——"You've been snoring all day and I've been sitting here all day"——"What a beautiful day!"——"Yes it's been a beautiful day"——"How strange!"——"Yes, strange . . . but not so strange either, you're just tired"——"What do you think of Billie?"——He chuckles over his pipe: "What do you expect me to say? that the frog bit your leg?"——"Why do you have a diamond in your forehead?"——"I dont have a diamond in my forehead damn you and stop making arbitrary conceptions!" he roars——"But what am I doing?"——"Stop thinking about yourself, will ya, just float with the world"——"Did the world float by the park?"——"All day, you should have seen it, I've smoked a whole package of Edgewood, it's been a very strange day"——"Are you sad I didnt talk to you?"——"Not at all, in fact I'm glad: we better be starting back," he adds, "Billie be coming home from work soon now"——"Ah Ben, Ah Sunflower"—— "Ah shit" he says——"It's strange"——"Who said it wasnt"——"I dont understand it"——"Dont worry about it"——"Hmm holy room, sad room, life is a sad room"——"All sentient beings realize that," he says sternly——Benjamin my real Zen Master even more than all our Georges and Arthurs actually——"Ben I think I'm going crazy"——"You said that to me in 1955"——"Yeh but my brain's gettin soft from drinkin and drinkin and drinkin"—— "What you need is a cup of tea I'd say if I didnt know that you're too crazy to know how really crazy you are"——"But why? what's going on?"——"Did you come three thousand miles to find out?"———"Three thousand miles from where, after all? from whiney old me"——"That's alright, everything is possible, even Nietzsche knew that"——"Aint nothin wrong with old Nietzsche"——"'Xcept he went mad too"——"Do you think I'm going mad?"——"Ho ho ho" (hearty laugh)——"What's that mean, laughing at me?"——"Nobody's laughing at you, dont get excited"——"What'll we do now?"——"Let's go visit the museum over there"——There's a museum of some sort across the grass of the park so I get up wobbly and walk with old Ben across the sad grass, at one point I put my arm over his shoulder and lean on him——"Are you a ghoul?" I ask——"Sure, why not?"——"I like ghouls that let me sleep?"——"Duluoz it's good for you to drink in a way 'cause you're awful stingy with yourself when You're sober"——"You sound like Julien"——"I never met Julien but I understand Billie looks like him, you kept saying that before you went to sleep"——"What happened while I was asleep?"——"Oh, people went by and came back and forth and the sun sank and finally sank down and's gone now almost as you can see, what you want, just name it you got it"——"Well I want sweet salvation"——"What's sposed to be sweet about salvation? maybe it's sour"——"It's sour in my mouth"——"Maybe your mouth is too big, or too small, salvation is for little kitties but only for awhile"——"Did you see any little kitties today?"——"Shore, hundreds of em came to visit you while you were sleeping"——"Really?"——"Sure, didnt you know you were saved?"——"Now come on!"——"One of them was real big and roared like a lion but he had a big wet snout and kissed you and you said *Ah*"——"What's this museum up here?"——"Let's go in and find out"——That's the way Ben is, he doesnt know what's going on either but at least he waits to find out maybe——But the museum is closed——We stand there on the steps looking at the closed door——"Hey," I say, "the temple is closed."

So suddenly in red sundown me and Ben Fagan arm in arm are walking slowly sadly back down the broad steps like two monks going down the esplanade of Kyoto (as I imagine Kyoto somehow) and we're both smiling happily suddenly——I feel good because I've had my sleep but mainly I feel good because somehow old Ben (my age) has blessed me by sitting over my sleep all day and now with these few silly words——Arm in arm we slowly descend the steps without a word——It's been the only peaceful day I've had in California, in fact, except alone in the woods, which I tell him and says "Well, who said you werent alone now?" making me realize the ghostliness of existence tho I feel his big bulging body with my hands and say: "You sure some pathetic ghost with all that ephemeral heavy crock a flesh"——"I didnt say nottin" he laughs——"Whatever I say Ben, dont mind it, I'm just a fool"——"You said in 1957 in the grass drunk on whiskey you were the greatest thinker in the world"——"That was before I fell asleep and woke up: now I realize I'm no good at all and that makes me feel free"—— "You're not even free being no good, you better stop thinking, that's all"——"I'm glad you visited me today, I think I might have died"——"It's all your fault"——"What are we gonna do with our lives?"——"Oh," he says, "I dunno, just watch em I guess"——"Do you hate me? . . . well, do you like me? . . . well, how are things?"——"The hicks are alright"——"Anybody hex ya lately . . . ?"——"Yeh, with cardboard games?"——"Cardboard games?" I ask——"Well you know, they build cardboard houses and put people in them and the people are cardboard and the magician makes the dead body twitch and they bring water to the moon, and the moon has a strange ear, and all that, so I'm alright, Goof."

"Okay."

31

So there i am as it starts to get dark standing with one hand on the window curtain looking down on the street as Ben Fagan walks away to get the bus on the corner, his big baggy corduroy pants and simple blue Goodwill workshirt, going home to the bubble bath and a famous poem, not really worried or at least not worried about what I'm worried about tho he too carries that anguishing guilt I guess and hopeless remorse that the potboiler of time hasnt made his early primordial dawns over the pines of Oregon come true——I'm clutching at the drapes of the window like the Phantom of the Opera behind the masque, waiting for Billie to come home and remembering how I used to stand by the windows like this in my childhood and look out on dusky streets and think how awful I was in this development everybody said was supposed to be "my life" and "their lives."——Not so much that I'm a drunkard that I feel guilty about but that others who occupy this plane of "life on earth" with me dont feel guilty at all——Crooked judges shaving and smiling in the morning on the way to their heinous indifferences, respectable generals ordering soldiers by telephone to go die or drop dead, pickpockets nodding in cells saying "I never hurt anybody," "that's one thing you can say for me, yes sir," women who regard themselves saviors of men simply stealing their substance because they think their swan-rich necks deserve it anyway (though for every swan-rich neck you lose there's another ten waiting, each one ready to lay for a lemon), in fact awful hugefaced monsters of men just because their shirts are clean deigning to control the lives of working men by running for Governor saying "Your tax money in my hands will be aptly used," "You should realize how valuable I am and how much you need me, without me what would you be, not led at all?"——Forward to the big designed mankind cartoon of a man standing facing the rising sun with strong shoulders with a plough at his feet, the necktied governor is going to make hay while the sun rises——?——I feel guilty for being a member of the human race——Drunkard yes and one of the worst fools on earth——In fact not even a genuine drunkard

675

just a fool——But I stand there with hand on curtain looking down for Billie, who's late, Ah me, I remember that frightening thing Milarepa said which is other than those reassuring words of his I remembered in the cabin of sweet loneness on Big Sur: "When the various experiences come to light in meditation, do not be proud and anxious to tell other people, else to Goddesses and Mothers you will bring annoyance" and here I am a perfectly obvious fool American writer doing just that not only for a living (which I was always able to glean anyway from railroad and ship and lifting boards and sacks with humble hand) but because if I dont write what actually I see happening in this unhappy globe which is rounded by the contours of my deathskull I think I'll have been sent on earth by poor God for nothing——Tho being a Phantom of the Opera why should that worry me?——In my youth leaning my brow hopelessly on the typewriter bar, wondering why God ever was anyway?——Or biting my lip in brown glooms in the parlor chair in which my father's died and we've all died a million deaths——Only Fagan can understand and now he's got his bus——And when Billie comes home with Elliott I smile and sit down in the chair and it utterly collapses under me, blang, I'm sprawled on the floor with surprise, the chair has gone.

"How'd that happen?" wonders Billie and at the same time we both look at the fishbowl and both the goldfishes are upside-down floating dead on the surface of the water.

I've been sitting in that chair by that fishbowl for a week drinking and smoking and talking and now the goldfish are dead.

"What killed them?"——"I dont know"——"Did I kill them because I gave them some Kelloggs corn flakes?"——"Mebbe, you're not supposed to give them anything but their fish food"——"But I thought they were hungry so I gave them a few flicks of corn flakes"——"Well I dont know what killed them"——"But why dont anybody know? what happened? why do they do this? otters and mouses and every damn thing dyin on all sides Billie, I cant stand it, it's all my goddam fault every time!"——"Who said it was your fault dear?"——"Dear? you call me dear? why do you call me dear?"——"Ah, let me love you" (kissing me), "just because you dont deserve it"——(Chastised):-"Why dont I deserve it"——"Because you say so . . ."——"But what about the fish"——"I dont know, really"——"Is it because I've been sitting in that crumbling chair all week blowing smoke on their water? and all the others smoking and all the talk?"——But the little kid Elliott comes crawling up his mommy's lap and starts asking questions: "Billie," he calls her, "Billie, Billie, Billie," feeling her face, I'm almost going mad from the sadness of it all——"What did you do all day?"——"I was with Ben Fagan and slept in the park . . . Billie what are we gonna do?"——"Anytime you say like you said, we'll get married and fly to Mexico with Perry and Elliott"——"I'm afraid of Perry and I'm afraid of Elliott"—— "He's only a little boy"——"Billie I dont wanta get married, I'm afraid . . ."——"Afraid?"——"I wanta go home and die with my cat." I could be a handsome thin young president in a suit sitting in an oldfashioned rocking chair, no instead I'm just the Phantom of the Opera standing by a drape among dead fish and broken chairs——Can it be that no one cares who made me or why?——"Jack what's the matter, what are you talking about?" but suddenly as she's making supper and poor little Elliott is waiting there with spoon upended in fist I realize it's just a little family home scene and I'm just a nut in the wrong place——And in fact Billie starts saying "Jack we should be married and have quiet suppers like this with Elliott, something would sanctify you forever I'm positive."

"What have I done wrong?"——"What you've done wrong is withhold your love from a woman like me and from previous women and future women like me——can you imagine all the fun we'd have being married, putting Elliott to bed, going out to hear jazz or even taking planes to Paris suddenly and all the things I have to teach you and you teach me——instead all you've been doing is wasting life really sitting around sad wondering where to go and all the time it's right there for you to take"——"Supposin I dont want it"——"That's part of the picture where you say you dont want it, of course you want . . ." ——"But I dont, I'm a creepy strange guy you dont even know"——("Cweepy? what's cweepy? Billie? what's cweepy?" is asking poor little Elliott)——And meanwhile Perry comes in for a minute and I pointblank say to him "I dont understand you Perry, I love you, dig you, you're wild, but what's all this business where you wanta kidnap little girls?" but suddenly as I'm asking that I see tears in his eyes and I realize he's in love

with Billie and has always been, wow——I even say it, "You're
in love with Billie aint ya? I'm sorry, I'm cuttin out"——"What
are you talkin about man?"——It's a big argument then about
how he and Billie are just friends so I start singing *Just Friends*
like Sinatra "Two friends but not like before" but goodhearted
Perry seeing me sing runs downstairs to get another bottle for
me——But nevertheless the fish are dead and the chair is broken.

Perry in fact is a tragic young man with enormous potentials
who's just let himself swing and float to hell I guess, unless
something else happens to him soon, I look at him and realize
that besides loving Billie secretly and truly he must also love
old Cody as much as I do and all the world bettern I do yet
he is the character who is always being put away behind bars
for this——Rugged, covered with woe, he sits there with his
black hair always over his brow, over his black eyes, his iron
arms hanging helplessly like the arms of a powerful idiot in the
madhouse, with the beauty of lostness pasted all over him——
Who is he? in fact?——And why doesnt blonde Billie washing
the homey dishes there acknowledge his love?——In fact me
and Perry end up we're both sitting with hanging heads when
Billie comes back in the livingroom and sees us like that, like
two repentant catatonics in hell——Some Negro comes in and
says if I give him a few dollars he'll get some pot but as soon as
I give him five dollars he suddenly says "Well I aint gonna get
nothin"——"You got five dollars, go out and get it"——"I aint
sure I can get any"——I dont like him at all——I suddenly realize
I can leap up and throw him on the floor and take the five dollars away from him but I dont even care about the money but I
am mad about him doing that——"Who is that guy?"——I know
that if I start fighting him he has a knife and we'll wreck Billie's
livingroom too——But suddenly another Negro comes in and
turns out a sweet visit talking about jazz and brotherhood and
they all leave and me and Jacky are alone to wonder some more.

All the muscular gum of sex is such a bore, but Billie and I
have such a fantastic sexball anyway that's why we're able to
philosophize like that and agree and laugh together in sweet
nakedness "Oh baby we're together crazy, we could live in an
old log cabin in the hills and never say anything for years, it was
meant that we'd meet"——She's saying all kinds of things as an
idea begins to dawn on me: "Say I know Billie, let's leave the

City and take Elliott with us and go to Monsanto's cabin in the woods for a week or two and forget everything"——"Yes I can call up my boss right now and get a coupla weeks off, Oh Jack let's do it"——"And it'll be good for Elliott, get away from all these sinister friends of yours, my God"——"Perry aint sinister."

"We'll get married and go away and have a lodge in the Adirondacks, at night by the lamp we'll have simple suppers with Elliott"——"I'll make love to you always"——"But you wont even have to because we both realize we're bugs . . . our lodge will have truth written all over it but tho the whole world come smear it with big black paints of hate and lies we'll be falling dead drunk in truth"——"Have some coffee"——"My hands'll grow numb and I wont be able to handle the axe but still I'll be the truth man . . . I'll stand by the drape of the window night listening to the babble of all the world and I'll tell you about it"——"But Jack I love you and that's not the only reason why, dont you see that we're meant for each other from the beginning, didnt you see that when you came in with Cody and started calling me Julien for that silly reason you told me about where I look like some old buddy you know in New York"—— "Who hates Cody's guts and Cody hates him"——"But dont you see what a waste it is?"——"But what about Cody? you want me to marry you but you love Cody and in fact Perry loves you too?"——"Sure but what's wrong with that or all that? there's perfect love between us forever there's no doubt about it but we only have two bodies"——(a strange statement)——I stand by the window looking out on the glittering San Francisco night with its magic cardboard houses saying "And you have Elliott who doesnt like me and I dont like him and in fact I dont like you and I dont like myself either, how about that?" (Billie says nothing to this but only stores up an anger that comes out later)——"But we can call Dave Wain and he'll drive us to Big Sur cabin and we'll be alone in the woods at least"——"I'm telling you that's what I wanta do!"——"Call him now!"——I tell her the number and she dials it like a secretary——"O the sad music of it all, I've done it all, seen it all, done everything with everybody" I say phone in hand, "the whole world's coming on like a high school sophomore eager to learn what he calls New things, mind you, the same old singsong sad song truth of death . . . because the reason I yell death so much is because

I'm really yelling life, because you cant have death without life, hello Dave? there you are? know what I'm callin you about? listen pal . . . take that big brunette Romana that Rumanian madwoman and pack her in Willie and come down to Billie's here and pick us up, we'll pack while you's en route, honey's on, and we'll all go spend two weeks of bliss in Monsanto's cabin"——"Does Monsanto agree?"——"I'll call him right now and ask him, he'll say sure"——"Well I thought I'd be paint-ing Romana's wall tomorrow but maybe I'd a just got drunk doin that anyway: sure you wanta do all this now?"——"Yes yeh yeh, come on——" "And I can bring Romana?"——"Yes but why not?"——"And what's the purpose of all this?"——"Ah Daddy, maybe just to see you again and we can talk about purposes anywhere: you wanta go on a lecture tour to Utah university and Brown university and tell the well scrubbed kids?"——"Scrubbed with what?"——"Scrubbed with hopeless perfection of pioneer puritan hope that leaves nothing but dead pigeons to look at?"——"Okay I'll be right out . . . first I gotta get Willie's tank filled up and an oil change too"——"I'll pay you when you get here"——"I heard you were eloping with Billie"—— "Who told you that?"——"It was in the paper today"——"Well we'll start off by getting into Willie again and dont bring Ron Blake, we'll be just two couples dig?"——"Yeh——and lissen I'll bring my surf castin rod and catch some fish down there"—— "We'll have a ball——and listen Dave I'm grateful you're free and willing to drive us down there, I'm down in the mouth, I've been sitting here for a week drinking and the chair broke and the fish died and I'm all screwed up again"——"Well you shouldnt oughta drink that sweet stuff all the time and you never eat"——"But that's not the real trouble"——"Well we'll decide what the real trouble is"——"That's right"——"Methinks the real trouble is those pigeons"——"Why?"——"I dunno, re-member when we were in East St. Louis with George, and Jack you said you'd love those beautiful dancing girls if you knew they would live forever as beautiful as they are?"——"But that's only a quote from Buddha"——"Yeh, but the girls didn't expect all that"——"How ya feeling Dave? what's Fagan doing tonight"——"Oh he's sitting in his room writing something, calls it his GOOFBOOK, has big wild drawings in it, and Lex Pascal is drunk again and the music is playing and I'm real sad and I'm glad you called"——"You like me Dave?"——"I aint got nothin else to do, kid"——"But you really have somethin else to do really?"——"Lissen never mind, I'll be up, you call Monsanto right away tho because we also gotta get the corral gate keys from him"——"I'm glad I know you Dave"——"Me too Jack"——"Why?"——"Maybe I wanted to stand on my head in the snow to prove it but I do, am glad, will be glad, after all that's right there's nothing else for us to do but solve these damn problems and I've got one right here in my pants for Romana"——"But that's so sick and tired to call life a problem that can be solved"——"Yes but I'm just repeating what I read in the dead pigeon textbooks"——"But Dave I love you"——"Okay I'll be right over."

32

WE PACK UP LITTLE ELLIOTT'S PATHETIC WARMCLOTHES and put food together and get the hamper all set and wait for Dave to come sadly in the night——And we have a big talk——"Billie but why did the fish die?" but she knows already they probably died because I gave them Kelloggs cornflakes or something went wrong, one thing sure is that she didnt forget to feed them or anything, it's all me, all my fault, I'd as soon be rusted by autumn too-much-think than be dead-fisher cause of those poor little hunks of golden death floating on that scummy water——It reminds me of the otter——But I cant explain it to Billie who's all abstract and talking about our abstract soul-meetings in hell, and little Elliott is pulling at her asking "Where we going? where we going? what for? what for?"——She's saying "And all because you think you dont deserve to be loved because you think you caused the death of the goldfish tho they probably just died on their own accord"——"Why would they do that? why? what kind of logic is that for fish to have?"——"Or because you think you drink too much and therefore every time you're feeling good on a little booze you give up and say your hands hang helpless, like you said last night when you were holding me with those hands blessing my heart and my body with your love, O Jack it's time for you to wake up and come with me or at least come with somebody and open your eyes to why God's put you here, stop all that staring at the floor, you and Perry both you're crazy——I'll draw you magic moon circles'll change all your luck"——I look her dead in the eye and it is blue and I say "O Billie, forgive me"——"But you see you go there talkin guilty again"——"Well I dont know all those big theories about how everything should be goddamit all I know is that I'm a helpless hunk of helpful horse manure looking in your eye saying Help me"——"But when you make those big final statements it doesnt help you"——"Of course I know that but what do you want?"——"I want us to get married and settle down to a sensible understanding about eternal things"——"And you may be right"——I see it all raving before me the endless yakking kitchen mouthings of life, the long dark grave of tomby talks under midnight kitchen bulbs, in fact it fills me with love to realize that life so avid and misunderstood nevertheless reaches out skinny skeleton hand to me and to Billie too——But you know what I mean.

And this is the way it begins.

33

IT SOUNDS ALL SO SAD BUT IT WAS ACTUALLY SUCH A GAY
NIGHT as Dave and Romana came over and there's all the
business of packing boxes and clothes down to the car, nip-
ping out of bottles, getting ready in fact to sing all the way to
Big Sur "Home On the Range" and "I'm Just a Lonsome Old
Turd" by Dave Wain——Me sitting up front next to Dave and
Romana for some reason maybe because I wanted to identify
with my old broken front rockingchair and lean there flapping
and singing but with Romana between us the seat is pinned
down and no longer flaps——Meanwhile Billie is on the back
mattress with sleeping child and off we go booming down Bay
Shore to that other shore whatever it will bring, the way people
always feel whenever they essay some trip long or short especially in the night——The eyes of hope looking over the glare of
the hood into the maw with its white line feeding in straight as
an arrow, the lighting of fresh cigarettes, the buckling to lean
forward to the next adventure something that's been going on
in America ever since the covered wagons clocked the deserts
in three months flat——Billie doesnt mind that I dont sit in
back with her because she knows I wanta sing and have a good
time——Romana and I hit up fantastic medleys of popular and
folk songs of all kinds and Dave contributes his New York Chicago blue light nightclub romantic baritone specialties——My
wavering Sinatra is barely heard in fact——Beat on your knees
and yell and sing Dixie and Banjo On My Knee, get raucous
and moan out Red River Valley, "Where's my harmonica, I been
meanin to buy me a eight dollar harmonica for eight years now."
   It always starts out good like that, the bad moments——
Nothing is gained or lost also by the fact that I insist we stop at
Cody's en route so I can pick up some clothes I left there but
secretly I want Evelyn to finally come face to face with Billie——
It surprises me more however to see the look of absolute fright
on Cody's face as we pour into his livingroom at midnight and
I announce that Billie's in the jeep sleeping——Evelyn is not
perturbed at all and in fact says to me privately in the kitchen
"I guess it was bound to happen sometime she'd come here

and see it but I guess it was destined to be you who'd bring her"——"What's Cody so worried about?"——"You're spoiling all his chance to be real secretive"——"He hasnt come and seen us for a whole week, that's in a way what happened, he just left me stranded there: I've been feeling awful, too"——"Well if you want you can ask her to come in"——"Well we're leaving in a minute anyway, you wanta see her at least?"——"I dont care"——Cody is sitting in the livingroom absolutely rigid, stiff, formal, with a big Irish stone in his eye: I know he's really mad at me this time tho I dont really know why——I go out and there's Billie alone in the car over sleeping Elliott biting her fingernail——"You wanta come in and meet Evelyn?"——"I shouldnt, she wont like that, is Cody there?"——"Yah"——So Willamine climbs out (I remember just then Evelyn telling me seriously that Cody always calls his women by their full first names, Rosemarie, Joanna, Evelyn, Willamine, he never gives them silly nicknames nor uses them).

The meeting is not eventful, of course, both girls keep their silence and hardly look at each other so it's all me and Dave Wain carrying on with the usual boloney and I see that Cody is really very sick and tired of me bringing gangs arbitrarily to his place, running off with his mistress, getting drunk and thrown out of family plays, hundred dollars or no hundred dollars he probably feels I'm just a fool now anyway and hopelessly lost forever but I dont realize that myself because I'm feeling good——I want us to resume down that road singing bawdier and darker songs till we're negotiating narrow mountain roads at the pitch of the greatest songs.

I try to ask Cody about Perry and all the other strange characters who visit Billie in the City but he just looks at me out of the corner eye and says "Ah, yah,hm,"——I dont know and I never will know what he's up to anyway in the long run: I realize I'm just a silly stranger goofing with other strangers for no reason far away from anything that ever mattered to me whatever that was——Always an ephemeral "visitor" to the Coast never really involved with anyone's lives there because I'm always ready to fly back across the country but not to any life of my own on the other end either, just a traveling stranger like Old Bull Balloon, an exemplar of the loneliness of Doren Coit actually waiting for the only real trip, to Venus, to the mountain of Mien Mo——Tho when I look out of Cody's living-room window just then I do see my star still shining for me as it's done all these 38 years over crib, out ship windows, jail windows, over sleepingbags only now it's dummier and dimmer and getting blurreder damnit as tho even my own star be now fading away from concern for me as I from concern for it——In fact we're all strangers with strange eyes sitting in a midnight livingroom for nothing——And small talk at that, like Billie saying "I always wanted a nice fireplace" and I'm yelling "Dont worry we got one at the cabin hey Dave? and all the wood's chopped!" and Evelyn:-"What does Monsanto think of you using his cabin all summer, weren't you supposed to go there alone in secret?"——"It's too late now!" I sing swigging from the bottle without which I'd only drop with shame face flat on the floor or on the gravel driveway——And Dave and Romana look a little uneasy finally so we all get up to go, zoom, and that's the last time I see Cody or Evelyn anyway.

And as I say our songs grow mightier as the road grows darker and wilder, finally here we are on the canyon road the head-lights just reaching out there around bleak sand shoulders—— Down to the creek where I unlock the corral gate——Across the meadow and back to the haunted cabin——Where on the strength of that night's booze and getaway gladness Billie and I actually have a good time lighting fires and making coffee and *gong* to be together in the one sleepingbag easy as pie after we've bundled up little Elliott and Dave and Romana have re-tired in his double nylon bag by the creek in the moonlight.

No, it's the next day and night that concerns me.

34

THE WHOLE DAY BEGINS SIMPLY ENOUGH with me getting up feeling fair and going down to the creek to slurp up water in my palms and wash up, seeing the languid waving of one large brown thigh over the mass of Dave's nylons indicative of an early morning love scene, in fact Romana telling us later at breakfast "When I woke up this morning and saw all those trees and water and clouds I told Dave 'It's a beautiful universe we created'"——A real Adam and Eve waking up, in fact this being one of Dave's gladdest days because he'd really wanted to get away from the City again anyway and this time with a pretty doll, and's brought his surf casting gear planning a big day—— And we've brought a lot of good food——The only trouble is there's no more wine so Dave and Romana go off in Willie to get some more anyway at a store 13 miles south down the highway——Billie and I are alone talking by the fire——I begin to feel extremely low as soon as last night's alcohol wears off.

Everything is trembly again, the trembling hand, I cant for a fact even light the fire and Billie has to do it——"I cant light a fire any more!" I yell——"Well I can" she says in a rare instance when she lets me have it for being such a nut——Little Elliott is constantly pulling at her asking this and that, "What is that stick for, to put in the fire? why? how does it burn? why does it burn? where are we? when are we leaving" and the pattern develops where she begins to talk to him instead of me anyway because I'm just sitting there staring at the floor sighing——Later when he takes his nap we go down the path to the beach, about noon, both of us sad and silent——"What's the matter I wonder" I say out loud——She:-"Everything was alright last night when we slept in the bag together now you wont even hold my hand . . . goddamit I'm going to kill myself!"——Because I've begun to realize in my soberness that this thing has come too far, that I dont love Billie, that I'm leading her on, that I made a mistake dragging everyone here, that I simply wanta go home now, I'm just plumb sick and tired just like Cody I guess of the whole nervewracking scene bad enough as it is always pivoting back to this poor haunted canyon which again gives me the willies as we walk under the bridge and come to those heartless breakers busting in on sand higher than earth and looking like the heartlessness of wisdom——Besides I suddenly notice as if for the first time the awful way the leaves of the canyon that have managed to be blown to the surf are all hesitantly advancing in gusts of wind then finally plunging into the surf, to be dispersed and belted and melted and taken off to sea——I turn around and notice how the wind is just harrying them off trees and into the sea, just hurrying them as it were to death——In my condition they look human trembling to that brink——Hastening, hastening—— In that awful huge roar blast of autumn Sur wind.

Boom, clap, the waves are still talking but now I'm sick and tired of whatever they ever said or ever will say——Billie wants me to stroll with her down towards the caves but I dont want to get up from the sand where I'm sitting back to boulder——She goes alone——I suddenly remember James Joyce and stare at the waves realizing "All summer you were sitting here writing the so called sound of the waves not realizing how deadly serious our life and doom is, you fool, you happy kid with a pencil, dont you realize you've been using words as a happy game——all those marvelous skeptical things you wrote about graves and sea death it's ALL TRUE YOU FOOL! Joyce is dead! The sea took him! it will take YOU!" and I look down the beach and there's Billie wading in the treacherous undertow, she's already groaned several times earlier (seeing my indifference and also of course the hopelessness at Cody's and the hopelessness of her wrecked apartment and wretched life) "Someday I'm going to commit suicide," I suddenly wonder if she's going to horrify the heavens and me too with a sudden suicide walk into those awful undertows——I see her sad blonde hair flying, the sad thin figure, alone by the sea, the leaf-hastening sea, she suddenly reminds me of something——I remember her musical sighs of death and I see the words clearly imprinted in my mind over her figure in the sand:-ST. CAROLYN BY THE SEA——"You were my last chance" she's said but dont all women say that?——But can it be by "last chance" she doesnt mean mere marriage but some profoundly sad realization of something in me she really needs to go on living, at least that impression coming across anyway on the force of all the gloom we've shared——Can it be I'm withholding from her something sacred just like she says, or am I just a fool who'll never learn to have a decent eternally minded deepdown relation with a woman and keep throwing that away for a song at a bottle?——In which case my own life is over anyway and there are the Joycean waves with their blank mouths saying "Yes that's so," and there are the leaves hurrying one by one down the sand and dumping in——In fact the creek is freighting hundreds more of them a minute right direct from the back hills——That big wind blasts and roars, it's all yellow sunny and blue fury everywhere——I see the rocks wobble as it seems God is really getting mad for such a world and's about to destroy it: big cliffs wobbling in my dumb eyes: God says "It's gone too far, you're all destroying everything one way or the other wobble boom the end is NOW."

"The Second Coming, tick tock," I think shuddering—— St.Carolyn by the Sea is going in further——I could run and go see her but she's so far away——I realize that if that nut is going to try this I'll have to make an awful run and swim to get her—— I get up and edge over but just then she turns around and starts back . . . "And if I call her 'that nut' in my secret thoughts wonder what she calls me?"——O hell, I'm sick of life——If I had any guts I'd drown myself in that tiresome water but that wouldnt be getting it over at all, I can just see the big transformations and plans jellying down there to curse us up in some other wretched suffering form eternities of it——I guess that's what the kid feels——She looks so sad down there wandering Ophelialike in bare feet among thunders.

On top of that now here come the tourists, people from other cabins in the canyon, it's the sunny season and they're out two three times a week, what a dirty look I get from the elderly lady who's apparently heard about the "author" who was secretly invited to Mr. Monsanto's cabin but instead brought gangs and bottles and today worst of all trollopes——(Because in fact earlier that morning Dave and Romana have already made love on the sand in broad daylight visible not only to others down the beach but from that high new cabin on the shoulder of the cliff) (tho hidden from sight from the bridge by cliffwall)—— So it's all well known news now there's a ball going on in Mr. Monsanto's cabin and him not even here——This elderly lady being accompanied by children of all kinds——So that when Billie returns from the far end of the beach and starts back with me down the path (and I'm silly with a big footlong wizard pipe in my mouth trying to light it in the wind to cover up) the lady gives her the once over real close but Billie only smiles lightly like a little girl and chirps hello.

I feel like the most disgraceful and nay disreputable wretch on earth, in fact my hair is blowing in beastly streaks across my stupid and moronic face, the hangover has now worked paranoia into me down to the last pitiable detail.

Back at the cabin I cant chop wood for fear I'll cut a foot off, I cant sleep, I cant sit, I cant pace, I keep going to the creek to drink water till finally I'm going down there a thousand times making Dave Wain wonder as he's come back with more wine——We sit there slugging out of our separate bottles, in my paranoia I begin to wonder why I get to drink just the one bottle and he the other——But he's gay "I am now going out surf castin and catch us a grabbag of fish for a marvelous supper; Romana you get the salad ready and anything else you can think of; we'll leave you alone now" he adds to gloomy me and Billie thinking he's in our way, "and say, why dont we go to Nepenthe and *priv*ate our grief tonight and enjoy the moonlight on the terrace with Manhattans, or go see Henry Miller?"——"No!" I almost yell, "I mean I'm so exhausted I dont wanta do anything or see anybody"——(already feeling awful guilt about Henry Miller anyway, we've made an appointment with him about a week ago and instead of showing up at his friend's house in Santa Cruz at seven we're all drunk at ten calling long distance and poor Henry just said "Well I'm sorry I dont get to meet you Jack but I'm an old man and at ten o'clock it's time for me to go to bed, you'd never make it here till after midnight now") (his voice on the phone just like on his records, nasal, Brooklyn, goodguy voice, and him disappointed in a way because he's gone to the trouble of writing the preface to one of my books) (tho I suddenly now think in my remorseful paranoias "Ah the hell with it he was only gettin in the act like all these guys write prefaces so you dont even get to read the author first") (as an example of how really psychotically suspicious and loco I was getting).

Alone with Billie's even worse——"I cant see anything to do now," she says by the fire like an ancient Salem housewife ("Or Salem witch?" I'm leering)——"I could have Elliott taken care of in a private home or an orphanage and just go to a nunnery myself, there's a lot of them around——or I could kill myself and Elliott both"——"Dont talk like that"——"There's no other way to talk when there's no more directions to take"——"You've got me all wrong I wouldnt be any good for you"——"I know that now, you want to be a hermit you say but you dont do it much I noticed, you're just tired of life and wanta sleep, in a way that's how I feel too only I've got Elliott to worry about . . . I could take both our lives and solve that"——"You, creepy talk"——"You told me the first night you loved me, that I was most interesting, that you hadnt met anyone you liked so much then you just went on drinking, I really can see now what they say about you is true: and all the others like you: O I realize you're a writer and suffer through too much but you're really ratty sometimes . . . but even that I know you cant help and I know you're not really ratty but awfully broken up like you explained to me, the reasons . . . but you're always groaning about how sick you are, you really dont think about others enough and I KNOW you cant help it, it's a curious disease a lot of us have anyway only better hidden sometimes . . . but what you said the first night and even just now about me being St.Carolyn in the Sea, why dont you follow through with what your heart knows is Good and best and true, you give up so easy to discouragement . . . then I guess too you dont really want me and just wanta go home and resume your own life maybe with Louise your girlfriend"——"No I couldn't with her either, I'm just bound up inside like constipation, I cant move emotionally like you'd say emotionally as tho that was some big grand magic mystery everybody saying 'O how wonderful life is, how miraculous, God made this and God made that,' how do you know he doesnt hate what He did: He might even be drunk and not noticing what he went and done tho of course that's not true"——"Maybe God is dead"——"No, God cant be dead because He's the unborn"——"But you have all those philosophies and sutras you were talking about"——"But dont you see they've all become empty words, I realize I've been playing like a happy child with words words words in a big serious tragedy, look around"——"You could make some effort, damn it!"

But what's even ineffably worse is that the more she advises me and discussed the trouble the worse and worse it gets, it's as tho she didnt know what she was doing, like an unconscious witch, the more she tries to help the more I tremble almost too realizing she's doing it on purpose and knows she's witching me but it's all gotta be formally understood as "help" dingblast it——She must be some kind of chemical counterpart to me, I just cant stand her for a minute, I'm racked with guilt because all the evidence there seems to say she's a wonderful person sympathizing in her quiet sad musical voice with an obvious rogue nevertheless none of these rational guilts stick——All I feel is the invisible stab from her——She's hurting me!——At some points in our conversation I'm a veritable ham actor jumping up to twitch my head, that's the effect she has——"What's the matter?" she asks softly——Which makes me almost scream and I've never screamed in my life——It's the first time in my life I'm not confident I can hold myself together no matter what happens and be inly calm enough to even smile with condescension at the screaming hysterias of women in madwards——I'm in the same madward all of a sudden——And what's happened? what's caused it——"Are you driving me mad on purpose?" I finally blurt——But naturally she protests I'm talking out of my head, there's no such evident intention anywhere, we're just on a happy weekend in the country with friends, "Then there's something wrong with ME!" I yell——"That's obvious but why dont you try to calm down and for instance like make love to me, I've been begging you all day and all you do is groan and turn away as tho I was an ugly old bat"——She comes and offers herself to me softly and gently but I just stare at my quivering wrists——It's really very awful——It's hard to explain——Besides then the little boy is constantly coming at Billie when she kneels at my lap or sits on it or tries to soothe my hair and comfort me, he keeps saying in the same pitiful voice "Dont do it Billie dont do it Billie dont do it Billie" till finally she has to give up that sweet patience of hers where she answers his every little pathetic question and yell "Shut up! Elliott will you shut up! DO I have to beat you again!" and I groan "No!" but Elliott yells louder "Dont do it Billie dont do it Billie dont do it Billie!" so she sweeps him off and starts whacking him screamingly on the porch and I am about to throw in the towel and gasp up my last, it's horrible.

Besides when she beats Elliott she herself cries and then will be yelling madwoman things like "I'll kill both of us if you dont stop, you leave me no alternative! O my child!" suddenly picking him up and embracing him rocking tears, and gnashing of hair and all under those old peaceful bluejay trees where in fact the jays are still waiting for their food and watching all this——Even so Alf the Sacred Burro is in the yard waiting for somebody to give him an apple——I look up at the sun going down golden throughout the insane shivering canyon, that blasted rogue wind comes topping down trees a mile away with an advancing roar that when it hits the broken cries of mother and son in grief are blown away with all those crazy scattering leaves——The creek screeches——A door bangs horribly, a shutter follows suit, the house shakes——I'm beating my knees in the din and cant even hear that.

"What's I got to do with you committing suicide anyway?" I'm yelling——"Alright, it has nothing to do with you"——"So okay you have no husband but at least you've got little Elliott, he'll grow up and be okay, you can always meanwhile go on with your job, get married, move away, do something, maybe it's Cody but more than that I'd say it's all those mad characters making you insane and wanta kill yourself like that——Perry——" ——"Dont talk about Perry, he's wonderful and sweet and I love him and he's much kinder to me than you'll ever be: at least he gives of himself"——"But what's all this giving of ourselves, what's there to give that'll help anybody"——"You'll never know you're so wrapped up in yourself"——We're now starting to insult each other which would be a healthy sign except she keeps breaking down and crying on my shoulder more or less again insisting I'm her last chance (which isnt true)——"Let's go to a monastery together," she adds madly——"Evelyn, I mean Billie you might go to a nunnery at that, by God get thee to a nunnery, you look like you'd make a nun, maybe that's what you need all that talk about Cody about religion maybe all this worldly horror is just holding you back from what you call your true realizing, you could become a big reverend mother someday with not a worry on your mind tho I met a reverend mother once who cried . . . ah it's all so sad"——"What did she cry about?"——"I dont know, after talking to me, I remember I said some silly thing like 'the universe is a woman because it's round' but I think she cried because she was remembering her early days when she had a romance with some soldier who died, at least that's what they say, she was the greatest woman I ever saw, big blue eyes, big smart woman . . . you could do that, get out of this awful mess and leave it all behind"——"But I love love too much for that"——"And not because you're sensual either you poor kid"——In fact we quiet down a little and do actually make love in spite of Elliott pulling at her "Billie dont do it dont do it Billie dont do it" till right in the middle I'm yelling "Dont do what? what's he mean?——can it be he's right and Billie you shouldnt do it? can it be we're sinning after all's said and done? O this is insane!——but he's the most insane of them all," in fact the child is up on bed with us tugging at her shoulder just like a grownup jealous lover tryin to pull a woman off another man (she being on top indication of exactly how helpless and busted down I've become and here it is only 4 in the afternoon)——A little drama going on in the cabin maybe a little different than what cabins are intended for or the local neighbors are imagining.

35

BUT THERE'S AN AWFUL PARANOIAC ELEMENT SOMETIMES in orgasm that suddenly releases not sweet genteel sympathy but some token venom that splits up in the body——I feel a great ghastly hatred of myself and everything, the empty feeling far from being the usual relief is now as tho I've been robbed of my spinal power right down the middle on purpose by a great witching force——I feel evil forces gathering down all around me, from her, the kid, the very walls of the cabin, the trees, even the sudden thought of Dave Wain and Romana is evil, they're all coming now——I leave poor Billie face in hand and rush off to drink water in the creek but every time I do something like that I have to run back to be sorry and say so, but the moment I see her again "She's doing something else" I leer and I dont feel sorry at all——She's mumbling face in hands and the little boy's crying at her side——"My God she should get to a nunnery!" I think rushing back to the creek——Suddenly the water in the creek tastes different as tho somebody's thrown gasoline or kerosene in it upstream——"Maybe those neighbors wanta get back at me that's what!"——I taste the water carefully and I'm positive that's what happened.

Like an idiot I'm sitting by the creek staring when Dave Wain comes striding down with one fish on the line and his big cheerful western twang as tho nothing unusual's happened "Well boy I spent a whole two hours and look what I got! one measly but beautiful pathetic as you'll see holy little rainbow sea trout that I'm now going to clean——Now the way to clean fish is as follows," and he kneels innocently by the creek to show me how——I have nothing else to do but watch and smile——He says: "Be prepared to be taken on tour of Farollone Island within next two years, boy, with wild canaries actually lighting on your boat hundreds of miles out at sea——See I'm tryna to save money for a fishboat of my own, I think fishing is bettern anything and I intend to entirely reorganize my life for this tho I see the stern image of Fagan shrieking with a Roshi stick, but you ought to see how fast you can bait up hundreds of herring and clean salmon in one and a half minutes, it's a fact, and you walk around in hickory shirts and wool knit caps——Man I know all about it and I'm writing a final definitive article on how clean hard work is the saviour of us all——When you're out there it's a very primal light, fishing is——You're a hunter——Birds find fish for you——Weather drives you——Foolish mind-hangs dissolve before utter fatigue and everything comes in"——As I squat there I imagine maybe Billie is telling Romana what happened in the cabin and Dave'll know in a while tho he seems to know a lot that's going on——He's hinted several times, like now, "You look like you're having the worse time of your life, that kid Elliott is enough to drive anybody crazy and Billie is sure a nervous little wench——Now here's the way you scale, with this here knife"——And I marvel that I cant be so useful and humanly simple and good enough to make small talk to make others feel better, like Dave, there he is long and hollow of cheeks from long drinking himself the past few weeks, but he's not complaining or moaning in the corner like me, at least he does something about it, he puts himself to the test——He gives me that feeling again that I'm the only person in the world who is devoid of humanbeingness, damn it, that's true, that's the way I feel anyway——"Ah Dave someday you and me'll go fishing in your abandoned mining camp on the Rogue River, huh, we'll be feeling better by then somehow gaddamit"——"Well we've got to cut down on the sauce a whole lot, Jack," saying "Jack" sadly a lot like Jarry Wagner used to do on our Dharmabum-ming mountain climbs where we'd confide dolors, "yes, and we drink too many SWEET drinks in a way, you know all that sugar and no food is bound to upset your metabolism and fill your blood with sugar to the point where you aint got the strength of a hen; you especially you've been drinking nothin but sweet port and sweet Manhattans now for weeks——I promise you the holy flesh of this little fish will heal you," (chuckle).

I suddenly look at the fish and feel horrible all over again, that old death scheme is back only now I'm gonna put my big healthy Anglosaxon teeth into it and wrench away at the mournful flesh of a little living being that only an hour ago was swimming happily in the sea, in fact even Dave thinking this and saying: "Ah yes that little muzzling mouth was blindly sucking away in the glad waters of life and now look at it, here's where the fittin head's chopped off, you dont have to look, us big drunken sinners are now going to use it for our sacrificial supper so in fact when we cook it I'm going to say an Indian prayer for it hoping it's the same prayer the local Indians used——Jack in a way we might even start havin fun here and make a great week out of it!"——"Week?"——"I thought we was coming here for a week"——"Oh I said that didnt I . . . I feel awful about everything . . . I dont think I can make it . . . I'm going crazy with Billie and Elliott and me too . . . maybe I'll have to, maybe we'll have to leave or something, I think I'll die here"——And Dave is disappointed naturally and here I've already routed him up out of his own affairs to drive down here anyway, another matter to make me feel like a rat.

36

B<small>UT DAVE'S MAKING THE BEST</small> of clomping up and down the cabin preparing the bag of cornmeal and starting the corn oil in the frying pan, Romana too she's making an exquisite big salad with lots of mayonnaise and in fact poor Billie is mutely helping her setting the table and the little boy is crooning by the stove it's almost like a happy domestic scene suddenly——Only I watch it from the porch with horrified eyes——Also because their shadows in the lamplight gone casting on the walls look huge and monsterlike and witch-like and warlock-like, I'm alone in the woods with happy ghosts——The wind is howling as the sun goes down so I go in, but I go out at once again madly to my creek, always thinking the creek itself will give me water that will clear away everything and reassure me forever (also remembering in my distress Edgar Cayce's advice "Drink a lot of water") but "There's kerosene in the water!" I yell in the wind, nobody hearing——I feel like kicking the creek and screaming——I turn around and there's the cabin with its warm interiors, the silent people inside all noticeably glum because they cant understand anyway what's with the nut wandering in and out from cabin to creek, silent, wan faced, stupefacted, trembling and sweating like midsummer was on the roof and instead it's even cold now——I sit in the chair with my back to the door and watch Dave as he lectures on bravely.

"What we're having is a sacrificial banquet with all kinds of goodies you see laid in a regal spread around one little delicious fish so that we all have to pray to the fish and take tiny little bites, we only have about four bites apiece and there's all kinds of parts of the fish where the bites are more significant——But beyond that the way to properly fry a freshcaught fish is to be sure the oil is burning and furiously so when you lay the fish in it, not burning but real hot oil, well yeh even burning, hand me the spat, you then gently lay the fish into the oil and create a tremendous crackling racket" (which he does as Romana cheers) (and I glance at Billie and she's thinking of something else like a nun in the corner) but Dave keeps on making jokes till he actually has us all smiling——While the fish is cooking, tho, Romana as she's been doing all day is constantly handing me a bite to eat, some *hors d'oeuvres* or piece of tomato or other, apparently trying to help me feel better——"You've got to EAT" she and Dave keep saying but I dont want to eat and yet they're always holding out bites to my mouth until finally now I begin to frown thinking "What's all these bites they keep throwing at me, poison?——and what's wrong with my eyes, they're all dilated black like I've had drugs, all I've had is wine, did Dave put drugs in my wine or something? thinking it will help or something? or are they members of a secret society that dopes people secretly the idea being to enlighten them or something?" even as Romana is handing me a bite and I take it from her big brown hands and chew——She's wearing purple panties and purple bras, nothing else, just for fun, Dave's slappin her on the can joyfully as he cooks the supper, it's some big erotic natural thing to do for Romana, she believes in showing her beautiful big body anyway——In fact at one point when Billie's up leaning over a chair Dave goes behind Billie and playfully touches *her* and winks at me, but I'm not of all this like a moron and we could all be having fun such as soldiers dream the day away imagining, dammit——But the venoms in the blood are asexual as well as asocial and a-everything——"Billie's so nice and thin, like I'm used to Romana maybe I should switch around here for variety," says Dave at the sizzling frying pan——I look over my shoulder and see at first with a leap of joy but then with ominous fear an enormous full moon at full fat standing there between Mien Mo mountain and the north canyon wall, like saying to me as I look over my trembling shoulder "Hoo doo you."

But I say "Dave, look, as if all this wasnt enough" and I point out the moon to him, there's dead silence in the trees and also among us inside, there she is, vast lugubrious fullmoon that frights madmen and makes waters wave, she's got one or two treetops silhouetted and's got that whole side of the canyon lit up in silver——Dave just looks at the moon with his tired madness eyes (overexcited eyes, my mother'd said) and says nothing——I go out to the creek and drink water and come back and wonder about the moon and suddenly the four shadows in the cabin are all dead silent as tho they had conspired with the moon.

"Time to eat, Jack," says Dave coming out on the porch suddenly——No one's saying anything——I go in and sheepishly sit at the table like the useless pioneer who doesnt do anything to help the men or please the women, the idiot in the wagon train who nevertheless has to be fed——Dave stands there saying "Oh full moon, here is our little fish which we are now going to partake of to feed us so that we shall be stronger; thank you Fish people, thank you Fish god; thank you moon for making our light tonight; this is the night of the fullmoon fish which we now consecrate with the first delicate bite"——He takes his fork and opens the little fish carefully, it's beautifully breaded and fried and centered in a dazzle of salads and vegetables and cornmeal johnnycakes, he opens a funny gill, goes under, removes a strange bite and projects it to my mouth saying "Take the first bite Jack, just a little bite, and be sure to chew very slowly"——I do so, oily delicious bite but nothing delicious any more in my tongue——Then the others take their little holy bites, little Elliott's eyes shining with delight at this wonderful game that however has started to frighten me——For obvious reasons by now.

As we eat Dave announces that he and I are sick from too much drinking and by God we're going to reform and see to it that we shape up, then he launches into stories as usual, ending in a talkative ordinary supper that I think will sorta straighten me out at first but after supper I feel even worse, "That fish has all the death of otters and mouses and snakes right in it or something" I'm thinking——Billie is quietly washing the dishes without complaint, Dave is gladly smoking after-dinner cigarettes on the porch, but here I am again mooning by the creek hiding from all of them each five minutes tho I cant understand what makes me do it——I HAVE to get out of there——But I have no right to STAY AWAY——So I keep coming back but it's all an insane revolving automatic directionless circle of anxiety, back and forth, around and around, till they're really by now so perturbed by my increasing silent departures and creepy returns they're all sitting without a word by the stove but now their heads are together and they're whispering——From the woods I see those three shadowy heads whispering me by the stove—— What's Dave saying?——And why do they look like they're plotting something further?——Can it be it was all arranged by Dave

Wain via Cody that I would meet Billie and be driven mad and
now they've got me alone in the woods and are going to give
me final poisons tonight that will utterly remove all my control so that in the morning I'll have to go to a hospital forever
and never write another line?——Dave Wain is jealous because I
wrote 10 novels?——Billie has been assigned by Cody to get me
to marry her so he'll get all my money? Romana is a member of
the expert poisoning society (I've heard her mention tree spirits
already, earlier in the car, and she's sung some strange songs the
night before)——The three of them, Dave Wain in fact the chief
conspirator because I know he does have amphetamine on his
person and the needles in a little box, just one injection of a
tomato, or of a portion of fish, or drops into a bottle of wine,
and my eyes become mad wide and black like they are now,
my nerves OO ouch, this is what I'm thinking——Still they sit
there by the fire in dead silence, when I tromp into the cabin
in fact they all start up again talking: sure sign——I walk out
again, "I'm going down the road a ways"——"Okay"——But
the moment I'm alone on the path a million waving moony
arms are thrashing around me and every hole in the cliffs and
burnt out trees I'd calmly passed a hundred times all summer in
dead of fog, now has something moving in it quickly——I hurry
back——Even on the porch I'm scared to see the familiar bushes
near the outhouse or down by the broken treetrunk——And
now a babble in the creek has somehow entered my head and
with all the rhythm of the sea waves going "Kettle blomp you're
up, you rop and dop, ligger lagger ligger" I grab my heat but
it keeps babbling.

Masks explode before my eyes when I close them, when I
look at the moon it waves, moves, when I look at my hands and
feet they creep——Everything is moving, the porch is moving
like ooze and mud, the chair trembles under me——"Sure you
dont wanta go to Nepenthe for a Manhattan Jack?"——"No"
("Yeh and you'd dump poison in it" I think darkly but seriously hurt I could ever allow myself to think that about poor
Dave)——And I realize the unbearable anguish of insanity: how
uninformed people can be thinking insane people are "happy,"
O God, in fact it was Irwin Garden once warned me not to
think the madhouses are full of "happy nuts," "There's a tight-
ening around the head that hurts, there's a terror of the mind

that hurts even more, they're so unhappy and especially because they cant explain it to anybody or reach out and be helped through all the hysterical paranoia they are really suffering more than anyone in the world and I think in the universe in fact," and Irwin knew this from observing his mother Naomi who finally had to have a lobotomy——Which sets me thinking how nice to cut away therefore all that agony in my forehead and STOP IT! STOP THAT BABBLING!——Because now the babbling's not only in the creek, as I say it's left the creek and come in my head, it would be alright for coherent babbling meaning something but it's all brilliantly enlightened babble that does more than mean something: it's telling me to die because everything is over——Everything is swarming all over me.

Dave and Romana retire again by the creek for a night's sweet sleep under the moon while Billie and I sit there gloomy by the fire——Her voice is crying: "It might make you feel better to just come in my arms"——"I've got to try something, Billie after all I've told you I cant make you see what's happening to me, you dont understand"——"Come into our sleepingbag again like last night, just sleep"——We get in naked but now I'm not drunk I'm aware of the real tight squeeze in there and besides in my fever I'm perspiring so much it's unbearable, her own skin is soaking wet from mine, yet our arms are outside in the cold——"This won't do!"——"What'll you do?"——"Let's try the cot inside" but maniacally I arrange the cot all screwy with a board on top of it forgetting to put sleepingbag pads underneath like I'd done all summer, I simply forget all that, Billie, poor Billie lies down with me on this absurd board thinking I'm trying to drive my madness away by self torturing ordeals——It's ridiculous, we lie there stiff as boards on a board——I roll off and saying "We'll try something else"——I try laying out the sleepingbag on the floor of the porch but the moment she's in my arms a mosquito comes at me, or I burst out sweating, or I see a flash of lightning, or I hear a big roaring Hymn in my head, or imagine a thousand people are coming down the creek talking, or the roar of the wind is bringing flying treetrunks that will crush us——"Wait a minute," I yell and get up to pace awhile and run down to drink water by the creek where Dave and Romana are peacefully entangled——I start cursing Dave "Bastard's got the only decent spot there is to sleep in anyway, right there in that sand by the creek, if he wasnt here I could sleep there and the creek would cover the noise in my head and I could sleep there, with Billie even, all night, bastard's got my spot," and I kick back to the porch——Poor Billie's arms are outstretched to me: "Please Jack, come on, love me, love me"—— "I CANT"——"But why cant you, if even we'll never see each other again let us our last night be beautiful and something to remember forever."

"Like a big ideal memory for both of us, cant you give me just that?"——"I would if I could" I'm muttering around like a fussy old nut inside the cabin looking for a match——I cant even light my cigarette, something sinister blows it out, when it's lit it mortifies my hot mouth anyway like a mouthful of death——I grab up another batch of bags and blankets and start piling myself up on the other side of the porch saying to Billie who's sighing now realizing it's hopeless "First I'll try to take a nap by myself here then when I wake up I'll feel better and come over to you"——So I try that, turning over rigidly my eyes wide open staring full fright into the dark like the time in the movie Humphrey Bogart who's just killed his partner trying to sleep by the fire and you see his eyes staring into the fire rigid and insane——That's just the way I'm staring——If I try to close my eyes some elastic pulls them open again——If I try to turn over the whole universe turns over with me but it's no better on the other side of the universe——I realize I may never come out of this and my mother is waiting for me at home praying for me because she must know what's happening tonight, I cry out to her to pray and help me——I remember my cat for the first time in three hours and let out a yell that scares Billie—— "All right Jack?"——"Give me a little time"——But now she's started to sleep, poor girl is exhausted, I realize she's going to abandon me to my fate anyway and I cant help thinking she and Dave and Romana are all secretly awake waiting for me to die——"For what reason?" I'm thinking "this secret poisoning society, I know, it's because I'm a Catholic, it's a big anti-Catholic scheme, it's Communists destroying everybody, systematic individuals are poisoned till finally they'll have everybody, this madness changes you completely and in the morning you no longer have the same mind——the drug is invented by Airapatianz, it's the brainwash drug, I always thought that

Romana was a Communist being a Rumanian, and as for Billie
that gang of hers is strange, and Cody dont care, and Dave's
all evil just like I always figured maybe" but soon my thoughts
arent even as "rational" as that any more but become hours of
raving——There are forces whispering in my ear in rapid long
speeches advising and warning, suddenly other voices are shouting, the trouble is all the voices are longwinded and talking very
fast like Cody at his fastest and like the creek so that I have to
keep up with the meaning tho I wanta bat it out of my ears——I
keep waving at my ears——I'm afraid to close my eyes for all the
turmoiled universes I see tilting and expanding suddenly exploding suddenly clawing in to my center, faces, yelling mouths,
long haired yellers, sudden evil confidences, sudden rat-tat-tats
of cerebral committees arguing about "Jack" and talking about
him as if he wasnt there——Aimless moments when I'm waiting
for more voices and suddenly the wind explodes huge groans
in the million treetop leaves that sound like the moon gone
mad——And the moon rising higher, brighter, shining down in
my eyes now like a streetlamp——The huddled shadowy sleeping figures over there so coy——So human and safe, I'm crying
"I'm not human any more and I'll never be safe any more, Oh
what I wouldnt give to be home on Sunday afternoon yawning because I'm bored, Oh for that again, it'll never come back
again——Ma was right, it was all bound to drive me mad, now
it's done——What'll I say to her?——She'll be terrified and go
mad herself——*Oh ti Tykey, aide mué*——me who's just eaten fish
have no right to ask for brother Tyke again——"——An argot of
sudden screamed reports rattles through my head in a language
I never heard but understand immediately——For a moment
I see blue Heaven and the Virgin's white veil but suddenly a
great evil blur like an ink spot spreads over it, "The devil!——
the devil's come after me tonight! tonight is the night! that's
what!"——But angels are laughing and having a big barn dance
in the rocks of the sea, nobody cares any more——Suddenly as
clear as anything I ever saw in my life, I see the Cross.

37

I SEE THE CROSS, it's silent, it stays a long time, my heart goes out to it, my whole body fades away to it, I hold out my arms to be taken away to it, by God I am being taken away my body starts dying and swooning out to the Cross standing in a luminous area of the darkness, I start to scream because I know I'm dying but I dont want to scare Billie or anybody with my death scream so I swallow the scream and just let myself go into death and the Cross: as soon as that happens I slowly sink back to life——Therefore the devils are back, commissioners are sending out orders in my ear to think anew, babbling secrets are hissed, suddenly I see the Cross again, this time smaller and far away but just as clear and I say through all the noise of the voices "I'm with you, Jesus, for always, thank you"——I lie there in cold sweat wondering what's come over me for years my Buddhist studies and pipesmoking assured meditations on emptiness and all of a sudden the Cross is manifested to me—— My eyes fill with tears——"We'll all be saved——I wont even tell Dave Wain about it, I wont go wake him up down there and scare him, he'll know soon enough——now I can sleep."

I turn over but it's only begun——It's only one o'clock in the morning and the night wears on to the wheeling moon worse and worse till dawn by which time I've seen the Cross again and again but there's a battle somewhere and the devils keep coming back——I know if I could only sleep for an hour the whole complex of noisy brains would settle down, some control would come back somewhere inside there, some blessing would soothe the whole issue——But the bat comes silently flapping around me again, I see him clearly in the moonlight now his little head of darkness and wings that zigzag maddeningly so you cant even get a look at them——Suddenly I hear a hum, a definite flying saucer is hovering right over those trees where the hum must be, there are orders in there, "They're coming to get me O my God!"——I jump up and glare at the tree, I'm going to defend myself——The bat flaps in front of my face——"The bat is their representative in the canyon, his radar message they got, why dont they leave? doesnt Dave hear

that awful hum?"——Billie is dead asleep but little Elliott suddenly thumps his foot, once——I realize he's not even asleep and
knows everything that's going on——I lie down again and peek
at him across the porch floor: I suddenly realizing he's staring
at the moon and there he goes again, thumping his foot: he's
sending messages——He's a warlock disguised as a little boy, he's
also destroying Billie!——I get up to look at him feeling guilty
too realizing this is all nonsense probably but he is not properly
covered, his little bare arms are outside the blankets in the cold
night, he hasnt even got a nightshirt, I curse at Billie——I cover
him up and he whimpers——I go back and lie down with mad
eyes looking deep inside me, suddenly a bliss comes over me
as the sleep mechanism takes sinking hold——And there I am
dreaming me and two kids are hired to work in the mountains
on the same "ridge" as Desolation Peak (i.e. Mien Mo Mountain again) and start with a cliffside river crew who tell us two
workers have apparently sunk in the cliffside snow and we must
lean over sheer drops and see if we can "dump them out" or
haul them in——All we do is lie there on crumbly snow a thousand foot fall to the river crumbling the snow off in slabs so big
you wouldnt know if men were trapped in em or not——Not
only that the bosses have special shoes on sliders that are holding them to the safe shore (like ski clamps) so I begin to realize
they're only fooling us poor kids and we could have fallen too
(I almost do)——(did)——(almost)——As observer of the story
I see it's just an annual ritualistic joke to fool the new kids on
the job who are then dispatched to the other side of the river
to slump off *more* snow from sheer banks in hopes of finding
the lost workmen——So we start there on a big trip, downriver
first, but en route all the peasants tell us stories of the God
Monster Machine on the other shore who makes sounds like
certain birds and owls and has a million infernal contraptions
enough to make you sick with all the slipshod windmill rickety
details, as "Observer of the story" again I see it's just a trick
to make us scared when we get there at night and hear actual
natural sounds of birds, owls, etc. thinking as green rookies in
the country it's that "Monster"——Meanwhile we sign on to
go to the main mountain but I promise myself if I dont like
the work there I'll come back get my old job on Desolation——
Already our employers have shown a murderous sense of

humor——I arrive at Mien Mo Mountain which is like Raton Canyon again but has a large tho dry rot river running in the wide hole and down there on many rocks are huge brooding vultures——Old bums row out to them and pull them clumsily off the rocks and start feeding them like pets, bites of red meat or red mite, tho at first I thought the eccentric old town bums wanted them to eat or to sell (still maybe so) because before I study this I look and see hundreds of slowly fornicating vulture couples on the town dump——These are now humanly formed vultures with human shaped arms, legs, heads, torsos, but they have rainbow colored feathers, and the men are all quietly sitting *behind* Vulture Women slowly somehow fornicating at them in all the same slow obscene movement——Both man and woman sit facing the same direction and somehow there's contact because you can see all their feathery rainbow behinds slowly dully monotonously fornicating on the dumpslopes——As I pass I even see the expression on the face of a youngish blond vulture man eternally displeased because his Vulture Mistress is an old Yakker who's been arguing with him all the time——His face is completely human but inhumanly pasty like uncooked pale pie dough with dull seamed buggy horror that he's doomed to all this enough to make me shudder in sympathy, I even see her awful expression of middleaged pie dough tormentism——They're so human!——But suddenly me and the two kid workers are taken to the Vulture People respectable quarter of town to our apartment where a Vulture Woman and her daughter show us our rooms——Their faces are leprous thick with softy yeast but painted with makeup to make them like thick Christmas dolls and dull and fuzzy but human expressions, like with thick lips of rubber muzz, fat expressions all crumbly like cracker meal, yellow pizza puke faces, disgusting us tho we say nothing——The apartment has dirty beatnik beds and mattresses everywhere but I walk thru the back looking for a sink——It's *huge*——An endless walk thru long greasy pantries and vast washrooms a block long with single filthy little sink all dark and slimey like underground Lowell High School crumbling basements——Finally I come to the Kitchen where we "new workers" are s'posed to cook little meals all summer——It's vast stone fireplaces and stone stoves all rancid and greasy from a month-old Vulture People Banquet Orgy with still dozens of uncooked chickens lying around on the floor, among garbage and bottles——Rancid stale grease everywhere, nobody's ever cleaned it up or knew how and the place as big as a garage——I push my way out of there pushing a huge greasy-stink foodstained tray of some sort hurrying away from the big stinky emptiness and horror——The fat golden chickens lie rotten upsidedown on littered stone slabs——I hurry out never having seen such a dirty sight in my life. Meanwhile I learn the two boys are studying a hamper full of Vulture Food for us and one of them wisely says "Blisters in our sugar," meaning the Vultures put their blisters in our sugar so we'll "die" but instead of being really dead we'll be taken to the Underground Slimes to walk neck deep in steaming mucks pulling huge groaning wheels (among small forked snakes) so the devil with the long ears can mine his Purple Magenta Square Stone that is the secret of all this Kingdom——You end up down there groaning and pulling thru dead bodies of other people even your own family floating in the ooze——If you succeed you can become a pasty Vulture Person obscenely fornicating slowly on the dump above, I think, either that or the devil just invents the Vulture People with what's left over out of the underground Hell—— "Beans anyone?" I hear myself saying as *thump!* I'm awake again! Elliott has thumped his foot just at that moment on the porch!——I look over there!——He's doing it on purpose, he knows everything that's going on!——What on earth have I brought these people for and why just this particular night of that moon that moon that moon?

I'm up again and pacing up and down and drinking water at the creek, Dave and Romana's lump figures in the moonlight dont move, like hypocrites, "Bastard has my only sleeping spot"——I clutch my head, I'm so alone in all this——I go fearfully casting about for control back inside the cabin by the lighted lamp, a smoke, trying to squeeze the last red drop out of the rancid port bottle, no go——Now that Billie's asleep and so still and peaceful I wonder if I can sleep just by lying beside her and holding her——I do just this, crawling in with all my clothes which I've put on because I'm afraid of going mad naked or of not being able to suddenly run away from everything, in my shoes, she moans a little in her sleep and resumes sleeping as I hold her with those rigid staring eyes——Her blonde flesh in the moonlight, the poor blonde hair so carefully washed and combed, the ladylike little body also a burden to carry around like my own but so frail, thinnish, I just stare at her shoulders with tears——I'd wake her up and confess everything but I'll only scare her——I've done irreparable harm ("Garradarable narm!" yells the creek)——All my self sayings suddenly blurting babbles so the meaning cant even stay a minute I mean a moment to satisfy my rational endeavors to hold control, every thought I have is smashed to a million pieces by millionpieced mental explosions that I remember I thought were so wonderful when I'd first seen them on Peotl and Mescaline, I'd said then (when still innocently playing with words) "Ah, the manifestation of multiplicity, you can actually see it, it aint just words" but now it's "Ah the keselamaroyot you rot"——Till when dawn finally comes my mind is just a series of explosions that get louder and more "multiply" broken in pieces some of them big orchestral and then rainbow explosions of sound and sight mixed.

At dawn also I've almost dimmed into sleep three times but I swear (and this is something I remember that makes me realize I dont understand what happened at Big Sur even now) the little boy somehow thumped his foot just at the moment of drowse, to instantly wake me up, wide awake, back to my horror which when all is said and done is the horror of all the worlds the showing of it to me being damn well what I deserve anyway with my previous blithe yakkings about the sufferings of others in books.

Books, shmooks, this sickness has got me wishing if I can ever get out of this I'll gladly become a millworker and shut my big mouth.

38

DAWN IS MOST HORRIBLE OF ALL with the owls suddenly calling back and forth in the misty moon haunt——And even worse than dawn is morning, the bright sun only GLARING in on my pain, making it all brighter, hotter, more maddening, more nervewracking——I even go roaming up and down the valley in the bright Sunday morning sunshine with bag under arm looking hopelessly for some spot to sleep in——As soon as I find a spot of grass by the path I realize I cant lie down there because the tourists might walk by and see me——As soon as I find a glade near the creek I realize it's too sinister there, like Hemingway's darker part of the swamp where "the fishing would be more tragic" somehow——All the haunts and glades having certain special evil forces concentrated there and driving me away——So haunted I go wandering up and down the canyon crying with that bag under my arm: "What on earth's happened to me? and how can earth be like that?"

Am I not a human being and have done my best as well as anybody else? never really trying to hurt anybody or half-hearted cursing Heaven?——The words I'd studied all my life have suddenly gotten to me in all their serious and definite deathliness, never more I be a "happy poet" "Singing" "about death" and allied romantic matters, "Go thou crumb of dust you with your silt of a billion years, here's a billion pieces of silt for you, shake that out of your shaker"——And all the green nature of the canyon now waving in the morning sun looking like a cruel idiot convocation.

Coming back to the sleepers and staring at them wild eyed like my brother'd once stared at me in the dark over my crib, staring at them not only enviously but lonely inhuman isolation from their simple sleeping minds——"But they all look dead!" I'm carking in my canyon, "Sleep is death, everything is death!"

The horrible climax coming when the others finally get up and pook about making a troubled breakfast, and I've told Dave I cant possibly stay here another minute, he must drive us all back to town, "Okay but I sure wish we could stay a week like Romana wants to do,"——"Well you drive me and come back"——"Well I dunno if Monsanta would like that we've already dirtied up the place aplenty, in fact we've got to dig a garbage pit and get rid of the junk"——Billie offers to dig the garbage pit but does so by digging a neat tiny coffinshaped grave instead of just a garbage hole——Even Dave Wain blinks to see it——It's exactly the size fit for putting a little dead Elliott in it, Dave is thinking the same thing I am I can tell by a glance he gives me——We've all read Freud sufficiently to understand something there——Besides little Elliott's been crying all morning and has had two beatings both of them ending up crying and Billie saying she cant stand it any more she's going to kill herself——

And Romana too notices it, the perfect 4 foot by 3 foot neatly sided grave like you're ready to sink a little box in it—— Horrifying me so much I take the shovel and go down to dump junk into it and mess up the neat pattern somehow but little Elliott starts screaming and grabs the shovel and refuses I go near the hole——So Billie herself goes and starts filling the garbage in but then looks at me significantly (I'm sure sometimes she really did aspire to make me crazy) "Do you want to finish the job yourself?"——"What do you mean?"——"Cover the earth on, do the honors?"——"What do you mean do the honors!"—— "Well I said I'd dig the garbage pit and I've done that, aint you supposed to do the rest?"——Dave Wain is watching fascinated, there's something screwy he sees there too, something cold and frightening——"Well okay" I say, "I'll dump the earth over it and tamp it down" but I go down to do this Elliott is screaming "NO no no no no!" ("My God, the fishes' bones are in that grave" I realize too)——"What's the matter he wont let me go near that hole! why did you make it look like a grave?" I finally yell——But Billie is only smiling quietly and steadily at me, over the grave, shovel in hand, the kid weeping tugging the shovel, rushing up to block my way, trying to shove me back with his little hands——I cant understand any of it——He's screaming as I grab the shovel as tho I'm about to bury Billie in there or something or himself maybe——"What's the matter with this kid is he a cretin?" I yell.

With the same quiet steady smile Billie says "Oh you're so fucking neurotic!"

I simply get mad and dump earth over the garbage and tromp it all down and say "The hell with all this madness!"

I get mad and stomp up on the porch and throw myself in the canvas chair and close my eyes——Dave Wain says he's going down the road to investigate the canyon a bit and when he comes back the girls will have finished packing and we'll all leave——Dave goes off, the girls clean up and sweep, the little kid is sleeping and suddenly hopelessly and completely finished I sit there in the hot sun and close my eyes: and there's the golden swarming peace of Heaven in my eyelids——It comes with a sure hand a soft blessing as big as it is beneficent, i.e., endless——I've fallen asleep.

I've fallen asleep in a strange way, with my hands clasped behind my head thinking I'm just going to sit there and think, but I'm sleeping like that, and when I wake up just one short minute later I realize the two girls are both sitting behind me in absolute silence——When I'd sat down they were sweeping, but now they were squatting behind my back, facing each other, not a word——I turn and see them there——Blessed relief has come to me from just that minute——Everything has washed away——I'm perfectly normal again——Dave Wain is down the road looking at fields and flowers——I'm sitting smiling in the sun, the birds sing again, all's well again.

I still cant understand it.

Most of all I cant understand the miraculousness of the silence of the girls and the sleeping boy and the silence of Dave Wain in the fields——Just a golden wash of goodness has spread over all and over all my body and mind——All the dark torture is a memory——I know now I can get out of there, we'll drive back to the City, I'll take Billie home, I'll say goodbye to her properly, she wont commit no suicide or do anything wrong, she'll forget me, her life'll go on, Romana's life will go on, old Dave will manage somehow, I'll forgive them and explain everything (as I'm doing now)——And Cody, and George Baso, and ravened McLear and perfect starry Fagan, they'll all pass through one way or the other——I'll stay with Monsanto at his home a few days and he'll smile and show me how to be happy awhile, we'll drink dry wine instead of sweet and have quiet evenings in his home——Arthur Ma will come to quietly draw pictures at my side——Monsanto will say "That's all there is to it, take it easy, everything's okay, dont take things too serious, it's bad enough as it is without you going the deep end over imaginary conceptions just like you always said yourself"——I'll get my ticket and say goodbye on a flower day and leave all San Francisco behind and go back home across autumn America and it'll all be like it was in the beginning——Simple golden eternity blessing all—— Nothing ever happened——Not even this——St.Carolyn by the Sea will go on being golden one way or the other——The little boy will grow up and be a great man——There'll be farewells and smiles——My mother'll be waiting for me glad——The corner of the yard where Tyke is buried will be a new and fragrant shrine making my home more homelike somehow——On soft Spring nights I'll stand in the yard under the stars——Something good will come out of all things yet——And it will be golden and eternal just like that——There's no need to say another word.

"SEA"

Sounds of the Pacific Ocean at Big Sur

Sea

Cherson!
  Cherson!
    You aint just whistlin
        Dixie, Sea——
      Cherson! Cherson!
        We calcimine fathers
            here below!
        Kitchen lights on——
            Sea Engines from Russia
            seabirding here below——
    When rocks outsea froth
      I'll know Hawaii
      cracked up & scramble
      up my doublelegged cliff
    to the silt of
      a million years——

Shoo——Shaw——Shirsh——
Go on die salt light
  You billion yeared
    rock knocker

Gavroom
Seabird
Gabroobird
Sad as wife & hill
Loved as mother & fog
Oh! Oh! Oh!
    Sea! Osh!
Where's yr little Neppytune
        tonight?

These gentle tree pulp pages
which've nothing to do
with yr crash roar,
    liar sea, ah,

were made for rock
tumble seabird digdown
   footstep hollow weed
  move bedarvaling
  crash? Ah again?
Wine is salt here?
  Tidal wave kitchen?
Engines of Russia
    in yr soft talk——

Les poissons de la mer
    parle Breton——
Mon nom es Lebris
   de Keroack——
  Parle, Poissons, Loti,
   parle——
Parlning Ocean sanding
  crash the billion rocks——

   Ker plotsch——
   Shore—shoe——
god——brash——

The headland looks like
a longnosed Collie sleeping
with his light on his
   nose, as the ocean,
  obeying its accommodations
 of mind, crashes in
  rhythm which could
  & will intrude, in thy
  rhythm of sand
  thought——
——Big frigging shoulders
on *that* sonofabitch

Parle, O, parle, mer, parle,
  Sea speak to me, speak
    to me, your silver you light
    Where hole opened up in Alaska

Gray——shh——wind in
  The canyon wind in the rain
  Wind in the rolling rash
  Moving and t wedel
      Sea
       sea
         Diving sea
O bird——la vengeance
  De la roche
      Cossez
      Ah

Rare, he rammed the gate
rare over by Cherson, Cherson,
we calcify fathers here below
——a watery cross, with weeds
entwined——This grins restoredly,
  low sleep——Wave——Oh, no,
shush——Shirk——Boom plop
Neptune now his arms extends
  while one millions of souls
    sit lit in caves of darkness
——What old bark? The dog
mountain? Down by the Sea
  Engines? God rush——Shore——
Shaw——Shoo——Oh soft sigh
  we wait hair twined like
  larks——Pissit——Rest not
——Plottit, bisp tesh, cashes,
  re tav, plo, aravow,
shirsh,——Who's whispering over
    there——the silly earthen creek!
  The fog thunders——We put
    silver light on face——We
      took the heroes in——A billion
      years aint nothing——

O the cities here below!
  The men with a thousand
  arms! the stanchions of

their upward gaze! the
coral of their poetry! the
  sea dragons tenderized, meat
  for fleshy fish——
      Navark, navark, the fishes
    of the Sea speak Breton——
    wash as soft as people's
dreams——We got peoples
  in & out the shore, they call
  it shore, sea call it
    pish rip plosh——The
      5 billion years since
      earth we saw substantial
        chan——Chinese are
          the waves——the woods
          are dreaming

No human words bespeak
  the token sorrow older
  than old this wave
  becrashing smarts the
  sand with plosh
  of twirléd sandy
thought——Ah change
  the world? Ah set
  the fee? Are rope the
    angels in all the sea?
    Ah ropey otter
  barnacle'd be——
    Ah cave, Ah crosh!
    A feathery sea

  Too much short——Where
  Miss Nop tonight?
Wroten Kerarc'h
  in the labidalian
  aristotelian park
with slime a middle
——And Ranti forner
  who pulled pearls by

　　rope to throne
　　　the King by
　　　　the roll in the
　　　forest of everseas?
Not everseas, *be* seas
　　　——Creep
　　　　Crash

The woman with her body
in the sea——The frog who
never moves & thunders, sharsh
——The snake with his body
　under the sand——The dog
　with the light on his nose,
　supine, with shoulders so
　enormous they reach back to
　rain crack——The leaves hasten
　　to the sea——We let them
　　　hasten to be wetted & give
　em that old salt change, a
　nuder think will make you see
　　they originate from the We Sea
　　　anyway——No dooming booms
　on Sunday afternoons——We
run thru the core of cliffs,
　blam up caves, disengage no
　　jelly or jellied pendant
　　　　thinkers——

　　　　　　Our armies of
　　　anchored seaweed in the
　　　coves give of the smell
of jellied salt——
　　　Reach, reach, some leaves
havent hastened near
enuf——Roll, roll, purl
the sand shark floor
a greeny pali andarva
——Ah back——Ah forth——
Ah shish——Boom, away,

doom, a day——Vein we
firm——The sea is We——
 Parle, parle, boom the
  earth——Arree——Shaw,
  Sho, Shoosh, flut,
  ravad, tapavada pow,
 coof, loof, roof,——
     No,no,no,no,no,no——
     Oh ya, ya, ya, yo, yair——
     Shhh——

   Which one? the one? Which
one? The one ploshed——
 The ploshed one? the same,
  ah boom——Who's that ant
that giant golden saltchange
ant magnifying my mountain
of feet? 'Tis Finder, finding
 the change in thought to join
  the boomer hangers in the
  cave a light——And built a
  house above it? Never fear,
     naver foir, les bretons qui
parlent la langue de la Mar
  sont español comme le cul
  du Kurd qui dit le maha
 prajna paramita du Sud?
  Ah oui! Ke Vlum!
     Glum sea, silent me——

 They aint about to try
it them ants who wear
 out tunnels in a week
 the tunnel a million years
 won——no——Down around
 the headland slobs for weed,
 the chicken of the sea
  go yak! they sleep——
 Aroar, aroar, arah, aroo——
Otter me otter me daughter me sea

——me last blue lagoon inside of
me, the sea——Divine is the
substance all over the Sea——
    Of space we speak &
hasten——Let no mouth
  swallow the sea——Gavril——
  Gavro——the Cherson Chinese
  & Old Fingernail sea——Is
ringin yr ear? Dier, dee?
  Is Virgin you trying to
      fathom me

  Tiresome old sea, aint you sick
    & tired of all of this merde?
this incessant boom boom
& sand walk——you people
 hoary rockies here to Fuegie
& never get sad? Or despair
like a German phoney?
Just gloom booboom & green
  on foggy nights——the fog is part
of us——
     I know, but tired
 as I can be listening to all
 this silly majesty——
    Bashô!
    Lao!
    Pop!
   Who is this fish
  sitting unsunk? Run up
 a Hawaii typhoon smash him
 against his rock——We'll jelly you,
  jellied man, show you essential
     jello of the sea——King
    of the Sea.

No Monarc'h ever Irish be?
 Ju see the Irish sea?
Green winds on tamarack vines——
Joyce——James——Shhish——

Sea——Sssssss——see
——Varash
——mnavash la vache
    écriture——the sea dont say
muc'h actually——

    Gosh, she,
huzzy, tow, led men
  on, Ulysses and all them
    fair headed moin——
    Terplash, & what difference
    make! One little white
      spark of light!
  Hair woven hands
    Penelope seaboat
    smeller——Courtiers in
      Telemachus 'sguise
      dropedary dropedary
      creep——Or——
    Franc gold rippled
    that undersea creek
where fish fish for
    fisher men——Salteen
    breen the wet Souwesters
      of old Portugee Prayers

    Tsall tangled, changed,
salt & drop the sand
  & weed & water brains
    entangled——Rats
    of old Venetian yellers
    Ariel Calibanned
      to Roma Port——
Pow——spell——
    Speak you parler,
in this my mother's
  parlor, wash your
undershoes when you
    come in, say thanks
  to foggy moon

Go brash, Topahta
offat,——we'll gray
  ye rose——Morning
  primord creeper sees
  the bird of paravision
dying tweet the yellow
mouthroof! How sweet
  the earth, yells sand!
    Xcept when tumble
boom!
    O we wait too
for Heaven——all
in One——
    All is there
in fair & sight

I'm going to wash now
  old Pavia down,
 & pack my salt
    to Either Town——
  Cliffs of Antique
  aint got no rose,
  the morning's seen
the ledder pose——
  Boom de boom dey
  the sea is me——
  We are the sea——
    It aint all snow

We wash Fujiyama down
    soon, & sand
  crookbird back——
We hie bash
rock————ak——
  Long short——
  Low and easy——
  Wind & many freezing
bottoms on luckrock——
  Rappaport——
Endymion thou tangled

dreamer love my thigh
——Rose, Of Shelley,
 Rose, O Urns!
  Ogled urns in fish eye

   Cinco sea the Chico sea
   the Magellan headland sea
——What hype sidereal did he put down
 bending beatnik sea goatee
 over old goat manuscripts
 to find the other side of Flat?
    See round, see the end of me?
Rounden huge bedroom?
   Awp hole cave & shwrul——
 sand & salt & hair eyes

——Strong enuf to make
   coffee grow in your hair——
   Whose planation Neptune got?
    That of Atlas still down there,
    Hesperid's his feet, Sur his sleet,
     Irish Sea fingertip
     & Cornwall aye his soul
     bedoom

Shurning——Shurning——plop
 be dosh——This sigh old learning's
 high beside me——Rough
  old hands have played out
  pedigree, we've sunk more boats
  than dreamer'll ever ever see
——Burning——Burning——The world
 is burning & needs waaater
——I'll have a daughter,
    oughter, wait & seee——
     Churning, Churning, Me——
      Panties——Panties——
    these ancient fancies are
     so girling——You've not seen
     mermaids in my actual sea

——You've not seen sexless babies
   with breasts of Majesty——
     My wife——My wife——
    Her name is Oh so really
        high life

The low life Kingdom where
we part out tea, is sea
 side Me——
     Josh——coof——patra——
 Aye ee mo powsh——
Ssst——Cum here read me——
  Dirty postcard——Urchin sea——
   Karash your name——?
 Wanta swim, sink or swim?
 Ears ringing again?
  Sea vibrate rhythm
crash sets off cave
  hanger blowers whistling
dog ear back——to sea——
  Arree——
     Gerudge Napoleon nada——
Nada

  Pluto eats the sea——
  Room——
  Hands folded by the sea——
  "On est toutes cachez, mange
le silence," dit les poissons de la
  mer——Ah Mar——Gott——
   Thalatta——Merde——Marde
de mer——Mu mer——Mak a vash——
   The ocean is the mother——
    Je ne suis pas mauvaise quand j'sui
    tranquil——dans les tempêtes
   j'cril! Come une folle!
   j'mange, j'arrache toutes!
   Clock——Clack——Milk——
    Mai! mai! mai! ma!
  says the wind blowing sand——

Pluto eats the sea——
    Ami go——da——che pop
    Go——Come——Cark——
    Care——Kee ter da vo
Kataketa pow! Kek kek kek!
Kwakiutl! Kik!
    Some of theserather taratasters
trapped hyra tchere thaped
  the anadondak ram ma lat
round by Krul to Pat the lat
    rat the anaakakalked
    romon t o t t e k
     Kara VOOOM
     frup——
        Feet cold? wade——Mind sore?
sim——sin——Horny?——lay the sea?
  Corny? try me——
       Ussens here hang no more
  here we go, ka va ra ta
plowsh, shhh,
  and more, again, ke vlook
  ke bloom & here comes
    big Mister Trosh
     ——more waves coming,
   every syllable windy

  Back wash palaver
paralarle——paralleling
parle pe Saviour

A troublesome spirit
hanging here cant make it
  in the void——The sea'll
only drown me——These words
  are affectations
of sick mortality——
   We try to make our way
  in self reliance, aid
    not ever comes too quick

from wherever & whatever
heaven dear may have
suggested to promise us——

But these waves scare me——
I am going to die
 in full despair——
 Wake up where?
   On second breath in life
   the atmosphere is dearer
   maybe closer to Heaven
   ——O Paradise——
Is the sea really so bad?
 Have you sent men
here for this cold clown
& monstrous eater at the
 world? whose sound
    I mock?

God I've got to believe in you
 or live in death!
 Will you save us——all?
    Soon or now?
 Send illumination
  to our drowning brains
——We're pitiful, Lord,
 we need yr help!
 Save us, Dear——
 (Save yourself, God man,
    ha ha!)
 If you were God man
you'd command these waves
 to very well Tennyson stop
   & even Tennyson
      is dear
         now dead
Leave it to the light
 Concern yourself with supper,
 & an eye

somebody's eye——a wife,
a girl, a friend, an animal
——a blood let drop——
 he for his sea,
  he for his fire,
   thee for thy desire

"The sea drove me away
 & yelled 'Go to your desire!'
——As I hurried up the valley
It added one last yell:-
   'And laugh!'"

   Even the sea cant stop me from
    writing something to read in my old age
——This is the chart of brief forms,
   this sea the briefest——Shish yourself——
After scaring me like that, Mar,
I'll excoriate yr slum——yr
 iodine weeds & slime hoops,
 even yr dried hollow seaweed
   stinks——you stink all over——
   Boom——Try that, creep——
   The little Monterey fishingboat
   glides downward home 15 miles to go,
   be home to fried fish & beer b'five——
   It guides the sea its bird routes——
   ——Silver loss forever outward
——From blue sky of human bridges
 to the massive mawkcloud sea center
   heap——to the gray——
     Some boys call it gunboat blue,
     or gray, but I call it
     the Civil War of Rocks
——Rocks 'come air, rocks 'come water,
   & rock rocks——
Kara tavira, mnash grand bash
——poosh l'abas——croosh
 L'a haut——Plash au pied——
   Peeeee——Rolle test boulles——
   Manche d'la rache——

The handsome King prevails
over boom sing bird head——
"Crache tes idées," spit yr ideas,
says the sea, to me, quite
appro priate ly——
    Pss! pss! pss!
    Ps! girl inside!
    Red shoes scum, eyes of old
sorcerers, toenails hanging down
in the barrel of old firkin cheese
the Dutchman forgot t'eat that
                      tempest
              nineteen O
                 sixteen——

When torpedoed by gunboat
  Pedro in the Valley
of a Million Fees?

When Magellan crosseyed
 ate the Amazonian feet——
And, Ah, when Colombo cross't!
When Drake sir francised the waves
  with feeding of the blue jay
    dark——pounded his aleward
  tank before the boom,
 housed up all thoughts of Erik
   the Red the Greenland caperer
& builder of rockdungs in New
    Port——*New*——yet——
 Oldport Indian Fishhead——
 Oldport Tattoo Kwakiutl Headpost
   taboo potash Coyotl potlatch?
Old Primitive Columbia.——
Named for Colom *bus?*
  Name for Aruggio Vesmarica——
    Ar!——Or!——Da!
    What about Verrazano?
he sailed!——
    He Verrazano zailed & we
statened his Island in on deep

in on dashun—
      Rotted the Wallower?
    Sinners liars goodmen all
   sink waterswim drink Neptune's
    nectar the zal sotat——
      Zal sotate name for crota?
     Crota ta crotte, you aint
     'bout to find (Jesus Christian!)
any dry turds here below——
     Why fo no?
      Go crash yonder rock
    of bleak with yr filet mignon teeth
     & see——For you, the hearth,
      the heart, the lock of hair——
       For me, for us, the Sea,
       the murdering of time by eating
       lusty cracks of lip feed wave
        at aeons of sandy artistry
        till nothing's left but old age
           newmorning primordial pain
         of sitters by
         the unborn
          bird
         of roses yet undone——

    With weeds your roses,
sand crabs your hummers?
With buzzers in the sea!
 With runners in the deep!
This Sceptred Osh, this wide leg
 spanning rock U.S. to rock
  Ja Pan, this onstable
  roller roaming all,
  this ploosher at yr gory
   dry dung door, this mouth
  of silverwhite arring to hold thee,
   this purger of conscience
   arra for thee——
    No mouse in here but's got
    a little glee——and

aft, or oft, the osprey
in his glee's agley——
   Oh purty purty ocean
      me——
      Sop! bring the Scepter down!
Again you've accepted me!

Breathe our iodine, filthy yr drink,
faint at feet wet, drop
  yr profile move it in the sea,
float weeded watery Adonais
  longs for thee——& Shelley three,
   that's three——burn in salt
with slow most change——
We've had no crack at eternity
in a billion years of trying——
   one grain of sand possesses
   3 thousand worlds of glee——
   not to mention me——
      Ah sea

    Ah si——Ah so——
shoot——shiver——mix——
  ha roll——tara——ta ta——
  curlurck——Kayash——Kee——
Pearls pearls in the yellow West
——Yellow sky to China——
Pacific we named here
  water as always meeting
  water——Pacific Pacific
   Pacific tapfic——geroom——
  gedowsh—gaka—gaya——
   Tatha——gata——mana——
   What sails used old bhikkus?
   Dhikkus? Dhikkus!
What raft mailed Mose
to the hoven dovepost?
  What saved Blackswirl
   from the Kidd plank?
  What Go-Bug here?

Seet! Seeeeeeeeeee
eeeeee——kara——
Pounders out yar——

Big Sur they call this sand
  these rocks this creek?
  Raton Canyon by name pours
  Coyote leaves & old Pomo bones
& old dust of Tomahawks
    into your angler'd maw——
    My salt maw shall salvage
    Taylors——sewing in the room
                    below——
Sewing weed shrat for hikers
  in the milky silt——
  Sewing crosswards
    for certainty——Sartan
  are we of Price Victory
  in this salt War with thee
  & thine thee jellied yink!
    Look O the sea here called
      Pacific Sea!
          T a k i !

My golden empty soul'll
outlast yr salty sill
——the Windows of my jelly eye
  & fish head muck look out on thee,
    slit, with cigar-a-mouth,
  some contempt——
          Yet I hie me to see you
——you hie thee to eat
    me——Fair in sight
    and worn, aright——
Arra! Aroo!
    Ger der va——
    Silly silent cities in the sea
  have children playing cardboard
mush with eignyard old Englander
    beeplates slickered oer with scum

of histories below——
No tempest as still & awful
　　　as the tempest within——
Sorcerer hip! Buddhalands
　　& Buddhaseas!
　What sails Maudgalyayana used
　　he only knows to tell
　but got kilt by yellers
sreaming down the cliff
　　　　"Let's go home!
　　　　　Now!"
　——leave marge smashed djamas
Maudgalyayana was murdered by the sea——
　　　But the sea dont tell——
　The sea dont murder——
　　　The seadrang scholars
　　　　oughter know that
　　　　　or
　　　go back to School

　　Hear over there the ocean motor?
Feel the splawrsh of it?
　Six silly centepedes here, Machree——
　　　Ah Ratatatatatat——
the machinegun sea, rhythmic
　balls of you pouring in
　with smooth eglantinee
　　in yr pedigreed milkpup
　　　tenor——
　　Tinder marsh aright arrooo——
　　　arrac'h——arrache——
　　Kamac'h——monarc'h——
　　　Kerarc'h Jevac'h——
　　Tamana——gavow——
　　　Va——Voovla——Via——
　　　　Mia——mine——
　　　　　sea
　　　　　poo

Farewell, Sur——

Didja ever tell him
about water meeting water——?
O go back to otter——
Term——Term——Klerm
Kerm——Kurn——Cow——Kow——
Cash——Cac'h——Cluck——
Clock——Gomeat sea need
be deep I see you
Enoc'h
soon anarf
in Old Brittany

21 August 1960
Pacific Ocean at Big Sur
California

THE GREAT REMEMBERER
By Allen Ginsberg

CHRONOLOGY

NOTE ON THE TEXTS

CHARACTER KEY

NOTES

The Great Rememberer
by Allen Ginsberg

Two noble men, Americans, perished younger than old white-beard prophets' wrinkled gay eye Archetypes might've imagined like Whitman. The death of America in their early stop—untimely tears—for loves glimpsed and not fulfilled—not completely fulfilled, some kind of withdrawal from the promised tender Nation—Larimer Street down, green lights glimmering, Denver surrounded by Honeywell warplants, IBM war calculators, selfish Air Bases, Botanical Mortal Brain Factories—Robot buildings downtown lifted under crescent moon—The small hands gestured to belly and titty, under backstairs decades ago, seeking release to each other, trembling sexual tenderness discovered first times . . . before the wars began . . . 1939 Denver's mysterious glimpses of earth life unfolding on side streets in the United States—Perfectly captured nostalgia by Jack *Visions of Cody* (Neal) . . . Peace protester adolescents from Cherry High with neck kiss bruises sit & weep on Denver Capitol Hill lawn, hundreds of Neal & Jack souls mortal lamblike sighing over the nation now, 1972.

Mortal America's here . . . disappearing Elevateds, diners, iceboxes, dusty hat racks preserved from oblivion . . . Larimer Street itself this year in ruins resurrected spectral thru *Visions of Cody*—And the poolhall itself gone to parking lot & Fun Adult Movies the heritage of Neal's sex fantasies on the bench watching Watson shoot snooker—

By this prose preserved for a younger generation appreciative of the Bowery camp & 'thirties hair consciousness destroyed by real estate speculators on war-growth economy.

I don't think it's possible to proceed further in America without first understanding Kerouac's tender brooding compassion for bygone scene & personal Individuality oddity'd therein. Bypassing Kerouac one bypasses the mortal heart, sung in prose vowels; the book a giant mantra of appreciation and adoration of an American man, one striving heroic soul. Kerouac's judgment on Neal Cassady was confirmed by later Kesey history.

"I saw the flash of their mouths, like the mouths of minstrels, as they ate."

High generous prose moments, I reread this book 19 years later—the Shabda (sound waves) passage, "like ants in orchestras." Hector's Cafeteria food description a Homeric Hymn. "All you do is head straight for the grave." Robert Duncan circa '55 was impressed by the passages reflecting shiny auto fenders in plate-glass.—"Lord, I scribbled hymns to you"—nobody else says anything like that, not Mailer Genet Céline . . . "hundreds of death-conscious boys."

I worship Jack's candid observation of inner consciousness manifested in solitude, the girl eating in Cafeteria, a complete world satori. Here as distinct from his critic P., Kerouac is present in the world solitary musing, observing actual event, "mind clamped down on objects" completely anonymous, in a single universe of perception with no mental manoeuvers or selfconscious manipulation of any reader's mind (he's writing for no reader but his own intelligent self)—completely *here*, watching the world—not generalizing in a study, but sketching solitude Mannahatta's cafeteria—"She just blew her nose daintily with a napkin; has private personal sad manners, at least externally, by which she makes her own formal existence known to herself . . ."

Great ringing historical lines: "I accept lostness forever. Everything belongs to me because I am poor." Complete prophecy Dream 1951–1973: "A Ritz Yale Club Party . . . hundreds of kids in leather jackets instead of big tuxedo . . . everybody smoking marijuana, wailing a new decade in one wild *crowd*" . . . in a single parenthesis, a whole American future style's prophecied. This book, then, an education on perceptions of the mind Person: "and I dig *you* as we together dig the lostness and the fact that of course nothing's ever to be gained but death." Thus a panoramic consciousness, "The wide surroundment brooding over him . . ." (K.'d been reading Melville's *Pierre*), "long ago in the red sun."

"The unspeakable visions of the individual . . . the joy of downtown city night . . . the red brick wall behind the red neons . . . the poor hidden brick of America . . . the center of the grief . . . America's a lonely crockashit . . . And so I struggle in the dark with the enormity of my soul, trying desperately to be a great rememberer redeeming life from darkness."

Thousands of children now, millions of children now, orphaned in America by the war, crying for the United States to repent and love them again.

The Tape: a new section of the novel, begins, if anybody doesn't know, how could they? Cody (Neal) telling Jack the story of what it was like summer 1947, Cody and myself hitched from Denver to New Waverly Texas to Bull Hubbard's (Bill Burroughs') marijuana garden farm in E. Texas bayou country; recollection for the great rememberer of our *Green Automobile* vow. Of course Cody wasn't entirely romantically frank with Jack—We vowed to own and accept each other's bodies and souls & help each other into Heaven, while on earth, One Person. And the incident of the bed never did get told—tho it dominates 30 pages of conversation: Cody and I had no mutual Texas bed to sleep together in, I was eager, so tried to build one out of 2 army cots with Huck's (Huncke's) help a miserable symbolic failure, sagged in the middle. "I couldn't stand him touching me," says Cody somewhere. He didn't help build the love bed, tho I pleaded.

The entire tape section's a set of nights on newly discovered Grass,* wherein these souls explored the mind blanks impressions that tea creates: that's the subject, unaltered & unadorned—halts, switches, emptiness, quixotic chatters, summary piths, exactly reproduced, significant because:

1) Vocal familiar friendly teahead life talk had never been transcribed and examined consciously (like Warhol 20 years later examined Campbell's Soup cans).

2) Despite monotony, the gaps and changes (like Warhol watching Empire State Bldg. all night) are dramatic.

3) It leads somewhere, like life.

4) It's interesting if you want the characters' reality.

5) It's real.

6) It's art because at that point in progress of Jack's art he

---

*Incidentally, Neal spent several years in jail a decade later, & lost his family type RR job he revered so stably for years, as result of giving a couple joints to a carful of Agents who gave him a ride to work. So he was an early "political prisoner."

began transcribing *first* thoughts of true mind in American speech, and as objective sample of that teahead-high speech of his model hero, he placed uncorrected tape central in his book, actual sample-reality he was otherwhere rhapsodizing.

Art lies in the consciousness of doing the thing, in the attention to the happening, in the sacramentalization of everyday reality, the God-worship in the present conversation, no matter what. Thus the tape may be read not as hung-up which it sometimes is to the stranger, but as a spontaneous Ritual performed once and never repeated, in full consciousness that every yawn & syllable uttered would be eternal . . . the tape coheres together with serious solemn discussion of their lives.

Jack Kerouac's style of transcription of taped conversation is, also, impeccably accurate in syntax punctuation—separation of elements for clarity . . . labeling of voices, parenthesizing of interruptions. A model to study.

Concluding we see the beauty of the tapes that Jack cherished, that they are inclusive samples of complete exchange of information and love thoughts between two men, each giving his mind history to the other—The remarkable situation, which we are privileged to witness thru these creaky tapes transcribed by now dead hand, is—of Kerouac the great rememberer on quiet evenings 1950 to 1951 with Neal Cassady, the great experiencer & midwest driver and talker, gossiping intimately of their eternities—here's representative sample of these evenings, and we can take as model their exchange and see that our own lives also have secrets, mysteries, explanations and love equal to those of feeble, seeking heroes past—Another generation has followed, perhaps surpassed, Neal & Jack conversing in midnight intimacy—if it hasn't discovered that "huge confessional night" then this tape transcript is fit model. If it's surpassed—more coherent these days—I doubt it!?! But then, this is ancient history—if History's interesting now that America has near destroyed the human compassionate world still surviving as in fragments of bewildering conversation between these two dead souls.

There follows an "Imitation of the Tape in Heaven," taking off from Black Preacher calling Jesus in the night, inspired rhythmic babble, gemmy little fragments of literature, by now K.'d obviously given up entirely on American Lit., and let his mind loose. Thus proceeds analysis of his fall from College Window innocence, & American innocence too—where the "alienation" is now obvious & frightful filled with Jelly Bombs Fragmentation Nazi Electronic Good American Monster Phoenix Assassination Central Dope Intelligence News Conditions—Back in 1951–52 Jack saw it as a change of insouciance, going into a bar . . . something as subtle as that . . . "There's no neighborhood any more"—and that's his first *Town & the City* tragic theme. "Beyond this old honesty there can only be thieves," and that means Nixon & Bebe Rebozo. So that "Looking at a man in the eye is now queer." A perfect expression (p. 300) in Whitmanic terms, of what went wrong with American males, muscle biceps tensely meet on the street: "Low panhandler homosexual dopefiend nigger Communist" paranoia.

Later an explanation for this journey across U.S. is given complete: "At the junction of the state line of Colorado . . . go moan for man . . . go thou, go thou, die hence; and of Cody report you well and truly"—What American poet ever had more sad & beautiful directions, commands from the God muse? more prophetic, yet more anonymously erranded?

Thence into the book, a New Neal after *On the Road*—That period is covered in *Visions of Cody* for those who'd ever wish'd a historic sequel—What happened to Dean Pomeray, settled and married—? Kerouac's golden dreams come true—and a prophecy:

"War will be impossible when marijuana becomes legal." How truly lovely the primitive faith, in depths of 1951 cop-lobbied national Dope Fiend Hallucination, that his private experience of grass would become, as it *did*, a national experience?

"*Everything always all right*"—afternoons together, Americans, working on the railroad—at that time no guilt, even the sticky hot tar and rail smoke soot a sort of golden afternoon's honest perfume—before the murder of Indians came to consciousness in America. Way before Neal's bust, this was just before Dulles & Ike & Everyone Spellman started Vietnam War Indochina.

Heavenly Cody soliloquizes: "Our common death in this skeletal earth & billion particle'd grey moth void one empty huge horror and glory isn't it awful . . . Adieu Sweet Jack, the air of life is permeated with roses all the time," he has Neal say and himself reply, "I heard you, I sure do know it now," to Neal's speech, "I love you, man, you've got to dig that; boy you've got to know." Whitman's Adhesiveness! Sociability without genital sexuality between them, but adoration and love, light as America promised in Love.

The New Consciousness is early pronounced here, an old consciousness already forgotten since the good grey bard's 19th century yore; and among these prophecies the reader finds Kerouac's completely *written* Peyote text, total explanations of states of consciousness, "This thing is the realization of suicide, your mind tells you how you can die, take your pick; I see"— perfect mind-changes of peyote recorded, a brilliant contribu- tion to the literature, and early O hippies, how early his tragic common sense and un-drunk humanity squinting undismayed dismayed at the cactus "with his big lizard hide & poison hole buttons with wild hair, grooking in the desert to eat our hearts alive, ach. . . . Cody, this is the end of the heart." Follows the funniest description of Mr. Peyote writ ever.

And after Peyote vision of their life together in moth-wracked joyful trembling stomach-ghost-horror glory—he begins to try nail down the exact places & visions he loved Neal in.* And "the great spindly tin-like crane towers of transterritorial elec- tric power wires . . . pagodas of Japan hung in a grey mist . . . marching to the beat of Bethlehem steel hammers" can still be seen year after year speeding north on Bayshore beneath San Francisco's hills, where Neal & Jack worked the railroad.

At last, reveal'd, Kerouac's memory of the time Cody fuck'd the car driving "pansy" they traveled east with—This reference alas was excised from *On the Road* thus removing one dimen- sion of American Hero and misleading thousands of highschool boys for decades—A vigorous description & very Shakespere- funny's given, tho Jack in the toilet watching quoting Céline, "It's not in my line," probably should have got into the act for

*The bus station photograph described p. 343, Neal in pinstripe suit—can be seen p. 22 *Scenes Along the Road*, Ed. Ann Charters, Portents/Gotham Book Mart, New York City, 1970.

his own happy good, not drunk himself to death later with sin-
ful visions like "at one point it appeared Cody had thrown him
over legs in the air like a dead hen" . . . ouch. . . . No wonder,
"Slambanging sodomies that made me sick." Well I enjoyed
both Cody and Jack, many times in many ways jolly bodily and
in soul love, and wish Jack had been physically tenderer to Cody
or vice versa, done 'em both good, some love balm over that
bleak manly power they had, displayed, were forced to endure
and die with.

"I'm writing this book because we're all going to die . . . my
heart broke in the general despair and opened up inwards to
the Lord, I made a supplication in this dream." This is the
most sincere and holy writing I know of our age—at the same
time for Pre-Buddhist Jack, a complete display of knowledge of
Noble Truths he soon discovered in Goddard's *Buddhist Bible*.
  Yet Jack had another 18 years ahead with Neal on earth, neither was dead ("Neal is Dead"), except this vision book was all
out effort to understand early in the midst of life, what Jack's
yearning and Neal's response and both their mortal American
energy was all about, was directed to—but only time could
tell, & both got tired *several* times—Jack went on to write not
only *Dr. Sax* but *Mexico City Blues* in the next year & then *The
Subterraneans* & *Springtime Mary (Maggie Cassidy)* and more
and more and more climaxed 5 years later with some fame, and
the brilliant Buddhist exposition *Dharma Bums*, and also *Desolation Angels* later, to keep the perfect chronicle going—"rack
my hand with labor of Nada"—and many poems—not to speak
of his *Book of Dreams* and giant as-yet-unpublished *Some of the
Dharma*, 1000 pages of haikus, meditations, readings, com-
mentaries on Prajnaparamita & Diamond Sutras, brain-thinks,
Samadhi notes, scholarship in the Void—reading Shakespere
& Melville all the while & listening to Bach's St. Matthew's
Passion evermore—

Saying farewell to Cody, Jack was saying farewell to the World,
both of them gave up several times—But at that 1952 time both
of them were at their wits' ends with the world and America—
The "Beat Generation" was about that time formulated, the
Vietnam War just about to be continued American bodied

(as 'twas already funded American dollar'd via opium push-ing France & French-Corsican Intelligence agencies)—Two years after completion of this book Neal lived in a quiet home, receptive and friendly but by then entered into a blank new insistent religiosity, "like Billy Sunday in a suit" epistled Jack, namely Edgar Cayce study—which reincarnation philosophy drove Jack to study Buddhism; a new phase not even recorded or mentioned in this vast essay on Early or Middle Neal.

I remember the sleepless epiphanies of 1948—everywhere in American brain-consciousness was waking up, from Times Square to the banks of Willamette River to Berkeley's groves of Academe: little Samadhis and appreciations of intimate spaci-ness that might later be explain'd and followed as the Crazy Wisdom of Rinzai Zen or the Whispered Transmission of Red Hat Vajrayana Path Doctrine, or Coyote's empty yell in the Sierras. Out of Burroughs' copy of Spengler Kerouac arrived at the conception of "Fellaheen Eternal Country Life"—Country Samadhi for Jack, country Ken & consciousness latent discov-ered in Mexico as our heroes crossed the border: immediate recognition of Biblical Patriarch Type in Mexic Fellaheen fa-thers: the Bible those days the only immediate American mind-entry to primeval earth-consciousness non-machine populace that inhabits 80 per cent of the world—"Jeremiacal hoboes lounge, shepherds by trade . . . I can see the hand of God. The future's in Fellaheen. At Actopan this biblical plateau begins—it's reached by the mountain of faith only. I know that I will someday live in a land like this. I did long ago." Heartbreaking prophecy. And intelligent Neal'd said, "What they want has already crumbled in a rubbish heap—they want banks."

Jack Kerouac didn't write this book for money, he wrote it for love, he *gave* it away to the world; not even for fame, but as an explanation and prayer to his fellow mortals, and gods—with naked motive, and humble piety Search—that's what makes *Visions of Cody* a work of primitive genius that grooks next to Douanier Rousseau's visions, and sits well-libraried beside Thomas Wolfe's *Time & River* (which Thos. Mann from his European eminence said was the great prose of America) & sits beside Tolstoi for its *prayers*. A La La Ho!

So we see the end of the American road is the U.S. boy's

conscious discovery of the eternal natural man, primitive, ancient Biblical or Josephaic Shepherd idiotically stark sanely presented on p. 452—A quote from the mustached Vice Regent Consult of Empire next to a quote from Jackey Keracky:

"False nonsense"—Acheson, 1952
"You've got to legalize the Fellaheen"—Duluoz, 1952

And why this paean to Neal? It's a consistent panegyric to heroism of mind, to the American Person that Whitman sought to adore. And now, "The holy Coast is done, the holy Road is over." Jack thought Cody'd gone back to California Marriage, would settle down be silent & die of old age—Little he knew the Psychedelic Bus, as if *On the Road* were transported to Heav'n, would ride on the road again through America, the Great Vehicle painted rainbow colored as Mahayana illusion with its tantric Kool-aid & Celestial passengers playing their Merry Pranks "Further" thru the land, "A vote for Goldwater is a Vote for Fun" sign painted on bus-side, en route to find sad drunken Jack, enthusiastic but speechless high bring him to Acid Apartment on Park Avenue crowded at midnight with 50 Prankster bus passengers all cynically expectant jester-dressed & starry eyed worshipping—The old red faced W. C. Fields Toad Guru trembling sly hungover sick potbellied Master tenderly came back to the city afraid to drink himself to death—A Park Avenue apartment the site for Great Union Reunion Kerouac Cassady Kesey & Friends all together at last once in New York under unofficial mock but real Klieg lights with microphones reverb feedback wires snaking all over th'electrified household living room floor 86th St. upper East Side—An American Flag draped over couch, on which shocked Jack refused to sit—Kesey respectful welcoming and silent, fatherly timid host, myself marveling and sad, it was all out of my hands now, History was even out of Jack's hands now, he'd already written in 15 years before, he could only watch hopelessly one of his more magically colored prophecy shows, the Hope Show of Ghost Wisdoms made modern Chemical & Mechanic, in this Kali Yuga, he knew the worser death gloom to come, already on him in his alcohol ridden trembling no longer sexually tender corpus—Anyway, O clouds over Tetons, great Rain clouds over Idaho, lowbellied cumulus over Gros Ventre rain!—the conversation in that brilliant lit apartment Manhattan 1967 was sparse halting sad disappointing yet absolutely real, & thus recorded on tape as Jack already did, as well as (new era technology 15 years later Spenglerean time) on Film! O rain spoils't thou man's toys & images? Washest Time? And then the Bright Vast Bus on the magic road went honking up to Dr. Leary's Millbrook tantric mansion, what eras're ushered in on us?

The last pages say, "All America marching to this last land." The book was a dirge for America, for its heroes' deaths too, but then who could know except in the unconscious—A dirge for the American Hope that Jack (& his hero Neal) carried so valiantly through the land after Whitman—an America of pioneers and generosity—and selfish glooms & exploitations implicit in the pioneers' entry into Foreign Indian & Moose lands—but the great betrayal of that manly America was made by the pseudo-heroic pseudo-responsible masculines of Army and Industry and Advertising and Construction and Transport and toilets and Wars.

Last pages—how tender—"Adios King!" a farewell to all the promises of America, an explanation & prayer for innocence, a tearful renunciation of victory & accomplishment, a humility in the face of "the necessary blankness of men" in hopeless America, hopeless World, in hopeless wheel of Heaven, a compassionate farewell to Love & the Companion, Adios King.

May 17, 1972—Denver————June 9, 1972—Rendezvous Mountain, Tetons, Wyo. ALLEN GINSBERG

Chronology

1922 Born Jean-Louis Kerouac on March 12 at the family home at 9 Lupine Road in Lowell, Massachusetts, the third child of Joseph Alcide Leon (Leo) Kerouac and Gabrielle Lévesque Kerouac, and is baptized at St. Louis-de-France Church on March 19. (Father, born 1889 in St. Hubert, Quebec, immigrated with his family to Nashua, New Hampshire, where he learned printing. He later moved to Lowell, where he became the manager and printer of *L'Etoile*, a weekly French newspaper, and sold insurance. Mother, born 1895 in St. Pacome, Quebec, also immigrated as a child to Nashua. Orphaned at age 16, she was working in a shoe factory when she married Leo Kerouac on October 25, 1915. Their first son, Gerard, was born on August 23, 1916, and their daughter Caroline was born on October 25, 1918.) Family speaks French-Canadian dialect at home.

1923 Father opens his own print shop in Lowell.

1925 Family moves to 35 Burnaby Street. Gerard becomes seriously ill with rheumatic fever.

1926 Family moves to 34 Beaulieu Street. Gerard dies on June 2.

1927 Family moves to 320 Hildreth Street.

1928 Kerouac enters St. Louis-de-France parochial school, where classes are taught in both English and French. Family moves to 240 Hildreth Street.

1930 Family moves to 66 West Street.

1932 Family leaves Centralville section of Lowell and moves to Phebe Avenue in the Pawtucketville section, where father becomes the manager of a social club. Kerouac attends St. Joseph's parochial school.

1933–35 Enters Bartlett Junior High School in 1933, where all classes are conducted in English. Begins keeping his first journals and records his achievements in sports. Develops a baseball game played with cards, marbles, and dice, and invents an imaginary league and fictitious players. Writes short stories, draws cartoons, and invents mysterious character "Dr. Sax." Reads extensively in school and at the public library.

1936   Merrimack River floods in March, causing extensive damage
            to father's print shop. Family moves to 35 Sarah Avenue.
            Kerouac enters Lowell High School in the tenth grade.

1937–39   Excels in sports, especially as a sprinter in track and a
            running back in football. Reads Thomas Wolfe, William
            Saroyan, Henry David Thoreau, Mark Twain, and others.
            Father sells his shop in 1937 and becomes a printer for hire
            while mother begins working in a shoe factory; financial
            strain is increased by father's gambling and drinking. Family
            moves to tenement at 736 Moody Street. Kerouac becomes
            close friends with Sebastian Sampas and discusses litera-
            ture, philosophy, and politics with him and a small group
            of friends (who for a time call themselves the Young Pro-
            metheans). On Thanksgiving 1938, scores winning touch-
            down for Lowell High School against local rival Lawrence.

1939–40   Graduates from Lowell High School on June 28, 1939. Re-
            ceives football scholarship from Columbia University on
            condition that he attend Horace Mann, a preparatory school
            in the Bronx, for a year. Lives with his mother's stepmother
            in Brooklyn and commutes to school by subway. Publishes
            his first fiction in the *Horace Mann Quarterly* and is intro-
            duced to live jazz in Harlem by classmate Seymour Wyse.
            Writes about jazz and sports for the school newspaper.

1940   Enters Columbia in September. Fractures tibia in his right
            leg during his second game with the freshman squad and
            spends months recuperating.

1941   Receives high grades in French and literature courses but
            fails chemistry. Spends summer in Lowell and in New
            Haven, where his parents move in August. Returns to
            Columbia in September. Quarrels with the coaching staff,
            quits the football team, and leaves school. Moves to Hart-
            ford, Connecticut, where he works as a gas station atten-
            dant and writes a short story collection, "Atop an Under-
            wood" (some of the stories are posthumously published
            in *Atop an Underwood: Early Stories and Other Writing*
            in 1999). Returns to Lowell when his parents move back
            to the city. Registers for naval aviation training after the
            Japanese bomb Pearl Harbor. Becomes a sports reporter
            for the *Lowell Sun* while waiting to be called up.

1942   Quits the *Sun* in March and goes to Washington, D.C., where he works on the construction of the Pentagon and as a short-order cook. Returns to Lowell, then joins the Merchant Marine and sails from Boston in July as a scullion on the army transport ship *Dorchester*. Sails along the Greenland coast before returning to Boston in October. (The *Dorchester* is sunk by a German submarine on February 3, 1943, with the loss of 675 lives.) Accepts invitation to rejoin the Columbia football squad, but quits after he is benched during the Army game. Stays in New York during the fall and begins affair with Edie Parker (b. 1922), an art student from Grosse Pointe, Michigan. Works on novel *The Sea Is My Brother* (published in 2011). Returns to Lowell in December.

1943   Fails examination for flight training and is sent in March to naval boot camp in Newport, Rhode Island, where he is committed to the base hospital for psychiatric observation after repeated acts of insubordination. Transferred to Bethesda, Maryland, where he is diagnosed as having "schizoid tendencies" and given a psychiatric discharge from military service. Joins his parents, who are now living at 94-10 Cross Bay Boulevard in Ozone Park, Queens, New York. Rejoins the Merchant Marine and sails from New York in September on the *George Weems*, a Liberty ship carrying bombs to Liverpool. Returns to New York in October. Divides his time between Ozone Park and apartment on West 118th Street that Edie Parker shares with Joan Vollmer Adams. Meets Columbia undergraduate Lucien Carr (b. 1925).

1944   Introduced by Carr to William S. Burroughs (b. 1917), Columbia undergraduate Allen Ginsberg (b. 1926), and David Kammerer (b. 1911), Carr's former scoutmaster who had followed him to New York from St. Louis. Sebastian Sampas dies on March 2 after being wounded while serving as an army medic on the Anzio beachhead in Italy. Works on *Galloway*, novel that eventually becomes *The Town and the City*. Carr fatally stabs Kammerer in Riverside Park on August 14, then visits Kerouac, who helps Carr dispose of his knife and Kammerer's glasses. Kerouac is arrested as a material witness after Carr turns himself in and is jailed when his father refuses to post bail. Marries Edie Parker in a civil ceremony on August 22 and is released after she obtains bail money from her family. They move to Grosse Pointe, Michigan, where Kerouac works in a ball-bearing factory. (Carr pleads guilty to manslaughter and serves two years in prison.) Sails from New York in October on the Liberty ship *Robert Treat Paine*, but jumps ship in Norfolk, Virginia, and returns to New York. On November 16 Kerouac estimates that he has written 500,000 words since 1939, including "nine unfinished novels." (One of these is published as *The Haunted Life* in 2014.) Edie returns to New York at Christmas and they move in with Joan Vollmer Adams in apartment on West 115th Street.

1945   Kerouac and Burroughs collaborate on *And the Hippos Were Boiled in Their Tanks*, a novel based on the Kammerer-Carr case (published 2008). Explores the Times Square underworld with Burroughs and Herbert Huncke, a drug addict, petty thief, and street hustler. Completes novella *Orpheus Emerged* (published in 2002). Separates from Edie during the summer. Helps care for his father, who has stomach cancer. Hospitalized in December with thrombophlebitis, a debilitating circulatory condition in the legs possibly related to his 1940 football injury; Kerouac also attributes his illness to his heavy use of Benzedrine and marijuana.

1946   Kerouac, Burroughs, and Ginsberg are interviewed for the Alfred Kinsey study *Sexual Behavior in the Human Male* (published in 1948). Father dies on May 17 and is buried with Gerard in Nashua. Kerouac continues work on *The Town and the City*. Agrees to Edie Parker's request that their marriage be annulled. In December Kerouac is introduced by his friend Hal Chase to Neal Cassady (b. 1926), a self-educated car thief and hustler from Denver who is visiting New York with his wife, Luanne.

1947   Travels to North Carolina in June to visit his sister, Caroline, and her second husband, Paul Blake. Leaves New York in July to visit Cassady and Ginsberg in Denver, traveling by bus to Chicago and then hitchhiking the rest of the way. Meets Carolyn Robinson, a graduate student at the University of Denver (she and Cassady marry in April 1948). Travels by bus in August to San Francisco, where Henri Cru (a friend from Horace Mann) gets him a job as a security guard in Marin City. Travels through California before returning to New York in October.

1948 Completes first draft of *The Town and the City* in May. Begins writing an early version of *On the Road*. Visits sister in Rocky Mount, North Carolina, in June after the birth of his nephew Paul Blake Jr. Meets writer John Clellon Holmes in July. Takes literature courses taught by Elbert Lenrow and Alfred Kazin at the New School for Social Research in New York. Cassady arrives in Rocky Mount while Kerouac is visiting his sister at Christmas and drives with him back to New York.

1949 Leaves New York in January with Cassady, Luanne, and Al Hinkle and drives to Algiers, Louisiana, where they visit Burroughs and Joan Vollmer Adams, who have been living together for several years. Continues on to San Francisco with Cassady and Luanne, then returns to New York by bus in February. Columbia professor Mark Van Doren recommends *The Town and the City* to Robert Giroux at Harcourt, Brace, who offers Kerouac a $1,000 advance in late March. Kerouac and Giroux work on cutting and revising the manuscript. Moves to Denver in May and rents house at 61 West Center Street in Westwood. Continues working on *On the Road*. Travels to San Francisco in August, then drives back to New York with Cassady, visiting Edie in Grosse Pointe along the way. Moves in with his mother at 94-21 134th Street in Richmond Hill, Queens.

1950 *The Town and the City* is published on March 2; it receives mixed reviews and sells poorly. Travels to Denver in May, then drives with Cassady to Mexico City, where he visits Burroughs. Returns to New York in August. Meets Joan Haverty (b. 1931) on November 3 and marries her in a civil ceremony on November 17. They live in a loft on West 21st Street, then move in with Kerouac's mother in Queens. Receives a long letter from Neal Cassady in December. (Kerouac will later say that Cassady's "fast, mad, confessional" letters inspired "the spontaneous style of *On the Road*.")

1951 Moves to a studio apartment at 454 West 20th Street in Manhattan with Joan, who is working in a department store. Begins new version of *On the Road* on April 2 and types it in three weeks on a 120-foot-long paper scroll. Separates from Joan and moves in with Lucien Carr and Allen Ginsberg. Denies paternity when Joan tells him she is pregnant with his child. Robert Giroux rejects the scroll version of *On the Road*. Hires Rae Everitt of MCA as his literary agent. Suffers severe attack of thrombophlebitis while visiting his sister in North Carolina. Enters Kingsbridge VA Hospital in the Bronx in August. Burroughs accidentally kills Joan Vollmer Adams in Mexico City on September 7 after she drunkenly challenges him to shoot a glass off her head. Kerouac leaves the hospital in September and returns to Richmond Hill. Begins rewriting *On the Road* in an even more spontaneous form (reworked version is posthumously published as *Visions of Cody* in 1972). Moves to San Francisco in December to live with Neal and Carolyn Cassady and their children at 29 Russell Street.

1952   Works as baggage handler for the Southern Pacific Railroad. Receives $250 advance for *On the Road* from Ace Books. Daughter Janet Michelle Kerouac is born in Albany on February 16. Kerouac begins affair with Carolyn Cassady. Drives with the Cassadys to the Arizona-Mexico border, then takes bus to Mexico City, where he stays with Burroughs. Writes *Doctor Sax*, May–June. Joins his mother and sister in North Carolina in July, then moves in with the Cassadys in San Jose in September. Works as a brakeman for the Southern Pacific. Begins keeping dream journals later published as *Book of Dreams*. Lives in a skid row hotel in San Francisco for a month because of the tension caused by his affair with Carolyn Cassady, then returns to San Jose in November. John Clellon Holmes publishes novel *Go*, in which Kerouac is fictionalized as Gene Pasternak, and "This Is the Beat Generation," an essay in the November 16 *New York Times Magazine*. Kerouac travels to Mexico City with Neal Cassady, then returns to his mother in Queens.

1953   Writes *Maggie Cassidy*. Meets with Malcolm Cowley of Viking Press to discuss the possible publication of his work. Travels in April to San Luis Obispo, California, where he again works for the Southern Pacific. Leaves job in May and sails from San Francisco to New Orleans as a kitchen worker on the S.S. *William Carruthers*. Returns to Queens in June. Writes *The Subterraneans*, October 21–24. In response to questions about his composition methods from Ginsberg and Burroughs, writes "Essentials of Spontaneous Prose."

1954   Leaves New York in late January to live with the Cassadys in San Jose. Works as a parking-lot attendant and studies Buddhist texts. Returns to his mother in Queens in April.

Hires Sterling Lord as his literary agent (Lord will represent him for the rest of Kerouac's life). Works on *Some of the Dharma* (posthumously published in 1997). Malcolm Cowley publishes essay in *The Saturday Review* in August in which he credits Kerouac with inventing the phrase "beat generation" and writes: "his long unpublished narrative, *On the Road*, is the best record of their lives." Kerouac visits Lowell in October.

1955 In January Alfred A. Knopf becomes the sixth publisher to reject *On the Road*. Joan Haverty takes Kerouac to court seeking child support, but his lawyer, Eugene Brooks (Allen Ginsberg's brother), succeeds in having the case postponed because of Kerouac's recurring phlebitis. Kerouac and his mother move to North Carolina, where he writes *Wake Up: A Life of the Buddha* (published 2008). "Jazz of the Beat Generation," excerpted from *On the Road* and *Visions of Cody*, appears in *New World Writing* in April. Travels to Mexico City in July. Begins *Tristessa* and *Mexico City Blues* before going to San Francisco in September. Meets the poets Kenneth Rexroth, Lawrence Ferlinghetti, Michael McClure, Philip Lamantia, Philip Whalen, and Gary Snyder. Attends poetry reading at the Six Gallery in San Francisco on October 7 where Allen Ginsberg reads from *Howl* for the first time. Visits the Sawtooth Mountains of Idaho with Gary Snyder in October. Rides freight cars through California. *The Paris Review* publishes "The Mexican Girl," another excerpt from *On the Road*. Kerouac returns to North Carolina and begins *Visions of Gerard* on December 27.

1956 Completes *Visions of Gerard* on January 16. Hitchhikes to California in March. Lives with Gary Snyder in a cabin in Mill Valley, where he writes *Old Angel Midnight* (posthumously published in 1993) and *The Scripture of the Golden Eternity*. Hitchhikes in June to Mount Baker National Forest in northern Washington. Works for two months as a firewatcher in the Cascade Mountains, staying in a lookout cabin on Desolation Peak. Returns to San Francisco in September before going to Mexico City, where he begins *Desolation Angels*. Ginsberg's *Howl and Other Poems* is published by City Lights Books. Kerouac returns to New York in November. Viking Press accepts *On the Road* for publication.

1957   Makes his final revisions to *On the Road* in January. (Vi-
            king had insisted that names and locations in the book be
            changed to avoid possible libel suits.) Begins affair with
            writer Joyce Glassman (b. 1935, later Joyce Johnson). Sails
            in February for Tangier, where he visits Burroughs and
            helps type his novel *Naked Lunch* (a title originally sug-
            gested by Kerouac for a different manuscript). Visits Paris
            and London in April before returning to New York. Moves
            with his mother to Berkeley, California, in May, but in July
            they move to Orlando, Florida, where his sister is now liv-
            ing. Visits Mexico City, then goes back to New York. *On
            the Road* is published on September 5, becomes a bestseller,
            and makes Kerouac a national celebrity. (In *The New York
            Times*, critic Gilbert Millstein calls it "the most beautifully
            executed, the clearest, and the most important utterance
            yet made by the generation Kerouac himself named years
            ago as 'beat,' and whose principal avatar he is.") Despite the
            success of *On the Road*, Viking rejects all of Kerouac's un-
            published manuscripts, including *Doctor Sax*, *Tristessa*, and
            Desolation Angels. Writes play *Beat Generation* (published
            in 2005) and novel *The Dharma Bums* in Orlando during
            the fall. Returns to New York in late December to give a
            series of readings with live jazz backing.

1958   Gives series of interviews, including one with Mike Wallace
            for the *New York Post*. *The Subterraneans* is published by
            Grove Press in February and receives almost entirely bad
            reviews. Buys house at 34 Gilbert Avenue in Northport,
            Long Island. Suffers broken arm, broken nose, and possible
            concussion when he is beaten outside a bar in Greenwich
            Village. *San Francisco Chronicle* columnist Herb Caen uses
            the term "beatnik" in print for the first time on April 2.
            Kerouac drives from New York to Florida and back with
            photographer Robert Frank. Moves into Northport home
            with his mother in April. Begins sketches later published as
            Lonesome Traveler. Neal Cassady begins serving sentence
            for marijuana trafficking in July (he is released from San
            Quentin in the summer of 1960). *The Dharma Bums* is
            published by Viking on October 2. Affair with Joyce Glass-
            man ends. Kerouac's health worsens as the result of years
            of heavy drinking and Benzedrine use.

1959   Records narration for improvised Beat film *Pull My Daisy*,
            directed by Robert Frank and painter Alfred Leslie. Writes

introduction for the U.S. edition of Frank's photographic collection *The Americans*. Grove Press publishes *Doctor Sax* as a trade paperback in April, and *Maggie Cassidy* is published as a mass-market paperback by Avon in July. Kerouac begins writing column for *Escapade* magazine. Moves to 49 Earl Avenue in Northport with his mother. Travels to Los Angeles in November and reads from *Visions of Cody* on the Steve Allen television show. *Mexico City Blues* is published by Grove Press. On November 30 *Life* magazine publishes "Beats: Sad But Noisy Rebels," article by staff writer Paul O'Neil attacking Kerouac and Neal Cassady.

1960   Works on *Lonesome Traveler* and *Book of Dreams*. Totem Press publishes *The Scripture of the Golden Eternity*. Avon publishes *Tristessa* as a mass-market paperback in June. Film version of *The Subterraneans*, directed by Ranald MacDougall, is a critical and commercial failure (Kerouac received $15,000 for the film rights). Spends summer at Lawrence Ferlinghetti's cabin in Bixby Canyon in Big Sur, where he suffers mental breakdown while trying to deal with his worsening alcoholism. Sees Carolyn Cassady for the last time before returning to Long Island in September. *Lonesome Traveler*, a collection of travel pieces, is published by McGraw-Hill on September 27.

1961   Meets Timothy Leary in January with Ginsberg and takes LSD. *Book of Dreams* is published by City Lights Books. Leaves Northport and moves with his mother in April to 1309 Alfred Drive in Orlando. Spends a month in Mexico City during the summer and completes the second part of *Desolation Angels*. In August *Confidential* magazine publishes "My Ex-Husband Jack Kerouac Is an Ingrate," article detailing Joan Haverty Aly's ongoing attempts to collect child support from Kerouac. Writes *Big Sur* in Orlando, September 30–October 9. Goes on an extended drinking spree in New York in the fall.

1962   Meets his daughter Jan, now 10, for the first time when they undergo blood tests in February, and is ordered to pay $12 a week in child support. Grove Press publishes the first American edition of Burroughs' *Naked Lunch* in March. *Big Sur* is published by Farrar, Straus and Cudahy on September 11. Buys house at 7 Judy Ann Court in Northport and moves there with his mother in December.

1963   Works on novel *Vanity of Duluoz* (a different work from
          unpublished manuscript of 1942). *Visions of Gerard* is pub-
          lished by Farrar, Straus and Cudahy in September and re-
          ceives poor reviews.

1964   Gives drunken reading at Harvard University in March.
          Sees Neal Cassady for the last time when he comes to New
          York City with Ken Kesey and the Merry Pranksters dur-
          ing the summer. Sells Northport house and moves with
          his mother to 5155 Tenth Avenue North in St. Petersburg,
          Florida. Caroline Kerouac Blake dies of a heart attack in
          Orlando on September 19; she is buried in an unmarked
          grave because Kerouac is unable to pay for a headstone.

1965   Suffers two broken ribs when he is attacked in a St. Pe-
          tersburg bar in March. *Desolation Angels* is published by
          Coward-McCann on May 3. Visits Paris and Brittany in
          June in an attempt to research his ancestry. Writes *Satori
          in Paris* soon after his return to Florida.

1966   Moves with his mother in the spring to 20 Bristol Avenue
          in the Cape Cod town of Hyannis, Massachusetts. *Satori
          in Paris* is published by Grove Press. Visited in August by
          Ann Charters, who is compiling his bibliography. (Charters
          will publish the first biography of Kerouac in 1973.) Mother
          suffers massive stroke on September 9 that leaves her para-
          lyzed. Kerouac briefly visits Milan and Rome to promote
          the Italian publication of *Big Sur*. Marries Stella Sampas
          (b. 1918), the sister of his Lowell friend Sebastian Sampas,
          in Hyannis on November 18.

1967   Moves in January with Stella and his mother to house at
          271 Sanders Avenue in Lowell. Completes *Vanity of Duluoz*.
          Gives lengthy interview to the poets Ted Berrigan, Aram
          Saroyan, and Duncan McNaughton for publication in *The
          Paris Review*. Sees his daughter Jan for the second and last
          time in November.

1968   Neal Cassady collapses and dies on February 4 in San
          Miguel de Allende, Mexico. *Vanity of Duluoz* is published
          by Coward-McCann on February 6. Visits Portugal, Spain,
          Switzerland, and Germany in March. Sees Burroughs and
          Ginsberg for the last time in early September when he
          goes to New York for the taping of William F. Buckley's
          television program *Firing Line*. Returns to St. Petersburg,
          moving to 5169 Tenth Avenue North with Stella and his
          mother.

1969   Completes *Pic* (published in 1971). Suffers cracked ribs when he is beaten outside a bar in early September. "After Me, the Deluge," article in which Kerouac disassociates himself from the New Left, appears in the *Chicago Tribune* on September 28. Collapses at home on the morning of October 20 and dies at St. Anthony's Hospital in St. Petersburg on October 21 from massive internal bleeding caused by cirrhosis of the liver. A Requiem Mass is held at St. Jean Baptiste Church in Lowell on October 24, after which Kerouac is buried in Edson Catholic Cemetery.

Note on the Texts

This volume contains three novels by Jack Kerouac: *Visions of Cody* (1972), *Visions of Gerard* (1963), and *Big Sur* (1962). All three were seen by Kerouac as forming part of *The Duluoz Legend*, a multivolume autobiographical saga recording the major events of the author's life.

Kerouac began composing *Visions of Cody* in 1951. He completed it in March 1952 while staying in San Francisco with Neal and Carolyn Cassady. The book was originally called *Visions of Neal*, and at one point Kerouac changed the title to *Visions of Enal*. Kerouac considered *Visions of Cody* one of his masterworks, viewing it as a superior telling of the events depicted in his breakthrough novel *On the Road* (1957) and a more definitive literary rendering of Neal Cassady, the central figure of both works. However, *Visions of Cody* met with initial resistance even from Kerouac's close friend Allen Ginsberg (letter, June 11, 1952), who mixed praise ("the inventions have fullblown ecstatic style . . . Where you are writing steadily and well . . . it's the best that is written in America, I do believe") with serious criticism ("It's crazy (not merely inspired crazy) but unrelated crazy"). Kerouac repeatedly submitted *Visions of Cody* to publishers, but the book did not appear in its entirety until 1972, when it was published by McGraw-Hill in New York with an introduction ("The Great Rememberer") by Ginsberg (first published in *Saturday Review* in December 1972), the text of which is reproduced as an appendix to this volume. (A British edition was published at the same time by Andre Deutsch.)

New Directions published *Excerpts from Visions of Cody*, an abridged version of 120 pages in a limited edition of 750 copies signed by Kerouac, in January 1960. Kerouac worked closely with New Directions publisher James Laughlin on the selections. Laughlin inserted a slip describing *Visions of Cody* as "the long novel . . . which is Kerouac's favorite but which is considered unpublishable at present." Kerouac contributed the following statement to the New Directions edition:

VISIONS OF CODY is a 600-page character study of the hero of *On the Road*, "Dean Moriarty," whose name now is "Cody Pomeray." I wanted to put my hand to an enormous paean which would unite my vision of America with words spilled out in the modern spontaneous method. Instead of just a horizontal account of travels on the road, I wanted a vertical, metaphysical study of Cody's character and its relationship to the general "America." This feeling may soon be obsolete as America enters its High Civilization period and no one will get sentimental or poetic any more about trains and dew on fences at dawn in Missouri. This is a youthful book (1951) and it was based on my belief in the goodness of the hero and his position as an archetypical American Man. The tape recordings in here are actual transcriptions I made of conversations with Cody who was so high he forgot the machine was turning. Dean Moriarty becomes Cody Pomeray, Sal Paradise becomes Jack Duluoz, Carlo Marx becomes Irwin Garden and so on in all of my work from now on, published and unpublished, (with the exception of the 1950 fictional novel *The Town and the City*). My work comprises one vast book like Proust's *Remembrance of Things Past* except that my remembrances are written on the run instead of afterwards in a sick bed. Because of the objections of my early publishers I was not allowed to use the same personae names in each work. *On the Road, The Subterraneans, The Dharma Bums, Doctor Sax, Maggie Cassidy, Tristessa, Desolation Angels* and the others are just chapters in the whole work which I call *The Duluoz Legend*. In my old age I intend to collect all my work and reinsert my pantheon of uniform names, leave the long shelf full of books there, and die happy. The whole thing forms one enormous comedy, seen through the eyes of poor Ti Jean (me), otherwise known as Jack Duluoz, the world of raging action and folly and also of gentle sweetness seen through the keyhole of his eye. Thanks to J. Laughlin for helping make this selection of 120 pages.

In addition to the publication of the abridged 1960 version, selections from *Visions of Cody* appeared in a number of magazines and literary journals during Kerouac's lifetime, as listed below:

"Neal and the Three Stooges": *New Editions* 2 (1957).

"October in the Poolhall": *Playboy*, December 1959, as "Before the Road: The Earlier Adventures of Dean Moriarty."

"Three Excerpts from *Visions of Cody*": *The Beats*, edited by Seymour Krim (New York: Gold Medal Books, 1960).

The April 1961 edition of *Escapade* featured a one-page excerpt from *Visions of Cody* as Kerouac's monthly column, "The Last Word."

"Joan Rawshanks in the Fog": *Transatlantic Review* 9 (1962).

"Manhattan Sketches," from the first section of *Visions of Cody: The Moderns*, edited by LeRoi Jones (New York: Corinth Books, 1963).

"October in the Poolhall" (excerpt): *A New Directions Reader* (New York: New Directions, 1964).

"October in the Poolhall" (excerpt): *Ice*, edited by T. Clark (London, 1966).

"October in the Poolhall": *The New Writing in the USA* (London: Penguin UK, 1967).

"First Night of the Tapes": *Transatlantic Review* 33/34 (1969).

"The Mad Road": *Madrugada* 1 (Spring 1970).

An audio version of Kerouac reading "Neal and the Three Stooges" appeared on the LP *Readings by Jack Kerouac on the Beat Generation* (Verve, 1960). The tape recordings whose transcriptions form the central section of *Visions of Cody* are no longer extant, having been lost by either Kerouac or Cassady.

The text of *Visions of Cody* printed here is taken from the 1972 McGraw-Hill edition.

Kerouac began *Visions of Gerard* on New Year's Day 1956 and finished it twelve days later, writing at the kitchen table of his sister Caroline's home in Rocky Mount, North Carolina. It was published by Farrar, Straus and Cudahy in New York in September 1963. (A British edition, also containing Kerouac's *Tristessa*, was published by Andre Deutsch the following year.) The original edition contained illustrations by James Spanfeller; while Kerouac was originally hesitant about including illustrations, he came to appreciate Spanfeller's drawings a great deal and purchased Spanfeller's "Gerard in the Window with Cat and Birds," hanging it on his living room wall. Spanfeller's sketches have been reproduced in this volume. The text of *Visions of Gerard* printed here is taken from the 1963 Farrar, Straus and Cudahy edition.

Big Sur, an account of the time Kerouac spent in Lawrence Ferlinghetti's cabin in Bixby Canyon during the summer of 1960, was composed in Orlando, Florida, in 1961. Kerouac completed the manuscript, typewritten on a teletype roll, over a ten-day period stretching from the end of September through the beginning of October. The book was published by Farrar, Straus and Cudahy in September 1962; a British edition was published by Andre Deutsch in October of the same year. The text of *Big Sur* printed here is taken from the 1962 edition.

This volume presents the texts of the original printings chosen for inclusion, but does not attempt to reproduce nontextual features of their typographical design. The texts are presented without change, except for the correction of typographical errors. Spelling, punctuation, and capitalization are not altered, even when inconsistent or irregular. The following is a list of typographical errors corrected, cited by page and line number: 14.36, Massachussetts; 39.18, stripteaster,; 44.13, Griffiths'; 65.3, Baloon; 72.24, silly-gigling; 85.7, ot weeds; 101.3, gymn; 108.26, seemed; 117.7, Alistair Sims; 126.25, pyschic; 132.32, times." I want; 146.1, Mezrow; 148.7, treestrunk,; 162.1 (and *passim*), Holliday; 187.38, its; 188.33., practic; 192.18, here him; 223.9, its; 226.8 (and *passim*), Petersberg; 253.9, or course; 289.13, Thev; 300.32, orginally,; 316.7, Fransciso; 316.17 (and *passim*), kleig; 319.39, Gaugins; 323.20 (and *passim*), Gherig; 325.23, Collier; 339.27, steets; 345.35, "Yes!" Look; 353.31, Irrelevant; 397.40, If was; 453.18,

comtemplating; 457.35, ("Lester; 463.1–2, Joesphine,; 493.11, commis-
serating; 497.7, this this; 519.4, exhilirates; 520.38, beside; 527.33, desert; 528.3, photopaly; 538.1, thrown; 539.25, it's; 543.10, mater; 544.29,
afteernoon; 554.13, *cricumstantibus*,; 557.7, irrelevencies; 584.20, at the;
599.22, antisepticsm; 611.38, believe; 614.10, girls; 614.21, bad; 622.25,
whith; 625.35, Alisteir; 626.2, books; 629.1, pint; 661.1, out; 671.22,
buy; 676.29, I kill the; 701.11, amphetomine; 710.8, uner arm; 742.25,
eternies; 745.32, Mathew's.

Character Key

Despite Kerouac's preference for using the real names of people he wrote about, Kerouac's publishers over the years, wary of lawsuits, insisted that he create fictional names for himself and the other figures depicted within the *Duluoz* cycle. Kerouac complied with those requests, and often changed these names from work to work. The identities of those portrayed in the novels included here are indicated as thoroughly as possible in the following glossary.

A. Quinn] A. A. Wyn (1898–1967), publisher and editor who founded Ace Books.

Allen Minko] Allan Temko (1924–2006), journalist and architectural critic. Temko won the Pulitzer Prize in 1990 for his architectural criticism published in the *San Francisco Chronicle*.

Ange Duluoz] Gabrielle-Ange Kerouac, née Lévesque (1895–1973), Kerouac's mother.

Armenagé Duluoz] Jean-Baptiste Kerouac (1849–1906), Kerouac's grandfather.

Arthur Ma] Victor Wong (1927–2001), artist and actor.

Aunt Anna] Emma Vaillancourt (1871–1967), Kerouac's aunt on his father's side.

Aunt Clementine] Leontine Kerouac (1882–1975), Kerouac's aunt through her marriage to Joseph Kerouac.

Aunt Marie] In *Visions of Cody*, Marie Harpin (1879–1958), Kerouac's great-aunt on his mother's side; in *Visions of Gerard*, Marie Louise Michaud (1878–1962), Kerouac's aunt on his father's side. Michaud is also referred to as Aunt Louise in *Visions of Gerard*.

Aunt Pauline] Claire Buckley (1894–1979), Kerouac's great-aunt on his mother's side.

Ben Fagan] Philip Whalen (1923–2002), poet.

Bev Watson] Elizabeth Holmes Von Vogt (b. 1932), author and sister of John Clellon Holmes.

Biff Buferd] Bob Burford (1924–2004), whom Kerouac befriended in 1940s Denver.

Billie] See Willamine "Billie" Dabney.

Bob Hindenburg] Bob Brandenburg, New York street criminal whom Kerouac befriended in the mid-1940s.

Boisvert] Robert Giroux (1914–2008), American publisher who edited Kerouac's *The Town and the City* (1950) for Harcourt, Brace & Company.

Buddy Van Buder] Peter Van Meter, friend of Kerouac from New York.

Bull] William S. Burroughs (1914–1997).

Carl Rappaport] Carl Solomon (1928–1993).

Cecily Wayne] Celine Young (1924–1972), with whom Kerouac had a brief affair while she was attending Barnard in 1944.

Charley Bissonnette] Charles Morrisette (1909–1987), first husband of Jack's sister Caroline (or "Nin").

Charley Low] Charley Mew, a merchant seaman friend of Kerouac's.

Cody Pomeray] Kerouac's close friend and muse, Neal Cassady (1926–1968).

Cody Pomeray, Sr.] Neal Marshall Cassady Sr. (1893–1963).

Curt] Curtis Hansen (1950–2014), son of Neal Cassady and Diana Hansen.

Danny Richman] Jerry Newman (1918–1970), recording engineer and founder of the record labels Counterpoint and Esoteric.

Dave Sherman] Frank Jefferies (1923–1996), a friend from Denver who accompanied Kerouac and Neal Cassady to Mexico in 1950. He also appears as Stan Shephard in *On the Road* (1957).

Dave Wain] Lew Welch (1926–1971), poet.

David Stroheim] David Kammerer (1911–1944), New York acquaintance of Kerouac who was stabbed to death in August 1944 by Lucien Carr. Kerouac wrote about the incident a number of times, including in *The Town and the City* (1950), *Vanity of Duluoz* (1968), and the 1945 novel he wrote with William Burroughs, *And the Hippos Were Boiled in Their Tanks* (published 2008).

Deni Bleu] Henri Cru (1921–1992), a lifelong friend of Kerouac. They met as students at Horace Mann in 1939.

Diana Pomeray] Diana Hansen (1923–1974), third wife of Neal Cassady.

Duke Gringas] Odysseus "Duke" Chiungos (1922–2007), football teammate of Kerouac at Lowell High School.

Earl Johnson] Bill Tomson (1929–1982), Denver pool hall friend of Neal Cassady.

Edgar] Armand Kerouac (1914–1999), Kerouac's cousin, a son of Leontine and Joseph Kerouac.

Ed Gray] Ed White (b. 1925), a Columbia friend from the 1940s.

Ed Laurier] Ed Saucier (1912–1962), jazz saxophonist who worked as a session musician for many years.

Ed Wehle] Ed Uhl, Colorado cattle rancher who once employed Neal Cassady. Uhl appears in *On the Road* as Ed Wall.

Ed Williams the Frisco Hipster] Ed Roberts, a San Franciscan introduced to Kerouac and Cassady by the poet Philip Lamantia (1927–2005).

Elliott] Eric Gibson (b. 1957), son of Jacqueline Gibson.

Elly] Edie Parker (1922–1993), Kerouac's first wife.

Emil Duluoz] Leo Kerouac (1889–1946), Kerouac's father.

Emily] Cathleen Cassady (b. 1948), daughter of Carolyn and Neal Cassady.

Evelyn] Carolyn Cassady (1923–2013), artist and wife of Neal Cassady.

Finistra] William Cannastra (1921–1950), a member of the New York Beat scene of the 1940s.

Freddy Strange] Freddy Strong, a San Francisco conga player and singer briefly befriended by Kerouac in the late 1940s.

Gaby] Melany "Jami" Cassady (b. 1950), daughter of Carolyn and Neal Cassady.

George Baso] Albert Saijo (1926–2011), poet.

Gerard Duluoz] Gerard Kerouac (1916–1926), Kerouac's older brother, who died of rheumatic fever at the age of nine.

G. J.] George J. Apostolos (1922–2010), childhood friend of Kerouac from Lowell.

Happy Bernier] Wilfred "Happy" Bertrand (1903–1985), who worked as a club bouncer in Lowell.

Harold Ginsberg] Harold Goldfinger (1906–1989), surrealist poet in postwar Greenwich Village; also referred to as Harry Levinski.

Harper] William Maynard Garver (1894–1957), New York street criminal who befriended the central New York Beat writers during the 1940s. Garver is also mentioned in Ginsberg's "Back on Times Square, Dreaming of Times Square" (1958).

Harry Levinski] Harold Goldfinger (1906–1989), surrealist poet in postwar Greenwich Village; also referred to as Harold Ginsberg.

Helen Buckle] Helen Hinkle (1925–1994), wife of Al Hinkle.

Helen Johnson] Helen Tomson (1925–1979), wife of Bill Tomson.

Henry Wunderdahl] Henry Funderburk, a San Francisco friend of Neal Cassady. Cassady met Funderburk while doing railroad work.

Huck] Herbert Huncke (1915–1996), street hustler and writer.

Ike] Dave Tercerero (1899–1954), Mexico City drug dealer first befriended by William Burroughs.

Irwin Garden] Allen Ginsberg (1926–1997), poet, author of *Howl and Other Poems* (1956).

Irwin Swenson] Alan Ansen (1922–2006), poet.

Jack Duluoz] Jack Kerouac.

Jamie] Jacky Rapinic (see Stanley Popovich).

Jarry Wagner] Gary Snyder (b. 1930), poet and environmentalist. He appears as Japhy Ryder in *The Dharma Bums*.

Jay Chapman] Jay Landesman (1919–2011), founding editor of *Neurotica*.

J. Clancy] John Kelly (1913–1966), writer who provided Kerouac with financial assistance in the early 1950s.

Jerry Fust] Geraldine Lust, a Barnard College friend of Joan Vollmer and Edie Parker.

Jim Evans] Bob Adams, Denver friend of Neal Cassady.

Jimmy Low] In part one of *Visions of Cody*, Charley Mew, a merchant sailor friend of Kerouac from San Francisco; in part three, Charley Ellisor, William Burroughs's neighbor from Texas (although the Jimmy included on the taped conversations is Mew).

Joanna Dawson] Luanne Henderson (1930–2009), first wife of Neal Cassady, who appears as Marylou in *On the Road* (1957).

Jody Mifflin] Rae Everitt, onetime literary agent of Kerouac.

Joe] Michael Fournier Jr.

Joey Rosenberg] Jarry Heiserberg, whom Kerouac befriended in 1960.

John Macy] John Kingsland (1927–1997), Columbia student whom Kerouac befriended during the 1940s.

John Parkman] John Hoffman (1930–1951), surrealist poet.

John Watson] Novelist John Clellon Holmes (1926–1988), author of *Go* (1952).

Jonesy] Les Thompson, a friend of Philip Whalen.

Josephine] Dorothy "Dusty" Moreland, painter.

Josh Hay] Joe May, New York acquaintance of Kerouac in the 1940s.

Julien Love] Lucien Carr (1925–2005), whose "New Vision" was an early formulation of Beat aesthetic philosophy in the 1940s. Carr worked for many years as an editor at United Press International.

June Hubbard] Joan Vollmer Adams (1924–1951), common-law wife of William S. Burroughs.

Justin G. Mannerly] Justin W. Brierly (1905–1984), Denver lawyer who took a mentoring interest in the teenage Neal Cassady.

Kay Blackman] Kay White, the wife of Phil White (see Phil Blackman).

Kevin Cudahy] Dennis Murphy (1932–2005), novelist and screenwriter.

Lanny Meadows] Tom Field (1930–1995), painter.

Layo Bernier] Leontine Bertrand (1905–1962), wife of Wilfred Bertrand.

Lex Pascal] Jay Blaise, painter.

Lionel] Seymour Wyse (b. 1923), whom Kerouac befriended at Horace Mann.

Little Zagg] Jack Melodias, aka Jack Melody, street criminal with ties to organized crime in New York. Kerouac knew Melody through Huncke (see Huck).

Lorenzo Monsanto] Lawrence Ferlinghetti (b. 1919), poet and publisher of City Lights Books.

Louise] In *Visions of Cody* and *Visions of Gerard*, Marie Louise Michaud (1878–1962), Kerouac's aunt on his father's side; in *Big Sur*, Lois Sorrells (b. 1935), with whom Kerouac had a love affair in 1960.

Lousy] Roland Salvas (1922–2004), boyhood friend of Kerouac.

Luke] Paul Blake (1922–1972), Kerouac's brother-in-law.

Mac] John Fitzgerald (b. 1923), Columbia student whom Kerouac met and befriended during the 1940s; also identified as McCarthy.

Mal Damlette] Al Sublette (b. 1931), a merchant seaman friend of Kerouac's.

Manuel] Manuel Santos, onetime business partner of Leo Kerouac. Santos worked alongside Leo at Spotlight Printing in Lowell.

Margaret Cole] Margaret Coffey (b. 1922), one of Kerouac's high school girlfriends.

Maria Calabrese] Maria Livornese (b. 1932) dated Kerouac briefly. She is the younger sister of Tom Livornese (called Tom Calabrese in *Visions of Cody*).

Marian Wilson] Marian Holmes (b. 1923), first wife of John Clellon Holmes.

Markan] Bob Malkin, a New York friend of Neal Cassady during the 1940s.

Matthew Peters] Peter Murray, sailor friend of Henri Cru (see Deni Bleu).

May] Mae Daly (1919–1944), a half sister of Neal Cassady.

McCarthy] John Fitzgerald (b. 1923), Columbia student whom Kerouac met and befriended during the 1940s; also identified as Mac.

Michel Duluoz] Joseph Kerouac (1881–1944), brother of Leo Kerouac.

Nardine] Mardean Butler (1928–2000), aspiring writer whom Kerouac befriended in 1950s New York.

Noel] Raoul Harpin (1915–1993), Kerouac's cousin on his mother's side.

Normie Krall] Norman Schnall (b. 1924), a 1940s New York friend of Kerouac.

Old Mike Fortier] Michael Fournier Sr.

Pat McLear] Michael McClure (b. 1932), poet and playwright.

Paul] Paul Blake (1922–1972), Kerouac's brother-in-law, also referred to as Luke.

Paul Lyman] John Holman, sailor friend of Henri Cru (see Deni Bleu).

Peaches Martin] Ginger Bailey (1928–2006), 1940s Greenwich Village folksinger.

Père Lalumière] Jean Baptiste Labossiere, a priest at St. Louis Parish, Lowell.

Perry Yturbide] Jamie Perpignan, San Francisco acquaintance of Neal Cassady.

Phil Blackman] Phil White, street hustler friend of Herbert Huncke (see Huck), hailing originally from Tennessee.

Pratman] Gershon Legman (1917–1999), writer who edited *Neurotica* with Jay Landesman (see Jay Chapman), 1948–52.

Robert Browning] Robert Lavigne (b. 1928), painter, illustrator, and set designer.

Roland] Herve Kerouac (1915–1971), Kerouac's cousin, a son of Leontine and Joseph Kerouac.

Romana Swartz] Lenore Kandel (1932–2009), poet.

Ron Blake] Paul Smith (b. 1943), musician.

Rosemarie] Natalie Jackson (1925–1955), who worked as an artist's model for Robert Lavigne (see Robert Browning).

Savas Savakis] Sebastian Sampas of Lowell (1922–1944), Kerouac's friend and first literary confidant.

Slim Buckle] Al Hinkle (b. 1926), a friend of Kerouac originally from Denver.

Stanley Popovich] John Rapinic, organizer of the Seven Arts Coffee Gallery Readings in New York during the late 1950s.

Subterranean Irene] Alene Lee (1931–1991); her 1953 love affair with Kerouac served as the basis for *The Subterraneans* (1958). Lee is also credited with typing the letters of William Burroughs and Allen Ginsberg published as *The Yage Letters* (1963).

Ti Jean Duluoz] Jack Kerouac (1922–1969), whose given name was Jean-Louis Kerouac. Kerouac was known affectionately to his family as Ti Jean, or Little John.

Timmy John] John Allen Cassady (b. 1951), son of Neal and Carolyn Cassady.

Tom Calabrese] Tom Livornese (1924–1990), a Columbia student whom Kerouac befriended in 1946.

Tom Watson] Jim Holmes (1926–2002), Denver gambler and pool shark.

Uncle Mike] Joseph Kerouac (1881–1944), Kerouac's uncle on his father's side.

Val Hayes] Hal Chase (b. 1923), Columbia University student whom Kerouac befriended in the early 1940s. Also referred to as Val King in the "Frisco: The Tape" section of *Visions of Cody*.

Vicki] Priscilla Arminger (b. 1924), also known as Vickie Russell, New York acquaintance of Kerouac.

Willamine "Billie" Dabney] Jacqueline Gibson (1927–1997).

Willie] William Seward Burroughs Jr. (1947–1981), son of William Burroughs and Joan Vollmer. Burroughs Jr. was the author of *Speed* (1970) and *Kentucky Ham* (1973).

Wilson] John Clellon Holmes (1926–1988), novelist, author of *Go* (1952).

Wyndham] Edward Stringham (1918–1994), New York friend of John Clellon Holmes.

Young Mike Fortier] Michael Fournier Jr. (1921–1991), childhood friend of Kerouac.

Notes

In the notes below, the reference numbers denote page and line of this volume (the line count includes headings). No note is made for material included in standard desk-reference books. Quotations from Shakespeare are keyed to *The Riverside Shakespeare* (Boston: Houghton Mifflin, 1974), edited by G. Blakemore Evans. For references to other studies and further biographical background than is contained in the Chronology, see Ann Charters, *Kerouac: A Bibliography* (San Francisco: Straight Arrow Books, 1973); Ann Charters, ed., *Jack Kerouac: Selected Letters, 1940–1956* (New York: Viking Penguin, 1995); Ann Charters, ed., *Jack Kerouac: Selected Letters, 1957–1969* (New York: Viking Penguin, 1999); Ann Charters, *A Bibliography of Works by Jack Kerouac, 1939–1975* (New York: The Phoenix Bookshop, revised edition, 1975); Barry Gifford and Lawrence Lee, *Jack's Book: An Oral Biography of Jack Kerouac* (New York: St. Martin's Press, 1978); Paul Maher Jr., *Kerouac: His Life and Work* (Lanham, Maryland: Taylor Trade Publishing, 2004); Dennis McNally, *Desolate Angel* (New York: Random House, 1979); Gerald Nicosia, *Memory Babe: A Critical Biography of Jack Kerouac* (New York: Grove Press, 1983).

VISIONS OF CODY

8.16–17 few feet over the Snake . . . as night falls] An allusion to events portrayed in Kerouac's 1959 novel, *Doctor Sax: Faust Part Three*, written in Mexico City in 1952. The plot centers on the efforts of the eponymous Doctor Sax to destroy the malevolent Great World Snake.

9.24 W. C. Fields] Stage name of William Claude Dukenfield (1880–1946), comedian and actor known for his work in vaudeville, on radio, and in films, including *It's a Gift* (1934), *You Can't Cheat an Honest Man* (1939), and *The Bank Dick* (1940).

10.3 Henry-Fonda-like] Stage and film actor (1905–1982) known for his portrayal of earnest, plainspoken characters in such films as *Young Mr. Lincoln* (1939), *The Grapes of Wrath* (1940), and *The Ox-Bow Incident* (1943).

16.37 Al Collins Purple Grotto] Al "Jazzbo" Collins (1919–1997), radio personality popular among 1950s hipsters. He began the decade at WNEW (New York) and finished it at KFSO (San Francisco), although he often claimed to be broadcasting from the "purple grotto" inhabited by fantastical characters such as Jukes the purple chameleon.

17.4 Louis-Marciano fight] On October 26, 1951, the American boxer Rocky Marciano successfully defended his heavyweight championship against former champion Joe Louis.

18.4 Bill Corum] Radio and television sportscaster (1895–1958).

19.21   "Moonglow"] Song by Will Hudson, Irving Mills, and Eddie DeLange, recorded by Joe Venuti and His Orchestra in 1933.

20.19–20   Aly Khan] Prince Ali Salman Aga Khan (1911–1960) served as Pakistan's representative to the United Nations during the late 1950s.

24.11   Myshkin-like] Prince Myshkin, protagonist of Fyodor Dostoyevsky's novel *The Idiot* (1869).

26.10–12   Proust's Combray Cathedral. . . . light from "outside"] See Marcel Proust, *Swann's Way:* "Its memorial stones . . . were themselves no longer hard and lifeless matter, for time had softened and sweetened them, and had made them melt like honey and flow beyond their proper margins, either surging out in a milky, frothing wave . . . or else reabsorbed into their limits . . ." In the same paragraph Proust describes the altar "purpled . . . with tints so fresh that they seemed rather to be thrown on it for a moment by a light shining from outside."

27.8–9   Sixth Avenue . . . Avenue of the Americas] The name change took place in 1945 through the efforts of Mayor Fiorello La Guardia.

27.16   "Mutt 'n' Jeff"] *Mutt and Jeff*, long-running comic strip created by Bud Fisher in 1907, though drawn chiefly by Al Smith.

28.15   Gea-like] Also Gaia, Gaea, or Ge; Greek primordial deity who birthed Earth and the cosmos.

28.38   LEE KONITZ] Alto saxophonist and jazz composer (b. 1927), associated with the cool jazz of the 1940s and 1950s.

29.13   Arnold Fishkin the Tristano bassplayer] Arnold Fishkind, jazz bassist (1919–1999). Lennie Tristano (1919–1978), jazz pianist and composer.

29.28   Manny's] Manny's Music, a musical instrument store on West 48th Street in Manhattan. It closed in 2009.

29.29   Symphony Sid] Sid Torin (1909–1984), jazz disc jockey and radio personality.

30.12   *Quo Vadis*] Film (1951) starring Robert Taylor and Deborah Kerr and directed by Mervyn LeRoy, adapted from the 1896 novel by Henryk Sienkiewicz.

30.20   *TEN TALL MEN*] Adventure film (1951) starring Burt Lancaster and directed by Willis Goldbeck.

30.38   George Handy's "The Blues"] The composition "The Bloos" (1946) by jazz composer and pianist Handy (1920–1997) was included in the multidisc compilation *The Jazz Scene*, released by Mercury Records in 1949.

31.1   Charlie Parker's] Jazz saxophonist and composer (1920–1955), often referred to as "Bird."

31.4   Herby Steward] Herbie Steward, jazz saxophonist (1926–2003).

31.20–21   Jimmy Foxx's] Or Jimmie Foxx (1907–1967); baseball player who played first base for the Philadelphia Athletics and the Boston Red Sox.

32.5–6   pre-Basil-Rathbone Sherlock Holmes on the radio] Prior to Rathbone, Holmes was played on radio by actors including William Gillette, Clive Brook, and Richard Gordon. Rathbone began his long run as Holmes in 1938 with the Twentieth Century Fox film *The Hound of the Baskervilles* and the following year with the radio program *The New Adventures of Sherlock Holmes.*

34.12   Nin and Gerard] Caroline "Nin" Kerouac (1918–1964) and Francis Gerard Kerouac (1916–1926), the only siblings of Jack Kerouac.

35.21   Pat O'Brien] Film actor (1899–1983) whose many films included *The Irish in Us* (1935), *Angels with Dirty Faces* (1938), and *The Fighting 69th* (1940).

38.4   *nappes*] French: tablecloths.

38.29–30   "A holy and . . . removed from sin"] 2 Maccabees 12:45.

38.31–32   MacArthur Old Soldier crap] See U.S. Army General Douglas MacArthur's remarks to Congress, April 19, 1951: "I still remember the refrain of one of the most popular barracks ballads of that day, which proclaimed most proudly that old soldiers never die; they just fade away. I now close my military career and just fade away."

40.28   Princess Margaret Rose] Sister (1930–2002) of Queen Elizabeth II.

41.2   Terry Gibbs] Jazz vibraphonist (b. 1924).

41.3   Birdland] New York jazz club founded in 1949; named for Charlie Parker, it was a popular hangout for the Beat writers.

41.11   *RÊVES*] French: dreams.

41.17   Rita] Rita Fournier (1917–2009), sister of Kerouac's childhood friend Mike Fournier.

42.16–17   relaxin at Kingsbridge! . . . Camarillos] An allusion to Charlie Parker's "Relaxin' at Camarillo" (1947), recorded after a six-month stay in Camarillo State Hospital in California.

42.37   Paul] Paul Blake (1922–1972), Kerouac's brother-in-law, also referred to under the pseudonym Luke.

43.13   Arthur Godfrey] Radio broadcaster and television entertainer (1903–1983).

43.26   Errol Flynn and Bruce Cabot] Flynn, Australian-born actor (1909–1959) known for swashbuckling roles in such films as *Captain Blood* (1935) and *The Sea Hawk* (1940). Cabot, film actor (1904–1972) who appeared in *King Kong* (1933) and many other films.

44.13   D. W. Griffiths' Feast of Belshazzar in *Intolerance*] A major set piece in the Babylonian sequence of Griffith's epic 1916 film.

46.8   *amant*] French: lover.

48.27   Louis-Ferdinand Céline] French novelist and physician (1894–1961), author of *Journey to the End of the Night* (1932), *Death on the Installment Plan* (1936), and other works.

49.19   Genet] Jean Genet (1910–1986), French playwright and novelist.

50.10   Leopold Bloom] Protagonist of James Joyce's *Ulysses* (1922).

52.12   June dying] In 1951, William Burroughs shot and killed Joan Vollmer in Mexico City, by some accounts while attempting to shoot a glass off the top of her head (see note 270.3). After eventually fleeing Mexico for Louisiana, Burroughs was convicted *in absentia* of manslaughter.

58.37–38   Pensacola Kid . . . Bat Masterson] Pensacola Kid, ring name of American light heavyweight boxer Henry Malachi; Willie Hoppe, American billiards champion (1887–1959); William "Bat" Masterson (1853–1921), western frontier figure who was a U.S. marshal, buffalo hunter, and gambler.

58.40   Old Bull Balloon] Or Old Bull Baloon; a composite character based on W. C. Fields and William Burroughs who appears throughout Kerouac's work.

59.2   Jelly Roll Morton] Professional name of early jazz pianist and composer Ferdinand Joseph LaMothe (1890–1941).

59.4   Theodore Dreiser] Novelist (1871–1945) best known for *Sister Carrie* (1900) and *An American Tragedy* (1925).

60.39   Xerxes' fleets] The fleet of Xerxes I of Persia (519–465 B.C.E.), or Xerxes the Great, invaded Greece during the Greco-Persian Wars.

60.40   Agamemnon] Commander of the Greek forces during the Trojan War.

62.38   Major Hoople] Principal character in long-running syndicated comic strip *Our Boarding House*, created in 1921 by Gene Ahern (1895–1960).

63.5   *Out Our Way*] Syndicated single-panel American comic strip first drawn in 1922 by J. R. Williams (1888–1957), known for its portrayal of rural life.

63.20–21   *True Confessions*] Magazine originally published by Fawcett Publications in 1922.

72.26   C.B.&Q.] Chicago, Burlington and Quincy Railroad, midwestern railroad operating under that name from 1855 to 1970.

74.25   *Saturday Evening Post*] American general-interest magazine published weekly, 1897–1963.

74.26   rubber tire ad] The image occurred in advertisements for Fisk tires, with the slogan "Time to Re-Tire."

74.36–38   Bela Lugosi . . . rainy castle] Lugosi (1882–1956), Hungarian-American actor who starred in *Dracula* (1931); the film's young hero was played by David Manners.

75.11 Popeye's] Muscular sailor hero created by E. C. Segar in the comic strip *Thimble Theatre* (later retitled *Popeye*) in 1929.

78.14 "Hallelujah I'm a bum] Folk song published by the International Workers of the World (IWW) in 1908.

83.15–16 *When lilacs last in the dooryard bloom'd*] First line of Walt Whitman's elegy (1865) on the assassination of Abraham Lincoln.

85.3 Rousseau-like] As depicted in the naïve paintings of Henri Rousseau (1844–1910).

90.25–26 Lana Turners . . . Ava Gardner] Turner, actress (1921–1995) known for such films as *They Won't Forget* (1937) and *The Postman Always Rings Twice* (1946); Gardner, actress (1922–1990) whose films included *The Killers* (1946) and *The Snows of Kilimanjaro* (1952).

95.38 D. & R.G.] Denver and Rio Grande Railroad.

96.2–3 *My Man Godfrey*] Film comedy (1936) directed by Gregory La Cava and starring William Powell and Carole Lombard; the plot concerns a wealthy man who takes a job as a butler during the Depression.

97.15 Indian love calls and Jeannette MacDonald] MacDonald was an actress and singer (1903–1965) whose vehicles included *The Love Parade* (1929) and *Love Me Tonight* (1932); she sang "Indian Love Call" as a duet with Nelson Eddy in the film *Rose Marie* (1936).

98.30 Miles and Lee Konitz] Miles Davis (1926–1991), jazz composer and trumpeter. For Lee Konitz, see note 28.38. Konitz was among the musicians on Davis's 1957 album *Birth of the Cool.*

99.9 old syphilis movies] Despite Kerouac's assertion that the movie in question was not "a Thirties film," his description suggests Edgar G. Ulmer's *Damaged Lives* (1933), a Canadian-American production.

100.24 Demosthenes pebble] The ancient Athenian orator Demosthenes (384–322 B.C.E.) purportedly overcame a stammer by speaking for a time with pebbles in his mouth.

106.5 Sad Sack . . . Genet's Alberto] Sad Sack, anonymous army private, protagonist of the comic strip *The Sad Sack*, created in 1942 by George Baker. Genet's Alberto, allusion to Jean Genet's 1957 essay "The Studio of Alberto Giacometti." Giacometti (1901–1966) was a Swiss painter, sculptor, and printmaker.

106.32–33 Orson Welles hall of mirrors in Frisco Park (*Lady from Shanghai*)] Much of *The Lady from Shanghai*, the 1947 film directed by and starring Orson Welles, was shot on location in the San Francisco Bay Area; it concludes with a shoot-out that takes place among the distorting mirrors of an amusement park fun house (re-created on a soundstage).

107.10 *Battleground*] War film (1949) about the Battle of the Bulge, directed by William Wellman.

109.5–6   Frank Sinatra's "April in Paris," Tony Bennet's "Blue Velvet"] "April in Paris" was written by Vernon Duke and E. Y. Harburg for the 1932 Broadway musical *Walk a Little Faster*; Sinatra released a single of the song in 1951. "Blue Velvet," written by Bernie Wayne and Lee Morris, was recorded by Tony Bennett in 1951.

109.22   *True Detective Magazine*] True crime magazine (1924–1995) created by Bernarr Macfadden in 1924, and featuring lurid and hardboiled subject matter.

110.25   Pic] Pictorial Review Jackson, the protagonist of Kerouac's posthumously published novella *Pic* (1971).

112.7   *H from the C*] An allusion to Kerouac's 1950 novel, *The Town and the City*.

113.33   the sea is my brother] Title of Kerouac's early novel, which was published in 2011.

115.15   N.M.U] National Maritime Union, American labor union founded in 1937. Kerouac was a member of the N.M.U. while working as a merchant sailor in the 1940s.

116.33   *Argosy*] Pulp magazine (1882–1978) founded by Frank Munsey.

116.37–38   Behold, your house . . . desolate] See Matthew 23:38.

117.7   Alastair Sim] Scottish actor (1900–1976) best known for playing the title role in *Scrooge* (1951).

120.3   S.I.U] Seafarers International Union, a confederation of maritime unions founded in 1938.

121.29   Blake's worm] See "The Sick Rose" by William Blake, in *Songs of Innocence and Experience* (1794): "O Rose, thou art sick! / The invisible worm, / That flies in the night, / In the howling storm, / Has found out thy bed / Of crimson joy; / And his dark secret love / Does thy life destroy."

122.26   Old Ghost of the Susquehann] See Part One, Chapter 14, of Kerouac's *On the Road* (1957).

124.15–16   *This Gun for Hire* with Alan Ladd] Film (1942) based on Graham Greene's *A Gun for Sale*, directed by Frank Tuttle and starring Alan Ladd as hired killer Philip Raven.

124.33–35   AFFAIRS OF STATE . . . Louis Verneuil] The comedy, written in English by French playwright Verneuil (1893–1952), opened on Broadway in 1950.

125.5   Garland] Robert Garland (1895–1955), drama critic for the *New York Journal-American*, 1943–1951.

125.18   *Vanity of Daoulas*] An unpublished manuscript begun in 1942, not to be confused with the later novel *Vanity of Duluoz* (1968).

129.30–31 Allen Eager and Gerry Mulligan] Eager, jazz saxophonist (1927–2003); Mulligan (1927–1996), jazz saxophonist and composer. Their collaborative album *The New Sounds* was released in 1952 on Prestige.

129.38 Thomas Mitchell] Character actor (1892–1962) who appeared in *Gone with the Wind* (1939), *Stagecoach* (1939), and many other films.

131.10 Mexican girl 1947] Bea Franco (1920–2013), whose brief love affair with Kerouac was detailed in *On the Road* (1957), where Franco is renamed "Terry."

131.25 P. & L.E.R.R.] Pittsburgh and Lake Erie Railroad.

134.8–9 Fred MacMurray and Barbara Stanwyck . . . at Xmas?] In *Remember the Night* (1940), directed by Mitchell Leisen and written by Preston Sturges, MacMurray as a prosecutor takes Stanwyck, a shoplifter, to meet his family at Christmas.

136.33 Five Guys Named Moe] Song recorded originally in 1943 by Louis Jordan (1908–1975).

137.19–20 Bing's "White Christmas"] Irving Berlin's "White Christmas" was recorded by Bing Crosby in 1942.

138.23 Ella, Mr. B.] Singers Ella Fitzgerald (1917–1996) and Billy Eckstine (1914–1993).

138.30 Lester and Hawk] Jazz saxophonists Lester Young (1909–1959) and Coleman Hawkins (1904–1969).

139.3 Prado's Mambo] "Mambo No. 5," composed and recorded in 1949 by Cuban bandleader Pérez Prado (1916–1989).

145.6–7 *Really the Blues*] Memoir (1946) by Milton "Mezz" Mezzrow (1899–1972), jazz musician and hipster prototype; the book was co-authored by Bernard Wolfe (1915–1985).

145.11 *Inside U.S.A.*] Nonfiction best seller (1947) by journalist John Gunther (1901–1970).

146.22–23 Little Orphan Annie] Title character of the syndicated comic strip created by Harold Gray in 1924.

147.25 "Lil Abner,"] Syndicated comic strip satirizing American rural life, created by Al Capp in 1934.

148.1 Billie Holiday] Jazz singer and songwriter (1915–1959).

148.25–26 no wonder he hit June and killed her] See note 52.12.

151.21 Peaches Browning] Browning (1910–1956) married the wealthy fifty-one-year-old Edward "Daddy" Browning at sixteen in 1926; she became notorious because of scandalous details made public during the divorce proceedings. She was married three times subsequently.

162.1–2 Billie Holiday's record of "Body and Soul"] Holiday first recorded "Body and Soul" with her orchestra in 1940. The song was composed in 1930 by Johnny Green, with lyrics by Edward Heyman, Robert Sour, and Frank Eyton.

163.10 "Them There Eyes"] Jazz standard (1930) by Maceo Pinkard, Doris Tauber, and William Tracey. Holiday's version was recorded in 1939.

163.15 "Good Morning Heartaches"] "Good Morning Heartache," jazz standard by Irene Higginbotham, Ervin Drake, and Dan Fisher, first recorded by Holiday in 1946.

168.16 "Stay With the Happy People"] Popular song by Bob Hilliard and Jule Styne.

168.17 Frank Morgan] Actor (1890–1949) best known for playing the title character in The Wizard of Oz (1939).

169.25–26 Coleman Hawkins' "Crazy Rhythm"] "Crazy Rhythm," song (1928) by Irving Caesar, Joseph Myer, and Roger Wolfe Kahn. Hawkins, accompanied by guitarist Django Reinhardt, recorded it in 1937.

169.34 Chu Berry] Leon "Chu" Berry (1908–1941), jazz saxophonist of the swing era.

170.11 Benny Carter!] Jazz composer and multi-instrumentalist (1907–2003).

170.40 Charlie Christian] Guitarist (1916–1942) of the swing era.

171.10 Scho-enn-berg] Arnold Schoenberg (1874–1951), Austrian-born composer.

177.17 Hopalong Cassidy] Western hero created in 1904 by Clarence Mulford and played on screen by William Boyd.

177.36–37 Glenn Miller "Moonlight Serenade"] The bandleader Glenn Miller (1904–1944) composed "Moonlight Serenade" with Mitchell Parish in 1939, recording it with his orchestra.

180.29 ARTIE SHAW] Clarinetist and bandleader (1910–2004).

180.32–33 "Gloomy Sunday,"] "Gloomy Sunday," composed by Hungarian pianist Rezső Seress in 1933, was recorded by Shaw in 1940 and by Holiday in 1941.

181.41 Notes From the Underground] Novella (1864) by Fyodor Dostoyevsky.

185.23 Gene Krupa's "Leave Us Leap,"] Krupa (1909–1973), jazz drummer and composer; "Leave Us Leap" appeared on the 1941 Columbia Records release Drum Boogie.

185.27 "Charmaine"] Popular song (1927) by Erno Rapee and Lew Pollack, recorded by Billy May in 1952.

185.30 Roy Eldridge] Jazz trumpeter (1911–1989).

185.35–36   "I Want to Be Happy"] Song by Irving Caesar and Vincent You-mans and recorded by the Glenn Miller Orchestra in 1939.

186.6   Dizzy] John Birks "Dizzy" Gillespie (1917–1993), jazz trumpeter and bandleader, one of the architects of bebop.

186.26   *Lester Young*] See note 138.30.

188.19–20   *Charlie Parker's "Lover Man"*] "Lover Man," song (1941) by Jimmy Davis, Roger Ramirez, and James Sherman; Parker's version was recorded in 1946.

189.27   *Flip Phillips*] Jazz saxophonist and clarinetist (1915–2001).

190.38   *"Honeysuckle Rose"*] Composed in 1929 by Fats Waller and Andy Razaf; recorded by Waller in 1934.

192.6   Coleman Hawkins and "After You've Gone."] "After You've Gone" (1918), by Turner Layton and Henry Creamer, was recorded by Hawkins in 1935.

193.12–13   *Josh White . . . "Bad Housing Blues"*] White (1914–1969) recorded "Bad Housing Blues," written with poet Waring Cuney, in 1941.

193.13   W.P.A.] Works Progress Administration.

197.33   *"I've Got a Love-ely Bunch of Coconuts"*] Novelty song (1944) by English songwriter Fred Heatherton, made popular in the U.S. by Freddy Martin and His Orchestra in 1949.

199.14   *Stan Kenton . . . "Artistry in Boogie"*] Kenton (1911–1979) cowrote "Artistry in Boogie" with Pete Rugolo, and recorded it on Capitol in 1946.

209.20   *Neurotica*] Journal of cultural analysis founded by Jay Landesman (1919–2011) in 1948, featuring contributors such as Gershon Legman, Chandler Brossard, Marshall McLuhan, Anatole Broyard, and Carl Solomon.

214.4   Jean Gabin] French film actor (1904–1976) who starred in *La Grande Illusion* (1937), *La Bête Humaine* (1938), and many other films.

214.22   Swinburne?] Algernon Charles Swinburne (1837–1909), English poet.

216.13   the murder] On August 14, David Kammerer was killed by Kerouac's friend Lucien Carr.

222.13–14   Prokofiev . . . "Nevsky Suite"] Sergei Prokofiev (1891–1953) wrote the music for Sergei Eisenstein's film *Alexander Nevsky* in 1938 and subsequently adapted the score into an orchestral and choral suite.

223.40–224.1   Charlie Ventura"] Jazz saxophonist and bandleader (1916–1992).

227.21–23   *Big* Blackie . . . Bull writes about in his novel?] The incident referred to involves a New York criminal figure known as Whitey, and is recounted in William Burroughs's *Junkie* (1953).

227.35   Damon Runyon] Fiction writer and journalist (1880–1946) known for *Guys and Dolls* (1932), *Take It Easy* (1938), and other collections.

233.3   the *Julien* novel] Kerouac and William Burroughs collaborated in 1945 on a novel that was published in 2008 as *And the Hippos Were Boiled in Their Tanks*.

245.26   *"Just One of Those Things"*] Song (1935) by Cole Porter.

246.13–14   Maurice Rocco, . . . Charley Spivak] Rocco (1915–1976), boogie-woogie pianist and composer; Spivak, trumpeter and bandleader (1905–1982).

263.5   *The Law of Mentalism*, by Sechnal] *The Law of Mentalism* (1902), self-improvement book written and published by A. Victor Segno.

270.3   "William Tell Overture"] Overture to the opera *Guillaume Tell* (1829) by Gioachino Rossini; later familiar as the theme to *The Lone Ranger* on radio and television. In the opera, as in the Friedrich Schiller play on which it is based, the legendary figure Tell is ordered by the tyrant Gessler to shoot an apple off his own son's head; later he uses his bow to assassinate Gessler. See also note 52.12.

272.34–35   Joe Williams] Jazz vocalist (1918–1999) best known for his work in the 1950s with the Count Basie Orchestra.

275.32   Lionel Hampton] Bandleader and multi-instrumentalist (1908–2002), known for his work on vibraphone.

279.10–11   *Irene Dunne in an old Cary Grant comedy)*] Dunne starred with Grant in the film comedies *The Awful Truth* (1937) and *My Favorite Wife* (1940).

279.13   "Just . . . one . . . of those things . . .] From "Just One of Those Things" (1935) by Cole Porter.

279.21–22   "Lover . . . in my eyes . . ."] From "Lover" (1932) by Richard Rodgers and Lorenz Hart.

282.36   Oscar Pettiford] Jazz bassist and cellist (1922–1960).

285.20–21   that little character with Barney Google] Snuffy Smith, moonshiner who was a regular character in the comic strip *Barney Google* from 1934 on.

285.28   James Mason] English actor (1909–1984) whose image as a suave and sinister aristocrat was established in such films as *The Man in Grey* (1943) and *Fanny by Gaslight* (1944).

286.13   Bud Powell] Jazz pianist (1924–1966), one of the architects of bebop.

286.16–17   twenty-five cent pocketbook "Marihuana"] Cornell Woolrich's 1941 novella was reprinted as a ten-cent Dell paperback in 1951.

286.20   Yma Sumac?] Peruvian singer (1922–2008) known for her exotic vocal effects on such albums as *Voice of the Xtabay* (1950) and *Legend of the Sun Virgin* (1952).

287.7   Hugh Herbert] Film actor (1887–1952) known for comic roles.

288.7   A. P. Hill!] Ambrose Powell Hill (1825–1865), Confederate general during the Civil War.

288.11   Bloom let the soap melt] In Joyce's *Ulysses*, Leopold Bloom buys a cake of lemon-scented soap which he carries in his pocket.

288.32   can Shelley be far behind] See the last line of Percy Shelley's "Ode to the West Wind": "If Winter comes, can Spring be far behind?"

289.27   Meade] Major General George Meade (1815–1872), Union commander.

289.29   ". . . enlightened by the vollied glare,"] See "The March into Virginia" in Herman Melville's *Battle-Pieces and Aspects of the War* (1866), line 34.

290.8   Moon Mullins] Title character of the comic strip created by Frank Willard in 1923.

291.26   WmRnHearst] Newspaper magnate William Randolph Hearst (1863–1951).

292.7   Saroyan] Fiction writer and playwright William Saroyan (1908–1981).

292.18   Gene Bearden] Major League pitcher (1920–2004) who played for the Cleveland Indians, the Chicago White Sox, and other teams.

292.32–33   Katzenjammer Kids or Animal Crackers or Zoo Parades] *The Katzenjammer Kids*, comic strip created by Rudolph Dirks in 1897; *Animal Crackers*, the title of two separate syndicated comic strips by the time in which Kerouac was writing; *Zoo Parade*, television program (1950–57) featuring zoo animals and hosted by the zoologist Marlin Perkins.

293.24–25   Cornelius Vanderbilt Whitney] Businessman and film producer (1899–1992) who also oversaw a prized stable of thoroughbred horses.

293.30   Rudy Vallee "A Pretty Girl . . ."] Vallée (1901–1986), Vermont singer who recorded the Irving Berlin composition "A Pretty Girl is Like a Melody" in 1935.

294.17   Operator 5's and Secret Agent X-9] *Operator #5*, later retitled *Secret Service Operator #5*, pulp magazine published from 1934 to 1939; *Secret Agent X-9*, comic strip created by Dashiell Hammett and Alex Raymond in 1934.

295.12   Thomas Wolfe's] Novelist (1900–1938), author of *Look Homeward, Angel* (1929), *Of Time and the River* (1935), and *You Can't Go Home Again* (1940); a major influence on Kerouac.

297.22   Émile Zola of the film] *The Life of Emile Zola* (1937), Warner Bros. production directed by William Dieterle.

299.33   Dagwood Bumstead] Husband of the title character of the comic strip *Blondie*, created by Chip Young in 1930.

300.16–17 "The Hour of Charm"] Radio program of the 1930s and '40s, hosted by Arlene Francis and featuring Phil Spitalny and his Hour of Charm Orchestra.

301.20 Doc Holliday . . . tips of Billy's ears] As in the fictional gunfight between American gunmen John Henry "Doc" Holliday and William "Billy the Kid" Bonney portrayed in Howard Hughes's film *The Outlaw* (1943).

302.40 Sherwood Anderson] Author (1876–1941) of *Winesburg, Ohio* (1919) and other works.

303.21 Henry Miller's] Writer (1891–1980), a Big Sur resident from the mid-1940s on, author of *Tropic of Cancer* (1934), *Black Spring* (1936), *Tropic of Capricorn* (1939), and other works. Miller wrote the preface to the 1959 Avon edition of Kerouac's *The Subterraneans*.

304.5 Mark Van Doren] English professor (1894–1972) at Columbia University with whom Kerouac studied. Van Doren was also the literary editor for *The Nation* (1924–28) and won the 1940 Pulitzer Prize for his *Collected Poems, 1922–1938*.

304.37 Major Hoople] See note 62.38.

306.12 Prince Albert] American brand of tobacco, introduced during the first decade of the twentieth century.

307.6 this lady with a clean handkerchief] Saint Veronica.

307.38–39 Alan Ladd, "Blue Something or Other,"] Ladd starred in the 1946 film *The Blue Dahlia*, directed by George Marshall from a screenplay by Raymond Chandler.

308.6 Popeye] See note 75.11.

308.15 SNUFFY SMITH!] See note 285.20–21.

308.21–25 eh *weyondon . . . et fre mon*] This passage, and the following two passages, combine Québecois with colloquial Franco-American: "eh come on, must we lean in such a moment? Stop . . . talking . . . you know, well you know, old boy, she'd have written you a letter if you'd've let her that poor lil' damned gal how beautiful she was and fuck if I ain't able to do it in the rear end and do my . . ."

308.27–28 *la musique . . . un moment?*] "the music the beautiful but stop now we have to stop a moment?"

308.31–32 *cest impossible . . . dire se desetangleta*i] "It's impossible to strangle yourself I mean to disentangle yourself . . ."

309.24 **GARY COOPER** . . . TOM MIX] Cooper, film actor (1901–1961) whose many films included *The Pride of the Yankees* (1942) and *High Noon* (1952). Mix, film actor (1880–1940) who starred in many Westerns.

311.11–12 *Milton Berle*] Comedian (1908–2002) in vaudeville, movies, and television.

311.27 Monroe Starr] Monroe Stahr, movie producer who is the protagonist of F. Scott Fitzgerald's unfinished novel *The Last Tycoon* (published 1941).

311.31 maggie and jiggs] Maggie and Jiggs, perennially quarreling married couple, the protagonists of *Bringing Up Father*, comic strip created by George McManus in 1913.

312.18 Danny Kaye] Actor, singer, and comedian (1911–1987).

312.32 Eddy Arcaro, . . . Ted Williams] Eddie Arcaro (1916–1997), champion jockey. Williams, baseball player (1918–2002) for the Boston Red Sox.

316.1 Joan Rawshanks] Identified in the original typescript as the movie star Joan Crawford (1904–1977). The point of departure for the section is Kerouac's observation of the filming of *Sudden Fear* (1952), directed by David Miller, on location on Russian Hill in San Francisco.

317.32 Leon Errol] Vaudeville and movie comedian (1881–1951).

319.18 the leading man] Jack Palance (1919–2006).

323.20 Lou Gehrig] First baseman for the New York Yankees (1903–1941).

323.36 Anna Lucasta] Play (1936) by Philip Yordan about a girl working in a waterfront bar, filmed in 1949 by Irving Rapper with Paulette Goddard.

323.40 Claudette Colbert of *I Cover the Waterfront*] Colbert (1903–1996) starred as a smuggler's daughter in this 1933 film, directed by James Cruze.

325.23 Collier brothers] Homer Collyer (1881–1947) and Langley Collyer (1885–1947), New York hermits and hoarders who were found dead in the Harlem brownstone where they had lived as recluses for many years.

326.8 Budd Schulberg] Novelist and screenwriter (1914–2009).

327.36 Nathanael West] The scene described occurs in West's novel *The Day of the Locust* (1939).

328.17 Hopalong Cassidy] See note 177.17.

331.29 Cecil B. De Mille] Film director (1881–1959) whose many films include *The King of Kings* (1927), *The Sign of the Cross* (1932), and *Samson and Delilah* (1949).

336.25 paterson williams the carlos poet] William Carlos Williams (1883–1963), poet, author of the long poem *Paterson* (1946–58).

338.7 Tiresias] In Greek mythology, blind Theban prophet.

338.38–39 Gashouse Kids] Gang of children in a series of movies including *Gas House Kids* (1946), *Gas House Kids Go West* (1947), and *Gas House Kids in Hollywood* (1947).

338.39   Denny Dimwit] Character in the comic strip *Winnie Winkle*, created in 1920 by Martin Branner.

342.25   Carlyle . . . Hero Worships] Thomas Carlyle (1795–1881), Scottish philosopher and historian, author of *On Heroes, Hero-Worship, and the Heroic in History* (1841).

343.36   Ruth in the Corn] See Ruth 2.

345.10–11   Marlon Brando . . . *Desire*] Tennessee Williams's *A Streetcar Named Desire* opened on Broadway in 1947 in a production starring Marlon Brando and Jessica Tandy; it closed in December 1949.

345.12   Abner Yokum] Title character of Al Capp's comic strip *Li'l Abner*.

345.31   Bartlebies] The reference is to Herman Melville's "Bartleby, The Scrivener: A Story of Wall Street" (1853).

345.32   Pulham Esquires and Victor Matures] *H.M. Pulham, Esq.*, novel (1941) by John P. Marquand, filmed the same year by King Vidor with Robert Young in the title role. Victor Mature (1913–1999), actor who starred in *My Darling Clementine* (1946), *Samson and Delilah* (1949), and other films.

347.20   Three Stooges] Vaudeville and film comedy troupe known for their slapstick humor.

348.27–28   *Count of Monte Cristo*] Novel (1844) by Alexandre Dumas.

350.13   Telemachus . . . Nestor's friend)] Telemachus, son of Odysseus in *The Odyssey*, visits Nestor while searching for knowledge of his father's fate. Nestor's son, Peisistratus, joins Telemachus in the search.

351.26   Chirico] Giorgio de Chirico (1888–1978), Italian painter.

354.4–7   "OBVIOUSLY, AN IMAGE . . . June 1942] The passage is from Eliot's essay "Andrew Marvell," published in *Times Literary Supplement*, March 1921.

354.33–34   Amos 'n' Andy] Radio program created by Freeman Gosden and Charles Correll in 1928; later a television series.

356.20–21   cuttin my way . . . fl-e-sh] The phrase is spoken by Fields in the 1935 film *Mississippi*.

356.32–34   *Les Paul echoey guitars . . . "Hold that Tiger")*] Les Paul (1915–2009), multigenre guitarist and luthier; he recorded the jazz standard "Tiger Rag" (also known as "Hold That Tiger") with Mary Ford in 1952.

356.35–38   Jelly Roll Morton . . . hold that tiger] "Tiger Rag" was first recorded by the Original Dixieland Jass Band in 1917; however, Morton (see note 59.2) long claimed to have authored the composition.

358.19   Nicholas Breton] English poet (1545–1626).

358.27   Joe Holliday] Jazz saxophonist (b. 1925), born Joseph Befumo.

359.16–17   Walt Winchell] Walter Winchell (1897–1972), gossip columnist and radio journalist.

360.6   Ben Turpin] Actor (1869–1940) best known for his work in silent comedies such as *A Night Out* (1915).

360.15   Liggens bandmen the honeyrippers] Reference to the hit record *The Honeydripper* (1945) by Joe Liggins (1915–1987).

362.22   schmecker] Heroin addict.

362.29–30   Pierre Louys] French poet and novelist (1870–1925), known for his erotic texts.

362.35   went wild! Theodora!] Allusion to the 1936 film *Theodora Goes Wild*.

362.40–363.1   "A Small Hotel," . . . "Long Island Zounds"] "There's a Small Hotel," song (1936) by Rodgers and Hart; "Zing! Went the Strings of My Heart," song (1934) by James F. Hanley; "Long Island Sound," composition by jazz saxophonist Stan Getz that first appeared on the 1949 Prestige recording *Stan Getz Quartet*.

363.4   Herman's band] Woody Herman (1913–1987), jazz clarinetist and bandleader.

363.5   Ray Eberle] Jazz vocalist (1919–1979) known primarily for his work with Glenn Miller.

363.14   André Gide] French author (1869–1951), winner of the 1947 Nobel Prize in Literature.

364.18   Lenny Tristano] See note 29.13.

364.36   Charles Laughton, as Captain Blah?] Laughton (1899–1962) starred as Captain Bligh in the 1935 film *Mutiny on the Bounty*.

365.14   Ippolits] Probably a reference to Ippolit Terentyev, consumptive nihilist in *The Idiot* who offers an extended argument for atheism.

365.15   Raskolniks] Raskolniks were seventeenth-century dissenters from the Russian Orthodox Church; the term suggested the name of Raskolnikov, the protagonist of Dostoevsky's *Crime and Punishment* (1866).

366.26–27   *Old Wives Tales*, . . . Arnold Bennett] Bennett (1867–1931) was the author of *The Old Wives' Tale* (1908).

367.35   Eliot's fog] See T. S. Eliot's "The Love Song of J. Alfred Prufrock," line 15: "The yellow fog that rubs its back upon the window-panes."

368.27   Buck Mulligan O'Gogarty] Malachi "Buck" Mulligan, character in James Joyce's *Ulysses* partly modeled on Irish poet and politician Oliver St. John Gogarty (1878–1957).

370.21   *Gangbusters*] *Gang Busters*, true crime radio program that first aired in 1935.

371.4 *Dragnet*] Radio program first broadcast in 1949; later a television series.

371.12 the cock of Shakespeare] See *Hamlet* I.i.157–164.

371.35 "Laura"] Popular song by David Raksin and Johnny Mercer, based on Raksin's theme for the 1944 movie.

371.36 David Rose] Pianist, arranger, and composer (1910–1990).

371.37 Thor Heyerdahl . . . Axel Stordhal] Heyerdahl, Norwegian ethnographer and adventurer (1914–2002) famous for his 1947 voyage on the raft *Kon-Tiki*. Axel Stordahl, music arranger (1913–1963) known for his work with Sinatra and American jazz trombonist and bandleader Tommy Dorsey.

371.39–40 "Brother, have you seen starlight on the rails?"] From Thomas Wolfe's short story "The Names of the Nation."

372.16–17 Frank Sinatra . . . "This Love of Mine"] Sinatra recorded "This Love of Mine" (composed by Sinatra, Sol Parker, and Hank Sanicola) with the Tommy Dorsey Orchestra in 1941.

373.16 Sid Caesar] Comedian (1922–2014) known for his work on the 1950s television program *Your Show of Shows*.

374.2 Devil or Daniel Webster's] "The Devil and Daniel Webster" (1937), short story by Stephen Vincent Benét.

374.23 Omar Khayyám] Persian poet and mathematician (1048–1131).

375.2–3 "War is the health of the State."] From "The State" (1918) by Randolph Bourne (1886–1918).

375.6 scrapple from the apple] "Scrapple from the Apple" (1947), composition by Charlie Parker.

375.9 Hackett and McPartland] Bobby Hackett (1915–1976), jazz trumpeter and cornetist; Jimmy McPartland (1907–1991), jazz cornetist.

375.21–22 Dalton boys] Outlaw gang of the late nineteenth-century American West.

376.35–36 "I looked into the mirror . . . has not loved for years. / "] From Allen Ginsberg, poem "345 W. 15th St."

376.37–39 "I came home from the movies . . . passenger ship"] From Allen Ginsberg, "345 W. 15th St."

377.13–18 "/ship to go to seas . . . in United States/."] From Allen Ginsberg, "345 W. 15th St."

377.33–35 "Two books on top . . . I cannot look"] From Allen Ginsberg, "345 W. 15th St."

378.3–4 "Then I heard . . . Mahogany Hall."] From Allen Ginsberg, "345 W. 15th St."

381.31 Brew Moore] Jazz saxophonist (1924–1973).

381.32 Jimmy Ford] Jazz saxophonist (1927–1994).

381.34 Sonny Stitt] Jazz saxophonist (1924–1982).

381.35 James Moody and his King Pleasure] Moody, jazz saxophonist and flautist (1925–2010). Pleasure, jazz vocalist (1922–1981), born Clarence Beeks, known as a pioneer of vocalese techniques on such recordings as "Moody's Mood for Love" (1952) and "Red Top" (1952).

381.36–37 Googe, . . . Vaughan] Barnabe Googe (1540–1594), English pastoral poet; Christopher Smart (1722–1771), English poet known for the ecstatic religious poems "A Song to David" and "Jubilate Agno"; Abraham Cowley (1618–1667), English poet; Henry Vaughan (1621–1695), English religious poet.

381.37 Sidney and George Herbert] Sir Philip Sidney (1554–1586), English Elizabethan poet known for *Astrophil and Stella* (1591); George Herbert (1593–1633), English religious poet.

382.34 Marty Glickman] Sports announcer (1917–2001) who was the longtime radio voice of the New York Knicks, Giants, and Rangers.

384.11–12 Ruth Brown] Popular singer (1928–2006) whose hits included "Teardrops from My Eyes" and "(Mama) He Treats Your Daughter Mean."

384.31 Betty Grable] Film actress and singer (1916–1973).

386.35 Sebastian] Sebastian Sampas (1922–1944), close friend and early literary confidant of Kerouac from Lowell.

388.13 Sarah Vaughan] Jazz vocalist (1924–1990).

388.17 Lionel Trilling] Literary critic and university professor (1905–1975) with whom Kerouac studied at Columbia.

389.39 King Cole] The King Cole Bar, cocktail lounge in the St. Regis Hotel in Manhattan, decorated with murals by Maxfield Parrish.

392.21 Gene Autry] Singing cowboy star (1907–1998) of radio, film, and television.

393.20 Clyde Beatty] Lion tamer and circus performer (1903–1965).

394.3–4 not a Modigliani . . . Breton genius] Amedeo Modigliani (1884–1920), Italian painter and sculptor known for his elongated portrayals of the human form. The "Breton artist" referred to is Yves Tanguy (1900–1955), born in Paris of Breton heritage, whose surrealist paintings also contain elongated and abstract representations of the human form.

396.17 Reich] Wilhelm Reich (1897–1957), Austrian psychoanalyst, author of *The Mass Psychology of Fascism* (1933) and *The Sexual Revolution* (1936).

397.19 Lou Little] Football coach (1893–1979), born Luigi Piccolo; he was head coach at Columbia, 1930–56.

399.19   Hurry up please . . . from T. S. Eliot] See Eliot's *The Waste Land* (1922), line 141.

401.2–3   Ibsen's *A Pillar of Society*] *The Pillars of Society*, 1877 play by Henrik Ibsen.

401.11   Rimbaud and his Verlaine] Rimbaud was involved in a tempestuous, and at times violent, romantic relationship with the Symbolist poet Paul Verlaine.

402.28   "The Hunt" Dexter Gordon and Wardell Gray] Jazz saxophonists Gordon (1923–1990) and Gray (1921–1955) recorded "The Hunt" live in 1947.

403.18   Ed Wynn] Vaudeville and radio comedian (1886–1966).

403.34   Slim Gaillard] Jazz musician and singer (1916–1991) known for his use of vocalese.

404.17   "Slowboat to China"] "(I'd Like to Get You on a) Slow Boat to China" (1948), song by Frank Loesser.

404.28–29   from the shores of Kitchigoomi] See Henry Wadsworth Longfellow, *The Song of Hiawatha* (1855), line 1: "By the shore of Gitche Gumee."

405.25–26   "Enlightened by the vollied glare"] See note 289.29.

405.39   Montesquieu, Abner Doubleday] Montesquieu, French social and political philosopher (1689–1755). Doubleday, U.S. general (1819–1893) purported to have fired the first shot of the U.S. Civil War.

408.6   Cozy Cole] Jazz drummer (1909–1981).

408.7   Max Roach] Jazz drummer and composer (1924–2007).

412.6   *guêles*] French: *gueules*, mouths.

413.38   "Close Your Eyes"] Popular song (1933) by Bernice Petkere (1901–2000).

419.2   Judge Bean] Roy Bean (c. 1825–1903), justice of the peace of Val Verde County, Texas, who held court in his saloon and became known for whimsical and arbitrary legal judgments.

421.9   B. O. Plenty] Disheveled character who figured regularly in the comic strip *Dick Tracy* from 1945 on.

423.18–19   "*Qu'elque chose pour la plage.*"] French: Something for the beach.

424.10   Dillinger] John Dillinger (1903–1934), famed bank robber of the Depression era.

433.6   Willard] Jess Willard (1881–1968), boxer and onetime world heavyweight champion.

434.7   "Idaho."] Jazz standard composed in 1942 by Jesse Stone.

434.29   George Shearing] British jazz pianist and composer (1919–2011).

434.32 Denzil Best] Jazz drummer and composer (1917–1965).

435.40 Eddy Dean and Peter Lorre] Eddie Dean (1907–1999), actor and cowboy singer. Lorre (1904–1964), Austrian-born actor known for his roles in *M* (1931), *The Maltese Falcon* (1941), and many other films.

439.17–18 Wynonie . . . Pudding,"] Wynonie Harris (1915–1969) recorded "I Like My Baby's Pudding" in 1950.

439.20 Jimmy Cagney] James Cagney (1899–1986), screen actor, star of *The Public Enemy* (1931), *Footlight Parade* (1932), *Angels with Dirty Faces* (1938), and other films.

439.29–30 Vaughn Monroe in the ghostly sky of the Western herd—] Vaughn Monroe (1911–1973) recorded a hit version of Stan Jones's song "(Ghost) Riders in the Sky" in 1949.

442.24–25 Fellaheen] This term, frequently employed by Kerouac, derives from the German historian Oswald Spengler's *The Decline of the West* (1918; 1923), a study of the cycles of world civilizations in which "fellaheen" denotes the equatorial and agricultural peoples who would come to direct the course of world history after the fall of Western civilization.

443.8 Tolstoy fable of the Cossack marshes] Leo Tolstoy's *The Cossacks* (1863).

443.23 Jack Benny] Comedian (1894–1974) whose career spanned vaudeville, radio, film, and television.

447.22 Calle de Los Niños Perdidos.] Street of the Lost Children.

450.8 Hedy Lamarr] Austrian-born actress (1914–2000) who starred in such films as *Tortilla Flat* (1942) and *Samson and Delilah* (1949).

452.31 "False nonsense."—Acheson, 1952] Dean Acheson (1893–1971), United States secretary of state (1949–53), declared in March 1952 that Communist claims regarding the use of germ warfare by United Nations forces in Korea were "false nonsense."

456.32 "Tutta tua vision . . . pur grattar."] See Dante, *Paradiso*, Canto XVII, lines 128–129: Make all your vision plain, and let them scratch.

457.35–36 Lester Young's . . . 1938] Young appeared on the February 1939 recording of "You Can Depend on Me" by Count Basie and His Sextet.

458.2 Maurice Chevalier] French actor and singer (1888–1972).

458.22–23 "Way Down Yonder in New Orleans"] The song (composed by Turner Layton and Henry Creamer in 1922) was recorded as part of the Kansas City Six sessions of 1938.

460.4 CHARLES ATKINSON] Charles F. Atkinson, whose translation of Oswald Spengler's *The Decline of the West* was published 1926–28.

462.18 'You Can Depend on Me,'] See note 457.35–36.

VISIONS OF GERARD

470.9 Avalokitesvara's] In Buddhism, an enlightened being (or *Bodhisattva*) of great compassion.

470.11 Womb of Exuberant Fertility] A phrase attributed to the Indian philosopher and poet Ashvagosa (80–150 C.E.), who offered it as a description of the universe itself.

471.12 Samsara] The Sanskrit term denoting the cycle of death and rebirth.

472.37 Raskolnik] See note 365.15.

473.4 "Doctor Sax . . . World Snake"] See note 8.16–17.

473.5 *Duluoz Legend*] Kerouac's overarching title for his volumes of autobiographical fiction; see Note on the Texts in this volume.

473.7 Nin] Family nickname for Kerouac's sister, Caroline Kerouac Blake (1918–1964).

473.14 Nirmana (appearance) Kaya (form)] Mahayana Buddhist designation for those instances in which the Buddha assumes human form.

473.15–16 Chillicosm] Or Chiliocosm; a term in Buddhist cosmology denoting the system of individual universes.

475.1 (Maha Meru)] Sanskrit for Great Meru, a reference to Mount Meru, which in Buddhist, Hindu, and Jain cosmology symbolizes the center of the universe.

476.28 Bardolph] A companion of Falstaff who appears in Shakespeare's plays *Henry IV, Part I*; *Henry IV, Part II*; *Henry V*; and *The Merry Wives of Windsor*.

482.22 Saturday Evening Post] See note 74.25.

484.21 Vilma Banky and Rogers Hornsby] Banky, Hungarian-born American silent film actress (1901–1991), star of *Son of the Sheik* (1926), *The Winning of Barbara Worth* (1926), and other films. Hornsby, baseball player (1896–1963) who played for the St. Louis Cardinals for much of his career.

487.40 *lacrimae rerum*] Latin: "the tears of things," derived from Book I, line 462, of Virgil's *Aeneid*.

488.5 President Coolidge] Calvin Coolidge (1872–1933), U.S. president, 1923–29.

488.31 Arjuna] In the Sanskrit epic *Mahabharata*, warrior prince whose dialogue with Krishna is recorded in the *Bhagavad Gita*.

490.3–4 "*Je vous . . . de grâce*"] French: Hail Mary, full of grace.

490.7–8 "*Le Seigneur . . . les femmes*"] French: Our Lord is with thee—blessed art thou among women.

490.10 "*Et Jésus . . . vos entrailles*"] French: And Blessed is the fruit of thy womb, Jesus.

490.17–18 "*Sainte Marie . . . de notre mort*"] French: Holy Mary, mother of God, pray for us sinners, now, and in the hour of our death.

491.23 INRI!] Latin acronym for *Iesus Nazarenus Rex Iudaeorum* (Jesus of Nazareth, King of the Jews), typically the inscription on the crucifix.

492.8 soil of Abraham] A reference to the Plains of Abraham, located in the Battlefields Park in Quebec City, Quebec. It was the site of the 1759 Battle of the Plains of Abraham, in which the French were decisively defeated by the English in the Seven Years' War.

494.34 *pitou*] Term of endearment in Quebecois, typically translated into English as "puppy."

495.7 "thou owest God a death"] See Shakespeare, *Henry IV, Part One*, V.i.126.

495.15 B. F. Keiths] One of a chain of vaudeville theaters founded by Benjamin Franklin Keith (1846–1914).

495.16 W.C.Fields] See note 9.24.

499.16–17 If his mortality . . . Augustine Page One] See St. Augustine, *Confessions*, Book One: "Man, that bears about him his mortality, the witness of his sin."

500.19 *azno*] Ladino: donkey or ass.

503.16 Boucher] François Boucher (1703–1770), French painter and engraver.

505.15 "*Mon Seigneur!*"] My Lord!

507.33 Diamond Light?] The reference is to *The Diamond Sutra*, a Mahayana Buddhist text that was a favorite of Kerouac's. It first appeared in a Chinese translation in the fifth century.

510.8 Rabelais and Khayyam] François Rabelais (1483–1553), author of *Gargantua and Pantagruel*; Khayyam, see note 374.23.

516.15 Edgar Cayce] Self-proclaimed clairvoyant and healer (1877–1945), founder of the Association for Research and Enlightenment.

520.19 Vaya] Or Vayu. In Hinduism, the god of winds.

522.2–3 Plains of Abraham] See note 492.8.

522.35 Frank Merriwell] Character created by Gilbert Patten (1866–1945) under the pseudonym Burt Standish. Merriwell's adventures, which became the model for American juvenile sports fiction, were the basis for a popular radio serial in 1934 and a series of films starting in 1936.

524.8 *blagues*] Jokes.

529.14 Rialto and Lamont] Billy Rialto and Laddie Lamont, vaudeville team.

529.15 Lois Bennett] Vaudeville and radio singer.

529.17   Muriel Pollock] American pianist and songwriter of Russian descent (1895–1971) who sometimes performed in vaudeville with Lois Bennett.

529.26   Miss Corinne and Dick Himber] Corrine Tilton, vaudeville performer. Himber, bandleader, composer, and magician (1900–1966).

529.29   'Getting Soaked'] Comedy review starring vaudevillians Bob Yates and Evelyn Carson, popular in the late 1920s.

529.30   Clarence Oliver] American singer and comedian.

529.32   Billy McDermott] American vaudevillian.

529.33   Coxey's Army] Protest march of unemployed workers led by Populist politician Jacob Coxey (1854–1951), which headed to Washington, D.C., during the economic depression of March 1894 to demand job creation.

529.39   Pathe News . . . Aesop's Fables] Pathé News, British producer of newsreels, 1910–70. Aesop's Fables, series of 445 animated film shorts created by Paul Terry, 1920–29.

530.10   Old Bull Baloon] See note 58.40.

531.36–38   "better be jocund . . . bitter fruit"] See Edward Fitzgerald, *The Rubáiyát of Omar Khayyám*, revised version, stanza 54.

533.38–39   Langford battered Johnson] On April 26, 1906, Jack Johnson (1878–1946) successfully defended the heavyweight boxing crown against Sam Langford (1883–1956) in Chelsea, Massachusetts.

539.36   "And time bids be gone"] See *Henry IV, Part Two*, I.iii.110: "We are time's subjects, and time bids be gone."

545.16   J.R.Williams] James Robert Williams (1888–1957), Canadian cartoonist known for cartoon series *Out Our Way* (see note 63.5).

550.4–5   "that bareheaded life under grass"] See Emily Dickinson, letter to Samuel Bowles, c. 1860: "That *Bareheaded life*—under the grass—worries one like a Wasp."

554.10–15   "*Suscipe, sancte Pater, . . . in vitam aeternam. Amen.*"] Offertory prayer from the Latin mass: Accept, O holy Father, almighty and eternal God, this unspotted host, which I, Thy unworthy servant, offer unto Thee, my living and true God, for my innumerable sins, offenses, and acts of negligence, and for all here present: as also for all faithful Christians, both living and dead, that it may avail both me and them for salvation unto life everlasting. Amen.

BIG SUR

561.10   Adam Yulch or Lalagy Pulvertaft] Yulch (1885–1950), lieutenant in New York's Nassau County Police Department who wrote well-regarded articles for criminology journals; Isobel Lalage Pulvertaft (b. 1925), British novelist best known for *The Thing Desired* (1957).

561.31–32   "I'll Take You . . . Kathleen"] Popular song (1875) by Thomas P. Westendorf.

561.37   "Road"] Kerouac's *On the Road*, first published by Viking Press in 1957.

564.7–8   St. Christopher] Patron saint of travel and travelers.

564.17   Ayahuasca] Psychedelic brewed primarily from the *Banisteriopsis caapi* vine, also known as yagé.

568.14–15   *affrayed* . . . *by a whip*] Edmund Spenser (1552–1599), English poet, author of *The Faerie Queene* (1590); in the early modern English employed by Spenser, "frayed" and "affrayed" would have been interchangeable designations for uneasiness or alarm.

570.6   Blakean groaning] As in the work of poet and artist William Blake (1757–1827); see "Infant Sorrow": "My mother groaned, my father wept / Into the dangerous world I leapt."

571.16–17   "Mountain of Mien Mo"] In *Book of Dreams* (1960), Kerouac recounts a dream involving the Flying Horses of Mien Mo: "'Mien Mo,' I think, remembering the name of the Mountain in Burma they call the world . . . those Flying Horses are happy! How beautifully they claw slow fore-hooves thru the blue void!" The reference is traceable to page 14 [or Note 16] in Paul Ambrose Bigandet's *The Life or Legend of Gaudama: The Buddha of the Burmese, Volume 1* (1858): "Our planet or globe is composed according to Budhists of the mountain Min-mo, being in height 82,000 youdzanas (1 youdzana is equal to little less than 12 English miles), above the surface of the earth, its depth is equal to its height." There is a further reference to Mien Mo in Kerouac's *Some of the Dharma*: "In Burma they think they live on mountain a million miles high named Mien-Mo (82,000 youdzanas high) (each y. is 12 miles) and that to the South is an island, Dzapoudiba, or, India—".

572.23–24   *Doctor Jekyll and Mister Hyde*] *Strange Case of Dr Jekyll and Mr Hyde* (1886) by Robert Louis Stevenson.

572.40   Bhikkus'] An ordained Buddhist monk.

573.17–18   Mexico City in 1957 . . . gigantic earthquake] On July 28, 1957, Mexico City was the site of an earthquake registering over 7 on the Richter scale.

574.14–15   Lankavatara Scripture] *The Laṅkāvatāra Sūtra*, Mahayana Buddhist text dating to the third century. It first appeared in a Chinese translation in the fifth century.

575.10   Vulcan's Forge] Vulcan, ancient Roman god of fire; smoke from volcanoes was often attributed to his forge.

576.37   Steve Allen Show] *The Steve Allen Show*, television variety show (1956–61) hosted by musician, comedian, and writer Steve Allen (1921–2000). Kerouac appeared in 1959, reading from *Visions of Cody* and *On the Road* to Allen's piano accompaniment.

578.9   Gauguinesque] As in the work of French painter Paul Gauguin (1848–1903).

578.20   Whore of Babylon] See *Revelation* 17–18.

578.21–22   weird Ripley situation] Reference to the newspaper series *Ripley's Believe It or Not!*, created by Robert Ripley (1890–1949), dedicated to odd and exotic information; the franchise expanded subsequently into paperback books and radio and television programs.

581.4–16   words of Emerson . . . spite at home"] The quotations in this section are from Ralph Waldo Emerson's "Self-Reliance" in *Essays: First Series* (1841).

581.26   "Steppenwolf"] Novel (1927) by the German-born Swiss writer Herman Hesse (1877–1962).

583.9   Bodhisattva's] In Buddhism, an enlightened being.

586.27   Eglevsky ballet] André Eglevsky (1917–1977), Russian ballet dancer who in 1958 founded the New York–based Eglevsky Ballet Company.

586.37   Bodhidharma] Buddhist monk of the sixth century credited with founding the Zen branch of Mayahana Buddhism.

587.7   Gandharvas] In Hinduism, *gandharvas* are male nature spirits and, in Buddhism, low-ranking heavenly beings (or *devas*). In a letter to Carolyn Cassady (May 17, 1954), Kerouac wrote: "We just think that we are dying when we die. It is like the castle of the Gandharvas, castles in the air . . . a world reflected in a mirror—the end."

589.4   *Éh vache*] Québecois expression of disgust.

590.3   Hui Neng] Dajian Huineng, highly venerated Zen monastic who lived in the seventh century.

590.6–7   You go out in joy . . . Thomas à Kempis] See *Imitation of Christ* (c. 1418–27), Book I, chapter 18.

591.24–25   Big Two Hearted River] "Big Two-Hearted River," short story by Ernest Hemingway with a trout-fishing background; included in the 1925 edition of *In Our Time*.

592.34   little twinkletoe steps like Babe Ruth] The distinctive home-run trot of baseball player Ruth (1895–1948) made him appear light on his feet despite his bulkiness.

595.37   Gerard] Gerard Kerouac (1916–1926); see *Visions of Gerard* (1963) in this volume.

597.28–29   Dharma Bum days] Philip Whalen, here Ben Fagan, appears as Warren Coughlin in *The Dharma Bums* (1958).

598.1   Stein and Pound and Wallace Stevens—] American modernists Gertrude Stein (1874–1946), Ezra Pound (1885–1972), and Wallace Stevens (1879–1955).

598.3–4 "When I leave town . . . back on the sauce"] See Philip Whalen, "20:vii:58, On Which I Renounce the Notion of Social Responsibility," in *Memoirs of an Interglacial Age* (1960), lines 1–2: "The minute I'm out of town / My friends get sick, go back on the sauce."

599.7 Chet Baker] Jazz trumpeter and vocalist (1929–1988).

601.3 Stravinski's dinosaurs] The 1940 Walt Disney animated feature *Fantasia* employed selections from Igor Stravinsky's *The Rite of Spring* (1913) as the soundtrack for an animated sequence depicting the evolution and extinction of the dinosaurs.

601.11 Second Patriarch?] Dazu Huike (487–593), student of Bodhidharma, the first patriarch.

601.15 Fubar] Military slang from World War II meaning "fucked up beyond all recognition."

602.16 Samuel Johnson] English poet, essayist, biographer, and lexicographer (1709–1784).

603.12 cityCityCITY] Short story originally published as "The Electrocution" in the August 1959 edition of *Nugget*; Kerouac's sole attempt at science fiction.

603.27 when no one cares like Sinatra sings] "When No One Cares," composed by Sammy Cahn and Jimmy Van Heusen, was recorded by Frank Sinatra in 1959.

603.30 Journey To The End Of The Night] *Voyage au bout de la nuit* (1932) by Louis-Ferdinand Céline (1894–1961).

604.7 Book of Songs] *Shih Ching*, the oldest existing collection of Chinese poetry, dating from the eleventh to seventh centuries B.C.E.

604.7–8 César Birotteau] *History of the Greatness and Decline of César Birotteau*, novel (1837) by Honoré de Balzac.

604.8 Satyricons] *Satyricon* or *Satyrica* is a classical Latin work often attributed to Gaius Petronius (27–66 C.E.).

604.9 Sir Philip Sidney] Elizabethan poet (1554–1586).

604.10 Sterne, Ibn El Arabi, . . . Lope de Vega] Laurence Sterne (1713–1768), Anglo-Irish novelist, author of *The Life and Opinions of Tristram Shandy, Gentleman* (1759–67). Ibn El Arabi (1165–1240), Sufi mystic and philosopher. Lope de Vega (1562–1635), prolific Spanish playwright.

604.11 Catulluses] Gaius Valerius Catullus (84–54 B.C.E.), poet of the Roman Republic.

609.18 Solemn Mass] *Missa Solemnis in D Major* (1819–23).

609.27 Raul Castro] Cuban revolutionary leader (b. 1931), brother of Fidel Castro.

611.33   Mae West] Stage and screen actress and singer (1893–1980), star of *She Done Him Wrong* (1933) and *I'm No Angel* (1933).

612.2   Subud] Spiritual movement founded in Indonesia in the 1920s.

613.28–29   Twelve Nirdanas] The Twelve Nidānas are the links in a chain of causation leading to rebirth, as expounded in section three of the *Visuddhimagga* of Theravada Buddhism, composed in the fifth century C.E.

615.5   Bashō] Matsuo Bashō (1644–1694), haiku poet of the Edo period.

615.6   Issa or of Shiki] Kobayashi Issa (1763–1828) and Masaoka Shiki (1867–1902), haiku poets.

617.10   Stan Getz] Jazz saxophonist (1927–1991).

618.8   Boswell's Johnson] *The Life of Samuel Johnson, LL.D.* (1791) by James Boswell (1740–1795).

619.22   Henry Miller] See note 303.21.

621.37   as Genet shows] Jean Genet (1910–1986), French playwright, novelist, and essayist. His 1946 book *The Miracle of the Rose* describes his experiences as a detainee at Mettray Penal Colony.

625.9   "Dark Brown,"] Michael McClure's long erotic poem was published by Auerhahn Press of San Francisco in 1961.

625.35–36   Aleister Crowley] English occultist (1875–1947).

626.2   a novel . . . Denton Welch] Denton Welch (1915–1948), English writer and painter; his novel *Maiden Voyage* (1943) is set in China.

626.32   Chan] Chinese school of Mahayana Buddhism known for meditative practice, known in Japan as Zen.

626.39   Devas] Benevolent supernatural beings in Hinduism and Buddhism.

628.34   Chiang Kai Shek] Chiang Kai-shek (1887–1975), Chinese political and military leader who after the Communist victory fled to Taiwan in 1949, where he ruled as president of the Republic of China.

629.17   Stanley Gould] New York bohemian (1926–1985).

629.35–36   Asuras Devadattas Vedantas] Asuras, power-seeking *devas*; Devadatta, Buddhist monk thought to be a cousin of the Buddha; Vedantas, foundational texts of Hinduism.

638.26–27   "The pathway to wisdom lies through excess"] See William Blake, *The Marriage of Heaven and Hell* (1793): "The road of excess leads to the palace of wisdom."

638.35–38   "*O mon Dieux, pourquoi . . . Aw 'shu malade*—] Québecois: O my God, why do you torture me this way—Father, Father help me—I am nauseous—I need to go to the bathroom but I cannot—so very sick.

641.16–17 Samadhis] A high level of meditation.

642.25 'Pataphysics] Philosophy defined by its inventor, Alfred Jarry (1873–1907), as "the science of imaginary solutions." *Evergreen Review* published a special issue devoted to it in 1960.

642.29 Theo Marzials] British poet and composer (1850–1920), author of *The Gallery of Pigeons and Other Poems* (1873).

642.29–30 Henry Harland] American novelist (1861–1905) who founded the magazine *The Yellow Book* in London in 1894.

643.5 Dame Mae Whitty] English stage and film actress Dame May Whitty (1865–1948), featured in *The Lady Vanishes* (1938).

643.27 "Sweet Sixteen"] Song (1938) by Roger Edens, originally sung by Judy Garland.

643.34 Milarepa] Jetsun Milarepa (1052–1135), preeminent Tibetan yogi and poet. The passages quoted are from "The Song of a Yogi's Joy" in *The Hundred Thousand Songs*.

645.20–21 Jean Harlow, Rimbaud and Billy the Kid] Jean Harlow (1911–1937), film actress who starred in *Red Dust* (1932) and *Red-Headed Woman* (1933); Jean Nicolas Arthur Rimbaud (1854–1891), French poet; William Bonney (c. 1860–1881), alias Billy the Kid, gunman and outlaw. Michael McClure's play *The Beard* (1965) depicts Harlow and Billy the Kid spending the afterlife together in a "blue velvet eternity."

646.5 Gallimard or Girodias] Gallimard, major French literary publishing house, founded by Gaston Gallimard (1881–1975). Maurice Girodias (1919–1990), French publisher, founder of Olympia Press.

646.7 Mexico City Blues] Kerouac's book-length poem (1959) consisting of 242 choruses.

646.39–40 Primo Carnera–Ernie Schaaft fight] Primo Carnera (1906–1967), Italian heavyweight boxer; American heavyweight Ernie Schaaf (1908–1933) fell into a coma and died following his bout with Carnera in February 1933.

650.10 Wallace Beery] Screen actor (1885–1949), star of *The Big House* (1930), *The Champ* (1931), *The Bowery* (1933), and many other films.

650.12 *Twenty Mule Team*] *20 Mule Team* (1940), Western directed by Richard Thorpe.

656.8 Erskine Caldwell] Novelist (1903–1987), author of *Tobacco Road* (1932) and *God's Little Acre* (1933).

662.2 Jerry Southern] Jeri Southern (1926–1991), jazz pianist and singer.

665.38 Van Dyck] Sir Anthony van Dyck (1599–1641), Flemish Baroque painter.

671.13–14   Claude Gallimard] French publisher (1914–1991), longtime head of Editions Gallimard.

672.21   Ah Sunflower"] See William Blake, "Ah! Sun-flower": "Ah! Sun-flower! weary of time, / Who countest the steps of the Sun, / Seeking after that sweet golden clime / Where the traveller's journey is done."

676.3–7   Milarepa . . . you will bring annoyance"] For Milarepa see note 643.34; the quoted passage is from "The Song of a Yogi's Joy" in *The Hundred Thousand Songs*.

678.4–5   *Just Friends* like Sinatra] "Just Friends," song (1931) by John Klenner and Sam Lewis, recorded by Frank Sinatra on his 1959 album *No One Cares*.

685.39   Old Bull Balloon] See note 58.40.

693.31–32   get thee to a nunnery] *Hamlet*, III.i.121.

695.35   Roshi stick] Lightweight wooden stick applied in Zen practice to alleviate drowsiness or loss of concentration while meditating.

698.15   Edgar Cayce's] See note 516.15.

702.5   Naomi] Naomi Ginsberg (1894–1956), mother of Allen Ginsberg. Naomi's lifelong struggles with mental illness were the subject of his poem "Kaddish" (1959).

703.20–22   Humphrey Bogart . . . rigid and insane—] The scene occurs in *The Treasure of the Sierra Madre* (1948), adapted by John Huston from B. Traven's 1927 novel.

703.40   Airapatianz] E. S. Airapetianz, Russian biophysicist and neurologist associated with the Pavlov Institute.

706.15   Desolation Peak] Located in Washington state's North Cascade mountains. Kerouac spent two weeks during the summer of 1956 inhabiting the peak as a fire lookout, an experience described in *The Dharma Bums* (1958), *Lonesome Traveler* (1960), and *Desolation Angels* (1965).

718.10–15   Les poissons . . . parle—] The fishes of the sea / speak Breton— / My name is Lebris / de Keroack— / Speak, fishes, Loti, / speak—

727.26–28   "*On est toutes . . . la mer*—] "We are completely hidden, eat / the silence," say the fishes of the / sea—

727.32–35   *Je ne suis pas . . . toutes!*] I'm not bad when I'm / at peace—in the storms / I shout! Like a lunatic! / I eat, I tear everything!

THE LIBRARY OF AMERICA SERIES

The Library of America fosters appreciation and pride in America's literary heritage by publishing, and keeping permanently in print, authoritative editions of America's best and most significant writing. An independent nonprofit organization, it was founded in 1979 with seed funding from the National Endowment for the Humanities and the Ford Foundation.

To subscribe to the series or to order individual copies, please visit www.loa.org or call (800) 964-5778.

*This book is set in 10 point ITC Galliard Pro, a
face designed for digital composition by Matthew Carter
and based on the sixteenth-century face Granjon. The paper
is acid-free lightweight opaque and meets the requirements for
permanence of the American National Standards Institute.
The binding material is Brillianta, a woven rayon cloth
made by Van Heek-Scholco Textielfabrieken, Holland.
Composition by David Bullen Design. Printing and
binding by Edwards Brothers Malloy, Ann Arbor.
Designed by Bruce Campbell.*